To Joan Moore

enjoy!

HOW YA LIVIN'

A Novel

Peace, love,
& light!

[signature]

June 2004

HOW YA LIVIN'
A Novel

JONATHAN LUCKETT

A Strebor Books International LLC Publication
Distributed by Simon & Schuster, Inc.

Published by

Strebor Books International LLC
P.O. Box 1370
Bowie, MD 20718
http://www.streborbooks.com

ISBN 1-59309-025-0
LCCN 2003112286

Distributed by Simon & Schuster, Inc.
1230 Avenue of the Americas
New York, NY 10020
1-800-223-2336

Cover art: © www.mariondesigns.com

First Printing June 2004
Manufactured and Printed in the United States

10 9 8 7 6 5 4 3 2 1

DEDICATION
For Zodie Makonnen

ONE

Four A.M. came way too fast! The alarm shook my ass out of bed as I struggled to keep myself from falling back into the warm confines of my comforter. But today was not a day to reckon with—no, today I couldn't just lie there and hit the snooze—not on this day. Today I was going on vacation!

So I held my head that was smarting from the buzz of the alarm clock and ran the shower. Then quickly got into my normal routine—teeth brushing and shaving my face and bald head with the Braun, and trimming my thick, dark goatee. I was turning toward the shower but then thought about it for one quick second—I was heading to the islands to play, so I should spend a minute more on grooming, 'cause things like that were important to me. So, I buzzed off what little chest and stomach hair I had, used the clippers (with guard!) to trim my pubic hair down to a thin layer just the way I liked it. Then got in the shower after admiring my taut form in the mirror. I liked what I saw. Firm, bronze-colored body, tight upper body with a hint of muscles, but not overdone, like some fucking jarhead. Tattoo-adorned— a thin tribal band on my left arm above my elbow; the colorful face of an Indian chief on my right shoulder—feathers from his headdress meandering down my arm to just below the elbow; and my latest acquisition—a five-pointed star, almost snowflake-like in form, sitting on my chest above my left nipple. Well-defined legs and a tight ass that sends the women wild (I'm just repeating what they tell me, so don't hate!)

The water running down my bald head, face, chest and arms felt sooooo good, I could have stayed there for an hour. But Air Jamaica was calling my name, "Trey, everyting irie, so get ya black ass down here, mon!" I wasn't about to miss out on any of that. It had been too damn long, ya hear me! Over a year since a real vacation for me. I mean, I've been traveling on business, don't get me wrong, but it isn't the same. This was the vacation that I'd been waiting for all year long. And today was the day. By noon I'd be on white sandy beaches! I couldn't wait.

I glanced down at my flat stomach and dark cock, grabbed the razor and the bar of soap, and went about cutting off the hair around my dick and balls. I loved that feeling of little to no hair down there…and the ladies loved it as well. I'm not sure if it was the fact that it made me more sensitive or not, but all I know was that it felt good to be fucking with smooth balls. With each scrape of the razor I thought about the possibilities awaiting me on that island—all of those dark and lovely honeys…six wonderful days…my dick began to swell as I thought of the delicious possibilities…

While toweling off, I recalled the conversation last night with my boy.

"Speak!"

"What up, dawg? How ya livin'?"

"Living large and in charge," I replied to the routine that hasn't changed in over 15 years. Vince and I are best friends, homies from way back! He's my man, the one person I genuinely look up to and love like a brother.

"So, my man, you ready?"

"Fuck no, what you think? I got my shit all over this mutha fucka—looks like a cyclone hit this place. But don't worry, my brutha, I *will* be ready!"

"I hear that."

"True dat!"

"So, my man, seriously, you gonna go down there to relax, right? Find your flow and do some soul searching?" I could hear Vince through the phone cracking up before my response was forthcoming.

"What you think? I'm gonna tag every ass that winks at me…I ain't playin'!"

"Dawg, listen to me—what you need to do is take it down a notch, find yourself one of those fine-ass Jamaican women, like Rachel on BET, with the long, dark hair, and thick like I don't know what, and romance the hell out of her. Do your thing, dawg, and she'll be like putty in your hands. Then bring her ass back up to the States and make her your wife!" He chuckled but not more so than I did.

"First off, this is *me* you talking to! Why you trying to play me like that? You know that ain't me. Shit. Wifey??? Fuck that, V. That's you, and listen, I ain't mad at ya, but that, my brutha, ain't me. Wife," I said again. "Nigga, please!"

It always amused me how two grown black men with close to seven years of post-graduate work between us still talked like we were from the ghetto—hoodlums, like rap stars or something. That's one thing I loved about Vince—put him in a work situation and he was all professional and shit, like another person took control of his voice—the way he said things, the manner in which he gestured; and his inflection sounded so damn *intelligent* and I dare say, *prophetic*. He was good at that shit—I mean, to a certain extent I am too—I have to be in my line of work, being an attorney and such, but I'm not like Vince. He's 'da man when it comes to shit like that. I guess that's why mutha fuckas pay to hear him speak! Anyway, some things never change between us, and this was one of those things—the way we spoke and vibed when we were around each other.

"I'm just saying, if it were me and I was heading to Jamaica for six days, I would be on the lookout. There's something about the islands that gets my juices flowing...when I'm around those beautiful beaches and sunsets it makes me feel all romantic inside. Make me wanna grab a honey and wine and dine her all night!" Vince was laughing now, but I knew his words were speaking the truth. That was the major difference between the two of us—the way in which we viewed the world. Vince was a serious romantic through and through—he still got plenty of play, but his approach was totally different than mine. Me, well, I'm just a stone-cold playa! I'm in to pussy, for real! The punany, plain and simple. I don't fuck around—when I see something I want, I go for it—no long-term romancing allowed! Just not part of my rules, ya see!

"I promise you this, Vince," I said, as I closed my garment bag filled with clothes for every possible occasion—my favorite dark, Italian-cut, three-button suit for the club; black, tight leather pants and stretch muscle shirt; a few button-downs, a thin pullover in case it got chilly; assorted jeans and shorts; and loafers and two pairs of sandals—black and tan. An unopened box of Lifestyles condoms (lubricated) lay in the upper right compartment of the garment bag. "I'm gonna relax and I'm gonna chill, but I *will* tag every fine piece of pussy I see. I ain't playing. This ole dick of mine is gonna get itself a fucking workout! Ya hear me!?!"

"You mean *more* than normal?" He laughed some more. Then we hung up after saying our goodbyes. I had to finish packing a second bag…

Both bags along with my leather carryon were currently sequestered in the trunk of my black M3. The engine was running and humming as I prepared to leave. I was dressed casual—over-dyed jeans, polo shirt—robin's egg blue, black leather jacket, and my fav Nikes, blue-tinted sunglasses perched atop my smooth dome—yeah, casual, yet stylish and fresh as only I could be—this I'm thinking to myself as I checked myself out in the full length in the hall before setting the alarm to the crib and jetting—after all, as I'm fond of saying—image is everything! No need to have the panties flying just yet. I mean, it wasn't even daylight yet. Yeah mon!

✖✖✖

Fast forward six hours. I was 43,000 feet in the air and cruising above Cuba at 545 miles per hour. How I know? 'Cause I'm a gadget freak and brought along my handheld GPS. I pointed that bad boy out the window (I was in the aisle seat with nobody beside me), got a fix on a handful of satellites (my shit got a 12 channel receiver!) and bam! My position was instantly calculated and displayed on a small LED screen. Kind of nice to know just where a mutha fucka is at all times!

Anywho…we'd been flying for several hours and the flight had been uneventful. Security at Baltimore-Washington International had been tight, but nothing overbearing—my designer belt buckle had set the metal detector off (what else is new!) and then they went through the pockets of my leather jacket because my Beemer key looked suspiciously fat under the X-ray machine. (Don't any of these fuckers drive a *luxury* car???) I was frisked by an elderly white guy (hourly employee, no doubt!) under the watchful eyes of a pair of National Guardsmen dressed in camouflage with their fingers on the trigger of their M-16 rifles. After that I chilled at the gate until boarding time, looking around like a hawk at my fellow passengers, trying to see if there were any fine honeys that I might get next to. Alas, no such luck. That was cool with me—I needed to save my strength for when I arrived in Mo Bay, ya know? I decided to call my other best friend, my boo, Erika, a.k.a. Sassy, even though it was before 7 a.m. Shit, she hadn't even called me last night to give me a send-off, so screw her if I wake her black ass up!

"Sassy, what's up, girl?" I said, booming into my cell.

"This better be a fucking emergency, I swear to God." I could hear her turning over in her bed. *Good, I got her at just the right time.*

"What up, boo? You forgot about your main man or what? Gonna let me get on a plane without any goodbyes? You know that shit ain't right!"

A stream of expletives escaped from her mouth, and I just had to laugh out loud. I loved it when she talked dirty to me. Erika and I have been down since I don't know when. At least as long as Vince and me. Actually, we had been friends since our college days, staying tight and sharing with each other the kind of things usually reserved for same-sex friendships. But Erika was down. She was cool. One of the fellas. I let her know that every chance I got.

"Look, baby girl, sorry to wake you, but I just had to holla at you before I go."

"No, your dumb ass just had nothing else to do while waiting at the gate! Am I right?" Erika responded.

"See, now I'm hurt."

"Well, fuck you!" She laughed. "Trey, I only got one thing to say to you, since you never listen to me anyway—are you listening?"

"Yeah, Sassy. Fire away."

"Trey, use protection. You hear me???" I laughed loudly as I grunted, and disconnected her dumb ass…

Okay—here I am just ranting and raving, going on and on about this and that, and I haven't even taken the time to properly introduce myself. Where are my manners? My mother would not be proud! So, here it goes…

My name is Trey Alexander. I'm 33 years old, living in Chocolate City (that's the nation's capital, D.C., for all of you who are not in the know!) I'm a divorce lawyer, admitted to the bar in D.C., Virginia, and New York. I work for a prestigious law firm in D.C.—and, no, I'm not going to tell you the name, 'cause some of you bitches just might call information and try to get my digits—I'm not having that! I'm originally from New York, Brooklyn, to be exact, and yes, that totally explains my cocky, in-your-face attitude and demeanor (fuck you, very much!) But to repeat what I've said habitually, "Don't hate the playa, hate the game!"

I've been in D.C. for about ten years—I came here to go to law school, Georgetown, thank you very much, and been here ever since. I love D.C.— love the atmosphere, the people, and most of all, the *ratio* of women to guys! When I got to this mutha fucka I said to myself, "This is soooooo me!" And here I am!!!! For real!

Anyway, I've lived in D.C. the entire time I've been here—right now I've got myself a stylish crib off 15th and U, a two-story condo with, check it— a doorman! Yeah! I'm moving on up, to the East side…you already know what I drive, but in case you haven't been paying attention, my ride is a sexy ass, black M3, courtesy of the firm. Yeah, late last year I won this high-profile divorce and child custody case for a prominent, white McLean plastic surgeon. The case was very complex and extremely nasty, so the Beemer was my bonus for winning. Listen, I love the ride and all, but to be truthful, when I think about it, I billed close to $100,000 on that case alone, so that's the least they could do!

Let's see—what else can I tell ya—last year I cleared $238,000 in salary. I'm not a partner, and that used to be a sore subject for me, but in the last nine to twelve months I've come to grips with the fact that Trey here does not intend to put in the hours that are demanded of an up-'n'-coming partner-to-be. My motto is and has always been—"work hard, play even harder!" And I live that maxim every day of my life. The firm gets its money's worth out of me; don't get me wrong. But when my workday is done, it is done, and don't talk shit to me about my professional gig. At that point it's Miller time, and Trey is ready to party! So, I'm cool with the salary and bennies they give me, my phat ride, crib in the city, and plenty of punany to chase after and keep me hoppin'! Now, I know the next question on your mind, so let's dispense with it right now: Girlfriend? Wife? Significant other, you ask? Not only "no" to those questions, but "fuck no!" Does that answer your question???

✖✖✖

Less than an hour later the clear, fresh aquamarine waters of Jamaica rolled underneath the belly of our jet as we approached Montego Bay. The lush hills of the island slipped beneath us as we landed into the wind. An ancient jeep that was painted just like the one on M*A*S*H (for those of you old enough—like me—to remember that show) stood off the main runway by a tin-slatted hut. As we deplaned onto the tarmac, the heat hit me square in the face and chest. Hard to believe that less than four hours earlier, I had been in forty-degree weather. "Welcome to Jamaica," a sign proclaimed as we made a right turn and headed for the terminal and (I hoped) air conditioning. I was here. The vacation was beginning! Ah yeah!

I'll dispense with the details. Suffice it to say, it took me close to two hours by bus to get from Mo Bay to my resort in Negril (located on the western part of the island). It was hot as hell and the roads were, pardon my French, fucked up! I mean half that island was in disrepair and the roads were in the midst of a serious reconstruction. That meant that every few minutes or so our Jamaican driver would have to downshift and maneuver around pot holes large enough for a horse to lie in. Along the way we saw some interesting sights—cows and/or steer (I don't know the damn difference!) grazing on the side of the road; a Pizza Hut and KFC that our driver was so damn proud of, he had to slow down and get on the fuckin' P.A.

system to announce; fishermen on the side of the road carrying fresh fish on a line; sellers of assorted fruits, beer, Bob Marley hats; bicycle tires or perhaps steering wheel covers (carried around their dark necks), and of course, ganja—yeah, these mutha fuckas actually ran alongside of our bus as we went through intersections trying to sell us this shit; a guy barefoot carrying groceries on top of his head…I thought I had died and gone to Africa!

There were five of us on the bus—two bruthas from Chicago who had gone to Howard and were therefore familiar with the D.C. area. And a nice, chatty, young, white couple named Lance and Chris from Louisiana. We got through the introductions and the normal chatter—first time to Jamaica? First time to this resort? Yada yada… But finally, we turned into our hotel complex and I breathed a sigh of relief. We were finally here. Yes, Lawd!

I thought check-in would be a breeze, but guess what? Our rooms weren't ready. I guess some things never change, regardless of what part of the world you are in. They invited us to leave our bags out front and relax in the dining room where a lavish buffet was in full effect. I was totally down with that. I sat with the H.U. bruthas and scanned the room for honeys as we ate…saw a few that definitely caught my eye. Everyone but us was clad in tee shirts, bikinis, colorful sarongs—sunglasses adorned their heads— carrying plates loaded with food to rounded tables. Open bar (this was an all-inclusive place, and I was not mad at anybody, you hear me!), so the Jamaican rum and other top-shelf shit was flowing! An hour later we were stuffed, and I was ready to lose my jeans, Nikes, and jacket, find a spot on the beach under one of them palm trees with plenty of shade and catch a snooze—after all, I'd been up since 4.

I sauntered over to the front desk where my H.U. boyz had already checked in and were following the bellmen to their room. I waved goodbye and waited my turn. Come to find out, there was a problem with my room reservation. Now listen, don't fuck with me after I've flown close to fifteen hundred miles and put these six days, five nights on my Visa—I had all the proper paperwork and documentation in my leather carryon—just give me a minute to get to it. No, that wasn't it, I was told—the crux of the matter was that the resort was under renovation. Funny—no one (especially my travel agent) had mentioned that *minor* point to me…an entire section of rooms (ocean view—*my* ocean view room, btw!) was closed, in addition to the main pool and disco!

Okay…here we go! It's about to get ugly up in here! OH HELL NO! I put on my best "don't-fuck-with-me-I'm-an-attorney" face and voice, kept my composure but told the cute, but tight-lipped Jamaican woman behind the desk that she (and this place) was about to have a serious problem if they didn't produce a comparable room A.S.A.P! She ducked into the back, presumably to consult her manager since the computer terminal at the front desk wasn't telling her shit—came out a few moments later (okay, more like five to ten minutes later), smiley face painted back on just right. This was what they were going to do—they had a sister resort literally right next door—she genuflected with a smile like she was Vanna fuckin' White— and it had some very nice ocean-front rooms that were available—I'd be transferred there—I'd retain the use of the privileges at this resort for the entire week, if I'd like—and, here's how they got me to ease up on a sistah pronto—for my inconvenience, they would comp me three days to be used the *next* time I came back here to Jamaica and to this resort!

Hmmmn, three days…suddenly things weren't looking that bad…but hold up—tell me more about this other resort, I inquired. I mean, what kind of place was this; what kind of amenities did they have? The Jamaican woman with her dark, perfectly smooth skin beamed a seductive smile as she leaned in toward me, knowing that she now had my full attention. Here's the thing—this place next door was really nice—and (she just *knew* from looking at me that I'd love this part), they had a nude side and a prude side…

Nude side! Did someone say, nude side!?! My mind raced for a nanosecond—let me see, does that mean nude honeys flocking by my open window as waves crash onto the white sand every few moments, I wondered??? Hmmn, tell me more, baby, don't let me interrupt you…

Pause—since y'all don't know me that well yet, let me say this right up front—I ain't never been no exhibitionist…okay? I mean, this brutha is comfortable, *very comfortable* with his body, but that doesn't mean I get into this naked, holistic, I'm down with nature, let my shit swing free, au naturel shit! I've been to a nude beach before—hasn't everybody? Actually, when I was growing up in NYC, my parents took me to Jones Beach one day and I wandered over the dunes to this spot where there were a whole lot of wrinkled white women with droopy tits and men with little dicks prancing around like spring chickens! Please! That didn't do shit for me. But the thought of being here, in Jamaica, for God's sake, with (and here's where my mind began to fuck with me)—Rachel-looking honeys with dark and lovely hair, big butts, luscious tits—and a smile that would kill a brutha— well, I guess I was just gonna have to take my chances. After all, I was on vacation. No problem, mon! Right???

Thirty minutes later I was in my new room—ocean-front, nude side— facing palm trees, white sand, aquamarine blue water, and honeys with bare titties and shaved pussies wandering by my open mutha fuckin' window, I kid you not—king-size bed, mirrored ceiling (hello!?!—did they create this mutha fucka just for me???) Things in an *instant* were looking up. Note to self—call travel agent when I get home—curse the bitch out, then send her a dozen roses! Three extra days for my trouble? Oh, no trouble, really! OH HELL YEAH! Trey in 'da house! Time to get naked, y'all! For real!

TWO

The breeze that swept in from the island beyond the beach made it perfect. It was one of those light breezes, the kind that tickles your hair and ears as it passes by, not enough to billow dresses or shirts, but with dazzling stars overhead and the full moon shining off to the west, its light cascading down onto the shore, illuminating palm trees and hammocks, it felt wonderful. The open-air disco was packed, every inch of planked floor taken up with frenzied dancers. The thump from the bass of rhythm and blues was intoxicating as men in comfortable linens and sandals, women clad in short or long flowing cotton skirts and tank tops, glistened with sweat as they twirled and dipped. The beat took control, forced movement even to those uninitiated as drinks flowed from well-stocked bars with efficient tenders.

Vince Cannon, Jr. sat on a high stool and watched from the teak bar, a long, solid, rectangular thing of beauty that butted against one wall facing the moonlit beach. A tall frosty drink with an orange and pink paper umbrella lay untouched in front of him. He observed his best friend, Trey Alexander, twenty yards away as he danced with his woman. He was overdressed, as only Trey could be—tapered, off-white sport coat and matching flat-front trousers; a thin, yellow V-neck sweater and loafers—a dark oblong stone attached to a cord that hung from his tanned neck. Trey was happy, that much was obvious. The way he smiled, his teeth shining from one end of the open-air room to the other. His woman—dressed to a T in a thin, slinky white and red dress with leopard skin-like patterns, high-heel red sandals, hair pulled back in a bun—threw her head back and grinned as Trey spun her around, a thin, sinewy arm outstretched toward the high ceiling. They danced well together, Vince had to give them that—the way they moved in sync with each other—it was as if Trey would silently telegraph upcoming moves to her without so much as a nod or a wink, and she would follow suit. For a moment, Vince felt a surge of pang in his heart—not jealousy—he was never jealous of Trey—they had known each other far too long and were way too close for that. Looking out over the sea of bodies, an ocean of writhing forms that undulated like the sea in a storm, he felt a twinge of envy—that said it best. And mid center, almost in the glow of spotlights and lasers that cut through the smoke and perspiration that hovered like mist above the heads, he spotted those two and locked onto their flow. The look that she had on her face right then, at that very moment as Trey reached for her, pulled her into him, and wrapped his arms around her half bare back as he kissed her longingly—yes, that look— when he pulled back from the kiss, her lips wet from him—said it all. At that moment Vince felt envy. Because of that look and the feeling that undoubtedly accompanied it—the feeling of pure, unconfined love—the way their eyes locked onto each other's and no one else's—the sea continued to bubble and foam, but to the two of them, theirs was an island, deserted save for them two.

Vince shifted in his stool, took a swig of the tall drink—felt the breeze as it ran past his glasses and through his dark hair, the ceiling fans turning out of sync to the D.J.-spun music, something from an old Prince jam, back in the day—old school, when he was still funky. The kind of groove that made you want to grab onto anything in sight and move—Vince lifted his glass in a toast as he caught Trey's eyes and grin. Trey made a fist and raised it above the crowd in triumph before returning his stare to the object of his affection. Vince shook his head with a laugh and then, as he caught her eye, smiled and nodded—yes, girl, you've found someone special, I know, and I can feel your ecstasy even from here.

Then it happened—just as the music downshifted and bodies parted, making for dry land—relief from tired feet. Trey and his lady came out of a spin and slowed down, his arm finding her waist, she leaning into him and them turning a quarter turn more before stopping on the floor. Vince watched silently, almost missing that moment as he signaled the bartender for a second drink. Trey kissed her silently, let his lips fall onto hers and absorb the warmth and love as they touched. And then he wiped the sweat that had formed on his head, hiked up a pant leg with a quick tug of his hand, and sank to one knee. It was a move that did not go unnoticed. Patrons were caught off guard; the music's beat moving way too fast for this to be part of any dance ritual. Even she played it off for a brief moment, laughing for a second before the smile was wiped from her face as she looked down and saw the seriousness in his eyes. Trey was staring up, child-like, the gaze unbroken as he searched her face slowly, memorizing each curve of her smooth dark flesh. He grasped her hands lightly; Vince sat up, then got off the bar stool as the music subsided—the D.J. realizing that a special moment was about to unfold—and so he panned the sound down until the room was still—the disco patrons pointing, looking, whispering, conversing and wondering about what was about to go down. Trey cleared his throat as Vince, mesmerized by the sight of his best friend on bended knee, took a step forward, wondering like the rest of the crowd, what was going on?

"Baby," he said in a soft, yet deep voice. It carried across the room and out onto the veranda by the beach. "I've reached a point in my life where I honestly can't go on." Trey paused for a moment. He was smiling up at her, noticing the beads of fear, not sweat, that formed at her brow. "It has taken me a long time to get to this place—and so, I've got no choice but to share with you what is on my mind…Okay?"

She nodded silently.

"Baby. You make me so incredibly happy. I can't begin to describe this feeling that I've had since you've entered by life. It's a feeling that I've never experienced before. I keep waiting for this dream to end—for me to wake up and sigh, but you know what? This is no dream. This is real—you are real. And this *love* I feel is real."

Vince turned his head away for a second to catch a glimpse of the crowd, wanting to know if anyone else in the disco was hearing what he had heard. He watched several couples as they nuzzled close to one another. Then he shook his head again, as if to say to himself and the others, yeah, this definitely is one hell of a dream—to think that my man Trey here would even *consider* this kind of thing...I mean, we're talking about *Trey*...but then he saw the tear that meandered down her cheek and heard his best friend continue.

"And so, I want to say this to you in front of all of these special people here tonight, as God is my witness—that I love you with all of my heart, and from this moment forward, I pledge to be *faithful*...

Vince had been standing by the bar, elbow on the teakwood when he processed those simple, yet powerful words. His pulse increased as the full realization of what was happening began to take shape. He shuffled forward, his eyes not able to leave the scene unfolding before him.

"I pledge to be the kind of man that is worthy to stand beside a queen." Trey was sweating, but he made no move to wipe the perspiration that layered his bald head. Vince blinked.

"And so, baby, tonight, I ask you the most important question I've ever asked anyone in my life..." The pang hit Vince again, like a left hook—it was a straight shot to the heart—powerful in its delivery. He watched as Trey's woman stood there—the look on her face said it all—that completeness that accompanies true, uncompromising love. Vince blinked again.

"Baby, I need to know whether you will be with me forever." Vince felt weak; the sweat that had popped out from his own forehead now meandered down his face through his closely cropped beard to his chin.

"Need to know, baby, whether you will consent..." Trey's hand was emerging from his pocket with a velvet-covered box. The onlookers had been dead quiet, wanting to grasp every breath, every single utterance. But when Trey produced that box there was a collective sigh that drifted throughout the room. He let go of her hand for an instant, the box was opened and at that moment a beam of light hit the diamond that was nestled inside, sending fragments of light out from the epicenter like a pebble that is dropped into a still lake...

Vince swallowed hard, felt the thump as it pounded against his chest, and blinked again…

✖✖✖

…And opened his eyes to a new dawn. He was lying on his side—a thick, pale-blue comforter pulled up to the nape of his neck. He sighed, felt his heart beating loud and clear as it danced inside his entire being. He lay still, feeling the pulse in his neck as it throbbed before settling down into a normal rhythm. He scanned the room with his eyes—first to the dark stained wooden chest where his wristwatch and thick college ring lay, then sweeping to the left and the half open bathroom door that lay beyond. He caught a glimpse of a shiny light blue bathrobe hanging from a hook on the inside. A ceiling fan turned sluggishly in the morning. An oversized tabby cat lay belly up and motionless at the foot of the bed.

Vince turned over, felt the large, thick mattress yield to his weight as he shifted to his left side and came face-to-face with Maxine. She lay on her side facing him, her eyes shut, dark, shoulder-length hair partly covering her soft face, the rise and fall from her breathing visible as the covers shifted around them. Vince loved to watch Maxi sleep—there was something so serene and peaceful about the way she slept, never twitching or moving—no, Maxi found her place and gave in to the feeling of slumber—allowing herself to be drawn into that deep, dark hole, swallowed up and consumed—a place that held not fear for her, but comfort. Maxi loved to sleep. And Vince loved to watch her doing so.

But now, on the cusp of this new day, Vince felt sadness that permeated his soul, replacing the feeling of tense anguish that had forced him from his dream state. It was slowly overtaking him—he could sense it, feeling it, the way a cup of hot tea that is drunk seeps in to stiff veins and warms one's entire being. Melancholy and downheartedness spread from limb to limb as he stared at Maxi's prone form and thought of yesterday…

It had turned out to be a wonderful day. Saturday morning spent running errands—bill paying, picking up some much needed supplies for the studio, stopping by the grocery store—much later in the afternoon, heading home, showering, changing, and then riding over to Maxi's. He took the Harley—his baby, as he was fond of calling her—a 1998 Fat Boy—purple with gray tank and trim—a custom paint job he had gotten done two years ago from a bike shop down in Richmond. He loved that thing, especially the way it sounded—88 cubic inches and Vance & Hines pipes that gave it a low growl and rumble every time he tapped the throttle. The source of much banter between Trey and him—those pipes. Trey swore his were louder. Of course, Trey was always dissing Harleys. That began last year when he went out and spent $25 grand on an Indian. Now it was Indian this and Indian that! The two of them loved to meet in Old Town in the evening after work, where the rest of the Hogs congregated, Trey pulling up with his beast, all of the Harley dudes stopping their conversation in mid-sentence when he downshifted to a stop—"damn, that's a fucking *Indian*!" Didn't see many of those on the road—not at all! Yeah, Trey loved that aspect—even got a tattoo on his arm—became an Indian convert for life! Vince had to admit, the bike was beautiful. But he was sticking with his Fat Boy. Nothing wrong with his girl. She would give that Chief a run for his money any day of the week!

Maxi had a small but cozy condo in Arlington by the courthouse. Vince had shown up in jeans and an oversized sweater that complemented his rich, dark skin; leather boots and jacket that together with his six-foot frame, muscles, closely cropped hair, and beard made him look rugged in a sexy kind of way. Maxi had chosen a pair of Levi's jeans and black stretch blouse that showed off her curves—she pulled her hair back and tied it down; her thin, black-rimmed glasses were set against her smooth dark face. One thing about Maxi—she didn't use a lot of makeup. Didn't have to. And Vince dug that. She splashed on some perfume, grabbed a light jacket that accentuated her leather boots, and was good to go.

They took her car into downtown around eightish—they felt like being around people but not in a dense crowd—so they settled on 18th Street Lounge for drinks—a hip, diversified place with acid jazz, plenty of comfortable couches, and great cosmopolitans. They found a nice quiet table by the window overlooking Connecticut Avenue, ordered a round of drinks—Maxi was a Johnnie Walker Black and Coke kind of girl—and Vince was in the mood for a cosmo. They talked about their work week and family—Maxi was from Detroit and spoke to her family regularly; Vince still had his parents here in D.C., and visited them each week, faithfully for Sunday night dinner unless he was out of town on a speaking engagement. The conversation flowed freely and without force—they had been dating for about a month now—so they were still circling around each other somewhat cautiously, but their guard had been lowered.

Maxi really liked Vince—for the first time in a long while she was with a man who didn't play games and was sincere. That's what defined Vince for her more than anything—the fact that he was so genuine. Most of the men she had dated since arriving here in D.C. two years ago were full of themselves and so full of shit. She had gotten so tired of the dating scene—going to the obligatory happy hours with her friends from work, meeting these knuckleheads—good looking, yet overly confident men who talked a big game, but always turned out to be nothing but big liars! Then she had met Vince one night at a book signing at the Barnes & Noble in Georgetown. He had seemed almost too nice at first—confident, but not cocky, intelligent, smooth in his delivery, the way he listened when she spoke—that was clearly his gift. He made people think as if they were the only one in the room when he spoke to them.

Vince immediately had dug her, too! They had exchanged small talk after he signed his book—*Finding Nirvana: A Quintessential Game Plan for Success*, for her. She had hung back—letting the rest of the small crowd that had gathered to hear him speak go to him—but they dispersed quickly. Afterwards, he had come up to her—remembered her name—that got him points big time—and asked her to join him for coffee at the Starbucks down the street. Nothing big, no fancy first date—just good conversation at a coffee shop on a Sunday night. She recalled how he had laughed when he told her that she had eyes just like Nia Long—and stroked her arm—he had sent chills down her spine when he did that. They had been seeing each other ever since.

For Vince—especially in the beginning, she had him all excited like a kid in a candy store—Maxi was something that didn't just come along every day. She was intelligent, had a good job, good looks—not a show stopper—not a hottie as Trey was fond of calling them—but, and most importantly, she was drama free—a definite keeper, no doubt about that. He liked her because he saw the potential in her—it was there during that first night at Starbucks as they chatted over Chai tea and Grande Latte—a future with this woman. In Vince's line of work as a speaker/writer—he met all kinds of women day in and day out. Most, unfortunately, were just not all that. On the surface they were nice—but if he dug down, like a diver who dips below the surface of the waves, he'd find the baggage and the drama that inevitably would push him away. Life was way too short to settle for stuff like that. And so, Vince would move on…thanks, but no thanks.

Last night, sitting there at 18th Street, sipping a really good cosmo, watching Maxi with her Nia Long eyes smile as they conversed, he felt good. That was the one thing about Maxi—they had fun together. Wherever they went, whatever they did, whether they decided to stay in and watch a DVD or go out to a club, they had fun. Good conversation; Maxi was not the kind of girl that bitched and complained about stuff—instead always upbeat and fun. And she was one of those self-sufficient women that impressed Vince a great deal. They weren't in each other's face 24/7, and Vince appreciated the fact that Maxi gave him his space. She had her own friends here—she hung with her girls and had some after-work activities—she was taking a photography class downtown and was really getting into that—spending a great deal of her free time with a Nikon slung around her shoulder, speeding up New York Avenue, M Street, or Wisconsin looking for stuff to shoot. If they didn't talk on the phone every day, no one had a melt down. *How refreshing*, Vince thought!

After 18th Street they went across Connecticut to Dragonfly, an eclectic sushi bar that played house and trance, and displayed weird Japanese-produced cartoons on its white walls. They finally got a table around eleven, ordered quickly because they both were famished—some really good sushi and sashimi, along with Coronas to wash the food down. The place was packed—a wacky kind of crowd in terms of dress and demeanor.

But neither Vince nor Maxi paid much attention to them—they talked some more—Maxi about this project she was working on at her job—she was a software developer for a small, Internet start-up in northern Virginia. Vince listened attentively as she described some of the problems they were having with their code. Then shifting gear, talking about stuff in general— what he was working on in his studio. She had only gone there one time and watched in quiet awe as he worked on his art.

A little after midnight, they drove to The Saint on 14th. A relatively short line had formed—they waited patiently for the bouncer to let them in. Maxi recognized a few folks—they exchanged their hellos. Once inside, Vince grabbed a Corona and water from the bar and found Maxi standing by a pillar overlooking the dance floor. The Saint was packed—mostly young, college-aged folks—black, white, Puerto Rican, Spanish, even Asian up in the spot this evening. The music was bumping, and after a few minutes of small talk, Vince led Maxine to the crowded dance floor. A rapid-fire succession of really good songs came on—nice grooves and bass lines—hip-hop and rap by Jermaine Dupri, Ja Rule, and Ludacris—they danced close together, Maxi moving with rhythm the way most black girls do—like they invented the shit! Vince grinned and followed along, doing his own thing, enjoying the feeling of grooving with his lady. They had fun and got a bit sweaty as they lip-synced along with the tunes—Jay Z., R. Kelly, and an upbeat new jam from Mary J. Blige that Maxi just loved.

By 1:30 a.m. they were heading home, Vince driving, Maxi a bit tipsy from the Black and Cokes she had downed. They made it back to her place without fanfare. When they arrived, Maxi kept the lights off and shades parted, turned on the stereo to WKYS—they were playing slow jams with little commercial interruption this time of night. She giggled softly as she shed her clothes, leaving a trail of her evening's attire around the living room. Vince watched as he undressed quietly. And then they lay down, right there on the carpet, and made love, stray flecks of warm street light-ing creating patterns across their bare bodies as they moved, not as quietly as they normally do—Maxi's inhibitions being smothered by the liquor—a warm, comforting feeling overtaking her and causing her moans and squeals to increase in pitch and intensity. In the background, Aaliyah's sultry voice: "...Rock the boat, rock the boat, work the middle, work the middle...change position...stroke it for me, stroke it for me..." Vince was enjoying himself completely, taking pleasure in the sensation of being inside her, making love to her face-to-face, eyes locked on each other as they thrust their flushed bodies against one another, Maxi's head resting in Vince's hands. They both felt the passion build and then spill over, over-flowing, Maxi crying out, and Vince covering her mouth with his as he joined her in orgasm. After a few moments of feeling the afterglow that comes from this kind of exquisite release, they lay together on the carpet for a while in silence, listening to the radio, old school songs with soulful melodies keeping them both awake. Some time later they climbed into her bed and fell asleep, Vince spooning Maxi tight, his hands covering her breasts as if they were precious gems, his pelvis nuzzling against her nude flesh, as they both settled down into that deep, dark hole, and dreamed very different dreams...

✖✖✖

In an instant, things can, and do change forever. And in this case, it was that image of a moonlit beach somewhere in paradise, Vince's buddy on bended knee—a sea of bodies huddled together, bonded in kindred spirits by this special moment—the look between lovers that would forever be frozen in time by his psyche—knowing unconditionally and without question what that look meant. What it said inescapably to him and to the others: this was the *one*. And that is what changed it, in an instant, for Vince. That knowing—that guttural, instinctual knowledge that is visceral—Maxi was *not* the one. In a sense, Vince had known that from the moment he had laid eyes on her at the book signing. Maxi was a wonderful girl—that was not even in question. She was successful, independent, and possessed good looks...also, brave, clean, and reverent! But at the end of the day, what mattered most to Vince, was that she was not the *one*. He did not love her. Not today, not tomorrow, and whether or not he *ever* could was also not the question—the fact remained—Vince needed and desired to possess that quality which he saw with pinpoint clarity in his mind's eye. Pure, unconfined love—the sea may continue to bubble and foam around him, but to Vince—he desired a woman that to the two of them, theirs was an island all unto themselves...

And so, on the cusp of this new day, Vince once again felt the sadness infuse his being until he was consumed, his soul overflowing with its soup. He rose quietly, began the shower and stood underneath, letting the hot water batter his face and neck, massaging his shoulders and back like a masseuse. He tilted his head back and closed his eyes, not from the spray, but from the injury, the wound that was smarting. He stayed in there a very long time, going over it again and again in his mind. But Vince was no stranger to the verse that rang inside of his head. This was a movie, which was all too familiar. He knew deep down inside exactly what he was searching for. Always hoping that he'd find it around the next corner, the next one who came along and smiled at him. He'd give each one a chance—that much was for sure—Vince, the kind of man who saw beauty in everything that crossed his path. It was there somewhere, if you just knew where to look and nurture it. But, sadly, at the end of the day, beauty alone did not bring him any closer to finding the one thing that kept him rising every day with a smile to continue his journey—true, unconditional love.

Vince dressed quietly, careful not to disturb sleeping Maxi. He said a silent prayer for her and for himself—that the two of them would one day find the happiness and the passion that made life worth living. That special something that was beyond the thrill of money, sex, or power.

Before he left, Vince bent down, kissed Maxi on her cheek—she opened her eyes briefly, those Nia Long eyes watching him silently for a moment before she smiled, turned and stretched like a cat before saying: "Vince Cannon, Jr., you were soooooo wonderful last night..." Then she closed her eyes and purred back to sleep, contentment etched into her face like an ancient hieroglyphic. Vince remained for a moment more, watching her settle back down into that place, free of fear and strife, before he climbed onto his motorcycle, still damp from the morning dew, and rode off into the rising sun.

THREE

First mutha fucking thing I did—no, it was not unpack! I slipped out of my clothes, took a quick shower to erase that airplane/travel smell, oiled my body up with lotion and sunscreen until my shit shined like I was in a bodybuilding competition…threw on a pair of designer swim trunks, a wifebeater, black sandals, the bad-ass sunglasses, and headed out to case the joint! Wanted/needed to get the lay of the land so to speak—I began with the open-air dining area where another lavish buffet was in full effect. I breezed through there like a movie star, head and chin up, fly shades on, pausing at the bar to order a Sangaster's original Jamaican rum cream. The dude behind the bar filled my glass with ice and rum cream—I took one sip and suddenly felt the reggae vibe as it coursed through me. Yeah, mon! Strolled around the grounds, checking things out—a few restaurants and bars—a 24/7 gym with free weights, Nautilus machines, duty-free store, tennis courts, squash courts, and basketball courts. I passed by this fine, Jamaican honey dressed in tight, pink bellbottoms and a matching, low-cut top that proudly displayed her lovely tits in a push-up bra! She said, "Welcome to Jamaica, mon!" I smiled while eying her lovely curves.

"Just get in?" she asked while sneaking a peek at my chest tattoo.

I smiled back. "Yes, I did—and loving it already."

"Prude side or nude side?" she inquired while resting a hand on a waist that was no more than 20 inches in circumference.

"Nude side," I exclaimed proudly, thrusting my chest out like it wasn't any big deal to me! "You gonna come by for a visit?" I asked all cockily.

"Oh," she said, softly, licking her lips seductively, while thinking of a comeback. Her nametag was attached to her flimsy top, but I was having a hard time concentrating on the lettering. "*They* gonna have fun with you!"

"Bring it on, I ain't *scared*," I replied, pronouncing the word "scared" like "scurred," the way Mystikal, that fly rapper from the dirty South had made famous in his song, "Shake Ya Ass." Then as she walked away with a wave of her hand, I was left standing there observing the rise and fall of her ass cheeks in those pink pants, thinking to myself, who were *they*????

✖✖✖

A sign proclaimed, "Nude Beach—No Photography!"—alrighty then! I had walked down to the beach, prude side first, observed the folks: black, white, Europeans, Jamaicans, and whatnot, baking in the sun. Folks looking good, I'll give them that. Walked past the watercraft—sunfishes, catamarans, kayaks, bicycles with huge oversized tires for use in the water, past the Jamaican locals who were selling wood carvings, trinkets, and jewelry on tables under the shade of palm trees—past rows of white plastic lounge chairs filled with holiday travelers lying out and just chillin'—until the sign slowed me in my tracks. Okay, here we go…

Walking past, I observed a number of couples lying about, butt-naked, mostly white, a few with some pigment to them, bushes neatly trimmed. Saw a lot of silicon—you can guess that I'm a self-proclaimed expert on titties, and can spot the fake ones a mile away—not that I'm mad at any of these ladies—do your thing, girls, I am not complaining!

The beach curved slightly to the left, and at the end off to the right was the pool area. I walked up the stone steps slowly eyeing those around me. The place was fairly well packed. A bunch of people, all butt-naked in the pool and by the swim-up bar area, checked me out as I strolled by looking for a place to chill and lay my things. I was still in my trunks and tee, but that was about to change. Through my shades I observed tits and much ass, and a few dicks, how could I not, and I have to say, I was impressed (with the tits/ass, *not* dicks)! Most of the women here, okay, let me say this—close to seventy percent, looked damn good! I mean, there were a few pigs; I'm not trying to be mean, just telling it like it is…but seriously, most looked okay in my book. The women were an average age of 35 I would say, and in good shape. The guys on the other hand were a mixed bag—some were fit, but most were carrying around a beer gut. I saw one brutha over by the edge of the pool sitting alone, lost in thought. Didn't pay him any mind. Past him was a hot tub the size of most YMCA pools. In the middle, was a whirlpool that currently held about eight people, all shaded and drinks in hand or close by.

I slowed my already unhurried gait and found an empty lounge chair with a good view of the festivities. My heart was thumping as I readied to remove my clothes—not from fear, just the opposite, in fact—my mind churning from the possibilities…endless possibilities. Bending down, I pushed my trunks off like they were an afterthought, balled them up and lay them under my lounge chair. The tee came off next and finally the sandals. Mutha fuckas were watching, I kid you not—oh yeah, they were checking a brutha out—seeing what I was packing. Now, let me stop you right there and keep it real. I ain't no Long Dong Silver; I ain't packing eighteen inches, no, not hardly—but my shit is nice; I've been told I've got a beautiful cock. It doesn't hang very low, but trust me, when you awaken that bad boy, that mutha fucka inflates to a nice length and solid girth. And that's when the ladies hold their hands over their mouths (and pussies) and exclaim, "Oh *my!*"

I glanced left, spied the towel rack behind the enormous hot tub that was empty this time of day. I casually walked to get a towel, shades on and nothing else, my shit tight and on-point! Mutha fuckas were clocking me, I swear to God, as I grabbed a towel and slowly sauntered back to my lounge chair. A few smiled, but most just *watched*…I gave them the show I knew they were craving…doing a very slight pimp roll, you know how *we* do…not too much leaning, but head up and chest out; stomach tight; arms flexed; a thick, expensive Breitling Blackbird on my left wrist; a thin, sterling silver bracelet on my right, each jingling as I walked by the onlookers. I flung the towel on the chair without missing a single stride; cut to the right and pool edge, bent down, one arm on the concrete and in one fell swoop, I gracefully entered the cool, refreshing water. Took my shades off for a moment as I submerged my head, then quickly returned the shades 'cause it was bright out! Swam over to the swim-up bar, mutha fuckas making a path for me as I went. Yeah, buddy! Who's mutha fuckin house is 'dis???

The bartender was a dark, Jamaican brutha with black shades on and a Hawaiian shirt. He was bopping to reggae music emanating from a boom box behind the bar. I nodded to a few couples as I edged over, ordered a rum punch, and said a few "Waz ups" to people who eyed me cautiously. Got my drink, took a sip and touched the bartender fist-to-fist, giving him dap. I nodded. "Respect," he replied.

I turned and headed back to my chair, being clocked by the women as I went. It felt real good. I mean, I hadn't been here five fucking minutes yet and mutha fuckas already knew I was the shit! Wait 'til I tell Vince about this. I suppressed the thought of running back to my crib (a.k.a. my room) and hitting him on the cell—naw, not right this minute, I'm a bit preoccupied…

A woman with a tight-ass body; deep, rich tan, and big titties that were obviously fake ('cause they defied gravity) was sitting on the side of the pool, while her man (or *someone's* man) massaged sunblock into her skin. He ran his hands over her neck and then descended to her mammoth tits, massaging those bad boys like he was a professional masseuse! She smiled as I went by, drink in hand.

"How you doing?" she asked in a New York accent, looking down over the rim of her designer shades. One leg was up on the edge of the pool, her perfectly shaved pussy was within spitting, or, more accurately, licking distance! The guy continued his massaging like he was on a mutha fuckin' mission! I was not mad at him!

"Livin' large. How YOU doing?" I replied as I stopped in front of her.

"Everyting irie." She threw her head back, long brown hair flowing down her back as she laughed.

"Oh, I didn't know you was Jamaican. Damn, girl!" I laughed with her and sipped my rum punch. Damn, that shit was good! "Listen," I continued with a grin, "if dude here misses a few spots, holla at me…Okay!?!"

"Damn," he said, removing his oily hands from her erect nipples to look at me for the first time, "been here five minutes and already working!" He was grinning; not that I was worried. Dude had a gut and would need a few of his buddies to take me on.

"You know how we do!" I responded while eyeing his honey. One thing about me, one lesson I learned long time ago—look a woman straight in her eyes when you're talking to her. Don't half-step it—none of this glance here, then there—no, that shit just doesn't work. Women love a brutha that will stare them down while he's speaking. Look right through them to their very soul. That shit turns them on. And that's just what the fuck I did—stared straight through this honey while I spoke to him, as if I was saying, "Yeah, I hear ya, my man, but it's *you* I'm talking to!"

"Just might do that," girlfriend replied, licking her lips in a way that I just know was done automatically, without conscious thought—like her lips had a mind of their own and were speaking directly to me.

"You do that, sweetie! I make house calls, too!" Taking another sip I moved on, feeling her eyes as they followed me away. I left the pool damn near the way I entered, with a flex from my upper body and a quick exit. I strolled back to my chair in slo-mo, drops of refreshing, pool water cascading down this bronze brutha's tight body, the weight of dozens of pairs of eyes upon my firm back, sexy tattoos, and ass. My package was right, ya hear! And it felt so damn good to finally be in Jamaica, on vacation. Yeah mon!

✖✖✖

You know, y'all, I probably should pause right here to explain something for a moment; a clarification, so to speak. One thing you need to know about me, when it comes to women, I am colorblind. I love women—all colors, shapes, and sizes. To me, the only color that matters is the color pink—that's 'cause pink is the mutha fuckin' universal color, ya hear? It may be different shades on the outside—white, black, dark, light, and whatnot, but it's all pink on the inside. Now, some of you are haters—you know who the fuck you are—yeah, I'm looking straight the fuck at you! And you're sitting there thinking to yourself, well, Mr. Big Shit over there thinks he's too good for sistahs. Naw, it ain't that at all. Don't get me wrong. I love me some sistahs. I've got nothing but love for my Nubian Queens; I'm serious. But at the same time, give me a blonde with big tits and a black girl's ass and I'm all in that shit, ya hear me??? I mean, I'm gonna fuck that pussy like it is going out of style. So don't hate 'cause I push up on a Latino, an Irish chick, or some corn-bread country thing with big tits and thick hair. I ain't mad at any of them. Long as they got pink pussies…I'm there! Enough said!

By now, the sun was beating down and attacking this black man's body from all angles. Okay! Every few minutes I had to leave the confines of my deck chair and immerse myself in the pool. My bald head was roasting, regardless of the sunblock that I had massaged into my skin. I had refreshed my drink a few times too many I thought already—them rum punches were kicking into overdrive, let me tell you. And it wasn't even dinnertime yet!

I had (mistakenly, I would later learn) taken a book with me to the pool. I rarely got time to read during my "normal" life in D.C. as an attorney and with my busy social commitments, I mean, hey, who has time to read? So I was viewing this vacation as a way to play catch-up on my fiction. I had picked up a few paperbacks at the airport Barnes & Noble, and the one I had begun on the plane now lay on my lounge chair. It was funny, but I had noticed that I was the only mutha fucka in the pool area who had brought a book with them. The book I was reading was entitled "White Teeth" by Zadie Smith—a black woman from England. I remember her from Oprah or some show like that saying something like, "Readers were better than sex!" I'm not sure what that was all about, but I'll tell you this—the book was all that! Anyway, I gotta give this chick credit—the book was damn good—I had totally gotten into the first seventy-five pages on the flight over, so naturally I took it to the pool with me…I mean, why wouldn't I? It had a distinctive red cover with bold white lettering on it. People kept glancing at the book when they walked by me. At first I assumed it was the cover that they were attracted to. Then I realized they had never seen a book in a nude pool area before!

For the first few hours I think I got about two pages read! I kept restarting the same paragraph over and over again. Just when things got interesting (in the book, that is), something in or around the edge of the pool would catch my eye! First it was Ms. Biggums with her Massage Daddy. Then I caught some activity over in the whirlpool—a few honeys were playfully splashing each other's tits with water while their boyfriends watched enviously! I mean, it was getting hard for a brutha to concentrate! And the heat was fucking with me. I decided to take a break and head to my room—time to put on another coat of sunscreen before I baked to a crisp, and see what I could see on the beach side…but before I left, I went to take a quick cool-me-off soak in the whirlpool, and do some quick intros to get acclimated…

I climbed in and swam over to a few folks. Most nodded in approval as I joined them. The fellas and I exchanged some "Waz ups," while the ladies looked on. I caught each of their gazes in turn and said, "Waz up, girlie? My name's Trey," or some variation of that theme as I got out of harm's way from one of the powerful whirlpool jets (that shit was way too close to a brutha's asshole, know what I mean?!) Small talk was exchanged: Just get down here? How you like it so far? (Wink, wink, grin, grin!), you know, shit like that, yada yada yada. A well-built middle-aged guy named Randy from Indiana with a shit-load of tattoos over 70 percent of his body was doing most of the talking at this point. He was loud, but totally cool. His wife, Cathy, was by his side, large tits with pierced nipples and a large tattoo on her navel plunging below to her shaved cunt (I didn't know it was shaved at this point, but trust me, I'd find out this little tidbit later on that evening.) Randy and I vibed right off the bat—he was a regular guy who dug his wife and was down here chilling and enjoying the sunshine, T&A, and reggae music. They owned a restaurant and tattoo parlor back home. I was not mad at them!

"Dude," Randy said in between sipping some kind of banana cream concoction that looked like cum, but smelled a whole lot better, "are you down here with the Lifestyles crew or what?"

"Hmmm?" I responded. Not clear on what he was talking about, I thought maybe he was referring to the condom company—perhaps they were down here doing a promotional bit, giving out condoms and shit…free samples? For real? Hit a brutha up 'cause I'm gonna be fresh out by nightfall!

"Lifestyles," Randy repeated slowly, moving closer to me to be heard over the two honeys across from us who were cackling like a bunch of black crows. "You know, the group?"

"Naw, never heard of 'em." I shook my head while watching the dark nipples surrounded by large, jiggling tits of the brunette in front of me.

"Lifestyles," Randy repeated, "they're a kind of national swingers group— they sponsored a trip to this resort for the past two weeks—you lucky guy, you happen to catch the tail end." He smirked as he checked my reaction over his dark sunglasses. His wife, Cathy, on the other side of me nuzzled against my side and her hand found my leg. She had a smirk of her own.

"You don't say?" I said, smirking now myself. At this point, everyone was just a smirking! "Swingers? You mean most of these folks here are…" I gestured with my hand while lowering my voice and keeping one eye on Ms. Jiggletits, letting the sentence finish itself.

"Oh, yeah," Randy said with a harsh laugh that I would learn was his trademark. He grinned and showed his teeth. "Oh yeah!" he said again while Cathy stroked me, knee to thigh. *DAYUM*, I thought to myself. Things keep getting better and better in this piece!

✖✖✖

I walked slowly back to my room, taking the scenic route. There was a tarmac-covered walkway that cut behind the beachfront and in between the two-story rooms, nicely littered with tall, shade-covering palm trees. A few chickens ran through the underbrush as I sauntered along, following the meandering path, my sandals and sunglasses the only articles of clothing on my person. This actually was a totally new feeling for me—the sense of ultimate freedom, the sun on my exposed flesh as I walked, talked, shook another's hand, took a sip, slept, read—feeling totally relaxed and at ease, as if I was a natural, and had been doing this for years. I admit I was a bit tired (jet-lagged, in a sense), but the rum had kicked in and mellowed me the fuck out. I felt the reggae vibe inside of me—it coursed through my limbs and veins even though I heard not a thing—but that was irie with me!

There were a few couples, mostly nude, who walked past me, nodding their welcome. I nodded back, caught up in my own little world. Farther down the winding path was my room. My room key jiggled on an elastic band around my dark ankle. The path wound to the right. I followed, suddenly noticing up ahead a splash of pink. My senses were heightened immediately, on alert—Defcom Three! It was the lovely Jamaican honey I had spoken with hours earlier. In her elbow she carried a metal vase filled with what appeared to be champagne. Two wine stems were curled between long, slender fingers. She was heading toward one of the rooms and it took her a moment to look up and see me. She smiled when she did, glanced down slowly (admiring the package), and then back up. We had stopped at the same place, in front of the same room. My room!

"For little ole me??" I said, batting my eyelashes.

"Doesn't look that *little* to me," she threw back. I laughed as I watched her observing me with a grin. "Just our way of welcoming our newest guests to our fine resort," she said, thrusting the vase in my direction. Her eyes sparkled, and I concentrated on them for a moment, letting my gaze seep in before lowering my stare to her wonderful dark breasts that strained against her tight, sequined bra. Barely covering that was her pink top. I glanced at her nametag—Jackie.

"Well, Jackie," I said, feeling myself growing, enlarging, engorging as I imagined that luscious, tight black ass covering my face and neck, tasting her luscious juices, "it's a good thing you are here," I remarked, lifting my sunglasses onto my bald head so she could see my eyes. I leaned against the doorframe and set down the champagne. Her face changed to a frown as if something was out of place.

"Is something wrong?" she asked, pursing her full lips together. She had on a pair of dangling earrings that sparkled in the sunshine. A thin, matching chain was around her neck. Complementing these, her belly was pierced with a single, knobby piece of silver that winked at me every time I peered down. Trick of light, I presumed.

"Most definitely there is, Jackie," I responded in my serious, attorney voice that I had perfected over the years. "And you arrived not a moment too soon. I was just getting ready to call the front desk." I unlocked the front door with my key and pushed on it, held it open, and gestured for her to enter. "Please, this way." Jackie looked at me for a moment; her eyes sparkled as she sized me up, trying to see if this was a ruse, a ploy to get her into my room. She stood her ground until I lightly touched her thin waist, ran my hand along her back and exerted small amounts of pressure. In unison, we crossed the threshold to my room. I set the glasses down on the dresser as her gaze swept around my room. I held the cold bottle of champagne by the neck in one hand, letting the cold drops of ice water run down my wrist.

"I'm sorry, Mr. …" Jackie paused.

"Alexander, Trey Alexander," I responded lightly, taking her hand in mine.

"Mr. Alexander then. Is it something with the accommodations?" she asked, twirling around the room to take in its contents. I used this moment to admire her beautiful ass. Two perfectly shapely balls packed in light cotton—I was about to lose my mind! She glanced toward the bathroom, then popped her head in for a brief moment before returning to the side of the bed. I let a moment of silence invade the space before responding.

"Isn't it obvious to you?" I asked, brushing my dick with the bottom of the bottle. The coldness made me flinch. I noticed that Jackie followed my movement with her eyes before responding.

"I'm sorry, Mr. Alexander, you're going to have to be more specific."

"*Indeed*," I said while moving within a foot of her body. She was quite beautiful. I glanced down into her sparkling eyes, which held my attention for a brief moment. "Actually, Ms. Jackie—the problem simply has to do with this bed." I paused while she looked over my shoulder to the well-made bed. She moved around me, tested the bed with her palms before straightening up and staring at me helplessly.

"I fail to see the problem. I'm sorry."

I sighed for effect. "The problem, Ms. Jackie, is *you*. And the fact," I exclaimed, moving within six inches of her, "that *you* aren't in it…"

In the time that it took for her brain to process that information I was on her in an instant—my mouth covered hers as I grasped her small waist, bringing her the remaining distance to me. She struggled (if one can even call it that) for a brief moment—her arms raised up to my smooth chest as if in protest—but that ceased as my tongue slipped into her mouth. She groaned as I wrapped my arms around her waist, taking a handful of ass with me along the way. My cock was fully hard now. I pulled her closer to me. Felt her warmth as she came to me, body-to-body, my pulsating dick against the thin fabric of her pink pants. My free hand went to her mouth, touched her face and traced the outline of her lips while I continued to kiss her. She pulled back.

"I…can't…" I gave her enough air to breathe before I ran my tongue around the edge of her mouth and then stuck it back between those divine lips. She licked at me, playfully at first, hands on my arms, as if trying to decide whether to pull me closer or push me away. "Seriously," she said, exhaling forcefully. I glanced down and could see her hardened nipples. I stroked her waist with my free hand, moved it up her belly, lightly touching the piercing before moving to the sequined bra. I ran a fingernail across the material, tracing circles over the exposed top part of her breasts, kneading the flesh with my hand. She moaned again and pulled me into her as she sucked at my tongue. Yeah, there wasn't going to be any further problems with this one…

My hand grabbed her tit and squeezed. Felt those lovely mounds of flesh. She let me squeeze and probe for a moment before she pulled back and ran a hand through her hair.

"Trey—seriously, I can't be doing this. I mean, I work here and…"

Okay—under normal circumstances I might have been tempted to hear this honey out—you know, it can be quite amusing to watch a woman all turned on and shit, pussy dripping, nipples distended, trying to explain why she shouldn't sit on your cock right this particular minute—but today's situation was different. Here I was fifteen-hundred miles from home, in paradise, I swear, standing, with not a stitch of clothing on, beside a beautiful, young Jamaican honey, with my dick harder than high school trigonometry— I wasn't about to let this shit get out of my sight! Nope. So I did what any playa in my situation would do. I pushed up on her; she backed into the closet that housed my clothes and the room safe—until there was no place left to go. I ran a hand down to the valley between her legs and felt for the damp space. It was there, just like I knew it would be. I bent down and kissed her harder this time, taking her upper lip in my mouth and sucking at it like fruit. I kept a firm grip between her legs, my fingers outlining her pussy through the fabric of her tight pants. My dick was pushing against her leg and she couldn't help but feeling it. But on the off chance she had a case of tactile insensitivity, I reached for her hand and brought it to my cock. She inhaled quickly and looked down as her fingers curled around the girth.

"Dayum! That..." she said, swallowing hard, "is one beautiful piece." (See what I mean, I don't make this shit up!) Her hand grasped the shaft and she squeezed it before moving to the head, which she massaged with her palm. "It's sooooo hard!"

"Yes it is, Jackie...look what *you've* done." I smiled while pulling her toward the bed. The door remained open. She glanced to the right as I let go of her hand. She went to the door and slid it shut, locking the bolt in place. I lay back on the bed, checking myself in the ceiling mirror the size of the bed itself. Slowly, Jackie moved back to the bed, a seductive grin on her face. My right hand held the champagne bottle while my left slowly stroked my cock.

"Damn," she exclaimed again, "boy, does that look good. *You* look good. Tattoos and all!" She leaned over me, one hand on the bed, and the other on my stomach. She lightly fingered my nipple, ran a hand across the newest acquisition—the star tattoo, spent a bit of time tracing the outline of the Indian Chief and his headdress—all the while licking her lips seductively. My cock was throbbing; I swear I could see that bad boy pulse!

"Stop playing, girl," I said with a smile. She tugged on my dick, ran a hand down to my clean-shaved balls, lightly squeezing the sacs. I managed to get the bottle open without too much effort. The cork flew off with a loud pop, startling Jackie, who bent down on the mat in front of the bed. Grasping my cock with her hand, she moved closer, lightly blowing on the shaft of my dick with her mouth. My eyes rolled back into my head, but not before I caught a shot of her and myself in the mirror. Damn, wish I had brought the camcorder! Her tongue touched the tip of my dick—she traced the outline of the head, leaving a trail of saliva in its wake. Then down the shaft she went, holding it gingerly, licking it like a child does a lollipop, reaching the base and my balls, giving them a playful tug before heading back up along the other side. With two wet swaths she painted my cock with her tongue, and I was not mad at her! She was incredible. I groaned and held her hair in my hand.

Jackie moved up, kissed my tight stomach, probing my belly button with her tongue before plunging her mouth, without warning, onto my dick. Her warm, wet mouth met my cock and it slipped inside effortlessly, parting lips and pushing her tongue aside in one fell swoop. She kept going down, my hand tightening the grip on her hair as her mouth took as much of me in as deep as she could. I hit the back of her throat, she paused, her eyes opened and she stared back at me, my cock buried to the hilt in her mouth. I took the bottle and ran it across her face. She flinched, but didn't lose any dick in the process—and then she went back to sucking.

"Yes, love, you are so amazing. My God!" I said, as she sucked my member with abandonment. "Shit, don't make me come yet, you hear me?" My words were lost in the sounds of her sucking—slurping, slobbering, suckling sounds that made me twitch in excitement. I reached behind her and unfastened her bra—her tits were fantastic—ripe, soft melons of fruit—small dark nipples that stuck out at attention at least a half-inch. I tugged at them with my fingers, squeezed the fruit, enjoying the feeling of natural flesh (no preservatives or enhancements here)—just 100% woman, soft, spongy titties that fit in the palm of my hand as if they were custom made just for me. Dark lovely nipples, hard as I twisted them between my thumb and forefinger.

"Your cock tastes so damn good!" Jackie exclaimed while leaning back to admire my taut, reclining form.

"You like?" I asked, knowing the answer. "Do I taste good, honey?" I said all baby-like. She glanced up and smiled, her eyes twinkling as she watched me.

"Oh yes, I love the way you taste, the way you smell. I could do this all day."
Hmmn, now there's a thought!

I took the opened bottle of champagne and poured some of the cold liquid onto my cock and stomach. Grabbed her hair and steered her mouth onto my champagne—laced cock. Have some bubbly, I thought to myself with a chuckle! She took it like a good woman should—without any complaints, and sucked me like this would be the last time for both of us. I felt myself stirring—that feeling, that pre-come sensation, which begins like a storm, deep in the bowels of my balls. I forced her off of me.

"What?" She had this look of disgust on her face, but I stroked her face and bent forward kissing her hard on the mouth.

"Jackie, you need to slow down. You are gonna make me come *hard* if you keep that shit up."

"Isn't that the whole idea?" she said, standing up and slowly unbuttoning her pants. Dayum!!!—Can I package this bitch up and take her ass back with me to America like Vince said, I wondered. I watched her perform a slow striptease. She slid her pants down, revealing a black g-string.

"Turn around," I ordered her. "Let me see that ass." Jackie was a soldier who knew how to follow orders. She turned seductively, her eyes never leaving mine. Her ass came into view—and what a sight it was to behold. Better than my wildest imagination: her black skin was flawless, without marks or blemishes. I held those lovely mounds of flesh, kneading them in my hands. Ran my fingers over her skin and to the cleft, then downwards, following the thin cotton fabric that disappeared as it reached around to cover her cunt. My fingers moved down and under, feeling her mound, which was wet with pussy juice. I pulled the cotton to the side, slipped a finger around her sticky pubic hair and then plunged inside, Jackie sucking in a breath as I entered her. A moment later I pulled a glazed finger out. She turned to me as I held my finger in front of my face, examining it for a quick second like a doctor would, before slipping it between my lips. I closed my eyes as I did this, for effect, of course, sucking on my finger hungrily before opening my eyes and offering up a single moan.

"Girl," I said, my eyes locked with her, "you taste *so* fucking good." Jackie's face melted right there. Putty in my hands!

I pulled her on top of me, running my fingers over her ass, tight thighs and knees before up her back and around to her lovely tits that hung inches from my face. I took each one into my mouth, licked them all over, paying special attention to the nipples that I bit lightly. She threw her head back and closed her eyes—I know this because I was watching her in the mirror—watching that ass that rotated as I massaged her cheeks, thrusting my hardened dick into her pelvis.

"Come here, Island girl. I've gotta taste you before we go any further."

I grabbed her by the waist and lifted her off of me, my muscles twitching and flexing as she slipped beneath me. She spread her legs and my mouth went to her stomach for a brief moment, ran a tongue over her belly before tracing a swath down to her canyon. Her dark skin glowed under me—then I came to her pussy. It was lightly covered with dark, curly hair. Her pussy lips were not overly big or fleshly, but she possessed a meaty clit that was presently elongated. I teased it with my mouth, blowing on it and then brushing against it with my closed mouth. Moving downward to her thin pussy lips, I twisted my head around her thighs, pressed my nose in between her wetness, then stuck my tongue straight out and let it forge a path. It found her cunt; she opened up with a groan as I probed her—licking voraciously as if I was a man who had been without a meal for far too long. Jackie was incredibly wet—her pussy juice meandered down her thigh before I caught it with the edge of my mouth, sucking the juice in and swallowing the liquid down in one gulp.

My head shook from left to right, her clit in between my lips. I tugged at it with my teeth as her lower body—hips, thighs, and ass—all began to shake. I had been eating her for thirty seconds before Jackie grabbed her ass with both hands, lifting herself off the bed as she came—her whole body trembling as she groaned.

"Ohhhhhhhhhh fuuuucccckkkk!" She pushed my head—then ground it into her pussy—grabbed my ears and tugged left and right—commanding my mouth to do her bidding, and I obliged like the good soldier that *I* was. When she was fully spent she collapsed exhausted onto the bed and held my head on her pelvis. My face was covered in love juice, nose and cheeks glazed with her cum, but I was happy, so damn happy.

"Damn, Trey, you suck a lady good!" I moved up her body and kissed her on the mouth. She sucked at my lips, tasting her own sap on my skin. Then I pulled away, leaving her wet and spent on the bed, legs parted and pussy pulsating in the afterglow of orgasm, as I went into the bathroom to grab a condom.

Trey came back ready for action. My shit was on-point and hard—encased in latex. Jackie had this glazed look on her face as I went to her. Her legs lifted and her arms found my ass as I guided my cock into her pussy. I threw my head back and sighed heavily as I entered her—what a lovely feeling, her tight pussy constricting around my cock—pulling me, sucking me inside. When I hit bottom I paused, kissed her lips and enjoyed the feeling of *not* moving, but just feeling us as one, me in her, her around me—her cunt tight like a glove, my cock buried to the hilt like treasure, deep inside of her fine body. And then I began rocking in and out, slowly at first, pulling that bad boy out until just the tip was showing, then plunging back in and to the hilt, hitting rock fucking bottom. My hands found her ass and grabbed her cheeks as I fucked her, first slowly with long, full strokes that made her shudder, then with increased momentum until I was jackhammering that hole, squeezing her ass as I pummeled her, the entire bed shaking as I worked my shit, Jackie grasping my ass as it blurred in a frenzy of fucking above her—her eyes rolling back into her head as I worked my shit!

"Yes, yes, yes, yes, yes, yes, yes…" she repeated over and over in time to my fucking. I could feel her cunt constricting on the down stroke. Her heart was beating; I could feel it, too, when my chest slapped against hers, our sweat mingling as one. I paused for a moment, placed my weight on top of hers, and hungrily devoured her mouth and lips.

It was time to turn her over. "Let me take you from behind, baby," I said gingerly. She grinned—no problem, mon!

I placed both hands on her ass, glanced up at the ceiling, loving the scene that met my gaze. Her head was turned to the side as she watched me. I rubbed my cock against her pussy lips and ass before slipping inside again.

"Oh, yeah," Jackie moaned as I quickly found my stroke again. I began rocking against her once more, all the while glancing down to watch my large cock appear and disappear among the lips of her cunt. Jackie was moaning now, her chest flat against the bed, her entire back and ass a thin layer of beaded sweat that turned me on as I moved. I continued to fuck her, ass cheeks firmly entombed in my hands. I slowed slightly, rotating my ass and hips so that my cock pushed against her cunt walls at different angles. This drove her crazy. She began to hum and moan, softly at first, then exploded with a yell as she came again, her hands reaching between her legs and rubbing the blur of flesh that was my cock and her pussy. In seconds I felt the storm winds blow and combine to hurricane strength—rising from the base of my cock, a tornado about to unleash its carnage. I raked her back with my fingers, twisting a nipple before gripping each cheek in hand and pumping with abandonment as I worked that thing, grunting as I went along. My head tilted back and I caught a glimpse of myself as I came—a split second of pain on my face as I unleashed into Jackie's lovely orifice—then the scene was erased as my eyes scrunched shut and my brain went on auto-pilot—I slammed in and out of that cunt as I continued to come—my mouth hanging open and something completely unintelligent emerging from my lips. The storm passed slowly. I felt myself spasm over and over again, Jackie's hand reaching up to grab my ass and pull me into her. I collapsed on top of her as the tide ebbed away.

"Oh my God!" I exclaimed, panting like as asthmatic, "that was so fucking awesome, I…" and then, for once, I was speechless, unable to continue the discussion. I rolled off of her and kissed her silently. She nodded to me and snuggled against my sweaty frame. No words were needed. Thank goodness. For once, I didn't have the energy for simple speech or dialogue.

FOUR

t is amazing what the smell of coffee will do for some people. For Vince, a good cup of coffee was worth the trip across town any day. He knew all of the coffee shops within a twenty-mile radius by heart. And he made sure that part of his daily ritual included stops at the various coffee establishments—sometimes only for a minute or two to sip at a cup in between tasks—other times, for longer periods of time, perhaps an hour or more, where he would take a legal pad or his laptop, prop up his feet on a chair or on one of the comfortable couches and get a solid amount of work done or creative energy expended, all the while the scent of ground coffee permeating the air.

He took the Fat Boy across the Memorial Bridge, which was relatively quiet this time of morning, down Constitution Avenue past the State Department, Fed, White House, and museums, then across Seventh Street to Independence Avenue. He loved riding through D.C. on his bike—the feeling of the open air and wind against his dark skin as he rode—something he found hard to describe. In a vehicle, one felt contained—protected—cut off—in a sense, from the road and what was occurring there and beyond its boundaries. But on a bike, you were immersed in the totality of the road and the elements—the smells, rolls of the earth, and its vivid colors—all of this, the very essence of life that jutted right up to the asphalt, suddenly attacking all five of your senses—the wind and sun on your face and skin as you rode; the vibrant colors not filtered by a windshield, doors, or windows; sounds not dampened; scents and odors, raw and uncut. Riding through D.C., Vince experienced people in their natural element as he roared by, catching them, photograph-like, stuck in mid-stride, mouth hung open, a dribble of syllables trickling out as he leaned into a turn and passed them. Owners walking their dogs, sniffing the air and barking as he moved swiftly past. Up Independence, beyond the various government buildings, the Capitol on his left as he increased throttle to maintain speed up the hill, loving the Boy as it hummed and groaned beneath him, the Vance & Hines singing their rumbling bass tune in the morning air.

Into Capitol Hill and near the various restaurants and bars like the well-known Hawk and Dove that catered to Hill staffers, and finally to the place which he frequented several times a week. Cosi stood at the corner of Pennsylvania Avenue and Third Street, S.E., a two-story building with a bunch of tables and chairs that were arranged around the entrance. Vince pulled to the curb and cut the engine. Several patrons glanced up from their Sunday paper—*Washington Post* or *Times*, as he climbed off and strolled in. Cosi was one of those places, especially this Cosi—hard to describe—but you knew it when you waltzed in—it was the airy, down-home, comfortable feeling. Call it atmosphere, or what have you, but it was something about the colors—warm earth tones—tall ceilings, eclectic art, which hung on brick walls, small tables and oversized couches, and heavenly smells that kept Vince coming back. He strolled up to the counter, helmet and gloves in hand, and smiled at the black girl behind it.

"Hey, beautiful, how goes it this fine, fine morning?" Vince asked, placing his helmet, a black half-shell littered with dozens of stickers—some nasty, but mostly just funny—a thing with bikers—on the counter.

"I'm fine—kind of tired—hung out last night with my girls until real late," she replied, moving a strand of hair from her eyes. "I knew I shouldn't have, but damn, there were some hotties up in that joint!"

"Yeah, where was this?" Vince was pulling out his money from his jeans, and she was ringing him up, all without either of them uttering a single word concerning his order—they both had done this many times before.

"This club up New York Avenue called Dream. You should see it, Vince;

I swear to God, this place is so awesome!" Her face lit up as she genuflected and spoke. "I mean, check this—this place has like, three levels, this huge dance floor, and two or three VIP sections—I can't remember which!" Vince grabbed his cup of coffee from a dark-skinned brutha with dreads whom he merely nodded to behind the counter.

"Yeah? Haven't heard of Dream."

"Oh my goodness—you need to check this place out. Vince, I swear! It is soooo nice. Wood and nice shit everywhere—I mean, this brutha, Marc Barnes, the owner, same guy who did Republic Gardens, put it down! Spared no expense. Everyone was up in that spot last night. All kinds of Ballers! I've never seen so many fancy rides in my entire life!"

"Really, Lisa?" Vince sipped at his coffee but made no move to leave.

"It's okay, go drink your coffee in peace. I'll holla at you later." The young girl shooed him away. He grinned at her, placed the change in a tip jar on the counter and headed for the couches in the back by the small bar.

There were only a few others in the bar this time of morning. He nodded to a white couple as he passed by, and found a comfortable couch that faced the front counter. He planted himself in it, placing his things on the low coffee table in front. Vince sipped his cup, flipped through the paper that lay splayed on the table. Nothing much of interest caught his eye. He used this time to kind of decompress and chill—to just think—Vince was a cerebral kind of guy, his mind was always ticking, things coming and going, information catalogued, stored away for later reuse—calculations and processing being conducted in the background, even during conversation. Vince noticed everything about someone—his or her dress, hairstyle, the fact that one eyebrow had been plucked a bit more than the other—the way a shirt hung just a bit too much over a waist. His eyes took in his surroundings, his mind trying to block the inevitable out of his brain, but it was hard—Maxi was there, just below the surface, and if he wasn't concentrating, or if he let his guard down for a second, she came bubbling back up to the surface. He let thoughts of her and last night invade his psyche; there was a part of him that missed her already, wondered if he was doing/feeling the right things—but then he shook his head—No, he was not going to do this to himself—he knew what he was doing and feeling was indeed correct. And so, he pushed Maxi and their short-lived relationship back down, below the waves, and concentrated on the present, the here and now.

Vince got comfortable, took off his leather jacket and leaned back. Then he decided to run to the bike and grab his artist pad from his saddlebags. He always carried around a pen and pad of some sort—there was just too many things swirling around in his head that he needed to jot down. And on mornings like this—Sundays, when there were few people up and about to bother or interrupt his thoughts, he worked best—whether composing his thoughts for an upcoming talk, or just sketching out some ideas for an upcoming art project.

He returned to his favorite couch, took a swig of coffee, leaned his head back, and stared at the ceiling. The piece he was working on at his studio required finishing. Vince was a sculptor of sorts—he took casts of people's faces, arms, or legs, made plaster castings and then painted over them. He had stumbled into this by accident years ago—he had always been creative and loved to spend hours as a kid in his parents' garage creating art from things most people threw away. He had come up with some pretty creative pieces and his parents encouraged him to take art classes and hone his skills. So he did—first, drawing classes, then on to pottery, which really didn't hold his fancy, although he did enjoy the feeling of working with clay and other malleable material. Then, almost by accident, he came across a plaster of Paris cast of a person's face—it was laying around in a bin at his art school class—his teacher told him he could have it. Vince took it home, stared at it for hours—the contours, bas-relief in each square inch of tissue—and then he had pulled out his paint set, grabbed a brush, and used his oil-based set to paint alternating swaths of color diagonally across the cast. When he was done he had a vibrant, colorful mask—something that came right out of an African tribal headgear—his teacher, parents, and friends loved it—his dad had had it mounted and framed; it still hung in the foyer of his parents' home today, a reminder to all of their son's creativity.

Over the years Vince had experimented more and more, pushing the envelope, not content to stay within the confines of "normal" art. What was normal anyway? The whole idea of being creative, the essence of why he did what he did—was to create things out of random nonsensical things—order out of non-order, and make them beautiful. And so, Vince discovered his passion—spending time in his studio huddled over castings of strangers or acquaintances—adding touches of paint and shadow to create something unique—a mask that told a story.

When he had first met Maxi a month ago, he had wanted to do a casting of her. She had agreed—reluctantly, at first, until he brought her to his studio and showed her his work. The process, while not painful at all, was messy, and required that a gel-like substance be applied to the subject's face and neck. You then waited for it to harden, and then it was pulled carefully off. Maxi was lukewarm to the idea of being his subject, but warmed when she saw his collection of masks—a assortment of colorful faces—caught in various expressions and effervescent shades of tint—some hot and exciting, like the subjects and their personas, others more subdued, shadowed, or darkened. Vince had done her casting about two weeks ago. The thing laid on his worktable at his studio, yet remained untouched. He had sketched out a number of color schemes to match her moods and facial makeup. But his work and travel schedule had precluded him from spending any real time on completing it. With the sudden turn of events—he wanted and needed to bring closure to this piece. One thing about Vince—he was constantly sketching out new designs and seemingly wanting to move on, but he hated to begin a new project until the others were completed. And now, as he sat in Cosi sipping his coffee, he thought about Maxi and the plaster cast sitting on his worktable surrounded by newsprint, and resigned himself to bring this part of his life to completion. Finish it, he told himself, and then mount it with the others—a collection of faces, many past lovers, those, he was sorry to say, who took *his* test, and had failed…

✖✖✖

The sound of the door opening caused Vince to glance up. He had been deep in thought for God knows how long—perhaps thirty minutes or longer. His pad laid on his lap—a woman's face, neck, and shoulders coming to life—the woman from his dream—Trey's woman—Vince attempting to capture those eyes, the look that spoke to him—the one that reached right under his skin, tugged at his insides until it reached the inner sanctum of his heart, and pulled on his heartstrings... Get it down on paper, if it were indeed possible, what was in his mind's eye. Difficult—even now, for the image was fading from the confines of his mind, evaporating like misty tendrils of smoke which are exhaled, and drift off into the ether.

A tall, dark-skinned woman stood at the counter—a shock of thick, black hair emerging from the back of her gray baseball cap. Dark-blue sweat suit and Avia running shoes. She ordered; turned for a moment in his direction, looked to the far end of the bar—where Vince was the only patron left; the white couple had left over fifteen minutes ago—and then turned back. Got her coffee—a tall, steamy thing, and a bagel, and took a seat at a table across from the long counter. Vince noticed a University of Maryland tee shirt underneath as she unzipped her jacket and pulled it off, placing it on the bar stool across from her. Vince spotted her long, yet muscular arms—they weren't overly big—but he could see that they were firm and without any traces of fat. She glanced in his direction for a moment, looked past him and then down to her bagel. Vince watched her as she began to eat it, forgetting for a brief moment the pad that lay in his lap. The woman pulled off her cap, took the ponytail holder out of her hair and shook her head, letting her hair go wild before tying it back up. The woman had high cheekbones—they were edges to her cheeks, and Vince found himself staring at her—not out of disrespect, or because he thought she was overly beautiful—but because she had an interesting face, and it intrigued him from an artist's point of view. He glanced down at his pad, flipped to a fresh new page, and quickly began to sketch the outline of her face, a dark face with well-defined angles to it—distinct lines that cut from the V in her chin to the edge of each cheek. Vince became mesmerized by the symmetry, the geometry of her face, glancing up as he drew—trying to capture and put on paper a vein of an idea that had formed in his mind...

She caught him staring. It was one of those awkward moments when a woman senses someone looking at her and glances up to find someone staring back. At that moment, Vince had been paused from what he was doing, mechanical pencil hovering over the coarse paper, as he stared at her chin, focusing on it and its lovely curves. Then onto her eyes, which in direct opposition to her strong facial lines were soft, oval orbs that shined when she paused from eating, and wiped away a crumb that had stuck on the edge of her lip. Yet, Vince wasn't smiling—he missed the opportunity for that fleeting connection—that microsecond of dead space—silence—before two people whose eyes had locked, turn away. For Vince, his mind was on a different plane—he was studying her, the way a scientist researches a particular subject—no, that wasn't quite right—in this case, that clinical detachment was missing—he was intrigued—and quite interested—but his intentions were about to be misunderstood.

The woman glanced down at her food and continued eating. She was reading something, Vince couldn't tell what—she sipped at her coffee—letting small mouthfuls of the hot liquid go down her throat with a single gulp. She was young. Vince put her in her early twenties—twenty-three at the most. She, obviously, was in good shape. He could tell from the way she sat, her fit and trim arms, the lines of her neck—he hadn't paid much attention to that before, but now as he looked closer he could see. Yes, she had wonderful lines in her neck—those ropy muscles and tight skin—sinewy, that's the word that came to mind as he stared at her neck—the way those lines plunged downward, toward her breasts—his eyes descended, following the lines, observing the rise of flesh, her breasts, pausing for a moment, watching with a sort of clinical detachment, then moving down again to her stomach and waist. She glanced up again, caught him staring for the second time—her stare remained—longer this time than the last. Vince, his mind in artist mode—mind racing, thinking of the possibilities here, yet once again on a different level than hers. Vince smiled at the woman—but her facial expression did not change. She shook her head—it was ever so slight, and then she went back to eating and reading.

Vince glanced down at the sketch on his lap. It was crude—in no way, shape, or form would anyone think this was a "good" sketch, but it wasn't meant to be—Vince was capturing ideas—the lines and symmetry of her face—chin and cheeks—the yin and yang between her lines and those soft, oval eyes—wondering all the while how to imprison all of this in plaster—confine it forever in the construct of a colorful mask. His mind sprinted with the possibilities—like a freshwater stream that rushes over slippery rocks—yes, he could use color here and splashes of hue there—he looked back at the sketch, and made a few impromptu notes. And then suddenly, he was rising from the couch as he finished the last of his still warm coffee in one gulp, slung the sketchpad to the table, and walked over.

She glanced up as he stopped in front of her table. Vince was smiling.

"Hello," he began, "I don't mean to bother you, but I've been sitting over there…" He gestured to the couch. "And I just wanted to say hello." He paused for a split second and then stuck out his hand. "I'm Vince Cannon, Jr." The woman watched him silently. Her eyes broke away from Vince's stare and glanced at his dangling hand. She let it hang there for a moment before speaking.

"I noticed you staring. Didn't your mother tell you it isn't polite to stare?" There was no trace of a smile on her face, nor a warming to her voice.

"Yes, she did, as a matter of fact." His hand rose a few degrees; he tipped his head to the side a bit and smiled, letting her see all of his perfectly straight white teeth. "So, touché! Now, are you going to sit there and not show this brutha any love??? Gonna just let my hand wave here in the breeze? That is definitely not right, is it?" He laughed. That got her to soften up just a bit.

"I'm Desiree." She placed her palm in his and they shook.

"Desiree. That is a lovely name. I apologize for staring. It's just that you have a very interesting face. Has anyone ever told you—you have wonderful lines?" Vince crossed his arms to his chest. Desiree cocked her head to the side.

"Wonderful lines? I'm not following." She put her coffee down and gave him her full attention.

"Yes, wonderful lines. Your face is very angular. I find that very distinctive—not something you see every day. The symmetry of your face is *intriguing*."

"Intriguing?" Desiree asked.

"Yes. And then there are your eyes—which are in direct contrast to your hard lines—I don't mean hard in a 'bad' way. On the contrary—your eyes have a very soft, almost dreamlike quality to them. Very distinctive."

Desiree stared up at Vince, watched him for a moment while she said nothing. She nodded slowly.

"Thank you."

"May I join you?"

"Listen, Vince," Desiree said touching her ponytail, "you seem like a nice guy and all, but here's the thing. It's Sunday—I'm sitting here chilling, enjoying the peace and quiet of the morning, not trying to get into anything with anybody and…"

Vince cut her off with a wave of his hand. "Oh, let me stop you right there—I'm not trying to pick you up or get your number. Actually, I'm an artist—what I am interested in doing is getting you to pose…"

"Listen, Vince," Desiree said again, "can I keep it real with you?" Before Vince could answer, she continued. He dropped his arms to his side and exhaled slowly. He could already see where this was leading. "See, this is what I never will understand—bruthas and their wack-ass pick-up lines. I mean…" And here she began to raise her voice. Lisa, leaning behind the counter, was watching her silently like a hawk. "I don't get it. How come bruthas can't come up with anything *original*. Damn! You know how many times this week *alone* some dude has offered to take my picture, hook me up with a portfolio, or make me a star! Damn, you bruthas need to get some original lines before you step to a sistah!"

Vince had listened to her without comment. He stood still, letting her say her piece. He was calm—no reason not to be.

"Obviously, you have the wrong impression about me, but that's cool. I was not trying…" Vince paused, then sighed. "You know what?" He shook his head forlornly. "Desiree, have yourself a very nice day. Sorry to have disturbed you."

He turned on his heels and went back to his couch. He picked up his sketchpad in one fluid motion—didn't even pause in mid-stride as he grabbed it, and exited out the side door. Desiree was watching him silently. She finished the last of her coffee, scrunched up her cup and got up to walk to the trash can, shaking her head. Lisa observed her, elbows on the counter, a women's magazine splayed in front of her. Desiree passed her by, paused, and then turned.

"Tell me something, sistah," she said to Lisa. "Are you feeling me on these wack-ass niggas who ain't got no game?" Lisa nodded sullenly. "I mean, I got nothing against a good-looking brutha who can converse, but if he doesn't have any rap, don't even waste my time!"

"I hear you," was all Lisa said in response.

"Listen, I'm not trying to disrespect these bruthas out here. But, damn, do you have to use the same ole tired-ass lines? 'Oh, baby, let me take your picture—you know you look like a model?—let me hook you up with my cousin, he's a director for MTV. For real.' Damn! All I want to do is come in here, get my coffee, sit here and chill, relax, not deal with that bullshit, you know?"

Lisa backed up from the counter, closed her magazine, and eyed Desiree carefully.

"I do hear you, my sistah, and it's none of my business, but you did come on kind of strong with my man there," she said, gesturing to the side door. Beyond the glass, Vince had finished donning his gloves, goggles, and helmet, and was firing up his Harley. The two watched him in silence for a moment.

"Please, he's just as tired as the next…nice-looking and all, sexy smile, but please! Get some brand-new lines!" Desiree grabbed the remains of her half-eaten bagel and tossed it in the trash. She donned her jacket—zipped it up and turned to leave.

"Like I said, none of my business," Lisa said in Desiree's direction, "but you might want to take a look at that over there," she said, pointing toward the far wall by the door. Desiree's eyes followed, stopping at a piece of art hanging on the wall. It was a mask set in the middle of an off-white canvas, with a thick, black lacquered border—with vibrant splotches of paint adorning the face—red, orange, green and blue spots that covered the surface—underneath, a reddish, brown stain that seeped below the surface and gave it a phantom-like sheen. The expression was one of joy—the lips were upturned, and accentuated—the eyes—although holes, burned bright with touches of brilliant acrylic paint—an eyeliner of sorts that rimmed the orbs and brought the mask to life. Desiree stared in silence—gathering her stuff and without breaking her stare moved toward the piece. The beauty of the mask drew her in—its raw, surreal quality was poignant. In the distance, Vince gunned the throttle, let in the clutch and rode away, the low growl from his engine suspended, like particles in the morning air.

Lisa let Desiree get within six feet before speaking: "A moving and very powerful piece, wouldn't you say?" She eyed Desiree, whose entire demeanor had changed. "He calls that one, 'My Secret Redeemer.'"

"Who?" Desiree asked even though her body shivered with the recognition of the answer, which loomed directly in front of her own face.

"The brutha who just walked out of here—the brutha with the tired-ass lines." Lisa eyed her for a moment more and then turned toward the back, leaving Desiree to stand in front of the mask, and contemplate its meaning, and its maker, alone…

FIVE

Say what you want about a brutha, but after cutting a damn fine slice like Jackie, I had no choice but to sleep like a baby! I mean, Jackie and I had lain there a few moments after our lovemaking session, staring up at our reflections in the ceiling mirror, her finger tracing a meandering course along my sweaty thigh. A light rain had begun to fall—Jackie informed me that at this time of year, it rained on a regular basis for short periods of time almost every afternoon in Jamaica—usually for less than an hour. So, I closed my eyes, catalogued away this wonderfully delicious image of the two of us, legs intertwined, her sexy body covered with a thin layer of sheen, the afterglow that comes from being totally fulfilled and spent, her straight white teeth that formed a beautiful smile as she waved to the mirror while holding my wilted cock, and that pierced navel, which continued to wink at me as her stomach rose and fell from her breathing.

I awoke a few hours later. Jackie was gone and the rain had stopped. And I was hungry! Checking the Breitling, I saw the dinner hour was upon us. So I took a quick shower, washed away the remnants of lovely Jackie from my body, and put on some fresh, clean clothes after buzzing my head and face for the second time that day. I decided that for my first night at the resort I needed to look fresh—you know I had to rock a phat outfit just in case there was any doubt as whose house this was for the next five days. So, I decided to slip on (and leave unbuttoned) my light-colored silk shirt along with a pair of shorts. I rounded out this ensemble with my black sandals. Dabbed on this new cologne that I was totally feeling. Grabbed my rose-colored shades and headed out to dinner and the promise of an adventurous evening.

As soon as I rounded the corner and walked into the open-air dining room I heard my name shouted. I felt like Norm from *Cheers*! *Damn, it's good to be me!*

I found Randy and Cathy sitting with some folks at a large round table. Randy for some reason high-fived me, as if he already knew what I had been up to before dinner. Cathy winked at me as introductions were made. They asked how my first afternoon had gone. I leaned in to to Randy and quickly provided the high-level on my encounter with Jackie. I left out the juicy details, 'cause I'm just not one of those bruthas who kisses and tells—ranting and raving all over this mutha fucka about what went down. Never done that shit, at least not to casual acquaintances. Randy freaked out, began laughing really loud and patting me on the back. Cathy leaned in to participate, but Randy just shooed her away with his hand. "He's telling me about that real cute Jamaican he just fucked!" The rest of the table, men and women alike, bobbed their heads rapidly as if I was the man—like, damn, we've *all* been trying to get with that fine piece since we first got here…how'd you turn that out so damn fast???

The food wasn't bad at all. It was served buffet style—fresh fish that was blackened or grilled, jerk chicken (you can't go anywhere in Jamaica and not get jerk *something*!), roast beef, a lot of pasta, various cooked vegetables, bread, salads and whatnot on separate tables, and desserts. One thing about me—I had been on a low-carb diet for a few months now—not that I needed to lose weight, but I liked to look my best, and watching my carb intake allowed me to stay lean and tight. I had decided long time ago, I would not reach mid-life with a gut or paunch—oh hell no! I was not gonna carry no beer belly or anything other than a tight bod. So, I loaded up on meats and fish, left the starches and breads alone, grabbed a separate plate for a nice salad, and drank about three tall glasses of ice water.

About halfway into our eating, Randy leaned into me to explain the *rules* to me.

"Trey, it's real simple. You see something you want while down here, you simply ask. I mean *anything*. And here are the rules—no means no. And yes, well, that means hell yes!"

I decided to play dumb and to make sure I absolutely got this part down pat; that there was no confusion on my part. "You mean, with respect to these 'Lifestyles' folks?"

"You got it!" Randy ratcheted down his voice, which was a real stretch for him. "Me and the ole lady came down here last year for the first time—met up with the 'Lifestyles' folks. We were kind of curious back then—you know, we'd talked about it, the whole idea of swinging…" He bent forward and lowered his voice a notch further when he said the word, "swinging," then flowed back to normal volume. "We'd never actually tried it until we came here. And boy, let me tell you…" He let the rest of the sentence hang in the air, as if it didn't need finishing. His wicked grin said it all—use your fucking imagination…

"Yeah?"

"Oh fuck yeah—Trey, let me tell you, it's so fucking easy down here—you literally just *ask* for it. I mean, how much simpler can it be?"

"Are you serious?" I had been scanning the crowd—my honey radar had been sweeping and beeping non-stop since I'd sat down. Women had been walking by with their sexy-ass selves, most wearing something seductive— something you couldn't really get away with back home. But here, it was a different story, no rules applied, and so they strutted around in their see-through tops, titties half exposed, booty shorts that showed plenty of ass, lingerie and body wraps that left little to the imagination. All grinning to each other as they took a second helping of food, smiling at cuz as they went by, checking out the silk and the shades, admiring the tattoos that peeked out from underneath my Versace shirt; some of them undoubtedly had witnessed the package at the pool and were now *fans*—just recognizing a brutha! Yeah, I was smiling and nodding to most of them, letting them know that I was down while giving Randy my full attention—that I was approachable—don't be *scurred*!

"You're telling me I can just walk up to these women even with their man

55

around and ask them if they wanna fuck?" I had this incredible look on my face, like damn, this has to be a dream, or have I really found heaven? Punany heaven???

"That's what I'm telling you! And no means no, remember that—don't take it personally at all; but yes, my man, means yes!" Cathy giggled at that last comment. She knew what we were talking about.

"Damn!" That about said it all. I was anxious as hell to try out these new rules. I mean, here I was—six hours into my first vacation day down in Jamaica—in fucking paradise, and things were about to get *live!* "Bring it on!" I exclaimed to Randy. He high-fived me again. I laughed and high-fived him back for good measure! All the way *live!*

✖✖✖

Don't ask me how, but we ended up at this piano bar much later on that evening. We had been laughing and carrying on at dinner, until I suggested that we check out the rest of the resort and see what we could see—so we headed out, Randy, Cathy, and me, a few others that I had met at dinner in tow—a caravan of sorts, going here, then there, to the beach (prude side), the various shops and restaurants, the disco (but it was way too early for anything to be jumping off in there yet), tennis/basketball/squash courts, before making it over to the nude side and the hot tub. This was where (I was told) everyone went later on in the evening.

We shed our clothes and got in. The hot tub was packed—probably a good fifty or sixty folks in there. The water felt damn good. We found an available corner where we could chill and take in our surroundings. People were hanging out under the stars, drinks in hand, laughing and carrying on, talking among themselves, touching, feeling, probing, and kissing. I spotted Lance and Chris, the couple from Louisiana whom I had met on the ride over to the resort. They, too, had had their room switched here. Quick introductions were made, and I was mesmerized by Chris's wonderful tits. They were large ripe melons with dark, taut nipples. Her body was a tight package with a nicely manicured pussy. Randy wasted no time and asked if her tits were real. Chris proudly proclaimed that she had just gotten them done less than six weeks ago. Everyone was impressed. They really did look life-like, I have to say. Randy then asked if he could touch them. Chris was fine with that. So we all got a turn squeezing her newfound friends, and let me tell you, those puppies were nice! Lance stood around all proud, and I could see why. I was not mad at him!

A few minutes later, Randy and I found ourselves on either side of Cathy, who wasted no time reaching for our cocks and stroking us to hardness under the water. My fingers quickly found her shaved pussy while Randy played with her pierced tits. Small rings were on the ends of each nipple. Randy tugged at them playfully, while I finger-fucked her in the water. Cathy arched her head back and came with a grunt as Randy kissed her neck. Cathy then returned the favor by taking my cock in her mouth. A few people turned, and conversations paused to watch this delicious act in the making. I lay back on the side of the hot tub, water dripping from my dark body while this chick took my dick in her mouth. It felt damn good. Randy was egging her on: "Go on, girl, take that snake in your mouth!" I just closed my eyes and enjoyed the moment. A friend of Cathy's came over to interrupt us, a small woman with dirty blond hair and perky tits; saying something about how good my cock looked from over there, and proceeded to take over, deep throating a brutha! I grabbed her wet hair as she sucked me, then Cathy moved in and together they licked the side of my shaft in unison, each taking turns putting the head in their mouth, licking and squeezing my balls, while a crowd of admirers watched the scene unfold. This to me was the ultimate, having two women servicing me at once. I have to say, as freaky as I can be, I've never been in a situation like this before—two women on me *and* in front of a crowd. It was a definite turn-on—the other guys who were paused in conversation, watching with envy as these two ladies went down on me, the look on their face said it all—you lucky bastard! Even the other women were checking out the scene—watching my dick get stroked, the shaft getting licked like a piece of sweet candy, witnessing it grow and blossom, my flat stomach, tight upper body, and tattoos moving/flexing as they worked me. And then I found myself pulling at Cathy's friend, a woman as yet un-named—she got on the edge of the hot tub and silently sat on my face. I reached for her perky tits and squeezed them while consuming her loveliness in my mouth. I tasted her sweetness, licked at her pussy lips and sucked her insides; Cathy grabbed my cock and jackhammered my dick with her mouth. The three of us; water bubbling underneath our hungered bodies that writhed as we touched, licked, and fed; bodies slicked with water, love juices, and desire as we played under a Jamaican moon; an envious crowd that longed to join in, but didn't dare interrupt this feast. I was the main course. And I had found heaven. No other way to describe it...

Later still we donned our clothes and made our way to the piano bar. A nice size crowd had assembled there, a few nice-looking ladies standing at the wooden bar being served by Jamaicans as folks sang along with the dreaded piano player. Randy sashayed up to the bar and ordered shots for the entire lot of us—a nasty concoction called a Flaming Bob Marley. Don't ask me what was in it—I sure as hell couldn't tell you. But I do recall that you had to light that mutha fucka on fire and drink it rapidly through a straw. Five of those later (Cathy made me do it!) I was feeling no pain. I was in rare form—I'm pretty sure of that—laughing, carrying on, and talking more shit than I normally do, but I don't remember the details. I know I didn't get up and sing, 'cause no amount of alcohol is gonna make me do that! But other than that, I can't say with 100 percent certainty what else did or did *not* happen. I do know this—at some point close to twenty-four hours since that alarm clock had shaken my ass out of bed in a world that now seemed blurred—long ago and far away—I managed to drag myself away from the Flaming Bob Marleys—"dragged" being the operative word here—back to my room where I collapsed in a heap on the oversized bed, and slept long and hard. Who knows what I dreamed of—it could have been of the lovely dark-skinned Jackie—her wonderfully unblemished ass that spoke to me and made my dick quiver; the two women who licked and sucked me while I lay back on the smooth tile under a colorful moon; or the hot Jamaican sun that sizzled my skin and turned me to a ripe, golden brown. All I know is that I slept, deep and without tension, the stress being sucked lovingly from me by new friends in a place that defied explanation but made life worth living—with a smile that I wore straight until morning...

✖✖✖

Day two! Mon, what can I say? The vacation had paid for itself twice over, and yet I hadn't even spent a full day on the island. What a place! I had assumed that I would enjoy myself once I got down here—I'm the kind of brutha who pretty well adapts to any given situation, like a chameleon that can change colors depending on its surroundings. I knew I was gonna have fun on this vacation—I mean, sun, fun, reggae music, rum, and dark 'n' lovely women! Come on! But what I experienced my first twelve hours on the island was not something I had planned for. But Trey always goes with the flow—never a problem, mon! When you think about it, most people have never (and will never) experience what I just experienced. So, what was it—was it my good looks, sexy body, engaging smile—seriously, was it those things that put me in these situations? Or was it my attitude, my carefree way of taking advantage of a situation and creating a very positive outcome? I thought about my encounter with Jackie: fucking her with abandonment, my caramel-colored body slapping against her lovely, chocolate skin until I had come *hard* in her cunt, and then onto the three-some in the hot tub, and how I had laid back while those ladies had grasped my shit, each one taking a fistful in hand and tag-teaming the head, licking me up and down as my eyes rolled back into my head from sheer fucking *delight*—how many people could only dream about something as wickedly good as that? And then I realized what I had always known—that there were those who meandered through life like a leaf floating in a stream; they were carried along by the current, never truly knowing where they would end up—and then there were those who *took* control—grabbed hold of the reins and told that pony where the fuck to go! That had always and forever would be me: directing, controlling, commanding, leading—and making things happen! Yes, Lawd!

So here I was, day two, sun streaming in through the open window, a

dark-skinned Jamaican with thick forearms and a colorful hat placing
wooden carvings on a table in between two palm trees, setting up shop for
the day. My head was pounding, like a hammer that smacked my bald head
every few seconds with no let up. Those fucking Flaming Bob Marleys. Did
I mention that I never wanted to see a flaming drink again as long as I live?
Did I? Please don't ever mention that brutha's name around me, again!
Okay?

So, I decided to deal with my hangover head-on, like a man. I pulled on
some running shorts and a tee shirt, threw on my Nikes and shades and
walked to the open-air gym. There I proceeded to sweat every drop of that
fucking liquor out of my body for the next thirty minutes. I ran on the
treadmill—two miles until I thought I was going to throw up or pass out,
whichever came first. But as I cooled down, I actually began to feel better.
My stomach was growling, a good sign. So I came back to the room, took a
shower, shaved, dressed, and headed to breakfast.

I ran into Randy and Cathy on the omelet line. I bitched about my hangover and how I was holding them personally responsible for all of the pussy
I had missed out on the previous night. Randy just laughed his loud laugh
and told me not to worry; that everyone drank way too much their first
night down here and then passed out. Anyway, as far as he was concerned,
I was already *way* ahead of the game, so stop bitching!

I had to agree with him on that one. Yeah, mon!

✖✖✖

The rest of the day passed uneventfully. I can say that without any sense
of disappointment. I had a wonderful day. Relaxing on the beach, getting
some reading done, enjoying the water as it lapped at my ankles while I
walked along the shore, consuming large quantities of rum punches made
by my man behind the bar who said "respect" whenever I nodded at him,
talking with folks, and just watching the festivities. Yeah, it was a great day!

I met another nice couple—Raul and Gabrielle, a South American couple
from the D.C. area. Raul was a middle-aged man who owned a construction
company, and constantly smoked Cuban cigars. Gabrielle, his wife, was a

good-looking woman with olive skin, full tits and dark nipples, rounded out by thick thighs and a full ass. She had a cute accent that fucked with me—most women with accents do. She was sitting with a bunch of naked folks at a picnic table under the shade of several palm trees. She didn't do a lot of talking at first—just kind of sat there and watched me as I was introduced to the group. I had walked by with my shades on when someone called my name. Apparently, I had been introduced to somebody there the previous night in the piano bar—but of course, all of what transpired after the Flaming Bob Marleys was just one big fucking blur to me!

I had gone back to my beach chair after chatting with them for a while. Lance and Chris were also on the beach chilling. I hung with them for a bit, just talking and enjoying the view of Chris's lovely new acquisitions. I was actually getting a fair amount of reading done when out of the corner of my eye I noticed some activity in the water. Gabrielle and two of her girl-friends were splashing around on a raft in waist-high water not far from where I lay. I put my book down to watch as the three of them decided to have a pussyfest—each one in turn eating out the other while a bunch of us watched them in earnest. At first I wasn't that interested—I've never been the kind of guy who gets into watching lesbian activities, whether in porno or in person—but when Gabrielle climbed onto the plastic raft and spread her dark legs for this black woman with a J.Lo ass, I definitely paid attention. Perhaps it was something about the way she threw her head back, dark hair dangling into the water as she moved her hips, the other feasting on her dark pussy lips—I don't know. But that shit turned me on! What can I say?

I spent a fair amount of time in the pool area as well, just getting a lay of the land, so to speak, seeing who was there, and whom I wanted to pursue. This real fine white woman with an hourglass body and wearing a frayed white cowboy hat drew my attention. She was lying in the shallow part of the pool on a lounge chair by the grotto or cave area. A bunch of men and women, all damn good-looking (I have to say), were with her. I walked by several times on my way to refresh my drink, and smiled or winked at her, checking out the thin patch of blonde hair just above her pussy, her nipples that spoke to me as I walked by—just profiling at this point, you know how we do—not being overly pretentious, didn't have to, really, but letting her know that I was interested.

I spotted Jackie walking by, clad in a white tennis skirt and lavender polo shirt. Damn, she looked fine! I got up from my chair and went to her, my dick tingling in excitement as I recounted those delicious images from the previous day. I grabbed her hand and asked if she was gonna stop by later to see me. She just gave me a seductive smile as she let go of my hand, told me that she was working and that I would just have to wait and see. I feigned disappointment, but she stroked my cheek and told me that I'd be okay. I told her I know that's right!

At some point in the afternoon (I can't tell you exactly when 'cause I left the Breitling in the room safe) it began to rain, just like Jackie said it would. A bunch of us ran for cover—I headed for my room and a nap while others waited it out in the hot tub. When I returned it was blue sky and fiery sun again, and I joined Raul and Gabrielle who were talking about this toga party that everyone was attending after dinner. I didn't even know how to tie a fucking toga, but the thought of all of us drinking, dancing, and carrying on, clad only in thin, white sheets turned me the fuck on! Gabrielle informed me that one of the Jamaican resort girls had been showing people the proper way to tie a toga over at the pool. I guess I had missed that during naptime. I swear, if I ran into Jackie again, I'd take her back to the crib and have her show me exactly what to do!

Guess what I learned—there are over a thousand different ways to wear a toga! I stood in front of the mirror for over a half-hour getting mine just right. You know I had to rock this party—and so, I made sure my shit was tight. First off, I didn't want the sheet to hang down very far past my balls. Oh hell no! I wanted to give honeys a show tonight. Let them see a bit of the snake as it sneaked a peek from under my toga. Also, it was *key* that my tattoos were prominently displayed. So, I managed to tie the two ends of the sheet together onto my left shoulder, draping the rest of the fabric down across my lower chest, and around my hips and ass. When I was done, I threw on my sandals, dabbed on some spankin' cologne, and walked into this mutha fucka like I owned the joint.

White folks got creative—I will give them that—some folks wore their shit in some whacked-the-fuck-out ways, but it was all-good. Ladies were the most creative, coming up with these designs that showed off their titties and asses. Some obviously decided to just say "fuck it" and not even attempt to cover much up. One skinny guy, for example, walked in wearing only a sock covering his dick. I got to give homeboy credit—his shit was on point—but not as tight as mine!

I cruised around the dining area where the toga party was being held, met the gazes of a few ladies who clocked me as I walked by. I grabbed a drink from the bar—at this point I was pretty much a rum punch-only kind of guy—and chilled. A few honeys walked up, showed me some love as they waited to be served. I was enjoying myself when I spotted Gabrielle and Raul. Raul had his shit hastily tied, like he really didn't give a fuck. Gabrielle had bikini bottoms on covered by some see-through flimsy thingy—her tits were bare and she wore high heels—that's about it! She came up to the bar and without fanfare reached for my dick underneath of my toga. Gave it a quick tug as she smiled hello. One of her girlfriends from the afternoon came up to us, and Gabrielle told her to check, in her words, "my nice package," which she promptly did. I was just standing there; drink in my hand, minding mine…two bitches feeling my shit. And it wasn't even 9 p.m. yet! DAYUM!

Gabrielle was whispering in my ear that she wanted to fuck me. She had this kind of devilish/seductive look on her face—an interesting glow in her eyes and full lips that pouted when she wasn't saying anything that made my dick hard. I leaned over and asked her what her husband would say. She told me to wait a moment and waltzed over to this table where Raul was sitting smoking a cigar, chilling with another couple. They conversed for a second and then waved me over. I shook Raul's hand and sat down. He leaned over to me and said in between puffs from his Cuban:

"You wanna fuck my wife?" I looked at him for a split second before responding. Gabrielle had taken a seat beside me and was watching the scene in silence, her lips turned into a sexy kind of pout.

"Matter of fact—I do." I was thinking about Randy's Rules as I replied. "But only if that's cool with you."

"It's fine with me. I ain't going nowhere. Go handle your business." He offered me a Cuban, which I politely declined. My mind was spinning, contemplating this place where folks were so *casual* about another man fucking their spouse. Not that I was complaining, you understand!

Ten minutes later (I would have made it five, but I didn't want to seem desperate, 'cause Trey is *never* desperate), Gabrielle and I were heading back to my crib. It was a beautiful night outside—just a light breeze coming in off the water, temperature just about perfect. No clouds in the sky, a nicely shaped moon rising. I took Gabrielle's hand as we descended the steps toward the beach and our rooms.

A bonfire on the beach beckoned us near. It lit up the night, spitting sparks up into the darkness. Over to the right of the fire were a bunch of hammocks strung out every ten yards or so between palm trees. Amazingly, the beach was empty, most of the resort guests at the toga party. Silently, I led Gabrielle to one of the white hammocks that swung lazily in the nighttime breeze. As soon as I stopped, Gabrielle was on her knees, and pulling my cock out from under my toga. She put my growing member in her wet mouth, and began sucking it as I hastily untied my sheet. She had a wonderful mouth; strong cheeks that sucked me in, swallowing almost my entire length. I enjoyed looking down while she sucked me off, her dark lips constricting my cock, while I grabbed a tittie in my hand and squeezed. Pinched her nipples as she worked on me. She paused, coating the side of my dick with her saliva as she glanced up.

"You have a big cock!" She stuck it back inside her mouth with a slurp, getting it all wet and engorged. At this point the toga was down around my ankles, and I was watching the shadows from the bonfire reflect off our bare skin, her head bobbing up and down, my one hand grasping her dark hair, guiding her rhythm, the other fondling her firm tit. I lay back onto the hammock, getting comfortable, adjusting my weight so that my cock was at mouth-level. Her bikini bottoms were still on, so I snaked my hand down around her ass and pushed the rayon fabric to the side. My fingers found her cunt: thick, dark, pussy lips that glistened with juice. I stuck two fingers inside. She sucked at me harder, one hand solidly wrapped around the girth of my dick, the other cupping my balls. She kept squeezing and rubbing my smooth sac lightly as she slurped and sucked on my dick. Her hand moved down to my asshole and lightly played with the hole. I felt myself tense and spasm in her mouth as she did that. I pulled out and laid her back on the hammock, the ropy material making imprints on her ass cheeks as I spread her thighs. Kneeling down on the still warm sand, I pushed the bikini to the side; I attacked her cunt with my mouth, wetting her hole with my spit. She moaned as I ate her thick pussy lips, which I tugged at with my teeth while her eyes rolled back inside her head. Her pussy tasted good—it had a musky kind of pussy smell that got me off. I dug that. I licked her from ass to clit, while sticking my thumb in her crack and pressing it around. Pushing her legs back and up into the air, I concentrated on her ass, probing the hole with the tip of my tongue while my thumb massaged her clit and wet pussy lips. She reached down and tugged on my fat cock, and I knew I needed to get inside her quick.

She was so damn wet, that slipping inside was the least of my worries. I glided in lusciously, hit bottom and then pulled all the way out, using the hammock's swing as my cadence. I paused again, bent forward, and grabbed the back of her head with my hands as I settled into the hammock, shifting my weight on top of her. I began slowly, letting her feel the full thrust of my cock as I fucked her, her hands tightly gripping my firm ass, then increasing the speed of my stroke, fucking her without tenderness, her head thrashing from side to side as she yelled out in that damn accent that made my dick spasm.

"Oh, fuck yeah, fuck me!"

"You like that?" I asked while sweat formed on my brow and nose. Off in the distant I could hear the bonfire spit and crackle as logs shifted in the sand. "You like my cock?" As I asked this I rammed her pussy hard and fast. The hammock rocked back and forth, powered by our movement—animal sex, primeval, raw, and powerful. Her cunt responded by contracting and pulling me into that sloppy, squishy cavern. A smile was painted across those sexy, dark lips. The limbs from both trees bowed inward as I fucked her with *determination*.

"Oh, yeah! Don't stop!"

But I did.

I paused in mid-stroke, pulling my shit out until just the tip was showing around those sticky, thickset cunt lips. Shifting to the side, I carried her along until she was on top of me, careful not to upset the balance and fall out. We giggled together, like kids in a schoolyard passing around a tiny joint, then I was grabbing her full ass and pulling her down on top of me, stuffing my cock deep inside of her hole once again.

"Oh, fuck yeah!" Gabrielle exclaimed again. She was sweating, her upper body and full tits swaying in unison to our rhythm, her dark nipples erect as I twisted them hard between my fingers. I pummeled her vigorously from below, arching my back off the hammock net to meet her pelvic thrusts. My body was writhing underneath hers, hands kneading her ass and swinging tits, grabbing at her mouth and sticking my fingers inside, her sucking at them hungrily like sugarcane as I stroked her pussy with my black cock.

Flipping her around, I just *had* to get a shot of that big, fine ass. She spread her legs wide, holding onto the hammock for support and balance as I stood by the edge of the net; her pussy lips hanging in front of me, all inviting, that fleshy aperture beckoning me in to play. I rubbed my latex covered cock all around her ass cheeks and hole, oiling her up, before thrusting into her waiting gap. She grunted as I filled her in one fluid stroke, one hand gripping her ass cheek, the other reaching forward and grabbing her hair, pulling her head sharply back. The sight of my large, dark cock slipping in between her butt cheeks was more than I was prepared to bear—several seconds after I entered her—a good ten strokes or so of good thrusting and fucking, the hammock vibrating as I worked her, palm trees on either side rustling in the gentle wind, I was pulling out, my hand reaching for my cock as the latex came tearing off, my other hand grasping for her chin and pulling her down onto the sand. I felt myself erupt and come almost suddenly, and I desperately wanted to see it on her face.

She opened her mouth; her eyes sparkled in the firelight in that devilish way that made my toes curl in the sand. I grunted as I came, spurting my hot, white cum onto her waiting face and parted lips. A stream of cum hit her on the tongue, shot straight to the back of her waiting mouth and went down her throat. A second shot splashed onto her full lips and formed a broken line between her chin, cheek and nose. I jerked my cock rapidly, base to head, the tip of my dick inserted into her cum-covered mouth as I continued to spurt my load, cum overflowing, not contained, and running down her chin in a delicious kind of way. She swallowed some with a smile, but the rest meandered down the valley of her full tits, coming to a final resting place on her belly. I looked down at the glazed path my cum had made on her damp skin: face to stomach, and bent down to kiss her on the mouth. She reached out and tongued me, sperm mingling between mouths and tongues as my cock slowly began to sag like an aging flower.

Behind us I heard applause—lightly at first and seemingly far away, then eruptions of sound: whooping, hollering, and plenty of high-fives. I turned around, seeing for the first time the crowd that had gathered by the edge of shadows, men and women alike, clad in togas, many gripping each other and tall drinks in hand, grins on their faces, thumbs upturned in the air. And as I reached for Gabrielle and took a bow, I spied in the midst of the crowd, Raul, her husband, clapping away with the others, a grin spread across his face as puffs from his Cuban rose into the Jamaican sky.

SIX

No matter how many times Vince spoke in front of a crowd, he always had butterflies before getting on stage. His father, an orthopedic surgeon at Children's Hospital in D.C., always commented how that was a good thing—the day you stopped getting nervous—that was the day you put down your microphone and found something else to occupy your time.

Vince stood behind the curtain staring out at the 400 or so folks who had assembled at the Le Pavilion Hotel in downtown New Orleans on a bright Friday morning—hard-working people just like him who had shelled out good money and taken off work to hear him speak. And regardless of where he was, New York, Atlanta, Boston, San Francisco, or The Big Easy, as he was right this very moment, he always felt the same pressure prior to getting on stage—these folks had come here today to hear something *profound*. They were here because they needed help in finding that one thing that eluded so many of us, regardless of race, creed, religion, or national origin—happiness and success. Therefore, Vince didn't do the mental calculations to come up with how much money he had just earned—no, instead, he did what he always did before walking on stage—he bowed his head, said a short prayer, and asked for the power to *inspire*…

A tall brutha dressed head to toe in Kente cloth stepped to the podium. The lights dimmed, conversations hushed.

"Good morning, my bruthas and sistahs. It is my distinct honor and pleasure to bring to the stage a man who among his many talents inspires, encourages, stirs, arouses, and motivates folk to do their very best. This is a man who has assembled all of the elements of leading a fulfilling and passionate life, and distilled it into a message that all of us can understand and learn from. Vince Cannon, Jr. hails from our nation's capital and has written the book—*Finding Nirvana: A Quintessential Game Plan for Success.* He is the president and CEO of his own company, a motivational speaker, avid motorcycle enthusiast, and accomplished artist. Please give a warm New Orleans welcome to Vince Cannon, Jr.!"

The stage grew dark. A jazzy rhythm began to take hold, softly at first, and then rose in volume as a barrage of lights and images bombarded the front screen. An African child; a sleek Learjet; a giraffe foraging for food in a tall tree; an air traffic control tower; a baboon and its mate; the interior of a high performance racecar; the winding, meandering Nile River shot from overhead; the World Trade Center in New York City; an enormous mansion; the Sphinx in Egypt; a pair of lovers walking hand-in-hand through Central Park; a rainstorm somewhere in the Midwest; a row of expensive cars, a crowded beach—thousands of other images—all cutting at breathtaking speed from one scene to the other—seemingly without any theme, rhyme or reason. And then as the music rose to a crescendo, a single image remained—a breathtaking sunset, fiery reddish orange—a fireball that consumed the entire screen. The crowd began to clap, softly at first, then more loudly, as they searched left and right for the speaker to emerge. And then, after waiting a few extra long seconds, Vince Cannon, Jr. walked on stage, dressed in a dark-blue, wool-and-silk, six-button, double-breasted peak-lapel suit, pale-gray silk shirt and matching silk tie, black leather lace-ups, thin, rectangular lens with wire-thin frames, hair and beard trimmed by the hotel barber an hour before. He strolled to mid stage to the enthusiastic applause of the crowd. He smiled, stuck his right hand in his pocket and waited for the applause to subside. *Okay,* he thought to himself as he flicked on the wireless mic attached to the lapel of his jacket…*here we go.*

"Morning!" he said, his voice bellowing across the high-ceiling ballroom.

"Morning," the crowd responded in unison.

"That's what I'm talking about! Folks wide-awake and raring to go! Welcome everyone. Before we get started let me say how delighted I am to be here—you are a good-looking crowd—I always love coming here, to New Orleans—there's something about this city that I find *magical*. The music, the food, the people..." that got more applause, "Yes, especially the people—there are some good looking folks here today! So forgive me if I lose my place from time to time; I will try to stay on track!" Laughter, then settling down. Vince put on a serious face.

"Let me ask you this—how do you define success?" He paused, took his hand out of his pocket and touched his finger to his lips as if deep in thought. He began to pace the stage, looking out over the crowd. Most were women, young and middle-aged, all colors, shapes, and flavors—no different than most of his workshops and seminars—he catered to women mostly, the backbone of the family who were searching for answers to improve/ enhance their lives.

"What is success? Is it happiness? Is that it? If you are happy, have you made it? Are you then deemed a success? Are you? How about owning a fancy car—does getting a new Cadillac Escalade, with a ten-CD changer, in-dash DVD, On-Star computer, and blazing steel rims make you successful? Huh??? Don't laugh, you know there are a bunch of you out there right now saying, 'Damn, how'd he know that's *exactly* what I want?'" Vince paused for the laughter, stared down at the tables, nodding at the folks who smiled back. He lumbered off the stage and began walking through the crowd, touching folks on the shoulder, nodding in greeting, smiling, shaking a few hands as he walked and continued his talk.

"Seriously, if that's your definition of success, that is fine with me. I did not come here to judge you or anyone else, so whatever you decide is fine with me. So, I ask again—what is success? Does it mean owning your own business? Finishing that degree you put off long ago? How about having two or three lovers at your beck and call? Is being a playa what success is all about? Huh? How about this? Are you successful if you earn three-quarters of a million dollars a year? Is that what happiness is all about?"

Folks were nodding their heads as if in church. Some were yelling out:

"NO!" or "YEAH, that's what I'm talking about!" Vince encouraged that kind of thing—he wanted his crowd to get into what he was saying—this was what it was all about—interacting with folk—bringing the message to the masses—and having a healthy debate about the topic at hand.

"Making seven hundred and fifty-thousand dollars a year—is that how success is defined for you? By the way, if any of you *do* make that kind of money, please see me during break—I need to get you my room key! I'm serious!" That elicited laugher from the entire room. Vince high-fived a woman upfront. She giggled and whispered to her friend nearby.

"Folks—I hate to break it to you, but I've got bad news—and you can write this down! I honestly don't know what success is. Why? Because success is measured differently by each person. So what is success to me might not necessarily be success to you. I will tell you this much, and you better pay attention to this, because here comes the profound part of my lecture—are you all—or as we say down here in N'Awlins—are *y'all* ready for the profound part?" Vince paused, hiked a leg on the seat of an empty chair, and stuck his hand in his pocket—*strike a pose*, he thought. He grinned and the crowd grinned back, nodding in agreement.

"Are y'all ready? I don't think those folks in the back are ready for the profound part yet." He dropped his head to his chin. In the back, folks were vigorously nodding their heads and shouting. Vince used the time to smile at the crowd, make eye contact with as many people as he could. He let his stare find each one—linger for a moment and seep in—give each one a moment of private time, his way of sharing himself with the audience. They responded and loved him for it. You could feel the energy and enthusiasm in the air.

"Okay!" Vince spun on his heels and made his way back on stage. He moved to the center. The crowd hushed. "This, my friends, is the most important part of my lecture—so pay attention—in the packet of materials in front of each of you, there is a blank pad of paper. Take that out and a pen. On a blank page I want each of you to draw a large circle. Go ahead; draw a circle on the paper, and don't be stingy—take up the entire page. Okay. Now, divide the circle into three equal parts—you can either draw a large "Y" inside the circle or an inverted "Y," like a peace sign—I don't care which you choose—just make sure that all three sections are the same size. Okay—everyone done?" Behind him the image of a large circle with an inverted "Y" inside—a peace sign—took up the entire screen.

"I don't know what success means to each one of you—but I do know this—there are three aspects or facets to being happy and successful. Without these three aspects to your life being in balance—you will never succeed and find happiness. This, my friends is a fact—we don't have time to debate it here this morning, but as you can see, I've taken the liberty of giving each of you a copy of my book, where at your leisure you can read at length my thesis and arguments.

"The first aspect to a healthy, successful existence is one's professional life—select one-third of the circle and write in 'professional life." This part deals with the professional aspects of our lives—whether we are a mathematician, CEO, astronaut, or executive assistant, each of us has a professional life—this aspect of our life deals with the things we do to earn a living—it includes all of the relationships that accompany our professional life, such as our boss, our assistant, if we have one, our colleagues, etc. Okay? Everybody with me so far? Good.

"The second aspect of a healthy, successful existence is one's personal life—select a second section in the circle and write in: 'personal life.' This part of our life deals with family and friends. Personal relationships—it includes marriage, children, parents and grandparents, and siblings. If you are single—it deals with searching for one's soul mate—the whole dating scene, looking for love, etc...Oh yeah, and sexual gratification falls into this area. Can't forget that part, can we?" The crowd members shook their heads.

"Last, but definitely not least is the third aspect to a healthy, successful existence—Self! Go ahead and write 'self' in the remaining space in your circle. Self deals with the care and feeding of ourselves—it is the mental, physical, and spiritual facets of our lives that we do to strengthen and enrich our own selves. It includes staying healthy—and that means, eating right and exercising. It also includes finding one's passion—whether we mean hobbies, or things that we are good at, things we love to do: things that stimulate us. Make us want to wake up the next day and do it again! Finally, it includes keeping one's mind and soul healthy—however you choose to do that—whether through prayer and/or positive thought.

"There you have it, ladies and gentlemen—three aspects to a healthy, successful life: professional, personal, and self. All three must be developed and in balance. Without exception." Vince paused to let his words sink in. He climbed off the stage and meandered among the crowd, which was silent, contemplating this idea.

"We all know people who have great jobs, and great home lives, but don't make time for themselves—they haven't concentrated on the 'self' aspect—and are they truly happy? NO!

"We all know people who have great relationships with their family and friends, have invested heavily in themselves, but not in their careers—are they truly happy? Have they made it? Do they consider themselves successful? NO!

"We all know people who have great jobs and wonderful hobbies, in fact, many times these hobbies consume their personal lives—but their home life suffers as a result—are they truly happy?" Vince shook his head gloomily.

The crowd answered in unison. "NO!"

"And many of you out there are parents, some of you single parents. Am I right?" Light applause. "And, Lord knows raising children, either with a partner, spouse, or alone is one tough job! But, let me keep it real for a moment—I know some of you out there are *consumed* with raising your children—hey, I know parenting is a full-time job, but some of you—and you know who you are—can't or *won't* find any time for yourselves. Are you truly happy? Are you successful? Answer it truthfully, y'all. The answer is NO!

"I challenge each and every one of you here today…" Vince said, pointing to the crowd and sweeping his finger from side to side in a wide arc, "choose any successful person you know, either now or in the past. Anyone—and I guarantee that they have these three facets of their life—professional, personal, and self, in balance. That, my friends, is the secret to success. *Define* these three elements in your own life—*develop* and nurture them—

74

and *balance* the three—and you, my friends, will find success and happiness!" Vince walked to the center of the ballroom underneath a huge, ornate chandelier. He held his hands up.

"Today we will accomplish great things—today, with the help of my assistants and me, you will draft a game plan for finding and sustaining a healthy, successful existence. You will a) define these three elements as they relate to your life, b) develop them so that you know exactly what areas you need to concentrate on, and c) begin to comprehend and understand how to balance all three. At the conclusion of today's session you will possess your own personal game plan, ladies and gentlemen—a game plan for a healthy and sustained successful life!"

Vince held his hands at arm's length, palms out to the crowd and smiled. The audience began to nod and then clap—lightly at first, then erupting into a booming thunderous applause, which swept through the large room. Vince nodded to the crowd as he smiled, touching a few folks in turn, as he made his way back to the stage.

✖✖✖

A short movie was shown while Vince stood at the podium taking a sip from some bottled water. The movie was a testament to his program—he didn't want to seem like an infomercial, or like something out of an Atkins Diet—some woman who had lost over sixty pounds and was standing there in Spandex going, "This program changed my entire life!" But the reality was that people responded to others who had lived through the program— had followed the steps outlined in his book and seminars, constructed a game plan, learned how to strike a balance, and were now reaping the benefits. So, instead of standing there telling people how great the program was, he showed these short testaments—that did the trick—got them enthused and ready to work.

A movement off to the side caught his attention. It was like a flash of lightning from a midnight storm—the sudden crack of light draws your attention in. Vince followed the movement—someone making their way to the front of the darkened room. The person didn't move as much as sweep in, like a rushing stream. He could see the hair—highlighted from the spotlights—it was long, frizzy, and wild; unkempt like a vine. A bronze color that seemed to change like the seasons as it moved—bronze, to golden brown, to a reddish brown. And then the figure stopped at a table with an empty chair to the left of center stage, and Vince was able to get a good look. The woman wore a white-laced blouse, bare at the shoulders; light brown; lace-front suede bell-bottoms with an elaborate embroidered pattern on the front; tan sandals, and a large Spanish suede-fringed shoulder bag. She found her seat, brushed her hair from her face with a quick flip of her hand, stared at Vince on the podium, and smiled. He smiled back, the movie ended, and the lights came up.

Vince moved to the center of the stage as the spotlight shone on him. His eyes swept out over the crowd—yes, they were ready, and he could see it in their eyes. They longed to soak up his knowledge like soft earth, and begin their own journey. He began to speak, tell them of how the rest of the day would shape up. How they would break into groups, facilitated by one of his assistants—and Vince himself would hit each group in turn, spend some time with them—give them a chance to develop their plan, share them with each other if they'd like—or with him.

The woman with the frizzy, wild hair who had just joined them crossed her legs, flipped through his book rapidly before setting it back on the table in front of her. She was nodding her head, as if she was moving to a tune that only she could hear. Vince snuck a glance in her direction—she caught his stare, glanced up and turned her head to him, matching her stare with his for a brief moment. Vince found himself studying her as he spoke to the crowd before they launched in to the next part of the workshop. She seemed very interesting—her look was one that reminded him of Lisa Bonet from *The Cosby Show*. She had that same sultry-sexy look. Her eyes never remained in one place for very long—always moving, searching, probing—except when she met your stare with hers—then she stopped and stared—didn't bore her eyes into you, but searched your innards, the window to the soul. Her clothes, too—bohemian in a sensuous kind of way.

He was glancing at her every few moments—actually trying *not* to—he was taking questions from the crowd—just a few hands had gone up, when he had asked if anyone had any questions, but his concentration was on her—the bell-bottom suede pants—tight- fitting that showed off her contours. She bent down to get something from her bag, her blouse rode up her back, revealing the top of dark, g-string panties. Then she was upright, giving Vince her full attention once again, smiling once more, aware that he was looking at her.

Vince was thinking about the conversation he and Trey had had many times before—there were two kinds of good-looking women out there—those who had beauty and good looks—and both men agreed that there were many of those around. And then there were those who possessed sensuality. Not everyone who possessed good looks was also sensuous. In fact, there were many good-looking, even fine women out there—but only a small subset were sensuous—being sexy wasn't something you were born with—it was something you learned, practiced, mastered, and then lived—this woman, whomever she was, had sensuality that she hoisted around her wherever she went. It was there in her eyes, and her smile that held a bit of deviousness to it. Her tongue that flicked out to wet her lips every so often. And regardless of her unkempt hair and funky clothes, Vince found himself aroused by her—not just in a physical sense—but because he could sense a whole lot more to this person beneath the surface. Like an iceberg. Yes, she was an interesting one…he'd keep an eye on her.

✖✖✖

The rest of the day flew by and before he knew it, Vince was wrapping up his workshop. It was close to four o'clock in the afternoon on a Friday in New Orleans—the day had been a good one—lots of folk had gotten something out of his seminar—he could see it in their faces as he walked around talking, shaking hands, looking at the personalized game plans that each participant had developed. The breakout sessions had gone very well—a lot of good discussion and dialogue—he had facilitated a number of them, moved between the different groups, meeting folks, spending a few minutes in private, getting to know individuals and the particular issues that had brought them here. At lunch, he had dined with about 20 participants, and had conversed with them about a number of issues—mostly personal but of value to everyone around the table—motivating oneself, how to make time for those goals that always seems just out of reach, and more personal questions—how did he, Vince Cannon Jr., keep it all together?

After lunch and during the afternoon sessions, he had looked for an opportunity—an opening—to try and get close to the bohemian woman, but it hadn't happened. Not at lunch nor afterwards. They had exchanged glances several times over the course of the afternoon—he had joined her group and fielded several questions. He was hoping she would speak up—at one point she looked like she was going to—moving around in her seat, poised to raise her hand. But, alas, it hadn't happened. And now, they were coming to a close—Vince was thanking them for their participation—urging them to continue on their journey toward sustained success—to keep in touch with him over email, to let him know how they were progressing. And then he stood and bowed to the crowd's lengthy applause before exiting the stage, determined to make his move—and not let the woman get away without grabbing a few moments of conversation.

The Kente-clad gentleman returned to the stage—told the crowd that a wine and cheese reception would immediately follow with Vince Cannon, Jr. available to sign his book and answer any questions that they might have. The crowd began to adjourn to the dining area where lunch had been served. Vince was standing backstage, watching the crowd from his vantage point. When it began to break, he moved—not wanting his movements to seem too hurried or frenzied, but quick enough to ensure that he got to her before she left. He advanced on the woman, who was gathering her things, scooping up the materials before her. He approached from the side as she bent down, rummaging through her shoulderbag, the sight of her lovely bronze shoulders and a hint of her breasts peeking out from the white-lace blouse, made his spine tingle. He touched her shoulder lightly. She flicked her head up quickly, sending her wild mane flying, a frown replaced by a smile as recognition seeped into her.

"I'm sorry," Vince said, "I didn't mean to startle you."

"That's quite all right."

"I was hoping that we could talk for a moment before the workshop ended. Are you planning on staying for the wine and cheese reception?"

"Yes. I was going to introduce myself if you hadn't come over..." The woman stood and Vince inhaled the scent of her perfume. He couldn't place it, but she smelled wonderful...the scent of flowers and other nameless things, intoxicating. The emcee touched his arm, and Vince turned, the spell, for a moment, broken.

"We'll be ready for you shortly. Would you like to freshen up before we begin? We have a few minutes."

"Yes, thanks." Vince turned back to the woman, the interruption a mere annoyance. She had collected her things and replaced her bag on her shoulder. She stood there, looking up at him silently.

"You need to go." It was a statement.

"Yes." Vince touched her elbow. "Don't go anywhere. Okay?" He was staring into her eyes, mesmerized by their color—hazel like that of her hair, which seemed to change in hue every few moments depending on the light.

"Wasn't planning on it." She smiled and he grinned back.

Vince ran to his room to freshen up and check his messages. When he returned, the reception was in full effect. Folks were mingling, glasses of California Chardonnay and Merlot in their hands while they nibbled on crackers and various cheeses. A table had been set up at one end of the reception hall for Vince. He took his place after shaking the hands of participants and began signing his book. It wasn't tedious work at all—even though it had been a long day, for Vince, this was what it was all about—being able to interact one-on-one with his fans, his readers, his seminar participants—spend a few precious moments with them alone—even if for just twenty or thirty seconds—hearing folks tell him what they thought of his book and his workshop, and how he helped to inspire them. The look in their eyes, the smiles on their faces, when he signed his book—writing out their name and some short, one-line message—"Shoot for the moon"; "Don't stop until you're completely there"; "Be proud of your accomplishments"; or his personal favorite—"Be passionate about everything you do, and amazing things will come…" And so, he was thrilled to see that most of the four hundred or so participants formed a line and waited patiently for their time to pay their respects and get their copy of *Finding Nirvana* signed.

By 6 the reception was winding down. A short line remained. Over the past hour or so, he had glanced up several times from scribbling his name and conversing with people to look for the bohemian woman. He felt like an adolescent back in high school—this was silly, he told himself, but the butterflies were fluttering around in his stomach when he spotted her off to the side, deep in conversation with two other women. He watched her for a moment, observing as she sipped her glass of Chardonnay before he resumed the signing of his book for the next participant in line.

Shortly after 6 she got in line. There were less than a dozen folks whose books were left to sign. When it was her turn she walked up to the table, clutching her frilly shoulderbag and his book in one hand, her wine glass in the other. She smiled as she set the book down.

"I'm pleased to finally meet you, Vince—I've been a fan since your book came out." She grinned, showing him her pearly white teeth and contagious smile, as she wiped her hair from her face. Vince grinned back and found himself stealing a glance once again at her lovely shoulders. It was their color and her smooth, creamy skin that he found eye-catching.

"Hello, it is always a pleasure to meet an old fan!" He smirked and she laughed. She stuck out her hand.

"My name is Angeliqué. I enjoyed today's workshop very much." Vince took her hand, enjoyed the feeling of touching her, the way it felt when their palms connected.

"Vince Cannon, Jr. It is my pleasure. What a lovely name. Angeliqué. That is…different. Very classy…with an air of mystique to it."

"Thank you. My mother named me after a voodoo priestess whom she was very fond of."

"Now that is something I find quite interesting. And are you continuing the tradition of practicing voodoo?"

"Well, that's a long story…" she replied as she smiled down at him. He began writing out her name and then paused, wanting to come up with something profound to inscribe. He glanced up.

"A voodoo priestess—hmmn…" He shook his head; she smiled as he composed a short note to her. He signed his name with a flourish, glanced back at her and passed the book delicately back to her. She read the inscription: "'I sense intense passion in your veins—channel that and you will go far… Best regards, Vince" She nodded her head silently and smiled before looking over at him.

"You are very good at what you do. You obviously have a gift for reading people and helping them on their way."

"Thank you. I hope you found today's session helpful. At a minimum, I hope it has given you much to think about."

"That it has. Listen, let me not take up any more of your time…" She glanced behind her at the line of remaining participants. Vince felt his pulse quicken. Their eyes exchanged a short burst of silent messages. His mind raced—there was much more to say to this mysterious woman with the voodoo namesake—but ten or so people remained in line—he couldn't do them a disservice by disrespecting them, focusing all remaining energy and attention on her. Yet…he didn't want it to end like this…it was now or never, he told himself. Seize the moment…

"Listen, you seem very interesting. I'd like for us to talk further. Can you wait a few more minutes—let me finish up here—we're almost done. We could grab a cup of coffee or dinner somewhere, if you don't have plans…"

"Yes. I'd like that."

"Good." He extended his hand and she took it. Again, he savored the feeling as their hands touched—the electricity that seemed to flow between their fleshes.

The next person, a black woman with short hair, wide eyes, and a smile came up and excitedly shook his hand. Vince beamed at his fan while he watched Angeliqué walk away, his thoughts not on this new person or what she was saying, but on the woman who lit him up…

✖✖✖

He found her to the left of the lobby twenty minutes later, standing alone by an oversized clay pot of wildflowers—their colors and fragrances, feral, like her hair, but beautiful nonetheless. She smiled when he approached her.

"I hope I haven't kept you waiting long," Vince said, relieved that she had decided to remain.

"Not at all," Angeliqué retorted.

"Wonderful! I have a few thoughts about dinner if you are still…"

"Can I interrupt you for a moment—before we get to that, I should let you know my, uh, fee—it's $200 for half 'n ' half; $300 for 'round the world… just so we get that part out of the way…"

Vince's face turned ashen; his jaw dropped, and he found himself speechless. "I'm…sorry. 'Half 'n' half'? Are…you…" Vince was having a hard time conjuring up the words. Unconsciously, he shook his head. It wasn't possible. It couldn't be. The thought of her as a—Vince couldn't even let the thought reach completion. Angeliqué let the silence invade the space between them for a moment before a wide grin overtook her face.

"IT'S A JOKE!" she said, pronouncing each word carefully. "Calm yourself! I am not in *any* sense a two-bit whore—besides, my stuff is way too *delicious* to be going for a mere two-hundred bucks!" Vince stared for a moment more before he broke into laughter; nevertheless, he wiped his forehead with his hand.

"Damn, woman, you got me that time! You don't know what just went through my head."

"I'm sure!" They both laughed, their gaze never straying from one another. "Now, you were saying?" Angeliqué continued.

"Okay, let's try this again—I was saying before I was so rudely interrupted…" Vince paused for effect and to grin before continuing. "I was hoping I could interest you in dinner with me—I have several ideas, not that I'm by any stretch of the imagination an expert in Creole cuisine— but I hear there are some good places around here."

"Actually, I took the liberty, while waiting for you to finish up, to make reservations. Hope you didn't mind. We've got an eight o'clock table at Brennan's, one of New Orleans' finest…I hope that's acceptable to you?" Vince stared down at Angeliqué, her fine features—frizzed hair that moved like the wind as she worked her neck, amazing bare shoulders, golden brown, like desert sand, those suede bell-bottom jeans with the embroidery on the front, hint of tan, flat stomach, her in-your-face-attitude—refreshing, like newly fallen snow—all of this swirling around him, his senses taking all of it in, inhaling all of her in one big gulp as if she was clean, invigorating air. Vince fought the overwhelming desire to reach down, scoop this lovely lady's face into his hands, and kiss her. Instead, he merely smiled and said, "That, my friend, is wonderful with me."

SEVEN

One would think that after a workout like the one just experienced with the lovely Gabrielle, I'd be spent! But for some reason, I felt completely revitalized—as if someone had injected *me* with a shot of adrenaline, instead of the other way around. I went back to my room, showered, to get that fuck-smell out of my pores, buzzed my head again (gotta keep the dome clean, ya know?), splashed on some more cologne, massaged a fair amount of lotion into my skin so that my shit would be *aglow*, then decided on what I was going to wear. The toga party was still in effect, however, my toga was sand-filled and nasty, the sheet having been used to wipe the cum off of Gabrielle's pretty face and body. So, I searched through my closet for a half-hour (like a girl) trying on this and that, just not being satisfied until I decided on a simple outfit to blaze. I chose my stone blue shorts as the foundation, and then turned my attention to a shirt. That took even longer—I mean, I went through six or seven different ones before I just said, "Fuck it!" and left my shit bare. Kept the top button to my shorts unbuttoned—kind of like inviting the honeys in without actually doing so—slipped on my brown sandals, the Breitling Blackbird, my silver necklace and bracelet set, a sharp pinky ring, and headed on out. It was still early and I planned on getting into some *more* fun before midnight!

I waltzed into the toga party feeling like a king. I mean, things were going so wonderfully well for me, I couldn't believe it. I felt so revitalized—really good sex always did that to me—like cleaning out the system, one felt completely refreshed and rejuvenated. I had come *hard* with Gabrielle, my favorite way to come, and my dick and balls still carried that totally spent feeling that would stay with me for hours. I was feeling good, on top of the world. And my first full day hadn't even come to an end yet!

A bunch of toga partiers were sandwiched together on the small dance floor while reggae music blasted out of ceiling-hung speakers. As soon as I walked in, the crowd spotted me (how could they not—I was one of the only mutha fuckas in there *not* wearing a toga!) A few rowdy partygoers started yelling and screaming, pointing my way—in seconds the entire crowd was cheering me. There was a small stage up front—the D.J. had positioned his equipment off to one side—when he saw me, he grabbed his mike and moved to center stage while calling for me to join him. I was playing it off at first, just standing back, smiling and waving to the crowd, my gleaming chest heaving from the play I was getting, my arms shining and flexing, tattoos looking good against well-tanned skin. But then I thought to myself, I'm the star of this show, so why delay any further—and so I rolled onto center stage. The roar became louder, almost deafening as I moved to the middle. Bitches were clocking me as I went—I waved to the moving, sweaty throng while grinning at Randy who was raising his fist into the air screaming my name—"TREY, TREY, TREY, TREY, TREY!" People were being worked into a frenzy. And I was not mad at any of them!

I reached for the mike and gestured for the crowd to chill. The sound fell quiet on my cue.

"Yeah…y'all…" I said, all Barry White-like, dropping my voice down several notches in pitch—the crowd went wild again. Again, I gestured for quiet and they responded.

"I'd like to thank God and the Academy…" Laughter erupted as I grinned and nodded silently to the toga-clad pack. A few women showed me their tits. I winked and licked my lips to each one in turn.

"But most of all…let me thank my co-star," I put a hand to my forehead to search the crowd, "where the fuck's she at?" A pause. "Y'all seen my CO-STAR?" My voice rose to a crescendo as I completed the sentence. Mutha fuckas were pointing to Gabrielle who was seated with Raul and another couple about mid-way from the stage on the right. I grinned, pointed to her and told her to get up. Reluctantly she stood and curtsied for the crowd. Gabrielle remained standing for a moment more while applause erupted around her. She threw me a kiss. The mob then went wild as I raised my fist in triumph, the heavy reggae beat began to rise, and I turned to exit the stage gracefully, like the star that I truly am!

✖✖✖

That's when I spotted her. And literally, in the time that it takes to blink, the blood drained from my face. Far back, but unmistakable among the toga-clad revelers—she stood there, distinct from others by her short dress—orange, low cut, and hugging her sensuous curves like a tight, leather glove. But it was the high cheekbones, distinctive even from where I stood, frozen in mid-stride—and her long hair, perfectly straight and jet black, running halfway down her back like that of a model—that caused my heart to miss a beat and jaw to drop like a stone. I knew I looked ridiculous up there on stage—the entire *congregation* watching my every move, the pain that formed at the top of my bald head and flowed like an avalanche down my face, neck, shoulders, and chest—and onto my firm legs that suddenly felt like Jell-O and began to tremble as such.

My knees buckled; I faltered and began to sway—the D.J., thankfully sensing that something was terribly wrong, reached out with his dark arm to right me—and I took refuge in his grip, flashed a fake smile, trying to play it off. Some might have assumed it was the booze taking control—that being the norm at a party like this, but the vast majority of the crowd knew something was indeed wrong. It was the look—I could see it on their faces—their smile wavered, laughs and catcalls waned as their eyes locked onto mine, everyone in the room trying to comprehend the shift, the sudden drop in temperature. Our eyes locked for a moment, hers and mine—and like flipping a switch, the pain appeared: severe and concentrated in my heart, like a knife, which is thrust into flesh and twisted in a sinister, gruesome way, ensuring maximum collateral damage. My throat constricted, I felt the air being extinguished, the lights dimming, fading fast, and for the first time in a long while I was *scared*, utterly terrified; my heart was thumping, reverberating in my ears so fucking loud I swore every partygoer in the place could *hear* my pulse. So many thoughts and images invaded my brain in that split second—like a movie jammed on fast-forward—they flashed by, details blurring as they raced by—and yet, I knew what I was seeing. And then the *realization* hit me like a crisp slap to the cheek—was this my punishment for living large on a cloud too high, consuming way too much, more than my slice? Down here for less than 36 hours and living *dreams* that only a fraction of us ever get to realize—who the fuck did I think I was—was that it? Was this God's way of letting me know I had gone *too* far—pushing me back down, and into place?

And then the wave passed—as quickly as it had surfaced—with the sudden awareness that the object of this unexpected ache was a delusion, like a desert mirage—it was not *her*. The pain dissipated into thin air, like tendrils of Cuban smoke—I was breathing once again, vision clear and focused, legs working as advertised—I displayed a smile to the crowd, once again raised my fist in a puny attempt to correct any misconception that had begun to form—this was *still* Trey's house, wasn't gonna let mutha fuckas think even for one quick second that it wasn't—these bitches were still sweating me like I was going out of style—yeah, in the blink of an eye, I was back—okay, sixty percent and rising—batteries recharging…

I found myself at the bar, a steady stream of fans stopping by to high-five me and say, "Waz up!" At this point, every mutha fucka in the spot knew my name. But I wasn't basking in the *glow* of the limelight. No. I stood there anxiously, wiping away the sweat that had formed on my smooth dome, ordered a drink after a few minutes of indecisiveness—finally deciding on a Bob Marley, and told the bartender to light that mutha fucka up if he dared—cause at this stage Trey needed *anything* with strong liquor in it. The bartender placed the shot in front of me and stroked his lighter—I sucked heartily at the straw, oblivious to the blue flame, and motioned for another. Out of my periphery I could see Randy and Cathy making their way over to the bar—Randy's boisterous voice leading the way—hand on my shoulder—"Dude, everyting irie? You look like you've seen a ghost!" I flashed another fake smile, grabbed the second shot before the Jamaican could reach for his lighter, and downed it, splashing some on my cheek.

"Naw, I'm fine…" I elbowed my way out of the bar crowd that was getting thick and annoying. I needed space and fresh air to breathe. Randy had this funny look on his face; I was putting distance between the two of us, but Cathy reached for him as he tried to go after me. I turned to him and gestured for him to stay. "Everyting irie, mon," I said, flashing a weak smile. "Trey back in control… True dat!

Randy stopped and nodded. He seemed to believe it. I turned to leave. The question was, did I?

✖✖✖

Back in my room, I splashed cold water on my face and tried to think—and will myself to calm down. This was out of character for me, and that's what really bothered me. The fact that my mind was on a separate path, not going with the flow—not with the damn program. That wasn't right, but nothing I could do would change the way I felt. And so, I stood in front of the mirror—stared at the image that reflected back. Took deep breaths. Patted my face with a towel and pushed the thoughts that were welling up inside of me away, like an annoying child.

A knock at the door broke my spell. I froze—listened to the sounds—movement on the other side of the wall, white noise and other distractions that made it hard to focus—but Randy's voice was unmistakable, cutting through the air like a knife. I made my way to the door, knowing with certainty that he was not going away.

"Dude, open up! Someone's here to meet you!" Banging, incessant knocking—and that deafening/raunchy voice that I had come to know—now the last thing I wanted to hear. I paused at the door, taking a deep breath, wiping my head with my hand as if that would somehow transform my appearance.

When the door opened I found myself face-to-face with *her*—orange dress no more than twenty-four inches away, smiling, her perfectly white teeth shining as her eyes sparkled, lighting up the darkness. She was gorgeous, no, that didn't even do her justice—her beauty, and in particular, her sensuality, was unparalleled—high, sculpted cheekbones; perfectly shaped nose; bright, unwavering eyes; dark, unfathomable hair; long, curved eyelashes; perfect breasts that peeked out from the confines of her dress…

"Trey, mon, this fine young lady was inquiring about the star of the show! Hope you don't mind, my man, know you wouldn't…" Randy was interrupted when she stepped forward, invading the narrow space between the doorframe and where I stood, thrusting a hand forward—I had no choice but to take it—electrons flying between us as our hands touched, I could feel the electricity surge, and under any other circumstances my whole aura would be glistening and shimmering, yet I could feel the temperature dropping again.

"I'm Cinnamon, undoubtedly your biggest fan!" She flaunted another smile—meanwhile Randy stepped up, a few drinks under his belt/toga, and feeling no pain.

"I'm sure you are, baby; all sugar and spice!" he replied, wrapping a tattooed hand around her lovely waist.

"…And," she said, eyes blinking, waving Randy's comment off like it was an annoying insect, "I just wanted to say how much I enjoyed your show."

I stood there, taking this all in, mind spinning, the normal Trey-comebacks being plucked from the far recesses of my crammed databanks and compiled, but at half-speed, way too fucking slowly. Randy, sensing my discomfort, stepped in, taking control.

"Trey, meet Cinnamon. Cinnamon, this is Trey. Mon, Cinnamon's visiting—only here for this one night—and guess what? She's heard about our nightly hot tub party—said she's definitely game, but only if *you* join the party tonight…" Randy was grinning ear-to-ear as if he had just delivered news that would save the nation. Cinnamon made no move to back up—her eyes sweeping over my bare chest and arms, taking in the tattoos, my unbuttoned shorts and tanned legs that gleamed under the night-lights. Cathy, standing behind her, locked her eyes on Cinnamon's scrumptious

ass, licking her rouge-touched lips, and undoubtedly thinking of the possibilities here…

"Give me a minute," I said finally, delivering the best that I could do
under the circumstances. The pain was there, just under the surface, like a
jellyfish—its long, perilous tentacles paralyzing every living thing in its
path—"I just need to *freshen* up." Randy cocked his head to the side, pursed
his lips as if this notion didn't compute. "Need just a minute…is that cool?"
I asked, smiling at Cinnamon. As an afterthought, I reached out to stroke
her forearm, as if this would add some sense of potency to my words.

"Oh yeah, that's *way* cool with me, Trey," she answered. Under any other
circumstances, I swear to God, I would *deposit* my tongue down the throat
of this goddess-bitch—this was a no-brainer; the woman was sweating me;
them panties were *soaked*, that much was obvious, I had already won the
prize. And yet, just reaching out to touch her had left my right arm feeling
beaten and bruised. I smiled regardless, shielding my trepidation, closed
the door slowly as Randy, Cathy, and our new companion, Cinnamon,
withdrew to the hot tub and the prospects of another made-in-heaven
connection.

I could hear their retreat: their laughter and footfalls echoing in my
ears long after they had left. With the lights extinguished, as if that
would somehow shelter me from harms way, I slid down the whitewashed
wall, gradually to the bare, cold floor. At some point I fell asleep, my figure
remaining in that spot—not moving, harried breathing, until this new
anxious self—one that I hadn't seen in a long, long time—met the new
dawn…

EIGHT

Angeliqué left Vince to go change and freshen up, with the promise to meet him at Brennan's at 8. For the next hour, Vince could barely contain himself. Images of her—her form, the context and content of her words replayed themselves a thousand times in his head. He practically ran from the elevator to his room, stripped off his clothes and jumped in the shower, the excitement and adrenaline coursing through his veins like a drug, intoxicating, warming his spirit. He thought about bringing flowers for her—pondered the thought for close to thirty minutes, even reached for the phone to give the concierge a call, then thought better of it. Didn't want to seem too excited. But then again…no, he decided…not yet…

Vince arrived at Brennan's by taxi at 7:45. The restaurant was located on Royal Street in the French Quarter, a block up from the famous Bourbon Street and a short walk from the Mississippi River. Antique shops and art galleries framed it on both sides. Angeliqué arrived a few minutes past eight—swept in, again, like the wind, looking sensational. She had showered and changed—with a renewed glow to her features. She wore a long flowing skirt of vibrantly colored tie-dye patterns, a matching blouse with oversized sleeves and a plunging neckline—her hair had been washed, conditioned, and combed back—it shimmered and shined halfway down her back. She wore large, silver hoops in her ears, and an Ethiopian cross dangled from a thin chain around her neck. She greeted him with a hug and Vince stole the opportunity to inhale the fragrance of her hair and skin—

once again the desire to kiss this woman was overpowering; instead, he savored their moment of closeness, before she pulled back and looked him over. He had changed into dark slacks and a camelhair sports jacket—with a dark turtleneck underneath; comfortable yet stylish loafers on his feet—Angeliqué's gaze swept over him before commenting on how good he looked. Vince returned the compliment, adding that he was dizzy from her perfume and scent of her hair. She displayed her wonderful smile as the hostess led them up the stairs to the second floor.

Their table was in a cozy room off from the main dining area—dark-red wallpaper, a few portraits in ornate frames, a fireplace, dual windows overlooking a garden courtyard below, just two other parties besides them already seated. An attentive waiter got their drinks—Angeliqué was staying with white wine—she made an off-handed comment about how mixing liquor with wine brought out the wildness in her—Vince made a mental note to file that precious info away. Vince, too, settled on a nice glass of not-too-dry Chardonnay. They began to talk, Vince giving Angeliqué his undivided attention.

"So, tell me about yourself?"

"Not much to tell," Angeliqué began.

"I find that hard to believe." Vince grinned.

"Well, I was born here in New Orleans—my father was French Creole and my mother is Cuban. I've spent my entire life here and love it—the people; my roots are here—the music, cuisine, and arts. I'm not a big-city kind of girl—I like to be left alone to do my thing. Here people let me do my thing…"

"I hear that. Go on."

"Like you, Vince, I'm an artist—painter mostly. I have a studio that is close by—walking distance actually—right smack in the Quarter, which I just love!" She paused to take a sip from her wine glass. "I run an art gallery—a small place, but it pays the bills, mostly my stuff and some friends—paintings, some sculptures, a few glass-blown pieces, stuff like that. But, I'm happy here—I am a social person—I love to go out and listen to live music—and if you're into live music, New Orleans is the place to be!"

"Tell me, Angeliqué, what brought you to the workshop today?"

"Well," she said, shifting in her seat and raising her glass again to her lips. Vince used the occasion to gaze at her features. He found himself mesmerized by her stare—those eyes seemed to look right through him—yet he was not uncomfortable by it—just the opposite—he felt himself warming every time her eyes found his. "I read your book shortly after it was released—happened upon it by chance one morning while strolling through one of our local book shops. Read it and became fascinated with the entire premise—this concept of yours—this holistic approach to happiness—using the circle as a metaphor—and the idea of balancing each of the three portions. It was definitely something I related to.

"For one, I found myself intrigued with the story—your story—your description of how you came to this place where balance rules your life—your journey with your art, your passion for motorcycle riding and writing; how you were not content to live the typical 9-to-5 routine and took steps to break from the mold—I found myself drawn to you in a way, and your story. You see—I would like to think that I'm cut from the same piece of cloth as you—we share a passion for life—that much is evident—and balance is something I strive for every day of my life."

"You sound like a very together woman," Vince said. He reached for her arm, stroked it without thinking. Let his touch linger for a moment. Angeliqué smiled, enjoying the contact.

"Thank you. In one sense, I guess I am. I am fiercely independent, passionate about many things—but there is a side of me that is in need of development—that, Vince, is why I came here."

"The fact that you recognize this…shortcoming…for lack of a better term—and you are ready and willing to tackle this head-on, and improve yourself—speaks volumes about who you are and where you are going. I am very impressed."

The waiter returned. Food was ordered—Angeliqué told Vince of Brennan's—they were famous for their turtle soup, which he had to try, and Bananas Foster—a dessert consisting of fried bananas dipped in rum and lit—world famous and to die for!

"There's another reason why I came."

"And that is…?" Vince asked.

"I was hoping for help in making sense of a relationship that went bad—a year and a half ago I was involved with someone. It lasted for close to a year. It ended suddenly and I'm over it—but I guess I've been searching for answers—what went wrong—why is it that two people who love each other can't sometimes find the strength to stay together—is it something about me that I need to focus and work on? I thought this workshop could help—after all, relationships are a big part of your circle." Angeliqué stopped, pulled at the bread and ate silently. Vince nodded while watching her, sipping his wine.

"Indeed. Tell me about this relationship." His voice softened, drawing her in. And Angeliqué smiled and began to talk, sensing his compassion and being okay with her wanting to vent her feelings, as if she were discussing her relationship problems with an old friend.

Angeliqué had met a man—a Creole from the north side of town at a gallery showing. He was handsome, educated, and married. He had courted her for a while—she was standoffish, having no desire to get in the way of an existing relationship—especially a marriage. But he was persistent, and well, he intrigued her. He seduced her—slowly through romance, flowers, late night phone calls, notes left on the steps of her studio—in the end, she gave in to the passion and her desires, and had an affair with him. She told herself that it would only happen once—but it was so good and intense, that she found herself going back for more. She became swept up with the *idea* of this relationship—this thing that never could be what she ultimately wanted it to be—but that didn't stop her from fantasizing about the two of them being together for more than just a few fleeting moments.

She turned to voodoo—a religion and way of life for her since she was small—using the charms, rituals, deeply spiritual practices as a way to enrich her life in the ways of love. To assist her in getting what she desired more than anything else—to possess what she needed to feel complete—this man—Angeliqué dug deep, called on the spirit of Ezili Freda, the goddess of love to help in this endeavor. She erected an altar of her favorite offerings—pink and pale-blue candles, jewelry, sweet cakes, perfume, cigarettes, images of white doves; took a lady bath using basil, sweet peppers, *zo-devan* powder, *Baume du commandeur,* and Florida water—the inside and outside of her tub basin traced in chalk with the *veve* or symbolic drawing of Ezili Freda. The bath, preceded and followed by an offering of a sweet dessert—rice cooked with milk and a sprinkling of cinnamon—then she withheld from bathing for three full days in order to allow the lady bath to take full effect. Afterwards, she fashioned a charm lamp made from a coconut shell, in which she placed a piece of sheep's brain (which took her a painstakingly long while to obtain), immersed in olive oil, cane syrup, honey, and petals of jasmine—the attributes of the sweet ingredients, Angeliqué explained, used to enhance the properties of attraction. A wick was then threaded through the center of a Queen of Hearts playing card, which was then floated on top of the oil. The lamp was refreshed daily, and burned continually until the charm worked...all of this Angeliqué did, with the single, unifying purpose of making her lover hers. And yet...

The food arrived—Angeliqué fed upon fresh redfish that was served blackened and with turtle soup. Vince ate a medium-cooked filet with horseradish sauce and cooked banana—it went against his better judgment and palate sensibilities, but once tasted, one single bite, and he was a convert for life—the meeting of sweet banana, creamy sauce, and beef was pure pleasure on his tongue. The conversation slowed, due to the food—it was wonderful, and both Angeliqué and Vince savored the silence, and the opportunity to stare across the white tablecloth at one another, watching as each ate silently, not afraid of the gaze—nor the bond that was rapidly being forged between them this evening.

After they had finished, Angeliqué made Vince order the flaming bananas dessert. While they waited, they sipped glasses of Chardonnay topped off by their waiter, and she continued with her story. She and her account captivated Vince. He couldn't help it, but the desire to reach out and stroke her forearm, grab her hand, and kiss her was overpowering.

"For close to a year, I practiced my voodoo, the craft that had been handed down from generation to generation—I was a serious practitioner and truly believed that my baths, altar offerings, and charm lamps would bring me what I desired. But, in the end, it did not happen. My rituals did nothing to deliver to me the man whom I desired, away from his wife. They rekindled their waning relationship, and moved away from here, as if this place and I were a curse."

Vince swallowed and took her hand. "I'm sorry," is all he said.

"Don't be." She made no move to let go of his hand. It felt comfortable between them. "I grieved for a period of time—blamed myself for all the wrong reasons—analyzed it from every angle—in the end, what suffered most of all was my craft—I became disenchanted with the whole concept of voodoo—as a religion and way of empowerment. I took a step back from that part of my life—that was hard, it's been with me my entire life...but I had lost my faith."

Dessert came, lighting up their faces as a match was struck and the rum ignited. Vince enjoyed the sweetness—Angeliqué nibbled a bit but let him consume the rest of it. They finished their dinner with rich smelling coffee. Hot and good tasting.

Vince spoke: "Angeliqué, you've shared something very special and personal with me tonight—thank you for that. Thank you for trusting and confiding in me. I wish I could provide you with a succinct answer—something poignant and prophetic that would take all that you have gone through and make sense out of it. Alas, I don't have such answers.

"In a sense, we all are searching for what you seek—completeness that we hope will come from finding that special one—our soul mate—I confess that I suffer from the same malady as you do—I, too, long for that special person. I'm still searching—and hopeful that she is out there and that I'll find her."

The check arrived. Vince paid while Angeliqué excused herself to the ladies room. Vince watched her exit the room, feeling her more deeply than he did a few hours before—the opening up, like a flower, causing him to see beyond her physical self—her beauty—to the deeper core—her strength, her essence, her being.

When she returned, he watched her silently as she moved—the colorful patterns of her tie-dye skirt shifting like a sea storm, the hint from her breasts—rising flesh that caused his skin to tingle, and her lightly colored hair bouncing seductively under the light of dimmed chandeliers.

"I have an idea," Angeliqué said to Vince as she rounded the table, touching his back, letting her fingers graze his neck and shoulders briefly. "Let's continue this conversation, that is, if you're up to it, in a more *intimate* location…someplace where we can finish this in peace…"

Vince caught her hand that had alighted from his shoulder blade. He found it in mid-flight and took hold, stopping her from moving away. She glanced down into his eyes. He returned her stare, passion smoldering under the surface of his corneas. "Nothing, Angeliqué, would please me more…"

✖✖✖

They walked along the streets of the Quarter—past the antique shops and art galleries of Royal, avoiding Bourbon Street and all of its clamor— the loud music, inebriated tourists gripping potent Hurricanes from Pat O'Brien's, bead-laden young folks, stopping to gawk at the female impersonators, strip-club dancers who hawked their wares on dirty, beer-drenched sidewalks, or out-of-towners who dared to bare their breasts for a pair of cheap, beaded necklaces, past the thumping bass of Cat's Meow, or one street down to the gay clubs where patrons slipped dollar bills into the tiny g-strings of male dancers. Angeliqué and Vince avoided all of this, choosing instead to take a more tranquil route, enjoying the peaceful night, and the moment where their shoulders and arms met, quite by accident, leading to an intertwining of fingers and hands. They remained this way, enjoying the connection, the joining of each other's warm flesh, and the sensation of being in close proximity to someone new, the feeling, electrifying and invigorating. Past Toulouse, St. Peter, Orleans, and St. Ann; then over to Dumaine and finally St. Philip. A quiet, residential block, an eclectic collection of colorful two-story homes, shutter-covered windows, balconies with ivy reaching up to the roof. Hushed conversation or the sheer beauty of relaxed silence—the excitement of just feeling each other as their clothes brushed up against one another.

They came to a two-story, newly painted building that sat on the corner, the first level taken up by an art gallery with wide panes of twin glass divided by a single oak door. The second level featured a wraparound balcony with wooden ceiling fans positioned every ten feet. A single gas lamp hung from the base of the iron balcony down to the front door, its flame wavering behind beveled glass. Off to the right, several yards before the building curved along the edge of the street, a side entrance, enclosed with a wrought-iron door. Angeliqué silently led Vince past the entrance to a garden hidden from the street. It was rectangular in shape, a courtyard of sorts that was surrounded by the building's four sides. Directly in front of them was a brick wall, with thick ivy clinging to red stone. Below the wall, an oval pond trickling water, lit from an overhead spotlight. Goldfish swam in between damp lily pads that sheltered a spotted bullfrog. On either side of the pond, medium-size trees had been planted. And beneath them, a concrete bench and wrought-iron round table and chair set. Vince was speechless.

"Please make yourself comfortable," Angeliqué ordered. Vince chose a wooden bench on a wall overlooking the pond. Across from him, light from the back windows of the gallery illuminated the garden. Overhead, windows cut into the second-floor brick were dark.

Angeliqué returned moments later holding twin stems of white wine. They toasted each other silently. She pulled up a lounge chair and reclined in front of him.

"My God, this place is beautiful," Vince remarked.

"Yes, it's been in my family for years. I'm very lucky to possess it. I love the fact that it's smack dab in the middle of the Quarter. So close to the action, so to speak, yet far enough away from prying, nasty tourists."

Vince laughed. "It's wonderful. I'd remain here day in and day out if it were mine."

"So, Mr. Cannon, your turn. Tell me about you and your art?"

Vince took the opportunity to tell Angeliqué about his passion, explaining his evolution as an artist. Most of it she knew already; he had covered this in his book, so he concentrated on what he had been working on recently—the life casting process, and the making and painting of masks. Angeliqué sat still while he spoke, mesmerized and intrigued by his creativity.

He then asked her about her art. She indicated that she had been an artist, specifically, a painter for most of her adult life. She had always gravitated toward representing the *veve* of the various voodoo spirits—normally traced on the ground during ceremonies using cornmeal, wood ash, powdered red brick, or even gunpowder—the elaborate designs creating geometrically complex and intricate patterns. Instead, she took these designs and put them on canvas, using the colorful hues and shades of the Haitian art as a backdrop. Soon, she tired of this and branched out, explored the creation of *veve* on alternate medium—settling on painting the detailed, highly structured patterns on the human body.

Vince sat enthralled as she spoke about her craft.

About six months ago, after experimenting with various patterns and colors for months, she held a show at her gallery. Word of her work spread quickly through the New Orleans art community—the painting of these intricate, hieroglyphics on moving, breathing flesh garnered her some interesting reviews, to say the least. A few months later, she held a second show—this time to a sold-out audience. Folks from as far away as Dallas/Fort Worth came to see her *veve*-covered bodies and live art.

Vince had a million questions. She smiled at him, as the words rushed from his mouth. As an artist, he was intrigued by her creative spirit and hungered to understand her process. As a man, feeling the connection between them, he longed to soak up more of her.

For hours they spoke in hushed tones, about everything—their childhood, growing up, school, adult life, failed relationships, likes, dislikes, favorite foods and colors. Angeliqué refilled their glasses several times over the course of the evening. The evening was perfect, the temperature just right—the glow from the city arcing above them created a comforting blanket of radiance. Before long, Vince was stunned to learn from his watch that it had passed 1:30 a.m…the time racing past them like a flock of bluejays.

Vince stood. He drained his glass and set it on the stone ground. Angeliqué stretched, her feet long since abandoned the confines of her sandals. Spontaneously and without thought, he pulled her to him, wrapped an arm around her lovely shoulders and back, moved in and kissed her lightly on the lips. She responded, reached for his face with both hands and returned the kiss. For a moment, they did not move, simply savoring the feeling of their lips pressed together, as one.

They parted and smiled.

"Thank you for a lovely evening," Vince said, his hands dropping down her forearms, fingers interlocking.

"Yes, if was wonderful to meet and spend time with you," Angeliqué replied. "I like you, Vince. I'm not afraid to say what is on my mind. You stimulate me, in more ways than you might think. I'd like to see you again."

"That, Angeliqué, would be my pleasure." He tipped her chin up with a finger and kissed her again. This time, their tongues met for the first time. She slipped a card into his palm. He glanced at it. It was for her art gallery.

"Come visit me tomorrow. I've got a show to do at seven. You can come early and watch me work. That is, if you'd like to?" The beam on her face was so seductive and sexy that Vince could only stand there and exhale slowly.

"I'd like that."

After he had left—she had offered to call him a cab, but Vince insisted on walking, the beauty of the evening and all of its glory invading his senses and giving him time to replay every delicious detail concerning their time together—Angeliqué went upstairs. She slowly removed her clothes, stood naked by the altar not far from her bed and made up her mind—no contest really—Angeliqué was determined that she would make love to Vince, felt the desire stirring in her, vibrating her body from the insides on out.

And for the first time in over a year, Angeliqué bent over her altar, whispered a short prayer to Ezili Freda, the voodoo goddess of love, and lit a pink and pale-blue candle before slipping into bed, and falling gently asleep…

✖✖✖

Vince awoke at noon, feeling more revitalized and refreshed than he had in a long while. He felt recharged and invigorated, as if every pore on his body had been scrubbed clean, leaving him brand-new. He remained in the king-size bed, covers pulled up to his chin, staring at the ceiling, recounting last night. He closed his eyes and memorialized every detail of the lovely Angeliqué—her hair, skin, face, smile, arms, legs, and toes; the way her lips curled up when she smiled and laughed, her gaze—deep, strong, and unwavering.

His thoughts were on flowers this particular morning, the desire to send Angeliqué a bouquet so overpowering that he could think of nothing else; the thump in his chest, overbearing. He slipped out of bed, booted up his laptop and went on-line, checked a few floral web sites for ideas, then turned to the hotel's concierge. He was on the phone with her for over half an hour, discussing arrangements and delivery options. His first thought was to get her a vase of rustic wildflowers—something from a country meadow that would denote her spirit—gerbera daisies, alstomeria, delphinium, lavender stock—or perhaps a colorful arrangement of lilies, snapdragons, carnations, and solidasters. On reflection, he began to consider a branch and plant arrangement—pussy willows, forsythia, kalanchoe, and ivy; or perhaps the striking snow-white calla lilies with their beautiful flowers and rich, green stems, a symbol of grace and elegance. Roses—another consideration, but one he quickly discounted…ordinary men bought their women roses—he was no ordinary man and this, my friends, was no ordinary occasion…

In the end, simple beauty won out and said it best—tulips—crisp, brilliant petals, stems that lifted and curved, soft pastels and bright hues—a vividly mixed color combination that the concierge personally guaranteed. Vince had them sent over to the gallery shortly after one.

And then he was on his cell—a longshot, he knew, but maybe, just maybe, Trey would pick up. He knew his best friend was tearing up the island of Jamaica this very second, leaving no stone, that is, skirt, unturned…

The call went to voicemail, and he hung up, disappointed. Vince knew what Trey would have said anyway. He could see his friend this very minute yelling into the phone—"Dawg, you mean to tell me you spent all that time alone with her and you didn't *HIT IT*????" Vince laughed out loud.

The next call was placed to Erika. It was early afternoon—hopefully, she was up. He desperately needed to tell *someone* about his evening and this amazing woman with the voodoo namesake. All about the astounding connection between them, their common interests, and approach to life. Unfortunately, this call too bounced over to voicemail. He hung up, crestfallen; suddenly he was famished—he showered and got dressed.

The rest of the afternoon was a blur—eating breakfast/lunch at the hotel's restaurant, getting an hour of running in, then relaxing, walking through the streets of New Orleans and the French Quarter, shopping at River Walk, and preparing for his second evening with Angeliqué.

He returned to the hotel, spent close to an hour selecting his suit—finally deciding on the dark wool pinstripe suit—simple and elegant sometimes said it best; a thin, black, crew-neck sweater he had picked up that day; and the black lace-ups. By 5:30, he was ready.

✖✖✖

Vince arrived at the gallery at 6. He went in and spent a few moments admiring the artwork. A number of paintings adorned the wall—most were Angelique's work—and for the first time, Vince was able to observe the *veve* rather than imagine them—the intricate, replicated patterns of the voodoo gods/goddesses on canvas—interpreted by Angeliqué and her brushes: the sailboat motif of Agwe and Lasiren, king and queen of the ocean; bulls head and horn patterns of Bosou, associated with the fertility of the soil; serpent lines of Danbala and Ayida Wedo, snake spirit and mistress of the skies; heart shapes of Ezili Freda, love goddess; cross and coffin figures of Gede, guardian of the dead. Wonderful stuff—the motifs back-dropped by vibrant colors—Haitian influence—reds, blues, greens, purples, and oranges, swirling around canvas, creating powerful statements.

A thin woman with short hair and dark vibrant skin walked up and touched his elbow. "You must be Vince. I've heard a lot about you. Angeliqué is expecting you." Vince beamed at the thought of the conversation between these two concerning him.

She led him to the back, where he could see the garden, displayed in its entire splendor in daylight through French doors, down a short hallway and up a set of stairs. At the top, a narrow hallway ran left and right. Vince was led to his right and he at last found himself in Angeliqué's studio.

Angeliqué was bent over a nude form on the floor. She glanced up and smiled when he entered. Off to the side, on the far wall, in the forefront of a large, six-foot square colorful painting, sat a nude man with well-defined muscles spread across his body. He was covered bald head to toe with light-red paint—the *veve* interlocking across every inch of his decorated skin.

"Hey, stranger! I'm glad you are here." She stared at him and grinned, then stood, her denim cutoffs layered with splotches of drying paint. A white tee shirt bunched at the waist was similarly covered with speckles and splotches. Her hair was tied back with a band. "I'd come over and give you a kiss, but I'd hate to mess up that fine suit of yours—check you out!"

Vince just laughed.

"Thank you soooooooo much for the beautiful flowers—I absolutely love them!" Angeliqué exclaimed while pointing to the tulip-filled vase on a coffee table.

"You are very welcome," Vince replied warmly, but his attention was drawn to the young woman on the floor. She reclined; head back, brown hair inches from the floor. Her darkly rimmed nipples were erect; trim body, firm legs and thighs, auburn skin also covered with a different pattern of *veve*. Her eyes roamed over his clothes and to his shoes, silent while Angeliqué stood over her, brushes in hand. Thin lines of wet brown and black paint were visible on her stomach—a star radiating out from her navel done in the design of a snowflake. Vince was stunned into silence by a shard of recognition that flowed through him. He couldn't put his finger on it, but something about this woman reminded him of…something…he just couldn't quite place it.

"Vince," Angeliqué said, "I'd like you to meet Jacques, over there, one of my male models, and this pretty thing here is Amber." Vince nodded his head to Jacques before turning back to the lounging Amber. She was staring at him while his gaze swept over her.

"Amber, a pleasure," Vince said with a smile. "You look vaguely familiar;

is it possible that we have met before?" The woman continued to stare at him for a moment before responding.

"No, I don't believe so," she responded softly. Amber turned her head, glanced up at the ceiling as Angeliqué bent back on her haunches and began applying paint to Amber's thighs. She worked silently for a few minutes as Vince stood and watched.

"You can take a seat if you'd like," Angeliqué remarked. We are almost done here—then I've got to get ready. Not much time before show time!"

Vince took a seat and let his gaze sweep across the room. It was large, airy and free of clutter. A number of paintings of various sizes adorned the walls. Off to Vince's right side was a large wooden worktable covered with paints, brushes, and artist's tools. Behind it, a picture window looked out on the courtyard garden below. In one corner was a small, dirty sink. Over by the male model, Vince noticed an altar of sorts—a small wooden table covered with a pyramid of lit, scented candles, of various sizes and colors. Several cloth dolls were propped up, along with a myriad of assorted things—coins, incense, cigarettes, playing cards, and sequin-covered bottles, one containing a doll's head. In addition, dozens of beads and beaded necklaces were strewn about the surface of the altar and adorned the dolls; a large metal cross and *paket kongo*—cloth packets bound with ribbons and other decorations, topped with feathers. A large embroidered rug covered the floor. An old brown leather couch and an oak coffee table were set against a wall facing dozens of paintings, some unfinished, which leaned against a bare wall. Vince noticed a copy of his book was sitting on the coffee table near a pair of burning candles and the colorful and fragrant tulips. The scent of incense filled the room.

"Angeliqué has been talking about you, Vince" Jacques said, shifting off of his stool. Vince's gaze swept to the man's large penis and testicles, which were shaven and painted with red *veve* of Papa Legba, guardian of the crossroad between the sacred and mortal worlds—the repeating patterns of red, intricate crosses, keys, and walking canes. He quickly looked up to the man's face.

"All lies, I'm sure," Vince replied with a smile. He unbuttoned his jacket and took a seat on the couch, stealing a quick glance over at Amber. From his vantage point, it was an unobstructed view to her painted thighs. She, too, was shaved, the thin, swirling lines of the *veve* decorating her sex in a manner that Vince found enthralling. Amber had dropped her gaze from the ceiling, checked Angeliqué's work and glanced over at Vince. She seemed totally at ease and carefree as her lips curled into a tight smile before returning her stare to the painter.

"I doubt it," Jacques continued. "We heard all about the workshop and your subsequent dinner at Brennan's. Actually, that's all we've been talking about." Jacques laughed and snorted.

"I know that's right," Amber said softly.

"Oh, the two of you need to be quiet and mind yours...both of you are just jealous." Angeliqué pivoted on her haunches and stole a quick glance at Vince while she grinned. "Wish you could be with a finely dressed man like Vince. Ain't that right, Jacques?" Jacques just smirked.

"Oh I know that's right!" Amber proclaimed, giving Vince a seductive smile.

"Okay, we're done here. Stand up, Amber, and you too, Jacques. Let me see the two of you together." Amber stood and stretched. Vince stared at her perfect form, her shapely hips, ass, and firm breasts. She was young—Vince judged her at no more than twenty-two. For the second time, a vein of recognition quivered in his mind, but once again, he couldn't seize it.

Jacques walked over to join Amber on the rug, the *veve* covering his skin undulating like a serpent. He reached for Amber, slid his arms around her thin waist; their hips joined and Vince was astounded to see the new pattern that emerged as their skins converged. Angeliqué was hovering around their bodies checking her handiwork, touching and probing with her brushes, ensuring everything was perfect. Amber's gaze swept around the room, not focusing on anything in particular. Then she settled on Vince sitting on the couch and smiled—it was an innocent grin—her standing there, her body bare, taut skin covered with the *veve* of a voodoo goddess, and yet, Vince felt something stir in him. He brushed the thoughts quickly from his head.

"It's show time," Angeliqué exclaimed, before exiting quickly from the room, as if she were riding on puffs of air...

✖✖✖

Four hours later he found himself standing with Angeliqué in the court-yard garden, the glow from the gallery bathing them in shadows. Angeliqué looked sensational in a pair of thin, form-fitting black satin pants, a see-through black top with solid sleeves and embroidery-like designs across the front, and a pattern-filled belt with a large, oval buckle made of silver. Added to this ensemble was a pair of hanging earrings of tiny stones strewn together in the shape of a pyramid, matching necklace; hair combed down her back. In her hand she held a flute of champagne. Vince toasted Angeliqué as her hand slipped around his waist.

"I'd say the show was an unqualified success!" Vince remarked. She grinned up at him and squeezed his sides.

How to describe the show—close to five-hundred, well-dressed people had shown up. There were five models, including Amber and Jacques. Each had been painted with a different, distinct *veve*. The models had been posi-tioned in different corners of the gallery, lit from above by track lighting, and for the first hour they remained in unmoving poses for ten to fifteen minutes apiece while folks crowded around, watching, staring, and admiring the body art. Angeliqué had moved between the crowd, Miles Davis' "Kind of Blue" playing softly in the background, encouraging the participants to touch her artwork, feel the *veve*, experience the *veve* as it moved and breathed—and people did not have to be told twice—fingers met bare *veve*-covered flesh, felt it as the models moved and breathed, while waiters served champagne and seafood hors d'oeuvres. Excited women and a few men drew their clammy palms across the taut chest and thigh muscles of Jacques as he stood there, his stare unwavering. Then later, pairs of bare models drew together for joint poses, male-female, female-female, male-female-male combinations that were strikingly erotic. Face-to-face, breasts and nipples covered with paint touching, or face-to-back, bodies pressed together, the crowd bearing down on the models, anxious to run a finger or hand across painted flesh. At one point Jacques reclined on the bare floor, Amber climbed on top of him, and lay her sleek festooned body over his—

they remained there, flesh upon flesh, the ending of one *veve* creating the beginning of another, a sea of decorated, undulating flesh, erotic, seductive, and enthralling to all who witnessed this performance.

To say the least, the crowd loved it!

Afterwards, Angeliqué stood mid-center of her models and bowed, said a few words about her art, the flashes from cameras of local newspapers and television stations reflecting off of gallery walls and ceiling. Her gallery assistants worked the crowd, and sold a number of pieces. Throughout the evening, Vince watched with deep admiration, enjoying the show and the closeness to Angeliqué who was never far from him. She introduced him to many of her friends and artsy acquaintances as a big-time author from up North, and he enjoyed mingling and networking with the crowd. All in all, everyone agreed, it was a very successful evening.

"So, Mr. Cannon, Jr., tell me honestly what you thought of my show," Angeliqué asked, nuzzling against Vince. He wrapped an arm around her shoulder, and gazed down into her eyes.

"It was incredible, Angeliqué. I've never seen anything that stirred me as much as what I saw here tonight. You have an amazing talent. There is no doubt that this is just the beginning of where your creativity can take you." Vince kissed her lightly on the mouth. His tongue invaded her mouth and she tasted him, grabbed hold and devoured him as if he were a piece of succulent lamb, marinated with heavenly spices. In the background, the sound of running water gurgling from the pond infused with the darkness.

When they finally parted, she held him by both hands and said, "Let's go back to my studio. There's something I want to do to you." Her eyes sparkled with mischief and of untold things to come.

"It's not gonna hurt, is it?" Vince asked with a smirk.

"That…is what I should be asking you…"

NINE

I'm back y'all…Yeah, Trey in 'da house! Livin' large and in charge! But, hold up—I see some of you haters out there—yeah, you know who you are—just standing there with your hand on your hip snickering—"last time we saw that fool, he wasn't talking very much smack!" Well, let me tell you something, *dickwad*—Trey is in control and back on the scene, ya heard? Back from a wonderful, crazy, mind-blowing, better-than-I-ever-could-have-imagined, sex-laden vacation that left me purring like a damn kitty! DAYUM! That shit was 'da bomb!

But, enough about the past! Fast forward to today. A lovely Wednesday morning and I was on top of the world. Just got back into town late last night. Felt like I hadn't been home in a month! My shit was all strewn around my crib—lots of dirty laundry, unopened mail, and shit to put away. But I left a message with Mrs. Feathers, who cleans and does my laundry, to swing by. My crib would be sparkling clean and my clothes laundered and put away by the time I got home from work tonight

So, there I was…driving down 16th on my way to work feeling totally refreshed and rejuvenated—top down, the drone from the M3 invigorating, permeating every nerve ending, Lenny Kravitz's jam—"Dig In"—playing on the in-dash CD player—the twelve Harmon/Kardon speakers cranked so that I could hear that mutha fucka's guitar wail as only he can! The thumping in your face rhythm from Lenny, my fingers hammered against the leather-clad steering wheel like a bass player. Me, shaded, in an auburn-colored, two-button, single-breasted suit, a light-blue cotton shirt, yellow and blue spotted silk tie, and leather lace ups. One word said it all—*sharp-sophisticate*! Okay, smarty pants, that's two words! Just singing away as if there was nobody sharing the street with me: *...once you dig in, you'll find you're coming out the other side...*

I downshifted as I pulled up to a red light. Off to my left, a lovely honey in a tight mini and vibrant yellow top with her titties jiggling underneath her sheer blouse came off the curb, watching me with a curved smile. Her hair was light and frizzy, standing off her head like an eighties fro, but I was not mad at her! She was looking good. Sistah was clocking me, I kid you not! As she got even with my bumper her smile was replaced by a frown as she *processed* the music and wrinkled up her nose at the rock-infused song. She shook her head slightly. I lowered the volume via the controls on the steering wheel.

"What's the matter, baby?" I said, clearing my throat and speaking above the engine noise. "Don't like my music?" I flashed a smile, showing her my teeth as I ran a hand over the lapel of my jacket.

"All that money," girlfriend replied, still shaking her head from side to side, the flash in her smile gone, "nice ride, threads, yet brutha-man still ain't got no sense!" She made it to the other side of the street, glanced back once more before turning her head and moving on, swaying her hips and fine ass 'cause she knew I was watching.

I swear to God the words: "Fuck you, be-yatch!" were forming on my tongue when I checked myself. Instead, I calmly replied, "Sorry, baby, if I'm not your *style*...but to each his own..." I guess she was expecting me to be sporting some hip-hop shit like Busta Rhymes or somebody. Pu-leaze! I tipped my head back and laughed as my eyes sparkled with mischief. I cranked Lenny back up while watching her sashaying up the street, attitude dripping from every pore of her being. My philosophy was simple—your loss if you don't dig my style. No harm, no foul. I put the M3 in gear and peeled away, leaving that sweetness on the sidewalk alone, with something to think about...

A few moments later I pulled into my spot in the garage on Pennsylvania

Avenue. It was a quarter 'til 8. I breathed deeply, listened to the electric whirl as the soft-top unfolded itself from the trunk, settling in overhead, and locking down. I grabbed my briefcase from the back seat and walked to the elevator that took me to the eleventh floor and my office. I was glad to be back, actually. Work didn't stress me. I loved what I did and was damn good at it. And so, I walked with a skip in my step, pushed the "up" button as I hummed softly and checked myself in the steel reflection. "Once you dig in, you'll find you'll have yourself a good time!" Trey back in the saddle, y'all. True dat!

✖✖✖

I flashed my signature smile as I swept into the reception area like a storm. Becky was at the front desk, headset over her blonde hair, smiling as I waltzed in.

"What's up, baby girl?" I said, running my palm over the teak reception desk. She glanced up, desire in her eyes as mine traveled down the front of her blouse to where those lovely mountains rose.

"You're back!" she exclaimed. "How was your vacation? Did you miss me?"

"Baby, it was wonderful, but you know I did. I couldn't help but thinking, how much better it would have been if you had been there with me…Oh, the things we could have done, my sweet Becky!" I replied, pursing my lips and then grinning.

"You are too much," she glanced around before lowering her voice as her stare found mine, locking on, "and *so* full of shit. But I'm glad you're back. We missed you around here."

"I'm sure," I said confidently.

"Perhaps you should invite me to lunch to *catch up*…"

I leaned over the desk and scanned her curves slowly before replying, "perhaps I should…" And then I had a sudden epiphany—a wonderfully, delicious thought of sweet, sultry Becky sprawled across my sheets, butt naked—and I felt myself getting hard at the thought of my chocolate-covered Johnson sliding between her smooth, white thighs. But then I caught myself—Trey's Rule Number 28—Don't fuck the help. Or put another way—Don't shit where you eat! I sighed heavily, my smirk replaced with a look of disappointment.

I strolled on, passing folks who welcomed me back and commented on my tan features. I just grinned and high-fived a few partners who were in the hallway conversing, coffee in hand. I came to another reception area—this one a bit smaller than the main one. My assistant was hunched over her desk, head between her legs, her dreads spilling across the white top.

"Whatchew looking at, girl?" I asked. She quickly popped her head up, sending her hair flying.

"Well, well, look what the cat dragged in…"

"Good morning to you, India!" I said.

"That's Ms. Jackson, to you!"

"Pardon. Morning, India Jasmine Jackson! Better?"

"Much." India smiled while wiping the dreads out of her face. "So, Trey, how was it? And don't leave any details out. You know you gotta give a sistah the *full* 411."

"India, all I can say is that it was off the chain! For real. It was all that and a bag of chips, I kid you not! Off the rocker!"

"For real?"

"For real. I'll fill you in later." I walked into my corner office with India trailing in tow. My office was large and spacious, and had a wide view of the street below. In the distance the Capitol could be seen to the left. A cream-colored leather couch was set in the middle of the room on a patterned throw rug. Across from the couch was a pair of thick upholstered chairs. A low, glass coffee table stood between the chairs and the couch. On the walls were various paintings—a large African plains scene on one wall and two smaller framed prints done by local black artists on another. Behind the chairs was a wide bookshelf with hundreds of books, mostly from my academic years. A high-tech looking Bang & Olufsen CD player/tuner was sandwiched on the top shelf—the remote laid at the corner of the coffee table. I loved my office. It was very much a part of me. It made me (and my clients) feel comfortable, and that was important in a job where I sometimes spent many hours walking them through the ins and outs of divorce court.

I put my bag down on the couch and went behind my desk that was situated in front of the large picture window. I sat in my chair, swiveled around to boot up my computer and glanced through my messages that were neatly arranged on the corner of my cherrywood desk. "So, what have I missed around here?"

"Not much. Oh, Calvin wants to see you as soon as you get settled."

"Yeah, okay. Tell him I'm on my way up in five." India retreated. "Oh, by the way, I got you something." I rose and went to the couch where my bag laid. India waited by the door with an excited look in her eye. She was dark skinned, about five-six, nicely shaped with thick, long dreads. India possessed a great smile. She had been with the firm for eight years. She knew her shit and could keep up with the best of them. She talked shit in front of me because I allowed it. But she was strictly professional. That was until she tried to nose into my business and I had to tell her where to step off!

I opened my briefcase and rummaged inside. "What the hell?" I exclaimed with a puzzled look on my face. "Where did I put that thing?" I paused for effect while watching her out of the corner of one eye. India squirmed around like a child.

"Stop playing, Trey!"

"Oh, here it is." My hand emerged, holding a small box wrapped in colorful paper. I handed it to her. She wasted no time ripping off the outer cover.

"Oh my goodness, they are beautiful!" She held up a pair of wooden earrings, dark triangles with intricate carvings on the face, done by hand by one of the natives.

"Yup, one of the locals carved those on the beach by my hotel. Saw them and thought of you."

"Oh, Trey, I take back every nasty thing I've ever said about you." India came over and hugged me. I feigned revulsion for a moment but then hugged her back.

"Don't get mushy on me, Ms. Jackson, or I'll fire your black ass. Now, listen up: I need an eight p.m. reservation at bluespace for this evening, table for three, our usual spot, and then give Vince and Erika a call reminding them of our little get together. Oh, and call that chick over at BET, what's her name? Oh yeah, Alicia something...tell her I need a pair of tickets to the Brian McKnight concert that they just announced on the radio—I need really good seats, like first couple of rows—if she can't deliver those I'm not interested...tell her there will be something real good in it for her if she does—something that involves lots of oral sex!"

"You so nasty!"

"I know."

"So, who you taking to that show?" India inquired.

"You so damn nosy. Anyway, who the hell knows? I've got two weeks to decide," I replied as I swept out of my office, leaving India standing there, admiring her earrings in one hand, and shaking her head. "Tell Calvin I'm on my way up!" I yelled as I rounded the corner, quickly out of sight.

✖✖✖

Calvin Figgs, ESQ., was my boss and 'da man. A managing partner with the firm for the past fifteen years, he had personally recruited me out of Georgetown, mentored me while I prepared for the bar; helped me to get a clerkship at the D.C. Superior Court under Judge Henry Jackson, Jr. before moving me over to the firm. That was five years ago. He had made sure that his pick worked extra hard—and hard work is what I gave him back. For the past five years I've been one of the rising stars at the firm, taking on the difficult and complex cases, many involving high-profile clients and celebrities. The hard work had paid off. Calvin, who is legendary in Washington as a shrewd attorney, art collector, philanthropist, and an "A-List" kind of guy, had taken me under his wing. I got to know his family and spend some time with him at his home. Now many of the sweet cases were passed my way, or at a minimum, I had been given the right of first refusal.

I took the steps up to the twelfth floor and found him in his corner office. Calvin's office was three times the size of mine and could have come out of the pages of *Architectural Digest*. The amount of teakwood amongst these walls alone would make any grown man cry.

Calvin looked up from his phone call, smiled and waved me to a chair. I took a seat in the red leather wingback chair facing the floor-to-ceiling windows. A number of art pieces littered his office—a few bronze sculptures, colorful paintings, and knickknacks that Calvin had picked up from his journeys around the world. He signed off, removed his headset and got up to shake my hand. I stood as a sign of respect.

"Good to see you back in the office, Trey," Calvin Figgs said, his voice clear and steady as the morning air. "How was the vacation, son?"

I smiled affectionately. "It was wonderful, good for the soul, Calvin. Just what the doctor ordered." Calvin grinned and went to the door, shutting it softly. He was tall and a well-built man, mid-fifties, in excellent shape, with short dark hair that was peppered with flecks of gray. A thin, closely manicured beard adorned his dark face. He had smooth lips and an engaging smile. A pair of designer reading glasses was perched on top of his head.

"Bullshit. Don't play an old school playa, Trey. Tell me how it really was!"

"Okay, you always were the man…"

"Damn skippy, and don't you forget it!" Calvin remarked, taking a seat across from me. He folded his legs, and ran a hand down the crease of his pants. Calvin's suit was immaculate. He was dressed as only Calvin could— dark Armani suit, crisp white shirt, silk silver patterned tie, and leather loafers. The man could put me to shame when it came to dressing—in fact, he's the one who taught me everything I know in this world about clothes and fashion.

"Well, Calvin, what can I say? I found paradise. I kid you not!"

"Go on." Calvin leaned forward, elbows on his knees while he steepled his hands in front of his face.

"I can't describe this place and do justice to it. All I can say is that…"

"Trey, brevity was never your strong suit. Just tell me how many?"

"Actually, sir, I lost count." I grinned.

"Hot damn! That's my dawg!" Calvin remarked. He high-fived me, then sat back. "You know I've got to live vicariously through you, since the Missus wouldn't appreciate me whoring around town."

"Don't even think about it, Calvin; you've got yourself a fine woman there."

Calvin and I chatted for a few minutes, but I could see that something wasn't quite right. He wasn't his normal jovial self. I cut to the chase.

"Calvin, what's up? You've got something on your mind. I *know* you," I said gently.

Calvin's look took on an air of seriousness. "Trey, we've brought in a new managing partner." He paused, letting the weight of that sink in.

"WHAT?" I said incredulously. Suddenly everything, including the trip to Jamaica was a distant memory. "You're the managing partner of this firm. Have been for fifteen years!" I wanted to fucking scream, but I kept my composure. Something was definitely not right here.

"His name is Bernard John Marshall. He's a rainmaker from Briggs McPherson out of New York City. A good guy. Lots of connections in the right places."

"You're a good guy with *loads* of connections in the right places." I stood and paced his office, never taking my eyes off him.

"Trey, it's not that bad. Things will change somewhat—they always do when a new partner is brought in, but you have nothing to worry about. Your assignments won't change. And…"

"Calvin." I stooped down on my haunches to be eye level with him. I spoke softly but distinctly. "Listen, this is me you're talking to. We go way back and you're like family to me. So please—tell me what the *fuck* is going on?"

✖✖✖

A knock at Calvin's door broke the spell. Both our eyes turned in unison. Calvin cleared his voice and said, "Come in." In walked Bernard John Marshall.

I fucking knew it was him, and instantly I hated the man. They say first impressions are everything. Bernard John Marshall strode in, and the first thing that I noticed was his grayish-black hair that swept back from his forehead, coated with a layer of gel. He reminded me of a gangster. *Goodfellas*, for God's sake. His face was thin and angular, not an ounce of fat anywhere on his cheeks or chin. He was jacketless. Thin body and tall; a flat stomach—obviously, he worked out. His white shirt was impeccable.

His tie: Neiman-Marcus, Private Collection (I know; I shop there.) He came to us, extended his hand to me as he grinned, showing me his perfect teeth. "You must be Trey Alexander. A pleasure. Bernard John Marshall." I watched his eyes as I took his hand. They were jet-black, motionless, and lacked any depth. They just stared back—this dead/dull kind of expression that spoke volumes. That's when I was sure I hated the mutha fucka. He was going to make my life a living hell. I could sense it.

"Calvin, morning to you." He smoothed out his tie with his bony hand. Calvin waved him to a seat.

"Morning, Bernie, I was just telling Trey that you had joined the firm."

"Wonderful. I've heard a great deal about you. I'm looking forward to us working together." I smiled and nodded, but said nothing.

"Calvin tells me that you've got an interesting deposition coming up." He paused while turning his head in my direction, those lifeless eyes neither darting left nor right. "Quentin Hues, Washington Wizards forward."

I took a breath. "Yes. Settlement agreement. Tomorrow morning if memory serves me." I knew exactly when the fucking meeting was and what the particulars of it were.

"Sounds interesting."

"How so?" I kept this deadpan expression on my face. I wasn't gonna give this mutha fucka shit. Not until Calvin and I finished our one-on-one. "It's your typical agreement. Division of property, etcetera, etcetera…not too terribly exciting," I said.

"Yes. Except for the fact that the property in question is valued at over five million dollars." Bernard was pokerfaced and I didn't like that one bit.

I shrugged. "The guy's a professional athlete. Been in the league for five years. What can I say? He signed a sweet deal with the Wizards. With New York before that." Bernard had been snooping around in my files, that much was clear. "I'm sure you knew that," I added scornfully. Note to self—have a *chat* with India, ASAP. We need to lock down the fucking office! I glanced at Calvin. He, too, was pokerfaced. At least his eyes were *alive* with movement.

"Sounds like you have things well in hand. I'll look forward to hearing how things turn out." Bernard John Marshall stood and shook my hand. "I'll let you two get back to your business. Again, good to meet you, Trey."

I stood. "You, too, Mr. Marshall."

"Please. Call me Bernard. Calvin."

"As you wish," I said ever so softly as my eyes flicked over to Calvin who merely nodded, yet remained silent.

TEN

Angeliqué was not about to waste any more time. She went to her altar, lit the candles and incense, returned to the couch where Vince had chosen to sit, lit those on the coffee table as well and extinguished the light. Warm air swirled in through an open window, causing the flames to flicker. Angeliqué silently handed Vince a wine stem, went to her worktable, grabbed her brushes and paints, and returned to the center of her studio where hours earlier she had worked on Amber. Shadows of her lovely form wavered on the surrounding walls.

"Take off your jacket and sweater," she commanded. Vince stood, removed his jacket and placed it on the ends of the couch. She watched as he took off his sweater, noticing the well-developed muscles of his stomach and upper body. He started for her but she spoke... "Come to think of it, take off your pants, too. We certainly don't want to mess up a perfectly good suit, now do we?" Her eyes had closed to mere slits, but Vince could still see the twinkle in her stare as she kneeled on the rug. He obeyed— came to her, the fabric of his black boxers pulled taut. His heart was fluttering. She reached for him, pulled him down onto the carpet and began adorning his chest with color.

At first, she used light delicate strokes, and then she abandoned her craft, deliberately cutting wide, uneven swaths across his neck, nipples, and stomach. Vince laughed, grabbed his wine stem and took a healthy swig; the amber-colored liquid spilled and meandered down his bearded chin to his chest. It mixed with the still-wet paint. Angeliqué laughed. She pulled the wine away from him and took a wild swig. Vince reached for her blouse and pulled upward—her arms raised without indecision and it came off. Underneath, she was braless. Next the belt and pants were removed. She was still painting him, applying red, brown, and orange paint onto his legs and thighs, the thick brush sweeping past his boxers, lingering for a few moments so that she could feel his flesh. He grabbed the brush from her hand, dipped the tip in red wet paint and applied a swath to her swaying breasts. She giggled and he repeated the movement again, applying circles until her entire upper body was covered.

Angeliqué began to wrestle him, attempting to pry the brush from his grasp. Vince was far more powerful, and won easily, although Angeliqué didn't give up without a fight. He directed the brush to her lower region, painting a wide path from one thigh to her knee. She had her head back and was laughing; suddenly she kicked out at him as he reached behind her and felt her ass. Vince maneuvered over her, and she reclined into a prone position; he placed the freshly dipped brush between his teeth and ran it across her neck, shoulders, and chin. Simultaneously, and without warning, he grasped each end of her g-string between his fingers. Her eyes widened briefly as she felt the fabric moving down her legs. And then she was naked, frowning because he was still covered. She thrashed out, attempting to reach for him, but Vince was too quick, squirming out of her reach. During the lull in the excitement, Angeliqué grabbed a bit of blue paint with her fingers, tricked him into coming near her—not that he needed coaxing—smeared it over his back and ass, before catching the rim of his boxers with her cupped hand and yanking *hard*. The boxers came off, Vince yelping as they tore down his legs and ankles.

And then Angeliqué was on him in a flash, her body moving like that of a cat, firm breasts hovering over his chest, her hair in her face and his, Vince's hands reaching for her, feeling the ripened mounds of flesh and squeezing, twirling fingers about her nipples, and consuming her mouth with his. Angeliqué savored the feeling of their mouths and bodies pressed together as one, the current that surged from her insides, pushing outward until she felt as if she were about to burst. They tasted each other, no-holds barred, giving into their desires, exploring each other with their mouths, tongues, hands, and fingers. Vince moaned under Angeliqué, his sex fully engorged and feeling as if he was ready to explode from the passion and excitement. Her thighs rubbed against his, her hips seductively rotating against his muscular legs, the heat between hers overpowering. Vince closed his eyes, desperately wanting to ensure that this was no delusion. Before he could open his eyes, Angeliqué impaled herself with Vince's hardness—riding him bareback, Vince a beautiful, black stallion, her legs splayed wide across his wonderful, decorated body, gripping the reins of his flesh, her head back, eyes shut, skin dripping with acrylic color and blending with their sweat as the candle flames flickered and fluttered, and Vince and Angeliqué gave in to their fervor…

They made love, intensely and passionately, the way true lovers do. Vince shut his eyes and concentrated on *feeling* Angeliqué, every nerve tip alive and dripping with sensitivity. His entire being seemed to be swallowed up by her, she riding him slowly, enjoying every delicious inch of his manhood, Vince smiling as her pelvis ground against his, and his arms reached around to hold her, feel her delicate flesh as his fingers glided across her paint-covered skin.

"My God, you feel so incredible!" Vince managed to say in between lunges of his hips. She smiled, then giggled, reached for the paint tray, swiped at the pile of bright orange paint with her fingers, and smeared it all over his chest, circling his nipples. As she continued to squirm against him, her hand snaked down his stomach to where they joined, and on her upstroke, she grasped hold of his member, wrapped her hand solidly around him and decorated it with the paint, before plunging back down on his stiffness. Vince grinned as she coated him with the sticky dye, reaching for her taut nipples as she threw her head back and laughed. Then she tilted to the side and they came undone, Vince following her lead, scooping her up in his powerful arms and laying her gently underneath him. She glanced down, wanted to witness him in all of his glory. She touched him, wrapped her hand around his penis again, and felt his pulse as she guided him back into her wetness.

"Oh, YES!" Angeliqué shouted, her voice rising in pitch as he slipped into her, his forearms resting near hers as he bent down and kissed her lips. Then his muscles flexed as he pushed up and moved arms length from her, his hips and ass below a frenzied array of movement as he unleashed his vigor into her. Angeliqué thrashed underneath him, her sweaty hips and thighs a blur of activity in response to his thrusts. She reached for his face, tugged at his closely cropped beard that she found so damn sexy, and gripped the back of his head as she watched him make love to her, the exquisite feeling of him alternately filling then draining her, so intense and overshadowing, that she felt herself flush. And then Vince paused, pressed his body against hers, the sticky pigment from his chest, stomach, and legs mingling with hers. They remained this way, quiet and frozen, the only sound coming from their harried breathing, each feeling the other's heartbeat, powerful and strong, as they listened to the wind as it rustled in from the open window.

Vince came off Angeliqué, knelt before her and let his gaze sweep from her tousled hair to her painted toes. How lovely she was! He reached for her, turned her over gingerly until she was on her stomach, her lovely ass rising like a crescent shaped moon above the now sticky carpet. He scooped up a handful of red paint from the tray, and silently lathered up her thighs, ass, and lower back until a solid coat of paint was evident. Angeliqué turned her head to the side and laid it in her hands while she watched him work his art. When he had smoothed out the coat of paint, smeared it around her flesh and massaged it in to her skin with his fingers, he reached for the bright blue acrylic, scooped up a small mound and applied a wide swath in a circle around her ass. Next, he grabbed some green paint and did the same, drawing a smaller, inner circle, closer to her canal. Lastly, he reached for the black paint, measured out two-fingers' worth as Angeliqué moaned and spread her legs sensuously for him. With the candles flickering in the background, creating dancing shadows on the walls, Vince smeared the black coloring over and around her sex, the tips of his fingers gliding in between the slippery folds of her molten core. He sat back finally, admired his handiwork, as Angeliqué lay there panting, a bull's-eye on her lovely, fine ass. Vince smiled a wicked grin, before guiding himself back inside of her.

He thrust against her decorated ass with abandonment, the passion within both of them riding high until it crested like a giant tidal wave—and they cried out, in tandem, consuming each other until there was nothing left to give, the passion wrung out, spent—the relief oozing out from pores and orifices like sap from a tree. And Angeliqué lifted her head slowly, turned toward her altar of burning candles and incense, recited a quick prayer of thanks to the love goddess of voodoo before closing her eyes and losing herself in this ecstasy of this man named Vince…

✖✖✖

The chime from the cell phone awoke them—Vince at first, then Angeliqué, who was nestled in his arms, paint-coated back to him, and under the warm confines of a blanket. The chime stung his senses—at first he was unaware of his surroundings, but one look at the disheveled bronze hair on his chest told the story—he smiled as he felt Angeliqué stir, stretching her legs and flexing her backside, which was nuzzled against him on the carpeted floor.

Vince extricated himself from the still half-asleep form of Angeliqué, rose and moved, naked, to the leather sofa where his clothes and cell phone laid. He answered on the fifth ring; his eyes stretched wide open as he scanned his paint-clad body, and recalled delicious images from the previous night.

"Hello?"

"Hey you." A woman's voice. Vince was staring at Angeliqué who had turned toward him, and was staring admirably at his nude form, her eyes not roaming but fixed in one position.

"Hey…" Vince did not recognize the voice.

"I'm…not…calling at a bad time, am I?" The voice raised in pitch. Angeliqué's stare had elevated to his eyes. She watched him silently, as he stood there naked, cell phone in hand. She knew it was a woman on the other end of the phone. No doubt about that. None whatsoever.

"No…not really." Recognition came to him and he unconsciously frowned. It was Maxi.

"You haven't called." A statement.

"…I've been busy with my workshop…" Vince was beginning to get uncomfortable. He attempted a smile at Angeliqué, but it came out flat and weak. She sensed his discomfort immediately.

"…Which was over Friday night. It's *now* Sunday morning. Forgot how to dial, or just busy?" Maxine was pissed and she made no attempt to hide her blossoming irritation. Vince had turned his body toward the still-open window. He glanced down at the garden-courtyard, which was bathed in sunlight. The trickling pond shimmered in the morning light. Angeliqué watched him as he moved toward the window, his back to her. She slipped out from beneath the blanket, rose, nude, like him, her body adorned with the battle-scars from last night's lovemaking session. She smiled with the recollection of them falling asleep with Vince still inside of her, the two of them on their sides, spooning each other as Vince held her tight and nuzzled his face against her warm neck. The feeling—indescribable. She had been in heaven. Still was…

"Listen, I'd prefer not to get into this right…" Vince paused as he felt Angeliqué's hand circle his waist. Before he could pivot on his heels, her warm body was pressing against him, and he felt her soft breasts bear down on his painted back, her pubic hair rubbing against his ass. He began to harden.

"Oh I see!" Maxi said, loud enough for Angeliqué to hear. "I guess this *isn't* a good time after all!" she said, all indignant. "Let me not hold you up, Vince!" He turned to Angeliqué, wrapping an arm around her waist and pulling her into him, relishing the warmth from her naked skin. He was fully hard now, as Angeliqué had taken his member in her hand and was slowly squeezing and tugging on his sex, a wicked grin spreading across his face.

"We need to talk, Maxi," Vince replied, taking a moment to exhale forcefully, his hand dropping from Angeliqué's waist to her lovely round ass. He took hold of it and squeezed. She moaned involuntarily. Vince turned away; concerned that the sound could be heard on the other end of the cell phone. "I will call you when I get a moment to talk—I'm heading to L.A. this afternoon, so it may be later on in the evening."

"Fine. Whatever." The phone went dead and Vince sighed, snapping his phone shut. Angeliqué moved in front of him, positioned herself dead center and in his space. His manhood was snuggled decisively between her painted thighs. She looked up at him with an iniquitous grin.

"Problems at home?" she said, faux-innocence dripping from her baby-girl voice like maple syrup.

"Good morning to you, too!" Vince said, his pulse slowly returning to normal...

✖✖✖

They showered together to remove the paint from their bodies. While the hot water pounded against their freshly scrubbed skin, they made love again, Vince taking her from behind as Angeliqué stood in the shower stall, her palms pressed against the dripping white tile, her head thrown back in complete utter delight, and her lovely bronze mane dangling down her back in a single coil of wet, stringy hair. Vince's hands went to her breasts, massaged her nipples and soft mounds, and held on as their bodies slapped together underneath the rush of steamy water.

Afterwards, they dried each other and dressed, and Angeliqué prepared a hearty breakfast for Vince—an oversized Creole omelet with cheese, tomatoes, and fresh crawfish that she had picked up from the market the previous morning; bacon, and strong coffee. He had to get back to his hotel—pack and get ready for his trip—his flight to Los Angeles left that afternoon, four p.m. to be exact, and it was close to noon now. And of course with security being what it was these days, he needed to give himself plenty of time at the airport. It was time to go...

And so...Vince and Angeliqué stood out in front of a closed art gallery on a brilliantly lit Sunday morning, on a quiet street named St. Philip, in the decadent French Quarter of New Orleans, a short, lovely walk from here to the Mississippi River, a wonderful breeze catching the leaves and causing them to quiver as Vince kissed Angeliqué tenderly under the flicker of an overhead gas lamp. No words were spoken; nothing further needed to be said. Sometimes, the language of lovemaking is more than enough...

✖✖✖

And later—much much later, Vince found himself staring out at the sprawl that is known as Los Angeles. His mind was racing—shuttles, hotels, food, business at hand, book signings, workshops, speaking engagements—and just as the flight attendants were preparing the cabin for landing—his mind pushed all of this irrelevant stuff to the side and made way for the *new* object of his affection—he was staring at the business card that had "Angeliqué Malevaux—Artist" in embossed lettering; his fingers rubbed the inscription as if doing so over and over, like Aladdin and his magic lamp, would somehow bring her to him this very instant; transcending time, and, more importantly, space—and he desperately wished that he could remember the voodoo god/goddess of love—Freda *somebody*—wished that he had been paying better attention when Angeliqué had mentioned these deities by name, so he could issue his request in prayer right now...

✖✖✖

And then, in an instant, Vince found himself running through the white terminal, the steady stream of luggage-clad passengers a nuisance on his corneas as he dodged old ladies and children holding Pokemon and Barbie dolls. Outside, sliding into a taxi and slinging his bags in behind him, shouting orders to the turban-clad cabdriver, rolling, and the city-side a blur as his foot tapped incessantly with mounting impatience. Eyes moving, shifting like sand in a storm as he glanced ahead, willing cars, trucks, and buses in front of him to part around him like the Red Sea, annoyance and irritation boiling under the surface, like a fighter ready to strike. Subsequently, he was descending into a tunnel and running along the tracks before the wind suddenly shifted, and the subway car arrived, its gleaming doors opening with a whoosh. In-a-rush passengers, pushing and shoving their way out like tuna trapped in a net, before the dust settled and he could see again. Vince breathed heavy, entered the train, moving again, from car to car, searching the backs of heads, necks, and shoulders, some all too familiar, until he was within arm's length, striking distance. Running now, knowing she was near—he knew it, could feel it, his skin tingling, synapses firing, and the smell of her, invading his senses, overpowering everything else, his legs weakening, blood pumping, rushing to tiring limbs, trying to hold up, under the escalating pressure. And Vince reaching out now, almost haphazardly, from one agitated individual to another, the snap of their head all-telling, yet Vince not giving up, knowing in his heart, that she was here…close at hand…

Finally onto the street—cool, refreshing air invading his lungs, away from the darkness and dampness that was making his skin *crawl*—turning the corner and yelling out in anticipation, the desire building like a tremor that metamorphoses into a rumbling earthquake. In the distance, a lovely form, hips and untamed hair swaying to an untold beat, synchronized with his rapidly beating heart, that in its own way, was attempting to break free from the confines of its chains.

And Vince finds himself reaching out, his fingers splayed, brushing against her hair as she turned, recognition lighting up her smile like the dawn. Vince falls to his knees, the tears erupting from his eyes as he comes face-to-face with his desires, opens his mouth to speak as she smiles, those perfect teeth and dazzling, sparkling eyes—and he begins to articulate his feelings to her, knowing that she may not comprehend—or worse, that she will be frightened, but having to go on nonetheless because Vince simply has no other choice…and so on bended knee he opens his mouth…prepares to say those simple, yet powerful words…yet nothing…*nothing* escapes from his lips…

ELEVEN

I arrived at the restaurant at quarter past 8. Pulled up to the front by a small crowd that had already formed under the signature sloping awning that rushed at folks from on high—plunging down like a ski slope before turning upward at that final moment and fanning out over the street; an awesome contraption of steel, mesh, and canvas, with neon blue at the tips spelling out the name of this eclectic establishment—bluespace. Me in my sexy-ass black M3, top down, clothes unchanged from earlier in the day, D'Angelo on the box—yeah, y'all, I was in *that* kind of mood—didn't want to hear nothing but old school funk, "Chicken Grease," to get me out of my own funk. The braided, *swoled* brutha did just that—I was singing along with the lyrics as I rolled up to the valet, checking out the patrons from behind light-purple shades even though it was dark outside, (you *know* by now how we do!), *Let me tell U 'bout the chicken grease...*

I handed the attendant a fifty, told him to keep it and my shit right out front. I pointed to a coned-off section that laid beyond the front door. He nodded rapidly as he squeezed into the heated leather seat. "Don't mess with my ride, *Holmes*," I remarked before heading inside.

A beautifully elegant Ethiopian woman named Nikki greeted me once inside the door. We hugged, I pecked her high cheek, commented on how damn sexy she looked, told her that if I had a piece of *injera* on me right now, I'd sop her up and eat her like a succulent mouthwatering portion of *zil zil*...Nikki just laughed, shook her head, and pointed upstairs to our usual spot.

How to describe bluespace? Art meets food. Jazz, colorful, vibrant images, and luscious dishes all coming together under one roof. Inside, the walls were whitewashed and curved, floor to ceiling. Multiple levels, with a balcony that ran the circumference of the place and allowed the patrons an unobstructed view of the floor below. A freestanding fireplace stood mid-center of the hardwood floor, open on four sides, a translucent chimney that carried the sparks and ash up to the sky. Multiple skylights were cut into the concave-shaped ceiling. Tonight they were open to the nighttime air.

The owner/designer, Scott Chase, had fashioned a unique light show and choreographed it to jazz. A ring of track lighting adorned the walls, mid-way between the floor and ceiling. Their beams were directed back onto the walls to display a vibrant show of patterns, colors and shapes. Scott Chase, a talented brutha with an eye for color and a taste for wonderful food, had married the two in bluespace. The place received rave reviews shortly after it opened. Reservations were hard to come by. Folks came from all over to see his light shows and sample his great cuisine. On the weekends, after twelve or one when the last of the patrons were gone, they'd clear the tables and turn bluespace into D.C.'s hottest after-hours spot—playing house, trance, acid-jazz, hip-hop, or old school, depending on the mood of the D.J. and the crowd.

I waltzed in, feeling my playa-vibe take over. That always happened when I was around well-dressed folks. Plus, the shit at work today had fucked my head up—left me with an annoying buzz going on inside of me—like a hunger that couldn't be satisfied; it hung just below the surface, out of reach, but letting me know that it was there.

I heard the sound of raindrops—slowly, imperceptibly at first, and then changing to a driving rain. The lights dimmed and for a moment winked out. Off to the right, a splash of purple and blue splayed across one wall. From the left, a swath of red and orange shot across the wall/sky, combining with the purple/blue in an explosion of color. Simultaneously, the beginning of a sunrise—a red hot/orange/indigo-colored horizontal line, bowed slightly, that rose slowly to the sounds of Boney James and his sax. Then, when it had risen almost to the top of the structure, the music changed, shifted to classic Pat Metheny Group—"Are You Going With Me?" The soulful, wind-inspired synths of Lyle Mays increasing in volume slowly until everyone was grooving along with the sound, as patterns erupted onto the walls from all directions—blue/greens, the colors of a Brazilian jungle, and its rich sounds—then shifting to the reddish brown and bronze earth tones of a California desert at twilight, the background noise of a rainstorm soothing and frightening at the same time. I had to pause in my step and watch, like everyone else, the scene mesmerizing and awe inspiring.

I reached the top step, folded my shades and put them away, and scanned the crowd, making eye contact with a few choice honeys who were seated with their men. Erika and Vince were already there. I grinned to them as I made my way over. Vince stood and hugged me. It had been a while—only a few weeks, actually, since I'd last seen my best friend in the flesh, because our schedules took us out of town, but it seemed like a lifetime. I missed my homey, and our drawn-out embrace told me he felt the same. He was dressed in a dark sports coat, tan slacks and loafers. He looked impeccable as usual and I told him so. I then turned and hugged Erika, kissing her on her cheek. What can I say about my home girl? Erika is the bomb, and she looked damn good as usual. Erika was tall, about five eight, thin, with smooth, caramel skin, black curly hair that she wore pulled back and resting on her shoulders. She wore a light-blue tank top, which accentuated her small, yet firm breasts and showcased her thin arms, an off-white knee-length skirt, a thick tan leather belt, and matching open toe shoes. Her face was beautiful—the suggestion of Asian descent, sculptured nose, thin lips and eyebrows, high cheekbones, and finally, just a hint of a cleft chin. We hugged affectionately. I had missed my girl, too! I pulled back, looked at her up and down admiringly while making animal noises. "Ummm, ummm, ummm! Damn, Sassy, you look fine. Don't she, Vince?"

"You know it. Classy as usual," Vince said, grinning and grabbing a sip from the wine stem in front of him.

"Fuck that, Holmes," I said, turning my attention once again to Erika who had taken her seat. "Baby girl, can a brutha getwithchew?" I licked my lips and she replied by swatting my arm. I just smiled and sat down. Trey's

Rule Number 13—don't fuck your friends, no matter how fine they are. For real!

The waiter came and I ordered a drink. Vince and Erika hadn't been seated more than five minutes. We got down to business.

"So, how ya livin'?" I asked around the table.

"Large and in charge," Vince responded.

"Me too!" Erika chimed in. We both shot her a nasty look.

"What?" She playfully hit me on the arm again. "I can't live large and in charge like the big boys?"

"Anyway…Damn, y'all," I said, kicking things off. "It feels like a lifetime since we've all gotten together."

"I know," Erika mused. "If you two would stop gallivanting all over God's green earth then maybe we could catch up on the *regular*."

"Oh no she didn't, Vince," I said, a feigned look of surprise on my face. Vince just shook his head silently. "Don't she know someone's gotta do it?"

"I guess she didn't get the memo," Vince remarked.

"Whatever," Erika said. "Anywho, I gather from both of your calls that there is a lot to cover tonight."

Erika, Vince and I had been doing this thing for over a year now—we'd come here to bluespace every other Wednesday to catch up, to find out what's going on in each other's lives—a lot easier having the three of us in one room as opposed to having separate conversations—not that that still didn't occur, mind you. I loved these times with Vince and Erika—they were my true friends—the ones I could share my innermost, deepest, darkest secrets with, and know that they would not judge me, regardless of my actions.

"So, whose turn is it anyway?" Erika asked. Vince and I turned to one another and said simultaneously: "Mine!"

"See," I said, placing my palms flat on the table. "This ain't right. You know it's my turn to go first this time." I looked to Erika for support; her face was scrunched up in a frown.

"I don't think so," Vince said calmly.

"Don't even try it, my man, you know it's my turn. Erika, help a brutha out, please?"

"Trey, you *always* try to weasel your way into going first. Damn, can't you let someone else go for a change?"

"That is not true. Vince, that's not true, right?" I looked to Vince for moral support, a man-to-man, brutha-to-brutha thing.

"True dat!" he said. "Now, can everyone kindly shut up, you especially, Trey, so I can say my piece? We're wasting valuable time here…" Vince said, looking at his watch.

"Sassy," I said, cutting my man off, "you notice how Vince always tries to act all grown up and shit? Like he's somehow a cut above the rest of us?"

"Yeah," Erika responded, eyeing Vince cautiously. "Who he think he is, anyway?"

"Exactly!" I joined in. Vince pressed his mouth shut and shook his head silently.

"Y'all are *so* damn childish! Anyway, as I was saying before being so rudely interrupted…I met *someone*…" Vince's eyes were sparkling and the table became silent.

"No shit?" I said, looking at Vince dumbfoundedly. Surrounding us, the light show was in full effect. Colorful strobes danced on and off to the sounds of Acoustic Alchemy, something upbeat and funky that left patrons tapping their hands and feet as swaths of colors—green flashes, oránge strobes, and yellow pulses danced and meandered across the ceiling and curved walls.

"Her name is Angeliqué, I met in her New Orleans during a workshop, and guys, she stole my heart…"

"Wait a second," Erika asked, holding up her hand. "What happened to Maxi? Am I missing something?"

Vince cleared his throat and for the next fifteen minutes proceeded to give us the details—beginning with his dream that led him to question his relationship with Maxi, onto his trip to New Orleans where he met Angeliqué, and their subsequent, whirlwind romance.

He spoke of their wonderful, romantic dinner; intense conversation in the courtyard of her gallery/home; the passion of this mysterious, voodoo goddess; her art, subsequent show, featuring *veve*-covered flesh; the way they made love on the floor to candlelight—painting one another with colorful hues, smearing each other's flesh with paint, and fucking with abandonment, the way new lovers often do.

Erika was enthralled. I sat there, asking questions when Vince got to the juicy part.

"That's my dawg!" I exclaimed, high-fiving Vince. "Dude, hope you captured that shit on video…please tell me you brought a copy home to a brutha?"

"Sadly, the tapes were confiscated at the airport." Vince looked dejected.

"Damn, I hate when that happens. But, dawg, sounds like you did okay— I guess my mentoring finally paid off!"

"Please," Erika said. "Vince, I'm happy that you met this woman. It sounds like the two of you hit it off immediately."

"Sassy, that's what excited me the most," Vince said, his eyes lighting up with remembrances of Angeliqué. "The speed at which we vibed. I mean, you know, I meet women every other day of my life, but something about her struck me as truly special."

"Here we go," I said, downing the last of my Corona.

"Ignore his ignorant ass, Vince," Erika mused, scooting closer to Vince and rubbing his shoulder. "I, for one, am very excited for you. I just have two questions for you: one, are you going to see her again, and two, what are you going to do about Maxi?"

"Dawg," I added quickly, "You know I'm happy, too, for you. Damn, you go, boy! Sounds like you got a tight woman on your hands."

"Thanks, man," Vince said. He turned to Erika. "To answer your questions—hell yeah! I'm gonna see her again. If I have my way, real soon. And two, I gave Maxi a call when I got home. She knew something was up—she called when I was just waking up with Angeliqué…not a good thing…"

"Damn!" I exclaimed. I didn't know which turned me on more—the sex or the drama!

"Yeah, but I was honest with her, as usual. Perhaps too much so. I told her that I wasn't feeling the relationship anymore. That while she was a wonderful lady and someone I had a lot of fun with, I just didn't see things panning out the way I wanted them to. She didn't understand—asked a lot of questions for which I didn't have a lot of answers." Vince paused to take a sip of wine and to rub his beard. "I don't know, Sassy—I know I'm doing the right thing. I can't put into words exactly how I'm feeling, but I know what I want…and Maxi, unfortunately, is not it."

"I hear you, Vince, and you should be commended for being a man and telling her how you feel—not dragging things out the way some bruthas do just so that they can get some every now and then. No woman wants to be led on and have things dragged out, trust me."

"Yeah, I guess." Vince was quiet, deep in reflection.

"Listen," I said, steering the conversation back to a more positive vibe, "all this talk about naked painted women, hoodoo-voodoo, and wild monkey sex reminds me, I've got a shit load to spill. So if the gentleman from the District is finished, I'd like to go next…"

"I can't believe this mutha fucka," Erika remarked, getting all indignant and thrusting her finger in my face. "Can't you see that your boy over here is both excited and hurting? Seems all you want to do is get to the blow-by-blow sexploits of your incredible vacation. Trey, that's low, even for you." Erika got up abruptly and excused herself to the ladies room. I was left staring at my boy Vince, who eyed me curiously from across the table.

"Dawg, you know I got your back on this one?" I said, hoping Vince wasn't angry with me. He smiled, giving me that grin that was his signature trademark, like a photo taken from his book jacket, and in that moment I knew everything was a-okay with us.

✖✖✖

The food arrived. I was famished. Erika was working on an oversized Caesar salad with fresh cheese and healthy-sized chunks of dark jerk chicken. Vince was in the midst of consuming thick, honey-glazed pork chops, alternating between admiring the presentation and remarking on the ease at which his knife cut through the meat as if it were butter. I had opted for the grilled Norwegian Salmon—I loved the way Scott Chase prepared this dish, with spicy mashed potatoes and fresh asparagus, which had been stir-fried in hot oil and spices. I know y'all will find this hard to believe, seeing how I'm a true playa, but with my interest in culinary delights—yeah, you *heard* me right—I had spoken with Scott months back, compared recipes, and was constantly trying to improve and share my new creations with him via email or in person.

Around us, laser beams of hued light danced across the whitewashed walls to the soulful voice of Billie Holiday's "God Bless the Child," while the bright faces of children from over two-hundred countries beamed overhead, a celebration of life, its most treasured gift.

It was my turn. Finally! And this brutha waited not one second more to dive into the carnal delights of my trip to Jamaica. I talked for forty-five minutes, sparing no minutiae as I recounted every deliciously sinful detail—from my getting down there, the problem with my room that turned out to be a blessing in disguise, from my chance encounter with the lovely Jackie, and her first taste of *Trey Steak*, an African-American *delicacy*, to me in the hot tub with mutha fuckas watching, green with envy as two ladies went down on me under a blanket of stars. Onto the days spent lying by the warm waters of the Caribbean watching a pussyfest unfold, or by the pool getting my dick sucked by some honey with fake tits and a shaved pussy—then fading to the toga party and the late night entertainment featuring Gabrielle, the South American honey, and yours truly in a hammock by a bonfire, while dozens, including her own husband watched and cheered us on. Yeah, Sassy, I kid you not, her mutha fuckin' husband!

Girlfriend and Vince just shook their heads while their mouths hung open...

And as I talked on, the lights around me strobed and pulsed as if alive. Swaths of orange fire burned high overhead while Erika and Vince were mesmerized by my recount. The melodic pianos of Jim Brickman, Keiko Matsui, and Joe Sample played on, while I found myself transported back to the shores of Negril and to paradise, where this Stella *definitely* got his groove back. The rest of my mind-blowing vacation became a colorful blur, running at high speed—bits and pieces, those lusciously delectable tidbits, which I'm sure will come to me from time to time in the future, but I swear the fine points are lost forever.

I closed my eyes, bringing to mind the white cowboy hat lady with the hourglass-shape body. Her name was Montanna; she and her husband, Chad, were out of Houston. Chad and Montanna, I explained after taking another swig of my Corona, took me to another level of Lifestyles pleasure—they taught me the difference between raw animal pleasure of the flesh, and connections that lead to a deeper, fulfilling lovemaking—that feeling of total, uncompressed passion that is expressed as a storm—one which wells up inside of you, and ejects itself from every pore during the severe explosion we all know as orgasm…

I recalled my final nights in Jamaica as memorable and special. At that point, I was a man wholly satisfied and at peace, the tranquility that comes from total fulfillment—I had been enjoying the pleasures of numerous women, but I had toned it down, no longer needing to go non-stop like a freaking Energizer Bunny—I had reached the summit, the Mount Everest of fucking; my mark was indelibly left on that special place—mutha fuckas whispered my name, pointing to me as I swept by, my dark cock swinging in the Jamaican breeze. At this juncture, *everyone* knew my name!

And then I recounted for Vince and Erika that final morning where I found myself in the whirlpool surrounded by my friends and lovers—old and new, as I waited for the Breitling Blackbird to turn 1 p.m., signaling my departure home. The sky was overcast—a telling sign, a rainshower was coming in from the west. New faces lined the pool and bar area—a lot of the folks whom I had come to know intimately were gone, back to their normal lives, the treasures experienced at this out-of-this-world resort packed away in the special recesses of their minds…never to be forgotten…

And yet, in a sense, nothing had changed. Those last moments by the pool when I exited the whirlpool for the last time, hugging my remaining friends, strolling back to my chair to collect my things, drops of refreshing pool water cascading down this sexy brutha's tight body, the weight of dozens of pairs of eyes were once again upon my firm back, sexy tattoos, and ass. Yeah, they were clocking a brutha, one last time…And I was totally feeling it—life and all she has to offer. I was livin', y'all. Livin' large!

✖✖✖

I finished up, took a deep breath, sighed, and sat back, a satisfied look on my mug. Erika was speechless. Vince was shaking his head slowly from side to side, a grin painted across his dark features.

"Dude, you should write a novel with that yarn," he remarked. We pounded fists. I downed the last of my Corona and signaled for another.

"Trey, that shit is incredible, even for you," Erika said finally, breaking her silence.

"Yeah, what can I say? You're right, Sassy. It's gonna be hard topping that shit. But you know this brutha's sure as hell gonna try!"

"True dat! You wouldn't be my dawg if you didn't," Vince exclaimed.

I paused for a moment, reflected on the one part that had been hidden from my recitation—and as I checked my friend's faces, I weighed whether or not I should mention that one, small yet indelible bit of info…realizing that I would be grated over the coals if it came out later that I had held this important fact back. And so, after pushing the lime into the bottle of my fresh, cold Corona, and tipping it upside-down as my thumb covered the opening, I took a long swig, wiped my mouth and sighed deeply before speaking. "There's one more thing I need to mention." I paused. Both eyes were locked on mine. Unintentionally, my voice dropped a notch in volume. "Something freaky happened down there; I need to share." That got Erika's and Vince's attention but quick!

✖✖✖

How do I say this—where do I begin? I found myself suddenly perspiring and wiped the beads that had formed on my brow. My dawg, Vince, and my boo, Erika, watched me silently.

"I, umm, saw someone down there…or I *thought* I saw someone." I paused and took another hit of my brew.

"Trey," Erika remarked, eyeing me curiously, "the suspense is fucking killing us!"

"Okay. Damn." Another breath taken. My mind whirled. Fragments from *that* night raced along the corridors of my mind, but at half-speed—me on stage, toga-clad, at the top of my form, my game, the crowd whipped into a frenzy and chanting a mutha fucka's name over and over again as I stood defiantly center stage—"TREY, TREY, TREY, TREY, TREY!" And then, I spotted her, and…that feeling…sinking…

"What up, Dawg?" It was Vince speaking. "You okay?"

"Yeah." I cleared my throat. Raised my head and scanned both sets of eyes before continuing. "I thought I saw *Layla* down there."

"No…Oh shit." Erika's hand had involuntarily gone to her face. Her mouth hung open.

"Yeah. *Layla.*" I let the *significance* of that sink in. And sink in it did. Like a big-ass rock! I watched Vince, whose face had twisted and taken on an air of deep concern. He said nothing, but the apprehension showed in his brown eyes. My eyes flicked over to Erika, whose own face was painted with distress. "They say," I continued, holding the table's rapt attention, "that everyone has a twin somewhere. Well, let me tell you something, I found Layla's twin, and she was *her* to a T, I kid you not!"

"Damn. Where and when did this happen?" Sassy wanted the facts.

"Remember I told you about Gabrielle, the honey I fucked on the beach in a hammock?" Once again I found myself transported backwards in time as I closed my eyes, back to that night, the ocean breeze on my face, sweaty chest, and withering cock, the applause from the crowd behind us, the eruption of sound: hooping, hollering, and plenty of high-fives, thumbs upturned in the air, and smiles, while Gabrielle and I took our bow. Then a dizzying fast-forward to the toga party, and me onstage, the crowd screaming and carrying on, and I standing there with this cocky, shit-eating grin on my face thinking: *There's no one on this planet right now who is feeling more alive and in control than I am.* The power that comes from having mutha fuckas throw their hands in the air because they *respect* your style… yeah, ride this beautiful shit for just a minute, while honeys whisper your fucking name…

And then, in an instant—like a car careening out of control, over the median, and into oncoming traffic—the wind was snatched from my lungs, the blood drained from every inch of my tanned skin, when I spotted *her*. A spitting image of her, of Layla, the woman I had once loved more than life itself, the one person I would have gladly lain down and died for. Without question…

Once again, Vince and Erika were speechless.

"For a moment, y'all, it was her. Same hair, same face, same eyes. I swear to God, I would have bet all of my 401K plan on that shit; I ain't playing!"

Short dress—I recall it well—some things you don't forget—orange, low cut, hugging her curves like a tight, leather glove. Curves I had once upon a time gotten to know like the back of my own hand.

"What did you do, Trey?" Erika asked softly. Her arm had come up and was massaging my back. The waiter had cleared our plates and refreshed their drinks. I had waved him away without a second thought.

"I stood there—frozen on stage—I couldn't breath. I felt…how can I describe this…sick, yeah, I felt sick, off-balance, like I was going down. But then, the feeling passed, thank goodness." I drained the Corona and set it down hard on the table. "I'll tell you this, I wasn't any good for the rest of the night."

"Layla," Vince said breaking his silence. He shook his head slowly. "Did you speak to her?"

"Yeah, well, I had to get the fuck out of there. Got back to my room where I could think. But my friends showed up at my door…with her." I shook my head in remembrance. "Her name was Cinnamon. And, God was she beautiful. Cinnamon wanted to party. Was there at the resort for only one night. And she wanted me."

"Damn," Erika said.

I looked around the table. Just the thought of that moment had taken a toll on me. My shoulders sunk down as I felt the weight of something just out of reach pressing down on me. The further burden of my situation at work added a vicious blow to my already bruised self. I shook my head sadly.

"The funny thing—as fine as she was, I couldn't bring myself to be with her. I remember her standing at my door, with that look of sheer fucking desire blazing in her eyes." I paused, shuddered involuntarily as I recalled the scene in vivid detail. "She wanted me, Dawg, no fucking question about that. Those panties were *soaked*, you hear me?" Vince nodded silently. "But I had to leave it alone."

"It's understandable," Erika said, rubbing my back again.

Yeah, I thought to myself as I tried to emit a cocky laugh. But it came out more like a shrug and a groan.

I *had* to leave it alone...

TWELVE

They finished up at bluespace by 10 and left to run home and change. Trey and Vince swung by Erika's place in Silver Spring, and together they rode down 16th Street to the waterfront, like wingmen from a fighter squadron. The night was perfect for riding—the temperature had not yet begun to dip into winter zone.

It was after eleven by the time they roared up Maine to H20. Insisting they make a grand entrance to the club, as only they could do, Trey rode point on the Indian, decked out in soft brown leather from jacket to boot, Erika gripping his waist, adorned in a pair of tight jeans, black leather jacket and boots, her hair swept back by a faded yellow bandanna underneath her helmet. Vince held the rear on the Fat Boy, shaking his head as Trey weaved in and out of downtown traffic, the stars shimmering and shining overhead as they rode.

By the time they had arrived, a crowd had formed on the sidewalk in front of H20, a rare sight for a Wednesday night. But Erika had remembered from listening to Donnie Simpson on WPGC earlier that day that someone famous—she just couldn't recall who exactly—was gonna be there for some kind of reggae after-party.

Trey downshifted, gunned the throttle for show, making a few women jump from the sharp rapport, smirked behind his helmet, and turned toward the sidewalk. All eyes were on them as he dropped his boots to the ground—and this was the part that excited Trey and Vince the most—when folks stopped in mid-conversation as they rode by—wondering just who those wild boys were—decked out in their leathers and fly shades on, the rumbling of hot chrome between their legs. Trey steered his machine past the now silent crowd that had parted to let them through, up under the awning where they came to rest, all eyes upon them. Normally, this space was off limits for any kind of parking, since it was directly in front of the club's front entrance. But Trey knew the owner fairly well, and had been here with the Indian and the Fat Boy too many times to count—so the bouncers became familiar with their motorcycles, and allowed them to park there. Plus, it was good for business. The owner knew from experience that folks loved to gawk at those two machines. They always attracted a crowd.

Erika dismounted first, taking Trey's hand to maintain balance as she swung her leg over the Corbin seat. Once both feet were back on solid ground, she smoothed out her jeans and removed her helmet, retying her bandanna tightly behind her. Trey and Vince also wore bandannas over their heads, and looked sexy as hell, she had to admit. Trey waved to a few acquaintances as he stowed his gloves and set the disc-lock. He then walked over to the bouncer who had let them through, hugged him briefly and slapped his back as he palmed a fifty into his hand. The brutha pocketed the bill and gave Trey dap. Erika just had to smile. She had to give her boy credit; he knew how to work it, no question about that.

In the few moments that it took to waltz into the club—there was a line, but Erika and company damn sure weren't about to wait to get into this place—she surveyed the crowd and had to smile. It never ceased to amaze her, she thought to herself while scanning the mostly dark faces—a source of much discussion between Vince, Trey, and herself—how women always had the same look on their faces when they spotted guys on their bikes. What was it about being a roughneck, possessing that living on the edge wild-streak that drove women crazy? It was funny—most women talked non-stop about wanting an educated, well-dressed man. Hell, they all knew that from personal experience, especially Trey—his ass worked downtown, he knew! Just waltz around Seventh Street, F Street, or K Street (Lawd, have mercy!) at lunchtime, shaded and Brooks Brothers-*down*, and watch the women as they stared at his fine ass! Them ladies loved them some well-dressed niggas! No doubt! But then, let Trey or Vince sport a leather jacket and pants, bandanna and shades, face unshaven, and come roaring by—oh, hell no, and sistahs would just about lose their minds! It was that sense of excitement mixed with danger—it could be seen in their eyes…

"Oh, I see, you ain't just any old nine-to-five man, you *ride?*"

"Oh, hell yeah, Shorty, I live to ride…"

"Hmmmn…I've *always* wanted to get on the back of a bike…"

"Baby, I'd just *love* to get you on the back of one right now! Girl, you just don't know…"

Erika grasped both Trey's and Vince's hands—the three of them loved to do this when they went out—kept folks guessing just who Erika was with—this one…or that one—or was that fine sistah with them both??? Dayum!

They waltzed into the club that served up Caribbean-inspired food and the best music Chocolate City had to offer (that is if you dug *anything* besides hip-hop and rap), up the winding stairs to the second floor, past the large dance floor, and raised upper-level area to the back VIP section and bar. Past hundreds of patrons who were sweating and grooving to the funkin', throbbin' sounds of the D.J., who had Cameo on the box—"Single Life," its bass line thump-slapping against their chests like heavy heartbeats. Trey grabbed Erika's hand and pulled her into the sea of bodies while belting out, *I'm living a single, single…life…* Folks parting around them like a waterfall surrounds suntanned flesh, watching them closely, wondering just who in the fuck was this leather-clad couple, colorfully bandanna-*down*, painted-on jeans (fellas, Erika was working them jeans!) while everyone else was dressed conservatively—as Erika and Trey moved to the rhythm as if tethered, yeah, they moved *that* well—her thigh slipping in between his legs as his arms wrapped around her thin waist, head thrown back, eyes closed, fingers and hands reaching toward the ceiling. Vince pulled in behind her into *his* slot, as if on cue—now mutha fuckas were really losing their minds—watching him slap against her ass with his pelvis as if he were fucking her right on this very dance floor, his hands on her hips as the three of them fell into their own sync-groove, like pistons on a well-oiled engine—the trio making a writhing sandwich, Erika being the *meat*, one hell of a sight—everyone in the club straining their necks to get a glimpse…

And then the music shifted, D.C.'s own Me'Shell Ndege'Ocello, "If That's Your Boyfriend (He Wasn't Last Night)," her sultry, sexy voice rapping over a bass-infused jam.

Folks who were tiring and beginning their exit from the dance floor turned in mid-stream as they recognized the melody and yelled, "That there's my song!" The floor filled again quickly, as Trey, Vince, and Erika disengaged and moved over to the VIP bar overlooking the harbor. The bouncer shook Trey's and Vince's hands in turn before fixing his hooded eyes toward Erika. They sparkled briefly as he looked her over. She was used to that and didn't pay him any mind. He waved them past and they took a seat at the bar, Erika between them, and ordered drinks from a Rasta bartender.

It was late, they all had to work in the morning, but there was still much more to discuss—Trey had just begun to touch on the newly unfolding drama at work, and Erika hadn't even shared any of her stuff yet—that was just like them too—usually, Trey and/or Vince spent most of the time consuming their precious *bluespace*-time reveling over their own exploits, rarely leaving enough time for her—actually, that was okay with her—she didn't possess the same need as they did to spill her guts and glory all over the table…but still…once in a while…damn…and as it turned out she actually had something of her own to share this time…

When their drinks arrived they toasted to each other, and Erika glanced around. The VIP section wasn't crowded—just a few well-dressed folks lounging on couches behind them, and a few seats at the bar taken up by well-dressed women. Erika smiled at them while watching Trey and Vince from the corner of her eye. Vince, to her left, was chatting with the bartender about some reggae star who had just completed a set downstairs. Trey, on her right, was swiveling around on his bar stool, nodding silently to the women at the bar, while simultaneously checking out a group of women on couches off to the side. He had caught the eye of a particular white woman; Erika noticed that immediately—Trey was grinning his usual grin, showing all of his perfectly straight white teeth, and tipping his glass in her direction—Erika was surprised that he was still sitting in his chair when she felt a tap on her shoulder. She pivoted around and looked into the eyes of a familiar face. Without warning, she felt herself flush.

"Erika."

"James." Trey and Vince turned in unison and glanced up at the man who stood behind Erika. They stared at him, synapses in their respective heads firing rapidly—Trey's smile was replaced by a frown as he looked the brutha up and down—sharp, two-button, single breasted wool suit and leather lace ups, gotta give him credit—whoever this mutha fucka was, he sure knew how to dress! And then recognition exploded in front of him—Trey knew this guy—saw him on a regular basis—on television—the local news.

"How are you? You look great." James bent down and pecked Erika on her cheek. She smiled but wondered if her boys could sense her discomfort.

"James, these are my close friends Trey Alexander and Vince Cannon, Jr. James works for Channel Four here in town."

"Nice to meet you two," James remarked, sticking out his hand to Vince first, as if sensing that Trey might not take it. Vince smiled ever so slightly and shook James' hand before dropping it quickly, as if he might catch a communicable disease from this guy. Trey made no move to shake James' hand; rather he just continued to stare into the brutha's eyes.

"Where you two know each other from?" Trey asked, his vision a laser point equidistant from James and Erika. James began to speak, but Erika raised her voice, signaling to James and everyone else within earshot that she was going to take this one.

"We met a few weeks ago at an embassy function that I attended recently…"

"Since when you attend embassy functions?" Vince had turned on his stool and was staring at Erika, boldly ignoring James who hovered closely behind her.

"Yeah, embassy functions? That's a new one on me," Trey quipped.

"Listen to you two—acting like my damn daddy!" Erika smiled and James laughed. He was the only one. "Anywho—we met, had a drink together, and got together a few times after that." She stared at Trey who was eyeing her curiously, and then over to Vince whose drink lay untouched beside his elbow.

"Got together a few times…" Trey repeated. He had cocked his head and was looking at James curiously.

"You have to excuse these two—we go way back and they tend to be a bit possessive—like I'm their little sister or something."

James swallowed involuntarily as he eyed Vince who was shifting in his bar seat. Vince placed his palms flat on the bar deck and used the opportunity to flex his large muscles. The moment was not lost on James.

"I understand." A pause followed by a short laugh.

"Do you?" Trey said, turning to face James fully. "I mean, we take Erika here very seriously. We don't let just anyone get close to her—I'm sure you know what I mean."

"Of course." James stepped back a bit as if to remove himself from within striking distance. He placed a hand inside his pocket and shifted uneasily in his shoes. "Well, I'm going to leave you alone. It was nice seeing you, Erika. Give me a call—I'd like to take you out again, that is, if it's okay with your protectors here?" He smiled and backed away before either Vince or Trey could respond.

"Mutha fucka," Vince whispered. "Sassy," he said while following James with his stare, "you better come clean right now! What's the deal with you and James?"

"I was going to tell you guys when my turn finally came around."

"Whatever, trick! Don't play us like that," Trey exclaimed. "What? It just conveniently slipped your mind that you're dating the fucking anchor from Channel Four news? I think not!"

"Both of you need to take a sip of your drinks and chill. Damn, I have nothing to hide. And I was going to tell you tonight. But Vince here's falling for a voodoo priestess, and Trey—well, with all of your monkey sex-acts, it's extremely difficult to get a word in edgewise!"

"Don't make me bitch-slap you!" Trey exclaimed, but his eyes were softening.

Erika took a breath. "K," she said, "Here it goes…"

✖✖✖

And so, for the next fifteen minutes, it was Sassy's turn to tell her tale—what she had been up to since they all had last met. She began with the embassy function—a fund-raiser that Caren, one of her friends from the hospital, dragged her to several weeks ago. Erika had been standing around a bunch of stuffy, uppity folks—pontificating about this and that when she spied James across the room, deep in conversation with a mixed group of people. She caught his eye as he was genuflecting with his wine stem—he smiled, she returned the smile, then turned her back on him. He disengaged himself from the group ten minutes later and came up to introduce himself.

"James was very confident in his approach. I liked that. I think it had to do with the fact that there weren't too many of us there," Erika said, rubbing her brown forearm to make the point. "We chatted about superficial stuff—I asked a few questions about news anchoring, 'cause I knew exactly who he was as soon as I spotted him."

"Cut to the chase, Sassy—you fucking him?" Trey asked, signaling the bartender for another round. Beyond the VIP bar the main floor was packed as Usher sang in the background.

"Did I interrupt your monkey ass when we were at bluespace?" She didn't wait for the answer. "Anywho, before I was rudely cut short..." She cut a quick glance at Trey who was pursing his lips and eyeing her inquisitively. "That night we had a very stimulating conversation. I was very much attracted to James and the fact that he wasn't trying to impress me with his 'hey, I'm on TV and I've got my own driver' bullshit. He is intelligent and can carry on an intellectual conversation. I like that. Plus, look at him." She smiled and patted Vince's forearm. "Homeboy is fine, you've got to admit it—he was wearing that suit!"

"Whatever!" Trey and Vince spoke in unison, then turned and high-fived each other.

That first night, forty-five minutes into their conversation, James pulled out a business card, scribbled his home and cell numbers on the back, and handed it to Erika. Without being asked, she had reached for his pen, requested another one of his cards, and written her home number on the back.

"Call me, James, and we'll go out," she had said while staring up into his clear brown eyes. And then she turned on her heels and exited the large room, leaving James with this shit-eating grin on his face!

Two days later, James called. They met at I Ricchi on 19th for dinner the following night. Spent two hours over some of the best Italian she'd every had, conversing about everything from where they grew up, gone to school, dating in the new millennium, African-American politics, and the hip-hop culture. They left I Ricchi and walked over to Ozio, an eclectic cigar bar on M Street, which caters to Washington's chic and elite. James got them into the third-floor VIP section where they lit up a pair of fresh Cubans, ordered Cosmopolitans made extremely well by a bartender named Nick from New York, and danced to hip-hop music. By eleven-thirty, after they had been dancing for thirty minutes straight (they were the only ones in VIP who were dancing, but Erika didn't care—she was thrilled by the way everyone was checking her and her new beau out, plus she loved the way James moved when he danced, especially after he had shed his suit jacket and loosened his tie)—she made up her mind right then and there. She was going to sleep with James—that night...

"WHAT???" Trey yelled, almost knocking over his drink onto the wooden bar and spinning around to see if James were still in the vicinity. Thankfully (for James) he was not.

"You've got to be kidding, Sassy," Vince remarked. "At that point you had been with the guy what, four maybe five hours? And you were already consenting to having sex with him?"

Erika took a sip of her drink slowly and then put her glass down. She eyed Vince first, then Trey before speaking. "This shit is hilarious! The two of you have got to be the world's biggest hypocrites! You, Vince—with your voodoo lady—how long did it take you before you were fantasizing about spanking that ass? Huh? I'd estimate no more than an hour—tops! And Trey. Don't even get me started on you—I mean, when you fucked that Jamaican girl the first day on your vacation, exactly how many *minutes* had gone by since you'd first eyed her? Five? Ten? Surely no more than that!"

Both were, for a moment in time, lost in thought.

"I can't believe this double standard our society has—I'm not stupid; I know it's always existed between men and women, but this is me we are talking about. Erika—and I'm a woman who has the same wants and desires that you men do. Well, maybe not the same as Monkey-ass over there," she said, cutting a sharp glance over at Trey. "But I get just as horny as you both do. I have sexual thoughts. A lot. And I want to get mine just like you do. And like the two of you I sometimes choose to act on my emotions when I want to. This is twenty-oh-four. I'm a big girl. And If I wanna fuck a brutha I just met, I'm gonna!"

Trey was snapping his head from left to right and back again, eyes closed, repeating the words, "no, no, no," over and over again.

Vince tried... "Sassy—I, we understand what you're saying..."

"No, we don't," Trey interrupted.

Vince sighed. "Sassy—I understand how you are feeling. But you know, it's different for a woman to be out there doing that kind of thing."

Erika cut him off. "Oh, I see. If a man sleeps with a woman he hardly knows it's okay, but if a woman does it, then she's a ho."

"Excuse me, Mr. Bartender," Trey said loudly. "Do you have any ho cakes for this ho right here?" Erika's hand rose up without warning and slapped him hard on his shoulder. Trey yelped and immediately hung his head.

"If I'm a ho, mutha fucka, then you are one bitch-ass slut puppy!" She had her fingers in Trey's face, and everyone in the VIP section, including the women at the bar had ceased their conversation to partake in the new drama going down. Vince calmly (and gingerly) took her hand away from Trey's face.

"People, let's not let this situation degenerate. Trey, if Sassy wants to get her groove on, then that's her prerogative. Okay? Look at it this way—she could have picked a worse nigga to ball. At least we know who he is and where to find him. He ain't going to do anything stupid or risk his precious career over messing with a woman, ya know?"

"Whatever. I can't believe you gave that nigga some. Damn!" Trey rose off his bar stool, grabbed his beer from the bar, and walked away.

"What's his fucking problem?" Erika asked, turning to Vince.

"He's very protective of you, Sassy, you know that. Always has been."

"Yeah, I guess." Erika's eyes began to soften. Actually, she found the whole scene kind of cute. A slow song had come on: Brandy, from one of her more recent CDs. Couples rushed toward the center of the floor for a chance to slow dance. "Oooh. I love this new jam. Dance with me, Vince. I need someone to hold me."

Vince smiled and reached for her. "Lead the way, Sassy, you sexy-ass ho!"

They were walking toward the dance floor as the lights dimmed and lasers began to strobe when his cell phone vibrated. Vince reached for his hip, flipped the phone open, glanced at the screen and grinned. "Uh, one moment, Sassy, I've got to take this." He took the call, and Erika watched his face change—a slow transformation, like candle wax dripping or slow-going molasses—Vince's eyes lit up along with his smile. "Hey you…" he began. Erika knew it was Angeliqué, the voodoo priestess—who else these days would make Vince beam like that? And so, Erika walked away to give Vince some privacy, and stood by the side of the dance floor. There she witnessed couples hold each other as if it were their last night on earth, while listening to that Brandy slow jam, the one she just loved, alone…

THIRTEEN

"**G**uess what I'm wearing?" That sultry, sensuous voice transported Vince back to the Quarter and the courtyard of Angelqué's home; a light breeze, the steady trickle from the oval pond lit from high above by a crescent-shaped moon. *Veve*-covered flesh that undulated to his light touch. A kiss, a tongue, a hard, distended nipple, and hair that bounced to Miles, *Kind of Blue*. He had no choice but to smile.

"I can't imagine…" Vince said, cupping the phone to his ear and heading for the balcony outside where he could continue his conversation in peace, "and the suspense is damn near killing me!"

"I'll give you a hint, baby," Angelqué teased. Her voice rose and fell as if in singsong. Vince found himself aroused and closed his eyes for a moment to experience the full effect. "Not much. I'm in my studio—lights off, my favorite jazz piece playing softly in the background, pink and pale blue candles burning, sweet cakes and a pack of unlit cigarettes on the altar, an offering—the spirit of Ezili Freda permeating the air like thick wonderful perfume…"

"Ummmmn, wish I was there." Vince found a spot overlooking the street. He could see the line of folks that extended beyond the overhang— partygoers, young folks, oblivious to the time of night, who were still waiting to get inside H20.

"If you were here, lover, you'd see that I've painted myself, my breasts that ache for your touch and your hot tongue; my forearms, thick with red paint and yellow dots; my pussy, which I shaved an hour ago after a long hot bath of basil, sweet peppers, and *zo-devan* powder—shaved her clean so that I could lather her with vibrant colors and feel every stroke of my brush—God, that's what did it, you know…that tiny little brush stroking my freshly shaved pussy—my eyes closed, thinking it was you stroking and eating me with your wonderful tongue. God, I'm so fucking wet, Vince. I'm sorry baby; I know it's late, but I had to call you and let you know that I was thinking of you…"

Vince turned away from the patrons who were sitting at tables on the dimly lit balcony, enjoying the nighttime air. Turned away so that he could hide his growing erection. That's what he admired—no, loved about her, his Angeliqué. The way she was at peace with her own sexuality—and the way she could communicate her thoughts and desires to him as if they had known each other for ten-thousand lifetimes. His thoughts whisked back to weeks ago, when the two of them had lain there on the carpeted floor, the light from a half dozen candles flickering off their naked forms, as Angeliqué slid on top of him in a flash, her body moving like that of a cat, her firm breasts hovering over his chest, her long wavy hair in her face and his, as he consumed her mouth with his—savoring the feeling as their tongues and bodies pressed together, the current that surged within until they were about to burst.

Vince could only imagine her there now, alone, and sighed.

"Vince Cannon, Jr., if you were here with me right now I'd give myself wholly to you—rub my shaved, *veve*-painted pussy against your bearded face until you tasted all of my voodoo love juice. And then I'd make love to you so good like I did that night, let you take me the way you did when we were together. Do you remember that, Vince?"

Vince was fully hard now and dizzy with the liquor of sensual dreams. "Oh, God, Angeliqué. What I wouldn't do to be there with you right this very minute…"

Angeliqué's voice softened. "I spoke to Ezili Freda tonight, Vince, 'cause I couldn't take it one second longer—told her I needed you back here, inside me where it's safe and warm. I heard her, Vince, heard her speak to me in the hot, scented bathwater, among the vapors and candle wax that dripped onto the porcelain lip of my tub." Vince heard Angeliqué take a long drag from a cigarette. He imagined her standing there, nude and painted, thin tendrils of smoke drifting upward as a dozen set of button-eyes from cloth and sequin-covered dolls watched her with their unwavering gazes. "She told me you'd be coming." Vince could hear Angeliqué's voice shift—it became hushed and far away. "Tell me Ezili Freda speaks the truth, Vince. Tell me you are on your way soon?" Vince heard the pleading in her dithering voice.

"Yes, Angeliqué. Ezili Freda is a wise ole voodoo priestess." He paused for a moment to look up at the clouds that were forming over Washington from the west. His heart was beating fast, and his penis was fully engorged. But this came down to more than raw sexual desire or the longing for soft warm flesh. Vince felt his muscles constrict, tightening around his chest walls. "Baby," he said softly, in a tone that surprised even him, "I am on my way soon…"

✖✖✖

Trey Alexander sauntered around H20, attitude permeating from every pore of his black body. Part of it had to do with his conversation with Erika—Trey knew he was being overprotective and a bit childish, definitely a double standard when it came to Erika and himself—but damn it, they went *way* back—they'd been friends for God knows how long, and so, it was okay if he was a bit overbearing at times. Besides, he knew that deep down Sassy loved it! But this was only part of the reason for his demeanor…

The other reason…Trey was dressed for attitude. He had donned his brown leather pants and matching boots before heading out on the bike. Underneath his leather jacket he wore a caramel-colored, tie-dyed, ribbed tank top that was tight-fitting and showed off his tribal band and Indian chief tattoos. And this was exactly the reason why his jacket was presently resting on the back of the bar stool over in the VIP section. So, he wasted no time strutting around the club's floor as if he owned the place—stopping to speak to whomever glanced his way. He wasn't getting very far considering all of the stares...

Folks, mostly women, were getting to observe him in all of his glory. He was feeling good—the few drinks that he and friends had had over dinner earlier had presented him with a nice warm buzz. Not that Trey needed anything to converse with folks...

He made it down to the first floor and navigated around the dance floor that was packed with dancers vibing to thumping, heart-pounding reggae. He headed for the bar, got the attention of another dreaded bartender, a sistah this time, and ordered a beer. He saw her checking out the "tats" and his soft leather pants, flirted with her for a minute, before moving on...

Back to the second floor, Trey circled the area, checking out the talent—not much this evening, it being a weeknight; a lot of folks though were staring and whispering as he walked by, bandanna still tied about his bald head. He loved this rough-cut look—so distinctively different than what he was used to—always suit-and-tie-down! This felt good—*because* folks were talking about him. He knew exactly what they were thinking: damn, he looks good—wish I could pull that shit off!

Trey made his way back to the VIP section where Erika was sitting alone nursing her drink. He moved behind her, stroked her hair and back with a light touch. She glanced over her shoulder and smiled when she spotted him. They didn't exchange words. The look between them said it all. He downed the rest of his beer and set the empty glass on the bar.

"I just hope that nigga's treating you well," he said.

"Yeah, James is cool. He's treating me just fine. No complaints so far."

"You know, Sassy, if it was just dick you were longing for, you could've come to me. I mean, what are friends for?" Trey smirked as Erika spun around and gave him a dazed look.

"Trey, have you forgotten how hard I slapped you the last time you pulled that shit?" She had a scowl on her face, but Trey could see that it was rimmed with a smile. He recalled back to the very first time he had ever laid eyes on Erika. That was almost fifteen years ago...

Trey recalled it vividly. He was standing on the main floor of the university library waiting for the elevator to take him to the third floor. A blue knap-sack half-filled with textbooks hung over his left shoulder. The elevator was taking forever to come. He was exasperated and almost decided to huff it up the stairs (located across the way on the other side of the stacks) when the indicator pinged and the doors slid opened. Trey stood aside to see if anyone would exit. When no one did, he entered the cramped elevator and pushed the button for the third floor. As the doors slid shut he raised his head and noticed her standing there. What he saw took his breath away— tall, creamy skin, wonderful dark hair, and a lovely curved mouth, but most importantly, firm, round breasts under a thin cotton polo shirt the color of lavender that clearly exhibited her taut nipples. Trey stepped back to the wall, faced her and stared. Even back then he was cocky, and while his mind whirled with something profound to say, she just stood there, glancing down at her sneakers. Erika felt his stare and slowly raised her head. Big mistake! Trey had a grin on his face the size of a football field! He was staring directly at her breasts and erect nipples; gazing upon them; fanta-sizing about their color, feel, and texture; wondering why on earth they were at attention in this elevator? Trey made no attempt to conceal the object of his affection. He took a breath and began to speak, seeing that he had her full attention now.

"My goodness. Aren't those puppies lovely? Are you a bit nippy or just glad to see me?" He thought he was being charming—and that women actually found this kind of shit appealing. Erika stared in disbelief at him for a split second, shock and anger written all over her face. Then her hand came up from seemingly nowhere and slapped him in the face so hard Trey's bony frame spun around, causing his forehead to crash into the steel back wall. His knapsack went flying as he yelped in pain from the sudden contact of Erika's open-fingered hand and the elevator's frame. The imprints of her digits were easily discernible on his light-skinned face, and would be for at least the next twenty-four hours. Not good, considering he had a track meet in four hours…

"Obviously manners are not your strong suit," she exclaimed calmly as the elevator door opened and she exited without so much as a backwards glance.

They became friends fairly quick after that first encounter…Erika felt guilty because of the mark that had been indelibly left on Trey's malleable face…And for his part, Trey never again tried anything fresh with his friend…

They both smiled with the remembrance…

"So, are the two of you regular *fuck buddies* now?" Trey asked, still standing. "James looks like he's already whipped!"

"What can I say," Erika exclaimed. "My shit is 'da bomb, you hear me?"

"Whatever. Just watch your back, Sassy. I don't want to have to bust a cap in some anchorman's ass, but I will if I have to. Just say the word!"

"Thank you, boo, sometimes you can be so sweet and endearing."

"And—other times?"

"Trey—you know you can be A-Number-One asshole without even trying." She smiled and reached for him, kissing him on the forehead. Trey returned her smile but said nothing.

"To be honest, we've only hooked up only twice—not that it hasn't been nice, because it has been—Stella got her groove back, ya know! But I'm just not trying to get all serious right this minute, you know?

"I hear that."

"Besides," Erika said, rubbing Trey's forearms for a moment, and lowering her volume, "James is acting kind of weird when it comes to sex."

He was preparing to sit down when he glanced around and caught the eye of the white woman from earlier in the evening.

"What did you say?" Trey asked, eyeing the woman, his thoughts shifting into high gear.

"Nothing much. Just that James is acting a bit weird about sex, that's all…" A frown had replaced her smile. Trey, unfortunately, was no longer paying Erika any attention.

"Sassy, watch my drink; I've got to take care of something for a minute." She nodded silently, looking beyond to the couches where the woman's party had congregated. It was okay with her. Trey probably wasn't the best person to talk to about this particular issue…now, if Vince would get the hell off the phone and come back…

Trey walked over, confidence exuding from his being like a blinding white light. The woman, who was sitting with four other women, glanced up and smiled as he arrived. In the background, the music was rocking, and the D.J. had just put on a record by Fat Joe and Ashanti, a jam that Trey just adored.

"Let me ask you a question," he said, without so much as a hello.

"Yes?"

"You know how everyone has that one song that they just love—that's their song, the one that makes them stop and groove regardless of what they're doing or where they are?"

"Yeah, definitely." The woman was gazing up at him, a sensuous grin on her face. She wore her brown hair shoulder-length, a beige skirt, knee-high black boots, and a tight, blue and tan striped shirt that was low-cut and showed off her ample breasts. Trey enjoyed standing over her and glancing down at her cleavage.

"Well, this here's my groove. So, I have no choice but to dance. Understand?"

"Absolutely." The rest of her friends had paused in conversation and were watching him closely, amused by his introductory line. Where was he going with this, they were wondering.

"So, my question is this—if you and I go out on the dance floor over there," Trey said, pointing to the packed area beyond the bar, "are you going to show this crowd how it's done, D.C.-style, and make me proud, or..." and here he paused for effect before continuing, "are you just going to move like a typical white girl and mess up my image? Hmmn? Baby, I need to know before we go any further!"

The woman was speechless and taken aback for a split second. At first she couldn't believe her ears, but the laughter and the "Oh no he didn't!" from several of her girlfriends told her that she had heard him correctly. She set her drink down on the coffee table in front of her, got to her feet slowly, smoothed out her skirt, and looked Trey square in the eyes.

"I guess we'll just have to find out exactly what *this* white girl has to offer, won't we, darling?" Her friends began to giggle and high-five each other. "You go, girl," one of them said. "Don't let that fool talk trash to you!"

Trey stared back, not in the least bit intimidated. He smiled, showing her all of his straight, white teeth. "Well then, whatchew waiting for, girl?" he said, holding out his hand. "Show me what you got!"

They walked hand in hand to the dance floor, past Erika who merely rolled her eyes when they went by. Trey led her to the floor, excused himself as he parted bodies to make way toward the interior of the dance area. They made it about ten feet in before he stopped and turned to her. The music was blaring and folks were shaking, sweating, and grooving. They began to dance and immediately Trey was impressed. The woman didn't dance like any of the white girls he had known. No, she moved like a sistah! He grinned widely; she smiled but said nothing, concentrating instead on showing this man how she moved. Trey admired her—here girlfriend was, in a sea of black folks, gyrating her hips and ass to the beat, moving her upper body, shoulders and neck with attitude and style like she was one of them. Trey increased his movement, determined to stay the course with her. She leaned in, grabbed his shoulder and pulled him to her.

"How's your image holding up so far, darling?" she said over the din of the music.

Trey grinned. "So far so good. Damn, I'm impressed. If I didn't know any better I'd swear you were a sistah. You damn sure move like one!"

"Things are not always what they seem. So watch yourself. You might learn something!" She pushed back, twirled around and dipped. Flipped her hair backwards while positioning her ass against his pelvis. Her arms extended to the ceiling as she glanced back and gave Trey a seductive smile—it spoke to him—it said, show me what you can do! He reached for her hips, pulled her into him, feeling her ass cheeks make contact with his awakening cock. They moved together, in unison, while his hands moved upward from her hips, past her ribs and toward her breasts. He paused when he felt the flesh begin to rise. She reached for his hands and squeezed before pulling away and spinning back to face him.

Trey observed her closely as she danced. She was enjoying herself, lost in the rhythm and thumping sounds. Then the song changed, Fat Joe to J. Lo and Ja Rule—and Trey and his newly found friend continued to dance. For three more songs they grooved, until the sweat was visible on her face, neck, and the valley between her breasts. Trey was having a hard time concentrating on little else. Plus, he was sweating as well. He could feel the drops of perspiration form under his bandanna and on his arms. So, he grabbed her hand and led her off the floor. She was grateful for the reprieve.

"Well, that wasn't so bad, now was it?" she said in his ear. Trey turned to her and grinned while placing his hand around her waist and pulling her into him snuggly.

"Not at all. I love the way you move."

"Thank you."

"No, thank you. My reputation remains intact!"

They moved back to the VIP section. Vince had returned and was chatting with Erika.

"Saw you out there, dawg. Looks like girlfriend was giving you a run for your money!" Vince said, smacking his bare shoulder.

"Yeah, Trey. It's a good thing you quit when you did—she was about to hurt you!" Erika added.

"Trick, please!" He bellowed. Trey turned to his dance partner. "Don't pay these haters any mind. Okay?" He patted his empty bar stool while grabbing a stack of square napkins. He gently dabbed the woman's forehead and neck. She watched him in an amusing kind of way, but didn't stop him until his hand descended toward her bust.

"Okay, I think I'm dry now."

Trey eyed her. "You sure? Any other *wet* spots?"

"You are something else, you know that?"

Trey just smiled. "What are you drinking?"

"Apple martini, thank you."

Trey ordered. "I don't even know your name—forgive me."

"I'm Allison." She stuck out her hand.

"Nice to meet you, Allison. These two knuckleheads here are Vince and Erika. Oh, and I'm Trey!"

Allison was reaching out to shake Vince's and Erika's hands when she heard Trey's name. She turned to him, the curve in her smile momentarily flattened ever so slightly. Erika noticed it.

"Uh oh, Trey, seems like your reputation has preceded you *this* time."

"What?" Trey was gazing down into Allison's face and upper body, his eyes sparkling with a million desires. Her breasts were right there...he was thinking, so close and looking so damn yummy...

Erika began to laugh. "I saw that look, Allison—if Trey would stop eyeing your boobies, he'd have seen it, too!"

"No..." Allison tried to speak.

"Hold on, Sassy," Trey said, breaking his stare from Allison and giving Erika the evil eye. "I was just admiring Allison's lovely frame. Besides, you know I'm a gentleman. Why you trying to go there?"

"Because, she knows you! Or she's heard about you. Isn't that right, Allison?"

All eyes turned to Allison who sipped her martini slowly, the drink weighing heavily in her hand.

"No, we've never met. The name's familiar, that's all."

"Bullshit," Erika quipped. "You may have never met him, but something caused the light bulb to glow bright."

Trey ignored Erika by moving closer to Allison. Erika snorted and turned her attention back to Vince. "So, Allison, have we met before? Seriously, I just *know* I would have remembered someone as lovely as you."

"Nope, honest." Allison glanced toward her friends and their table.

"So, what do you do for a living, Allison, besides looking so damn fine?"

Allison laughed while rolling her head back. Trey watched her thick brown hair as it glided down her back. He also noticed her ropy neck muscles go tight, watched her full breasts as they rose, then fell. He felt himself becoming aroused, and imagined her on his mattress at home, legs splayed, body laced with sweat from their intense lovemaking—wanting to bed this woman in the worst way.

"Trey, do we have to talk about work? I spend twelve to fourteen hours a day busting my ass—I'd much rather talk about something else right this minute, if that's okay with you."

"Baby, that's cool with me." Trey reached up to stroke her shoulder and play with her hair. Allison involuntarily shut her eyes for a brief moment before turning to him.

"Listen, I have to get back to my friends, but thank you for the dance and for the drink."

"Hey, so soon?" Trey asked, his palms held outstretched like a preacher. "I'm just getting to know you, and there's more ground to cover." He flashed his trademark smile and Allison returned it with one of her own, thinking to herself, this one is really smooth...be careful...

"Tell you what, let me go check on them and I'll join you in a few. Okay?" Trey stood over her and watched her eyes as they swam back and forth following his stare. He dropped his gaze again to her breasts and waist. Continued the vein of a thought concerning the two of them in his bed. Tonight. Jamaica and all it had to offer was a distant memory. He needed to move hurriedly.

"Sure, but don't keep a brutha waiting too long..."

"Gotcha. Be back..." She slid off the bar stool and strolled back toward her table leisurely, knowing Trey's eyes were on her ass, but no way to avoid it, so she smiled to herself, and gave him the show he longed to see...

FOURTEEN

"How's Angeliqué?" Erika asked excitedly.

"How'd you know I was talking to her?" Vince asked.

"Nigga—please! I only had to look at those puppy dog eyes that drooped as soon as you said hello!"

Vince smiled as he rubbed Erika's shoulder. "Angeliqué is doing fine. She misses her boo. Can you blame her, all that good lovin' I threw down!"

"Nigga, *please* is right!" Trey said, turning in his stool after completing his stare of Allison's slow stroll. Vince ignored his best friend and continued.

"We spoke about me coming back down to New Orleans real soon to see her." Erika noticed the fire in his eyes—the way they blazed as he spoke of her, the voodoo priestess whose fire had stoked his heart, melted his core like molten lava.

"You go boy," Trey said, giving Vince dap. "Go handle your business, ya heard?"

"You know that!" Vince was nodding his head slowly, a decision already made. He turned his attention back to Erika.

"Sassy, you were saying about James?" Erika turned to glance at Trey who was eyeing her curiously.

"What, why you all up in my business?" She smiled and then laughed. "I was just saying that James and I are cool."

"You had mentioned something that wasn't quite right." Vince encouraged her to go on.

"Naw, everything's cool."

"Obviously *not*," Trey interjected.

"Do we have to have this conversation right now?" Erika asked, suddenly feeling self-conscious.

"Yeah, we do! What's the matter—cat got your tongue now that I'm present?"

"Trey, shut the fuck up and let Erika say her piece—without *commentary* from your black ass!" Vince's speech was forceful, but the glint in his eye let Trey knew he was asking for some understanding here. Trey nodded silently. Erika sighed.

"All I said was that James was acting kind of weird when it came to sex." Erika paused, realized that it was much more difficult to discuss *this* thing that had been bothering her for over a week now with both of them staring her down—individually, there was no problem. She could talk with Vince about this, no problem, and even with Trey, one-on-one. The difficulty arose when both of them were present. But, there wasn't a whole lot she could do about it now. So, she pressed on.

"We've only hooked up a few times so far—two to be exact."

"Go on," Vince said.

"I really enjoyed myself with him. James is a good lover—he takes his time, is romantic and knows how to please a woman."

Trey was sitting there thinking to himself, *well, what's the fucking problem then*, but decided to keep his thoughts to himself.

"That first night when we went to dinner, then over to Ozio, I was, for the first time in a really long time, *feeling* a man. James wasn't pretentious like most niggas I meet—he wasn't trying to impress a sistah. He was just being himself, and I dug that. A lot. I found myself letting my guard down with him and just decided to go with the flow. And I wanted him. And I knew he wanted me."

Trey turned uncomfortably in his seat.

"We left Ozio and went back to his place 'cause I told him I wanted to go there. Decided that night I wasn't going to play any games—I told him what I wanted. *Him*."

"You go, girl!" Vince exclaimed. Trey said nothing. Erika felt herself loosening up as she recalled the details of her night.

"Yeah, I remember us dancing up in the VIP section, smoking cigars, drinking Cosmos, and just chillin', having a grand ole time. I put my lips to James' ear and whispered that it was time to go—back to his place. I've never seen a nigga pay a tab so damn quick!"

Vince and Erika high-fived each other.

"When we got to James' place, he was very much the gentleman. He already knew by this point that he was going to have me—that was a foregone conclusion. Homeboy could have just waltzed into the crib with lil' ole me in tow, grabbed my hand and pulled me into the bedroom. Honestly, fellas, at that point, I would have gone. Willingly."

Erika paused, and checked Trey. He looked at her, eyes unblinking as he mouthed the word "ho" slowly. They both grinned.

"Takes one to know one, be-yatch! Anywho—as Trey here is fond of saying—'them panties were *soaked*,' ya know? But James was playing it cool; he put on some smooth jazz, lit a few candles and some incense and dimmed the lights. Very romantic. I wasn't expecting that."

"Damn," Vince exclaimed, "that nigga does have some sense. Maybe he's salvageable after all. So, Sassy, wherein lies the problem?"

"Well, Vince, as I said, James took his time. He undressed me very slowly and sexily, taking the time to touch me and not rush things. I was very turned on."

"Yeah?"

"Oh yeah. Homeboy had skills! We began kissing and groping, you know, and then he started to…you know…perform oral on me."

"You let a nigga you don't even know go down on you, Sassy?" Trey belted out, then immediately regretted it. Both Erika and Vince eyed him with disdain. He quickly lowered his head.

"And here's where the problem began," Erika said softly.

"What happened?" Vince asked tenderly.

"Don't get me wrong. James was good. Very good. No, damn *spanking* good—okay? I mean, he made me come *twice*. Tongue and all. I am not mad at him!"

"Doesn't sound like a problem to me."

"Hold on—after that, of course a girl's gonna reciprocate. I wanted to give him pleasure. I mean, he was still fully dressed. I tried to take off his pants, unbuckle his belt, but James stopped me…"

"Uh-oh, that brutha's a faggot—see I told you!" Trey shouted.

"Shush!" Erika whispered. "James is no faggot—I could tell he was aroused—damn, I could see his dick sticking up straight through the fabric of his suit pants. I wanted to feel him, wanted to taste him the way he tasted me. Wanted to feel him inside of me. I told him so."

"And?"

"James said that he wanted to focus that first night on pleasing me. I thought that was sweet, but honestly, all his tongue had done was make me want his dick even more. Does that make sense?"

"Yeah, it does," Vince said, with caring in his voice. Trey rolled his eyes.

"I swear to God, I was tugging on his shit for five minutes—we practically were wrestling on his couch before I finally gave in—he wasn't going to let me fuck him."

Vince cleared his throat and thought for a moment. "Sassy. I don't necessarily see a problem in James' actions. When you think about it, there is nothing wrong with what he did—wanting to focus the evening's attention on pleasing you. Actually, what he did was down right admirable—letting his pleasure take a back seat to yours. In a way, he was sealing the deal for the next time, not that he needed to do that—but in his own way, he was saying to you, baby, pleasing you is my first priority. Not a bad thing, if you ask me."

"I hear you, Vince, but think about this," Erika said. "Sex is about communication and connections between two people. What makes love-making so special is that it allows two people to touch each other in a very intimate way. The whole point is not to make one person *come*; it's not a task to complete; it sure ain't no damn competition, like a fucking race, but a way of bringing two people closer together in mutual pleasure and a flurry of passion."

"Okay, point taken. But so far I don't agree with your assessment of there being a problem. So go on. What happened next?"

"Well, it was late and James was done, as far as he was concerned. He cleaned me up, kissed me tenderly on my lips—damn, I still remember how good that shit felt, and took me home." Erika paused to remember the sweet details. "I got busy at the hospital; James was tied up at the station, so a few days went by. I wanted to put some space between us anyway, so that I could figure things out. James was calling almost every day, but we didn't hook up again until the following week. Our second date was very nice— James prepared dinner for me…" Trey snapped his neck so quick both Vince and Erika flinched.

"Oh no he didn't!" Trey declared, getting off the stool to make his point. "Nigga's gonna mooch off my shit—I knew I should have *copyrighted* that play—now everybody's gonna try that shit at home! And fuck it up! There is only one chef supreme pussy-licking big daddy connoisseur playa in this mutha fucka, you hear me!?!"

"Yeah, Trey, you 'da man. Everyone in Chocolate City knows that. Even Allison!" Erika quipped.

Vince howled.

Trey spun around in his seat to check out Allison, who was seated on the couch, engaged in laughter with her friends. She caught him staring, glanced his way and smiled. He waved sheepishly.

"Anywho—as I was saying before being rudely interrupted—James cooked me dinner—nothing that would compare to one of Trey's mouthwatering masterpieces, but the brutha was trying—can't fault him for that. We ate, drank some very nice wine…"

"Where this nigga live anyway?" Trey asked.

"Reston."

"Figures," Trey retorted. Erika glanced at Vince, then continued.

"Alrighty then. We drank some nice wine—more of the same, candles, incense, and smooth jazz. He had gotten me some really pretty flowers…"

"Isn't that special!" Trey quipped. "Mutha fucka's a regular Martha Stewart with balls—well, that remains to be seen!" He sneered. Erika was not amused.

"Trey, fuck you!" She swiveled in her stool and faced Vince who was silently shaking his head. "Once again James was the perfect gentleman, but this time, after dinner and a few more drinks, he led me upstairs to the bedroom. We undressed—both of us, simultaneously. It was an incredible turn-on. Then we made love."

"Cool," Vince said. "So far so good!"

"Yeah, it was wonderful. It felt really good to be with a man who was that romantic. As I said, James wasn't the kind of lover who rushed himself. He took his time, attended to my needs first, but this time, afterwards, he let me have my way." Erika had a devious look on her face. Vince grinned and even Trey had to crack a smile.

"Go 'head—handle your business, girl!"

"Yeah, but here's the thing. I don't know if I should be making an issue of this or not, but…" Erika's voice trailed off.

"What? Sassy, as you're fond of saying, the suspense is fucking killing us!" Vince said.

"I know." She chuckled. "The thing is, James didn't *come*. Not once. Not during me giving him a blowjob, which I damn sure know how to do, thank you very much! Not during sex, which incidentally involved several positions besides plain old missionary." Trey eyed her curiously. "What? You don't think this here girl got skills? Please! I know how to do the *do*!"

"All right. So did you talk about it?"

"Well, I mentioned it. I mean, there we were going at it for close to an hour and he still hadn't come. He finally stopped after I came God knows how many times, and proceeded to wash us off. He apologized, stating that it was the condom, which was 'interfering'; I think was how he put it. Under normal circumstances I wouldn't have thought twice about it—but with what happened the first time, I became suspicious. After that evening I found myself thinking about it a lot. Don't get me wrong. I'm enjoying the hell out of sex with James. But until I figure out what the deal is, I'm not sure I want to mess with James any further. I just don't want to start something that might spell trouble down the road." Erika downed the remnants of her drink and sighed, placing her palms on the shoulders of her two best friends. "Whatever the case, the nigga's been calling me every day like clockwork. You know my shit is 'da bomb!'" Erika grinned and nodded like a boxer who had just knocked down his opponent.

"I don't know, Sassy; sounds like a faggot problem to me," Trey quipped. Erika cut him a nasty glance.

"Sassy, don't pay that nigga any mind. I think everything's cool—just give the brutha a bit more time. I have a feeling things will work themselves out," Vince reasoned while stroking Erika's back.

Erika sighed. "Well, we'll see…"

✗✗✗

Allison was gone. Trey noticed it as soon as Erika had finished telling her tale—the thing between her and James—the "sexcapades" of Sassy—damn, what was the world coming to? Sassy getting her groove on???? Who would've thunk it? Anyway, more pressing matters were upon him. Trey jumped off his stool, grabbed his half-empty Corona, and headed for the main floor.

Trey walked slowly, yet confidently, scanning the crowd for the white girl. He wanted her. Something about her smile—the way her hair fell on her shoulders and back when she laughed; and those titties—firm, masses of warm flesh that he desired between his fingers and lips.

He came to the winding, curving staircase. Glanced downward, watching folks as they sauntered up and down, taking their time, the reflection from the mirrors ensuring everyone had a view. He started down, gripping the metal as he took a swig. He came to the bottom and saw her, Allison, her back to him as she donned her coat and headed out the front door.

Trey hit the bottom step with both feet, ran past the large, thick dark-skinned brutha bouncer who eyed him with curiosity as he hit the glass door with his palms. It swung open and he was suddenly outside, the midnight air feeling wonderful on his skin.

"Allison!" he yelled. She had gotten about fifteen yards when she turned, and Trey had to smile. The way she pivoted in those black boots, her dark hair swinging in an arc, ass tight within the boundaries of her short skirt, her breasts held within the confines of her blue and tan top, jiggling with the movement made by her sudden turn—made him appreciate being a man. He jogged over to her. Her friends waited a short distance away.

"Hey, girl. Leaving so soon?" Trey flashed a smile and ran a hand over his bandanna. It was damp from sweat so he removed it. Allison gazed up and admired his handsome face and bald head.

"Yeah, gotta get ready for the a.m. You know I'm not as young as some of those folks in there—girl can't hang like she used to."

"Please, I bet you'd give them all a run for their money." He moved closer. "Listen, I know it's late and all, but I was really hoping we could spend more time together. I like you, Allison, you've got...spunk...I dig that." Trey looked down into her eyes and smiled, gave her that look—can Allison come out and play with me—the one he had perfected over the years...innocence with a touch of mischievousness tossed in for good measure.

"Trey, I wish I could...honestly. Perhaps another time." She turned to move. Trey caught her arm gently with his hand and stroked her forearm. He was taking in the whole package—form, fly clothes, hair, eyes, scent, everything. He wanted her. Now. Time to go to general quarters...

"Let me take you home, Allison. My ride's parked right here," he said, gesturing to the hunk of engine and gleaming chrome. The Indian made a statement and he watched her eyes brighten. "Allison," he said, dropping his voice and moving in, as close as they had been earlier on the dance floor, "I really want to get you on the back of my bike—you just don't know!"

"Is that right?" Allison said, enjoying the closeness and the raw sexual energy that pulsed in the air. She glanced up, admiring the bald head, his pretty eyes, that engaging smile—damn, he was fine, no question about that, but off limits...

"Oh yeah. You, me, those sexy black boots—I could keep mine on if you'd like..."

"Really? Hmmm. I think I'd like that." Her voice had dropped to a whisper as she glanced down at his leather pants and boots, noticing how well his clothes fit him. Trey still held her arm. His fingers were splayed—feeling her skin through the shirt; eyeing her breasts—couldn't help himself—not that Allison seemed to mind. In fact, Trey was convinced that she was thoroughly enjoying this exchange. He moved in—maneuvered his thigh next to her ass, extended his leg and connected. Let her feel him, know that he was engorged, inflamed, excitement in the air like electricity during a storm. She stood her ground—making no attempt to move, staring up at him and his eyes as he watched her, enjoying the fact that his gaze roamed all over her body, the flirting between them delightful, like the midnight air. She was no fool—Allison knew what he wanted. "Trey, darling. It's late—I'd love to stay here with you, but I really can't." Allison twisted to her girlfriends who waited patiently for her to finish up. "I've got to leave—my girls gotta go."

"Like I said, giving you a ride is no problem. In fact, I'd thoroughly enjoy it!"

"Another time—another place." Allison disengaged herself, ran a hand through her hair, and made ready to leave.

"Then give me your number. Let me make sure you find yourself home safely tonight."

Allison bit her lip. Indecision was written on her brow. She glanced back at her friends. "Tell you what—do you have a card, Trey? I'll call you."

Trey was already reaching into the back pocket of his leathers—he *always* carried a card. Like condoms. Shit, Trey never went anywhere without them. He handed one to her. Allison took a moment to read it.

"Trey Alexander," she read, "Esquire. I like that. Can I call you 'counselor'?"

"Please do—real soon—tonight preferably." He bent down and kissed her cheek—let his lips linger on her skin a little longer than necessary. Allison made no attempt to pull away. Then he straightened up, flashed her one more smile before spinning on his heels and heading for the front entrance of the club. He left her the way he liked to do all of his women— leave them quick—standing there, contemplating him, this man of mystery with the dazzling eyes, great looks, tattoo-adorned brown skin, and a devilish smile that drove most women (and some men) wild with the possibilities…infinite possibilities…

FIFTEEN

All six-foot-six, two hundred thirty-five pounds of dark chocolate-complexioned Quentin Hues, Washington Wizards forward, graduate of UConn, former resident of New Jersey, husband and soon-to-be divorcee turned and smoothed his three-button blazer when Trey swept into the reception area. Quentin had been bent over the reception desk, preferring to wait there as opposed to being ushered into Trey's office directly, a ploy, Trey knew damn well, to give Q. time to chit chat with Becky, the blonde receptionist with the pretty teeth, smooth shape, and fake titties. When he strolled in, Trey hugged him, brutha-style, and gave him one of those, "Dawg, I'd hit it if I were you" looks and winked at Becky before ushering him down the hall. While walking they exchanged small talk. Q. and Trey had known each other for a little under a year now. They had been introduced to each other at some bourgeois function held at Jordan's Restaurant over in the new Ronald Reagan Building. Trey loved to attend those soirées—it gave him an opportunity to network with folks—an absolute necessity in his business—plus, and far more importantly, pussy adored sports, money, and power—and Trey *treasured* pussy above all else.

They came to a wood-paneled conference room door. Trey had briefed him on the agenda on the way over…negotiating property settlement between a client and their spouse could be a nasty business—especially when it involved big items such as mansions, speedboats, and penthouse suites. Luckily, Quentin hadn't amassed that kind of property in his short

NBA career. Plus, he had only been married a little over a year. This wasn't going to be too difficult. All in a day's work for Trey Alexander, Esquire, no doubt!

Trey pushed the heavy door open and strolled in first. He stared over at the oversized window, where a white woman wearing a smart navy blue suit stood with her back to him. Her brown hair was tied back with a single blue band. He cut his gaze over to the immense mahogany conference table. At the very end sat a thin, extremely attractive young woman. Trey took in her russet-colored skin, her half-black, half-Indian features, and the dark hair that wound down her back in a single braid. She was twenty-three years old. Her eyes were fixed not on Trey, but on Quentin, her husband, behind him. Her mouth was set in a firm arrangement. She neither gave off positive or negative vibes—she just existed, in this time and place, a necessary evil, unfortunate that it came down to this—waiting patiently for this meeting to commence and be done with. Trey thought to himself: *Damn, Dawg, you let that honey get away?* And then he remembered the maxim—regardless of how fine a woman thinks she is, somewhere, some-place, there's a man who's tired of her shit!

At the exact moment that Quentin walked in behind him, his eyes fixed on his young wife, soon-to-be ex, the woman at the window turned. Trey's heart skipped a beat when he recognized Allison, the woman from H20, the night before.

"Morning, Counselor," Allison said, extending her hand and staring into Trey's startled brown eyes. "I'm Allison Matthews, attorney for Mrs. Aponi Hues. I trust you are well-rested and are ready to get down to business!"

✖✖✖

Vince kept his eyes closed, the large mug of steaming coffee held under his nose as he inhaled the scent of the freshly brewed liquid. He imagined the vapors as tendrils of smoke, which raised up like cobras, winding like a mountain stream before finding their home—his nostrils, slipping within as he took a breath—meandering through his insides, gliding downwards as they headed for his center, feeling his core heat up with each mouthful. And then he placed the mug to his lips and took a sip—instantly warming as the liquid shot down his throat like a raging waterfall, and Vince shook his head slowly, thinking to himself, the old adage is indeed true: wake up and smell the coffee—it would do all of us some good...

Vince opened his eyes and set the mug down on the coffee table. It was Sunday morning, about elevenish, Cosi at Penn and Third a hubbub of activity, folks streaming in and out, business booming, tables and chairs both inside and out filled to near capacity. Luckily, Vince had arrived before the morning "rush" and was able to get his favorite spot—the low couch in back—a yellowish-green eclectic thing that was clean and comfortable. Vince leaned back, observing the ceiling before glancing around at the patrons, magazines or Sunday papers tucked under their arms, then scanning outside to his gleaming Fat Boy that was parked out front like a pit bull, guarding the entrance.

Vince was in a great mood—the week had been a good one—productive; his book, *Finding Nirvana*, was doing well, not bestseller material...*yet*, and Oprah wasn't banging down his door...*yet*, but okay for someone who was new to the publishing game. He pulled out his Palm Pilot and made a few notes—next week, he'd concentrate on getting *Nirvana* reviewed in a few more papers—that was important. Plus, he had yet to take his seminar to Philadelphia or Boston—he'd work on that in addition to trying to set up a book signing or two while he was in town. Then there was his trip back to New Orleans. Vince smiled to himself as he thought about Angeliqué and the conversations that had been heating up between the two of them lately. She was some woman, Vince mused. He definitely needed to get back down there soon—he missed Angeliqué, her touch, kiss, and the whole *vibe* that surrounded her like a thick fog. That voodoo vibe—electric, mysterious, eerie, and yet, comforting. She was something else—that was for sure.

Vince glanced up and saw Lisa, the Cosi cashier, walking toward him. She looked tired.

"Coffee okay?" she asked as she cleared a few empty cups from the table next to him. They had spoken when he had first arrived.

"Fine, as usual. Business is kicking, I see."

"Yeah, I wish it would calm down; I'm tired as hell." She produced a weak smile as she used a rag to wipe down the table.

"You look it, Lisa. What's up? Burning the candle at both ends again?" Vince asked, grinning at her.

"Vince, you know how *we* do. Shoot—last night, my girls and me checked out this spot called the VIP Club. Have you been there yet?"

Vince shook his head.

"Oh, Vince, this place is the bomb! It's on F Street across from Platinum. This place is all that! I'm not playing. Check out who was in there..." Lisa said, her eyes becoming animated as she spoke. "Jermaine Dupri and Jagged Edge. Supposedly, they're in town shooting some video. Ummn, then Lisa Raye was there and also Missy Elliott, but we didn't actually see her. But the rest of them we did."

"Damn!" Vince exclaimed. "Sounds like it's the new hot spot. What happened to Dream? I still haven't made it there yet."

"Oh, that place is still the bomb, too. Especially on Friday nights—shoot, you can't even move in that place, it's so packed." Lisa chuckled to herself.

"So, what time did you get in this time?" Vince asked with a smirk.

"Vince, you don't even want to know—all I got to say is that it is a damn miracle that I'm here right now!"

"I hear that."

"Oh, by the way, your secret admirer keeps asking about you." Lisa turned toward the front, saw the line of customers growing and groaned to herself. "Shit, I gotta go, Vince."

"Wait," Vince exclaimed, reaching for her arm. "What secret admirer?"

"Tell you in a minute—let me handle these folks before my black ass gets fired!"

Vince sighed and let go of her hand. She winked at him as she skipped away toward the front. *Ah, to be young again,* Vince considered. Staying out to all hours of the night and then having the energy to get up and go to work the next morning—he had to hand it to Lisa. He couldn't do that shit—not anymore. He, like Lisa, had lived that life, once upon a time—

when hanging out in trendy clubs and new joints was the most important thing in his sphere. But that was then, when one could survive on three hours of sleep. And this is now—Vince had grown, matured, gotten to the point where going to the club wasn't the end-all. There was more to life than drinking Cosmos, doing shots, and exchanging numbers in dimly lit, smoky, D.J.-infused spaces. Then his thinking shifted to what Lisa had last said before scampering away—he had a secret admirer. Vince wondered whom she was talking about. He hadn't been here in a few weeks with his travel schedule and everything else going on. One of her friends or perhaps a customer?

Vince shook it off—Lisa would fill him in later, when she had the time…if she could remain awake long enough to tell him…

✖✖✖

Vince had been reading for a while and had lost track of the time. He glanced up from his book, a new Eric Jerome Dickey urban-drama that he just loved—picked up his coffee mug, stared down into it and saw shiny bottom—empty—and put it down with a sigh. His eyes lifted toward the front. A line of customers formed all the way to the door. Lisa was busy ringing up orders. The Fat Boy remained where he had left it. Folks were reading their papers, in no hurry—a lazy kind of Sunday—the best kind, Vince considered. No place in particular to go—nothing of importance that required his immediate attention. This was the way Sundays were supposed to be. A good book, a great cup of coffee, and a comfortable couch…

Vince scanned the line of patrons as he stretched his legs and yawned. A young woman stood out from the rest of the pack—baseball cap, dark hair emerging from underneath her hat, navy blue leggings, running shoes, white Nike tee shirt, and smooth dark skin. Her turn to order just then, she moved up, spoke briefly to Lisa, glancing up at the menu while laying her wallet on the counter top. Her head turned in his direction and Vince recognized her from the last time he was in here—the woman whom he had spoken to briefly. The woman whose face he had sketched—strong, angular lines, the geometry of her face that he had found intriguing…her name, however, escaped him.

Vince watched her collect her bagel and steaming cup of coffee. Lisa glanced at him, nudged her chin in the woman's direction before turning back to the next customer. Vince was momentarily caught off guard—was Lisa trying to tell him something? It seemed that way. And then the woman was strolling toward him, eyes locked on him—Vince looked away, not uncomfortable, but confused for a moment. Was she coming to talk to him?

"Hello. May I join you?" she said before Vince had an opportunity to process the rest of his thoughts.

"Yes, of course. Please have a seat," he said, smiling. The woman took a seat opposite him in a small, yet comfortable chair. She put down her bagel and cup and proceeded to hold out her hand.

"Hi, I'm Desiree. We met a few weeks ago—actually, I was quite spiteful to you, and I wanted to apologize."

Vince took her hand and shook it. "Vince Cannon, Jr." He watched her break apart her bagel, popping a sliver into her mouth.

"The artist. I've been admiring your piece over on that wall," she said, gesturing toward the far wall by the door.

"One of my favorite pieces." Vince smiled.

"It's very good. You're very good. I had no idea you were actually telling the truth." Desiree eyed him and smiled. "About being an artist—sorry, but it's true." She took a sip of her coffee and laughed. "Do you know how many bruthas I've met lately who *aren't* full of shit? Zero or very few—you're in the minority, Vince, let me tell you. You should be proud."

"Thank you. I am. I've always thought that telling the truth gets you farther along than telling a lie, even a little white one."

"I hear that—can you tell some of these bruthas out here, please?" Desiree took another sip of coffee before continuing. "Anyway, I wanted to apologize for my behavior last time—you were being nice and I wasn't… I'm sorry for that—you seem like a good guy and obviously a very talented brutha."

"Apology accepted. And I do understand. There are a lot of full-of-shit folks out there—it's really too bad because it gives those of us who are genuine a bad name." Vince closed his book and put it down. He eyed his coffee cup forlornly, frowning because it was empty but not having the desire to stand in that long line up front. Desiree continued to consume her bagel and sip her coffee while watching him silently. Vince looked up as one of the Cosi people walked over carrying a large mug of steaming coffee. He set it down on the table and said to Vince, "Compliments of Lisa and the house." Vince thanked him and glanced over to Lisa who was ringing up a customer, but smiled briefly and winked. Vince waved and mouthed, "thank you," to her.

"Wow, that was nice," Desiree said. "You've got the hook-up around here"

"Pays to know the help, you know?" Vince said.

"I guess so."

Vince took a sip and savored the flavor of the strong brew. "So, Desiree— you know what I do—I can't say the same." Desiree wiped her mouth with a paper napkin and Vince watched as she raised her hand to her lips— smooth dark skin, fine lines, strong, yet not overpowering muscles and ligaments and she worked her arm in the simple act of reaching for her mouth.

"Well, let's see—I guess you can call me a perpetual student—I'm about half-way through a part-time master's program in early childhood education, and I also work at a Montessori school in the District."

"Very nice!" Vince exclaimed. "A woman who extols the virtues of higher education while giving back to society. I dig that."

Desiree smiled while picking at the crumbs of her half-eaten bagel.

"Yeah, for a long time finding what I wanted to do was a struggle—I thought I wanted to do something in marketing or advertising, but after taking Marketing 101 I decided to look somewhere else."

"Many people spend most of their adult lives meandering around— lost—trying to figure out exactly what it is that makes them feel good— what is the perfect job that gives them that absolute joy. Most people, unfortunately, never find their true passion."

"True. Have you? Found your passion?"

"Hmmn…that's a good question—and be careful—because I'm known for not giving concise answers." Vince smiled and sipped at his coffee.

"Meaning you like to talk?" Desiree quipped.

"Exactly!" Vince said. "Anyway, to answer your question, yes, I believe that I'm one of the lucky ones—I've discovered my passions."

"And they are???" Desiree asked with a wicked grin.

"Well, my art, for one—being creative—developing something that is beautiful and lasting with your hands is something that provides me with endless joy. I know that sounds clichéd, but it's true."

"Yes, I can see that just from looking at that piece over there—one can tell it was done with lots of love."

Vince nodded, his thoughts whisked back to the creation of that piece, "My Secret Redeemer," the vibrancy of colors—reds, oranges, greens, and blues mixed with the chestnut reddish-brown stain that seeped below the surface of the mask, the upturned lips, and eyes that burned bright with excitement, anticipation, and passion…

"Art can be a true enabler—it allows one to go beyond the normal bounds that hold us back—it facilitates the creation of something truly amazing and in many cases, transcending…it allows us to speak in a tongue which is universal, and that is what gives art its power—the ability to transcend cultural and language barriers, cut through the political morass and speak to us here…" Vince paused to point to his chest. "In our hearts."

"I feel you, Vince." Desiree nodded while studying his face.

"Yeah, my art is without a doubt my passion. But it's not the only thing."

"Wow—more than one passion in life—you *are* one of the lucky ones!"

"Yes, I am. I also write and talk to folks about things—I guess you could call me a motivational speaker, although I really don't like that term because in my mind, it limits what I can do. I have this vision of Les Brown or Anthony Robbins doing these infomercials, and that's *not* what I'm into!"

"That's deep—motivational speaker. So, what do you speak on?"

And so, Vince proceeded to tell her about his life's work—when you broke it down, deconstructed it down into the various piece parts, what Vince was truly about was helping folks find their happiness. Through his seminars and workshops, his book, *Finding Nirvana*, and talking to people like he was doing now, Vince was helping folks, one step at a time. Defining those three important aspects of one's life—*professional, personal, and self*—developing and nurturing them, the way a gardener tends to soil, and balancing them so that no one element pushes any other too far out of whack. At the end of the day it was all about balance, baby…

Desiree listened intensely. She found herself enjoying the conversation with someone who had something positive to say. Lately she found it the exception to the rule to come across a black man who could carry on a conversation without staring at her breasts or commenting on her looks—don't get her wrong—Desiree was like most women in that she enjoyed compliments as much as the next gal—but there was a time and a place for that, ya know?

She told Vince about her family that still lived out West in Southern California, and how she had come East to be on her own and nurture herself. Vince talked about his move from working for the *man* to being in charge of his own destiny—and the joy and pain of working for oneself.

"Anything else, Mr. Renaissance Man?" Desiree asked, beaming her broad smile around the interior of Cosi. "I mean, you are an accomplished artist, writer, speaker—damn, most bruthas out here can only list their ride as their claim to fame!"

Vince for a moment was taken aback—he was ready to open his mouth and respond, but found himself pausing, almost by accident, as he stared across the space at Desiree, drinking in her features—flawless skin, those angular facial lines, warm, sensitive eyes, and the striking dichotomy between her dark chocolate complexion and her straight white teeth.

"Uh-oh," Desiree said, putting her coffee cup down with a thud as she felt the pause in conversation open up. "Maybe I spoke too soon—are you about to prove me wrong, Vince?"

"What?" Vince asked, using the interruption to sip from his mug.

"I mean, the way you were staring and all—and after I just concluded you were different." Desiree shook her head and finished the last of her coffee. She gathered her trash as she eyed him curiously.

"Desiree." Vince said her name slowly. "I see you are sensitive around this issue, and that's too bad—I was looking at you thinking how first impressions can be deceiving." Vince reached for the newspapers, folding the sections within themselves before sliding his book inside of the papery folds.

"How so?" she asked.

"Honestly? You're more than a pretty face, Desiree—you have considerable depth to you, and I find that appealing, especially in, and don't take this the wrong way, one so young. That's something you don't find every day. But my first impression of you—at least what I came away with from that first exchange we had weeks ago—was of a young, attractive, streetsmart, but shallow woman. But as I talk to you here today I see that I was wrong. You are more than just a pretty face—and I am enjoying talking with you; please don't read more into it than that. I'm sorry if my thinking about that caused you some discomfort. It was not my intention." Vince smiled as he ran a hand across his closely cropped beard. Desiree watched his movement in silence for a moment before speaking.

"Thank you, Vince. I enjoy talking to you, too. I hope that we can continue to do this. And I'm sorry for overreacting. It's just I get tired of men having nothing more to let loose than comments about my looks."

"Understood. Tell you what—I promise not to say anything further about the way you look as long as you keep your comments about my good looks to yourself. Deal?"

"Excuse me, but what comments? I haven't said anything about how good you look…"

"See," Vince interrupted, "that's what I'm talking about right there!" Vince exclaimed, while pointing at Desiree. She swatted away his hand as she laughed.

"Whatever—I can say whatever I want, Mr. Vince, whatever your last name is…"

"Cannon."

"Yeah, I can say whatever I want, Mr. Cannon, Jr. so there!"

"Alrighty then!" Vince checked his watch. "Damn, where has the time gone—it's close to two p.m."

"Are you kidding me?" Desiree asked, checking her own timepiece, as if Vince's were telling lies. "Damn, boy. You sure can talk!"

"Whatever!" They made ready to leave, grabbing their things and depositing their trash. Vince winked at Lisa who was eyeing them as they headed for the door. She wore a smirk on her face and Vince just knew that he would owe her the full 411 next time he returned.

Outside, the sun was high in a cloudless sky. Desiree donned a pair of sunglasses and glanced up, feeling the warmth nuzzle against her skin the way a cat does its master, as Vince made his way to the Fat Boy.

"Oh no you don't ride a *bike!*" Desiree cried out. Vince feigned injury.

"What? A renaissance brutha like myself can't be down with a hog?"

Desiree ignored him while circling the machine, gawking at the gleaming chrome, fat pipes, and wide leather seat.

"Oh, cat got your tongue now?" he inquired.

"Damn, Vince—you don't know what a Harley does to me," Desiree said, continuing to stare the way a kid does when a jet plane passes overhead. "It makes me all squishy inside!"

Vince grinned. "Squishy is good. Very good, Desiree."

"I'll say!"

"Perhaps I'll give you a ride one day."

"Damn, Vince, don't play with me. You give me a ride on this thing and there's no *telling* what I might give you!"

"Oh really? What makes you think you got something I even *want*?" Vince added wickedly.

"Oh please—I see how you look at me—don't even front, Mister. You know you want these goods." Desiree cocked a hand on one hip and lowered her stare so she could give him the eye.

Vince sucked his teeth as he swung his leg over the seat. He adjusted his goggles, donned his helmet and fired up the Boy as Desiree watched him silently. He gunned the throttle several times causing her to jump back. He was playing with her and loving it. He nodded to her and prepared to leave.

"Hey, wait a minute, Vince—aren't you going to ask a girl for her digits?"

Vince removed his hand from the throttle, lowered his goggles and leaned toward Desiree. "Right now I'm having impure thoughts concerning you and my ride—and so I'd rather leave it alone. Keep that perfect gentleman image of me inside your pretty head instead. Okay." He grinned.

"No, not okay," Desiree said as she rummaged through her wallet and pulled out a card, handing it to him. Vince took it and glanced at it before stuffing it into the back pocket of his jeans. "Call me, Vince Cannon, Jr. Okay? I want to collect on that ride, damn it."

"Oooh, I really dig it when you talk dirty to me, Desiree."

"I'm serious—in fact, hold up…" Desiree reached for a flip phone that was attached to her hip. She opened it and looked at Vince. "Okay, boy, give me your digits."

Vince sighed, glanced around at the patrons who were swarming in and out of Cosi.

"Come on, I don't got all day!" She grinned at him. Vince pursed his lips and gave her the info she was requesting. She punched his number into her phone, bit her bottom lip while playing with the cell, storing his name along with the number. "Cool—so now if I don't hear from a brutha in a reasonable period of time, I'll just call him my damn self! See about collecting that ride."

"You do that."

"I'm gonna."

"Later, alligator!" Vince let out the clutch while throttling up. Desiree stood on the corner shaking her head, muttering to herself, "I can't believe he just said that…"

SIXTEEN

The night air was crisp and clear. Erika fell in step next to James silently, glancing upward at the tiny pinpoints of stars that blazed down upon them as they ran. Out here, away from the bright lights of street corners and neon-lit establishments, one could truly see heaven. Erika sucked in a lungful of fresh air and exhaled forcefully, pumping her arms as she extended her legs to match the rhythm of James' stride. They ran together, side-by-side, past huge, aging oak trees that towered over wide asphalt streets, James' idea actually, he having called her on her cell about three hours ago, as he was finishing up at the station.

"Hey, beautiful—here's a thought—a quiet relaxing evening at my place—some Thai takeout, perhaps a DVD movie, we could get a run in, then take a shower together…whatdathink? Bring your stuff and you can stay over. Cool?"

"Way cool!"

Erika smiled to herself. It really didn't take much to make a sistah happy. A good man with a sense of humor, intelligence, good conversation; a romantic, good in bed—scratch *good*, make that *great* in bed, God-fearing, mom-loving man—that wasn't asking too much, was it? James was different than so many of the men she had been dating lately. He didn't try to impress her with rides in his fancy car, taking her to the hippest spots, and working the VIP *thang* every damn day—no, the point was, James didn't have to do that. He possessed a sense of humor, was a great listener, always asked about her day and what was going on in her life—and didn't pontificate on and on about how he was a celebrity. He talked about things that were important to her, and not how much *cabbage* he made or how big his dick really was…Thank God!

They ran on in silence. This was something that they had discovered they enjoyed doing together. It was important to Erika to work out on the regular. Sistah-girl wasn't getting younger—none of us were—and the only way to maintain a tight body was to work it every chance she got. But with a j.o.b., especially with her insane hours, it was increasingly difficult. James, it turned out, had the same problem. His hours were unpredictable, to say the least, so he tried to get to the gym when he could. But to be in great shape required discipline and commitment. The proverb, "I'll get to it when I can," was just not good enough.

And here was another thing that made her smile and thank her lucky stars—she and James could run together without having to make conversation. Sometimes it was nice to just be in one's presence without all of the dialogue that accompanied most relationships. After a long day at the hospital, tending to patients, running around doing this and that, dealing with those damn doctors (Lord, they were worse than attorneys, Erika knew that for a *fact!*) this was exactly what the doctor ordered—peace, a little space, and tranquility out here among the elements, her man at her side, jogging a few miles, working her muscles, feeling her heart throb with every step and breath, pumping her arms as she pulled ahead of James with a grin, then settling into that rhythm that all runners strive for—that point in your run where you forget about the pain in your legs and chest, overlook the fact that your ankles may be starting to swell, disregard the heaviness in your arms—and just let your stride carry you onward, your breathing becoming regular like a smooth sine wave, the stress from the day escaping from your pores like puffs of air whisked off into space. It was just her among the elements, wind in her ponytail-tied hair, stars navigating overhead as her feet touched ground to a beat only she could hear. It was comforting and restful. And having James there was the perfect end to an otherwise ordinary day.

They turned onto an even wider street, felt the incline pull at them as they increased their pace, James glancing over to Erika and winking before directing his attention straight ahead. Erika glanced at her watch and saw they had been running for close to forty-five minutes already. She was jazzed, feeling good, her heart pumping loud and clear, the blood that rushed through her veins and arteries was clean and fresh. Anticipation of the coming evening tugged at her insides, directing little pin pricks of enchantment to that spot between her thighs, the form-fitting Lycra shorts which she wore accentuating the sensation. She stole a glance at James— his firm body snug in a pair of tight-fitting running pants and tank top, the sinewy muscles of his arms and torso covered with a thin layer of sheen, and looking good enough to eat. Speaking of eating, Erika felt her stomach bark. James must have heard it rumble.

"I'm hungry," he said.

"Me, too."

"Cut left at this next intersection—we're less than a half-mile from home."

Five minutes later, after sprinting the remainder of the way, they were bent over and panting on the back upper deck of James' palatial home—a large, five-bedroom, multi-level brick home with manicured lawn, three-car garage wider than her own living room and dining room *combined*, upper deck that spanned half the length of the house, feeding to a mid-tier deck that housed a circular wrought-iron table with matching chairs and an enormous gas grill—which in turn led to a lower deck that housed a twelve-person hot tub. A gentle rolling hill led away from the deck to a thick tree line several hundred feet away. The space was dark save for a few halogen spotlights that shined their light on the deck surface. Erika stretched her legs while James did squats to keep his muscles from seizing up. A moment later he led her inside to the kitchen where he dialed a local Thai restaurant that delivered. He placed their order—chicken with chili sauce, pad Thai noodles with curry shrimp, and an order of grilled calamari. Forty minutes until. Perfect. Time enough for them to shower and to play...

James' bedroom was upstairs and at the far end of the house facing the tree line. Erika undressed silently while James stepped into the master bath—a huge room with dual skylights, a step-up Jacuzzi tub with so many jets she needed a calculator to count, shower stall with twin brass shower heads and clear glass doors. She heard him start the water as she slipped out of her Lycra running pants and glanced at herself in the full-length mirror in the corner by the obscenely wide flat-screen monitor and stereo cabinet. James, like most men, was an electronics freak—he loved him some gadgets— and he had it all here—satellite receiver, DVD, VCR, dual cassette deck, 33-band graphics equalizer, Dolby 5.1 tuner and preamp, home theater speakers, remotes too numerous to count. And this was all in the bed-room—you should see his set-up in the family room downstairs! The lights pulsed and flashed in different colors and hues as she scanned her figure from top to bottom, her naked flesh rosy from the recent workout. James called to her from the bathroom.

"Shower's ready..."

Erika joined him. He stood with his back to her, head tilted back, letting the water pummel his face, neck, and shoulders. He felt her move behind him, he reached down and behind, pulling her into him. Squirmed against her pelvis, running both hands along the contours of her thighs and ass. Grinning with delight.

"I'm so glad you are here," he said gently.

"Me, too, thanks for the invite."

James turned to face her, glanced down while reaching for her breasts and giving them a tug. Erika closed her eyes, tipped her head back and into the stream of hot water, and let the water cascade down, dousing her hair. James reached for the body wash, this citrus and basil smelling gel that according to the label, "turns a shower into a wonderful pampering experi-ence..." It came out as a gel, but turned into this rich foam shaving-like cream. Erika had brought it over a week ago and left it there, consciously marking her territory—letting any other bitches that might come around know that she had been there. James loved the stuff—he used a loofah pad to soap her up until not one square inch of caramel skin showed through— beginning with her ankles and thighs, working his way upward, spinning her around to get at her back and ass, then back around again, to her stomach and breast area, neck and face—stopping just below the eyes. Then he used his fingers as if he intended to massage each molecule of foam into every single pore, circling around her areolas, tracing the outline of each clavicle, feeling the rise of flesh as it transitioned from thigh to buttocks—James fully hard now, his member swinging against her foam-covered stomach, and Erika, eyes still closed, reached out to take it, covering it in the palm of her hand, and rewarded him with a playful squeeze.

"Turn around, baby," James commanded. Erika did not have to be told twice. Pressing her elbows against the large square tile, she rested her head against the wall and felt the water beat against her skin. It felt so damn good. The smell of citrus and basil was in the air. Her skin tingled. Her muscles relaxing with every second spent under this waterfall. And then James silently spread her legs, ran the back of his hand from the crack of her ass to her vulva, flipped his palm up and retraced his steps, allowing his fingers to linger among the slippery folds of her sex.

"Ohhh, James," Erika whispered, "That feels really good." James was silent in his response as he pressed himself against her warm backside, the foam layer between their skin providing ample lubrication. James rotated his hips slowly while moving his hand around and cupping her breasts, pinching the nipples that stuck out like thumbtacks. He used his fingers to feel her, and this is what Erika really liked—most bruthas went straight for the promised land—gave the nips a quick hello before traveling south and aiming for the wet spot. But Erika—like most women, dug foreplay. That meant, knowing not only where the spot was, but more importantly, how to get there…

James had wonderful hands—he used them wisely, always taking his time, playing her body with his fingers as if she were an instrument, never rushing, never ever in a hurry. He always got to where he was going, and when he did, Erika was ready. He touched her there now, the epicenter of her womanhood—felt her open to his touch, slipped a finger inside while his other hand reached for her neck and played with her thick hair. Erika moaned. James worked his finger inside of her, slowly at first, then, sensing a change in her rhythm and feeling her drive against his pelvis with her ass, he increased the momentum, using his thumb and forefinger to grasp her clitoris, tugging at it, pulling it from side to side, spreading her lips, pulling them apart and then to one side, all the while kissing her along neck and wet cheek.

It didn't take Erika long—in moments, after the anticipation of seeing James again after a short hiatus of several days, *knowing* the pleasure that was in store for her, awaiting his touch as they ran side-by-side, expecting the release but not knowing exactly when it would occur—finally feeling him totally as he explored her sensuously, doing to her precisely what she liked to have done, and at the tempo that was right for her—Erika arched back and felt her entire being vibrate as she *came*. That wonderful feeling of discharge, the expulsion of everything that is *bad* and infusion of everything that is *good*, all in the same breath—the sensation that is undeniable and indescribable, an orgasm which is intense, all consuming, and satisfying…Thank you, Lawd!

✖✖✖

They lay on his wide bed with the thick bluish-green comforter—this fluffy, wonderful feeling bedspread that reminded Erika of what it must look like beneath the waves—muted colors of sea green that morphed into bluish-black—that kind of out of focus sensation that one gets when immersing themselves underwater—vision blurred, but color and hue lovely and discrete.

James was still wet, clad in a thick white terry cloth robe with the initials JWC on the breast. Erika wore a matching robe that hung to her ankles, her dark hair unencumbered and still wet from the shower moments ago. She lay near him, her hand propping up her face; the folds of her robe open, allowing an unobstructed view of one breast. James' robe hung open, too; a light coat of chest hair lay wet and matted against his cinnamon skin. Boney James played on in the background, his sultry sax sounds permeating the air like fog. Several scented candles burned, creating the only light in the bedroom, save for the cockpit-like glow from the electronics on one wall and the sliver of light that seeped from the bathroom door, making an angular statement on the off-white carpet.

Erika reached for James, lightly played with his chest hairs, before tracing a path with her fingernail down his torso to his stomach, circling his navel, untying the loose belt that held the folds of his robe in place, spreading the terry cloth apart, like butterfly wings, setting him free. Silently, as James watched from a half-sitting, half-prone position, she reached for him, felt his already engorged state, and slipped him into her waiting mouth.

Erika took her time, in no rush, tasting the head, nibbling at it like it was a tasty strawberry, enjoying the flavor, then running her tongue along the shaft, circling this piece of manhood that was strong and firm. She backed away, the sheen from her saliva noticeable even in the dimly lit room, grasped him in her hand, studied it from her close vantage—marveling at the way no two looked identical—James had one that was of average length, but was beautiful, a true work of art—the head, smooth and not overly bulbous—and Erika enjoyed rubbing the spot where the soft piece of skin downturned into a generous lip of flesh with rounded edges. The girth was something she enjoyed, too—big enough to fill her up, but not overbearing in a way that made things uncomfortable. The most enjoyable thing she thought was the way his penis laid on his stomach now, curving slightly upward like a banana, not enough curvature to cause discomfort— just the opposite in fact, she loved the way it felt inside of her, especially when she was on top and leaning in to him, that probe of manly comestible, curving inside of her and rubbing against her womanly walls in a loving and comforting sort of way.

Erika returned her mouth to him, sucking him in quickly with an audible slurp, and gripping the shaft, hearing him wince. James shifted and lay back, face to the ceiling, eyes closed, enjoying this feeling that overtook him. She sucked him good, using long, full strokes, allowing James to go as deep as he could before reaching the back of her throat—and then pulling back out—James controlling the motion with his hips, Erika holding on and directing the show with her glazed hand. She very much enjoyed the sensation of fellating James—knowing as sure as there was a tomorrow that this was a feeling that he truly loved. As she continued along with this rhythm, Boney James in the background on a groove that made her toes dance, she matched her beat to his own, and closed her eyes, taking pleasure in making him feel good. A nagging thought suddenly appearing in the annuals of her mind without warning—tonight would James *come*? Would he finally come, once and for all? It had been close to five weeks. That was a long time not to have an orgasm. They had talked about it—briefly— James telling her not to worry—once again reassuring her that it was the condoms. But there had been a lot of sex within those five weeks. But no orgasm for James. And then, before she could make sense of these thoughts, lay it out for full inspection, and analyze further what was really going on, the doorbell chimes rang, a low-pitched, electronically enhanced sound that floated up to the bedroom. James, who had been squeezing her damp hair between his fingers as she sucked him, gently pulled her away, and sat up.

"Hold that thought, beautiful," he said, catching his breath and closing his robe quickly, "dinner's about to be served..."

Five minutes later he returned with the food. Loaded onto a large wooden tray, the three entrees were set on fancy china, the fragrance of curry shrimp and piquant chili sauce suspended in the air, tall glasses of Coke filled with ice, cloth napkins, salt and pepper, utensils, everything they would need to commence their little feast. James arranged the plates on his comforter, telling Erika not to worry—*whatever* got on the sheets, he said with a sneer, could be washed off.

Erika inquired if his fat erection had subsided by the time he made it to the door. James smiled and replied that, no, the delivery guy, who just happened to be gay—gay and a Thailander, imagine that—did indeed notice his "pickle in his pocket" as James put it, and after handing over the brown bag of food to James, cocked (no pun intended) his head to the side and asked if he could be of *further* service. James politely declined and closed the door. Erika squealed with laughter!

The food was tasty and hit the spot. The calamari was perfect—grilled, not fried—not too spicy, but with a kick that made Erika's mouth tingle. They lay on the bed, still clad in their robes as they ate, James occasionally feeding her with forkfuls of the chicken immersed in chili sauce—he had given up on using chopsticks after seeing that it took far too much effort to keep from dropping the morsels of food onto his comforter. Erika chowed down on the pad Thai noodles with shrimp, one of her favorite dishes, washing the seafood down with her Coke. Boney James had been replaced with Norman Brown's CD—his soft guitar licks inhabiting the room like an old friend.

They made small talk as they ate—James talked about his day at the studio, and a story he was working on that intrigued him—a piece about a black kid, high school age, who had just been accepted to Stanford University on a scholarship. The rub was that the kid and his family were homeless— the piece would primarily be about how the family had come to be in this predicament, and more importantly, how in this day and age, people from all walks of life still lost their homes every single day. Erika listened as he talked; then they switched gears, and she spoke about her day—as with many people Erika talked about what was bothering her at work—mostly office politics and such—this person trying to backstab another to get ahead. How petty some folks were—how personalities made or broke many situations—and turned one's experience at work into something pleasurable or something that was dreaded, like surgery. Erika thought about Trey, and how in the blink of an eye his situation had gone from wonderful to extremely shitty—with his mentor being replaced by some slick-back newbie, trying to get in everyone's business and upset the balance of the firm.

When they were done about thirty minutes later, James cleared the plates, loading everything up onto the wooden tray and carrying it back downstairs. Erika seized the opportunity to stand and stretch her legs, run her fingers through her still drying hair, and re-tie her bathrobe. She was full, feeling good—the combination of run—shower—orgasm—food had left her feeling peppy and totally alive. She pranced over to the stereo, changed CDs again—this time to something a bit more uptempo—selecting Donnell Jones, snapping her fingers as the first jam came on. She began to move her hips, mouthing the words along with the singer. She bent down, examining James' collection of music and DVDs. Several titles caught her eye—a few blockbusters—*The Matrix; Training Day; Gladiator, M:I-2.* Next to those were a dozen or so DVDs that were placed in the shelf backwards, their titles not showing. Erika pulled a few out and studied their covers— *Indecency; The Uranus Experiment 2; Devil in the Flesh; Shag-A-Rama!* A frown replaced her smile. *Shag-A-Rama?* Her fingers went to other titles— *Anal in the Amazon; Black Cocks, White Pussies; Assume the Position;* and *Unusual Objects.* Erika stared in awe at the explicit cover photos. James—a closet freak? This was totally unexpected. She heard him enter the room, spun around, feeling her face flush from embarrassment. His eyes met hers and he smiled.

"See you found my collection," he mused. His fingers fumbled with the sash at his waist. He unloosened it, letting the folds of his robe hang free. Erika could see his penis swinging free, but beginning to swell.

"Yeah. James, what is this stuff?" she asked, anxiety filling her voice.

"What's the matter, baby? A little porno scares you?" James' tone had changed and Erika shivered involuntarily. He went to her, wrapped his arms around her terry-cloth-clad frame and pulled her into him. He kissed the top of her head and she immediately felt warmth. He glanced down at her. "Everything cool? If it bothers you I can put it away."

"No, it's just…"

"I thought it might be fun to watch one. Together." James pulled back from her and smiled, untying his sash as he went. His robe fell to the ground and Erika saw he was fully hard. "Anyway, don't we have some unfinished business to…uh, finish?" She nodded silently, her mind spinning, wondering what James was up to. She had seen him this excited before— hell, he was always excited when *she* was around—but something about this time—she couldn't put her finger on it exactly—but it just seemed different. Silently, she watched as James selected a DVD and inserted it into the player. He lay back on the bed, holding out his hand for her to join him. She did, keeping her robe on as she knelt by his waist, reaching for his penis. James placed a pillow under his head so he could remain propped up, facing the large screen. Erika ran her hand around his shaft, cupped him in her palm and began to jerk him, feeling the thickness expand with every tug she gave. Her mouth reacquainted itself with his member, taking him in her mouth, as much as she could stand, as her eyes scanned the TV set, as

James worked the remote. Scenes flew past rapidly, and then he settled on one, as Erika continued to blow him. James massaged her shoulders and neck with his left hand, then reached for her hair and grabbed it, letting her mane slide in between his fingers. She increased the tempo, her head sliding up and down as if on a string, a puppet, her eyes never leaving the screen.

The scene was of a thick black woman, equipped with a killer body—large, firm breasts, J. Lo ass, strong legs and strong arms—an equally impressive brutha underneath of her—the woman and man sixty-nining each other as they wriggled and moaned for the camera. His cock was being consumed by the woman on screen—she was taking him entirely in his mouth until only his testicles showed; for his part, his face was completely covered by her lower body, which thrashed around as he ate her voraciously, his fingers spreading her ass cheeks apart so he could reach and consume more of her.

James bucked his hips slowly; spoke softly to Erika, letting her know how much he was enjoying her doing this to him. He reached again for the remote, pressed a button or two—the scene fast-forwarded to where the black woman had returned with a white vibrator, the brutha lying back on the bed, legs splayed wide, matching the grin on his face. Erika watched with a detached sort of fascination—on the one hand enjoying the fact that her man was so excited and stimulated by what was going on—on the other, bothered by this scene—not that it was disgusting or anything—but it struck her as somewhat odd that *her* man would find this sort of entertainment stirring.

The black woman on the screen reached for the bedside table and some lube—spread some on her fingers and proceeded to rub the gel on the brutha's ass and around the dildo. Then she, without any fanfare, inserted the tip of hard plastic into the brutha's orifice, while stroking his dick with her dark hand.

At this point James had taken a hold of Erika's head with one hand, and using the palm of his other to push her downwards, increasing the tempo of her sucking. He was moaning incessantly now, not attempting to conceal his pleasure. Erika increased her grip, lightly gnawed at the head, teasing him with her tongue and teeth before rubbing his balls with her fingers and brushing against his ass with her digits.

On screen the brutha was in heaven—back in the real world James was, too—both women fellating their men deeply, except on screen the girl was plunging the white vibrator in and out of the brutha's ass while she worked her oral magic. Erika found the scene disturbing, to say the least. What, she wondered, did James find erotic, about a man with a dildo up his ass???

And then, James issued a low growl, his legs and the rest of his body tightening, and Erika felt her mouth fill with semen. It caught her completely off guard, but she did her best not to show her surprise. James was holding her head in both hands as he spasmed, and Erika had no choice but to let him fill her mouth with his seed. She jerked his penis with her hand, her mind on autopilot, feeling the waves recede as he began to wither between her lips.

"Oh God!" James moaned. His head fell backwards, and Erika moved off him, bringing her hand to her still closed mouth. She glanced at him while heading for the bathroom. His eyes were fluttering rapidly, eyeballs rolling back and forth in their sockets, lost in their own little world.

Once in the bathroom, she ran the water, spit his seed down the sink, and washed out her mouth. Rinsed again before she ran the hot water, grabbed a hand towel, and lathered it up. Returning to the bedroom, Erika cleaned up James in a lovingly sort of way, washing him with the warm cloth. He moaned softly, but was otherwise silent. She took the remote from his limp hand, shut down the television set and went back to the bathroom. When she returned, James had crawled underneath the comforter, turned on his side and was snoring peacefully, his chest rising and falling slowly with every steady breath.

Erika blew out the candles and slipped beneath the covers, coming to a rest behind him. She ran her tongue inside of her mouth and swallowed a taste of James—thinking about the scene that had just unfolded in real life and on screen…wondering to herself as she wrapped a leg and arm around his sleeping form—was it she who had made him come tonight—or was it the couple in the video? This was the single solitary thought that would haunt her until daybreak…

SEVENTEEN

I couldn't believe my freaking eyes—Allison, lovely fair-skinned Allison, homegirl from the night before—same honey who barely nine hours previously was allowing me to dab little droplets of sweat from between her luscious breasty melons—across from me—in the flesh! Now here I was, my jaw dragging against the goddamn floor—not a pretty sight, considering I was decked out in my usual smart office attire—a four-button robin's-egg blue suit, crisp white cotton shirt, navy blue silk tie with thin slivers of yellow meandering down the face of the fabric, and to complete the *coup de grace*, light-brown lace-ups—the kind of ensemble I usually reserved for those upscale social settings, but it just so happened I was in one of those *moods*—you know how *we* do, when you feel like making mutha fuckas snap their heads around as you walk by—don't even trip, y'all, you know you get that feeling just like I do every so often…and so, I quickly shut my trap, smiled at Allison and Quentin's wife (whom I had never met), and gestured for my client to take a seat.

I was giving Allison the eye, all the while grinning but thinking to myself—bitch, I can't *believe* you pulled this shit on me last night—playing me like I was some kind of fool, but before I could let my thoughts go to completion, she was introducing me to Quentin's wife, soon-to-be ex, Aponi Hues, a tiny little thing, lovely as she could possibly be. I took her all in as she stood to reach out and shake my hand—thin waist, tight body, no traces of aged fat here—that's what I'm talking about, y'all, medium-sized firm breasts that didn't need the support of a bra underneath her button-down white blouse, a sculptured face, dark hair in a single braid, dark eyes that stared right through you—all-in-all a very nice package! Quentin, you go, boy, I am not mad at you. Dawg, if that were mine, I'd hit that ass every fucking chance I got! And as I gripped Aponi's hand, smiled, and thought about what she must look like naked, I had to check myself—Trey's Rule Number 4—never, ever, fuck your client—that, my friends, is a no-no. That shit can get you disbarred! But then, in the blink of an eye, I analyzed the situation, examined it from all angles, as if I were a physician probing the innards of an anxious patient—and came to the logical conclusion that in this *particular* situation, Rule Number 4 did *not* apply! Lawd Have Mercy! After all, Aponi was not my client! Ah, sookie sookie now!

Allison was bending down to open her briefcase and scatter some legal papers across the shiny conference room table, and I was clocking her every move. Her navy blue suit looked damn good on her, hair pulled back, girl-friend trying to look all business-like, and *succeeding*, and I'm sitting there thinking about last night at H20 and how damn good she appeared, titties spread before me like a pair of succulent fruit that were waiting to be snatched off a vine and devoured. And then my lips downturned into a frown—was Allison off-limits also? Did Trey's Rule Number 4 apply to opposing counsel as well? I'd have to check the rulebooks for a decision, y'all—let me think…naw, Allison and *any* opposing counsel were cool, I hastily concluded—and so I wasn't about to let this stop me from tagging that ass. Just then Allison looked up, her gaze meeting mine for a brief moment—and in that instant an encoded message for me and me alone seemed to transmit across the ether that hovered between us silently, and my smile was quickly erased—it was clear that whatever had transpired between us in the club the night before was *past tense*…and would stay in the past—Allison was about to get down to business. Strictly business.

Damn it, y'all, I just *hate* when that happens!

Allison cleared her throat and ran her palm over a ink-filled legal pad. "Good morning, gentleman. As you know my client has filed for divorce in the District of Columbia. One of the first matters that needs to be attended to is the separation of marital assets and property. Per normal legal procedure, I've asked Mrs. Hues to take an inventory of said assets and property in the hopes of speeding up this process." Allison proceeded to pass out several sheets of paper that were stapled in the upper-left corner. "Of course, we expect that Mr. Hues will review this list, or if it is counsel's wish, he can generate a list of his own for our review." Allison paused and smiled at Quentin who merely nodded silently. Her gaze flicked over to me—I let my stare find the bridge of her nose and hover there for a moment without saying shit. I wanted this little hussy to feel my indignation over last night. I still could not believe that she played me! Girlfriend knew all along who I was—that's what Sassy had been referring to when we made our introductions—she had seen the way Allison had paused for a split second when I told her my name. She had known I was opposing counsel. So that's why she had decided to leave the *dick* alone. Okay, two can play that game. I decided to play tough with her—spare no punches—was ready to say, "of course we will be furnishing our own fucking list—you think we're going to take the word of some skanky ho?" —but then decided that this probably wasn't the most appropriate thing to say in front of my own client, considering the "ho" in question was still his wife…

"That's fine, Ms. Matthews, let my client review this. If there's a problem or if he'd prefer to produce his own list then we will, of course, let you know." I sat back, satisfied. Looked at Quentin who was studying the list with a furrowed brow, deep in thought. I glanced over at Aponi to my left— she remained motionless, her eyes moving between her attorney and me. Her breath was steady—the slow rise and fall of her breasts was mesmerizing to me. *But,* I told myself, *this is business—and business comes first.*

Allison grabbed a pair of thin reading glasses and slung them on while flipping to the second page. Damn, she looked sexy in those black frames! I imagined her lying in my oversized bed, the *Wall Street Journal* strewn around her naked form, save for those sexy glasses…

"As you can see, gentlemen, while there are lots of items on this list, my client is prepared to make this process far more palatable for Mr. Hues. She is *only* interested in the deed to the primary residence…" Quentin sucked in a quick breath and exhaled forcefully. I involuntarily reached out for Q.'s hand. Allison paused for a moment and glanced up before continuing. "The residence in question located in Raritan Township in New Jersey being turned over to my client."

"No fucking way!" Quentin spoke low and with a growl. He had turned his body to face his wife. Ignoring Allison, he reached out past me and pointed to his wife. "You've gotta…"

"Hold it!" I said forcefully, while gently pulling Quentin's arm down. I had spoken to Q. on the way over here about the possibility of this happening. It always did. Quentin was like most youngbloods in the NBA—he had made mad loot quickly—he was still young—twenty-seven—and rapidly had gone about making his mark by amassing a small collection of material things—a jet-black Land Cruiser ($68,000), a silver Jaguar XKR convertible ($90,000); two twenty-thousand-dollar Harley Davidson motorcycles (which he rarely rode); a top-floor condo overlooking the Georgetown Harbour ($1.6 million); and a three-million-dollar mansion in New Jersey that his wife had just put her dibbs on. Not to mention the jewelry, video, satellite, and high-fidelity electronics, mounds of CDs, matching Jet Skis, furniture, a small recording studio—probably costing over one-hundred grand in equipment alone—because Quentin (like many of these niggas out there) thought he could rap, and a small mountain of cash for God knows what. Quentin had gone over his own list three weeks ago with me, item by item—so I knew exactly what was what—and I had told him in no uncertain terms—in situations like these, the wife usually goes for the main home—fuck the cars, the bikes, the boats and rest of the shit—electronics weren't invented for women anyway—they don't know the first thing about using a remote! I had braced Q. that this might happen. Asked him to maintain his cool if it did…let me take the helm…I was ready for this shit—had rehearsed it many times…so I took a breath and went on.

"Ms. Matthews—I fail to see how your client has any legal rights to this home. If my memory serves me," and here I paused just to make a point by glancing up at the ceiling for a brief period of time, "Mr. and Mrs. Hues were married two years ago in May. Unfortunately, Mr. Hues had purchased the home in question back in September of 2000, several months after he signed with the New York Knicks. That was 2000, Ms. Matthews, two solid *years* before he married Mrs. Hues here." I paused, gave her one of my "how ya like me now" smiles before glancing over at Aponi who remained tight-lipped. I had to give homegirl credit—she was playing things way too cool—she was calm and held her demeanor a little too well. This concerned me—I expected her to go "ghetto" on us at any moment now—break out of the seat, pointing, spitting, and telling us just what the fuck she and her posse were gonna do—that's what was usually the case with some women—but Aponi seemed to be different. This would require further thought.

"My client," I continued, "has every legal right to continue to own the main residence, live in it, sublet it, or do whatever he sees fit. Your client, regardless of the fact that she was married to Quentin, unfortunately has no legal right to it."

I took a breath before continuing. Allison stared impassively at me. *Good, I got your fucking attention now, be-yatch.*

"My client," I continued, "Ms. Matthews, is prepared to split all assets and property that was amassed *during* the marriage, amicably and equitably, but not one day before. That is not only fair, Ms. Matthews," and here I sat forward, pivoted left, and gave Aponi my full attention, "and Mrs. Hues…but that *is* the law." I sat back, confident and satisfied, giving my client, Quentin Hues, Washington Wizards star forward, a quick clutch of his forearm while I grinned my ass off at Allison!

✖✖✖

Like in the movie, *Titanic*, I was on top of the world!!! But Allison Matthews, counsel for Aponi Hues, was about to bust my bubble. The skanky ho wench!

"Mr. Alexander," she said, way too calmly, while glancing around the room, smiling that devilish smile that had made my dick quiver last night. "Do you happen to have a laptop handy that I could use?" My eyes narrowed—a laptop???? Just what the fuck did she want/need with a laptop?

"I'm sorry?" I said gingerly, buying time to allow my analytical mind to run scenarios through my brain at gigaflop speeds. Quentin was searching Aponi's eyes for a clue. There were none, and this, more than anything, bothered me.

"A laptop—do you have one handy?" Allison asked again, producing a shiny CD-ROM from her leather briefcase. She held the disc case in her hand, moving it ever so slowly between lovely fingers. My mind was pounding in anticipation—this was the Yin and Yang of law that gave me the adrenaline rush that was as good as sex (well, *almost* as good as sex)—the not knowing what was to come next—sparring with an able partner and learning to anticipate their tactics—like a tough game of chess where the most able players think eight to ten moves ahead—pawns overtaking rooks when one isn't expecting it…

"Hold on. Give me a sec." I reached for the PolyCom in the center of the conference table and quickly dialed India's extension. She picked up on the first ring.

"It's me—can you bring a laptop over to the Peace Room? Yes, thanks." I smiled at Allison and Aponi. "Aptly named, don't you think?" I sat back, took a moment to compose my thoughts, cut a quick glance over at Quentin who was sitting at the table quietly, save for the vein in his temple that throbbed to some hushed rhythm. Allison smiled, took a moment to jot down a few notes on the pages of her legal pad. Aponi, on the other hand, took the opportunity to get up and stretch her legs by moving to the large window. I used the occasion to check out her ass—it was nice, round and firm, no hint of jiggle, momma's been good to her, that's for sure—the package wrapped up in a pair of tight, shiny black pants with a thick leather belt with an oversized ornate buckle. Under any other circumstances I would have zeroed in on the contours of her sexy young flesh, the kind that hadn't begun that decomposition of sensuality that ultimately brings every woman down—the sexy curve of her ass cheeks which intersected the cleft where her (undoubtedly tight) pussy lay—but not today—today, at this exact moment I *needed* to know what the fuck was on that CD…something wasn't right. That was for sure.

India arrived three minutes later. She set the laptop down in front of me, smiled and departed silently. I flipped the clamshell open, powered it on, and swiveled it around for Allison to use. She nodded to me while inserting the CD into the drive.

"Mr. Alexander," she said softly, as she waited patiently for the computer to boot up, her full attention directed on me, "are you aware that the only reason for the demise of the marriage between Quentin and Aponi Hues is your client's *infidelity*?" I felt the weight from a steel I-beam that is used to build skyscrapers come crashing into my solar plexus, knocking the wind out of me. While I couldn't see my bald head, I knew without a shadow of a doubt that beads of sweat were bursting forth from my pores. I felt myself turning pale.

I managed a weak, "excuse me?"

"Infidelity." Allison said the word with fluidity, style, and grace. Like she had practiced it a million times before this morning's meeting. I snapped my head over to Quentin who was holding his breath and looking straight-forward. *Oh shit*, I thought to myself, *this is going to be one fucked up day...*

✖✖✖

Allison had finished fumbling around with the laptop and swiveled it around to face Quentin and me, her index finger poised over the keyboard. She checked her legal pad for a moment—as if she needed to be reminded about what was to come next. Without preamble she unleashed on us.

"Mr. Hues has on, at least three occasions that we are *aware* of, committed adultery..."

"What?" Quentin yelled. I put my hand on his forearm and gestured for him to be silent.

"Yes, adultery—and memorialized it onto digital format for all of eternity. Not too smart, considering the fact that his wife found the evidence on his laptop." Quentin was turning ashen. Aponi's mouth was frozen into a tight curve. "Yes, his laptop." And with that Allison hit the <Enter> button with her manicured index finger—and in a split second the screen was filled with moving images of Quentin and his extremely well-hung cock being pampered, licked, and sucked by some nameless white girl. Allison turned the sound up with a flick of her thumb so we could all hear him talking his dirty trash to this little slut. I blinked and all I could think about was stupid mutha fuckas who filmed their own versions of home porno, and then lived to regret it…

Now it was Aponi's turn to unleash.

"You mutha fucka! I thought you loved me!" she exclaimed, rising out of the seat as she extended her hand in his direction. I was already out of mine, forming a human shield between her and my client. "Instead you were fucking these *bitches*? You dirty mutha fucka!" Traces of spittle were deposited at the corners of her mouth. Her nipples were hard, that was apparent, and even in the midst of her fury, she was still quite beautiful. Quentin had pushed back from the conference room table and was standing, staring down his wife. He was silent for a moment before it was his turn to go off.

"Bitch, if you weren't always shopping and spending my goddamn money trying to be Gucci-down, perhaps I'd pay more attention to you!"

"Calm down, Q.," I told him, raising my hand to ensure he didn't decide to charge left toward his wife. Allison had risen and had gone to console her client, who stood her ground, and was huffing and puffing like a raging bull.

"Fucking bitch!" Quentin hissed, loud enough for everyone in the room to hear. "Why the fuck don't you go back to Limited Too where I found your dumb ass…"

"FUCK YOU, nigga!" Aponi spit, flinging her hands in the air. "You're the dumb mutha fucka here—taped your stupid ass and left it on the computer for me to find?" Aponi's face turned into a snarl. "Who's the stupid mutha fucka now, huh, nigga?" Her arms were across her upper body as if she were hugging herself. Quentin was a mass of rage that I would have trouble controlling in a moment. The boy was huge.

"Quentin," I said, calmly, looking first at him and then at Allison, while punching redial on the PolyCom. "India, please come escort Mr. Hues to my office—NOW." I pointed my finger toward him and glared at his eyes. "Quentin!" I repeated. Quentin bowed his head as he backed up toward the door. India flew into the room like a storm. She knew from my tone what was up. This wasn't the first time a meeting between feuding couples had turned ugly. She reached for Quentin's arm and gently nudged him toward the door. His eyes flicked from Aponi to Allison to me. I nodded silently as he left the room. The door closed and I spun to face Allison, who was still touching Aponi's shoulder.

"First off, that was a stupid stunt, counselor!" Allison opened her mouth to speak but I raised my hand and cut her off before giving her the opportunity. "That was really great for drama, but it didn't serve either of our clients' interests. Secondly, that disc doesn't mean a damn thing, and you know it. That could be anyone on that tape! Hell, nowadays anyone with a camcorder and some low-cost editing software can make a pretty convincing movie."

"You saying that's not Quentin on that screen?" Aponi yelled.

"I have no idea, Ms. Hues. But that is not what should concern you right now—this should—that movie was confiscated from property that does not belong to you. That's stealing. Further, it *may* contain data that is potentially damaging to my client's career and reputation. Therefore, as soon as I leave this office I will file an injunction against you with the Superior Court of the District of Columbia ensuring that the contents of that disc not be played, shown, inspected, copied, transmitted, or altered in any way."

"You can't do that," Allison exclaimed. "The contents of that disc were produced during the marriage and therefore is marital property, and…"

"Oh yes I can—and I *will*—you better listen to me, Ms. Hues, and listen carefully because I am not playing games here—I don't want to escalate things to the point where they get ugly, but you and your lawyer have brought us to this place, not me. I have no intentions of sitting here and allowing my client to be defamed. Your attorney pulled a stupid move—unfortunately for you, you're the one who will have to live with the consequences."

I reached for the laptop and snapped it shut while maintaining eye contact with Aponi. The sound of plastic impacting reverberated throughout the room.

"The penalty for violating a court-ordered injunction is quite high—you will go to jail, Ms.. Hues, I promise!" I paused to let that sink in. "And if you even *think* about doing something stupid with that disc or any other copies that you may possess, I would think long and hard before you act, Ms. Hues. I promise you, this has the potential to turn ugly like that," I snapped my fingers, "if you don't keep your head straight.

"This meeting, Ms. Matthews, is over. I strongly urge you to counsel your client on these matters. The law, whether you agree with it or not, is on my client's side. We will be in touch!"

With that, I scooped the laptop under my arm and exited the Peace Room, holding my breath and not letting it out until I was on the other side of the thick conference room door, and out of sight...

EIGHTEEN

Vince lowered the sketchpad to the deeply stained worktable and dropped the mechanical pencil as well. He rubbed his beard and scratched at his cheek. The drawing that stared up at him wasn't quite right—Vince couldn't put his finger on it, but it just wasn't the kind of sketch that he was feeling this minute. He sighed, glanced around his studio, and decided that a short break was in order.

It was a little after seven. The sun, he could see from the high windows, was beginning to set. The room in which he stood was an oversized loft, perfect for an artist such as himself. It had high ceilings and aging brick walls that held character and ancient whispers in the darkening mortar. Four high windows were cut into adjoining walls, each one high enough that he had to stand on a stool to reach the sash. A small fireplace was built into one corner of the room; a small pile of wooden scraps laid unburned inside the hearth. A cheap futon laid in the center of the room, one that he had picked up at Ikea a number of years ago—just in case he worked far into the night or just got too tired to head home—not a rare occurrence lately...

On the long wall opposite the two windows and in front of a low coffee table hung his collection of masks—they were suspended in rows from floor to ceiling. There were close to two dozen of them—masks of various shapes, sizes, patterns, and colors. Each one representing someone whom had touched him in some small, yet significant way. A lover, a friend, family member, or even stranger—someone whom had made a lasting impression on Vince's psyche.

The floors of this space were concrete, but Vince had taken a colorful throw rug that contained wisps of red, orange and purple, and placed it across the center of the room, giving the room a touch of class. Along with his masks and a few other knickknacks, it made the space feel lived in and homey. That was important since he spent a great deal of time here, working, thinking, and being artistic and creative.

Vince left the sketchpad on the worktable and walked over to the coffee table, reaching for his cup of java. He sat down on the futon, ran a hand over his hair and reached for his cell on his hip. After taking another sip of coffee, he flipped open the phone and dialed the number he knew all too well.

He was staring at his latest piece as he waited for the connection to be made—the one of Maxi—it hung off to the right about halfway up the brick wall. Vince was happy with it—the mask had come out quite nice—at first it had taken him a while to complete—not knowing for sure what color scheme to apply to the surface of plaster. The lifecasting itself had gone quite well, and the bas-relief that had stared back at him had been unnerving, to say the least. But Vince wasn't sure how this piece was to be finished—a solid dark color—no, that wasn't quite right, since it didn't match Maxi's mood—multiple colors then? Diagonal stripes, thick or thin swaths of alternating color? That was a thought—but he didn't think it would work here. In the end, a tie-dye kind of pattern—bursting out from the epicenter— radiating outwards, the darkness of deep rich browns and reds leading to the lightness of pale gray and yellows. And for the finishing touches, Maxi's lips—those sensuous pieces of flesh that Vince remembered all too well, outlined in a vibrant day-glow kind of orange smear, standing apart from the rest of the mask like a lone Joshua tree in a forgotten desert.

Vince heard the familiar voice and grinned to himself.

"Hey you."

"Hey."

"Angeliqué baby. Que pasa?"

"Sorry, lover boy..." And that's when Vince began to suspect that he wasn't talking to whom he thought he was. "...she's not here right now."

"Oh. My bad. I thought this was Angeliqué," Vince mused. "Guess not."

"No harm—most people confuse our voices. This is Amber. And you are Vince." Not a question, Vince noticed, but a statement.

Vince smiled. "Amber, hello. How'd you know?"

"Not too hard," Amber said, "she's only been talking about you non stop...kind of hard to concentrate on anything else..."

"Really?" Vince was intrigued. He directed his mind back to New Orleans for a clue as to the identity of this woman—and then suddenly it hit him like a palm to the forehead—she was the young woman whom he had met when he'd gone to Angeliqué's studio the night of her show—the beautiful model, bare, reclining on the floor—head tilted back, brown hair inches from the ground, darkly rimmed nipples erect, trim body, firm legs and thighs, auburn skin covered with a hauntingly beautiful pattern of *veve*. Vince saw all of her with razor-like clarity—and recalled the way he had been stunned into silence by a shard of recognition, which flowed through him now. He was silenced once again by the thought.

"Are you there?" she asked after the pregnant pause.

"Yes, ah, I'm right here."

"Soooooo—only you, me, and several thousand miles of optic cable between us..." Amber laughed and Vince felt himself flush.

"Yes. So true."

"Cat got your tongue, I see," she mused. "Not to worry. Guess you were expecting someone else—but listen, go ahead; why don't you throw down your rap, the one you were going to use on Angeliqué, on me instead—let me try it on for size!"

"Hmmn, there's a thought. But I better not."

"Why," Amber teased, "afraid I'm going to poke holes in your shit?"

Vince laughed. "Naw, nothing like that."

"You sure? I don't mind. I don't have anything else to do tonight!"

"Sorry to hear that, but tell you what—can you just *mention* to Angeliqué that I called? That would be best."

"Oh yeah, I can do that, Vince. Not a problem."

"Cool," Vince said, warming to this woman immediately.

"Yeah, cool," Amber responded, warming to him, too.

Vince was ready to say something else—feeling himself wanting to continue the conversation, launch onto another plane, another topic that had already formed on the tip of his tongue and was ready to take flight—when his cell beeped. He frowned, glanced at the tiny screen and the unfamiliar number, and put the phone back to his ear.

"Amber, can you hold one sec—I've got another call coming in. Don't go away, okay?"

"Sure, not going anywhere."

Vince clicked over and said hello.

"Mr. Cannon, Jr.?" a familiar voice asked.

"Yes?"

"Hey, Vince. It's Desiree! What's up?"

Vince smiled. "Hey you. How ya livin'?"

"Not bad considering…waiting for a brutha to give a sistah a call back and a ride on that beautiful bike. Ya know???"

"Desiree. Sorry, boo. I've been busy and…"

"Yeah, yeah, yeah. Tell it to one of those *uneducated* women you obviously are confusing me with, okay?"

"Damn, Desiree." Vince's thoughts went to that of Amber on the other line. "Listen—I'm on a call right now. Can I call you in a minute?"

"A minute?" Desiree responded, "or do you mean, tomorrow or next week? Don't keep a sistah waiting!"

"I got you, Desiree. I'll call you back." Vince switched back over with a sigh. "Amber? You still there?"

"Yeah, where am I gonna go? Besides, I'm waiting to hear some words of wisdom from you, seeing how you're the writer/philosopher here." Amber laughed and Vince found himself grinning along with her, momentarily forgetting Desiree and her *drama*.

"Writer/philosopher? Where'd you get that from?" Vince asked.

"Please. I'm staring at the cover of your book right now." He heard a rustling noise in the background. "Nice photo, by the way. I dig that jacket. Black suits you well, Vince."

"Thank you, Amber. Okay—you got me on the writer bit, but philosopher? I don't think so."

"Don't be modest. I've been reading you. And I have to say I'm impressed."

"Really?" Vince mused. He wouldn't admit it, but any time someone had something positive to say about his book, he absolutely loved it. Vince never got tired of hearing folks talk about his book. Never!

"I've only recently begun reading it, but yeah, it's good. I'm digging the part about how you found your passions, and how one goes about finding theirs. That has really got me thinking about what makes me tick—and what turns me on."

Vince thought about that. He recalled their brief time together in Angeliqué's studio—watching her as she lay silently as Angeliqué applied the finishing touches of paint to her body. The *veve* glistening as it dried on her smooth skin. And Amber watching him watching her, a peculiar expression on her face.

As Amber continued to speak, Vince listened and found himself intrigued by her words. "Yes—to be truly happy in life, we all need to seek out those things that we're one hundred percent passionate about—and pursue those."

Vince and Amber continued to speak on the subject that Vince loved— helping folks find their way to true happiness. They spoke for close to fifteen minutes—the time whisking by like some amusement park ride, Amber asking many questions, truly captivated by his words, and Vince responding, giving her little anecdotes from the book and his seminars. Vince was enjoying the conversation and impressed that Amber had taken the time to get into his book and explore the essence of his ideas.

"So, Amber, please continue to read the book and let me know of any questions or comments you might have. I'd love to help out in any way I can."

"That would be cool—I mean, like I know the author and got the hook-up, you know?"

"Exactly!" Vince smiled. "This is a journey—one I seriously believe will bring a lifetime of joy. So, enjoy the ride! Anywho—I'm not going to take up any more of your time, Amber. It's been a real pleasure speaking with you."

"Likewise, Vince."

"Take care and hope to talk with you soon."

"You too. Bye." Amber's sweet voice lingered in his ear long after the connection went dead. Vince sat there, thinking about her, replaying the conversation in his head, remembering Amber as he first saw her, reclining on the floor, a certain air of innocence and purity surrounding her being like a shroud. But then he smiled as he thought about certain words and phrases she used this evening, and the way she laughed—and Vince knew that just beneath the surface, there was raw, untapped sensuality, ready to burst forth from her pores like a geyser. Vince smiled. He could feel it. Vince could sense it. He knew...

✖✖✖

It was after eight when Vince returned Desiree's call. The sun had set; the evening was dark and moonless. A pot was brewing, sending a comforting aroma into the room.

Desiree answered on the third ring.

"Hey you. I'm returning your call. It's Vince."

"Greetings," Desiree said with a laugh.

"So, what's up? What are you doing?"

"Not much—finishing up some reading," she said. "How about you?"

"In my studio, trying to do some sketches, but not really feeling any of them—the spark of creativity refuses to light tonight," Vince mused.

"Wow—you have a studio?" Vince could hear the excitement in her voice.

"Well, yeah—you don't think I create my masks on the dining room table, do you?"

"I don't know—I guess I didn't consider it, that's all. Your own studio—now that is the bomb!"

"Thanks."

"So, what kind of sketches are you doing? Nudes?" Desiree chuckled.

"No, not nudes! Get your mind out of the gutter! Damn. I'm doing facial sketches—trying out some ideas for a new mask that I want to do. But I can't quite get it right—this is what happens sometimes—you have an idea in your head—you can see it when you close your eyes, but translating it onto paper or plaster is something else indeed."

"I think that is so cool, that you actually go through this process of creating your art," Desiree said, "as opposed to just flinging paint at a square of canvas and hoping the results turn out great."

Vince laughed as he poured himself another cup of the steaming liquid. "No, I don't just fling paint at canvas, but there's a thought! Thanks…"

"So," Desiree said, her voice getting softer, "perhaps I should come over there *now* and give you something to sketch. Whatdayathink?" She ended her sentence with a sexy kind of laugh—but Vince knew she was dead serious about her proposal.

"Hmmmn, there's a thought. But don't you teachers have to get up early? I mean, it is a schoolnight after all."

"Why don't you let me worry about that, Mr. Artist? I'd like to see you again, and it seems like you need some *inspiration*…I think I can provide some of that." She chuckled again; as she did, Vince had a number of thoughts swirling around in his head—he did like her look—he recalled her face from the coffee shop and how that first time he had spotted her he had focused on the lines and symmetry about her face. A face possibly suitable for one of his masks…

"Listen, that's cool with me. Let me give you the address and you can come on down now. That is if you're truly serious?"

"Give me the digits and find out!"

Vince gave her the information and hung up, a smile forming on his face as he did so.

✖✖✖

She showed up thirty minutes later. Vince opened the door and invited her in with a wide sweep of his hand. He took her coat, kissed her on her cheek while admiring her tight jeans and form-fitting white top that revealed her thin, dark waist. He offered her a cup of coffee, which she accepted, as she went to the wall to view his collection of masks.

"These are incredible," Desiree said as she stared in awe at his art. She marveled at the colorful patterns that were laid across the faces of plaster. Desiree had figured that Vince was a weekend artist—one who dabbled when he had the spare time, no more—but looking at the collection set in front of her, she knew she had been wrong.

"Vince, have you sold any of these?" Desiree asked, lightly stroking the raised plaster of several masks, then turning to stare at him.

"Some—I have a relationship with several galleries in town. But to be honest, I'm my worst critic—I never think they are good enough to be sold to the public."

"Well," Desiree said while taking a seat on the futon, "I'm here to tell you they are. Without a doubt. Boy, you could make some serious loot with these!"

Actually, Vince had been thinking long and hard about pursuing the sale of his art. Up to now, it had not been a priority of his to find more buyers for his masks. Vince knew that the interest was out there—all he needed to do was pursue this seriously, make some phone calls, let folks know he was ready to sell, and the tide would carry him onward and upward…no doubt about that.

"Thank you. Yeah, I need to get some of these out there and hung in galleries."

"For sure—you have real talent!" Desiree took a sip of her coffee and put the mug down. She rose, walked over to his worktable and the sketches that laid in a heap. She glanced through them, taking her time, admiring his work. Vince watched her silently.

"These are very good—what are you talking about?"

Vince rose and joined her, taking his cup with him. "I don't know—I can't put my finger on it, really—I just am not feeling any of them."

"What are you trying to do?" Desiree asked.

"Trying out some designs for my next mask. I'm going for a new look and want to try it out on paper first." Vince stood next to Desiree inhaling the scent of her perfume. It was sweet and heavenly. His eyes scanned her body—her leather boots, jeans that fit her like a glove, the roundness of her ass, her curvy hips and waist—thin and flawless, the tight-fitting tee, swelling of her breasts, strong yet sumptuous neck and shoulders, hair that was soft, dark, and pulled back, highlighting the features of her smooth face. Desiree was a good-looking woman—no, that didn't do her justice. Desiree was *fine*. She was young and her body was flawless, age having yet to play its cruel trick with her form. Vince felt the desire stir in him. He pursed his lips and thought about her, wondering how she moved, unencumbered by clothes, watching as her hips rotated ever so slightly as she shifted weight while reaching out to grasp another sketch, eyes flickering over to him and sensing him observing her silently. And she played the game back, twisting her lip into a smile and creating a sparkle in her eyes, grateful for his stare and interest.

"I should do you," Vince said, without preamble. It came out wrong, he realized, and laughed. "That didn't come out the way I planned. Sorry."

"No," Desiree said, pausing to look at a sketch before she turned to face him. She was inches from Vince. She could touch him easily by raising her arm just slightly. "Don't play that shy routine with me now—tell me what's really on your mind, Vince."

"Desiree," Vince said smoothly, raising his hand to her shoulder. "I didn't mean it that way."

"You said you should do me. What did you mean then?"

"I meant I should do a lifecasting of you," Vince explained, lowering his hand to her waist. "...For a mask," he said as she leaned into him. "You, Desiree, will be my next subject."

NINETEEN

Quentin was furious! I found him pacing the length of my office. India had gotten him a cup of coffee—it lay untouched on the coffee table, its tendrils of shifting vapor rising toward the ceiling. I came in, shut the door and flung my jacket onto the back of my chair.

"Q-Dawg—please tell me that ain't you on tape…brutha please!" I stood before him, hands on my waist, thinking about how fucked up this case had just become.

"Man?" His voice cracked like that of a frog. I thought to myself, *oh, Lord; this shit ain't good at all…*

"Okay—tell me this—we went over this a month ago—I asked you specifically, remember—were there any other women? And you said, 'no.' Remember that, Quentin?"

"Yeah." Quentin sat down and grabbed the coffee, spilling a bit on the table and his wrist. "Shit! Sorry." I went to my credenza and grabbed a tissue to wipe up his spill.

"Dawg—I'm not here to judge you. If you had extramarital affairs that's okie doke with me—but if I'm going to provide the best legal advice and get the best arrangement for you, I need to know the truth. Understand?" He shook his head sourly. None of this shit mattered now.

"Yeah, I'm sorry, Trey. I fucked up. I know it. I didn't think that this would come out. Fuck!" Quentin held his head in his hands. He looked so pathetic hunched over, this oversized guy, larger than life, sitting in my chair, realizing the errors of his ways—but unfortunately, too late…

"Q., how is it possible she found the tape? I mean…"

"It wasn't a tape—I shot it on DV, true, but copied it straight to my hard disk on the laptop and erased the tape."

"Yeah, well, so far so good," I said, with a hint of scorn in my voice, "but obviously she discovered it anyway. Right?"

"Man, I don't know how the fuck she found it. I had all that shit on a separate drive, used PGP to encrypt that shit and…"

"Dawg—if I want technical talk, I'll phone the firm's IT department."

"Sorry—I used this program that scrambles the data. You need a password to get to it."

"Okay, cool. So what happened—you taped the password to the screen?" I grinned but Q. wasn't laughing with me.

"Naw—I know I password-protected that shit. I don't know—sometimes I forget to log off or unmount the disk." Again I was shaking my head. Quentin stood and went to the window, staring down at the street below. "I guess it's possible that I left the drive in a state where she could view it without my password, like after I had already put in the password and just left the machine on. It's not like I shut the fucking thing down every day. Fuck! I don't know what happened, Trey. Obviously, I didn't leave the shit out for her to find. I'm not that stupid!"

I was ready to say something smart but held my tongue. Again, thoughts of Paris Hilton, R. Kelly, Pamela Anderson, and other celebrities who had found themselves in this very same mess sprang to mind.

"Okay. Let's leave this alone. We're not solving anything by focusing on what *may* have happened. The fact is, your wife found it, has copies of it, and Lord knows how many. Hopefully she hasn't shown it to too many folks. We have your career and reputation to think about."

"Fuck!" Quentin exclaimed, his fists clenched by his side.

"Where's the laptop now?" I asked.

"At my crib."

"Here? In the Georgetown condo?"

"Yeah, it's been there since I moved out six months ago." I pondered Quentin's words. Either his wife had known about her husband's infidelity for six months and said nothing or…

"Q. Has Aponi been to your crib since the two of you separated?" He turned from the window to stare at me.

"Naw, Dawg."

"Q.?" The look in his eye told me he was lying.

"What? Okay, yeah, she was there one time—she came to town with some of her friends a few weeks ago and we met to try and work things out." Right. I could just imagine how *that* went down. My mind was whirling with so many questions. Things were getting complicated by the second.

"Okay. Listen to me. Go home. Get some rest. You have a game in two days. Let me ponder all of this stuff and call you with any questions I may have. You gonna be around? I'm going to need to get in touch with you round the clock. Leave me your cell. I have a feeling her attorney's going to be hounding me."

"Yeah. No problem. Can you do anything about the disc?" he asked timidly.

"Don't worry about that—I scared the shit out of them—told them I'm filing an injunction with D.C.'s Superior Court. Told your wife she'll without a doubt do jail time if those images get into anyone's hands."

"Can you do that?"

"Damn Skippy! This is serious, Q. You don't want that tape floating around. Your career could suffer because of it. Nobody likes a playa who flashes his shit in front of a camera, especially when he's married. If we don't strike and strike hard, that shit *will* wind up on the Internet! Trust me, Dawg, you don't want that…" I put a hand on Quentin's shoulder. "But don't worry, Q., Trey is in 'da house, and on point—I got you covered. Things will work out in the end—you might have to give up that house of yours, though—that may be the only way out of this nasty little mess."

"Fuck," Quentin said, but it came out as a whisper.

Yeah, I thought to myself, *that's what got your dumb ass into trouble in the first place…*

✖✖✖

It always amazes me just how many freaking voice-mail messages I get when I'm not in the office—the amount is staggering. And that doesn't count the messages that India Jasmine Jackson takes for me—for those folks who don't want to be connected to my voice mailbox, or who are technologically challenged, or who would rather speak to a live female. Whatever!

The day after the fiasco with Quentin Hues, it was about two p.m. when I arrived back in the office after some pretty good sushi. I flung my jacket onto the back of my chair, sat down, unlaced my shoes to let my feet breathe, and punched the button on my phone and heard the female voice say in that recognizable tone: "You have *eight* new messages." Eight? In less than an hour? How the fuck was that possible? And so, I proceeded to listen and delete, listen and delete, listen and delete, when in walks Bernard John Marshall. He did not look pleased.

"Bernie."

"It's Bernard." He took a seat. I stared into his hard eyes, my mind relatively calm, not racing, not trying to anticipate or figure him out. Why bother? I'd find out soon enough.

"Bernard." I didn't have time or interest in small talk. Not with this prick who had stolen Calvin's job.

"This *thing* with Quentin Hues."

"Settlement conference," I corrected.

"Didn't go too well, I presume." I stared at Bernard. He obviously had done some reconnaissance work and gotten the 411. "You filed an injunction in Superior Court."

"Yes. Yesterday afternoon." I had done exactly what I said I would do. Make no mistake. When I say I'm gonna do something, I do it, especially when it comes to law.

"Not a good move, in my opinion."

"Really? Well, *Bernard*, right now my concern is to ensure that this *thing*, as you call it, does not tarnish my client's reputation. The best way to ensure that, in *my* opinion, is to file an injunction."

"By filing an injunction you are doing just the opposite—you draw attention to this thing—instead of focusing on…"

"Excuse me, Bernard," I said, cutting him off. I clasped my hands together, fingers interlocking on the smooth desktop. "I'm pretty busy right now. I sure don't have time to deconstruct every aspect of this case, or any other I'm working on, with you. Perhaps Calvin should have mentioned to you how I operate." I stared at those dead blue eyes, wanting to reach across the desk and strangle his fucking neck until the color drained from his face—but, don't get me wrong—I'm not a violent man...honest!

"And, Trey, let me tell you how *I* operate," Bernard replied calmly, but underneath the unruffled exterior, it was clear that a fire was brewing. "As the new managing partner, it is my responsibility and right to review the strategy of all attorneys in this firm, and to ensure that they are conducting themselves in a manner that is consistent with the overall objectives and direction of this law firm." Bernard paused for a moment to let me take that in. "On a personal level, let me say this—I really don't care how busy you are or whether in your past life you and Calvin discussed every aspect of each case or not. I reserve the right to come in here whenever I damn well please and ask whatever questions I see fit. Furthermore, if, in my humble opinion, I think you are heading down the wrong path, I will let you know. That is my job, counselor. That is my right." Bernard's voice had not increased in volume a single decibel. But it had changed in cadence and in pitch. He was pissed. I could almost see the steam rising off his head. "Are we clear, counselor?"

I was ready to fire back—first off, I don't need this fucking job—I'm damn good at what I do, and can find another gig anywhere in this town—I bring a shitload of money into this firm—second—I retain some pretty heavyweight clients—so fuck Bernard John Marshall and the horse he rode in on! But then, at the exact moment I was readying to unleash on BJM, my phone rang; I checked the caller ID and saw it was Vince. I glanced up and told Bernard politely, but firmly, "Bernie, I gotta take this one, okay???"

✖✖✖

Five days later, I get a call from guess who? Allison Matthews, Esq., of course. I'd purposely avoided calling her—part of my strategy these past few days—make her wonder what was going through this brilliant legal mind of mine—she already knew I wasn't kidding about the injunction—she and her client had already been served—that much I knew. That had happened on Friday just in time for the weekend. I love it! It was now Tuesday afternoon.

"Counselor, I've been waiting for your call," Allison began, cool, calm, and collected, just like at H20 a week before. My thoughts went back to that evening and I had to smile.

"Ms. Matthews, what a pleasant surprise. Is this to discuss business, or are you calling to collect on that ride I promised you? I'm still interested in getting you on the back of my bike, you know…" *Yeah,* I thought to myself, *on the back of my Indian, legs splayed wide across the hard leather, back arched against the backrest, lovely breasts bare to the elements…*

"I'm sorry, Mr. Alexander, but right now, all you and I have to discuss is business."

"That is a shame," I responded.

"I was hoping that by this point we would have completed our settlement issues and moved on…but I guess not."

"Well, counselor, the unfortunate deviation in the schedule is your doing, not mine."

"Look, Trey, you know damn well that the injunction isn't going to stick in any court—why are you wasting our time and your own?" I could hear Allison getting hot.

"Really? I don't see it that way."

"Let's examine the facts—your client is an adulterer—that much is true. He was stupid enough to tape himself with three women that we know of, and then left the evidence around for my client to find—not the sign of a genius…"

"I'll give you that one, Allison," I quipped, "…*if* it can be proven that is my guy on the disc, which remains to be seen."

"Okay—let's put that aside for a moment. Your client has effectively relocated here to Washington and away from New Jersey where Aponi was born and raised, and made her home."

"Agreed. But the house was his free and clear before he ever laid eyes on your client. He may owe her part of the furnishings acquired during the marriage, but nothing else regarding that premises."

"Look, Trey. I did not call to argue the merits of this case with you…"

"No? Then what did you call me for?" I asked in a smug tone.

"I want to see this thing settled just as quickly as you do. This is a strain on my client, and I'm sure on yours as well…"

"Yes it is—especially when he's in the public eye and being accused of adultery."

"Counselor—can we meet and get this issue behind us? I feel confident that the two of us—you and me—no clients around to complicate things, can make this happen—our cool heads will prevail. I'm certain of it." I had to smile. Allison was good—she was speaking to me, attempting to get back on my good side—after that staggering left hook that came from out of nowhere—and ladies and gentlemen, it was working.

"Okay Ms. Matthews, that sounds like a good idea. Let me check my calendar." I swiveled in my seat and glanced at my Outlook calendar on the screen.

"I was thinking tomorrow or the day after. My schedule is light," Allison was saying.

"Hmmn, the next two days are not good for me," I said, "in court. Let me see…"

"Friday then?" Allison was being more than accommodating—that was evident. And why shouldn't she be—we could have settled this thing last Thursday if it hadn't been for that *thing*. Why was everyone calling Quentin's screen debut a *thing*? Even I had called it that a few times…

"Hmmn, Friday. Oh, that's right, I'm heading out of town this weekend, leaving on Friday. No, that's not going to work." I could hear Allison controlling her breathing on the phone—the frustration was registering loud and clear. My lie about going out of town was to box her into a corner—give her little alternative but to see me one evening after work. "Here's a thought, Allison." My mind was racing—I could ask her to dinner, regardless of what she had said a moment ago about there only being business between us. Get her away from the office one night, perhaps pick her up on the bike—no, she'd never go for that—could meet her at the restaurant via the bike—bring the extra helmet—then she'd have no reason not to take a quick spin—no, she won't go for that either—she'd see right through that charade…

"I have this thing that I do once a month—it's kind of like volunteer work—you'll probably find this hard to believe," I let out a short laugh, "but I assist at a women's shelter here in town. Once a month I cook for the ladies—it's a thing I've been doing for close to a year now—they love it 'cause the food is the bomb, even if I say so myself, and I enjoy it because I get to hone my culinary skills on some fairly demanding folks."

"Why do I not believe you?" Allison asked. "This sounds like some kind of ploy to get me to think more highly of you." She was laughing now.

"What? A guy like me can't give back to the community? Is that what you're saying?"

"Not at all—I just don't buy that *you* would give back to the community, that's all." More laughter transported me back to H20 the week before.

"Well, I guess it shows how little you know about me. Anyway, here's the deal—I'm going to be there tomorrow evening from about four until eight-thirty or so. Why don't you stop by? You can have dinner with us, see me in action, if you doubt what I say, and most importantly, it will give us a chance to talk about the Hues." I was grinning to myself, knowing that she was ambivalent about doing this—on the one hand, wanting to get this case over and done with; on the other, not wanting to spend any social time with me because of a perceived conflict of interest. I loved putting Allison in this spot; it served her right for messing with me the way she did…

"Trey, I don't know…" Allison said uncertainly. I could hear the wheels spinning…

"Allison. This is not a date—I heard what you said about keeping it strictly business, loud and clear—but if we don't do this tomorrow, then it's next week before I'll have time to sit down with you." I let that thought hang in the air, like smoke from incense.

"I don't know…"

"Tell you what—here's the address of the women's shelter. It's not far from the U Street Corridor." I gave her the address and heard her scribble it down. "It will be fun. Plus I can always use another set of hands. You do know how to find your way around a kitchen, don't you?"

"Yes, Mr. Alexander, I do. We'll see," she muttered.

I decided not to push it any further. "Okay. Hope to see you tomorrow evening. Good day to you, counselor," I said, signing off.

"And to you as well."

TWENTY

I pulled my coal-black Cadillac Escalade up to the inconspicuous home of The Nona E. Taylor Women's Center at a few minutes to four on Wednesday. I double- parked my *other* phat ride with the gleaming rims—put the hazards on, and got out. It was a beautiful day. I glanced up at the heavens, took in the blue sky and cool breeze that caressed my bald head and face, and thanked God for another lovely day. Walked to the back to begin unloading the food and supplies I had brought from home.

The Nona E. Taylor Women's Center was housed in a four-story brick house on a well-lit and neat street in Northwest D.C. All well kept row houses, each one different in terms of size, color, and façade, giving the block that down home "neighborhood" feeling. In fact, one would be hard pressed to even pick the Center out from any other residential property, save for the small brass plaque that hung next to the doorbell, which was located up the stone steps on the second floor.

I used my remote to unlock the back and grabbed the first of a dozen large trays and Tupperware containing various dishes and ingredients. Walked up the stairs and hit the buzzer with my elbow and waited. A heavy-set woman came to the door a minute later, glanced through the lace that covered the beveled glass and opened the door.

"Trey Alexander, look at you!" I flashed a smile at Yolanda Taylor, founder and director of the Center. "Put that tray down and give me some sugar!" I obeyed and went to her willingly, feeling her bosom meld around my own body. Yo and I had known each other for two years—I met her through a friend; she had been searching for someone to do some pro bono work for the Center—I wasn't looking to get involved, but this friend urged me to give Yo a call, just to hear her story—and I did so after weeks of him hounding me—and I'm glad I did.

Yolanda was the color of chocolate syrup, possessed twisting dreads, a soft, youthful face, and a heart the size of her black coffee thighs.

"How ya livin', Yo?" I said, standing back to look at her.

"Life's a blessing, Trey, you know that."

"Yes, I do."

"Come on in. I've got sixteen women with hearty appetites—they are ready for you, boy."

"Any good looking ones, Yo? I could use a fall project right about now," I said, eyeing her with a smirk.

"Boy, you know I'll pop you, you mess with my girls."

"Just checking, Yo. Maybe next month."

"Boy, you too much!" I observed her smile—the way her full lips curved upward and showed her teeth—that wonderful smile and the way her eyes narrowed and held a tinge of sadness in them. Yolanda's sister, Nona Elizabeth, had been in an abusive marriage for a number of years. After two years of violence and neglect, after Yolanda tried repeatedly to get her younger sibling to leave and get the help she desperately needed, Nona's husband shot her dead one evening, in this very house, because he had come home several hours late from work, and dinner wasn't served hot, to his liking...

He was now serving a life sentence for first-degree murder at a correctional institution in Tennessee. Yolanda had purchased the house from the estate and turned it into a shelter for battered women, vowing never again to find herself in the position of not being able to extend a hand to another woman in need.

Yolanda had told me that story one fall day, the two of us strolling around the neighborhood, a cloudless sky overhead not unlike today, and me thinking to myself, I have no choice—I *need* to give something back to these women, *hope*—and what better way than to serve them. Me: Trey Alexander, with all of my superciliousness.

I handed Yolanda the tray, told her she better not drop it, and retreated to get the others.

Fifteen minutes later, all of the food was in the first floor kitchen and the Escalade was parked safely in the alley out back—Yolanda had graciously offered to let me use her spot so I could keep an eye on my shit. I strolled in the back door, wearing jeans and boots, and a thin pullover black sweater. Without fanfare I donned a heavy cotton personalized apron from *Williams-Sonoma*, one of my favorite stores, and a matching bandanna, and went to work.

The Center's kitchen was fairly large and functional—not equipped with all of the latest appliances for any kind of serious cooking, like mine, but it would do. The range was gas, thank God, and Yolanda had put in a double oven a few years back. A large, center island made of wood was where I did most of the food preparation work. This meal was something that I planned meticulously several weeks in advance. I thought long and hard about the menu, always vying for something different, a theme, if I could swing it, not wanting to just feed these women, but dazzle them with culinary excellence. That's what food was anyway, at least in my mind—more than just nourishment or sustenance—a means of teasing one's pallet, tempting the senses with wonderful aromas and tastes. I had settled this month on an age-old holiday favorite—a beef tenderloin roast, pan-fried with rosemary and garlic, served with deep-roasted fall vegetables, a salad, freshly baked bread, and for dessert, several scrumptious pies that I would bake here. All of the ingredients I bought myself—never asking for contributions or financial assistance—not that I needed it—plus, the whole idea was to give these women one night a month of dining in style—Trey style!

It's hard to explain—I've tried over the years, with my friends staring at me in awe when I tell them what I do, once a month, this way of giving back to the community—and they all have the same reaction—nigga please…you? The Trey we know? Cooking for a Women's Center??? PU-LEASE!

The truth—my job is filled with long hours and mountains of stress—for months I had been searching for something to help me release the tension (besides sex). I thought about something physical, and do work out on a regular basis. In fact, Vince and I try and get to the court for a game of pickup basketball when we can. But that isn't enough. No, I wanted something that wasn't so damn cerebral…practicing law meant that you were always on your toes—dancing with your opponent, the game of chess—surveying the kaleidoscope of moves—eight to ten steps ahead. Always thinking, or outthinking your opponent. It became tiring. But quick…

Cooking—it releases one from the normal confines that holds us to our daily lives—cooking allows us to dream, to experiment. When I cook, I forget about my problems or those of others. In the kitchen, it is as if I am in some other place that only I hold the reigns to. I feel free, alive; creating the way I know Vince must feel when he fashions a piece of art—a testament to those who have come before him, a celebration of the past and present.

And, on a more superficial level, I cook and serve because I *can*. I consider myself one of the lucky ones. I've been educated and found a trade that I'm damn good at, and they pay me a sizeable salary for my wares. I'm lucky—I've had choices all my life—some folks are not that fortunate. Or smart. Or gifted. Or, for whatever reason, find themselves in this shelter, at this sanctuary, on this quiet street, for just one day or a week, because someone close to them took their dignity away…

I began with the roast and the pies, since they would take the most amount of time. Some of the dishes I'd already prepared at home, such as the piecrusts and the bread. Some of the women from the Center came downstairs to meet and watch me work. There were all kinds here—a sanctuary from the "elements", a calm in a storm—Yolanda's warm smile and nonjudgmental heart comforting—black women, Latinos, a few white women, all ages and sizes from a barely legal girl impregnated by her young overconfident boyfriend to a middle-aged, educated white woman with thick red welts on her cheeks and neck.

I made small talk as I set the beef roast out on the counter surface, and tied the rosemary sprigs lengthwise along the meat with kitchen twine in two-inch intervals. I rubbed the meat down with garlic and seasoning while

I fielded questions from the onlookers—how old I was, how'd I learned to cook that good, how much money could a lawyer make, and was there a missus waiting for me at home...

Switching gears to the pies for a moment, since they needed to bake for a good forty minutes or so—I had settled on two of my favorite—wild blueberry-peach pie made from wild Canadian blueberries that I had FedExed to me the day before, and a mixed berry tart, using the leftover wild blueberries, fresh raspberries, blackberries, and strawberries. Treats, I just knew the ladies would love.

I pulled out the previously made dough, kneaded it among my black hands, while a young Latino with a thick accent, a dazzling smile, and twin black eyes watched me curiously.

"Papi, I hope your hands are clean!"

"Didn't you see me just wash them after handling that meat?"

"Naw."

"Pay attention then." I went back to my work as she sucked her teeth, but made no move to leave.

I proceeded to roll the dough into thin slivers, using generous amounts of flour and getting much on my black apron. Oh well, that's what aprons are for. The Latino snickered in the corner while I sucked my teeth at her. Grabbing a fresh mound of dough, I divided it in half and pressed each half into two pie dishes. I then grabbed a steel bowl that I had brought from home, and used it to combine the wild blueberries, cut peaches, cinnamon, and sugar into the pie filling. I divided this evenly between the pie dishes and then carefully draped the rolled-out pie dough over the filled pie dishes, trimming the edges, brushing the tops with heavy cream and sugar, and ending with cutting three slits equidistant from each other with a sharp knife. Perfection!

I had also planned on serving pasta—Capellini, or angel hair pasta, with fresh tomatoes and basil. I brought a large pot of water to boil and fetched the ingredients for this dish—plum tomatoes that I had already diced, cut basil leaves, ground pepper, and virgin olive oil. I loved pasta dishes—they were one of my favorites—the sauce was something I was always trying to improve upon.

Then back to the roast—I heated a large oval skillet with vegetable oil and began browning the roast, about four minutes each side. The kitchen filled quickly with the aroma of the rosemary and the cooking meat—Yolanda and a few of her ladies came to take a peek just as I was transferring the meat to the top oven where it would roast for a good twenty to twenty five minutes. Meanwhile, I directed my attention to the sauce that would cover the meat like a warm blanket—dry red wine, minced shallots, and soft unsalted butter, boiling the concoction for ten minutes until it was reduced to less than half a cup. Soon now, I would be pouring this lovely sauce over the beef for a mouthwatering meal. The anticipation, I could see, was growing.

The water boiling, I threw in the fresh capellini, checked on the roast and my pies, which all were coming along nicely. I yelled for Yo to set the table. She replied back from the next room that they were already on it!

At 5:45 pm, the ladies and I sat down to dinner. The oversized table fashioned from several pieces of rich oak was covered with a yellow cloth and fresh flowers that Yo had collected this morning on her rounds to several florists. Yolanda used her good china—this being a special occasion, and I did the honors, waiting for all of the ladies to be seated at the table before serving each entrée with a flourish.

Yolanda said grace. It was customary and obligatory—not to be messed with or hurried in this house. As I glanced around the oversized table I took in each woman—their attire—nothing formal—this not being the place or the time for that—most of these ladies had escaped with what they could carry or worse, what they had on their backs—nothing more—some came to the table barefoot and in jeans—others, a simple dress or pair of leggings. Regardless, they were each beautiful in their own way—they held their head up with pride, bruises and all. I grinned as I faced each woman in turn and felt satisfaction—I was pleased that I had chosen to spend my evening with these courageous ladies—women who found the strength to stand up and say, "enough is enough", and search for a better life…

Yolanda thanked me for my efforts. This was the one time where I found myself humbled. Humbled because my part in all of this—preparing tonight's meal, was the easy part. What these women faced every single day was difficult, and something, I wondered if I could cope with as well.

After grace, we began to eat. The food, if I may say so myself, was the bomb! The beef tenderloin roast was to die for, the vegetables, roasted to perfection, the capellini, well, what can I say—I have overheard folks say I make the best spaghetti sauce west of Sicily! We broke bread, the ladies and I, and feasted like there was no tomorrow. Even the security guard, a middle aged, oversized black man named Ernie, threw down. I made sure he got a plate and sat down with us. We made small talk—never speaking of one another's tragedy—there was a time and a place for that, but not tonight. No, on this evening it was about other, lighter things—the weather, shows on TV, any interested cases I could share—and of course, in my business, there were always interesting cases to discuss...

I glanced at my watch. 7:15. I wondered if Allison would show. For a split second I thought about sharing the unfolding drama between Quentin and his wife with the group—but that would be bad form—especially if Allison did indeed show up. Yolanda asked about my friends—she had met Vince and Erika before when they had come by to help months ago—and so we caught up on that, the latest gossip, what she was doing with the Center—never revealing too much about her personal life—as if that, too, was off-limits, or in some way offensive to her girls.

I served the pies around 7:30 while Yolanda poured strong coffee. The wild blueberry-peach pie was the hit of the evening—when I carried it over to the table, held snuggly between my oven mittens, the purple-blue-yellow filling was overflowing from the bursting slits and meandering down the golden brown pie crust like lava. The aroma struck everyone at once—it damn near brought a hush to the room. Of course, I snatched the opportunity to present this delicacy to the group with the most pomp and circumstance I could muster. Not an ordinary dessert—no, ladies, this one was commissioned especially for this group. Be careful, ladies—several spoonfuls of this delectable pastry and you undoubtedly will be hooked—an addict for life!

I sat back, stuffed, wiping my baldhead with my hands, sipping coffee, looking around at the satisfied faces. Feeling good about my life and where I found myself this particular moment. At the top of my game, in the zone—a successful attorney, clients whose life in the majority of cases genuinely improved, due to my talent and skill…great friends, my health, a sex life that most men would give their left nut for, a fly crib, phat rides…and at the end of the day—I was a good man, regardless of the shit I pontificated on endlessly about every day, because I gave back—I made these ladies smile, even if for just a fleeting moment, like a pebble dropped into a pond, the ripples fan out for a meager moment, and then the waters grow still again…

And then, out of nowhere, I felt this sudden rush of emotion—it began down low, in the bowels of my stomach, and rushed like an avalanche through my veins, turning my blood into ice water, smarting my heart.

The sad truth: I was alone. I didn't have the comfort of warm flesh, a partner, or lover for more than a fleeting hour or so—a soul mate who could take the chill away when I felt cold. I glanced around the table; some women were holding hands while conversing. There was laughter. There were hugs. And I felt my eyes water and sting as the tears began to well under my eyelids. Using my forearm and elbow, I quickly wiped them away, mindful that no one here would spy my weakness, and think less of me.

I was a lucky man, true—successful, talented, good looking, with many things that I could call my own. No question that there were many blessings in my life. But I was alone…

I turned my head and glanced toward the kitchen. Beyond the back door and windowsill lay my ride. I got up quickly, began walking towards it, as my vision distorted into a kaleidoscope of shifting patterns and colors…

TWENTY-ONE

Desiree lay back on the futon, eyes closed, waiting for Vince to begin. She was breathing regularly, which surprised Vince, since she was, at this point, shirtless.

"Is this going to hurt?"

"Please! Do you think I would have gotten all these other folks to pose for me if it did?" Vince responded, sweeping his arm toward his collection of masks. He glanced down at Desiree, took in her dark skin, the black laced underwire bra that held the two mounds of lovely flesh barely contained. She was spilling out, the roundness of both breasts perfectly symmetrical above the lace. A hint of nipples could be seen if one looked very carefully, but Vince didn't want to get caught staring.

The surface of the futon was covered with a clean off-white dropcloth. Her hair draped behind the back of the couch; it laid still, like her hands that remained in her lap.

"Can I get you anything before we begin?" Vince asked softly.

"No, I think I'm fine. I'm anxious to begin."

"Good. You're going to do just fine—I can tell." Vince smiled as he gathered the lifecasting materials at his feet behind her. Desiree glanced over at him, her eyes flicked upward; they danced for a moment before settling on the ceiling, and growing out of focus.

"Let me pull back your hair." Vince gingerly took the length in his hand and tied it back with a red bandanna. It covered her from the beginning of her hairline halfway back. "Don't want to get any mess on your lovely hair."

"It's okay—I'll just make you wash it." She gave Vince an impish grin.

"I just might hold you to it."

Vince moved behind her, bent down and said quietly, "Let's begin."

He reached for an oversized jar of petroleum jelly, raked two fingers worth of the gel onto his digits and slowly began applying it to Desiree's face. He worked slowly, methodically, stroking her face beginning with her forehead, and applying a thin layer of jelly to her skin. Desiree closed her eyes and smiled, moaned for effect and said: "Oooh, this is nice—I didn't know massages come with the package!"

Vince paused for a moment, looked into her eyes and said, "Depends on the package, darling…now hush!"

He continued—spreading a coating of Vaseline on her cheeks, rubbing the gel into her skin and around her cheekbones, using both fingers at once to knead the bridge of her nose. Vince worked slowly, taking his time, watching Desiree as he worked, leaning over and reaching for her chin, coating that angular rock of bone and flesh with gel until she glistened like a beacon. Once he was done, Vince stood back, admiring his work. He forked out another two fingers of Vaseline and reapplied his digits to her face, smoothing the blob of gel and creating an additional layer. He rubbed her eyelids gently, careful not to get any on her eyelashes; worked his way down around her nostrils, highlighting her full dark lips with the gel as if it were lip gloss, caressing her mouth as if she were his lover. Vince watched her as he worked, gazed at the rise and fall of her breasts, her eyelids that fluttered like leaves in an autumn breeze, her tongue that peeked out as if she were a mouse in a quieted house, searching for morsels of food.

Next Vince applied the alginate; the gel-like substance that once applied would harden within six to eight minutes. He spoke softly as he worked, explained the process as he went, telling her how he had mixed it with warm water and that she would feel a lukewarm sensation on her skin as he applied it. She was doing well, Vince told Desiree, reminding her that if she needed to move or stretch, now was the time to do it. Desiree was relaxed, Vince could tell—she had succumbed to this artist—allowing him to do what he wished in the name of art and creativity.

Spreading the alginate didn't take much time at all—he began with her forehead, used the fleshy tips of his fingers as a brush, painting her with the substance that would form the base of the mask. Vince next covered her cheeks and nose, leaving the nostrils for last. He encased her chin with the material, then told her to hold still and not to worry as he applied the gel to her lips. Lastly, he covered her nostrils with the gel, after inserting two short straws for her to breathe.

At this point her entire face was covered with the white substance. Vince bent down, studied his handiwork, told her that she was doing great, and that there were only a few minutes left to go. He rubbed her shoulder with his elbow, moved down her forearm, then moved close to her ear and pointed out that his hand was inches from her breasts. Desiree's arm came up as she tried to swat him away. Vince just laughed.

Behind the futon, on the floor, in a metal tray was a bunch of one inch wide plaster strips. Alongside the tray was a bowl of warm water. Vince reached for a strip, dipped it in the water and applied it to Desiree's face, gingerly laying it across the drying alginate. He explained to Desiree that the plaster would give the mold that he was creating more weight and actually speed up the drying process. He asked again if she was okay—she raised her hand and waved.

Applying the strips was one of Vince's favorite parts—it always brought back thoughts of those old Mummy movies that he'd watched as a kid. Vince used different sized strips that he had precut to lay over the alginate. He'd apply a strip to the hardening substance, and apply light pressure so that the plaster would bond more quickly. About three minutes after he began, her face was covered with plaster bandages, and the process was near completion.

"Okay, Desiree—you are doing great—now, we wait, let me see…" Vince reached for her face and stroked the cast lightly. He could feel that in some places it was already hardening. "About two more minutes and we will be through. Cool?" He smiled and glanced down her torso again. Damn—she was a fine woman, no question. Trey would love to be here right now— God he could imagine just what his boy would do to this woman in her compromising situation…

Three minutes later he tested the mold with his fingers and satisfied, told

Desiree to sit up slowly. He reached for her hands and placed them carefully against the mold. Then grasping her forearms, he pulled her to him, telling her to bend forward and let the weight of the cast come off in her hands. He used his fingers around the edges and guided it into her hands. The mold came off easily and without any fuss. He held it within his hands, and gingerly carried it over to his worktable where he inverted it and placed it on top of a folded towel. He returned to the futon with a warm facecloth lathered in soap, and tenderly began to wash Desiree's face. He got off as much as he could. Then, when most of the Vaseline had been removed, Desiree stood up and went to the worktable, a towel curved around her neck as she marveled at the mold that lay before her.

"My God, Vince, that shit worked!" she exclaimed as she studied the casting that lay on the table. It was always eerie for the model to see for the first time the cast—witnessing the clarity and detail that the lifecasting process afforded. "Wow, that's me—no two ways about it! Damn!" Vince smiled, rubbed her back and told her that she could finish washing up in the bathroom. There wasn't anything more to do until the mold was completely dry—a day or two away.

Desiree returned a few minutes later—even though she wore no makeup, the glow had returned to her face and neck. She joined Vince once again in front of the worktable, staring down at the mold of her features. Vince rubbed her bare back. She reached over and kissed him on his cheek.

"This has been so exciting for me, you just don't know. I'm thrilled that you are creating a mask of me."

"For me, too, Desiree—every mask holds a unique experience—this has been fun—and actually, once the mold dries the real fun begins, because that's when the creative juices take over and art burst forth!"

"I can't wait," she said.

"You'll be part of the process. I promise," Vince said.

"I wouldn't have it any other way!" Desiree responded. They stood there, the two of them, marveling at the creation on the table, each wondering where this piece of plaster would carry them.

✖✖✖

Three nights later, when Desiree arrived back at Vince's studio, the plaster lifecasting was hung in the center of a four-foot-square canvas and displayed on an easel, which stood in the center of the room, illuminated overhead by a single halogen lamp. Vince greeted her with a hug and a kiss to her lips…a kiss that lingered for a moment before he pulled back, glancing downward, happy to be seeing her once again.

"Good to see you, girl," Vince mused, his smile lighting up the darkened interior.

"You, too, my brutha." Her gaze swept past Vince to the easel and her likeness in bas-relief, under spotlight. "Damn, Vince, this is the bomb!" She rushed past him, left Vince standing by the open doorway, and screeched to a halt by the unfinished mask. Running a hand lightly over the face of the plaster, she found herself catching her breath and touching her own flesh, comparing it to the plaster and marveling at the similarity—the lines and depressions, captured as if redrawn perfectly by the hand of a divine spirit.

"Vince," she said softly, "I can't believe how good this came out. I mean, it is so damn lifelike."

"Yes, that's one of the things that attracted me to the lifecasting process—the way it captures the *essence* of a person's being—many folks who see themselves for the first time captured and memorialized in plaster find it quite unnerving."

"I can see why," Desiree said, stepping back from the easel.

"Of course," Vince said, "we are only halfway through—the best part, as far as I am concerned, is yet to come."

"And that is?" she inquired, turning to him.

"Creating art," he said, joining her by the mask. "Filling the crevice of plaster with paint, allowing the mask to breathe; to take wings and live."

"I feel you."

Desiree glanced at his worktable that was covered with dishes of colorful paint. Vince took her hand and led her to the table.

"This is what I was thinking—let me know your thoughts—you said something last time about flinging paint onto a canvas in a haphazard kind of way. Well, I was thinking that we could put a single color on as a base and then try that—see what comes of it!"

"Are you serious?" Desiree exclaimed, walking back to the easel and touching the mask. Vince eyed her silently. She stepped back, then returned to the worktable. "Yeah, I'm feeling that! Yeah, that'll work!"

"Alrighty then," Vince exclaimed. "Let's do this."

They selected a color for the base of the mask—Vince suggested something bright, to match Desiree's mood and personality—orange or red. She was feeling something of a darker color—a muted brown or jet-black. They settled on indigo. Vince used a wide brush to apply the paint while Desiree watched. He applied two coats to ensure that the paint saturated the plaster and soaked into the material's crevices. Once that was done, he reached for a clean brush, something thinner than the last one. He told Desiree that they should select a bright color, dip the brush into the paint and then fling it onto the mask, creating their art. Desiree asked that he begin the process, for she didn't want to mess up the mask with her *inexperience*.

Vince grinned and dipped the brush in some orange paint, stood about two feet from the easel, and lightly snapped the brush in the direction of the mask. Little streams of paint, colorful blobs of orange hit the mask's surface like raindrops, the heavier one cascading down as if tears. He concentrated on the eyes first, then selected a crimson red color and flung the paint at her nostrils and mouth. A blob of paint made contact with the plaster just to the right of her plaster lips—then it smeared and dripped down toward the chin. Desiree was enthralled.

"Let me do some, Vince!" He handed her the brush and stepped out of the way. She selected a greenish-blue hue first; then a pale-yellow shade, flinging the paint with abandonment, giggling like a schoolgirl as drops of paint attached themselves to her mask. Thirty minutes later they were done. The mask was awash with color—streams of paint, pinpoints of various shades adorned the plaster turning the once virgin mask into a dazzling creation of fine art. They stepped back together, admiring the creation. Vince was pleased. Desiree stood and gawked, silent at first, then raising her voice as she pointed to the various areas of still drying paint.

It was close to nine p.m. when Vince moved the easel over toward the high windows where the mask could dry. He cleaned up his workspace and washed up while Desiree made a pot of fresh coffee. They relaxed on the futon, staring silently at their creation. Desiree was impressed, Vince could tell. For his part, he was feeling it, too, and her as well, the time spent together over the past week as they gave this mask life giving him a fresh insight to this young woman. They sipped their coffee and talked, enjoying each other's company. Suddenly Desiree put her mug down and jumped up.

"Vince, I know you're going to think I'm crazy, but I've got an idea."

"Speak!" he commanded her, but winked as he laughed.

"What if…" she exclaimed, waving her arms in the air in an animated sort of way, "what if we did a casting…oh never mind!" Desiree slumped to the couch and reached for her cup. Vince stopped her.

"No, go on. I want to hear this."

"Okay. What if…I was thinking…we could do a casting…of my torso. There. I said it!"

"Torso?"

"You do know what a torso is, don't you?"

"Yeah, I recall that part of the anatomy from my freshman biology class— course, that *was* a long time ago!" Vince put his mug down on the coffee table and looked at Desiree. She was motionless, watching him for a reaction. He nodded slowly.

"I *could* do that."

"Vince, here's the thing—I was thinking—we do a torso casting, say from here…" She held her hand just below her neck, "…to say about here…" and used her other hand to trace a line slightly below her navel. "You could then take that casting, paint it the same way as we did tonight, and then somehow either attach it to the mask or better still…" She paused to ponder this point for a moment before continuing, "mount it on a frame like the others but leaving this space of perhaps four inches between the mask and torso. What do you think???"

Vince eyed her—watched her irises dance among the pupils. Excitement dripped from her pores like sweat. Vince grinned.

"Damn, girl, I like it! I honestly do!" He stood, went to the still drying mask and observed it silently. Turning to Desiree, he said, "Yeah, I like it a lot!"

Desiree was nodding her head rapidly.

"So, you're cool with me taking a casting of your…" He paused to consider the right word. "…*unclothed* upper body?" Eyebrows raised, waiting for a response.

"Well, hello! I'm the one who suggested it!"

"Cool. Just checking."

Desiree stood, drained her coffee in several gulps and slammed the mug down.

"Vince, let's do this!" she exclaimed while her eyes glittered. "Let's do this shit right the hell now!"

TWENTY-TWO

Ernie strolled in fifteen minutes later with Allison Matthews in tow. I was in the kitchen supervising the clean-up—one thing about Yolanda—she did not play when it came to chores around the center—she didn't ask for much in return—it cost the ladies nothing to stay here since most of her funding came from state and federal monies, the remainder handled by private donations. But she was adamant about everyone pulling their weight—a house this size meant that there were always things to do—cleaning, cooking, laundry, etc…The deal was that when I came every month to do the cooking, the ladies would clean up after supper.

I had my back to the wooden island, orchestrating the women putting what little remained of the meal into Tupperware bowls. There was a lot of dish washing to be done; the dishwasher had been filled ten minutes ago and a wash started. The young Latino lady named Carmen was eyeing me curiously as I directed the troops, she being by far the most voluptuous of the bunch was attempting to flirt with me. I was standing there, arms folded, thinking to myself—under any other circumstances, I'd give this girl the ride of her life…

And then Allison strode in.

She wore a devilish smile—like the one she flashed that first night at H20 when I had strolled up to her and gave her a taste of Trey's game. She wore a black suit—slim pencil skirt with a center slit and matching jacket, nylon-less showing off her nice legs, black pumps, and a blouse of graphic design done in black and white—black diamonds amidst a sea of alternating black, then white waves. Hair pulled back, all business-like, and large gold hoop earrings that came down nearly to the bottom of her jaw. A black leather bag hung from her shoulder. Allison looked quite beautiful and I fought the urge to go to her and kiss her on that sensuous mouth of hers.

"Hey, Ms. Matthews," I said, grinning while I wiped my hands with a kitchen rag.

"Counselor," she replied, nodding at the women who stared curiously at her. "I wanted to see if you really could cook—or if you were just yanking my chain." She smiled for a moment and then held out her hand to the others, introducing herself to the women in the kitchen. Carmen eyed her as she shook her hand, then said, "Are you his wife?" as she gestured toward me.

"He wishes!" Allison said and I feigned injury.

"Hmmn. Girlfriend then?" Carmen continued.

"No, not girlfriend either. We are working together on a legal case."

"Hmmn," Carmen replied again. She was staring at me, licking her lips, consciously or unconsciously, I don't know. "You got a woman at home, Papi?"

"Who wants to know?" I shot back. "Besides, no one here could handle these goods!" I exclaimed, hands on my hips. Yolanda, who was in the next room, let out a short yelp while the rest of the ladies rolled their eyes.

"Hmmn," Carmen grunted before drying her hands and leaving the kitchen in a huff.

"So, Allison," I said, turning my full attention to her, "can I get you a plate—there's still some excellent eating left."

Yolanda walked in, shook hands with Allison and said, "You really should grab a plate; Trey didn't hold back this time—tonight's meal was a real treat."

"No thank you," Allison said.

"No?" I asked, feigning surprise, "after all the smack you said about me, you're not even going to try my cooking—oh no, we can't have that."

"No, really, but I do believe you—since there are witnesses present, and that's the only reason."

"Whatever!" I snorted. I began to grab my utensils, dishes/bowls, and leftover ingredients, and made ready to put them in the back of the Escalade. "Well then, don't just stand there looking all pretty; give me a hand with these things!" Allison obliged as Yolanda leaned against the doorframe and smirked at me while shaking her head. She knew what I was up to—it was as plain as day to her.

A few minutes and several trips later, all of my things were securely stored in the back of my ride. Allison and I were standing by the back bumper staring at the sky, the colors of sunset—reddish-orange purple tinge—painting the sky like swaths from an enormous brush. A light wind had picked up, rustling the leaves on the trees. It was going to be a beautiful night.

"Care to grab a cup of coffee, Trey?" Allison asked. "I was hoping we could talk about our case."

"I have a better idea—why don't you follow me home. I've got to drop these things off—I don't want them to stay too long in the back seat. Let me drop them off at home and then I'll put on a pot of coffee that will make Starbucks shiver.

"I don't know…"

"Allison—are you always this indecisive? Listen, I don't bite, okay? Follow me home—I live three minutes from here. We can have the food put away in five, I'll fix you a plate and a cup of Joe, and we'll discuss our case." I moved toward the front of the SUV. "Where you parked? Let me pull around front and then you can follow me." I hit the remote and opened the door, got in and shut the door before Allison could say anything or argue the point further. I watched her through the mirror as I started the engine and slipped a Maxwell CD into the changer—indecision was etched on her face. The power windows came down and I leaned out and said with a smile and a wink, "Honestly, I don't bite, baby…unless you like it like that!"

✖✖✖

All this time together and I haven't provided you all with the details of my crib—shame on me! As I mentioned when we first met, I live in D.C.

right off of 15th and U Street. It's a bad crib—two-story condo on the ninth and tenth floor of this really upscale building, walking distance from Republic Gardens, Bar Nun, and Utopia. Parking is underground and we've got our own doorman. Oh yeah, you know by now how we do!

Allison followed me in her silver Nissan Altima as we pulled into the garage. I wound down to the P-2 level, parked in my spot and directed her to visitor parking. I grabbed a cart by the elevator and began unloading my stuff. A few minutes later, after Allison had joined me, we were done and riding up in silence.

The gleaming doors opened onto my floor. I let Allison pass, checking out her ass and tight legs as she moved past me, before pushing the cart to the right and toward my condo entrance. I unlocked the door, opened it, and stepped aside, letting Allison enter first.

I still recall the first time I walked into my condo two years ago—the building's renovation had just been completed and the paint on the walls and ceiling was still wet. My breath was taken away by what I saw.

When you walk in, the first thing you notice is the enormity of the open space and slanted ceilings. The first level is made up of the living and dining rooms with a large open-air kitchen to the right, the latter separated from the former by teak countertops. There are dual skylights cut into the slanted ceilings. Large sliding-glass windows are cut into one wall with a cement balcony beyond. Like my office, colorful African-American art adorns the walls. As you walk in, you immediately step down into the sunken living room—a thick buffalo-brown couch and matching love seat are off to the left by the window. Directly across from the couch on one wall is a huge wide-screen TV and state-of-the-art stereo system. A thick, dark-brown throw rug sits diagonally in the middle of the living room. To the right is the kitchen. Moving further to the right of that is the dining room, equipped with a cherrywood table set for eight, a clear vase containing fresh flowers in mid-center, the fragrance permeating the air.

Allison drew in a breath as she glanced around. "Wow," she managed to say after a moment.

"Yeah, kind of takes your breath away at first, doesn't it?" I asked, being sincere.

"Sure does—how long have you been here?"

"Two years—found it by accident and damn glad I did—can't imagine living anywhere else."

"It's beautiful." I had painted the walls of the living room a light golden brown; the dining area was a rich red, and the kitchen off-white. It worked, though.

"Have a look around while I put this stuff away." I watched her walk toward the back rooms and then up the winding staircase to the upper floor. I was done putting everything away by the time she returned.

"I have to say, Trey, I am impressed. This place is beautiful—and you've really done a wonderful job decorating it, although I can't believe you did all this by yourself—you *had* to have some help—a woman's touch, no doubt—there's no way you came up with all of this on your own."

"See, herein lies your problem, Allison—you just refuse to believe how great a package I am," I said grinning from ear to ear. "I mean, you can't accept the fact that I've got skills in the kitchen, regardless of the fact that we just left sixteen very satisfied women. Second, you come into my home…" I said, holding my arms out wide, "a home that I decorated with my own two hands, *without* assistance, and yet you still refuse to acknowledge the obvious—what is staring you straight in the face!"

"And what might that be, counselor?" Allison asked, taking a seat on the couch and crossing her legs.

"Simply that I am, without a doubt, the most amazing specimen of a man that you've ever met—past, present, and future, baby!" I threw my head back and laughed at the vastness of my own ego—even I had to chuckle at that one—then went to the kitchen to pour some wine. I put on a pot of coffee to brew and returned with two bluish wine stems filled with Luna Di Luna Merlot-Cabernet. The wine was a dark purple against the colored glass. Allison accepted the wine with a nod and took a sip.

"Oh my, that's nice."

"Yes it is. As requested, I'm brewing some coffee. Now, let me fix you a small plate of food." I turned toward the kitchen.

"Trey, don't go out of your way, really." I stopped in mid stride and spun around.

"Woman," I began, walking toward her. "You are plucking my last nerve—you will try some of my food, you hear me, you will. I've gone to a lot of trouble—at least have the decency to take a bite!"

Allison frowned. "Okay, I didn't realize you were so sensitive…"

"Women!" I said in an exasperated tone, but smiling as the word escaped my lips. I observed Allison remove her jacket and drape it on the arm of the couch. Her thin tank sweater was sexy in that it showed off her curves and slender arms. I was looking at her breasts underneath the sheer material, fantasizing about her nipples and what they must look like unencumbered by a lace bra.

I pulled out some leftovers to fix a plate for Allison—a small portion of the beef tenderloin and a generous helping of the angel hair pasta, made with the fresh tomatoes, basil, and my special sauce. I could have zapped the food in the microwave and saved some time, but that just wouldn't do. I pulled out a skillet to braze the beef, and a bowl to boil water for the pasta. I poured the pasta sauce in a smaller skillet and began to warm it under a low fire.

"Come here," I said to Allison, who rose off the couch and came to the kitchen willingly, her glass of Merlot-Cabernet in hand. Her shoes were off and I took in her red polished toenails. Nice. She slid next to the countertop where she could watch me, crossing her legs and curling her toes on the tile. "So," I said, while turning the beef and stirring the pasta sauce in the skillet, "let's talk about the case."

"Okay. As I was saying on the phone, Trey, I really think that this issue can and should be resolved without much fanfare. I mean, your client is a successful basketball player. My client was married to him for two years. She's not looking to clean him out—only to get what's fair and equitable…"

"The main residence is not fair game, Allison," I said, turning to stare directly at her. "We've gone over this before—the residence was bought *before* he married her."

"I understand that. But don't you think that this latest development changes everything?"

"No."

"Well, I do." Allison took a sip of wine and placed the stem on the counter. "Come on, Trey—the guy's screwing other women under his wife's own nose and then gets caught. This changes everything—the Hues would still be married if it weren't for his infidelity, for God's sake!"

"Not according to my client," I quipped.

"Trey—let's stop playing games here—my client is out of a perfectly good marriage. Now she's only looking for something that she can call her own. The main residence is located in the area of Jersey where she grew up—she has family there. Your client doesn't. He no longer lives in the area. He no longer plays for New York. There is no reason for him to keep that house. If my client wasn't asking for it, he'd probably have it on the market in no time!"

"Perhaps, perhaps not." I continued to stir the sauce and watch the beef tenderloin with a close eye.

"Why are you dragging this out? This I don't understand. We have solid evidence of your client's infidelity and no court in the land is going to enforce your hastily filed injunction—you'll see. Then we'll be in a position to ruin your man's reputation, hell, the tabloids and talk shows will make a field day out of this—all because he refused to play fair."

Allison shook her head and moved across the tile to the range where I was standing. She leaned against the counter and looked up into my eyes. "Is that what you want, Trey? A sensational trial—lurid tales of infidelity, wild interracial sex caught on tape by the star forward of the Washington Wizards himself?"

I stopped stirring the sauce and put the wooden spoon down on the stove. "Allison—are you aware that Quentin is in high-level talks with Pepsi for a multimillion- dollar endorsement deal? No? Well, he is. And what do you think is going to happen when the good folks at Pepsi get wind of this *thing* you're speaking of? I'll tell you what's going to happen. There will be no endorsement deal. Period. End of discussion. And you don't have to possess a degree in mathematics to know that zero divided by two is still zero." I paused to let this sink in. Took a sip of my wine before continuing.

"This deal, if I had to guess, and I'm taking into account other players who have had similar endorsements, will run on the average of five to ten million dollars for a relatively unknown like Quentin. He's no Michael Jordan, but the boy has skills, is good-looking, and commands a presence in front of the camera. Now, for the sake of argument, let's say he gets eight million. Eight divided by two is four—that's how much money your client will be entitled to." I took another sip, swished the wine around my gums before swallowing. Allison was watching me intently.

"Four million dollars, Ms. Matthews—not bad cheddar for the former Mrs. Hues who didn't do shit to earn it…"

Allison began to protest but I held up my hand.

"Hold it—I know what she's entitled to. What I'm saying is this—go public with this *thing* and everyone loses—my client and yours. Especially yours. My client's reputation will be tarnished. Yes, that much will be true. He will lose any chance of future endorsement deals. He may lose his contract. But he will, at the very least, have a skill that can be put to good use in some other city, on some other day when the smoke clears. Your client, on the other hand, has nothing other than her good looks. She's a young girl with no education and no plans for getting one—Quentin was her plan. Her way out. Screw with Quentin and his future, and she cuts off the hand that feeds her…Not a good strategy, Ms. Matthews, nor would I want to be the attorney who counseled her client on that course of action… "

Allison was silent. I glanced down, watching her toes curl. I concluded that she must do that when she's nervous. She, too, was looking down—then her head raised and she exhaled forcefully. "So, Mr. Alexander, what do want?"

I took a moment to turn over the beef tenderloin. It was sizzling in the pan, sending its wonderful aroma around the kitchen. The pasta sauce was beginning to slowly bubble, so I turned off the heat and moved it to the back burner.

"Simple—the disc and all copies destroyed, and a signed statement from your client, and anyone else that she may have shared her story with, that they will not discuss the contents of that disk—ever. And I mean *ever!* In turn—she gets the main residence. Then, we divide up the remaining assets as normal, and our clients go their separate ways. If the endorsement thing comes to fruition, then your client gets half, no questions asked. More than fair. If not, no harm no foul. With me so far?"

"Yes." Allison was staring off into space—I could see the wheels turning. This was a good deal and she knew it.

"Yes what? Is this acceptable to you? Do we have a deal?"

"It's acceptable to me. I, of course, have to run it by my client…"

"Wait a second, Allison—I thought you wanted to resolve this quickly—just the two of us—isn't that what you said to me yesterday? So let's resolve it. Right now. No clients, just us lawyers, as you indicated."

Allison walked across to the counter, picked up her wine stem, and took a long sip. I watched her tilt her head back and swallow. Watched her close her eyes for a moment as she enjoyed the wine warming her insides. Opening them, she stared straight at me and said with a wicked grin, "Okay, counselor, you've got yourself a deal."

"Excellent. I trust I can count on you to get me that disc and all copies ASAP. And we'll need to get your client and anyone else she talked to about Quentin's wanderings into my office at once."

"I'll take care of it. You have my word on that."

"Good. I knew you were reasonable, Allison." I scooped up a spoonful of sauce and placed the tip of the wooden spoon to my lips. I scrunched up my eyes and groaned. "Oh my God, this is soooo damn good!" Allison stood there with a smirk on her face. "What?" I asked, "you don't believe me?" I dug up another spoonful, blew on it, and walked over to her, my left hand underneath the spoon so I wouldn't drop any on the tile floor.

"Prepare to be dazzled," I said, as I reached her. Allison put down her wine glass, leaned back on the counter, arms extended on either side. She closed her eyes.

"Fire away," she said, and opened her mouth. I was giggling as I extended the spoon toward her open orifice.

"Open wide," I said. The spoon touched her bottom lip and I tilted upward, watching as a bit of the sauce slid sensuously into her mouth. She began to swallow, her lips closed on one another causing the spoon to shift on its axis slightly. Before I could react, a blob of sauce slid off the spoon and dropped, rebounding on her thin sweater above her left breast, and then dropped to her dark skirt right above the center slit. "OH SHIT!" I yelled. Allison's eyes snapped open in horror. She dropped her chin and glanced down.

"OH FUCK, Trey! Fuck, this is my favorite top!" Allison spun away from me as her hands went to the fabric. "Goddamn it!"

"Allison, NO!" I yelled, dropping the spoon on the counter and grabbing her hands. "Don't touch it—listen to me—you'll make it worse." I ran to the sink, grabbed a paper towel and ran back. I lightly dabbed the towel on the fabric of her top and skirt, soaking up the mass of the sauce. Allison had this look of horror on her face.

"I can't fucking believe this—sorry, I can't believe this shit—this is one of my favorite outfits…" She reached out to grab the towel from me, but I moved my hand back, resisting her.

"Allison—listen to me—this is what we are going to do." I bent down so she was eye level with me. "Follow me—we're going upstairs. I'm going to give you an oversized tee shirt that you're going to change into…"

Allison began to shake her head and protest. I reached up and lightly grabbed her chin.

"No, Allison—you're going to take these clothes off now and I'm going to clean them. I've got this stuff that works wonders on stained fabric that can't be washed—but we need to do it now before the stain dries." I bunched up the sauce-laden paper towel in one hand and grabbed Allison's hand with the other. I gestured for her to follow me. Silently, with a dejected look on her face, she did.

TWENTY-THREE

A fire burned leisurely, but not without silence, the flames spitting flickers and sparks into the brick-lined chimney. The lights were extinguished—no need for them, the firelight providing ample light and comfort to Desiree who lay topless and prone on the blanketed floor, and for Vince, who knelt over her, a smile lodged on his face. The oversized jar of Vaseline laid beside him. His fingers were covered with it and he paused as he admired her form—smooth dark skin, perfect breasts that swelled to chocolate peaks, a thin curvy waist and seductive navel, which like sexy lips, seemed to speak to him when he probed and massaged her brown flesh.

Taking his time, Vince coated her skin, rubbing her neck and clavicles, descending to her breasts, rubbing around the base of her mounds, then taking the nipples in his hands, between fingers, lubing them up, feeling them become pointy and hard as Desiree worked hard to control her movement and her soft moans, the fire dancing behind them creating patterns on the walls and ceiling. Moving downwards, to her flat belly and navel, massaging and coating her taut skin with jelly until her entire body shined. And then as Desiree watched him, speaking softly and with short-ness of breath as he worked, Vince proceeded with making a casting of her torso—for him, the very first time he had attempted this—the thought had been rolling around in his head for months, but not having the right person to try it with, he had put it on the back burner. Angeliqué would be

the perfect person to *experiment* with—but, well, Angeliqué wasn't here…
and hadn't returned his call from the previous week…but Desiree was and
so the opportunity had presented itself…

The alginate went on next, and Vince enjoyed spreading the gel over her
body—his fingers and palms reacquainting themselves with her lovely flesh
and nipples—before applying the plaster strips and waiting for those to dry.
He had her sit up and move to the futon when he was done, as she had done
before, wanting to ensure that her breasts be properly *represented* in the
plaster, not giving gravity a chance to interfere…

When they were done—the alginate and plaster hardened, he could
strike the firm cast with his knuckle and be rewarded with a hollow
response—Vince had Desiree sit forward as before so that he could remove
the casting. He did this gingerly, since the cast was twice the size of his
usual masks. Desiree watched silently as the cast came off, revealing her
still perky breasts (Vince had opened the windows earlier to ensure the
room remained nippy—no pun intended)…He carried the cast with both
hands to his worktable and laid it out so that it could dry. Desiree followed
him, unconcerned with her topless state, astonished once again at the ability
of the lifecasting process to capture the essence of human flesh. Together, they
stared in silence at the casting, reflecting on its meaning and the innumerable
possibilities once paint was applied.

Revisiting the futon a few moments later, Desiree sat back and Vince
returned moments later with a bowl of warm soapy water and a warm washcloth. Kneeling in front of her, he asked, "May I cleanse you?" Desiree
nodded, her eyes sparkling like the fire burning behind them. He reached
for her with the washcloth and using slow, gentle strokes, removed all
remnants of the alginate and petroleum jelly, and then washed her the way
a parent does his or her infant. She followed him closely with her stare,
watching him as he cleansed her, and Vince silently admired her form and
splendor, rubbing her flesh, feeling her the way a lover does. And finally,
when she was all-clean, and Vince decided that he could no longer stand
being mere inches from her body without taking her—a piece of succulent
fruit that longed to be consumed—he reached for her mouth with his own,

and took her, right then and there—his tongue invading her mouth, teeth scraping against enamel as the intensity between them ignited like a flame, hands finding breasts, soft to the touch as he kneaded them between fingers, Desiree responding to Vince by giving herself to him without question, leaning in, opening up, his hands on her thighs, rubbing the tight denim, grasping her legs, she reaching for his back and pulling him to her, mouths on each other, latching on, connecting—tongue to tongue, mouth to mouth, flesh to flesh—and she reaching back, grasping for his shirt and pulling upward, until it came off and landed on the floor several yards away from them. Then them resuming their connection of flesh—mouths finding one another again, and now, breasts to breast, nipples to nipples, as he pushed his weight against her, his breath hot on her neck. He found the cleft between her legs, the sweet spot, and rubbed her there, as she moaned and guided his hand, as if he needed the help, which he did *not*. Her jeans came down, peeling like a cornstalk, until they, too, like his shirt, laid crumpled on the floor. Clad in only her black panties, she looked uncompromisingly beautiful, with the firelight flickering off her naked form. And then, without further ado, using a slight tug from both hands, her panties slid downwards—thighs, then knees, then ankles, and then off into space, and he parted her legs like the Red Sea, using both hands to spread her wide, her head flung back and eyes closed, as he lowered his head and found the epicenter, her molten core.

Vince fed like a cat, lapping up her milk, her sweet juice, licking her folds that quivered with excitement as his hand rushed along her skin, gliding across every inch of softness, making his way from her neck to her ankles, ensuring he explored every delicious inch of her being as she held her legs in the air. Desiree opened her mouth and told him what she was feeling, let him know that this loving was so damn good—exciting her soul, making her yell out in ecstasy, the passion infusing her interior and whipping her into a frenzy. By the time he had pulled back to take a breath, Desiree had come twice—the juice of her sex glazing his mouth and chin, and painting her thighs and ass with its sinful wake.

Vince returned moments later, naked, his manhood erect and wrapped up tight in a latex condom. He knelt before her, kissed her passionately before leaning forward and entering her effortlessly. Desiree moaned on contact, reaching for him, pulling him to her, ensuring she was filled up completely, his balls pressed solidly against her vulva. As firelight danced off their undulating form, Vince found his rhythm and settled into a groove, grasping for the spot where her neck and chin rested against the futon, holding on, pumping against her, feeling her squeezing him and sucking him in, her sex like a vortex, swallowing him, consuming him with her passion. They found their groove together and moved to it, a song they both knew; Vince reaching for her breasts and squeezing, bending forward and consuming the areolas with his mouth, painting a wide swath with his tongue. Desiree felt so good to him, her body so tight and well defined, almost body-building material—Vince was turned on just by glancing down at her lovely form, observing her curves and the way she moved to him, thrusting against him as he impaled her with his cock—the feeling wonderful and yet, Vince thinking to himself, isn't it amazing how the simple act of loving in a singular kind of fashion—something that is repeated over and over again, a million trillion times over the course of a lifetime, can be so unique and utterly *individualistic*, as if he were experiencing this feeling, like an adolescent, for the very first time.

Vince paused and pulled out slowly, groaning as he did, then guided Desiree over, her knees on the futon, breasts and chest pressed against the back of the couch as he re-entered her and pummeled her with newly found enthusiasm. Desiree shrieked, reached back and pulled him into her, screaming his name, demanding he fuck her good and even harder than before, and Vince complying, closing his eyes, giving in completely to this woman, ensuring that this *experience* would be one that she would remember, recorded in the journal for all times, even though he knew he couldn't last much longer, the feeling much too sweet, like nectar, way too intense for him to continue any longer, and yet, wanting to hold out—not for her, but for himself—the feeling so *intense*, as good sex always turns out to be, but then in the end, giving in, resigning himself to the feeling that began rising from the base of his sex and shot through him like an avalanche—carrying with it all of the energy and passion of a sudden thunderstorm in summer.

Vince came—one minute he was contemplating the mere existence of an orgasm and whether he could hold out for a few minutes longer—and then it was *here*, now—and Desiree, in an instant, joined him, her entire body vibrating, fingers, hands, legs and thighs—each part of her body reacting as if it were a guitar being strummed—the flesh heaving, as if it had a mind of its own, shaking as she unleashed her passion—the two of them, their waves slamming against each other, Desiree's head thrown back and her eyes rolled back, her voice hoarse from screaming and moaning— "Oh God, Vince, I fucking came!"—the tendrils in her digits tight, the muscles in her neck and shoulders—taut like a bow.

And when he had ceased his thrusting, and slowed to a stop, Desiree sighed, one gigantic breath that was expelled as she turned to him, feeling him exit her warm, wet place, and together flopping onto the futon…

Finding each other,
Wrapping legs and arms around one another,
As if they were twine around a Christmas package,
Resting their heads on each other,
As their heartbeats slowed,
And they reveled,
In the afterglow,
Of wild, unrestrained sex…

TWENTY-FOUR

ifteen minutes later Allison and I were back where we left off—in my kitchen. Only now, Allison was clad in an extra-large gray Georgetown University sweatshirt. She was leaning against the counter watching me as I poured her more wine. I smiled fiendishly, handed the glass to her and toasted her silently with my own stem. I observed her taking a sip before I took one myself. She placed the glass down on the counter and sighed.

"Allison—I told you, the stains will come out—trust me. I just checked on it—they're almost gone. Give it thirty more minutes and you won't even know a stain was ever there. I swear!"

"I hope so."

"You'll see. So…" I said, putting my stem down and walking over to her. I reached for her glass, placed it on the table, and then before she could react, I reached for her waist with both hands and hoisted her up onto the counter. "You'll be safer here—trust me!" Her legs parted as I pulled back and I spied a hint of white panties. Allison frowned at me for a moment but then smiled, grabbed the wine and took another swig. I watched her, my eyes never leaving hers. Then I let them roam downward. She looked damn sexy sitting there on my counter, clad in an oversized sweatshirt, legs smooth and sculpted, toenails painted, a hint of white cotton visible when she rocked backwards or arched sideways to put down her wine glass.

"Allison," I said, wiping the smile off of my face. "We are going to try this again," I said, turning toward the stove and the still uneaten pasta sauce. I grabbed the spoon, stirred it in the skillet as I heard Allison say, "No, Trey," emphatically.

I ignored her purposely; stirred it a bit more, took a taste—satisfied, I loaded up another spoonful and carried it gingerly over to the counter.

"Trey! Remember what happened the last time!" Allison exclaimed.

I reached her, lifted my chin to her and said, "Open wide!"

"No." She shut her mouth and rocked backwards. I flicked my eyes down and gazed at her panties. The part where the fabric met skin was oh so smooth…Allison closed her legs with a smirk.

Raising the spoon to her lips, I again said softly, "Allison, open." This time she did. I moved in, her legs parted and I found myself nuzzled between her thighs. She arched backwards, the sweatshirt riding up—unconcerned, she grabbed the wine stem and took a swig, rolling her eyes back as she swallowed. Her mouth opened and I slid the spoon partway in. She swallowed, opened her eyes and said, "Damn—I take back every bad thing I've ever said about you, Trey—give me some more!"

I flashed a smile while moving in once again with the spoon. Touched her bottom lip, tilted upward, waiting in anticipation for the tip of her tongue to come out, probing the air cautiously, seductively, the motion reminiscent of a serpent.

"OUCH!" Allison bellowed. I glanced down. A blob of sauce had landed on her inner left thigh—a mere inch from her pantyline. Allison's eyes were wide. She said nothing. I didn't speak. Instead, I gazed at her parted legs and that spot of red delicious sauce. Glanced back up. Allison was watching me silently. Without warning, I kneeled down, my eyes never leaving her. Shifting my gaze, I found myself eye level with her crotch, the spot of homemade sauce inches from my nose. My heart was racing. The blood, I could feel, coursed through my veins like a water hose on full. I leaned in and touched my lips to that spot. Felt, more than saw Allison open her legs ever so slightly. Tasted my creation—my mouth opening slowly, the blob of pasta sauce in contact with my tongue, its mass smearing my lips as if gloss. I glanced up briefly, made eye contact with Allison—and before any words could be spoken, my gaze dropped back down. My nose followed, brushing against the centerline of her panties. Slowly and methodically, I moved my nose around her crotch, rubbing against the cotton of her panties, inhaling her scent. I had opened my mouth, sucked up what remained of the sauce, and swallowed it in one gulp before running a wet tongue over her flesh by the side of her pantyline, licking up any lingering remnants of my delicious pasta sauce.

My head tilted upward, searching her face—Allison was watching me silently, her eyes unwavering, lips unmoving, neither a smile nor a frown painted upon her mouth. Then both her hands found my head, palms connecting with flesh, and I understood what needed to be done.

Beginning at her ankles, my hands grasped her lower legs and moved upward, slowly feeling the smooth flesh. Reaching her knees, I paused, felt around the bone with my fingers while my head moved from left to right and back again, my nose brushing against the dampening cotton fabric of her panties. Reaching behind her knees, I felt for the hollow space and tickled her flesh before moving upward to her thighs. Then grasping them with my hands, I spread her legs wide and felt her arch backwards, while simultaneously lifting my chin, forcing my nose into the cleft of her center. I heard Allison groan as my mouth reached the edge of her now damp panties. My teeth found the fabric, gripping it, and tugged it aside.

Eyes opening, I saw her core, the axis of my desire and hers—Allison's lovely pussy—thin outer lips, a small entrance to her love tunnel—light brown pubic hair that radiated out from that spot, but controlled—cut, trimmed, like a well-kept lawn. At the bottom of her inner vulva, a single drop of juice—wetness, poised at the slit and gleaming like freshly fallen snow. Following her flesh lines upward to the top of her sex, darker than the rest of her skin, the convergence of pussy lips and hooded knob—and set in the middle—a thin, golden loop which pierced the center of her clit, with a tiny dark green stone that swiveled around the loop of metal, like an earring or a piece of artwork.

Not being able to contain myself one second more, I moved in—my lips colliding with hers, my tongue flicking at the drop of freshness as if it were salt, sloshing it around the tip of my tongue before, in one slow movement, I licked her sex from bottom to top. Allison responded by groaning. She gripped my head tighter and I attacked her pussy with all of my mouth—slowly at first, using my tongue as a probe to pierce her cunt like a fork does raw meat, alternating with wide swaths from my wet tongue across her lips and inner thighs—but then abandoning any semblance of slow, coordinated movement, losing myself inside of her sex—ditching any strategy that called for working her into a frenzy—no, at this point we were too far gone for that mess. *Fuck that*; I wanted to taste Allison, *NOW*! And so, I grabbed her thighs, hoisted her legs back toward the counter and like one devours an oyster, I took Allison's entire cunt into my waiting mouth, slurping it up in one giant gulp, swishing it around like sushi, shaking my head rapidly and violently, feeling the clit piercing between my teeth—then exhaling and opening my mouth, allowing her engorged pussy to slide out, like a baby from a birth canal, all shiny with spittle.

Drunk now with the liquor of Allison's sex, I reached for the wooden spoon, drew it across her pussy lips before she could react, sketching a red swath of warm sauce, painting her hole in all of its glory. The spoon found her clit, decorated her pierced clit with more paste before I moved it down her cleft, spinning the wood in my hands, watching it glide from one pussy lip to the other, leaving sauce in its wake. Then finding the hole and probing lightly, around the edges, lightly dancing along the opening, like a gymnast does on a balance beam, one foot in front of the other, hands held wide, before turning/diving into the vortex—sticking the wide mouth of the sauce-laden spoon deep inside of her.

The end of the spoon stuck out a good six inches in a perverse sort of way. Head held back, Allison was too far-gone to notice. And I wasn't telling…

Turning my attention to her clit, I flicked my tongue along the thin gold ring as Allison squirmed on top. Tugged at it with my teeth—side to side, up and down, inserting the entire thing into my mouth, sucking at it like it was some kind of hard candy that tasted so damn good, vacuuming up the sauce, tapping the ring against my teeth and tongue until Allison was bucking her hips and moaning incessantly. I raised my hand to her clit and rubbed the piercing with my thumb. Ran it lengthwise along her pussy lips and the embedded spoon handle, gripping the end, moving it around inside of her pussy, yanking on it and watching her give birth to it before I discarded it on the tile floor like trash. Then my tongue reacquainted itself with her cunt as I replaced my thumb where the spoon had gone, twisting my hand clockwise and feeing her insides swell around me. Allison squashed her thighs against my ears hard, making a mess—sauce and pussy juice combining, splashing against my nose, cheeks, and hand. And for a moment I heard my ears ring before I pried apart her thighs and slurped her cunt once again into my waiting mouth, not caring about my chin, which was covered with sauce and Ally juice. My dick was straining against my jeans. I let one hand snake down to feel myself. Hard as a stone. I was ready.

The next few minutes were a blur to me. I stood up, hands reaching underneath the sweatshirt and finding her lovely breasts as I assaulted her lips with my mouth. Our tongues intertwined and twisted around one another like branches on a vine. Slipping my hands underneath her bra as if my skin was lotioned, my fingertips found her nipples firm. Grasping them, tugging at them, I ground against her wet pussy with my hips. And then, my jeans were down—whether through Allison's help or not, I don't know. What is clear is that my dick found her opening like a missile finds its target, and I pressed home, into her wet slit as she sucked in a breath and reached for my back. I slid in, tip to balls, Allison's cunt expanding as I greeted her with my member, filling her up completely. I came to the end, paused for a microsecond and then began pulling out, the feeling of her pussy constricting around me so overpowering that I thought I might come quickly, like a high-school kid. And then Allison was pushing me away—my dick plopped out, shiny and wet, as she reached for it with her hand and gave it a firm tug.

"Wrap it up, Trey," she said seductively, her eyes shimmering with anticipation, "and then you can fuck me…"

TWENTY-FIVE

Images of candles flickering against dark skin, and Miles' horn cutting through the haze of incense and cigarette smoke rushed through Vince's psyche as he sprinted down the jetway to the waiting DC-9. His garment bag cut into his left shoulder, yet he smiled—remembering Angeliqué as she flung cool paint against his flushed skin. The way they made love that night on the floor of her studio was indescribable—the sudden rush of feelings and emotions simmering against their colliding flesh in a delicious kind of way—almost causing his step to falter with the intensity of it all. Vince reached the jet, flashed a grin to the flight attendant who greeted him as he took his seat in first class.

It had begun with a fleeting thought as he lay in his bed the night before unable to sleep, the trick the mind plays on itself as one stretches his or her limbs under the weight of covers—and for Vince, he found himself imagining Angeliqué as he shifted around in his bed, her lovely form caressing him lightly from above, the way the covers did to his nude, pulsing form, causing him to swell with anticipation, and with pain. And that feeling, at the edge of that place where consciousness crosses over the divide and sleep takes over, was haunting. Yet just before he slipped into the fathomless pit, he found a thought and forged it into cold, gleaming steel—Vince decided that night that he would go to her, just as she had prayed to Ezili Freda, the voodoo goddess of love, the one who was fond of pink and pale blue candles, that he would.

So here he was. Eighteen hours later. Heading south on a whim…

The plane made a slow roll skywards as the force of the engines pushed him back into his leather seat. He glanced outside his window as the city of Washington veered away to the right. Soon blue sky and sunlight was streaming onto his dark face, causing him to squint. He thought about what he was doing—heading to New Orleans to surprise Angeliqué. He hadn't seen her in a while—they'd talked on the phone—less frequently than when he'd first returned, but every time he heard her voice—the breathless way she called his name or used vulgar language to describe how she was feeling, and more importantly, what she intended to do to him once he was back in her town, made him crave her even more.

Vince was heading to New Orleans on a Friday afternoon to surprise Angeliqué. She had no clue that he was coming. He hadn't told her. His heart and mind raced with the possibilities of surprising her later that night. It tickled away at him and made him excited.

The jet banked left and followed the meandering shoreline southbound toward Angeliqué's home. Vince tilted his head back and closed his eyes. Immediately Desiree's smile replaced the picture of Angeliqué's wild, frizzy hair. The thought chilled him. He had spent an evening with Desiree just a fortnight ago. She had made him laugh over dinner at this West African place on 18th Street. As they sipped martinis and filled their bellies with spicy food, Desiree talked non-stop about her friends and their crazy drama. The one whose man was caught cheating with a woman from his church, or the other who told Desiree in a hushed tone that her cat was fond of licking her under the covers, and that she was growing to enjoy it way too much! Vince sat there and laughed as Desiree told him these stories and more, and he found himself thinking about her and their relationship—barely two weeks old. He enjoyed Desiree—she was good-looking, smart, and feisty—girlfriend definitely had plenty to say—there wasn't any dead air between them—and yet, he recognized after making love to her recently and spooning her body in his, that the *feeling* that he felt when they were together was *different* than that which he recalled between Angeliqué and him.

Not better, not worse…just *different*.

Vince tried to sort out the data that were his feelings and analyze the results. He was having trouble seeing it clearly. But what his heart was telling him so far was this: He enjoyed his time with Desiree. She was fun to have around, like Maxi (he reminded himself), then pushed that thought down, out of sight. Desiree was intellectual and could always be counted on for a lively debate. The sex was nothing to shake a stick at either—hell, there were no problems in that department, with her young, tight body and her angular features that caused him to stare sometimes without saying a word. But, as he pondered the similarities and differences between her and the voodoo lady he recalled how down in New Orleans Angeliqué had stirred something deep inside of him…something that had remained in his heart and in his soul, to this day…

He remembered the way he felt staring into Angeliqué's eyes as they dined at Brennan's, the way she moved as they walked hand-in-hand down Toulouse, her hip lightly bumping against his as they moved, the sophisticated, yet sensuous way Angeliqué carried herself as her wild hair caressed her face and neck—almost with a mythical, surreal quality, Vince thought. Was that right, or was this some kind of hoodoo-voodoo shit that he was conjuring?

His mind whirled as the plane leveled, the flight attendant bringing him a rum and Coke with a smile that Vince returned, momentarily suppressing thoughts of Angeliqué, Desiree, and even Maxi, as he made small talk about the weather and the coming of winter.

Then they were back—those three women who tugged at Vince's heartstrings in different ways. He allowed himself to remember with vivid recall the times he had spent with Maxi—the way she smiled, and her eyes that lit up a room. The way they moved as they danced in sync, that night at The Saint, in time to the music that seemed to wrap around them and sweep them away. Those sweet images came and went, replaced by those of Desiree—her thin, smooth form in his studio as he hovered over her with fire in his eyes, preparing for the lifecasting. Then, days later, flashes of the two of them playing chess as they conversed, Desiree clad in an oversized

University of Maryland sweatshirt and not much else, the rising swell of her sweet, bare ass uncovered as she reached over to capture one of Vince's knights.

But it was Angeliqué Vince's psyche kept returning to—it was something about her that was *different*. When he was with her, he felt something else—he couldn't put a finger on it, but he noticed his pulse quicken with the thought of gazing upon her again tonight—the stirring in him, radiating outward, warming with its fire-like intensity.

Like a sudden thunderstorm that swoops in from out of nowhere and darkens the sky, Desiree came flooding back into his thoughts, pushing the voodoo lady aside.

Here she was, a chocolate-coated vibrant young thing who looked damn good on his arm, and was at his beck and call. What was there not to like? But, he had had similar thoughts regarding Maxi, too. Vince had made a quick getaway from her only months after they began dating because it didn't feel right, because she was not the *one*—and Vince was afraid that he was about to do the same thing to Desiree. This time he needed to make sure—there had been several times recently when he wondered if he had done the right thing in letting Maxi go. He had been thinking about that just the other day, pondering those thoughts and letting them marinate as he watched Desiree prance around his studio as she shoveled Chinese takeout into her waiting mouth; he even picked up the phone and dialed Maxi's number after Desiree had left, fully satisfied from the food and the sex—the call went to voice mail and Vince sighed with relief but left a short message anyway because he knew she'd see the number on Caller ID.

Maxi hadn't returned his call yet.

With a whoosh Desiree was replaced by thoughts of Angeliqué. It was a powerful sensation that began in his toes and rose upward until he felt his spine tingling in anticipation.

Was it all a dream? Vince asked himself again. Or did Angeliqué possess some kind of supernatural power that she wielded over him, waving her wand from a thousand miles away to command him with a strength that he felt even from here? Was it the Creole magic, the spells and incantations, the ritual prayers to voodoo priests and priestesses, the altar in the corner of her Quarter studio, littered with dolls and candles, playing cards and chicken claws, that drew him to her?

This trip, Vince knew, was his way of finding out.

He wasn't about to make further changes to his social life until he was sure. Not yet. No need to rush things. He had acted hastily last time. He had lost Maxi in the process. Did he regret that? Perhaps. This time he needed to slow his roll.

Vince thought about the way he was acting, juggling these women as if they were balls that he tossed up and arced into the air—he knew it wasn't right—Trey, of course, would be proud, Vince acting like the true dawg that Trey hoped he'd grow up to be, but that wasn't him—never had been. Vince appreciated women. He treated them with respect and as equals with feelings.

What was he doing then, keeping Desiree on hold, in effect, while flying off to spend the weekend with some other woman?

Vince brushed the thought aside as the flight attendant refreshed his drink with her painted-on smile.

✖✖✖

The night air caressed his back—it was a wonderful sensation, to be back in New Orleans this time of year, the rest of the country hunkering down for winter, and yet, here in Louisiana, the flowers were still in full bloom, and birds were still singing, not yet having left for warmer pastures.

The flight had been uneventful. He had caught a taxi from the airport to his hotel, unpacked, taken a quick shower, and put on fresh clothes. He selected a pair of black baggy trousers and a gray mock turtleneck—then changed his mind, replacing the mock with a button-down gray silk. Black loafers completed the ensemble, but it took Vince another fifteen minutes to decide whether he wanted to wear socks or not—in the end, he opted for loafers sans the socks, and headed out to his woman.

His first stop was to the concierge desk where he was directed to a florist three blocks away. Vince picked up some carnations, vibrantly red, and proceeded to Angel…é's home.

He walked leisurely through the French Quarter, taking his time—it was close to eight o'clock—the sun had just gone down, but the sky was clear. The forecast that evening called for light winds and low sixties—he had thought about bringing a jacket, but left it back in the hotel room instead. He walked past shops and restaurants, enjoying the light breeze as it billowed his silk shirt, and the live music that emanated from open bars; the throng of young people that traversed Bourbon, searching frantically for beads—Vince followed them for a bit before heading onto a side street where it was peaceful.

He had thought about calling ahead, after all, this was a Friday night, the beginning of the weekend, and there was always the possibility that she wouldn't be home. But Vince weighed his options heavily in his head, ultimately deciding not to call—he'd just show up and take it from there.

Vince turned onto St. Philip, and immediately felt the pang of anxiety that coursed through him. As he passed the two-story homes with their shutter-covered windows and balconies draped with twisting ivy, Angeliqué's corner studio/home now coming into view, he felt angst—butterflies fluttering inside his stomach, and he exhaled slowly to calm his breathing. His grip tightened on the flowers he carried. He paused to check himself. This was ridiculous, Vince told himself—he looked fine; besides, he was going to visit someone whom he had shared something special with. There was no reason to feel apprehensive.

Nevertheless, Vince crossed the street, fading deeper into the shadows of the night. Light from the gallery windows flooded the street and he wanted to make sure he wasn't seen—not yet. Sounds from various night creatures were more pronounced here—away from the masses of yelling, inebriated people. Vince came to a stop directly across the street from the broad expanse of glass. He peered in, noticed that the place was empty save for a lone woman who sat at a desk toward the rear of the building, her head down as she attended to some paperwork. He scanned the interior walls, observing from the shadows Angeliqué's art, the *veve* of the voodoo spirits—

the elaborate designs surrounded by colorful hues and shades of the Haitian art.

Vince took a breath and crossed the street, cutting a diagonal line toward the gallery entrance. He spotted the courtyard entrance off to the right, a heavy wrought-iron door that hung open. He headed for that.

Coming upon the entrance, he slowed his gait and peered inside to what lay beyond. The courtyard was bathed in shadows; it was exactly as he remembered. The red brick wall was covered with thick ivy and he could hear the trickling of water from the oval pond. Vince reached for the black metal and then stopped dead. To the left by the table where he had laid his wine stem months before, he saw them—a couple caught in embrace. The shock of frizzy hair was unmistakable. Angeliqué was facing Vince, but shielded from view by the other person whose head she was grasping gingerly between her hands. Angeliqué kissed the person—it was not a long kiss, but what Vince witnessed froze his heart.

Angeliqué was in the arms of a woman.

TWENTY-SIX

I'm always down for a party, y'all! So when Q called me on Tuesday talking about how he was having this thing for his birthday on Saturday evening at Home, and that he had put me on the guest list I said, hell yeah, you know I'll be there. Home is this spot that's patterned after some of the new trendy clubs in South Beach, with actual beds and shit—I kid you not—and you have to reserve those bad boys—but it's all good, 'cause some fine-ass honeys roll in there looking for someone to share their covers with. And you know this brutha ain't mad at any of them!

I got there close to midnight. Not one to arrive early, I made damn sure I pulled my shit up to the curb just as a big-ass line was wrapping itself around the block. They had been promoting the hell out of this party on the radio all week—talking about how all of these ball players, rappers, and video stars would be there. Oh yeah, Quentin got it like that—he's young, good-looking, and on his game—with the exception of his little legal troubles, he'd be on top of the world. But Q wasn't one to let the soon-to-be-former Mrs. Hues bring him down. Not on his birthday. No! So he rented out Home on a busy Saturday night, invited everyone who was anybody, including the entire Wizards team and his former teammates from New York, and made sure all of Washington D.C. knew about it. And judging from the way the bouncers were handling the crowd, only fly looking folks were being allowed in. They were acting like this shit was Studio 54, pointing to this fine honey over here in the short red dress with the thigh-high boots, and that fine sistah over there with her painted on jeans and Victoria's Secret sequined bra, letting them and others like them in, while telling the rest of the folks to push the hell on back! Oh well, I hate it when that happens!

I had thought about bringing someone with me to this shindig—thought about that shit for all of five seconds, before deciding that flying solo was best. As I'm fond of saying, "Why bring sand to the beach?" Ya know???

I waltzed in, past the mad throng of people, after making sure my ride was safely tucked away, sandwiched between a bright yellow H2 and a midnight-black 740il. I had decided to dress down tonight, opting out of my normal fly attire—slick designer suit and power tie that are my trade-mark—instead going casual: brown suede pants that were hand-made for a brutha, a silk print shirt open halfway down my chest, and lizard boots the color of an African desert. Oh yeah, y'all, I was looking *funky fresh*, ya heard me, not at all like the high-priced divorce attorney that I am—but that was the whole idea. It was a Saturday night, and I was in the mood to play—Trey in Play, y'all. Grrrrr!

I found Quentin on one of the upper floors, VIP section of course, look-ing dapper in his well-tailored suit, sipping on Hennessy and toting a fat Cuban. These niggas crack me the fuck up—they all smoke cigars like they invented the shit, acting all serious like they're connoisseurs—please! You know damn well not one of them bruthas knows a humidor from a matador! Believe that!

"Yo what's up, Mr. Clean?" Q. yelled in a loud, boisterous voice while eyeing my threads. Around him the music swirled, *Clipse* belting out their latest jam, and not more than six feet away was some hip-hop producer extraordinaire whose name escapes me, lounging on a velvet couch surrounded by honeys and video hoes, looking exactly the way he does in his music videos. I gave Q. a hug as I shouted above the thumping sounds.

"Happy birthday, my brutha, how ya livin'?"

"Sheeit! You know how we do! Check you out," he said, grasping my silk shirt gingerly. "Dayum, bitches gonna lose their mind up in here when they see your shit!"

I grinned as I palmed my bald head. It felt as smooth as a baby's ass. "Q., dawg, you *know* how we do. I'm gonna handle my business, just like I know you will handle yours...it's what us bruthas gotta do!" Quentin grinned while pulling me toward the couch to introduce me to the producer. I shook hands with the man, nodded to the girls to his left and his right even though no one moved to tell me their name. That was cool—I wasn't trying to mess with brutha man's stable.

"So, you're Q.'s lawyer?" he asked me as he laid down a joint in an onyx ashtray on the coffee table where his legs were crossed. He wore baggy jeans, an oversized Phillies jersey, and white Air Force Ones. He eyed me curiously from under his Phillies baseball cap.

"That's right."

He pushed one of the honeys off the couch—gave her a slight nudge as he leaned in and whispered in her ear—a lovely thing, young, Latino, with big tits that glistened under the house lights, and a succulent ass barely contained in low ride jeans. He motioned for me to sit.

"Yeah, your boy's been telling me about his legal shit. I sure hope you can hook a brutha up. "

"Yeah, well, I'm gonna take real good care of Q. No worries." I grinned at Quentin who pointed at me for a split second before hooking the waist of some honey who giggled as she was reeled in. The Latino chick retuned with a brandy snifter half filled with Hennessy. She handed it to me silently. I grinned and mouthed a "thank you" to her.

"Word," the producer said while taking a deep drag on his joint. We chatted for a few minutes about what he was up to—he had just returned from Brazil where he had shot a video with the various rappers and hip-hop artists whom he was working with. I asked him about the biz and which celebrities he had spotted up in here tonight.

Moving on, I sashayed through the crowd, grinning to women as I glided by. A lot of folks I knew or at a minimum had seen before—if you socialize as much as I do, you can't help but run into the same mutha fuckas day in and day out. It's like that in this town. I made small talk with many of the players—Jordan, Stackhouse, Dixon, Laettner, Sprewell, Harrington; paying my respects, you know, I pick up a lot of business by mingling with these cats—it was all about networking, and if your shit was good (and y'all know mine is tight), then folks are gonna talk. I don't care who you are—black, white, rich or poor, sooner or later, you're all going to need a divorce lawyer.

Heading downstairs to the main level, I moved past the main bar, scoping out the talent—I was determined to get some pussy tonight—it had been a few days and the pipes needed to be flushed...I needed to be cleansed. But not one to rush things, I make sure I check the place out first, see who is there, and more importantly, let them see me in all of my glory. I grabbed the hand of some unsuspecting female and led her to the dance floor silently. Did my thing out there moving my body like it was a serpent—all sensuous-like, letting them know that a brutha could move. She was grinning from ear to ear as we danced to the new Snoop cut, and I could see out of the corner of my eye that people were talking about me. Oh yeah— let the hushed conversations begin—"who's that?—Oh, I hear he's some big-time attorney—look at him prancing around here like he owns this damn place—yeah girl, but he *is* fine, look at him—and I bet he can get us into VIP—shush—here he comes, maybe he'll ask *me* to dance!"

An hour later I was sweaty from shaking my stuff on the dance floor. I had pocketed four cards from various honeys—not bad—one every fifteen minutes—a bit slow for me, but hey, the night was still young. Besides, I wasn't ready to leave with anyone yet. So, I bid farewell to my latest dance partner, told her I'd give her a call next week to do lunch, and headed back upstairs to VIP where it was less crowded, and the big ballers played...

I spotted a low couch that was being shared by two women. I took the corner edge after freshening up my drink, and made small talk with them. One was a Wizards dancer. She was short and squat but had a killer body in her skin-tight polyester black pants and wife beater. The other, her friend, a tall statuesque redbone "model" from New York was clad in a pair of smart tan slacks, matching boots, and an off-white top that fit her torso to a T. It seemed that everybody was a model these days—I swear, every other woman I met nowadays did some kind of modeling. Well, that was cool with me. They both were fine as hell, so Trey here had no problem resting his ass with them for a minute. They were asking me about what I did, and that got us into a conversation about high-profile divorce cases—I was sharing with them some juicy stories from around the water cooler—and they were starstruck, just sitting there listening to a brutha talk casually about some well-known people who were going through some nasty shit, courtesy of their spouses.

Off to the right, something caught my eye. It was less the movement than the splash of color on this fine-ass frame that caught my attention—I glanced up, in mid-conversation with the lovely ladies, and had to pause in what I was saying. It took me a split second to look her over—her fine, chiseled features; perfect skin, shiny hair done in a thin braided ponytail that went halfway down her back, a pair of tight trousers that were an explosion of color: red, blue, indigo, and green—a kaleidoscope that shone off her package like a beacon—and a loose fitting white top with a plunging neckline that was worn midriff. Topped off by a pierced navel that sparkled and looked sexy as hell. This chick looked like a piece of mouth-watering candy, gliding along on pointy toed boots, with her three girl-friends in tow. Aponi Hues, Quentin's soon-to-be ex-wife had just made her grand entrance. Looking like she owned this spot, looking like she damn well belonged, which she damn well did *not*!

"Uh-oh," I said in a low voice to the redbone honey model who had her wrist leisurely hovering along my thigh. She stroked me absentmindedly as she leaned in, hooked on every bit of wisdom I was imparting this particular evening. I had already decided that I was going to take this honey home and fuck the living shit out of her, just as soon as I finished my drink. But just as I spotted Aponi everything changed. I glanced around searching for Quentin. I knew he would not be amused. Aponi's grin said it all as she waltzed in past a dozen players who eyed her with disdain—they knew exactly who she was and what she was up to. Aponi was here to fuck with a brutha, on his birthday, no less.

Dayum—things were about to get ugly up in this piece...

"What's wrong?" The redbone, whose name eluded me, whispered in a harried voice—names come and go with me—they stream in my ears and head right back out again unscathed. Her hand had ceased to pet my suede-covered thigh. I gingerly patted her hand and moved it closer to my crotch as my stare locked with hers—she read my meaning loud and clear.

"Nothing to be alarmed by, darling," I said, all debonair-like. "Don't look now, but the birthday boy's ex just walked in, and knowing Quentin the way I do—he's a client—he's gonna be none too pleased."

"Ouch," she replied, leaning into me, letting me feel the warmth and fullness of her breasts. My hand snaked from her knee to her inner thigh and squeezed as we nuzzled up against one another. I was getting hard quick, and my mind and pulse raced—delicious images sprinted through my psyche as I planned the culmination to this redbone's seduction. I would fuck this honey on my dining room table. Yeah…*Tonight*. I'd splay her legs over my shoulders while kneading her nipples in one hand and fingering her clit with the other.

But I couldn't fantasize in peace. Off to my left I spied Quentin talking to a female, glancing down at her sweetness and licking his lips as he would in anticipation of a juicy New York strip—I watched him at the exact moment that he spotted Aponi—saw as his words died on his lips, his mouth down-turned into a frown as he set his drink down—the woman whom had hung on every word a moment ago suddenly forgotten. He left her standing there without a second thought and breezed past me, the anger boiling in his veins.

"Uh-oh," I repeated, setting my own drink down on the coffee table in front of me as I smoothed out my pants and readjusted my erection. "I need to go handle this—don't go anywhere, Precious—okay?" Redbone looked at her friend who just shrugged.

Aponi was moving toward Quentin as if he didn't exist. She casually threw her head back and laughed at something one of her friends had said as she neared. I stood up, calling Quentin's name as he made a beeline for his wife. I could see his hands clench and knew there was about to be trouble. I heard him address Aponi above the drone of the music even though I was ten yards behind him.

"Who the fuck let you in?" Quentin bellowed to Aponi who brushed past him like he was a mere annoyance. One of his teammates had reached Q. before me and was tugging on his arm, begging him to back off. Quentin just shooed him away as if he were a fly. When Aponi didn't answer he stepped in front of her, blocking her way. Before anyone could react, he had placed his hands on her shoulder blades, pushing her sharply back.

"This is my party, *bitch*, and nobody invited your ass!" he hissed. Aponi smacked his hands away, her face turning into a snarl.

"Boy, you better get your big ass outta my face before I have you arrested, mutha fucka." Her friends were by her side raising their manicured fingers into his face. "I've got as much right to be here as any of these hos," she quipped, flipping her hand up into the air. She looked Quentin up and down before sidestepping him and bumping into a woman whose drink went crashing to the floor.

"Bitch, watch it!" the woman hissed, but backed away, not wanting to be in the direct line of fire. Aponi didn't have time to turn and react before Quentin had grabbed his wife by the hair and yanked *hard*, pulling her head to the side as if she were some sort of ragdoll. Aponi screamed, as all hell broke loose. Hands and fists started to fly, and bodies were pushed as I reached Quentin and grabbed his hand, yelling for him to calm down. He released Aponi's hair as he eyed me, a terrible snarl that had replaced his normally sedate face. His wife's hand, or someone else's hand, reached up and slapped Quentin across his face. I heard the report and watched in shock as his head flew back from the force. I maneuvered myself in between Aponi and her ex—feeling her body pressed against me as I struggled to keep Quentin from beating the shit out of his own wife—and going to jail for assault and battery.

Several of his teammates were successful in pulling him backwards, but not without a great deal of effort—I've got to say this—when a brutha is pissed, it takes a whole *village* to calm him down—that's no lie. And Q-Dawg was pissed as hell. Having his ex interrupt his party was one big-ass mistake.

I used the moment to grab Aponi by the arm and lead her away from Quentin. Her girls were all in my face now, yelling for me to get off of her.

"Hey!" I yelled to get their attention, "I'm a fucking attorney, Quentin's attorney in case you don't recognize me." This got Aponi's attention but quick. She stopped her struggle, ceased wiggling beside me in an attempt to escape my grasp as I led her through a hallway and into another room. Folks parted for me as if I were Moses. "Calm down, Mrs. Hues, just calm on down," I said to her once I could see she was regaining her composure. She kept glancing behind us, her stare wide-eyed. She was genuinely terrified—this I knew with one hundred percent certainty. It was as if the thought of Quentin, all six-foot-six, 235 pounds, lunging at his own wife who was at best 98 pounds when *wet*, never entered her mind until a split second ago.

"You've got to get out of here—you hear me?" I said, close to her ear as I continued to grip her by the elbow. "It's not safe," I added as I locked stares with her. "Get your girls to take you home now."

Aponi was shaking her head as I led her down the back stairwell. "Naw, me and my girls just got here—besides, they've been talking about this party for over a week." She glanced over her shoulder as her friends followed us down. There was chatter between them that was lost on me.

"Well, you can't stay here—I'm serious. Quentin is sure to follow and I don't think I can control him when he's this upset." We had rounded a landing and stopped for a moment so Aponi could catch her breath. Her girls were on her, hands at her back and hair, asking if she was okay. Aponi shrugged them away, bent down and started to cry. I looked at the girls helplessly.

"Can't you take her home?" I asked the one closest to me.

"It's her car—ask her," she replied, gesturing to the other. That one was fidgeting like a junkie, and I could tell she had no intentions of leaving any time soon. Aponi glanced up, wiped the tears away with the back of her hand, and centered her gaze on me.

"That mutha fucka's gonna pay for grabbing me. Believe that!" My heart began to plummet as she reached for her cell phone and punched in 911. I snatched the phone from her before she could complete the call.

"Fuck it, " I said, as much to myself as anyone else. I reached for Aponi and lifted her up. Her mascara was smeared and she wiped at the corner of one eye with a finger, making it worse. I smiled to her sheepishly, thinking to myself, she still looked fucking good, even though she just had gotten a beat-down. "Listen to me, Mrs. Hues—you are not going to call the cops. Not here and not now. You are going to get out of this club and go home where you can think about your own actions first." I led her to a fire door that warned of alarms and fines if opened in anything other than an emergency. I turned to her friends who remained by the bottom stairwell. "Y'all can go back to the party. I'll take Mrs. Hues home. We need to talk anyway about the legal ramifications of what she just did." I eyed Aponi seriously as I said this, her stare locked on mine, but saying nothing. I was lying my ass off as only Trey can do—hey, that's why I'm so good at what I do, and get paid the big bucks—I knew damn well that my words were baseless—Aponi had done nothing wrong. She definitely suffered from the disease known as poor judgment, but hey, so did a lot of folks these days. Besides, poor judgment wasn't against the law, last time I checked.

Her friends conversed with Aponi as I watched. She was okay, she knew they wanted to stay; she was no longer *feeling* this place and needed to get out. Yeah, she'd be cool with me. They looked me up and down as I shrugged.

For my part, I was pissed. Not only had I just given up some seriously fine pussy, but I didn't even know the honey's name or number. Damn! I thought about running back up there, leaving Aponi alone for a moment, but knew that wouldn't do. Quentin was upstairs, he would spot me immediately, would demand to know where Aponi was. I wasn't ready to deal with Q. yet—not until I talked to Aponi, and calmed her down. Going to the police and filing charges were the absolute last things my client needed right now. His dumb black ass knew not just how much trouble he was in…

✖✖✖

I placed my hand on the cold steel of the emergency exit door, sucked in a breath and pushed…

Nothing. No sound, no alarm.

It figures, I thought as I took Aponi's arm and ran down the darkened alley toward the lights of the street. We reached the sidewalk, cut left, slowed to a brisk walk as I stopped dead in my tracks.

"Shit."

"What?" Aponi asked, staring up at me.

"My car—it's back the other way—in front of the fucking club."

My mind raced. I searched left, then right, trying to make a decision.

"Stay here," I commanded. "Let me run and get the car—I'll be back in a flash. Don't leave, Mrs. Hues—we need to talk."

"Fine, but stop calling me Mrs. Hues—that's the last thing I want to be called."

I returned five minutes later, having to drive completely around the block since the street where Aponi was standing was one-way. She remained in the shadows until I honked the horn. She ran to the passenger side door of the M3 and got in.

"Nice ride," she remarked as I fell into late-night traffic.

"Okay," I said, willing myself to calm down from the rising anger I felt at this woman for interrupting for me what was destined to be a sure fucking thing. *Literally...*

"Where to?"

Aponi was quiet for a moment, her gaze staring straight ahead. "Hello?" I said, "Where to? We can't just ride around all night." Actually we could, but I wasn't a freaking babysitter—that's the last thing I had counted on this Saturday night.

"I don't know—I can't go back to the hotel. Quentin knows where I'm staying. He'll come there for sure. I know him." I could see the fear in her eyes as she glanced at me. I swallowed hard. *Great*, I thought to myself. *Trey tries to be the nice guy and look where it gets him.*

"Look, I'm sure things will be fine. Let me drop you off there, I'll give him a call on the cell, talk to him, explain that the last thing he wants to do is come to the hotel and confront you." Aponi was shaking her head.

"Shit, you don't know Q. He's beyond reason when he's upset. You saw the look on his face; you saw how he tried to kill me!"

"Mrs. Hues—Aponi, please. Quentin isn't trying to kill anyone—he's pissed because you showed up to his party, unannounced and clearly uninvited. That's wasn't a particularly smart thing to do considering the allegations of infidelity you've lobbed at him." Aponi jerked her body around in the seat and squared off at me.

"You've got to be kidding me—my husband's fucking hos in my own home, *our* home, and his dumb ass puts the shit on tape. You don't think I have a right to fuck with him by going to his party? Shit, if he didn't want me to show up, he should've had it at a private location, and not announced the shit on KYS-FM!"

She had a point there.

"Okay—listen, Quentin is not trying to hurt you. I know this. I know Q. He's upset and rightfully so. This is a very bad time for both of you," I said, my mind jumping to Allison Matthews and what she would say if she found out that I was with her client "unsupervised." "You need to take a step back, Quentin, too, regroup, think about what you want and what you are planning to do. My counsel to you, as an attorney, is to do nothing rash— think long and hard about your actions before you involve the police or the legal system because you may regret the outcome."

I was trying to sound all legalese and scare her. The thing was, Aponi was already scared, and royally pissed off to boot! A dangerous combination…

"So," I said, softly, as I made a right onto Constitution, not knowing where to take her. "Where's your hotel?

"Four Seasons, but we're not going there. I'm telling you that right now!"

Aponi's chest heaved as my eyes flickered quickly over her delectable form. There she was: sitting all snug in my tight ride, breath all harried, hair out of place, and makeup in need of serious refresh, but looking so damn sensuous that I felt a wave of pleasure course down my back and shoot for my legs. I sighed deeply as I cut a right onto 17th Street and headed for my crib…

TWENTY-SEVEN

In the less than ten minutes that it took me to drive to my condo, I weighed the pros and cons of fucking Aponi. I was still very horny—I mean, my shit had been interrupted literally moments before I was ready to make my move—take that redbone home and give her some *Trey Steak*, you know, the kind that comes with the special sauce (and I'm not talking A-1), or better yet, not even wait until we made it to my crib—no, take her ass by the hand, head to the nearest bathroom where once in a stall I'd pull them panties down by my teeth and fuck her doggie style—think I wouldn't?

Instead I found myself babysitting my client's ex—a fine piece of ass, no doubt, but to make matters worse, the client of the attorney I had just recently fucked. Not good...on the other hand, look how fine she was, sequestered in the soft leather of my M3, obviously enjoying the ride and her knight in shining fucking armor, that being *moi*. No, this is a mistake, I'd already gone too far with Allison, and this could spell trouble. Yeah, but look at it this way—SHIT! My dick was calling the shots here, and under normal circumstances that would be okey-doke with me—but tonight things were getting thicker by the moment. For real!

Damn, damn, dayum!

That's what Aponi said as she crossed the threshold and saw my crib for the first time. That's what I whispered as I followed her sexy black ass into my condo.

"Your place is off the heazy," she said, awestruck like a teenager. "You must be making mad cheddar as a lawyer. I hope you are charging the shit out of my lame-ass husband."

"I'm doing okay," I said awkwardly as I smiled, flashing her my white teeth. "Come in and make yourself comfortable," I said, closing the door behind us. She moved into the sunken living room and squatted on the couch, leaning back, showing me those perky young breasts. Her taut nipples were visible under her top. "I have to tell you," I said, "I don't think this is a particularly good idea, you coming here, seeing how your husband is my client, and your attorney won't be pleased." I was both hoping she'd take the hint and leave, but also stay. *Well, at least I made the disclaimer, for the record*, I told myself.

"You got anything to drink up in this piece?" she asked as she threw off her shoes, and folded her legs underneath her, making herself right at home. I returned a moment later with two glasses and a fifth of Johnnie Walker Black. Pouring two fingers, I handed her a glass and raised mine to hers.

"What are we drinking to?" she asked, and then continued, "Oh, I know, how about to niggas who fuck with mutha fuckas and get theirs in the end."

"Mmmn, I was thinking something a bit less...I don't know...*violent* sounding..."

Aponi shrugged and tipped the glass to her lips. I followed, silently. The liquor stung, and if I were smart, I would have realized that it was serving as a warning to me—of things to come—uncomfortable things—but you know my dumb ass didn't pay attention to the signs. I just let the hot liquid shoot down my throat and warm my belly as I eyed Aponi from a few feet away, the way she glanced my way as she drank, her initial serious stare replaced by one of devilish intent. I sighed, thinking things were about to heat up if I didn't take control...

"You know what, Aponi, it's getting late," I said, checking my watch, noting the time. It was close to 2 a.m. "It's been a long evening for both of us. I suggest we get some sleep. I've got a spare bedroom you can sleep in. Why don't we turn in and we can talk in the morning when both of our heads are clear."

"I don't know what you're talking about," Aponi said, downing the last of her drink and reaching for the bottle, pouring herself another one. "I'm feeling fine—my head is clear. Don't know about you…" she said as she took another swig.

"Okay, cool." I finished my drink in one gulp and reached for the bottle, pouring another myself. This little young thang wasn't gonna show me up in my own crib! Oh hell no!

"You don't look like a lawyer," Aponi said, eyeing me curiously.

"How so?"

"Check out your dress—suede pants, those boots—please! You look more like a model or a playa to me." Aponi smirked and I smiled back.

"I guess I should take that as a compliment." I could see her eyes were beginning to glaze over. Her fingernails were tracing circular patterns along her thigh. The movement was not lost on me. The battle raged within me—should I or shouldn't I? I was having trouble deciding. And Aponi wasn't making it any easier. I felt myself lengthening inside of my pants with every breath I drew, and I reveled at the sensation. This was a dangerous game I was playing, right? I took another sip and lost my train of thought as I swallowed hard.

I stood up and stretched, downing the rest of my drink. Aponi watched me silently. "Let me get you something to sleep in. A tee shirt or jersey," I said, heading for the spiral staircase. "The spare bedroom is right down that hallway," I said, pointing toward the opposite side of the room. "There's also a spare toothbrush and other toiletries that you might need in the bathroom next to the bedroom. Be right back," I said as I climbed the stairs. Aponi followed my movement but said nothing. I felt my pulse quicken as a thousand different scenarios raced through my head. The redbone was gone. Replaced by a young half-Indian, half-black vision of loveliness that fucked with me without even uttering a word. I reached the top step, sighed deeply, still undecided as I moved out of sight.

✖✖✖

Once inside the confines of my bedroom, away from the chick that was messing with a brutha like it was going out of style, I reached for one of my many jerseys and came to a decision. As I held the garment between my hands, looking at the colors, New York's colors, stuffing that one away and grabbing another, the purple and gold of Miami Heat, I decided, right then and there, to leave Aponi alone. For once I was going to think with my head—the big one; not the little one—and do the right thing. I was gonna leave it alone. As horny as I was, and let me tell you, I reached down and gave the big guy a squeeze; I swear to God I thought I heard him groan, I shook my head sadly. With resignation written all over my mug, I realized that in a few moments I'd be back here jerking off, while a lovely goddess lay one floor beneath me, her perfect body untouched by age and imperfection. But this was what was best. I knew that. Knew it from the moment I spied her at Home, knew it from the moment she slid into my phat ride. Leave the shit alone, I decided, before things got out of control and all fucked up.

I glanced at myself in the mirror to the right of my oversized bed, patted the package, *my* package, and winced as I felt it full of life. I sighed heavily as I moved out of my bedroom to return to Aponi.

✖✖✖

I was at the top of the winding staircase and preparing to step down when I glanced toward the couch. Aponi wasn't there. I paused. Felt my heart skip a beat. Where was she?

Glancing over the railing, I searched the living room area (not there), the dining area (not there) and the entrance to the kitchen (doubtful she would be there). I took a step down, paused again, and called out her name.

No answer.

I called her again.

I caught the movement below me, behind the interconnections of wrought iron. I stared downward, toward the junction of living room and hallway, and saw her glide into view. She was totally nude, her fine body shining with the glow usually reserved for angels or queens. I kid you not—

I hadn't seen anything that close to perfection in a long, long time. Her hair had been wet down and rebraided. Her breasts were perfect round orbs of loveliness with taut dark nipples that were already distended. The smudge of mascara was gone. My eyes roamed downward to her sex, which was shaved clean, save for a pencil-thin line that ran straight down to her pussy. Aponi glanced up at me. Our eyes locked, the stare unwavering. I was speechless. She, too, said not a word. She drew in a breath; I watched her breasts rise as she did so. Then she spoke.

"I don't need anything to sleep in."

I nodded silently, the garment falling from my hand effortlessly. It floated down to the floor below me.

"Trey," she began, nothing moving save for the rise and fall of her chest from her breathing, "let's stop this charade. Temptation has been with me all my life, but I stuck to my vows, as a wife should, even when my husband disrespected me in my own house." She glanced down at herself for a moment, hands down by her sides as she lost herself in silent thought. "I did what I was raised to do. But that ends tonight. I'm no longer Mrs. Hues, Trey. I'm no longer married to *him*."

Aponi took a step forward into the light, and the totality of her loveliness consumed me in a single gulp.

"Tonight I get what's been missing for a long, long time," she whispered, glancing up at me with a seductive smile. My heart was beating so fast I thought it would short-circuit my insides. "Tonight I get what's mine…"

✖✖✖

"Okay, one last time, Quentin," I said, eying him over the steaming mug of coffee as I sat on the couch in my office. Quentin Hues sat across from me, the rage from the weekend's affair long gone, replaced by a look of anxiety. I checked the Breitling and saw we had three minutes left. "I'm telling you for the last time, I want you to walk in there, sit down quietly, study the grain in the conference table, and not say a fucking thing…you hear me?"

"Yeah."

"Quentin—you have a lot to lose. Your wife could walk in here this morning and charge you with assault. I doubt that's going to happen—I talked to her Saturday evening and hopefully got through to her. But you know you fucked up. Fucked up bad. Now, it's time to put this behind you and move on. You're a ball player, at the top of you game. Don't let this thing bring you down. Are you listening to me?"

Quentin tipped his head up and sighed. "Yeah, Trey, I hear you."

"I sure hope so. Q.—let me handle my business. Okay—your job is to sit there and not say shit. We're going to dispense with the settlement agreement this morning and get the hell out of there. Agreed?"

"Yeah."

I stood, smoothed over my tie and buttoned my jacket. "Let's go," I said as I put down my coffee mug and headed for the door.

✖✖✖

Allison Matthews turned from the oversized window when we came through the door. She was not amused to see either one of us.

The scowl on her face shone like a searchlight.

I said "good morning" to her and she returned what sounded like a grunt.

Aponi Hues was sitting at the opposite end of the conference room table, same as before, dressed conservatively with her hair pulled back. Her hands were folded in front of her on the table, and she looked so damn good just sitting there, like fresh sunlight that warms your skin. I tried not to focus on her, but I couldn't help it. My eyes roamed over her face, lingering for a moment as thoughts from Saturday night invaded my mind. She stared back at me and smiled.

I sat quickly to hide my growing erection.

"Mrs. Hues," I said, making quick eye contact with her before turning my attention to her counsel. Allison cleared her throat and began.

"I trust this won't take very long, gentlemen, since I'm sure we all have better things to do." Allison's cold stare attacked me as these words wafted from her lips.

I wanted this over and quick. But I was having trouble concentrating. My mind raced—wondering if she *knew*.

Did Allison know?

Scenes from Saturday night invaded my brain and I was powerless to stop them.

Aponi, her lovely caramel breasts hovering inches from my face as I devoured them, one delicious inch at a time.

Those hard nipples, that elicited squeals when I pinched them.

The way she lay on my bed, head turned back as she watched me work, and the single slow lick beginning at the crack of her crescent-shaped ass, traveling downward until I tasted her sugary core.

The way she licked my balls and tugged on my shaft until I came.

The way we did it, over and over again until we were both sore...

Allison's words snapped me back to reality. "My client has made me aware of recent events that transpired this past weekend. These events concern *everyone* in this room."

Oh shit...

Allison continued. "The fact that Mr. Hues has assaulted my client, his wife, in public, is inexcusable and, frankly, counselor..."

"Ms. Matthews," I said, "let me..."

"Excuse me," Allison exclaimed, interrupted me, her ice-cold stare cutting deep, "I believe I have the floor. As I was saying, your client's behavior is inexcusable and against the law. There is no excuse for this kind of behavior and I am not interested in entertaining one. Are we clear?" Allison didn't wait for an answer.

"My client has further informed me that if it wasn't for the fast actions of counselor Alexander here, who knows what further harm may have come to her. For that, Mr. Alexander, we are grateful."

I did a slow exhale.

"*However*, let me be clear—your behavior, *counselor*, in terms of advising my client was less than professional. You should have called me, regardless of the hour, since she is my client, not yours."

I nodded silently.

"We could press charges this very morning; I hope you have made Mr. Hues aware of this fact."

"I have, Ms. Matthews."

"Good. We have decided not to. We will move forward and put this unfortunate business behind us. Agreed?"

"Yes." Quentin looked up and nodded. He quickly dropped his head back down.

"Mr. Hues, look at me, because I want there to be no misunderstanding on this point—if you ever lay a hand of my client again, I will personally make it my life's work to see you incarcerated for a very long time. Do I make myself clear?"

Quentin cleared his throat and said, "Yes, ma'am."

"Good." Allison smiled, pulled two documents from a manila folder, separated them, and slid them across the shiny surface to Quentin and me. "A revised copy of the settlement agreement, the terms that Mr. Alexander and I discussed last week. I trust you will find that everything is in order."

I scanned the multi-page document and told Allison to give me a moment to read it. I glanced right; Quentin stared at the table as ordered; I then snuck a peek left—Aponi watched me and smiled. I turned my head back to the document as Allison's stare alternated between Aponi and me. I felt my temperature begin to rise.

I read on. So far everything looked as we had discussed.

Cool. A few more minutes and then we could leave this room that had suddenly become very stuffy...

I finished reading the settlement agreement. Everything that we had discussed and agreed to was there. I nodded to Allison, then slid the non-disclosure agreement I had drawn up over to her for her review and signature.

The CD-ROM, the one featuring Hues & Ho in their debut perform-ance, was turned over to me.

There was silence as all parties completed the signing of documents.

Allison put down her pen and stood up. "That's it then."

"Yes," I said, relieved that this meeting was over.

She didn't know...

Thank you, Lord!

Aponi stood, walked over to me and took my hand. I shook it as we both smiled. There was a sparkle in her eyes. My heart was beating, and I wondered if Allison could hear the sound. Aponi brushed past Quentin without a word. I turned to leave, but Allison stopped me.

"A word, counselor?"

"Of course. Quentin, could you wait outside for a moment?" Quentin stood and exited the room silently. I shut the conference room door and faced Allison.

"Come here, Trey," Allison gestured. I maneuvered around the huge table, wondering if Allison was planning on giving me a kiss or another tongue-lashing. I walked up to her and gave her my best Trey-smile. That's when her hand flew up and smacked me dead in my face. HARD. The report seemed deafening.

"You son of a *bitch*," Allison hissed at me as I held my cheek in hand. "You think I don't know what you did with my client—your client's wife. You *fucked* her, Trey—I know it as sure as I am standing here."

I was stunned into silence. I reeled back, my mouth opened in shock, but nothing, no words or sounds emerged.

"As an attorney, I am astounded that you would blatantly violate the ethical behavior that as a lawyer you swore to uphold." Allison leaned in to me. "And, as a woman, the very same woman who shared her body with you not more than a week ago, Trey, I am aghast; no, that word doesn't do justice to the way I feel right now." Allison reached up and grabbed her hair with both fists. Her eyes were mere slits. "You have no fucking idea how this makes me feel. I can't even…" She paused, wrung her hands tightly, and looked as if she were readying to beat them against my chest. I moved back, out of range.

"You know what—fuck it, Trey." She grabbed her things and straightened her jacket. Allison sidestepped me and headed for the door. Her footfalls echoed loudly. As she rounded the table she stopped, spun on her heels and nearly lunged back to where I was standing by the window. Her trembling finger found my face.

"If you ever touch my client again or even get close enough to *breathe* the same air as she, I swear to fucking God I will take this matter to the D.C. Bar. I'll make sure you never practice law in this town again."

"Allison," I said, my hands coming up in self-defense, "let me…"

"NO, Trey!" Allison quipped, shutting me down, but quick.

"And if you even think about uttering a single word to me ever again, I'll…" she said, jabbing her fingers into my chest. "I know this—I won't be responsible for my actions…"

Allison moved quickly to the door.

"I thought I was getting to know you," she said, her voice lowered as her hand rested on the doorframe. "I thought I caught a glimpse of the kind of human being you were, but you know what? You're not even human," Allison whispered before exiting the room.

"You're a snake, Trey," I heard her say as the Peace Room door slammed, reverberating in my ears. "Nothing more than a fucking *snake*!"

I looked down at the floor, dejected. I was losing steam, like a deflating balloon. My head throbbed and my face, well, it hurt like hell. I heard the door open, and looked up, expecting to see Quentin Hues. Instead, Bernard John Marshall walked in, a smirk painted on his face.

"Judging from those choice words from opposing counsel," he said, a smug tone to his voice, "not to mention that handprint on your face, my assumption is that things aren't going too well…"

TWENTY-EIGHT

The monotony of repetitive motion from the Elliptical Trainer was soothing. Vince's legs were moving rapidly, knees rising up and down as he pumped his arms in time to the music in his ears, a DMX CD. He had begun with something a bit more mellow—some smooth jazz he had brought along, but the jazz just wasn't cutting it. Not now—he needed something with "in-your-face" lyrics and hard-hitting drum and bass hooks—DMX *delivered...*

Vince thumbed the volume until his ears hurt. Ignoring the pain, he wiped the sweat that popped from his brow with a forearm and increased the pace of his workout.

Fuck the pain. I need this...

Vince still couldn't believe it—was it a dream? Was what he had witnessed real? For a moment he closed his eyes and thought hard, as if the action would somehow erase what was etched into his retinas and his mind— Angeliqué in the arms of a woman—kissing her the way she had done to him...

Vince shook his head in disgust and moved faster against the rising strain in his chest.

No, this was no dream.

What he had observed was real.

Vince had watched for no more than several seconds—feeling the earth under his feet begin to heave. He dropped the carnations, partly due to the need to reach out to steady himself, partly because the fragrant flowers suddenly felt heavy and alien in his hand.

Vince had turned on his heels, sucked in a breath as he moved away from the courtyard entrance, increasing his pace until he was sprinting like he was back in college. How he made it back to the hotel was a mystery. But he did.

And here he was, going on sixty minutes on the machine, feeling as if his lungs were on fire, but not caring, as if sweating out the pain would somehow make what he was feeling go away.

But it didn't.

Nor did it make the image fade from his mind's eye.

That scene was locked in his psyche and not going anywhere soon.

Thirty minutes later, he stumbled off the Trainer, gulped down four cups of water and toweled off his face. He returned to his hotel room where he showered and then sat on the bed unable to contemplate his next move.

What to do?

Vince experienced a variety of emotions, from raw, uncut anger to intense hurt. He stared at his cell phone, a million thoughts traversing his cortex— should he call? No, definitely not. At this point he had nothing to say.

This surely wouldn't work—"Hey baby, you're not gonna believe this, but I was in the area and decided to stop by—guess what I saw?"

No.

Perhaps he should call home—speak to his boy, Trey.

Nope. Trey would only make light of the situation—"Damn, dawg, if it was me, I'd bum-rush the both of them and bend one over while making the other lick my balls..."

Perhaps, Erika—he dialed her number but hung up when it went straight to voice mail. She probably was working tonight. Besides, he wasn't sure he was ready to talk with her or anybody else right now.

His stomach began to grind—checking his watch, Vince saw that it was coming up on 10 pm. He was famished.

Ten p.m. on a Friday night in the Big Easy...alone...

So much for surprising his woman.

Vince snatched up the phone with a heavy sigh, and ordered room service before he made himself sick.

✖✖✖

Vince awoke at 7. He tried to sleep in, attempted to roll onto his side, squeeze his eyes shut and make the pain and hurt go away, at least for another hour more, but it didn't work like that. He lay there instead, staring up at the pattern etched in the ceiling for close to forty-five minutes before he cursed out loud and got up.

The first thing he did was call the airlines. He changed his return flight to later on that afternoon, a 2 p.m. departure. That was the earliest non-stop out of this town; Vince wasn't in the mood to fly to Atlanta or Charlotte and sit around in a terminal waiting on a connecting flight. So he put the charge on his AMEX Blue and hung up the phone.

Next he threw on a pair of sweats and a tattered Howard University tee shirt, and ran for an hour. The Quarter was miraculously empty this time of morning. Vince headed for the river, past stone churches, an open square that was home to several hundred pigeons, closed restaurants, and antique shops. A few folks were out enjoying the air. Vince neither eyed nor spoke to any of them—he ran to clear his head and his heart. For twenty minutes or so, it worked.

Returning to the hotel, Vince showered and changed into a pair of jeans, a light sweater, and a comfortable pair of Nikes. Grabbing some breakfast at the hotel restaurant downstairs, he contemplated his next move before making up his mind. Glancing at his watch, he saw he had enough time.

He quickly packed his clothes—actually stuffing them back into the garment bag was more like it. That took fifteen minutes. Vince was back on the street, showered, clothed and fed, and ready to do what he needed to do by 10:30.

He arrived at her residence fifteen minutes later. The street was as quiet as it had been the night before. The gallery was closed, and the wrought-iron gate to the courtyard was shut and locked. Vince peered into the gallery window, saw no signs of activity, and without fanfare rang the bell.

It took about five minutes for the door to be answered. He saw the gray sweats and the Saints jersey before he could make out her face. She came to the door, squinted through the glass as she brushed the hair from her eyes. Recognition lit up her face as the door swung open.

"Vince?"

It was Amber.

He smiled weakly, sensing again that they had met someplace before. "Hey you—ummn, Amber, how are you? I hope I didn't wake you?"

"Well," Amber replied, looking past him skyward before returning his gaze with her own, "actually, I was sleeping, but it's cool—what time is it anyway?"

"Almost eleven."

"Oh, well, it's Sunday—girls are allowed to sleep in on Sundays, ya know what I mean?" Amber smiled and Vince felt his apprehension decrease a notch.

"Listen, is Angeliqué around? I was hoping to speak to her, ummn, for just a moment." Vince shook his head slightly, knowing his words weren't on point as they usually were.

Amber eyed him curiously. "Wow—you know—she's not here. She—ah, left a while ago. That's a drag that you missed her. I can't believe you're here, Vince. You really should've called to tell us you were in town." Amber smiled as he shifted uneasily on his feet. Amber sensed his discomfort when he didn't respond immediately. "Hey, is everything okay?" she asked, touching his forearm. Vince stared down at his sneakers for a moment, deciding how best to answer the question. "You want to come in?" Amber asked. "I can throw on some coffee. You look like you could use a cup."

Amber reached out for Vince's arm, and guided him gently inside.

✖✖✖

The scent of coffee was strong. Vince took a moment to shut his eyes and inhale the sweet scent, letting it invade his body and still him. He took a sip and savored the hot liquid as it warmed his insides. Amber was facing him.

They sat in the first-floor dining room, a large art-filled room facing the courtyard. Sunlight streamed in creating bright diagonals on hardwood floors. A gray Siamese cat stretched—as she eyed the visitor curiously.

"So, Vince Cannon, Jr., famous author, philosopher, and motivator, what brings you to our fair city?" Amber asked, setting the mug into her palms.

Vince was silent as he watched the cat move. He took another sip before responding. "Well, I was hoping to surprise Angeliqué." Vince paused, seemingly lost in thought. "Looks like I'm the one who got surprised." His forehead creased and Amber's eyes grew narrow.

"What do you mean?" Her eyes locked with his, but her stare was soft and serene. Vince sensed comfort in her gaze. He sighed heavily and told her.

"I showed up here last night—unannounced." Vince paused to let that sink in. "I came here, hoping to see Angeliqué. I saw her last night all right." Vince emitted a short laugh. "Yeah, she was here—with a woman. They were kissing…"

Vince took another sip of coffee and leaned back watching Amber. Her face had changed—the smile was gone, replaced by a frown that seemed to radiate outwards. Her limbs appeared to hang from her frame. She was not the same woman whom he had watched recline on the floor months earlier, the *veve* covering her body like some exotic pelt.

"Oh my God—I don't know what to say, Vince. I'm sorry." She reached for his forearm across the table and stroked it.

"You don't need to say anything. I guess I came here to try and make sense of this whole thing. To speak with her before I left, seeing how there's no reason for me to stay now."

Amber was deep in thought. She sighed to herself before speaking.

"Vince, listen, I'm sure there isn't anything that I can say that will erase what you're feeling right now. But I want you to know this—Angeliqué, how do I explain this?" Amber glanced up at the ceiling before continuing. "I know she is feeling you—I know this because she speaks of you often. She's always commenting on how she misses you, and how special that night was to her."

"Well, she sure has a funny way of showing it," Vince quipped.

"Vince, you have to understand Angeliqué. She's not like most people—

JONATHAN LUCKETT

she follows her own drum. She's the kind of person who lives very much for today—I think she's been hurt deeply before and thus doesn't put too much stock in tomorrow. This person, this woman you saw her with—I don't think it means much…"

"Amber—with due respect, come on! She was kissing the woman. What does that tell you?"

"Vince," Amber struggled to find the words, "I think Angeliqué is the kind of person who possesses an extremely social and personable soul. I think she connects with folks on a variety of levels. She connected with you. Very much so. But you're not here—and she had no idea when she would see you again. I believe Angeliqué takes things one day at a time—she lives for today, because that's what feels safe for her."

Vince pondered her words. "Whatever the case, it doesn't change what I saw, and it doesn't change how I *feel*." Vince drained his mug and set it on the table.

"Again, I'm sorry."

Vince patted her hand as he stood up. "I'm not gonna take up any more of your time. Thanks for the coffee and the conversation—it's what I needed, Amber."

"Vince, why don't you stay for a while? I know Angeliqué will want to see you. She *is* missing you badly…"

Vince shook his head. "I don't think so."

"Please?"

Vince shook his head as he smiled at Amber.

"How about this then—where are you staying? Perhaps Angeliqué can swing by to see you when she returns."

"I'm staying at the Fairmont, but it doesn't matter—I'm going home in a few hours."

Amber was silent in thought. "Oh, I thought perhaps you were here through the weekend."

"I was," Vince said softly.

As he headed for the door, he said, "You know what? You are wise beyond your years. I admire that. And you have a perspective on life and on people that I find refreshing. Whatever you do, don't change."

Vince reached for the door.

"Will we see you again?" Amber asked nervously.

"I honestly don't know. But I do hope that you and I can speak again. If nothing else I find your words and presence comforting."

"I'd like that."

As Vince emerged into the brilliance of a Louisiana morning, Amber reached for him; he turned as she leaned in, kissing him lightly on the cheek. Vince stared at her for a moment, taking in the lines of her face as they both smiled, before heading deeper into the Quarter, away from unruly tourists searching for beads, blues, and beer…

✖✖✖

She swept in to the lobby of the Fairmont, her skirt billowing as if caressed by an autumn breeze. It was the hair—bronze and unkempt that got the attention of the male attendant at the desk.

"May I assist you?"

"Yes, I'm looking for a Mr. Vince Cannon, Jr. Can you tell me what room he's in?" Angeliqué asked. She raised her sunglasses onto her head and wiped the hair from her face.

"We aren't allowed to give out room numbers for our guests, but I can ring him for you. Just a moment," the clerk said, flashing his best smile at the pretty lady. Angeliqué returned the smile weakly and then glanced at her watch.

Twelve-eight p.m.

The clerk consulted a computer screen for a moment before frowning. "It appears that Mr. Cannon has already checked out."

Angeliqué bit her bottom lip. "When? Can you tell me how long ago he checked out?" she asked, her voice rising in pitch.

"Looks like you missed him by oh, fifteen minutes or so." The clerk adjusted his tie and said nervously, "I'm sorry, Miss. Perhaps I can be of further assistance?" But when he glanced up, the pretty lady had vanished into the wind…

TWENTY-NINE

Thursday night, nine p.m. at the stylish Tryst in Northwest D.C., and the coffee bar was jumping. Not a free table in the house. Thankfully, Erika and her crew of three had secured a table prior to the evening rush—actually, they'd stood at the bar drinking Cosmopolitans for close to forty-five minutes before spotting a group that was leaving, and bum-rushing the table before anyone else could claim it!

It had been close to a month since Erika and her girls had gotten together. Chalk it up to conflicting schedules—school, work, and their *mens*—so it was nice to finally have all of them sitting together in the same room—regurgitating conversations over and over by phone or e-mail just didn't cut it, and got old but quick!

They had a cramped table by the window overlooking 18th Street. Adams Morgan was filled with youthful crowds, even though winter was rapidly descending upon the city. Folk streamed past their window—shades and hues from various countries the world over, and it made Erika feel proud to be living in a city that had diversity as its middle name.

"Girl, I just love your hair!" Tianna, a thick boned, rich chocolate sistah said to Naomi, a leggy woman the hue of creamy butterscotch. She ran a hand over her shortly cropped brown hair, marveling at its texture.

"Thank you!" Naomi said, all smiles.

"Yeah, girl," added Angie, a squat Cuban with dark eyes and matching hair, "what happened to make you lose those twists?"

Naomi shrugged. "I don't know—change of pace, I guess."

"Well, it looks good on you, girl," Erika said, patting her hand. "And I bet your man is loving this new look of yours, am I right?"

Naomi's look turned serious. "Who? Michael? Please! I sent that bama packing after I caught his black ass two-waying some ho at one in the morning. You know a sistah don't play that!" She high-fived her girlfriends in rapid succession.

"I know that's right!" Tianna exclaimed. "What is wrong with these bruthas anyway?

"Oh please, don't get me started, mamí," Angie said, "'cause they're ain't enough hours in the day!"

"I feel you," Erika declared, laughing as she reached for her martini.

"Besides," Naomi continued, holding up her pinky finger, "the nigga wasn't much use to a sistah anyhow! You feel me?" Squeals of laughter rolled around the table as folks turned to see what all the commotion was about.

"Oh no he didn't," said Tianna, a look of shock on her face.

"Oh yes he did!" Naomi responded. She waggled her finger, and the girls cracked up again.

Things became quiet as the four turned to their drinks. Angie glanced at Erika and spoke. "So, girlfriend, how are things with that anchorman of yours? Don't think I don't watch Channel Four every damn day to get a glimpse of his fine-ass in those dapper suits!"

Erika smiled while running her fingers lazily through her hair.

"Ummn…what can I say? The brutha is fine, right?"

"Oh yes he is!" Tianna said. "Don't let me get that sexy ass man alone—I'll show him what real love is about—you know what they say—'the darker the berry…' "

"Trick, you *best* stay away from my man, unless you want a beat-down!"

"So, girl, seriously, how are things???" Naomi asked.

Erika cleared her throat as she thought about the best way to answer that question… honestly.

The truth—on the one hand, things with James were picture-perfect—he was the consummate gentleman, sending her flowers, taking her out to lunch, cooking for her, and above all else—listening to her—not dominating their conversations with discussions of "me, me, me," but being genuinely interested in her and how she spent her day. That got him major points. So, what was there to complain about? Erika had a man who attended to her every need, was caring and smart, good-looking (oh yes, thank you, Lawd!), and great in bed…save for that little problem…

Erika sighed.

"What's wrong, Erika?" Naomi asked, concern etched on her face.

"Nothing." Erika sighed again. "Things with James and me are fine. He took me away this past weekend. Planned the whole thing and made it a surprise—it was sooooo nice!"

"Really? Do tell…"

"Well, he called me up on Thursday night saying that he was taking me somewhere for the weekend and to be ready Friday afternoon. So, I was packed and waiting when he shows up in this *bad* stretch limo around four! Yes!" She grinned. "Can you believe it? We were then driven to this quaint bed & breakfast in Annapolis two blocks from the harbor. It was so romantic."

"Oh my goodness, that brutha is bad!" Tianna exclaimed.

"You got that right—can some of James rub off on Hector?" Angie asked, cutting a glance over to Erika.

"Ummmn, I don't know about that. Anywho—you should have seen this place—the room was so nice—king-sized, four-post bed, fireplace, window over looking this beautiful garden, drinks in the ornate living room, and being waited on hand and foot all weekend."

"Damn!"

"For real. James took me to dinner at this wonderful seafood place over-looking the harbor. Afterwards, we walked Main Street and window-shopped while we held hands." Erika paused in remembrance. "It was all so romantic and just what a girl needed, you know?"

All smiles around the table.

"We had a wonderful weekend. It was so nice to get away and just spend time with him. It was as close to perfect as perfect can be…" Erika sipped her martini and glanced out the window. Naomi watched her silently before speaking.

"So…why do I get the impression that something's missing?"

"I don't know," Erika responded, but the words seemed washed out like a faded sweatshirt.

"Erika," Tianna asked, locking her gaze on her friend's, "what's the real deal—we're your girls—you can tell us."

Erika put down her drink and sighed. "See, y'all are gonna think I'm tripping if I tell you." She frowned as her mind wrestled with how much detail to spill.

Angie smiled as she reached for the back of her hand. "It's okay, girl—we're not here to judge, you know that."

Erika sucked in a breath. "Okay. I don't know how to explain this, so I'm just going to come out and say it. All right?" Nods. "James is a great lover—we have a great time in bed. But he can't come!" Erika looked away for an instant before settling her eyes on each woman in turn. "There, I said it."

"What you mean, he can't come?" Tianna asked. "Like he can't get it up?"

"He can get it up all right—that's not the problem. No, James' trouble is that he can't orgasm. We've been together for several months now—the sex is the bomb—I'm getting mine, for real, but he doesn't come. And it's really getting to me." Erika took another sip, and then downed the rest of her drink. She caught the attention of the waitress, and swirled her hand about, signaling another round.

Naomi asked, "Have you spoken to James about this?"

"Yeah. I've mentioned it several times." Erika recounted how she first approached James early on in their relationship, and his measured response to her—not to worry; that it was the condoms; yada yada yada. But Erika knew that wasn't it. During the previous weekend, in the private confines of the B&B as a fire crackled and sparked, Erika lowered herself onto James sans a condom and rode him bareback—it was the first time, but they had been dating for a while now, so she trusted him, and more importantly, she needed to be sure. On that Saturday night, Erika made sweet passionate love to James on the four-post bed, reveling in the warmth and glow from the fire, as shadows danced across their writhing forms. The feeling that she experienced from having him inside of her unencumbered, unsheathed, was out of this world—she lost track of how many times she came that evening—but one thing was clear—regardless of how much James panted and moaned, he failed to ejaculate that night…

And that fact, coupled with the disturbing incident at his home with the videotape left her feeling, well, less than a woman.

"I don't know," she continued, "part of me says that it's not a major problem. I mean, we've only been dating a few months, and besides, I know it's not anything I'm doing." She paused, glancing around the table to read her friend's expression. "But lately, I'm wondering if it *is* me—that maybe I'm doing something wrong…"

"Trick, please!" Tianna said, cutting her off with a wave of a hand. "Look at you—you're a beautiful sistah who is definitely in control. Listen to me—it ain't you. Know this!" she said, jabbing a finger in Erika's direction.

Erika smiled. "I know, I know, but it does makes you wonder, right?"

"I agree with Tianna," Naomi said. "I hate to say it, but there are a lot of bruthas out there who can't deal with an intelligent, sophisticated sistah whose got her shit going on. For some, it's a major turn-off—they're used to these silly hos with their only claim to fame being the fact that they can shake their ass on cue!"

"Tell it, mommy!" Angie shouted.

"I'm serious. With due respect to James—you may be dating a brutha who is used to dealing with women who aren't his equal. His past relationships may have been with immature, demure girls filled with low self-esteem. For some guys, it's a power trip—they love being in control. It might be that now that James has met his equal, it's messing with his head—the big one and the little one!"

Erika laughed as her cell phone rang. She reached for her purse, pulled out the cell, and flipped open the clamshell.

"What up, boo—how ya livin'?" It was Trey.

"Fine—what's up with you?" she asked.

"Chillin'…how come you ain't answered my calls—damn, a brutha's gotta track you down?"

"Naw it ain't like that, but I've been busy." The girls chatted among themselves as Erika stole a sip from her martini glass.

"Whatever, ho. Where you at?" he said.

"Out with the girls—why?" Erika excused herself, walked toward the door, and leaned against the thick glass, pushing it open. Cold air blast onto her face causing Erika to shiver. "Hurry up, Trey, it's cold as shit out here. What's up?"

"I need to talk with you, that's what's up! I've been calling you for two days. Damn, boo, you didn't get my messages?"

"Trey, I can't talk. Not now, and probably not later," she replied, checking her watch. "I have a feeling we're going to be here for a while."

"Erika," Trey said, the seriousness in his voice coming through the connection loud and clear, "we need to talk—some shit's come up. I need ya, boo."

Erika hugged herself as the wind whipped around her frame, flinging her hair about. "How about tomorrow? I don't have to be at the hospital until six. We could do lunch if you're not too busy."

"How about later on tonight? You could swing by the crib after you finish your business with your girls."

"Trey, I can't. It's getting late, and I haven't seen my girls in over a month. I don't want to cut our get-together short. Let's shoot for tomorrow, okay? I promise you my undivided attention."

"All right," Trey responded, the disappointment obvious in his inflection. "When and where? Make it someplace we can talk."

Erika head for the door and pulled on it. "How about B. Smith's. I'll make the reservation."

"A'ight—if it can't be tonight I guess tomorrow's gotta do. Don't be late!"

"Whatever! You are not the boss of me!" Erika clicked off as she moved to their table and sat down. Her mind raced, back to the conversation at hand—James. Should she tell her girls about the incident that remained in the forefront of her mind, out in the open where it messed with her every chance it got—that James had come...once...and the circumstances surrounding that episode?

No.

She wasn't ready to share that aspect of her personal life with her girls just yet...

THIRTY

Vince glanced around quickly before taking a seat at the dark wood bar. The bartender, a busty brunette with a pierced eyebrow, took his drink order and sashayed away, swishing her hips from side to side. Vince failed to notice the move. He was lost too deep in thought.

It was a Wednesday night, a few minutes to eight at e-City, a thriving spot in Tysons Corner that catered to the after-work crowd—mostly ex dot-comers and IT folks. He took a swift look at his watch, hoping no one would notice his anxiety.

Would she show?

Unknown.

She had finally responded to his calls with a short-to-the-point response on his voice mail. Yes, she would meet him.

Vince sipped his Corona and brushed away the appetizer menu with a flick of his wrist. He swept his glance around again. The place wasn't very crowded. A few pockets of casually dressed people sitting around tables talking loudly. Not too many black folks in here, but no one was giving him the eye, which was good.

Stop feeling trepidation, he told himself. *There's no need…*yet, he couldn't stop the emotions he was feeling.

The last few weeks had played havoc on his emotions. They had been on a roller coaster of ups and downs since New Orleans. And why shouldn't they? The image of purity that he had held was gone—shattered by the realization that the woman whom he was falling for was gay. Or bi. Whatever her orientation, it didn't fit in with his plan. And that troubled Vince. Deeply.

Purity—that wasn't quite right. Angeliqué was far from pure. Vince knew that. But there had been something about her that had drawn him in, the way water spirals down a porcelain sink. The attraction, he had suspected, was very much mutual. They had connected on some deeper level; he knew that. So, why then, had things gone so horribly wrong?

Angeliqué had been calling for two weeks now. Attempting to connect with Vince. Trying, he presumed, to explain her behavior...

As if that kind of thing could be explained.

He had yet to return her calls. Vince hadn't fully sorted out his feelings. Besides, what difference would it make? Things had fundamentally changed. The image he held was shattered.

That's all that mattered now.

Then there was Desiree to consider. Was this thing with her just a mini-vacation for him—a jaunt with a feisty young woman, full of spunk and energy, but lacking a deeper connection that was needed for anything more than what they had now? Vince didn't know. And that was part of the problem...

Someone moved up beside him. Vince turned and found himself face to face with Maxi.

✖✖✖

It was the eyes he noticed first. Nia Long eyes. Dark and piercing; lovely orbs that cut right through him.

Vince felt himself shiver.

"Hey you—you made it."

"I said I would," Maxi said, placing her handbag on the bar stool beside him. Vince looked her over. She wore a fashionable beige leather jacket with whipstitch and dark blue jeans. Underneath the jacket, a crocheted cardigan was tight, showing off her breasts. Her hair was pulled back tight and shiny. Perched atop smooth dark cheeks was a new pair of designer glasses—thin, lightweight frames the color of titanium. Vince stared for a moment too long.

"Wow, check you out, Maxi, you look wonderful!" Vince reached over to kiss her. He was aiming for her lips, but Maxi turned her face, presenting him with her cheek instead.

"Thanks," she said, and sat down. Vince pivoted toward the bar, got the attention of the bartender by holding up two fingers. She came over and smiled at them.

"What can I get you?" she said, slipping a square napkin onto the smooth bar surface.

Maxi opened her mouth to speak as Vince leaned in.

"Get her a Cosmopolitan, if you would," he said, grinning at Maxi. The bartender said, "Sure," and reached above for a martini glass.

"Actually," Maxi said, raising her voice a notch, "I'll have an Absolut Heaven." Vince cut a glance over to her. Maxi shrugged. "It's my *new* drink."

Vince leaned back, feeling dejected. Thirty seconds into their reunion and things were not going well. "So, Maxi, thanks for meeting me. I hope you've been well."

"I have, Vince. And you?" she asked, smoothing her hair.

"Fine. Good, real good, thanks for asking." Vince was fumbling and he knew it. It always amazed him—here he was—a professional motivational speaker—he did this shit for a living—getting up in front of people and talking about issues he was passionate about. But, put him in a personal situation like this—and Vince felt himself on shaky ground…

"So, Maxi—I need to say something first. Get it out of the way," Vince said, turning to give her his full attention. "I am sorry for the way things ended." Maxi opened her mouth, but Vince raised his hand. "Let me finish—there are a hundred ways to break up with someone; I chose a shitty way to do it with you. I'm sorry for that, Maxi. There isn't any excuse for my behavior." Vince paused, reading her face, looking for signs. She stared back at him, not communicating anything with her expression, waiting instead for him to go on.

"Maxi, it's hard to explain the place I was in back then—sorting through the various emotions, trying to ascertain what I was actually feeling. I have to tell you, it was a blur to me, and I was confused. Not really knowing for sure what it was I was searching for." He paused to take a sip of his beer.

"You don't have to do this, you know," Maxi said. "I've had time to get over what transpired between us, and what's done is done. I'm not the kind of person to dwell on the past. You, of all people, should know that."

"Yes, you are indeed correct."

"I'm not going to lie to you, Vince—you hurt me. I thought that what we had was special. And I thought we had come to the same place, feeling each other the way we did—I guess I was wrong."

Maxi's drink arrived and she took a sip. "Ummm, this is good," she remarked.

"That's just it, Maxi," Vince exclaimed, "I don't want you to think that I wasn't into you, because that's the furthest thing from the truth. I *was* feeling you." He dropped his voice a notch. "I still am…"

"Vince, I'm not sure what you want me to say."

"I don't want you to say anything, Maxi. I'm here to say I am sorry. And that I hope we can move forward. Be friends or move down whatever road our relationship chooses to take us."

Maxi smiled, but Vince could tell it was the kind reserved for those situations when you felt sorry for someone. "Listen, Vince, you are a wonderful guy. And I enjoyed the time we spent together. But as you said, you were confused and not clear about what it was you were searching for. Well, I don't have that problem." Vince cringed. "I don't mean to be harsh, so forgive me for sounding that way. But I *do* know what I want. And I need a man who is on the same wavelength as me. As I said, you're a great guy; you just need to sort through your issues and then you can move forward." Maxi took another sip and gathered her things. She reached for her purse and dropped a twenty on the counter.

"Hey, you leaving so soon?" Vince asked, staring at the money. "I thought perhaps we could have dinner and catch up."

"Another time, maybe. I've got plans and have to run." Maxi stood up, and bent down to run her palms over her thighs. Vince glanced at her bent-over form. Red g-string panties peeked out from the back of her jeans. Vince felt a twinge of jealousy. Maxi was lovely, no denying that. He had fucked up. He had acted prematurely and it had come back to haunt him. She straightened up and smiled at him. "It was good seeing you, Vince. Stay well, okay?" she said, reaching out to stroke his beard. He returned a weak smile.

"At least put your money away; I'm the one who invited you."

"No, I insist, Vince." She pivoted away from the stool as Vince reached for her arm.

"Would it be possible for us to get together one day soon?" he asked, trying not to show the desperation in his voice that he felt in his heart.

Maxi turned back to him. "Tell you what, I'll give you a call one of these days. Bye, Vince; I really have to go." Vince watched her leave, before turning back to the bar and eyeing her drink that remained largely untouched. He sighed heavily as his cell phone chirped. He grabbed it, cut a glance at the Caller ID, and pressed the phone to his ear in a rapid motion.

"Yeah?" he said in a gruff voice.

"Vince. It's Angeliqué" she said slowly. "Hi, I've been trying to reach you for…"

"Give me a call back in five minutes, would you? I'm in the midst of something," he said, before snapping the phone shut without saying good-bye. He took a swing of his Corona and rose off the bar stool, heading angrily for the restroom.

Outside, Maxi had rounded a corner of the building before pausing besides a wall. Pressing her back into the concrete, she tilted her head up to the sky as she reached for her phone. She drew in a deep breath as she punched in a number.

"Hey girl, it's me," she said forlornly a moment later.

"Hey—so, spill it—how did it go?"

"As you figured—he apologized profusely and basically wants me back."

"I knew it! *Please* tell me you didn't fall for that playa shit, Maxi."

"No," Maxi said, "I followed your orders to the T."

"Good. You do not need no man who is wishy-washy."

"Yeah, but you should've seen him—he looked so damn fine," Maxi said, shaking her head with the memory of him sitting at the bar looking too cute. She began to move toward her car.

"Forget that—how about you? Did you dress the bomb, like I told you?"

"Oh yeah, his eyes practically fell out of his damn skull!"

"Good enough. Let him contemplate that shit!"

Maxi sighed as she opened her car door and got inside, starting the engine.

"Seriously, Maxi—you've already moved on. Don't head backwards," her friend opined.

"Yeah, I know. I know I'm doing the right thing," Maxi said, "but answer me this: Why then, do I feel so damn awful???"

✖✖✖

The tan Lexus coupe accelerated past the intersection as Vince steered the automobile onto the Beltway. He slid in a CD—something smooth— George Duke—to ease his mind. He was pissed. Not at Maxi, but at himself. He should have left it alone. Calling her was a mistake. He had fumbled the situation with her and came out looking like a fool.

A desperate fool.

Vince shook his head miserably. Why didn't he just stay away? He had Desiree and things with her were going fairly well. Why, then, did he feel the need to dredge up the past by trying to reconnect with Maxi?

Angeliqué, that's why.

Ever since he had spotted her in the arms of another woman, Vince had felt that nothing in his life made much sense. Here he was, seemingly heading in one direction, so he thought, but then the rug had been pulled out from under his feet, and he had gone flying, landing flat on his black ass, glancing around, dazed and confused.

Stop it, he told himself. *Get it together. You are Vince Cannon, Jr. There is no need for this shit. Lord, if Trey could see you now, he'd shake his head in disbelief and disgust. So stop tripping over something that wasn't meant to be. Something that never even got started…*

The chirping of his cell phone brought his thoughts back to the present. He cleared his throat and answered the phone.

"Me again." It was Angeliqué.

"Hey," Vince answered, softer this time.

"Is *this* a better time?" she asked cautiously.

"Yeah, it is." He thought about apologizing for his earlier behavior, but then decided against it. He was still fuming from his encounter with Maxi, and images of Angeliqué and her female lover didn't appease his mood one bit.

"So, I've been trying to call you—I guess you know that," she said. "Vince, I want to talk to you. We haven't spoken since prior to you coming back down to New Orleans. I am sorry, Vince, for what happened. I never meant to hurt you; I hope you know that."

Vince had rehearsed this conversation over in his head a million times. But all that he could come up with now for a response was a half-baked grunt.

"You have a right to not want to see or speak to me, but I hope that you won't do that."

Vince was silent.

"Vince, are you still there?" Angeliqué asked.

"Yes, I'm here. And I'm listening."

"How are things with you, Vince?"

Vince emitted a short chuckle. "Angeliqué, please. Is that it? Are we done talking about your encounter with the female?"

"The female—she happens to be somebody to me. I said I'm sorry for hurting you. But I'm not sorry that it happened. Terry is someone who is special. She is a wonderful human being. I'm not sure there is anything further to say."

"Oh, I get it. So I guess all this talk about how much you missed me was just bullshit, right?

"No, it's not bullshit, Vince..."

And I guess," Vince said, interrupting her, "that what we had, what we felt that weekend doesn't amount to shit!"

"Vince," she interrupted gently, "You can't expect me to sit here and put my life on hold for someone whom I have no idea if I'll even see again. Yes, we vibed—yes, we had a wonderful time. I don't deny any of that at all. But if you're expecting me to sit here and wait around for something that probably will never amount to anything, well, I think you've got the wrong girl."

Vince's mind whirled. This was not what he expected...

"Vince?"

"Yeah."

"I'm thinking about heading up to Washington for a few days. Think we could get together?"

"Well, Angeliqué, you had an opportunity to be with me, but instead, you decided to spend it with your tongue down some female's throat. So why the sudden interest in seeing me?" Vince was livid and no longer interested in hiding his growing anger.

"That's not fair, Vince, and you know it—I had no idea that you were coming down. If I'd have known..."

"What? You'd have made plans to *fuck* her after I left???"

The phone grew silent. Vince knew he had gone too far, but made no move to correct his mistake. A moment passed. Then another. Vince heard Angeliqué sigh and knew she was still on the phone.

"Vince, I'd like to know if you'll see me when I come to Washington. It's a simple question. 'Yes' or 'no' will suffice."

Vince grew still. His mind raced as he processed her words. He felt torn—on the one hand, what he had witnessed in New Orleans had snapped in two the bond he shared with Angeliqué. On the other, he desired to see her again, if for nothing more than to try and rekindle the flame, even though that didn't seem like much of a possibility now.

"I don't know, Angeliqué," he said.

"Okay, Vince. I understand."

Vince's chest rose and fell heavily. What a night—first Maxi and now Angeliqué. Too much drama for one man to take. Then all of that swept away, like a sudden onslaught, replaced with images of Angeliqué and him in her studio, their bodies caressed by candlelight and dripping with paint as he melted inside of her on the floor...

Vince smiled with the memories. Although short-lived, it was a wonderful time that they had shared.

Vince closed his eyes as he tried to erase the present and move backwards, into the past...

THIRTY-ONE

B. Smith's restaurant in Union Station is open-air and vast. Perfect for whatever Trey needed to discuss with Erika. She arrived at 11:45 a.m. sharp, and was seated at a table for two by the enormous floor to ceiling panes of glass overlooking the street. Their table was across from a large pillar, in a section behind the main dining-room area; it offered up privacy, yet one could still see the main section from where they were seated. Erika had just ordered a drink when in strode Trey, still shaded in his rose-colored glasses, bald head shining as always, his charcoal-gray, double-breasted suit impeccable, with a light-blue shirt and matching silk tie, polished black lace-ups, and sterling silver cufflinks that sparkled as he moved. B. Smith's was already busy with the lunchtime crowd—waiters scrambling about to fill drink orders and returning with appetizers and entrees—but even with all the commotion, folks still paused in conversation as he strolled by. Trey had it like that. Everywhere he went, people noticed him.

He came up and gave Erika a peck on the cheek before sitting down.

"Hey, Sassy, check you out. Girlfriend's looking fly as usual." Erika smiled. She wore dark jeans, a tan sweater, and matching boots. A choker adorned her neck with an Indian head nickel hanging from a single leather cord.

"You too, boo. Only about twenty women checked out your entrance this time!"

Trey cocked his head to the side, peering around the column as he adjusted his tie. "For real? Only twenty? Damn, I must be losing my touch!" A waiter came up beside them and took Trey's drink order.

"So, what is the big emergency, Trey? I mean, damn, a girl doesn't call you back within twenty-four hours and you go all mental. What's up with that?"

"Please—it ain't like that! Besides, I thought you were my boo—I mean, if you don't want me to share my innermost secrets with you, then forget you, I'll go find someone else." Trey removed his shades and pocketed them in his breast pocket. "Hmmn, I'm famished—let me see if they got any soul food up in this mutha fucka!"

"Trey, please—stop acting so damn ghetto—you know this is a nice spot!"

"That remains to be seen." The waiter brought Trey's drink and set it down on the table. Trey glanced up. "How's the salmon today, my man?" he asked.

"Very good, sir. I highly recommend it!"

"Well then, that's what I'm gonna have." Trey folded his menu and handed it to the waiter with a flourish.

"Excuse me," Erika quipped, cutting a stare at Trey. "But, what happened to 'ladies first'?"

"Oh, my bad."

Erika shook her head as she sucked her teeth. The waiter gave her an apologetic shrug. "I'll have the glazed pork chops."

"Excellent choice," the waiter responded.

"Oh, and bring my boy here some manners if you would," she declared.

"I'll see if we have any left in back," the waiter said as he moved off.

"Everybody's got jokes," Trey quipped.

"So, Trey. Seriously, what's up?"

Trey cleared his throat. "Not much—actually, a whole lot—it's been a crazy-ass week. Let me tell you." Erika nodded. "Where to begin...let's see. Oh yeah, I didn't tell you, since you didn't return my *phone calls*, but there was some serious drama last Saturday night at Home."

"Really?"

"Oh yeah—you remember Quentin Hues; he plays for the Wizards. He's a client."

"Yes, you told me."

"Yeah, well, he was having a birthday party there and we're all up in the VIP just chilling when in waltzes his wife, soon-to-be-ex with her girls like she owns the spot! All hell breaks loose, a fight ensues, and guess who has to handle the situation?" Trey is grinning as he breaks off a piece of warm bread.

"Let me guess?

"You got it, baby! Me—Trey to the rescue—Red Cross up in the shit!"

"What?" Erika asked.

"Oh yeah, *moi* had to escort the lovely fine-as-she-wanna-be Ms. Hues to safety." Trey was glancing down at his nails as he pursed his lips. Erika smirked.

"Oh boy—let me guess—safety being the backseat of your ride? What'd you do, Trey? Please don't tell me you took advantage of your own client's wife? Trey, please!"

Trey grinned but said nothing.

"Oh my God, Trey, this is fucked up, even for you—Quentin's wife?" Erika shook her head fiercely.

"What? The girl needed a ride out of there but quick—she was about to get a beat down from her own husband. I'm a hero, and all I get is static from you? That's messed up!" he said, spreading his hands wide.

"Trey, please. Sleeping with your client's wife is unethical. How can you look Quentin in the eyes after doing something like that?"

"Whatever! Besides that brutha's a bigger ho than me, believe that! Anyway, get this—we had our meeting a few days later to finalize the settlement agreement, right? Quentin and me; his wife and her attorney, Allison—you remember that honey from H20—I told you about that situation, right?"

"You mean the fact that you *fucked* her, too! Yeah, you mentioned that. Trey, you're incredible. The only one *not* getting fucked is Quentin—when are you going to show him the pipe? You might as well give him some, too!"

Trey laughed. "Ha, ha, that's a good one—listen up—Allison figured out that I'd been boning Aponi, so she went ballistic on me. Like I owe her a fucking explanation or something. Like we had something going on…Please, we fucked. *Once.* Hello. It doesn't mean she's ready for an engagement ring."

"Trey," Erika said, reaching for his hand. "You are going to do what you want to do. You always have. But listen up. One of these days, your whoring around is going to come back and bite you in the ass. For real, man. You need to slow your roll, ya hear me?"

"Whatever, Erika—I'm doing my thing, ain't hurting nobody. Besides, and you probably won't believe this, but I wasn't trying to fuck Aponi. In fact, I was hoping she'd just let me drop her off back at her hotel. But let me tell you, she was sweating a brutha, and well, I had no choice but to tap that ass!"

Erika eyed Trey but said nothing.

"Anywho—can we get to the topic at hand? The real reason for this get-together?"

"Sure, Trey—it's your party..."

The food came. They ate in silence for a few minutes before picking up where they had left off.

"So, the firm's got their ten-year anniversary party coming up in two weeks."

"Okay," Erika said, savoring the flavor of the chops.

"Yeah, this is big—huge. I mean, they're making a very big deal about this—black-tie and everything. Renting out Sequoia on the waterfront for this party. Can you imagine? Shutting down Sequoia on a Friday night for a private party? Sheeit!"

"So your firm is the bomb; they got it like that...what else is new?"

"Girl, you don't understand. This is serious—everyone is expected to attend. I mean, to not show is a career-limiting move, I kid you not."

"Okay," Erika said, "so obviously you're gonna go—you've been burning up the phone lines to tell me *this*???"

"Erika," Trey said, wiping his mouth with the cloth napkin, "if you weren't my girl, I'd reach over this table and smack you dead in your chops, and I don't mean those on your plate! You don't get it, do you? I need a date! I *have* to show up with a fine honey on my arm—I've got a reputation to uphold. This is all about image, for real—I can *not* go solo."

"So, get a date. I'm sure you can come up with someone to accompany you in less than fifteen seconds, all them females you know!"

"Erika, I'm serious. Man, this is bugging the shit out of me. Who am I going to take? It can't be just any ole ho...no, girlfriend's gotta have class, look damn good, and be able to carry on a conversation with folks—I mean, the partners are going to be there in force." Trey reached inside his jacket pocket and extracted a folded piece of paper. He flattened it on the table and glanced up at Erika. "I've been giving this a great deal of thought. In fact, I've been thinking about nothing else for the past week."

"You're kidding," Erika asked incredulously.

"Nope. In fact, look at this. I had India put together a spreadsheet to help me prioritize my options. Here," he said, sliding the printout over to her. Erika picked up the paper and looked it over, shaking her head.

"Trey, you *are* for real. Poor India...you don't pay her enough!" She glanced over the list. There were close to three-hundred names accompanied by notes—distinguishing characteristics or tidbits of data that would help Trey recall them all, along with phone numbers if he possessed them. "What—what is this?" Erika asked.

"What does it look like? A list of the eligible women. At least those I can *recall*..."

"And?"

"And nothing. I'm having trouble figuring out which one to take. I mean, some of them aren't a good fit for this particular affair. Others probably won't even speak to me 'cause I haven't exactly maintained a *relationship* with them, ya know?"

"Meaning, they haven't heard shit from you since you fucked them?"

"Basically." Trey smiled sheepishly. "Listen, I didn't come here to get a lesson from you on relationships or how to treat women. Okay? I'm soliciting your help because I don't know what to do. I was strongly considering Allison—good-looking, intelligent, fellow attorney, but at this juncture I doubt she'd want to accompany me...There's Aponi, but she's too young and unpolished."

Erika frowned as she shook her head. "You've got to be kidding me! I'm not going to help you with this." She shook her head firmly.

"Boo," Trey said, all smiles, "I *need* your help. Come on, give a brutha a break—please?"

Erika sighed as she glanced down at the sheet. "What about what's her name? The one you met at the Congressional Black Caucus—the tall one? Regina or something? She was nice."

"Naw—I ran into her a couple of months ago. She didn't speak when I said hello. She's still pissed because I never called after our wild night."

"It's no wonder. Okay, let me think." Erika consulted the list. "How about this one: Monica. Says here, 'fine ass and great at her job.'"

Trey snatched the paper and glanced over the list, shaking his head. "Great at her job—yeah, that chick gave a great *blowjob*—that's about the only 'job' she's any good at! Besides, last time I called her she told me she'd gotten engaged."

The two poured over the list —Trey pulled out a pen to make notes; Erika scanned the list and asked Trey pertinent questions. But, fifteen minutes later, no luck, they hadn't reached any conclusion.

"You know what, Erika? There's something very wrong with this picture when *yours truly* can't find a single decent woman to take to a goddamned party. I mean, really! I wouldn't be making an issue of this except for the fact that it is such a big deal!" Trey exclaimed, shaking his head. The waiter cleared their plates, and they both ordered coffee.

"Can I be honest with you, Trey?" Erika asked, but didn't wait for a response. "I think you need to step back and think about what this means… put it in its proper context. What this says to me is that you may have been *intimate* with loads of women, but you hardly know any of them."

Trey's stare locked on Erika's for a moment. For a minute neither spoke. Erika didn't glance away; she wasn't frightened. Erika knew this conversation was long overdue.

The coffee came. Trey and Erika sipped theirs in silence as he reviewed his list. Suddenly Trey's eyes sparkled. "Ah sookie now—I've got it!"

"Yeah?"

"Oh yeah. Hang onto your panties, Erika and check it—you could go with me."

"Me?" Erika asked, her eyebrow rising. She was shaking her head as Trey grabbed her hand.

"Of course, boo—it's perfect. We've known each other for years—and we look *damn* good together, you've got to admit. You are intelligent and can carry a conversation. This way I don't have to trip for the next two weeks trying to figure out who to take!"

"I don't know…" Erika was saying.

"Say you'll go with me, boo. Please? I need this. I can't go solo, and let's face it—none of these women are present tense. They're all past tense!"

"So, what you're saying is that I'm the one you go to when your other hos say no?"

"Naw, baby, you know it's not like that. You're my boo. Honestly, I didn't consider you until this moment, but the more I think about it, the more it makes wonderful sense. You're the one. You're perfect. Besides, we'd have a lot of fun. What do you say?

Erika sighed. "Trey," she said, "Give me some time to consider this, okay?"

"Meaning what? You have to check with James first to see if it's all right?"

Erika was ready to fire off a response when a movement caught her interest. She glanced to the right; Trey witnessed her change of appearance, as if a fist had suddenly connected with flesh. It was swift and complete. He turned his head, and in that moment, his entire world came to a grinding halt. Trey paused in mid-sentence. Erika was still attempting to process what she saw as her eyes opened wide. They flicked back to Trey for a split second before zeroing in on the object of her attention.

The hair was still long and jet-black, patting her shoulders and back in waves as she moved; the high cheekbones, evident even in profile; the curves to her hips, still shapely and in motion as she traveled the length of the dining room; her face turned to her companion, another woman—but all eyes were on *her*. And Erika could understand why—she was still, after all of these years, *breathless*. Trey's jaw dropped as his eyes literally bugged out. The change in his appearance was drastic. In an instant, he had aged ten years. He looked visibly sick, and Erika knew that inside, he was dying.

"Oh shit," Erika whispered as Layla, Trey's ex-girlfriend, the ex-love of his life, and the woman who had *ruined* him, sauntered on by, unaware that she had been spotted by either of them…

THIRTY-TWO

Another dreary day—skies devoid of blue, a steady wind that whipped branches around, announcing the coming of winter. Vince had awakened early; a restless night had forced him from his bed around seven. He had tried to sleep in, attempting to drown himself in the silence and darkness underneath the heavy comforter, but that didn't work. So he rose, and grudgingly went for a run.

He returned an hour later. Glancing around the first floor of his home, a three-story row house a few minutes from Children's Hospital, Vince noticed that there were papers from the previous three Sundays that had yet to be read. Taking in the laptop that laid on the coffee table, he remembered the loads of unanswered e-mails. The cordless phone was positioned snug in the cushion of his couch. Phone calls from several bookstores in Philadelphia and Newark had yet to be returned.

What was he doing?

He was never like this, letting his work pile up.

Last night—a Friday night—he remained at home, even though Trey had begged him to come on out—First Fridays at some spot downtown. You know Trey wouldn't miss those for the world. But Vince declined, saying he had too much work to do—which was true. Only thing, Vince hadn't accomplished anything. Desiree had phoned, too, asking if he wanted some company. He had refused her invitation as well, telling her the same lie he had told Trey. Instead, Vince had sat on the couch all by himself, nursing a

Corona in front of his television—channel-surfing the entire evening, watching stuff he could care less about until midnight rolled around, when he finally gave up and went to bed.

It was now after 9 a.m. the following day and his stomach growled something fierce. Unfortunately he hadn't the energy to fix himself something to eat. So he reached for the piled-up papers and began to go through them. Vince still wore his tight running pants and a Morehouse sweatshirt. His sneakers remained in the foyer by the door.

The doorbell broke his concentration. Vince glanced at the front door and frowned. He was not expecting anyone. He put down the paper and rose from the couch, smoothing out his hair and reaching to scratch at his beard. He knew he looked like a wild man this early in the morning. He hoped it was just FedEx or somebody like that.

Vince opened the door and found himself face-to-face with Amber.

She was all smiles.

Behind her stood Angeliqué, holding up a bag from Krispy Kreme.

Amber's stare traveled down slowly to his feet before bouncing back up. "Nice pants," she quipped while brushing past him into the house. That left Angeliqué and Vince standing alone.

"Peace offering," she said, handing him the donuts. Angeliqué grinned and Vince felt his heart break.

✖✖✖

He sat in his kitchen, refreshed from a quick shower, watching them work. Angeliqué was putting on coffee; Amber was slicing cheese for omelets. They had insisted on commandeering his kitchen; and who was Vince to put up a fight?

Angeliqué wore a pair of faded jeans, low riding and tight, with pointy black boots and a thin dark sweater. Adoring her head was a Kangol hat. Amber was clad in a pair of oversized sweatpants and a form-fitting cotton tee. Her feet were bare. Vince was still reeling from their surprise visit.

"When did you get in?" he asked.

"Last night. We caught a non-stop and were in D.C. by eight p.m."

"And how did you find me?" Vince asked incredulously.

"That was easy," Angeliqué mused, eyeing him from the stove where she stir-fried onions, green and red peppers, tomatoes, and garlic. The vapors wafted over Vince and he felt his stomach somersault. "You're in the phone book—a smart move if you're into stalkers."

"Hmmn," he said. Vince still was unsure of how to play this. Good cop or bad—that was the question. On the one hand, watching them in his kitchen filled his insides with a feeling that he hadn't experienced since New Orleans. But that was tempered by the conversation he and Angeliqué had had a few nights earlier. And the images from New Orleans remained...

"And what if I wasn't home?" he asked.

"Oh, I guess we'd be scarfing down these donuts all by ourselves," Amber said, flashing a smile in his direction.

"Right. Well, I am glad to see both of you." Vince stood and went to Amber, who leaned in and gave him a hug. He moved over to the range and slid behind Angeliqué who was busy at work. She tilted her head up and nuzzled her neck against his. They embraced and kissed gingerly.

"Pass those eggs, Vince, and step back," she said. "It's about to get ugly up in here!"

Thirty minutes later their plates were clean. Omelets and fresh coffee, followed by glazed and jelly-filled donuts had each of them holding their stomachs.

"Damn, after a meal like that I need a nap!" Amber exclaimed.

"I hear that," Vince responded as he cleared the dishes.

"Vince," Angeliqué said as they watched Amber stretch, "I was hoping you would show me your studio."

He glanced over at Amber who said, "You two go ahead, I'd like to stay here and crash on the couch for a while. If it's cool with Mr. Cannon, Jr. over there?"

Vince grinned. "Make yourself at home, but excuse the mess—my maid quit just last week; I haven't had time to replace her!"

"Yeah right..." Amber said, ambling toward the couch.

✖✖✖

She was silent for a long time. Vince observed her from the futon as she contemplated his wall of masks. Angeliqué moved slowly from one end to the other, studying each one in turn, his masks that each told a story: passion, happiness, anger, sadness. Angeliqué turned to him with a solemn face.

"Vince, these are incredible. I don't know what to say."

"Thank you." He sipped a mug of coffee as he watched her.

"I didn't know what to expect, but you are really good! You have a God-given talent. Are these hanging in any galleries?"

"Not really," Vince said. He'd been thinking long and hard about making some contacts in the art world so that he could begin selling his pieces. At this point, he had one hanging in Cosi on Capitol Hill, and another in Utopia on U Street.

"Well, you definitely should," Angeliqué said, joining him on the couch. She leaned against him, taking a sip from her mug. Her frizzy hair blanketed her shoulders, resting on her sweater. Some of her mane fell on Vince. He eyed her silently as her body pressed into his, concentrating on her straight nose, her rich skin, those cheekbones that rose as she spoke. His mind transported him back to New Orleans, and the very first time— when the two of them had made passionate love that night, the way she had made him feel, out of this world, unparalleled, the passion gushing forth from them both like a geyser. Without fanfare, Vince reached for her face, and placed his lips to hers.

Angeliqué responded by facing him; in a moment their limbs were intertwined like their tongues. They were silent—words did not do justice to what they were feeling. His hands raised to her face, lightly caressing her cheeks and lips, probing her mouth, then feeling her nose, running fingers over her eyelids as he pulled back to gaze upon her. Then he bent forward and kissed her again. Moments later, Angeliqué was atop him, straddling Vince as she squirmed out of her sweater. Her breasts heaved with her breathing, as Vince reached for her pointed nipples.

Cupping her breasts, he felt her warmth transferred between their skin.

They kissed ravenously, as if they had been denied sustenance for too long. Glancing upward, Vince watched her from his vantage point below, her eyes that had closed to mere slits, her body that writhed like a serpent as his hands traversed her torso toward her thighs.

Vince lifted her off of him with his powerful arms and returned her to the futon. He stood up and removed his sweater as she watched. Then his jeans slid down his legs, revealing tight briefs that barely contained his engorged state. Angeliqué reached out to stroke him through the fabric of his underwear, taking her time, running a lazy finger up the shaft as the heel of her boot slowly raked itself against his shin.

Reaching out for his buttocks with both hands, she pulled him to her until he was sandwiched between her thighs, his shins pressed up against the futon's skin. After massaging his ass for a moment, Angeliqué slowly peeled off his briefs as her stare locked with his—a devious smile painted on her face. When he had stepped free of his underwear, and stood naked and engorged in front of her, then and only then did she drop her stare, gazing at his member that bobbed inches from her face.

She took him into her mouth, grasping the shaft with an expert hand, tugging on the flesh as she sucked him in, and Vince shut his eyes and threw back his head, reaching out for support because he already felt himself growing weak. She nibbled lightly around the head, using her hand to guide his wand against her teeth and lips, as her tongue flicked against the hole before lowering herself to his sac, lightly squeezing the flesh as she took each testicle into her mouth.

Vince moaned and reached for her breasts, squeezing them between his fingers. His hand snaked down smooth skin to her navel before plunging south, beneath her jeans, searching for the damp cotton of her panties. He flopped out of her mouth, spittle adorning his shaft like a glaze as Angeliqué wriggled out of her jeans. Moments later she was fully nude, and Vince had to stand back and marvel at her form. She lay back on the futon lengthwise and curled her finger at him, beckoning him to enter.

Vince didn't need to be told twice!

He entered her effortlessly as Angeliqué wrapped her ankles around his back, her fingers raking his forearms that flexed as he moved. He began slowly, but increased his rapid thrusting, watching himself go in and out below thin brown pubic hair, as her golden navel seemed to contort with each drive.

She was a constriction around him, her neck nuzzling against his as they made love, panting, eyes closed, both waiting for that feeling to waft over them, those passionate sensations that soaked their essence and consumed them once, twice before, down in New Orleans, when the spirit of voodoo priests and priestesses hovered over them like fog.

But it did not come.

Not for Angeliqué nor for Vince.

Beads of sweat pooled in the valley of her back as Vince took her from behind, her unkempt hair like a scraggy vine as he rushed against her flesh, her thrusts meeting his head-on as their bodies blurred.

But that exquisite feeling, the delicious high that comes from consuming one's sensuality like a drug, remained elusive.

Both of them grunted and groaned as Vince attacked Angeliqué with his fervor, as if accelerating their frenzy might somehow boil their spirits, incite violence inside of them, riot the senses to the point of complete and unadulterated ardor—racing past the point of no return, bursting through the wall, to the end...

But as they came simultaneously, streaking through the tunnel toward the sunlight that blazed in, drawing them to the finish line, Vince and Angeliqué separately discovered that it was not what it could have been...

Not at all what it *had* been...

They disengaged, slowing their quickened heartbeats, and retreated to separate ends of the futon. For several moments neither spoke, as if they needed the silence to complete the tearing down of the cocoon that had shielded each one from the other's view.

Vince rose naked off the couch. Angeliqué did not follow him with her stare. Instead she began to don her clothes.

After several minutes of running water, Vince returned. Angeliqué was fully clothed and studying the wall of masks.

"Can you do me?" she asked softly.

"Hmmn?" Vince had his back to her, his attention at his workbench and the torso life-casting of Desiree. The plaster had long since hardened, and yet he studied the rise of her flesh from taut stomach to the peak of her supple breasts, running a hand along its texture as he recalled the real thing: soft, smooth, dark chocolate skin.

"A mask," Angeliqué said, "I was wondering if you can do one of me?"

"I don't know," Vince responded, his mind a million miles away, suddenly feeling the distress that had been heaved onto his shoulders. His fingertips alighted from the plaster as he turned away from the workbench and back to her—reflecting on what just had transpired between them, and all that had *not*. The finality of it all caused him to tremble at his core. "We'll have to see," he said. Angeliqué turned and nodded, but as she gathered up her things to go, she already knew what his answer would be.

THIRTY-THREE

Standing in my kitchen off of U Street, staring down at the swirl of coffee, I allowed myself to remember—*her*. I recalled for the first time in many years three singular events—ribbons of celluloid in my mind which had been locked away tight, unable to surface because my psyche would not allow it—for fear of dredging up an ocean of emotions, intense anger and something much worse. But this time, I allowed it to happen. I gave in to the sudden and severe cramps that scraped at my gut after seeing her there in the restaurant, knowing that these thoughts were long overdue. So I sucked in a breath, shut my eyes tightly, and *remembered*…

I vividly recall the rain—the steady drone of a downpour, drops as big as bumblebees free-falling vertically; there was no wind, no sideways pressure to cause the deluge to rake across uneven ground—no, it was a simple, yet complete storm. I recall the roar of the showers and the heavy swish-swish of my wipers as they fought gallantly to keep up, yet to no avail. This was no contest, and I remember thinking—God help anyone who is caught in this torrent—I almost laughed out loud as I took a turn with some effort, braking cautiously because I knew my ride could hydroplane at any moment, sending me and my shiny auto careening headlong into the timbers if I wasn't careful, so I concentrated on the yellow lines painted on slick asphalt at 1:17 a.m.—I recall that, too —the bright aquamarine LEDs that seemed to wink every minute, as I turned down the stereo in order to gain further concentration—all of these things occurring serially and in rapid succession—

my dark hands gripping the wheel tightly as I guided the car into the turn, braking slowly and carefully, the LEDs noting the time, my hand reaching for the volume knob on the stereo, and almost laughing out loud at the absurdity of this storm—and that was when I saw *it* and instinctively jammed on my brakes, causing me to skid to a stop.

Two cars, one by the side of the road, its hazards pulsating into the night, cutting the rain at oblique angles, and headlights shining onto a second vehicle—the other, ten yards away from the first, its body turned at a right angle to the road, an entire third of its body an accordion against a thick dark tree. My eyes flicked rapidly over the scene as my heart raced—then leveled against a form huddled on the ground leaning over something else—I strained my eyes to discern details, but the rain was blotting them out like ink spots. I pulled over and mechanically exited my vehicle without even thinking about what I would do. I was no doctor, but something in me commanded that I help.

I raced around the front of my car, my shoes squishing in the soft earth, mud splattering the cuffs of my suit pants as I came up to the person kneeling on the ground. Beneath her lay a woman—no more than eighteen, eyes closed, as if in deep sleep, mouth hung open slightly. The rain was relentless, and it was clear that no conscious person could stand the force of the raindrops slapping against their warm flesh without flinching. My eyes cut back to the woman hunched over the prone form—the long jet-black hair grabbed my attention first. I recall the way the rain pummeled her head and flowed down her back, causing her hair to shine and glow, but I didn't have time to appreciate the details—she turned her head and stared up at me—and our eyes connected—and this I will *never* forget—I saw something in there that caused my heart to stir—compassion and pain, the yin and yang that radiated out from those dark orbs as she blinked away the rain, communicating more with her stare than mere words ever could. I so wanted to keep my stare locked on hers; marveling at her high cheekbones that were rosy, and drink in the rest of her beautiful features, but the situation would not allow it.

"What can I do?" I belted out, kneeling down as I reached inside my jacket for my cell phone.

"She's unconscious and bleeding," the woman beside me yelled. "I tried my phone but can't get a signal." She was holding the young woman's head between both hands. Underneath, I could see dark red swaths painting grass stems. I glanced around frantically as I pulled out my cell and checked the signal.

Nothing.

"We need to move her!" I shouted, already deciding on a plan of action. The woman glared at me, raindrops beating her soft face and shoulders. She flung the water away with a quick shake of her head, and wiped her dark hair backwards. Her eyes never left mine—ours were locked as if in some kind of dance, and even among the storm-chill I felt the warming sensation—the first of many—an oozing of heat that radiated out from my core—just being within arm's distance seemed to quiet me. I sensed she felt the same because her glower seemed to soften, as if drawing strength from me, this stranger, forced her to not shut down. She dipped her stare momentarily to the unmoving form before returning it to me. She nodded slowly, and together we lifted the unconscious woman off the sodden ground.

✖✖✖

That night was the first time I had laid eyes on Layla, and from that moment I was hooked...

There was something about her, something so profoundly different from the other women I had dated, that I found myself completely and utterly *sprung*.

Yeah, y'all, I had fallen *hard*...

Layla and I had spent the next five hours together, a first date of sorts in the emergency room as they worked on the young woman, the two of us talking in hushed tones, getting to know one another, until the hours crept onward and I found Layla's head gently resting on my shoulder as she napped on the cold plastic chairs, her feet folded underneath her. I recall how she finally stirred around 6 a.m., as sunlight slowly crept along the worn carpet toward our row of chairs, Layla leisurely stretching a golden arm before opening her eyes and glancing upward into mine, where our

339

stares once again locked. There was no awkward moment of not knowing where or with whom she was with; no split second of vertigo where eyes grow wide—no, there was simple purity in her gaze, as if she had awakened knowing exactly where she wanted to be. Instinctively I had reached out to brush her dark hair from her cheek—I can't explain what possessed me to do that—it wasn't so much a physical act as a spiritual one—as if in that moment our souls connected—and Layla watched me silently, her dark eyes unblinking as I whispered that the young girl was out of surgery and in recovery—the doctors were guarded, but thought that she would make it. Layla blinked and smiled weakly before closing her eyes and nuzzling back into the warmth of my shoulder. An hour later we said our goodbyes in the parking lot of the hospital.

I recall driving home and using every second to vividly remember the sweet details of our chance encounter.

✖✖✖

How long ago did that fateful event occur that changed my world? Six, no seven years…

In some sense it seems like only yesterday. In another, it is as if decades have passed by, like when one attempts to recall the details of their child-hood and find that the window that they are glancing through is murky and cracked.

The second set of images that suddenly flooded my psyche caused me to reach out to the counter top for support. Lately when I glance at that counter top delicious images of Allison and the wooden spoon leap to mind. But this time, that did not happen. I felt myself grow weak as if my knees were about to buckle. My stare was fuzzy. My coffee mug seemed to swim in and out of focus as if it were alive. I wasn't looking—I was remembering…

Layla and I were at a hotel in New York, Upper West Side overlooking Central Park. We had come here on a whim; the weekend rate had set me back over a thousand bucks, but I didn't give a damn! I was with my lady, and that was all that mattered.

We had spent the day doing some touristy stuff—shopping on Fifth Avenue, taking in the Museum of Natural History and the Hayden Planetarium, and then back to the hotel for a quick nap before dinner in Brooklyn Heights overlooking the water and Manhattan skyline. Afterwards, we had cabbed it back to the hotel where Layla had shooed me into the bathroom for a long, hot shower. I had come out refreshed; my skin scrubbed clean, my senses singing in anticipation for what was to come. I remember waltzing out of the steamy bathroom and into a candlelight-filled bedroom. Layla was standing by the large window glancing downward to an expanse of park below. She had her back to me—when she turned, my breath was arrested.

I'll never forget the pose she held—Layla standing there, one hand on her hip, the other reaching out to stroke the wall, clad only in white lingerie: a beautiful laced bra that held her lovely breasts, a pair of match-ing g-string panties. A thin dark line of pubic hair could be seen through the translucent material. On her feet was a pair of spiked black heels. Her hair was straight down her back and shiny. Her eyes were dazzling orbs that sparkled at me as she smiled. For a moment neither of us said a word. I drunk in her features, the sensual stare that cut though me like a blade, and made my entire frame shudder.

I'll never forget that night, for that image, especially that pose is indelibly etched into my psyche. Also is the rush of emotions that I felt that evening—similar to that morning in the emergency room when our eyes locked—more a spiritual and soulful connection than on a physical plane—God, yes, my woman was beautiful—but it was her inner beauty that imprisoned my heart that night. And for the first time in my life, I felt something that I had never experienced before. There I was, standing before a breathtaking beauty—her sensuality reaching out to bathe me like a serpent does with its forked tongue, and what I felt deep inside was *not* the hardening of my sex, but the rush of emotions that made my eyes water. I was completely and utterly inebriated with someone to the point of total immersion...

That's when I knew.

I loved this woman, with all that my heart and soul was capable of...

✖✖✖

Suddenly the scene shifted. It was like one of those lovely days in Jamaica, ultra blue sky that would suddenly deepen and turn gray. Thick dark clouds rushing in bring torrential rains, but for only a short while…

My mind was enjoying the movie it was replaying—it had been a long time since I'd allowed the film to be shown again, but when the images shifted I felt as I had that fateful night on stage in Negril, a throng of partygoers belting out my name in unison as I spotted the woman at the back of the crowd and felt the temperature drop. A sudden chill overtook my body as a new scene replaced the old—one that I was not ready to see again.

I moved quickly to the living room, as if the act of physical movement would cause my brain to refocus.

It did not.

The image remained—Layla standing a foot away from me, hands drawn to her sides, tears streaming down her mascara-smeared face, as she told me her secret. And I remember backing away, as if she were some alien being, a monster that could do me harm, thinking to myself, *Oh my God, this isn't happening to me, this isn't possible, this is a sick joke. A minute from now we'll be laughing and carrying on as we always do. I'll reach out for her, she'll come to me, we'll embrace, becoming one, and everything will be okay…*

But it didn't end up that way.

I remember reaching up, almost instinctively, and slapping Layla hard across her face, as if in some small measure my action would serve to erase what she had just told me.

But it did not.

To this day, nothing has…

✖✖✖

A phone call thankfully saved me. It was Vince.

"What up, playa, how ya livin'?" he said.

"Waz up," I responded, but without the usual enthusiasm. Vince, I could tell, immediately picked up on my unusually weak demeanor.

"Hey, dawg, you okay?"

"Yeah."

"Come on, man, this is me you're talking to—what's up?" Vince asked.

"Naw, I'm cool," I said, attempting to muster up the energy that was needed to get through this call.

"A'ight—listen, Angeliqué and Amber are in town. I really want you and Erika to meet them. I know it's short notice, but we're heading over to bluespace later and would love for you to meet us there."

My mind raced. Pushed down into the depths of my brain were the fleeting images of Layla standing before me, swirling downward like a toilet flushed. I prayed they would stay there, but I knew they would not.

"Yeah, uh, that's cool. What time are you thinking?" I asked, wiping away the perspiration that had beaded on my bald head.

"I don't know," Vince said. "Probably around ten or eleven. Cool?"

"Yeah, that's cool," I said again, my mind still whirling from the blow of that last reflection.

"A'ight, listen, I really want you to meet them, so no excuses, playa!" Vince was trying levity, but I just wasn't feeling it. We clicked off. A moment later the phone rang again. I didn't even bother to check the Caller ID, knowing that it was probably Vince again, forgetting to tell me something.

"Speak!" I said, injecting a bit of the usual Trey-authority.

"Hi, is this Trey?" A woman's voice, heavily accented, vaguely familiar.

"Yes?"

"Hey," she responded, "this is Gabrielle, you probably don't remember me, but we met down in Jamaica a few months ago."

A flood of recognition hit me. Lovely Gabrielle, the honey whom I had fucked on the beach to the applause of an entire resort! And in that second, my mind flipped, literally, like a switch being thrown. No longer were there any lingering thoughts of Layla and her secret—those having been replaced by luscious Gabrielle—her rich olive skin, large tits, tight pussy, and talented mouth. Oh yeah, y'all, this call was exactly what Trey needed right about now!

"Hey, you!" I exclaimed, "Of course I remember you; how could I not!" Gabrielle giggled as we chatted for a few minutes, catching up and shit.

"So, listen, the reason I am calling," Gabrielle said in a breathy voice, "is because there's a party tonight at the home of this couple we know—very nice people, Lifestyles folks who just love to party. Anyway, I was thinking it would be great if you could come—come to the party and then hopefully come a few more times tonight, if you know what I mean!" Gabrielle was laughing and I could just envision her straddling my engorged dick. Again...

"Baby, I am definitely down for a party—especially if your fine ass is gonna be there!" I said, feeling my jeans go taut as my manhood stirred.

"Oh, Trey, that's great—I can't wait to see you!" Gabrielle gave me the details and I quickly jotted them down. Hanging up, I was giddy again— my old self—racing around the crib, wondering what I was going to wear to a party where mutha fuckas got naked! I'd have to shave my balls and bring a roll of condoms! Oh yeah, y'all...Trey's back in the saddle, y'all, for real!

True dat!

✖✖✖

I found the address easily, thanks to Mapquest. It was a nice-looking brick Colonial in a well-kept neighborhood just outside the Beltway in Silver Spring. Who would have guessed that mutha fuckas were about to get buck wild in this crib, sandwiched between PTA and soccer-mom homes. I parked a few houses away and walked leisurely up the stone steps to the door. After much deliberation I had decided on a dark suit, Italian cut, and a fine white silk shirt halfway undone. I didn't know these people save for Gabrielle and Raul, her husband, so I wasn't sure what to expect. But I wasn't one to take chances. You never knew when sexy-ass honeys were gonna show up, so I erred on the side of caution, and dressed contemporary with a bit of Trey-flair as only this brutha can do.

Come on, y'all, you know by now how we do!

I rang the doorbell, and glanced down at my black lace-ups that I had polished an hour earlier. I checked the Breitling: 10:18 p.m. Gabrielle told me the party started at 9, but fuck that! I wasn't one to show up on time for any damn thing. I thought for a moment about Vince and his friends heading to bluespace.

The door opened and I was greeted by a thirty-something blonde with long hair down her back, thin, and nice looking. She smiled with straight white teeth. The woman was dressed in a long colorful dress and heels that accentuated her small breasts and shapely ass.

"Hi," I said, flashing her my best Trey-smile. "I'm Trey Alexander, a friend of Raul and Gabrielle," I said, extending my hand.

"Oh, yes, we've been expecting you. Gabrielle had some very flattering things to say about you." She invited me in with a sweep of her hand, and I could have sworn that I spotted her gaze take a quick detour to my crotch.

And why not, if girlfriend's already heard about me???

I was led through a hallway, past the dining area and a formal living room, into the main living space. A large family room opened in front of me. It was tastefully decorated in pastels and plenty of eclectic artwork. The room was dim, but I spotted about twenty people at the far end by the floor-to-ceiling glass doors that opened onto an enclosed patio. Beyond was a strand of thick dark trees. The majority of the crowd had their backs to me. Most were half dressed or nude, the former wearing patterned sarongs that immediately took me back to Jamaica. Others were clad in leather—I spotted a few dudes in chaps, and some females in some very sexy black leather bodices with shiny steel rings. At least a handful of those I spotted wore collars.

My host introduced herself to me. She was Terri; her husband she pointed out was Bruce, a muscular guy, clad in brown leather chaps, zebra briefs, and otherwise bare-chester, who was the object of the crowd's attention.

Bruce stood before a nude woman who was bound by thick leather straps to a pair of eyebolts that descended from the ceiling. I could see that her feet, too, were tied together, ankles bound with thick rope. He bent down but whatever he was doing was lost on me.

Terri asked if I'd like to get more comfortable. I was contemplating her request, at the same time taking in the intriguing scene before me. Before

I could answer, she took hold of my hand with a sly grin and drew me away toward a staircase. I allowed her to lead me, following her as my stare dropped to her well-formed ass that moved seductively underneath fabric, her hips swaying rhythmically as we climbed. I asked if Raul and Gabrielle were here yet—she nodded and said she would take me to them momentarily.

We reached a carpeted landing and turned a corner. Terri led me into a darkened bedroom, which was lighted by a single candle. It cast a ghostly orange flicker about the room.

"Some of our guests find this to be more comfortable," Terri said as she handed me a folded blue sarong with a white fish motif adorning the cotton fabric. "It's up to you, of course, but I'd hate to see you wrinkle a fine suit." Terri grinned and I could see that her eyes were blazing as she looked me over.

"This will be fine," I said, holding the sarong.

"Give me your things then," she said, "I can hang them up for you." Terri made no move to leave. In fact, she promptly sat on the bed and folded her legs in front of me. I stood there for a split second, feeling the rush of adrenaline that was swimming through my veins. Again, thoughts of Vince popped into my head. Oh well, I guess homeboy would have to wait…Then I began to undress.

Terri sat there, watching me disrobe. Her eyes were tiny black slits that seemed to dance in their sockets. She didn't try to hide her stare nor avert her eyes. Just the opposite, in fact. It was clear that she took great pleasure in watching me remove my jacket, and lay it flat on the bed. Next, I unlaced my shoes, and as I slid them off my feet I unbuckled my belt and pants. My eyes were locked with Terri's, whose breathing had noticeably increased in intensity. She watched me unbutton the rest of my shirt, and pull it out and away from my trousers before removing it, placing it on the bed beside her. I could feel Terri's stare brush over me as she took in my tattoos, well-defined muscles, and bronze skin. I paused for a moment, counting silently to myself as I laid my hands on my pants.

"Waiting for something?" Terri asked, her voice slightly above a whisper. I responded by slowly allowing my pants to fall to the floor. I stepped out of them, removed my socks and handed them to Terri, who placed them over my jacket. Standing in front of her, clad only in my boxers, my dick became semi-hard under candle-lit illumination. Without further fanfare, I bent down and slid my boxers down my thighs.

Terri let out a sigh as she gazed upon my manhood. I took a step forward and handed my boxers to her. Terri took them silently and tossed them aside.

"Feel better?" she asked, cocking her head upward to meet my stare momentarily before returning to my well-engorged member.

"Much," I responded. I could see Terri's nipples poking through the thin fabric of her dress. I fought the rising temptation to reach out and grab them, not wanting within the first five minutes to blow my load, so to speak. Instead, I let my arms drape by my side.

Terri leaned forward, the neckline of her dress turning downward, allowing a nice shot of her cleavage. She came within a foot of me and I swore she was going to grab my dick.

"Gabrielle told me about your wonderful cock," she said, eyeing it with a smirk. "Perhaps I can get a taste of it myself later on tonight." She licked her lips and then blew gently across the head of my dick that was standing straight upright. It quivered in response to her breath.

I smiled. "I'd like that." Terri handed me the sarong; I wrapped it around and secured it snugly over my hips. I glanced down; my erection was like a Christmas tree draped in tinsel—the sarong did little to cover my meat. I sighed heavily, and Terri laughed.

"Let me take you to your friends," she said, patting the *package* gingerly before taking my hand and guiding me out of the room.

✖✖✖

As Terri and I returned to the main floor, moving slowly toward the mass of people huddled around Bruce, I spotted Gabrielle. She turned as we made our way over, flashing a huge smile as she noticed me. She rushed over and flung her arms around my neck.

"Hey, baby, long time no see," she said, pecking me on the lips before moving in to hug me. I flashed a smile as I held her at arm's distance, looking her over.

"Let me look at you," I said, taking in the white leather bra and g-string she wore along with a matching choke collar. Large holes were cut in the front of the bra allowing her cherry nipples to poke through. Her hair was pulled back and placed in a ponytail. "Damn, this gotta be D.C.'s finest!" Gabrielle gushed and winked at Terri.

"Just get here?" she asked.

"Yeah. Terri was kind enough to get me situated," I said, showing off my sarong.

"And it looks good on you!" Terri asked me if I wanted anything to drink. I told her a beer would be fine, and she headed off, leaving Gabrielle and me alone. Gabby leaned in and whispered in my ear: "So, Trey, I hope you are well rested—there are a bunch of people here who are anxious to party with you."

"You mean my reputation precedes me?" I asked in mock amazement.

"Oh, yes! Some of these couples were in Jamaica when you and I did our thing—remember?" Gabrielle asked with a grin.

"How can I ever forget," I replied, touching the corner of her mouth. She beamed seductively.

Our attention shifted to Bruce. We moved closer—beside his feet was an opened steel case. Bruce knelt and seemed to be rummaging around in it for a minute before he stood up, holding something in his hand—long, thin, and black, with what appeared to be a wide leather tip at the end. The woman in front of Bruce eyed him curiously as he waved it ceremoniously in the air and then placed it on a table nearby. I noticed that the woman's thighs were red. Bruce reached for her ankles and undid each rope. Then he bent down and fastened a cuff to each ankle. The cuff was tied off with rope to two eyelets in the floor behind Bruce. He pulled each rope tight and abruptly the woman was dangling at a forty-five degree with both legs spread wide.

The small crowd surged forward.

"Oh, you're gonna love this part," Gabrielle said as she took my arm.

"Where's Raul?" I asked, feeling myself growing hard for a second time as I eyed Gabby's lovely ass cheeks.

"Oh, he's around," she said, casually, "probably found some woman's face to use as a sperm dump!" Gabrielle's arm wrapped around me, and I wasted no time in placing mine around her. My hand found her right hip and descended slowly to cup her ass. I squeezed the flesh and grinned.

DAYUM.

The woman strung out and tied in front of us had a shaved pussy, I noticed. Bruce took his instrument and lightly began to tap around her thighs, using slow yet deliberate taps, not too hard, but enough pressure that everyone could hear the "pop" of leather on flesh.

He used a circular motion, beginning on the right thigh, moving clockwise toward her sex, but bypassing it, moving upward instead, tapping on her navel before moving on and descending to her inner thigh.

The woman was silent, but she was moving slowly with every tap he made.

Bruce moved closer to her sex, until he began tapping on her cunt, using the flat leather tip of the wand to slap against her pussy lips. The woman began to moan, almost imperceptibly at first, but then with increased volume. The crowd around us was silent. They were intently watching Bruce work. He was a master, working his magic for the woman, his slave, and for the crowd behind him. He neither turned nor looked in their direction, his attention totally focused on this woman and his craft.

Bruce moved closer, changing the angle of the wand until the flat head was facing downward—abruptly he slapped her pussy *hard* with an audible whack. The woman let out a short, piercing yell. Bruce moved to her side, facing us for the first time, then sent the leather wand back down on her reddening sex-box, causing her to thrash. The woman reflectively closed her legs but quickly opened them again as Bruce laid the wand on her clit, moving it in circles for some seconds before whacking her skin again.

"Oh, I love this," Gabrielle said, reaching down to stroke the front of my sarong. "Seems like you do, too!" she exclaimed as we exchanged glances.

"No, baby," I said, looking into her eye, "I'm just happy to see you."

"Yeah, whatever. You'd say anything right now!"

Out of the corner of my eye I spied a sistah heading toward us. She grinned at me and turned her attention quickly to Gabrielle.

"Tell me this is the chocolate bad ass you've been talking about?" she said. "Please tell me this is him!"

Gabrielle nodded. I looked her over—she was a large sistah, I'd guess close to 175 pounds, with rich dark skin and full dark lips set in a pretty face that reminded me of that fine ass Angie Stone, with large full breasts that clung to her colorful sarong. I could see her thighs peeking out from the folds of the fabric. Her ass was huge, jiggling as she genuflected at me.

"Nina, this is Trey," Gabrielle said. "Trey, my girlfriend Nina."

Nina stuck out her hand. "Oh, Trey, I've heard some things about you!" she said, flicking her eyes up and down my frame. I smiled and winked.

"All bad, I'm sure," I said.

"And you know that!"

"Nina," Gabby said, pulling her closer, "Trey and I were just about to go and get more *comfortable*," she said, eyeing me for a second. "Care to join us?" Before I could interrupt, Nina's mouth was spreading wide in a grin. I was scanning the body of this chick, wondering how I'd manage with all that woman under her sarong! I'd never been with a big girl before. Honestly, y'all know I'm only used to the finest honeys this side of the Atlantic—but then I caught myself and pondered this new thread for a moment—before concluding that, at the end of the day, pussy is pussy—it's all pink inside, ya know…so perhaps I'd give this big girl a ride, try her on for size, so to speak!

Yeah, that might work…

"Oh hell yeah," Nina said as she quickly grabbed my arm. Gabrielle took the other and I found myself again being led away, Bruce and the woman's shrieks fading from my consciousness as I focused on the next phase of my adventure…

THIRTY-FOUR

Bluespace was packed, even at this time of night, but thankfully, Vince had called ahead. So getting a table didn't require much of a wait. They had arrived around 11:30, Vince and Amber; Erika had called from her cell to say she was on her way and would arrive shortly—Trey hopefully would show any moment now—he said he would stop by, but Vince knew how Trey could be. The only unknown variable was Angeliqué. She had left shortly after they had returned from his studio, saying that she had some errands to run and some people to see—Vince had assumed she would return a few hours later. But she had been missing all day. He was feeling a bit of anxiety about that, but figured she, like Trey, would show eventually. She was aware of the get-together later on that evening at their spot.

Amber told him not to worry—Angeliqué was a big girl and could take care of herself.

Vince didn't doubt that for a second.

The colors of bluespace shifted around them as Vince led Amber to their booth upstairs. Dazzling colors—vibrant reds, oranges, greens, purples, and blues—colors that like a lava-lamp coalesced together like some living organism and slid down the curved white walls as the music of Floetry coursed around them. It was an intoxicating slow groove—"Say Yes," that mixed with the lightshow making an emotional statement. And then, as the colors blinked out and the restaurant was bathed in darkness for a moment, the music rose sharply, thumping bass-infused beats of hip-hop replacing the soft sensuous melody, as a half-dozen music videos were displayed on each wall, but out of focus—the fast-cutting imagery lighting up the interior of the space, like lightning, causing folks to clap.

Amber was enthralled as she slid into the curved sofa seat. Vince admired her silently. She was indeed beautiful. Her brown hair was tied back. No makeup adorned her auburn-colored skin. There was no need for it. Her eyes shined as she soaked up the atmosphere. She wore jeans, a thick mocha-colored sweater, and boots—her thighs and ass hugging the denim fabric as if they were family. Vince recalled the way she had looked just a few hours earlier.

She had asked to see his studio. Apparently she and Angeliqué had talked about his collection of masks.

Angeliqué had left Vince and Amber alone—they were hanging lazily around his house when she asked if he could take her to see it. Vince had agreed.

Thirty minutes later, Amber had stood in front of his mask-covered wall. Like the others, she had been spellbound by his art. She found his latest piece—the mask and torso lifecasting of Desiree—vibrant raindrop-splashes of color over an indigo base, most intriguing.

She had asked many questions—who was this person? What was she like? And questions about the actual process. She had stroked the paint-saturated plaster sensuously before spinning on the heels to face him.

"Have you ever done an entire body?" Amber had asked cautiously as she turned to stare directly at him. Vince had contemplated the question as he put down his coffee mug to return her stare. He felt something fluttering inside of him, excitement and sexual energy that slowly began as an expanding vortex. "No," he replied, "not yet. I've been toying with the idea for many months—but it's fairly involved—lots of material, and of course, lots of time on the part of the model."

Amber had considered this for a moment as her fingers alighted from the plaster of Desiree's breasts.

"Then let me be the first…"

✖✖✖

Amber had lain comfortably, the futon mattress spread out on the floor of his studio, several blankets covering the fabric as he prepared her for the full-body lifecasting. She was as beautiful as he had remembered, that first time seeing her in New Orleans, when he hadn't adequately taken the time to really focus on her features, for fear of upsetting Angeliqué, but this time, there was no such trepidation. She lay on her side, nude, one leg bent, the thickness of her smooth, unblemished thigh and tapered legs enthralling. Her hair hung free. Her cheekbones, eyelashes, curved mouth, breasts, and sculpted ass—all works of art. No *veve* covering her bare skin this time, like a full-body tattoo, nothing standing in the way between him and her splendor.

It was the beauty of her youthfulness that appealed to Vince.

But it wasn't just that—after all, Desiree was young—it was Amber's body. Thick in the right areas—thighs and ass—meat on her bones, as his momma was fond of saying. Curvy sensuous hips that led to a small waist, tapering back out to a voluptuous upper body. Her flesh wasn't taut the way Desiree's was—it wasn't pudgy either, but as he coated her skin with jelly, his fingers found depth everywhere he pressed and massaged—and Vince dug that.

He had taken his time. The process had taken a lot longer than he anticipated—yet, this was a lazy Saturday, he had nowhere to go—and neither did Amber. Painstakingly, he had applied the petroleum jelly to her skin as if he were a professional masseuse; Amber closing her eyes, purring like a kitten as she shifted to ensure every inch of her body was well lubricated. They had talked the entire time, conversation flowing easily, as if they were good friends sitting across from each other at a comfortable Starbucks sipping hot lattes, instead of what they were—a breathtaking woman reclining nude upon his studio floor while his hands caressed the supple flesh of her breasts, neck, shoulder blades, and ankles.

When Vince had completed her upper body and legs he had paused as she shifted to lie flat, parting her legs slightly. Vince gazed down at her sex, a thin line of dark pubic hair above her clit, the rest of that place otherwise manicured clean. He felt himself growing hard again—the fourth or fifth time today, or was it sixth or seventh? Vince had lost count—once again he fought the rising tension between his own thighs.

"Here," he had said, holding out the tub of jelly to her, "perhaps you should finish up…"

Amber had stared back at him unblinkingly. "Don't know why, Vince," she had said amusingly, "you seem to be doing such a fine job…"

Erika's arrival at bluespace brought Vince back to reality. He hugged Erika, and Amber smiled as they were introduced. Erika sat as drinks were ordered.

"So," Erika said as she removed her leather jacket, settling across from them, "aren't we missing some people?"

"Yeah," Vince said, "Angeliqué is out doing her thing, but promised to meet us here later; and your boy, Trey, well, Lord knows where that fool is!"

"Please—it's a Saturday night—I'm sure His Highness is fondling some hootchie momma this very moment!"

"Shit, he better show—I'm not playing with his dumb ass this time."

Erika turned to Amber. "Don't pay us black folks any mind—we're just messing around. It's good to finally meet you, girl—I've heard a lot about you."

The two began to converse as Vince ordered some hors d'oeuvres for the table. Erika learned that Amber was originally from Texas—born in Houston, and spent most of her life being raised by her great-grandmother.

"I never knew my real parents," Amber said as she sipped a beer. "My mom gave me up when I was barely two weeks old. She had medical problems and couldn't care for me, so I was told. And I never met my father," she added somberly.

Erika patted her arm. "I'm sorry—I'm sure that was very hard on you."

"Yeah," Amber replied, as Vince listened, "it was, but you get used to it— Her voice trailed off. Vince rubbed her shoulder. They had spoken at length about this topic hours ago. Amber smiled weakly. "It's cool, really. I'm not looking for sympathy. As I explained to Vince earlier, I came to the conclusion that this is my life—I can either feel sorry for myself or accept it and move on—I've chosen to live my life. This is the one that God has given me. It could be a whole lot worse."

"Wow," Erika exclaimed, "I love your attitude—so many people choose to feed into the negative aspects of what's been handed to them, but not you! You go, girl—a beautiful woman who's got her shit together!" She raised her beer to Amber. The two clinked their glasses together.

"I'm gonna like you!" Amber said with a smile.

"Me too, girlfriend," Erika responded, "me too!"

THIRTY-FIVE

We took the stairs, down instead of up this time, Gabrielle on point, me in the middle, Nina taking up the rear. Gabby came to the landing at the bottom of the stairs and stopped. Terri was at the bottom, stark naked with a frosty Corona in her hand. I took in her features, her small tits, each nipple pierced with a thin silver loop, and hairless pussy. My dick did a quick convulsion. I felt Nina's body pressing against mine. I tried to descend to the bottom step, but Gabby wasn't budging. I felt Nina's hot breath in my ear.

"Sexy-ass mutha fucka," she whispered, and I felt her grind her pelvis into my ass. I half-turned to the left.

"You have a foul mouth," I offered.

"You haven't seen *shit…*"

A beer was passed to me, I accepted it, thanked my hostess, and we were moving again. We found ourselves in a narrow hallway, candles suspended from the wall every few yards. We passed by several doorways, some open, others closed. We sauntered on and came to an open door on the right. Gabrielle was peering in and held up her hand, glancing back at us with a grin.

"Looks like I found my husband," she said to Nina and me before moving on. I made my way to the door and peered in. Raul was standing buck naked on a narrow bed, legs spread with a smoldering cigar in his mouth. A demure white woman knelt beneath him as he jerked his cock onto her face. The woman remained motionless but her C-cup tits were jiggling from the bed's and Raul's movement. Raul glanced over and grinned. He took his hand off his cock for a moment, gave me a salute, then went back to what he was doing, slapping the woman's face with his meat. As I moved on I witnessed her smirk as she opened her mouth, readying for Raul's juice to flow.

Gabrielle had gone to the end of the hallway and disappeared into one of the rooms. Nina and I followed, and discovered her stretching out on a queen-size bed bathed in candlelight. On the bedside table was a wicker basket filled to the brim with condoms.

"Gonna stand there," Gabby asked in a low voice, "or you gonna join me? I glanced quickly at my watch, noting the time: It was a few minutes past 11. A little voice in my head asked if I was supposed to be somewhere else right now? I quickly brushed the thought away—at this point I neither recalled nor gave a shit. I turned my attention to the girls who were settling onto the bed, and let my sarong drop to the floor. I stood there, my dick swaying in front of me like a beacon, letting them feast on the *package*.

Gabrielle had unhooked her bra and placed it on the night table. She then slid her g-string down and stretched out on the bed, spreading her legs. Meanwhile, Nina unwrapped her sarong and let it fall. Her breasts were dark fruits with thick nipples that hung free and looked appetizing as hell. I've got to tell y'all—even though I've never been with a big girl before, the sight of those melons was making my dick harder than it already was. Or maybe it was the sight of Gabrielle's fine ass bod three feet away.

Who knew???

I knelt on the bed and stroked Gabrielle's olive-skinned leg. Ran a finger from her ankle up to her thigh before flattening my hand and gliding it lightly across her shaved pussy. I could feel the wetness on my palm. Gabrielle's eyes never left me.

"She's ready for you, Trey," Gabrielle whispered. I responded by kneeling down and letting my tongue connect with the flesh of her knee, kissing it all over sensuously before tracing a wet swath up to her thigh. Gabby spread her legs wider as my hands found her breasts. I kneaded them lightly, then squeezed each one in turn and pulled at her nipples.

"You know what I like, Trey," she whispered again, head thrown back, her eyes closed. Nina was fully nude now, and came around the bed and squatted behind me. Her hands found my back, stroking me up and down before reaching around and grasping my shaft. She began to jerk me off slowly with both hands as she rotated her big titties into my back, sucking on my earlobe. My tongue found Gabby's hole—she held her legs apart and I moved in, tasting her nectar. Her syrup was sweet, just as I had remembered it. I scooped a bit of it up on my tongue and swallowed hungrily, before lowering my face to her pussy. My chin connected with her cunt lips, and I rubbed my face in her box, first my lower jaw, then lips, nose, and eyelids. Gabrielle was squeezing her thighs against my ears, but I didn't care—I increased my tempo, thrashing my head from side to side as I thrust out my tongue, cunt lapping Gabby as I tweaked her nipples. Nina had managed to maneuver beneath me and taken my cock in her mouth. I let out a gasp as her full lips enveloped my entire length –slurping it in and sucking it to the back of her throat as if she were a porno star. This sistah could suck a dick! I glanced down—Nina's eyes were locked onto me as she sucked. I shifted, allowing my hand to find her spongy melons. I palmed each one in turn before returning my attention to Gabrielle. Her cunt was drenched now. I returned to her orifice and probed her innards with my nose. Moving it rapidly from side to side, Gabby began to moan.

"Oh yeah, do it like that, damn, that's it!" she said between heavy breaths. "Oooh, Trey, you gonna make me cum, dammit!" I increased my tempo, fucking her with my tongue, stabbing her clit with my nose, grasping her pussy lips gingerly between teeth, sucking her in to my mouth, swishing around her entire love hole as I felt her convulse and come.

"Ohhhhhh fuck!" Gabrielle moaned, clamping her thighs tight against my ears as she reached out to grab my shoulders. Her nails dug into my flesh, but I didn't care. I slowed my movement, feeling her orgasm peak, then subside, the waves of pleasure receding. I placed my tongue on her still-throbbing flesh at the apex to her core, feeling her pulse and the heat transferred to me. I reveled in making a woman feel good. I glanced up. Gabby was smiling with eyes closed. She opened them, caught me staring, and squeezed my shoulder.

I beamed like the true playa that I am.

Nina shifted and my dick plopped out of her mouth, hard as a rock and glistening with her spit. I moved onto my haunches and sat up, guiding Gabby with my hand. She got on all four as I slipped on a condom. I glanced down. Even in the twinkling candlelight, I could see her asshole glistening with desire. I felt a twitch run the length of my shaft. Gabby's head was turned, watching me. I palmed both ass cheeks, spreading them wide as I entered her still-wet pussy, well lubed from my tongue and her orgasm. I filled her quickly, grabbing her waist with both hands, pummeling her as I watched my cock jackhammer her box. Nina slid underneath us and cupped my balls with a hand as her mouth connected with our flesh—shaft and pussy—her tongue painting a coat of wetness as Gabby and I fucked. The scene was surreal—I tipped my head back, studying the pattern of flickering candlelight on the ceiling for a moment before closing my eyes to concentrate on the feeling alone—Gabrielle's tight pussy, Nina's hot tongue, my black cock—three people coming together in a delicious fashion, the same way a scrumptious pie is prepared, each ingredient added to the bowl and devotedly mixed by hand, creating a creamy batter that drips with goodness.

Reaching forward, I grabbed Gabby's tits in hand and kneaded her flesh. Glancing down I watched Nina work her magic on Gabby's cunt and on me. Deciding it was time to give this sistah some *quality* time, I pulled out of Gabby and maneuvered on top of Nina. Her flesh was heaving as I spread her Hershey thighs, her stomach warm against my own tight body. I grasped my cock in hand, waved it around her cunt, spreading those black velvety folds before lowering my weight and thrusting inside of her.

Nina gasped as I entered her. Immediately she lifted her thighs in a motion that surprised me. I felt her pussy suck on my cock and I was amazed at the tightness of this chick's cunt. I grunted as I fucked her, smiling down as Nina thrashed her head from side to side.

"Fuck me, boy!" Nina belted out, as her eyes squeezed shut. Gabby positioned herself over Nina's face and lowered her pussy onto her mouth. She reached for me and we tongue-kissed as I rocked above Nina's flesh, her stomach and ass vibrating as I thrust in and out. Off to my right I caught a moment and cocked my head to the side. A man had entered the room and was watching us. He, like us was nude, thin, but well-toned, his cock in hand as he stroked it slowly. He grinned when we made eye contact, but said nothing. For a moment he stood there and I was trying to figure out what he was up to, but Nina was grabbing my ass and digging her fingernails into my skin as I fucked her.

"Harder," she commanded, and I forgot the guy by the wall as I lifted her thighs. I reared back and slammed all of my weight into her cunt, hearing her scream with delight as I hit bottom. "Oh yeah, that's what I'm talking 'bout!" she squealed, as I stuffed my dick into her hole, pressing my entire weight against her. I rested for a moment, grabbing both titties between fingers and tracing circles around her nipples with my tongue. They were large, distended things, with dark areolas that looked so fucking good. My mouth found them appetizing and I teased Nina by biting her nipples.

"Fuck me from behind," she directed. Gabby, who was bobbing to a rhythm all her own disengaged herself from Nina's mouth and I flipped Nina over. I palmed both cheeks. My hands barely covered a quarter of her ass, but something about it drew me near. I felt her pussy, which was hot and throbbing. I ran a finger over her anus, which from this vantage point was puckered at an upturned angle.

I reached for some lube and anointed my condom-covered dick. I slid into her pussy effortlessly and pummeled it as I contemplated the expanse of ass before me. Gabby had lain down and spread her legs so Nina could feed again. A quick glance to my right showed that the man was still there, his thin dick angled upward as he stroked it. Spreading Nina's ass with my thumb and forefinger, I probed her anus with a lubed digit before pulling out and teasing her backdoor with the head of my dick. Nina glanced back, perspiration adorning her face. Her eyes were on fire as if she were possessed.

"Take my ass, boy," she said, breathlessly, "that shit is yours!"

I positioned myself and barreled forward, feeling her ass open up to receive me. Nina let out a squeal; it was loud and high pitched. She lurched forward as I hit ass-bottom, then I felt her meet my thrust with her own, her cheeks a wave that bum rushed to and fro like the tides, a shuddering wall of thigh and ass-flesh as I slapped against her.

Gabby held Nina's head in her hands. Her thighs adorned her face, tremoring along with Nina whose body seemed to convulse in spasms. "Oh God, I am coming!" she yelled, before chomping down on Gabby's cunt, and reaching back with one hand to spread her ass cheek for me. I gripped her ass as firmly as I could, digging my nails into her flesh as I felt my own orgasms about to spout. I grunted and slapped against her as if there were no tomorrow, pummeling her as if she weren't even human—just an orifice that I was trying to plug, her ass some kind of repulsive, alien thing, and it was my job to snub it out. Nina was alive—I could feel her come, her entire frame shuddering, the waves unleashing from one end of her body to the other, her anus tightening up, as if it would fight to the end, not giving up until this last moment. I heard Gabby pant and then shriek. The pressure was building in me, too—my balls, already heavy, sperm-laden, ready to blow. I tilted my head back, eyes squeezed shut, my mind on autopilot, my lower body commanded by a separate microprocessor—one that controlled the simple act of fucking, the quickening in and out—and then I was coming, sperm spewing forth from my engorged state, rushing into Nina's ass, filling my condom with my juice as I cried out, mingling with the shortening moans from my lovers, Nina and Gabby.

✖✖✖

I flopped down on that ass, spent. Resting my entire weight on Nina, I felt the warmth of her body and that of Gabby. The three of us were exhausted. For a long while none of us moved. My breathing was timed to Nina's underneath me.

Hers was in time to Gabrielle's.

"That was so nice…" A female voice—that much I registered but beyond it nothing else. My entire focus was on my cock, which was still cocooned in Nina's asshole. It withered, yet she refused to give it up. I felt my sap drain from my balls, and as I reached around and palmed Nina's tits I found myself kissing the back of her neck.

It felt so damn good, I'm not gonna even front!

The candles continued to flicker and the entire scene was so surreal—like Jamaica—I closed my eyes, and concentrated not on the sounds of breathing or heartbeats, but what I was feeling. The rush that comes from passion-filled sex, the excitement from tasting someone new for the first time, entering them, feeling them swell to fit you, riding your sex, fucking you, and then coming with you. I opened my eyes and glanced over at Gabby. Her eyelids fluttered briefly, and she smiled at me before extricating herself from underneath Nina's body. I remained inside of Nina, feeling no need to get off of her. I spread my legs and pushed in deeper, feeling Nina's ass quiver with movement as I readjusted. Gabby came behind me, bent down and caressed my ass. I felt her reach for my balls and squeeze before hugging me with her body. I smiled, relishing the feeling of warmth and gratification.

I felt her hands on my ass again. Felt her fingers gliding along the crack of my ass. Felt her stop as she reached my opening. I tensed slightly, but sucked in a breath and reminded myself whom I was with. This scene was cool with me.

Fingers lightly probing my ass. The feeling—tense and exciting at the same time. Breasts rubbing against my back making my dick hard. Nina wiggling underneath me.

Then Gabby was gone, and I felt the air cool on my back. With my eyes closed I waited for her to return.

A pressure on my anus jarred me to open my eyes. As my head did a slow roll, turning in her direction, I felt something penetrate me. I gazed back in horror and jerked off of Nina as I saw the man's face inches from my own.

"WHAT THE FUCK!" I yelled, my forearm raised and pushing him off of me with a strength that I didn't recognize. He flew back and hit the wall with a thud.

I was on my feet, Nina scrambling off the bed as Gabby popped her head in the door.

"You fucking faggot!" I screamed, crossing the few meters of empty space to the guy and knocking him to the ground with a clenched fist. "WHAT THE FUCK ARE YOU DOING???" I yelled again. Gabby was on me in an instant, her breasts heaving against my back as she pulled me away and toward the door. My eyes were slits, foam leaping from my mouth—I didn't see or hear anything—I was a bull—out of control.

Then I heard myself utter: "That faggot tried to fuck me…" as I was dragged into the hallway. A crowd of people appeared, eyes-wide, Raul brushing past me and into the room. Terri was rushing toward us and then past me. Gabby was pulling me up the stairs, Nina at my back, as I thrashed like a caged animal.

"I'm no fucking faggot!" I hissed, reaching the top stair, folks petrified, a nigga out of control, backing up instinctively as I passed, fearing I'd lash out. "YOU FUCKING HEAR ME—I'M NO FAGGOT!"

I have no idea how I got my clothes nor how I left the house, but at some point I found myself on the Beltway heading south, the steady drone of tires on asphalt and orange-lit LED sobering. The weight of what had just happened came crashing down upon me, causing me to almost wreck. Everything that had been so good suddenly was erased by a singular event that was all bad…

"FUCK!" I yelled to the empty interior of my ride, my heart dropping to new depths as images of Layla rushed into my head, fusing with the recent events of tonight, forming a solid twisting mass of repulsiveness that refused to leave me alone.

THIRTY-SIX

The remainder of the evening—that is to say, for the next two and a half hours, Erika, Vince, and Amber huddled together, laughing like recently reunited high school friends. Vince enjoyed seeing Amber relaxed and in her element, taking pleasure in the closeness that comes from great conversation among good friends. Erika took to Amber immediately, drawn to her as if she were a long-lost cousin. The bluespace staff left them alone— except for the drinks that continued to arrive with clockwork precision, long after their plates of food had been wiped clean and cleared away.

It was 2:15 a.m. when they said their goodbyes. Vince and Amber stood outside in the chilled air, their breath rising as she clung to his elbow, huddled together watching Erika's brake lights fade into the stillness of the gray winter morning.

Neither Angelique nor Trey had showed...

...Or called...

✖✖✖

It was Erika who made the call.

"Put me through to that *fool*, please!"

India Jasmine Jackson laughed out loud.

"Listen, Trey," Erika began without preamble, "you've got a couple of friends who are extremely pissed at you right now..."

"Damn, Sassy—what did I do? It's not even ten a.m.," Trey replied. He glanced at his wristwatch on a dull Wednesday morning—the threat of snow hung in the air.

"Last Saturday, bluespace—you were supposed to show—Vince had *visitors* from out of town—remember?"

"Oh shit! Boo—let me tell you, I had one hell of a night…"

"Trey!" Erika exclaimed, cutting him off in mid-sentence. "Save it—we're meeting at bluespace tonight at eight. I strongly suggest you be there—that is if friendship means anything to you anymore…"

"Erika, come on…"

But she had already hung up.

✖✖✖

Trey was already seated at a first-floor booth at bluespace when they arrived. He was nursing a Corona, and had a tired look in his eyes. He stood up, gave Vince dap and Erika a rushed hug.

"You look like shit," were the first words out of her mouth, directed at Trey.

"I love you, too…"

"I'm serious, Trey. This whoring around is obviously catching up with you. Look at you—I bet you haven't slept in days."

Vince was eyeing his best friend curiously, yet silently. Trey sighed.

"Look—things have been extremely hectic in my life as of late. Work sucks and…"

Erika held up her hand. "Okay—let me stop you right there. See, this is what always happens. We get together, after weeks of not seeing you and the first thing that occurs is that you dominate the entire conversation, and no one can get a word in edgewise. Well, that stops today. We're here because your boy needs you. He needs us. So shut the hell up and listen!"

Trey cut a glance over to Vince who removed his glasses and rubbed his face. They looked at each other for a moment.

"So, Vince," Trey said, "how ya livin'?"

Vince returned a weak smile. "Been better, dawg. I have to tell you, I'm disappointed that you didn't show Saturday night." Vince eyed Trey. "Not only did you not come, but you didn't even call. We were waiting for you."

Trey took a small swig of beer. "Sorry, dawg. Something came up—I thought you'd understand."

"Yeah—well, that's the thing, Trey. It seems like something's always coming up with you. I mean, I don't feel like a priority in your life any-more." Vince's eyes were unblinking.

"I second that," Erika said, putting down her Corona. "You have high expectations of your friends, Trey, especially from your boy here and from me. When you need us, you call and expect us to come running. Funny thing is, we usually do."

Vince nodded silently.

Erika continued. "But lately, the whole vibe among the three of us has shifted—in recent months, it's all about you. Trey 150 percent, instead of the usual 90. I for one am growing tired of it. Seriously tired."

"Damn," Trey uttered.

Vince cleared his throat. "Erika's right, dawg. And you need to hear this. There's a lot of shit that's gone down in the past few weeks regarding both Erika and me—I don't think you have any idea what we've gone through. We need you, dawg—we need the old Trey back. You feel me?"

Trey was silent for a moment. His stare moved from one best friend to the other. He wore a downturned expression on his face.

"I don't know what to say—I guess I've always been a bit selfish. Lately probably more so. I'm sorry, y'all. For real!"

"Yeah," Vince said, "well, to tell you the truth, we've heard all of this before. I guess I need to know whether this is what we can continue to expect from you or not." He glanced over at Erika and then back at Trey. "Whether we can count on you as a true friend."

Trey put his beer down. "Okay, guys. I hear you. Honest I do—and you have my full attention. From now on…"

Vince smiled, then sighed deeply as he put down his beer.

ìI didn't want to tell any of you this but you know several weeks ago when

I went down to New Orleans to surprise Angeliqué? Well, I'm the one who ended up getting surprised. I found her in the arms of another person." He paused to stare hard at Trey before shifting his gaze to Erika. "In fact, I found her in the arms of a *woman*."

"What?" Erika exclaimed. Trey opened his mouth to speak, but then thought better of it.

"Yeah. A woman."

"Why didn't you tell us, Vince?" she asked.

"I don't know—I guess I was in shock. I returned home, mad as hell. I needed some time to sort things out. I needed time to think."

Trey shook his head forlornly and said, "Go on."

"Then she and Amber came up last week. It gave us some time to talk—I thought that perhaps there was a chance between us." Vince paused to down his Corona and signal the waitress for another round. "But now I know that it was not meant to be."

"I'm sorry, Vince," Erika said, rubbing his back with her hand.

"We made love one more time, at my studio, but it wasn't the same. My heart wasn't in it and I could tell neither was hers." Vince sighed as he shook his head. "I mean, it's weird going from what we had—the intensity, the passion down in New Orleans that first time to this. This time it was just physical. Devoid of anything emotional."

Trey cleared his throat. "Did the two of you talk about it? About what happened?"

"We tried," Vince responded, "but it was clear to me that this is who she is. Angeliqué, I guess, has this need to be a free-spirited person. Tied down to no one. I don't think she saw *us* even as a possibility..."

Erika asked, "Is that why she didn't show Saturday night?"

Vince nodded. "I'm sure that has everything to do with it. After we made love—correction, make that after we had sex, 'cause it sure wasn't making love—she left. Amber was still at my house chilling. We ended up spending the entire day and night together. Actually, there's a separate story there."

"Oh, I really like her, Vince."

Vince smiled.

"Don't tell me you tapped that too?" Trey asked.

Erika eyed him and Trey shrugged.

"No, Trey. I'm not like you. But guess what did happen? She asked to see my studio, so I took her. Once she was there, she asked if I'd do a full-body casting of her. And I did!"

Vince smiled. Erika was grinning.

"Wait a minute," Trey exclaimed. "You're telling me that one minute you're boning Angeliqué, the next moment you've got her friend butt naked in your studio? Damn, bro, there is hope for you yet!"

"Trey," Erika said, "not everything is about sex, you know. Oh, forget it—you'll never understand. I talked to Amber Saturday and it wasn't like that at all. She felt extremely comfortable being with Vince and actually thought up the idea of doing a full-body casting herself. And from the way she described it to me, Vince here was the perfect gentleman, as only I've come to expect from him."

Vince grinned. "What can I say?"

Trey grunted.

"I will say this," Vince continued, turning to Erika, "I'm really feeling Amber. She's so down-to-earth and cool—I mean, don't get me wrong—I'm not trying to jump into anything with her, especially on the coattails of this thing with Angeliqué but I can't help feeling the way I do. I truly enjoy being with her. I feel as if I can be myself, you know, just let go and say and do what I want.

"When we were in the studio doing her lifecasting she was so relaxed. We talked for hours about everything—her upbringing, her moms giving her up for adoption, her interests, my book, and my passions—all in this manner that I can't put into words, other than to say that there was this *vibe* between us. I could feel it, and I really believe that she felt it, too."

"Vince," Erika said, "let me ask you something—where does Desiree fit into all of this? Correct me if I'm wrong, but it seems like you're juggling two to three women, depending on how you count them, in your life right now. Don't you think you should figure out what you want and who you're interested in pursuing?"

"That's the thing, Sassy, I'm trying to do that. I had no intentions of pursuing anything with Desiree—it just kind of happened. And I'm enjoying myself. She's young, smart, got plenty of attitude, but in a good way…she looks damn good and sexy, but I don't know; I just don't see her hanging in there for the long term."

Erika nodded, thinking to herself, *I've heard this before…*

"Then I met Angeliqué. To be honest, I was swept off my feet; I admit it. I definitely saw myself settling down with her. But it never got off the ground. When I saw her with another woman, I just went cold inside. Whatever I was feeling for her died right then and there."

"I feel you, dawg," Trey said. "See, that's why I don't even front with these honeys…I've been down that road before, you know. I tried the whole, let-me-commit-to-you-and-no-one-else thing and I got burned big time! Ya hear? So no more of that shit for me!"

Erika sucked her teeth.

"Nigga, please! That was what? Five years ago? What are you saying, Trey, that you're never gonna trust another woman? That you're never gonna give love another chance?"

Trey eyed her but said nothing.

"That's messed up," Erika pronounced.

"Anywho," Vince said, bringing the conversation back to him, "things are pretty much done with Angeliqué. And then there is Amber. We clicked, we vibed. I don't know how she feels about me or whether she even senses the chemistry that's forming between us or not, but it sure feels different than the ones before her. There's something very special about that woman."

Erika nodded.

"You'd know what I'm talking about Trey if you had shown up…" he said.

"Ouch!" Trey responded.

The three were silent for a moment, watching the light show that was erupting around them. A hypnotic refrain from Prince, falsetto vocals wafted over them.

I wanna be your lover.

Erika broke the silence first. "That reminds me, Vince; Amber mentioned several times in conversation the fact that she has no idea who her parents are. I asked her if she was interested in finding them, and she said she had been thinking about that for the past year. So, I was telling James about her..."

Trey cut a sharp glance her way.

"What? Anywho—James knows this gay couple that runs this service that reconnects adopted children with their parents. Do you think Amber would be interested in finding her birthparents? James seems to think that he could get them to do some research for her gratis, since they've been bugging him to do a story on their firm for months now."

Vince smiled. "Hmmn, I dig that idea. I think she'd be down for that. Let me run it by her and see what she thinks."

"Hold up," Trey exclaimed. "Is James going to plaster her story all over the airwaves? If so, you need to consider whether or not that's in her best interest, or, for that matter, in the best interests of the birthparents, assuming they can be found."

"I asked James about that—he said he wouldn't do anything without getting the approval of Amber first. But I don't think he's interested in this from a news story point of view—he was just offering up a favor to help a friend of mine out."

Vince grinned and said, "Cool."

"Actually, I hope she is interested. I'd kind of like to help, myself," Erika said. "I'm feeling her, too, Vince—she's good people, and after James and I spoke it got me excited about the possibilities. At least it's a place to start."

"Thanks, boo, I'll give her a call and holla back."

Vince sat back and sighed, a contented look of on his face. Erika smiled back at him.

Trey exhaled loudly. Vince and Erika cut a glance over to him.

"Well?" Erika asked. "We both know you've been dying to open your big fat mouth all evening. I think we've tortured you enough already. What do you think, Vince?"

"Yeah, I say let the brutha speak!"

"See, y'all ain't right. But since you offered—check this shit out!"

Trey proceeded to give them a blow-by-blow account of the previous

Saturday night, working backwards from being "assaulted" as he put it, by a "faggot mutha fucka," to the sexual romping he and Gabrielle had with her homegirl Nina!

Vince and Erika were in shock, hearing how the evening had gone down, watching his face turn into a snarl as he described the "assault." Both knew how Trey felt about this kind of thing—Trey not at all comfortable with being approached by men, especially those showing a sexual interest in him. They had witnessed his reaction to gay men coming onto him before, and it wasn't pretty.

"Oh *NO*!" Erika cried out, but in a soft, whispery voice as if air were being forcibly let out of a punctured tire. Vince snapped his head in the direction of her stare. Trey was the slowest to react. He turned toward the front of the restaurant where two women were being led to a table nearby. His face contorted into pain as the realization of whom he was seeing seeped into his pores, making him sick. The color drained from his face in an instant.

"Shit!" Vince exclaimed as he made eye contact briefly with *Layla*, Trey's ex-love of his life...

Trey could not speak. He remained motionless as Layla paused for a moment, touching the elbow of the woman with whom she was with. Beads of sweat had popped out on the surface of his bald head. His mouth was suddenly pasty.

Layla glanced away for a moment, whispered something to the woman, and then approached their booth. Trey attempted to rise, but found his legs and hands would not work.

Layla stopped short a yard from their table. She smiled, white perfect teeth lighting up the room. She was in a word, stunning. From the sleek little black dress she wore which hugged her curves, to her cascading shiny hair, and bright lip gloss.

Erika was the first to speak.

"Layla."

"Erika. Nice to see you. It's been a long time."

"It has."

"Vince, hello."

"Hey."

Layla turned her attention to Trey who still had not moved or breathed.

"Trey. I just want to say hello. You're looking quite good."

Trey was silent. His stare was riveted to hers. She smiled feebly at him, testing the waters, yet he did not return the gesture.

"You're not going to say anything, Trey, not even a hello?" she asked.

In that moment Trey erupted from the table, his body exploding from the side of the booth like dynamite, frightening Layla to the point that she lurched back instinctively, her hand rushing up to her chest. Vince and Erika flinched in the same moment. The tabletop pivoted, bottles clanking and falling sideways, splashing cold liquid onto the surface, running in a sudden stream toward the wood floor.

Trey was inches from the side of Layla's face when his lips parted. She turned her head ever so slowly, their eyes locking as his expression morphed into a hideous snarl.

"Stay clear of me, *bitch*!" he hissed before pushing past her, toward the front entrance of bluespace.

A throng of folks waiting for their table ceased all conversation and parted quickly as he strode past them, and into the night.

It was over in an instant, a snap of fingers, a mere three blinks of an eye. But when the dust settled, Trey had left Erika, Vince, Layla, and the rest of the bluespace patronage shaking their heads in utter disbelief...

✖✖✖

"Can I talk to you?"

Layla, visibly flustered, glanced up into the eyes of Erika, and nodded.

Erika turned on her heels and headed for the curved teakwood bar by the side of the main entrance. Layla rose and followed. They found seats and ordered drinks. The lightshow facing them was enchanting.

A myriad of sunrises were displayed, rosy pinks and fire-reds, following the curved walls as the music rose, and for a moment, neither Layla nor Erika spoke, enthralled with the visual scenery.

Layla took a gulp of her apple martini and turned to Erika.

"Just what the *hell* happened back there?" she asked.

Erika tasted her own martini and nodded silently to the bartender before turning her attention to Layla.

"What are you doing?" she asked.

"What do you mean?" Layla asked, eyes blinking.

"I'll repeat—what are you doing? Here for one. A few weeks ago it was B. Smith's."

Layla's eyes grew wide.

"Oh yeah, you might have *thought* you weren't spotted, but you were. So come on *girlfriend*, don't play me. What are you doing?"

"Nothing."

"I *know*…" Erika whispered.

"What?" Layla stared at her deadpan.

Erika leaned closer. "I said, I know. Trey told me, told us," she said, gesturing back towards Vince who sat alone in their booth.

Layla's lip trembled.

"I'm not sure—"

"Listen, Layla," Erika said, "once upon a time you and I were friends. You may have forgotten, but I was your biggest supporter, your biggest fan. But that all changed because of what you did to Trey."

"What I did? Let me tell you…"

Erika cut her off.

"And you can sit there with this 'I-don't-have-the-slightest-idea-what-you-are-talking-'bout' attitude if that rocks your world, but I'm hear to tell you," Erika said, pausing to slowly glance down the front of her dress, from her full breasts that strained against the silk fabric to her curvy thighs and well-toned legs, "I know, Layla, I *know*."

Layla exhaled slowly and reached for her drink. She looked away, sipped at her drink. Erika watched her silently while she sipped at hers.

"He's changed, you know," Erika said. "Completely. The man you knew left five years ago—destroyed, I'm sorry to say. He will never love again, thanks to you. The old Trey you knew and loved is dead. Gone and buried."

Layla took a gulp and swallowed hard. Erika witnessed her wince as the liquor shot down her throat.

"I still love him," she whispered, turning to face Erika, her eyes wet with tears. "Haven't stopped, even after all these years…"

Erika set down her martini and gripped her hand.

"It's too late, Layla, believe me when I tell you this." Flecks of sunrise flashed in Erika's eyes as she stared at Layla. "The Trey you knew is dead. Leave it alone. And leave him alone. No good can come from this."

A lone tear meandered down Layla's right cheek. "But I still love him…"

"Please," Erika begged, "Layla, please don't do this to him. Don't do this to him or to yourself all over again."

Layla cried silently.

Erika turned away with a sigh. She downed her drink and shook her head, thinking just how bad things were about to get…

THIRTY-SEVEN

Erika lowered herself into the steaming bath, her eyes fluttering with delight as the jasmine-scented hot water infused into her tired pores.

It had been a rough day. *Another* twelve hour shift. The third one this week. Covering for Janice, whose child was out with the chicken pox.

Thankfully, it would end soon.

It better…

She had come home at nine, microwaved some leftovers, threw on her worn sweats, and slumped onto the couch, too exhausted to even give herself a pedicure.

Perhaps this weekend.

James had called thirty minutes later saying he wanted to come over. Erika politely refused, citing sleep deprivation, but James was insistent.

Erika, being too tired to argue, gave in. He was now lying on her bed in the next room, channel surfing.

Glancing around, Erika had to smile. Her boom box was on top of the vanity sink—her favorite Luther CD spinning. Several candles were positioned around the tub. A stick of incense burned not far from her feet, sending delicate tendrils of perfumed smoke wafting over her.

Erika leaned back and closed her eyes, lowering herself further until her shoulder blades dipped beneath a sea of bubbles.

Ah yessssssssssss! Her bath tonight felt wonderful. As she shifted in the tub, little waves caressed her neck and breasts, soothing her.

All in all, it was a perfect end to an otherwise shitty day.

Then without warning James burst in, a tormented scowl of on his normally smooth face, ruining all that Erika had fashioned in an instant...

✖✖✖

"Just what the fuck is *this*?" he yelled, holding up a large dildo the color of a Snickers bar.

Her dildo.

Her *buddy*.

Erika sighed. At that instant there were a thousand separate thoughts that lit up the living matrix of her cortex. She sucked in a breath. "Where did you find that?" she uttered slowly, eyes glaring with sudden intensity.

"That's not the point," James said, a bit flustered, "the point is—"

Erika stood as rivers of foamy suds cascaded down her taut body. She extended a finger toward the door.

"GET OUT!" Erika screamed, her eyes blazing. "Get the fuck out of my apartment. NOW!"

James did not move—his stare dropped momentarily, eyes scanning her wet body that was slick and shiny from the jasmine bath gel. "Erika, wait," he said, gulping air as he weighed the dildo in his palm, "we need to talk about this..."

Erika placed a hand on her hip and pursed her lips.

"Let me tell you something," she said. "You come into my house, rifle through my shit, and then have the nerve to throw what you find in my face? Oh *hell* no! I don't think so!"

Erika sat down abruptly, immersing her entire torso in the bathwater as a wave of bubbly suds rose up and over the lip of the tub, spilling onto the bathroom floor. James retreated like a toddler afraid of a frothy wave rushing toward the shore. "You need to leave!"

"Erika," he said in a kinder, gentler voice, "just explain to me why...*why* do you need this?"

Erika turned her head to stare at him in disbelief. James wore a sorrowfilled expression, as if he were constipated or suffering from deep abdominal pain. His eyes roamed over the jelly dong, considering it the purest form of evil.

"Why do I need that? Why do I need *that*?" she asked incredulously. Erika laughed. "Because it feels fucking good, you nitwit!"

James swallowed as his eyes lowered to the floor.

"You know what, James?" she said. "You have a lot of fucking nerve coming in here with your porno tapes and your…how do I put this delicately… your sexual idiosyncrasies…"

"Wait, hold up," James exclaimed, raising a hand, "*idiosyncrasies*?"

"Well, James, some might call them 'dysfunctions'…"

"I beg your pardon?"

"Please, don't get me started, because *you* don't want to go there, trust me!"

"No," James said, shouting as he moved closer to the edge of the tub, a fierce look about him, "let's go *there*…say your piece, Erika."

She sneered, nodding. "Okay…Let's just say that people who live in glass houses shouldn't throw stones. Translation—niggas who possess weird sexual hang-ups don't have the right to say shit to dildo-toting sistahs! Now GET THE FUCK *OUT*!"

✖✖✖

"Ah shit, Sassy!" I exclaimed, while grinning from ear to ear, "You da mutha fucking man, ya hear me?" Erika cut a sharp glance my way, but I continued to laugh anyway. I took a quick sip of my Grey Goose apple martini—oh hell yeah, y'all—the firm was picking up the Christmas party's tab—open bar, dinner and shit, so you know this nigga wasn't about to drink anything but top shelf!

Here we were, two weeks before Christmas, me, clad in a decadent black tux, looking sexy as hell, if I may say so myself, staring on in disbelief at my date for the evening; Erika, my boo, dressed as only she can in this sexy-ass red dress that came down two inches above her knee, plunging back, ribbons of silk crisscrossing down the front of her torso, holding her perky titties in place. White pearls, hair down and done to a T, diamond studs, eyes glimmering. I kid you not—if Erika wasn't like family—I'd wax that ass for sure right now!

"Tell me you're shitting a brutha!" I yelled as a table of partners and their wives nearby glanced our way.

"Trey! *Please*!" Erika whispered. "You need to keep your ghetto-talking ass down—those are your co-workers, in case you've forgotten." Erika took me by the elbow and ushered me away from the wood bar toward the railing overlooking the main dining room of Sequoia.

Together we glanced downward at the horde of people—the firm's finest—partners, associates, support staff, and their spouses, girlfriends and whatnot, all feasting on beef tenderloins, baked turkey, and candied yams. I spotted a few of my boys—office mates who I hung with when at the office—we exchanged smiles and chin nods.

Erika was by my side. I placed my hand on the small of her back.

"For real, girl, you look so damn good tonight," I said with a smile.

I meant every word.

Most of the women here were wearing formal gowns. Politically correct to-the-floor ensembles that were safe, yet fashionably boring. Erika stood out like a beacon of pulsating light.

"Whatever, Trey. You're just horny. And don't think I won't slap you silly if you try some stupid shit with me!" She grinned and I had to shake my head.

"So," I said, "getting back to the story at hand. Are you telling me this nigga went through your shit and found your vibrator?"

"Trey, please, keep your voice down," Erika scolded. "Yeah, can you believe it? The asshole tried to say he was looking for some Scotch tape!" Erika shook her head slowly. "Please, do I look like a fool?"

I laughed. "So?"

"You haven't heard the good part yet," Erika said, and I noticed that the smile on her face faded. She took a sip of her martini and became somber in her expression.

"James told me he loved me." Erika paused to let that sink in.

"What?" I exclaimed. "That nigga's so pussy-whipped it ain't even funny!"

Erika became silent for a moment. She bit her bottom lip before continuing. "I don't know Trey—all kidding around aside, I am really confused by this whole situation."

I led Erika over to a small table by her elbow away from prying eyes. We sat. "Go on," I said.

"I don't know, Trey. On the one hand, I've got this wonderful guy in James. He is very attentive to me, worships the ground I walk on, and is a very good lover. I am getting satisfied, you hear me. I've got no complaints. Well, if only that was true."

"Yeah, I mean, the guy has a fucking problem. And I mean literally, a *fucking* problem!" I had to snicker at my own humor.

Erika smiled weakly. "No, you are right—he does have a problem. Or maybe problem is not the right word. James can come. He has on a few occasions. But it is the circumstances of his orgasms that has me worried."

Sassy," I said, taking her hand in mine, "I'm gonna tell you this straight up, Trey-style. James is a faggot. No two ways about it. He gets off by having shit up his ass!" I eyed her seriously for a quick second. "Okay, poor choice of words, but you know what I mean."

"Trey, he's not a faggot, and stop using that word. It's very disrespectful."

"Please, boo. I call it as I see it. The boy's got problems, okay? There are so many bruthas out here who don't have issues with their plumbing—take me for example. You don't see me making excuses for why I can't come. Please—the day my dick doesn't work is the day I slit my own throat. Believe that!"

Erika shook her head sadly. "You are so messed up, Trey, do you know that?"

I feigned hurt.

"Can we get serious for a moment?" she asked. "I've got a great man in James who adores and loves me. And I'm sitting here being nitpicky over some shit that perhaps doesn't even matter. I mean, who out there is perfect? Who do you know that doesn't have issues?"

"Me!" I said quickly, unblinking.

"Boy, you are tripping, you hear me? I'm serious, Trey. I think that people spend their entire lives searching for Mr. or Ms. Perfect, when the fact of the matter is they don't exist. We need to learn to accept people for who they are—imperfect human beings, with faults and idiosyncrasies. Perhaps, I should accept James for whom and what he is—a great guy who has some hang-ups. I mean, who doesn't?"

"Trick, did I stutter? I said me!"

Erika smirked. "Please! You've got more issues than Imelda's got shoes. Look at you—you can't commit because you're all fucked up inside!"

"Damn, Sassy, don't sugarcoat it, girl…"

Erika ignored me. "Psst. You jump from bed to bed, as if fucking every Toni, Dina, and Harriet will make you more of a man. When what you really need to do is settle down—find yourself a good woman and get married!"

I looked at Erika as if I'd just been shot.

"Trick, you are straight trippin'! This kid ain't never getting married. And I'm never settling down. You forget that I tried going down that road once, and look where it got me. Hell the fuck no, Sassy, fuck *that* and fuck *you*!"

I sucked down the last remnants of my martini and quickly glanced around for a waitress to bring me another.

"Whatever, Trey. You can say what you want, but I know you. I know you are hurting inside." Erika leaned closer. "I know that because I see how you react when Layla's around…"

"Please!" I said, loudly. "That ho can come and go—it don't mean shit to me!"

"That's why you ran out of bluespace the other night like a dog with its tail between its legs. Nigga, don't play me."

I glared at Erika but remained silent.

"She still loves you, you know?" Erika said, lowering her voice a notch. "Layla told me so."

"What?" I shook my head in astonishment. "It's been five fucking years. The bitch needs to get over me. Dayum!" I stood up abruptly. "I'm getting another drink. You need one?"

Erika nodded once, as her stare never left mine. I blinked once before turning away.

"No," Erika said quietly, "it is *you* who needs to get over her..."

✖✖✖

I was washing my hands in the men's room sink when I heard the door open. I glanced up as I grabbed a towel to dry my hands. In waltzed Bernard John Marshall. I felt the temperature slither down several degrees.

Through the mirror we made brief eye contact. He was silent as he moved to a urinal. I quickly checked my tux and bow tie, ran a hand over my bald head, and headed for the door. I made it six paces when I heard him speak.

"I'm very impressed..."

I paused and turned slightly to glance his way.

"Excuse me?" I asked.

Bernard flushed and went to the sink. He turned on the water while eyeing me through the mirror.

"I said I'm impressed. Your date, Mr. Alexander. She is not at all what I expected." He smiled and I felt my face flush. I clenched my right fist and wanted nothing more than to bash his face in. I hated this mutha fucka with a passion.

"Excuse me?" I replied again, turning fully to face him.

"She's quite lovely. I guess I was expecting something else." Bernard pulled out a comb, ran water through it, and methodically slicked back his hair.

"Meaning what?" I said, a taste of venom on my lips.

He stopped combing, and turned to face me. "No need to get hostile, counselor. I thought your tastes ran in, shall we say, different waters..." Bernard smiled, showing me his teeth. His eyes were dead orbs that spoke volumes about the man.

I advanced toward him, my teeth clenched. "If you have something to say to me, Bernie, why don't you go ahead and stop pussyfooting around."

"It's Bernard, and I don't like your tone." He wiped away the grease from his comb with his fingers, ran them under the water as he eyed me. "I guess that opposing counsel from the Hues case wasn't interested, right?"

I stood with a deadpan expression; the only thing moving was my jaw.

"Oh, come now, Trey, you know what I mean—what was her name? Allison somebody, if my memory serves me." He grinned again.

"You're an..." I said quickly, and then caught myself. I silently counted to five before exhaling through my nose.

Bernard crossed the distance between him and me quickly, stopping a mere foot from me.

"A *what*, Mr. Alexander? If you have something to say then say it. To paraphrase you, 'stop pussyfooting around.'"

I remained silent.

"That's what I thought," he said with a sneer.

Bernard brushed imaginary lint off of his tuxedo. "In case you haven't figured it out yet, Trey, I don't like you. I think your vast ego far outshines your mediocre work."

I blinked rapidly.

"And I so do hope you show me your true colors soon. I trust it won't be too long a wait. People like you can't help themselves..."

"People like me???" I said incredulously. "Just what..."

"Enjoy the party, counselor," he said as he breezed past me, his shoulder grazing the fabric of my expensive tux.

The conversation was over.

I remained alone, staring down at the bathroom tile, attempting to control my breathing...and my surging anger...

✖✖✖

Vince Cannon, Jr. was helping clear the dishes when his cell phone chirped.

"Go ahead, honey," his mother said to him smiling, "your father can finish up here." Vince's dad gave his mother a brooding stare as she walked away.

It had been a while since Vince had spent time with his folks. For years he had never missed a Sunday dinner at their home in Northwest D.C. But over the past few months Vince's visits had begun to slip, missing the weekly meal on a more frequent basis. His parents understood—lately his book tour and seminars had been kicking up a notch or two. Just recently, he'd spent time in Philadelphia, New York, and Trenton doing one-day seminars and book signings. He had Boston, Atlanta, and Tampa booked for next month.

Vince glanced at the cell phone and felt his heart rate spike.

"Hello?"

"Hey you." It was Angeliqué.

"What's up?" he said, moving from the dining room with the massive oak hutch that had been in the family as long as Vince could remember, to the living room. He took a seat on a love seat by the window, hearing the clanking of plates in the background as his father moved around the kitchen grudgingly.

"I'm fine," Angeliqué said. "I just wanted to say hi, since you and I haven't spoken since we got back."

"Yeah, well, I'm sure you've been as busy as I have."

"Perhaps—I have to tell you, I was pissed that you did the casting of Amber."

Vince was silent.

"But I'm over that now."

"Okay," Vince said unsurely.

"And I hear it came out really nice. You'll have to send us a photo when it's complete."

"Will do," Vince responded.

"So, what has kept you from calling?" she said, a touch of sarcasm.

Vince emitted a short laugh. "What can I say? I've been busy. This past week I was out of town doing some one-day seminars."

"Cool, how did they go?" she asked.

"Very well. I conducted a few book signings as well. It's always nice to get out and meet the folks who support you."

"I hear that. Well, I just wanted to make sure that you and I were still cool."

"Yeah," Vince said, "why wouldn't we be?"

"You know—that weekend in D.C. didn't exactly go as planned, did it?"

Vince considered that for a moment.

"No, I guess not."

"Our time spent together didn't match what we had in New Orleans. I had hoped to rekindle what we felt when you and I first met, but it didn't work out that way. I know that now, and so do you."

"Correct." What else was there to say?

"I guess what I'm trying to say Vince is this: I want us to remain friends. You are an exceptional person, and you touched me in a special way. I don't want to lose that, Vince. I don't want to lose you as a friend."

Vince sighed. "You won't, Angeliqué. You won't."

He heard Angeliqué expel a breath. "I'm so glad to hear you say that. I was worried." Vince heard her giggle and his thoughts were transported back to that first time, when they walked the Quarter after a tantalizing dinner at Brennan's, their shoulders and arms brushing against each other as they sauntered past antique shops and blues clubs, fingers intertwined like vines. Vince recalled with vivid clarity that first time they made love in her studio, colors splashing across their bodies as they painted each other, creating art, making vibrant, passionate love. It was a moment Vince would soon not forget.

They talked for fifteen minutes more, getting caught up in each other's lives. The conversation grew friendlier by the minute, as if crossing this hurdle, deciding to remain friends, now enabled them to continue their friendship unencumbered.

Vince asked about Amber.

"She's been asking about you. I take it the two of you hit it off in Washington?"

Vince felt himself flush.

"She's good people—like you, Angeliqué, she's got soul."

"You trying to butter me up, Vince?"

"Naw, girl…not me."

"Alrighty then. Well, I'll be sure to tell Amber you asked about her. And Vince, don't be a stranger, okay? I dig talking to you on the regular."

"I feel the same, Angel, I feel the same…"

✗✗✗

His cell rang thirty minutes later. Vince was sitting in the living room, shooting the breeze with his parents.

"I don't get this many calls," his father quipped while shaking his head, "and I'm a damn physician!"

Vince rolled his eyes at his mother as he glanced at the Caller ID number. A 718 area code.

A number he did not recognize.

"Hello?" he said.

"Hi, may I speak to Mr. Vince Cannon, Jr.?" a female voice said.

"Speaking."

"Hi. I got your number from Cosi on Capitol Hill. I was inquiring about your artwork. Is it for sale?"

Vince smiled.

"Well, as a matter of fact it is. I've been working with some local galleries in the area, and should have most of my art on view shortly."

"That sounds great. I have to tell you, I was very impressed with the piece you have hanging in the Cosi shop. I don't think I've seen anything quite like it before." Vince listened to her voice—smooth, sensuous in its delivery.

"Thank you. That is one of my favorite pieces."

"Let me tell you my situation. I've purchased a new home and am looking for eclectic art to furnish it with. The more colorful and passionate, the better."

"I hear that," Vince exclaimed.

"And, I'm particularly interested in art done by those of color. You feel me?"

"Very much so," Vince said, grinning. He focused on her voice again—a quiet timber, but one which exuded power—a woman who knew what she wanted, and was used to getting it... Who was this woman???

"Great. I'd like to see your other work. I'm in the market for some pieces fairly soon."

"That's fine. What is your schedule like? I have a studio located in D.C."

"I'm flexible this coming week. How about tomorrow, sometime during the day?"

"Fine by me. Shall we say two p.m.?"

"Works for me. Give me the address."

Vince did.

"So, I will see you tomorrow at two o'clock. Looking forward to it, Mr. Cannon. Or may I call you Vince?" she asked in a voice that took Vince's breath away.

"Please call me Vince," he said in his rich, motivational speaker voice that drove the women wild. "And what may I call you?" he asked.

"You may call me what my friends call me," she responded in a singsong voice. "You may call me Raven…"

✖✖✖

Calvin Figgs, Esq. spotted the change in my demeanor immediately. He and his lovely wife were huddled around a batch of senior partners and their wives, Calvin doing what he did best, playing the game, showing these white folks that he still knew how to hang with the best of them. It was good to see Calvin; lately he'd been in the office on average only three days a week. We hadn't had an in-depth conversation in a while. He stood there, looking dapper as usual, wearing that tuxedo like he was a damn model; his wife of twenty-five years by his side, looking like a spitting image of Lena Horne, with her fine self. I was not mad at either of them!

He excused himself and came over, kissing Erika on the cheek.

"It is so good to see you again, Erika," he said. Calvin's hair and thin beard were manicured to perfection, and it pleased me greatly to see another black man who took pride in his looks as much as I did. He shook my hand and smiled as he said, "Counselor, looking good as usual!"

"Thank you, but I don't hold a candle to you. Check you out! The O.G.— Original Gangster!"

Calvin grinned. "As my daughter is fond of saying, 'Don't hate the playa!'"

His smile turned serious. "What's the matter, Trey, I can see that something's on your mind. Not enjoying yourself this evening?"

"The party's fine, Calvin. It's that asshole Bernard. I'm about to put my size-twelve foot up his ass, for real!"

Calvin grinned at Erika. "Would you excuse us for a moment? I need to school this youngster for a minute."

Erika smiled. "Please do. You know he needs all the schooling he can get."

"Ain't that the truth," Calvin quipped as he led me away.

Together we walked to an outside section that had been enclosed in a huge white tent. Due to the cold weather, few people were sitting there, even though the restaurant had provided tall gas heaters spaced every few yards apart. We found a table under one, unbuttoned our jackets, and sat down.

"What's going on?" Calvin asked.

"It's Bernard. He's a world-class fucker."

"Tell me something I don't already know!"

"Calvin, this guy is something else—he's all over my shit—putting his nose into every case I'm working on, questioning my judgment and everything."

"He is the managing partner of the firm, Trey. As such he does have the right to monitor the progress of partners and associates."

"Calvin, please!" I exclaimed. "Monitoring is one thing—but this guy takes 'micromanagement' to a whole new level!"

Calvin nodded.

"And that's not all. Tonight in the men's room he made a comment about Erika not being my type. Then he tells me that he doesn't like me, that my work is just 'mediocre,' and that he's just waiting for me to mess up."

Calvin shook his head.

"Here's the clincher, Calvin—the fucker then says to me: 'I can't wait to see your true colors soon. People like *you* can't help themselves.'"

Calvin scratched slowly at his beard, but said nothing. I waited for him to speak.

"Well?" I said, irritably.

"Trey, listen, my advice to you is to keep your head down and watch your back. Bernard is gunning for you; there is no doubt about that. I'm not sure why you've gotten under his skin, but you have."

"Can't something be done about him? Can't *you* do something? I mean, come on, Calvin. I've been busting my ass for five years around here. I'm valuable. I bill more than some of these lily white partners, and I'm fucking in demand, you know that."

"I do."

"But???" I said, trying to maintain my composure.

"Trey, things are changing around here in case you haven't noticed. The management is taking the firm in a new direction. That's why they brought Bernard in. That's why I'm out."

Calvin paused to let that sink in.

I stared at him in disbelief.

"What do you mean, you're out?"

"Just what I said. I've served my purpose here. It's time to move on."

"Are they forcing you out?" I asked, my voice barely above a whisper.

"Trey, it's complicated. They acknowledge my value to the firm over the years. And with my contacts around town, they'd be committing suicide if they just cut me loose. So no, they aren't forcing me out. But it's been made clear that my time is up—it's a new day around here."

"Damn…" I said. What else could be said? "Calvin, I'm so sorry this is happening to you. Of all people," I said with more sincerity then I've shown in months. "Are they going to take care of you at least?"

"Yes, they are. It would be insulting if they asked me to leave without making it worth my while. Between you and me, I'm being handsomely compensated. But you know what the best part is?" he asked, smiling.

I shook my head.

"My wife is ecstatic. She gets to spend time with me again. To be truthful, my long hours have been straining our relationship for too long to remember."

"What? You can't be serious?"

"As serious as a heart attack. You know the life of a partner—you have no life. Try being a managing partner. You must bump it up by an order of magnitude or you don't survive. I did what I had to do—I loved this firm. I put my heart and soul into it. It became my family, my life. In doing so, I sacrificed what I had had with Linda."

I sat there, staring off into space.

"Damn," I repeated.

"You know what they say, Trey. When one door closes, another one opens. That adage is so true, I can't begin to tell you. Frankly, this is the best thing that could have happened to me. I was feeling stagnant for years, not knowing that I was in a funk, not knowing how to get out of this mess that I had built for myself. Now I'm free. Unchained, unencumbered."

Calvin grinned. "I'm pursuing new endeavors, like teaching. Georgetown Law is very interested. I've met with the dean and he's offered me an adjunct faculty position. I'm also thinking about doing some writing for some law journals."

"DAYUM, Calvin!" I shouted, slapping his shoulder. "You are da man! Good for you. Damn good for you." I dropped my voice a notch. "Fuck these mutha fuckas, you hear me. Walk away with your head held high. You don't need these bitches. You will come out on top!"

Calvin's smile evaporated as he leaned closer to me. "Trey, listen to me. I know things are hard right now. But you need to watch yourself. Things are different now—I'm not going to be able to shield you from Bernard and his wrath. He's connected, senior management believes in him, and as I said, he's gunning for you. You need to keep your nose clean, and make sure you are on point 24/7. And Trey, above all—don't give him the satisfaction of losing your cool in front of him. That's what he's waiting for. Waiting for you to act like a nigger…"

Calvin stared at me.

Silently I stared back, swallowing as I nodded my head slowly, contemplating his words and their meaning.

Like a nigger, Calvin had said.

Yeah, I thought, *Calvin had Bernard pegged…*

THIRTY-EIGHT

V ince glanced at his watch: 1:45 p.m., fifteen minutes remaining until the woman named Raven would arrive at his studio. What would she be like? Vince didn't know. But the conversation last night gave him a sense of what to expect.

He had put on a pair of jeans still warm from the iron, lavender button-down shirt, and a pair of leather boots he normally reserved for riding. He took extra care to trim his beard and mustache, not wanting to look like a wild man. Not that Vince ever did. Not even on a bad day…

She arrived promptly at 2. Vince buzzed her in and heard the knock on the door a minute later. He opened it, and what he saw took his breath away.

Raven stood there, clad in a red wool coat, matching wool hat and mittens, holding a steaming Starbucks cup.

"Vince?" she asked.

"Yes, you must be Raven," he said with a smile.

He opened the door wider and stepped aside so she could walk in, glancing at her as she strode by.

He felt his heart beat faster as he witnessed her hips move. Raven stopped mid-center of his studio, glancing around. Her attention was immediately focused on his wall of masks.

"Very impressive."

"Thanks. Let me take your things." Raven unbuttoned her coat and slid out of it. She removed her hat and mittens and handed them over with her purse. Vince took the opportunity to look her over.

Raven had long dark hair that was tied back. Brown eyes were piercing and always moving. She wore tight jeans that showed off her long legs, firm hips and ass, a rusty brown sweater containing full breasts, and tan boots. Her smile was what captivated Vince the most. Her lips curved up in a sensuous kind of way as she extended her hand to him.

"It's nice to meet you and put a face with the name."

"Same here," he said. "Can I offer you something?"

"I'm good," she said, holding up her cup.

"Cool. So, welcome to my humble studio," he said, holding his arms wide. "Feel free to look around."

"Thanks." She moved over to the wall, studied the pieces hanging there for a few minutes before moving across the room to the worktable that held the unfinished full-body casting of Amber. It lay on the table like a half-finished mummy, the plaster of Paris already smoothed by Vince's hands, awaiting paint.

"My goodness," Raven said, walking over and lightly touching the casting, "this is amazing."

"Thank you. I did that particular piece just a week or so ago. I'm still trying to decide on a color scheme. As you can see, it's my first full body casting."

Raven nodded.

"So," Vince said, "you mentioned on the phone that you recently purchased a home and are looking to furnish it with some art."

"Yes. I'm looking for pieces that stir my emotions every time I gaze upon them."

"I feel you."

Vince observed Raven as she returned to the wall of masks. She moved slowly, examining each one, shifting closer until her nose almost touched the paint-covered plaster, taking in each piece, letting the colors invade her space. Vince was silent as he sat on the futon sipping at hot coffee.

"These are wonderful," Raven mused. Vince was silently watching her. His stare took in her features—long black hair, parted in the middle, and tied back with multicolored rubber bands, caramel cheekbones, sensuous lips that parted ever so slightly to reveal a pink tongue as she concentrated on his art. A good half-dozen silver bracelets adorned her left wrists, glinting as she moved to sit on the futon beside him.

"Have you priced out each piece?" she asked.

"Well," Vince said, "these masks go for between seven hundred fifty and a twelve-hundred dollars apiece." He paused to watch her, then added: "I hope you find them reasonable."

Raven was silent as she sat forward. Her hand went to her mouth, the bracelets jingling as she moved. After a moment she sat back.

Vince cleared his throat and spoke. "Art prices are always so subjective, don't you think? I mean, what the artist sees as value…"

Raven held up a hand, her bracelets clanking as they moved up her forearm. "No need for explanations, Vince. I believe artists should be paid for their craft. "

Vince watched her, not trying to eye her directly, but enjoying the closeness as she studied his art. A number of thoughts went through his mind as his stare flicked over her features. She was indeed a beautiful woman. Her dark hair shined and Vince dug the way she had it tied down her back. Her jeans were tight, revealing nice curves, the rise of her breasts hypnotic. Her lips were wet from her tongue. How old was she? Raven appeared to be around his age, but one could never tell. Was she dating? Married? He glanced down—numerous rings covered both hands, so it was difficult to tell. Vince caught her sipping at her coffee. "Mmmmn…" she exclaimed almost absent-mindedly. Vince grinned.

"I take it you are a coffee connoisseur."

Raven eyed him with a smile.

"Ain't nothing coming between me and my coffee," she said.

Vince nodded, feeling the temperature rise a few degrees.

Raven stood up abruptly. She went to the wall and pointed to four masks. "I'm interested in these," she said decisively.

Vince stood excitedly. "Let me take those down and put them together so you can decide."

Raven shook her head. "I'm interested in all four. That's not a problem, is it?"

Vince swallowed hard. "No. Of course not."

"Will four grand cover it?"

Vince blinked. "Why yes," he said, not knowing what else to say.

"I thought so," Raven said, and Vince swore he saw her eyes twinkle. She turned back to the wall of masks while Vince pulled them off the wall one by one, leaning them in a row on the floor. Raven studied her acquisitions carefully, bending down onto her haunches so she could get eye level with the masks.

Vince was silent as he stepped back. She stood, turning to him, and sighing heavily.

"Shopping always makes me hungry," Raven said with a teasing smile.

Vince beamed.

"There's a damn good Chinese place nearby..."

"You treating?" she asked with a sly grin.

✖✖✖

They sat across from each other, silently enjoying their food. Vince had ordered Hot Crispy Beef. Raven had selected the Szechwan Shrimp. He forked a sliver of the crunchy beef into his mouth, eyeing Raven as she helped herself to a helping of his entrée.

"Hungry?" he teased.

"What? A girl can't get her eat on?"

Vince smiled. They sat at a small table for two by the window overlooking a busy intersection. Automobiles whizzed past, spewing exhaust. People huddled together in an open bus stop across the street, bundled up against the cold. The threat of snow hung in the air like cigarette smoke.

Forty minutes earlier Vince had wrapped up each mask in newsprint while Raven had run to the bank. She had returned twenty minutes later with a cashier's check for the entire amount. Vince carried the packages to her black Range Rover before they locked the car and walked the three blocks to the restaurant.

"So," Vince said, wiping his mouth with a cloth napkin, "tell me about yourself. What do you do? Where are you from?" he asked. "The whole nine!"

Raven reached for the cup of green tea and sipped slowly. She placed the cup down gingerly and shook her head with a sigh.

"What?"

"Let me ask you something, Vince," she said. "Do you ever get tired of the back-and-forth games people play; this ruse, for lack of a better term; this self-marketing hype where I tell you of my significant accomplishments, and you nod your head vigorously while telling me yours? And it goes back and forth, deeper and deeper as the bullshit mounts?

'I did my undergraduate at Vassar!'

'Oh really? My post-doc work was done at U Berkeley.'

'Oh my, one of my frat brothers is a U Berkeley graduate—perhaps you know of him. Chad?'"

Raven shook her head sullenly. "At the end of the day, what does it all amount to, Vince? Nothing. People meet, they dance, they perform this ritual whose sole purpose is to search for their perfect mate. And when they don't find him or her, what do they do? They move on to the next person, regurgitating their résumé all over again to the next poor slob who will listen."

Vince had been eating slowly, digesting what she had said. He put his fork down, a bit taken aback.

"I didn't mean to hit a sore point, Raven. I was just wondering…"

"Vince," she said, interrupting as she stabbed a piece of shrimp and baby corn, gesturing in his direction. "Let me ask you this: What are we all searching for?"

Vince eyed her. "What do you mean?"

"Just what I said—what is it that men (and women) are searching for?"

Vince reflected. He knew the answer to this one. He'd written a book about it, for God's sake!

"Love. I think in a nutshell folks want to be loved. They want to fall in love, and remain in a long, nurturing relationship, where they can feel safe and be themselves."

"Well stated. But answer me this. How do we find love?"

Vince smiled as he glanced at his watch. "Well, I'm not sure if there are enough hours in the day to answer that one."

"Why not? It's a simple question," she quipped, eyeing him closely.

"I think not. Love is complex. It's mysterious. It may be simple, but it remains extremely elusive to most, and therein lies the rub."

Raven reached across the table to grab another helping of Crispy Beef. She slipped a piece of the crunchy meat into her mouth and chewed while her stare never left his.

"I'm not sure how we went from 'tell me about yourself' to 'what is this thing called love?'" Vince said. "I was just interesting in getting to know you…"

"Vince," Raven said, putting her fork down, "are you listening? I know you hear me, but are you really *listening?*"

Vince sat back, feeling a trace of annoyance filter into his bloodstream. "I *thought* I was listening, Raven."

She beamed, erasing any ill will he was feeling at that moment. "May I school you?" She didn't wait for a response. "See, love is not, contrary to popular opinion, an emotion, which can be turned on and off, like a switch. No. It's not something that grows, like a dandelion. Nope. Love is innate. Love, my new friend, is *chemical.*"

Vince looked surprised. "Chemical?"

"Yes," Raven said, smiling. "Do you really think that when two people meet and exchange their bios it brings them any closer to falling in love?"

"Yes, I do," Vince said. "Call me old-fashioned, but I believe in connections. I believe in the power of communication, of people connecting on a plane of mutual respect and understanding, and…"

"Vince—it's chemical, plain and simple. Spending time with someone, getting to know them better—that's all well and good—but at the end of the day, it's like it's been preordained. Whether two people fall in love has everything to do with chemistry. Some elements mix. Others don't. And all the forcing in the world won't change that simple fact. It's high school chemistry."

Vince stared at her. "So, what are you saying, Raven? Don't waste your time getting to know someone? Stop communicating because there is no point?"

"No…"

Vince barreled forward. "I should think not. No, Raven. Love may be chemical—and I'm not convinced that it is, but I'm not one to throw our tried and proven, yet perhaps old-fashioned ways to the curb. For me, I still treasure sitting down and talking to a woman, getting to know her, finding out what makes her tick. To me, Raven, there is a certain feeling I get, deep in my gut, when I'm sitting across from someone I fancy, and I'm still learning about what their likes and dislikes are, that overwhelming sensation that is hard to describe—happiness, excitement, anxiety, and passion, all fused into one, making your stomach twist into a knot because of the infinite possibilities you see sitting across from you. That feeling, that first inkling that you may be in *love*…"

Raven sat back, folding her arms across her chest. She stared silently at Vince for a bit, nodding absentmindedly. She reached for her tea and took a sip, placing the cup down before speaking.

"Obviously I'm sitting across from a romantic…"

"Card-carrying member for life, baby!" Vince grinned.

"I'm not mad at you, Vince. I guess I'm just tired of the whole scene—answering myriad questions about this and that when, fundamentally, it doesn't matter."

"Then I won't ask any more questions."

"Yeah, right. Like I don't know that you're dying to know more about me!"

"Please, honey," Vince quipped, "do I look pressed?"

"You're a man, right? Then you're pressed!"

Vince laughed. "You've been watching too much Oprah!"

"You know what I dig, Vince? I live to be unconventional. Out of the ordinary. Like, instead of sitting here going through the motions, I want to think outside of the box. Dare to be different, regardless of what society says the rules should be. You feel me?"

Vince nodded, unsteadily.

"Let's you and I become the people we've dreamed of being. Let's not talk about it; let's just do it! Show me, Vince, who you can be!" Raven's eyes lit up and Vince found himself aroused at the prospect.

"Go on," he said.

"Don't you sometimes want to be somebody else? Take on a new persona? Well, here's your chance. I don't know you; you don't know me. What a perfect opportunity to start with a clean slate."

Vince paid the check and escorted Raven out the door. The cold hit them in the face, hard. Raven wove her arm through Vince's and nuzzled close to keep warm.

"I've got an idea, if you're game," she said as they turned the corner, away from the traffic noise.

"Shoot."

"Let's hang out tomorrow night, if you don't have plans. The rules are simple: You aren't Vince and I'm not Raven. Tomorrow night, we reinvent ourselves, and we see where this chemistry thing takes us."

"I'm down," Vince replied enthusiastically.

"Cool. How about I pick you up at seven?

Vince raised his eyebrows. "Okay. Where are we going?"

"It's a surprise, but don't worry; I don't bite. Unless of course you want me to…"

Vince smiled, but said: "I have to admit I'm a bit confused…"

"It's simple, Vince. I don't want to hear about us—you and me—who we are or where we've come from. I'm not interested in accomplishments. Frankly, resumés bore me. Instead, I want to see where this can take us. Think of this as a grand adventure where the wind is nipping at your heels, and you have no idea where this safari will lead."

"So, if we don't talk, then what do we do?"

Raven's eyes sparkled like diamonds. "It's an adventure, man. We do whatever we choose to do…"

✖✖✖

"Hey you, it's Vince. Is his Highness in?"

"Oh Vince," India Jasmine Jackson said in an enthusiastic voice, "what is up, my fine Nubian brutha? How are you?"

"Can't complain. You?"

"Still waiting for you to propose…"

"It's in the mail, baby!" Vince exclaimed.

"Yeah right. Let me connect you."

Trey got on a moment later.

"How ya livin'?" he asked.

"Large and in charge. You know how we do!" Vince responded.

"Cool. So what's up, my nigga?" Trey asked.

"You got a minute?"

"For you? Always…"

Vince thought about the irony of that—perhaps one could teach old dogs new tricks…

"Listen, I met this woman today. She came over to purchase some of my art."

"Congrats!"

"Yeah. So, check this out. We're sitting together afterwards having lunch, and I ask her the usual questions—where she's from, what she does, etcetera, and she like bugs out! Starts talking all this crazy shit about how she's not interested in any of that—how that's tired and played out. How she lives to be unconventional and shit. How she likes to think outside of the box."

"Hmmmn," Trey said, thinking out loud. "How this chick look?"

"Trey, she's amazing," Vince said. "Long legs, long hair, curves in all the right places."

"Solid. So, give me the specifics. What exactly did she say?"

Vince recounted the details of their conversation. Trey interrupted f requently, asking questions; Vince clarified as best he could.

When Vince was done with his explanation he sighed deeply. "Tell me what this shit means, dawg."

"See—it's a good thing you called the *master*. 'Cause your dumb ass would be floundering if it weren't for me."

"Yeah, whatever, Master Bator…"

Trey chuckled at that one. "It's simple, really. This chick is sending you a message—and you best pay attention. She wants you, dawg, and she wants you bad. But she can't come out and say it—not that she seems that shy, based on what you told me, but she doesn't want to come off sounding like a ho. Oh yeah, she wants you in the worst way. She's fucking with you, telling you all this 'think outside of the box' and 'I'm unconventional' shit!"

Trey laughed. "Nigga, please! She's signaling just how bad she wants you to fuck her!" Trey giggled. "What you need to do is show up in a pair of tight leather pants and some boots, with a riding crop in hand and spank that ass as soon as she glances your way. That'll teach her to fuck with a brutha!"

"Trey, I don't know…"

"Nigga, please don't make me school you *again*! This chick is signaling to you exactly what she wants. She's looking for a man who is unconventional; she's practically begging you to be that man, 'cause she's tired of mutha fuckas with the same old tired-ass lines—translation—take the bull by the horns and fuck that horny little beast!"

"Trey, not everything is about sex."

"Oh Lord! Am I speaking to Erika or my boy? Dang, what am I going to do with you, Vince? I'll tell you what. Let me go on this date tomorrow and I'll give her a ride she'll never forget."

"That's okay, partner; I can handle this one myself."

"Make sure you do. Seriously, dawg, this woman is asking for you to amaze her—show her what you are made of. So show her a man that she's yet to see. Vince Cannon, Jr., what you gonna do?"

"I don't know, Trey. I mean, I don't know if I can waltz in there, acting like some rap star or someone whom I'm not, acting like I take no prisoners, just to impress her. That's really not me—I've got my own approach, and it's a bit less…*flamboyant*…"

"Vince," Trey said, raising his voice, "fuck that! We see all the time how women pass up the smooth romantic types for those ruffneck bad boys. That's why I'm so successful with the ladies, dawg, cause I give them what they really want—a sense of excitement and the freedom that they've *yet* to experience. As only I can do—Trey style!"

"I don't know…" Vince repeated.

"Listen, Vince, I gotta go. I've got a client coming up in five. But take my advice. Don't mess this one up. She sounds like she's a hell of a ride. So ride that shit—go in there like you own that mutha fucka! That shit is already yours. So, sweep her off her feet. Take her and spank her ass without asking permission. I guarantee you won't be disappointed. Just don't forget in the midst of all your enthusiasm to videotape that shit for me and the rest of the fellas to see! For real, playa!"

✖✖✖

His next call was to Erika. She picked up on the third ring.

"What up, Sassy? How ya livin'?"

"You tell me; you're the man."

"I'm good, but I need some advice."

"Shoot."

Vince described his dilemma for Erika. He told her of his encounter with Raven and her challenge to him.

"I'm digging this woman, Sassy, and I want to impress her. But I don't know if I can be someone I'm not; you know what I mean?"

"Yes, I do. I don't get why she's got you going in circles anyway. It seems as if she's just playing a game with you, and you've got to decide if that's a good thing or not."

"If I understand her correctly, she's tired of the same old thing—tired of meeting men and recounting for them her life story over and over again."

"Yeah, well, welcome to the club, bro. I mean, we all go through that shit. It's part of the mating ritual; you know that as well as any of us. How does she expect to get to know someone? By osmosis?" Erika laughed.

"Yeah, I think so. She says it's all chemistry."

"Whatever," Erika exclaimed. "You can do what you want, but my advice to you is this: Don't start off a relationship with game-playing. That's not healthy. You don't need to be anyone but yourself. Vince, you are already cool with being who you are. You are comfortable in your own skin, and you've got nothing to be ashamed of. You're good-looking, intelligent, creative, and have a great career. So, why spend time trying to be someone that you're not?"

"Good point. I tend to agree with you, Boo. That was my first thought—why should I play this game and try to be someone else? But at the same time, she seems very cool, and I think she just is looking for something different. And I think I can give her that."

"Hmmmn," Erika said, with not a lot of conviction in her voice.

Vince was silent for a moment. "Trey says I should…"

"Hold it, Vince. Why you listening to his monkey-ass? It'd be one thing if he had a lock on love and relationships, but he's the last mutha fucka you should be listening to!"

Vince could imagine her shaking her head. He smiled.

"Yeah, you got that one right."

"I mean, please—when was the last time Trey had a meaningful relationship with anyone? A year ago? Two? Try five!"

"I hear you…"

"Vince, this woman may be cool and all, but tread lightly. Don't commit yourself until you know more about her. Something sounds fishy to me, and us girls have got a sixth sense about these things."

"Okay, Ma, you're the expert…by the way, how are things between you and James?" he asked.

"Who? Oh please! Don't get me started, okay???"

✖✖✖

A dozen separate scenarios occupied Vince's psyche. For the next eighteen hours he thought of little else. How to impress the mysterious and sensual Raven?

That was the question.

Show up, clad in a lime-green pimp outfit with matching wide brim hat and platform shoes, courtesy of (who else?) Trey Alexander?

Pretend he was a rapper, and arrive in a limo with a pair of ghetto-fabulous girls on either arm?

Perhaps he could take on the persona of a plastic surgeon who does all the elite locals and politicians' wives?

Or a movie star in town for a film shoot?

No. Vince wasn't feeling any of these.

The problem was simple. Vince wasn't like Trey. He couldn't just waltz into a room and take charge, pretending he was someone else. It wasn't in him. Never had been.

His cell chirped around noon as he contemplated his options.

"Vince," a vaguely familiar female voice said.

"Yes?"

"It's Raven."

Vince smiled. "Hey you."

"Change of plans," she said, in a voice that chilled him with its sensuality. "I've got to take care of something. Why don't you just meet me at the spot later on tonight? Around tenish would be cool."

Vince frowned, but then realized that arriving by himself would give him some options he had yet to consider.

"Yeah, that's fine. Where shall we meet?"

Raven gave him the address.

"Did you say Philly?" Vince asked, suddenly sitting upright, "As in Philadelphia, Pennsylvania?"

"That's right." These words were delivered in a singsong upswept voice that hinted of deviousness. "I trust that won't present a problem, will it?"

Vince's mind raced. "No…not at all, Raven. The adventure, then, begins at ten…"

"Looking forward to it," she said.

"Likewise," was Vince's response.

THIRTY-NINE

The spot was named Bluezette. Vince found it shortly after 10:30. It was a small place, sandwiched between a men's shoe store and an Italian restaurant. As he drove by slowly, he could see the front bar and adjacent space was filled to capacity with patrons sharing holiday cheer. He drove on and found parking two blocks over.

Was he ready to see Raven?

Yes.

Vince knew exactly what he was going to do.

Reaching behind him, he pulled out a thin walking stick.

He checked himself in the rearview mirror before readying to head out. Vince had opted for a dark single-breasted suit with a contrasting turtleneck underneath. His dark gray overcoat was buttoned against the deepening cold. He eyed his hair and beard; everything looked good, so he exited his car.

There was a large glass door leading to the entrance of Bluezette. Vince paused by it, reached into his breast pocket and pulled out a pair of black designer shades. He donned them, checked to make sure his sight was completely impaired, and slowly went inside.

The warmth and sounds assaulted him. He stopped as soon as he felt the door shut behind him. There was music—acid jazz that invaded his senses, up-tempo bass lines, funky synths that gave it a kind of techno groove. Vince moved his head slowly to the beat while his body remained motionless, the cane steady by his side. He could hear bits and pieces of conversations—a table of women directly to his right—black women, there was no doubt about that. A smattering of talk to his left also, yet most of the chatter came directly from in front of him. The bar area, from what he remembered when he did his quick drive-by.

Someone came up to him and touched his elbow.

"Hello," a warm, friendly female voice said. "Welcome to Bluezette. Do you need, ah, a table?"

Vince smiled and nodded. "Yes, that would be nice. I'm supposed to be meeting someone here, but don't seem to *see* her."

There was a short pause.

"That was a joke," Vince said, softly, leaning in the direction of the woman. He grinned, and heard her laugh. "Can you assist me? I'm *blind*."

"Of course," the woman said quickly. "We have tables both here and upstairs. Do you have a preference?"

"Not really. I'm feeling the music, so wherever I can hear it best," he said. The woman took Vince by the arm and led him forward.

"Let me take you upstairs then. The live band's there."

"Wonderful," Vince said. "Lead on, pretty lady." Vince could sense her smile.

He was led past the bar, up the stairs, and then reversing direction toward the front of the building.

"I've never been here before," Vince said to the woman.

"Oh, you'll really like it. We're actually well known for our soul food, and we have the best martinis this side of the Mississippi, if I may say so myself."

"I hear that."

"And I think you'll like the band. They're a combination of neo-soul, smooth jazz, and spoken word. They're called The Verve."

"Sounds good," Vince exclaimed.

The band, Vince could tell, was positioned in front of him. He was led to a table off to the left side of the stage. The woman helped him into his seat and bent close to his ear. "Your waitress will be with you shortly. I hope you enjoy your evening."

"Thank you for your kindness," Vince responded, glancing up in her direction.

Vince sat back into his chair and concentrated on his surroundings. It was extremely difficult not being able to see…he, like most people, took for granted being able to use his visual faculties to their fullest. But tonight he would be forced to refocus his energy into what was left of his available senses—his touch, his hearing, and his smell. It would be difficult. Just walking past the bar and up the stairs took effort. He was conscious of every step he made, cautious not to bump into anyone, or hit them with his cane. He found that he was already mentally tired, his brain being forced to process much more data than normally, and from less used sources—the other senses abruptly turned up high.

A waitress brushed past his shoulder. He could sense her standing on his right. Vince glanced up, not being able to see a thing in front of him.

"What can I get you?" she asked, her voice a deeper, richer sound than the first woman who had led him here.

"I hear you've got great martinis."

"We do indeed."

"Can you make a mean apple martini?" he asked.

"Trust me, ours are the best! You won't be disappointed."

"Then I'll take one."

The music was rising as a keyboard solo went into overdrive. Vince bopped his head to the beat. He loved listening to live music. He loved the energy. Too bad that tonight he couldn't watch the band do their thing…

His drink arrived five minutes later. The waitress put it down beside him. Vince glanced up. "Tell me your name," he asked.

"It's Nechelle."

"Pretty name, Nechelle. I'm Vince. Listen I'm supposed to be meeting a woman here; her name is Raven. She has long dark hair, very striking. If you spot her, can you send her my way?"

"I'd be delighted to."

The waitress left and Vince tasted his drink. Damn good!

He detected shadows and slivers of light that seeped into the sides of his glasses. Vince glanced left, then right as the music died and claps erupted around him. He joined in, moving his head to try and discern the shapes and patterns that hovered around his head. There was hushed conversation around him; his senses clearly picked up the clanking of bottles and glasses; chairs being scuffed along the hard floor. The scent of apples was strong, as was something light and perfumed. Vince took it all in, amazed at how much one could pick up if you just concentrated on the senses available to you.

The music began again. A slow, steady groove, this time, just drum and bass. Vince turned his attention toward the source. Folks around him began to clap in time to the beat. He took another sip of his martini, placed his glass down and joined in. A woman began to sing. Her voice was sweet, low-pitched, and pure. It reminded him of India Arie. He leaned forward, concentrating on the sound. She wasn't speaking any words, but just scatting along with the melody, her voice like a surfboard, riding the wave, the highs and lows, and Vince was tempted to yank off his glasses and peer out at this woman, but fought the urge to do so. What did she look like? If her voice was any indication, she was a goddess...

The music shifted, abruptly upbeat as the rest of the band joined in, and suddenly the woman was rapping, her voice lifting up above the din of the music—sharp lyrics talking about strong black women, the foundation of the family. Folks were yelling as if in church. Vince was moved. He smiled to no one in particular. Cocking his head to the side, Vince suddenly realized something.

The voice on stage was familiar. Very familiar. Could that be Raven up there?

Vince fought the urge to peek above his shades.

The music downshifted and slowed, and the woman's voice became soft and light again. This time she began to sing, and Vince was blown away by the purity of her voice. Like others around him, he was mesmerized by her song. When she was done, the crowd erupted with thunderous applause, and Vince found himself out of his chair and standing, not sure if he was the only one giving her and the band a standing ovation or not, but not caring what others around him thought. He was moved, and he wanted this woman and the band to know it.

As the applause died, smooth jazz came on, while the band took a break. Vince sat down, gingerly feeling his way across the table for his drink. He took a sip, realizing that his martini glass was empty. He felt something between his lips, reached for it and mouthed the sweet cherry, swallowing it down heartily.

"Is this seat taken?" a soft, sensuous voice asked.

"That depends," Vince responded with a tilt of his head. "I'm actually saving this seat for a very beautiful woman. So," Vince said, with a smile, "are you beautiful?"

"You tell me."

"Well," he said, straightening up, "we'll have to see…sit down for a moment, please."

The scent of perfume wafted over him. The woman leaned close, something of hers brushing against Vince's forearm. "So, what do you think?"

Vince's hands crept over the table surface until he found her arm. He traced a finger along her skin toward her wrist. When he came to her hand he took it in his. Then he began moving his hands up her bare forearms feeling her skin on his fingers. She did not resist his touch.

"Nice skin," he said, leaning toward her. "Let's see about the rest of you…"

Vince grinned. His fingers reached her shoulders, feeling the fabric soft underneath his touch. Using both hands, he reached for her clavicles, and followed the contours of her neck upward until he came to her face. His fingers traced the outline of her jaw and chin, glazing over the soft tissue of her mouth. Remembering Raven when she visited him for the first time at his studio, he touched the flesh of her lips, feeling her upswept smile.

Moving upward, he ran a finger over the bridge of her nose, cheekbones, and eyes, upward still, tracing the crease in her forehead.

The waitress arrived, touching his shoulder. Vince turned his head to her, but did not take his hands away from the woman beside him.

"Nechelle, I'll take another apple martini. And whatever this lovely young lady desires."

"The same."

Vince heard her footfalls as she moved away.

"Reached any conclusions?" the seated woman asked.

"Too early to tell. I mean, you are indeed beautiful, that much is clear—

but whether or not you're the one I'm looking for remains to be seen."

"Oh really?"

"Don't take it personal, but I am waiting for someone special…"

"And just who is this chick, the object of your affection and attention?"

"Are you listening to me?" Vince mused. "I know you hear me, but are you actually *listening*?" Vince grinned.

"I see…"

His hands reached the top of her head, gliding over hair, smooth and silky. Downward, a single, thick braid ran halfway down her back.

"Ummmn," Vince moaned, "very nice."

"So can I stay?"

"Answer a question first. Was that you up on stage? Tell me that sultry, sexy voice belongs to you."

She leaned closer, taking his hands in hers, fingers interlocking.

"You're very perceptive. I dig that."

Vince smiled. "One of my many talents."

"And the others?" She leaned in, close enough for Vince to feel her breath on his neck. Her perfume invaded his olfactory senses, causing him to inhale deeply. His fingers rested in hers, both sets of hands lying on her lap. Vince could feel the warmth of her skin radiating into his.

Chemistry…

"Well, let's see…"

Vince's mind raced back to the conversation he had shared with Trey. He could hear him now—take charge, dawg, be completely in control, and above all else, take no prisoners…

"I've been told," Vince said, with a sly grin, "that my tongue possesses a mind of its own."

"You don't say?"

"I do."

Vince released his fingers from hers and traced the contours of her legs downward, cupping her calves in his hands, feeling the power contained there.

"A good-looking brutha with a talented tongue—damn, I'm sure you're in demand."

"Naw, it ain't like that. I have an exacting palate. It's very particular about who and what I eat…"

"I see."

"Nice legs, by the way. Well toned, but not too muscular. I like that."

"I'm glad you approve."

"Let's review—you're a beautiful woman, obviously talented. So, I guess you can stay…"

"Thank goodness."

"Tell me. Is singing your main profession?" Vince asked.

"Like you, I've got many talents…"

Vince smirked. "I'm sure you do."

She leaned closer, taking his head in her hands, and kissed Vince gingerly on the mouth.

When she pulled back a moment later, Vince asked, "What was that for?"

She replied, "For being *unconventional*…"

✖✖✖

Raven led Vince outside. The cold assaulted them, and they reached to each other for warmth.

"Take the glasses off." It was a command, issued without malice.

Vince had no problem complying. He stared at her for a moment, not saying anything, reveling in the closeness that they shared. Her eyes sparkled, and her hair shined, even in the streetlights of evening.

Raven was draped in a luxurious fur coat that hung inches from the ground. It was thick-haired and deep brown. Vince estimated its worth at fifteen-thousand dollars *minimum*.

"It's good to see you again," he said softly.

"It is good to be seen," she replied, reaching for his arm and wrapping hers in his. "There's someplace I want to take you to. Since we're in this mode of thinking outside of the box, and on this grand adventure."

"I'm game wherever you take me."

Twenty minutes later he parked on a side street and followed Raven for a short walk. They came to a building with a neon sign in the window announcing live dancers. Vince glanced at Raven who merely smiled as she paused in her step so Vince could get the door.

The interior of the club was small, but cozy. It actually had atmosphere. Vince had been to a number of strip clubs in his day, but this was a first. Missing was that seedy, almost dirty feel—this place had class. Most of the thirty or so patrons were seated on low couches or love seats. There was actually art on the walls. Funky music emanated from ceiling-hung speakers.

"This your day job?" Vince asked jokingly.

"You wish." They found an empty couch with a low coffee table positioned in front. They sat and glanced around. There were a few other couples enjoying the show. A number of women, clad in various stages of undress, meandered through the crowd, talking to patrons. Vince spied the main stage, up front, a raised square platform with mirrors behind and on the ceiling. A tall thin dark-skinned woman gyrated her hips to 50 Cent's "In Da Club." She was fully nude, and her body was exceptional.

A waitress came and they ordered a round of Coronas. Raven sat back and glanced at Vince.

"You gonna keep that coat on all night?" he asked.

Raven smiled, her lips curving upward into a sensuous grin. She removed her coat and Vince's eyes almost popped out of their sockets.

She wore a black with white trim half-shirt and matching panties. The top was stretched across her breasts, displaying perky nipples underneath. The panties were tight and short, baring ample amounts of flesh. Vince looked her over. Her stomach was flat, and her legs shined. Vince was speechless.

"You don't mind, do you?"

"You're kidding, right?" he responded, moving closer until their shoulders touched. "Damn, woman, you are fine!"

"Thank you."

Her eyes flirted over to the patrons, and observed the other dancers for a moment. A few had taken to dancing on the low tables in front of the patrons. Vince watched Raven silently. He sensed something in her, a bit of anxiety mixed with excitement.

"Everything okay?" he asked.

"Everything's cool." The beers arrived, and Raven took a long swig.

"You sure?" he asked, eying her as she took another wild gulp.

Her eyes sparkled as she nodded. Placing the bottle down, she stood up, pressing her hands to her torso and stomach. Vince couldn't help but admire her beauty. She placed one pump-clad foot on the coffee table and reached out with her hand. Vince leaned forward, taking her hand as she climbed up, using him for support. Raven glanced down at him and smiled. Vince was in shock.

The music shifted, 50 Cent to Beyonce, as Raven began to move. There may have been other activity going on in the club, but at that exact moment, no one seemed to notice. It was as if all attention had shifted to Raven. Vince could feel the temperature change. Conversation had been cut short that quickly!

Raven began a slow dance, moving her hips seductively as her arms went over her head. Eyes closed, head angled upward, she moved not like a stripper, but a woman who was in tune with her sexuality, enjoying the thrill that one receives from displaying her wares for all those hungry to see. Vince was alive. Although she hadn't removed anything yet, he was thoroughly enjoying the scene unfolding before him.

A brunette with fake breasts and an assuming smile came up to the table, holding something in her hand. Raven glanced downward and smiled; the woman reached for her ankle and slipped a lacy garter belt up to her thigh. She then placed two crisp dollar bills between the lace and her skin. They exchanged a few words that were lost on Vince. As she moved away, Vince stood, reaching for his wallet.

Slipping a twenty into her garter belt, Vince stood back and enjoyed the show. Raven pirouetted on her high heels, giving him her back. She tilted her head upward, letting her hair free fall down her back. Vince marveled at the sculpted back muscles that led to a perfectly shaped ass. Orbs of flesh peeked out from the edges of the fabric; she spun around before he could study it further, and moved in, until mere inches separated them. Raven flipped her hair forward, letting it fall over Vince's head and face. He glanced upward, their eyes and smiles locked.

"Enjoying the show?" Raven asked seductively.

"More than you know…"

"Should I keep going?" she asked, her hands gliding over her breasts and resting at the bottom edge of her top.

"Only if you want to."

Raven smiled. "I'm feeling particularly *frisky* tonight…"

"Then do your thang, girl. No one here is mad at you, least of all me!"

Raven turned away from him, and Vince sucked in a breath as her arms crossed over her stomach and in an instant her top was lifting up over her head. She glanced back, eyes sparkling, teeth flashing before she turned, and Vince got to see her in all of her unadulterated loveliness.

Her breasts were solid orbs of jiggling flesh that shook as she moved. Vince resisted the urge to reach for them. It was something he wanted to do very badly. Instead he sat back down.

Immediately, a graying man in his fifties approached the table. He smiled up at Raven, words were spoken, and he handed a folded bill to her. She curtsied and placed the bill in her belt.

More patrons lined up. Vince smiled at Raven as her eyes widened for a brief moment before tending patiently to each customer. For some she held on to their shoulder as she waved her hair in their faces; for others she presented them with her ass inches from their face.

After about fifteen minutes, Raven had a nice wad of cash protruding from the lace around one thigh. Vince stood again, the table finally to himself, and approached Raven. The music shifted from hip-hop to reggae. The thumping bass lines were hitting Vince squarely in his chest. Raven held onto his shoulders as she gazed downwards. Her nipples were hard; a thin sheen of sweat adorned her skin. Vince couldn't remember being more turned on.

He sucked in a breath and exhaled forcefully.

"Take your panties off," he said surely. He eyed her; unblinking as she stared back.

A moment passed.

Then another.

Slowly, methodically, she slid down her panties while Vince remained inches away from the core of her sexuality, the place where toned thighs came together, a half-inch-thick track of pubic hair on otherwise shaved skin. Without thought, Vince licked his lips. He glanced up, smiling, before returning his gaze to her sex. Raven backed away, fully nude now, the music infusing renewed passion and energy into her being.

She spun on her heels, and bent over, her ass and thighs a mastery of craftsmanship. She spread her legs slightly, and Vince sucked in a breath, marveling at her bare sex and the rest of her package, a work of art that spoke to him with her pure lines and soft curves.

Vince turned to see a throng of patrons, folded bills in hand lining up. He sighed as he returned to his seat, thankful for being able to hide his growing erection.

Thirty minutes later when Raven stepped down and donned her clothes she had earned slightly fewer than four-hundred dollars.

Vince grinned as she sat back, their shoulders touching as she placed a cold Corona to her lips and chugged the entire bottle.

Vince placed his hand on her thigh and whispered in her ear.

"That was truly incredible. *You* are incredible."

She turned to him and grinned.

"I can't believe I actually went through with it. I've wanted to do that for so long, but never could summon the nerve until tonight."

"What changed?"

"Seeing you in Bluezette tonight. You were unconventional. Never in my wildest dreams did I think you'd come up with what you did."

"You said, 'Think outside of the box…'"

"You amazed me," she said, her hair falling onto his shoulder. Vince made no effort to move away.

"The feeling is very much mutual, I assure you." Vince downed his beer. "Listen, as much as I love watching you, I'm tired of sharing your beauty with these other patrons. Let's get out of here—call me selfish, but I want you all to myself!"

Raven stood and donned her fur coat as the graying gentleman returned.

"Leaving so soon, Miss?" he asked, clutching a sheaf of bills in his hand.

Vince stood, taking her hand.

"Show's over, my man. Thank you for your patronage…"

Raven grinned as the gentleman handed her the bills; she stuffed them into her purse; all eyes were upon them as Vince led the elusive dancer from the club.

✖✖✖

They were silent as Vince drove. It was a quarter past 1 in the morning. The heat was turned up high; the volume in the car on low.

An old Joe Sample CD was playing. Raven closed her eyes briefly and let the melody carry her.

"Where to, sexy lady?" Vince asked, breaking the silence.

"Turn right at the next light."

"Cool." Vince's mind whirled. He wondered where this evening would lead. Raven was subdued, and that worried him. He wasn't sure if it was the lateness of the night or something else.

"Another right," she said.

Vince steered his car up Chestnut as directed. They went three-quarters up the block before Raven said: "Pull up in front of that awning."

Vince did as he was told.

He put the car in park and glanced to his left. The Omni was a five-star hotel in the midst of Society Hill not far from Independence Hall and the river.

Raven was stepping out of the car as a bellhop approached Vince's window.

"Checking in, Sir?"

Vince glanced quickly between him and Raven, who turned to the man and said cheerfully, "Room 1004."

The bellhop nodded as Raven took to the revolving doors, escaping the cold quickly as Vince followed mutely.

The ornate foyer was desolate of people this time of night. Off to the left, behind the registration desk, a lone attendant nodded to Vince. Raven's heels echoed on cold marble as she walked ahead of him. She cut to the right, toward a bank of elevators. Vince caught up as the doors hissed open.

"Everything okay?" he asked, when they were safely inside. Raven, who was clutching her fur with one hand, let it fall open. She smiled at him.

"Why wouldn't it be?" she replied with a devilish grin.

Vince exhaled, feeling his heart beat loudly in his chest. "You were incredible tonight. I don't think I've ever been more impressed."

Raven eyed him curiously but said nothing. She turned to the elevator controls and their reflection that shone back at them from the mirrored doors. Her hand reached up, pressing a button, and the elevator jolted to a stop. Vince felt his heart flutter as Raven turned to him. She took a step forward.

"I'm feeling *unconventional* right about now. How about you?" Before Vince could respond, her lips were pressed onto his, their mouths opening in unison as tongues fluttered against each other for the very first time. Vince reached for her, wrapping an arm around her body and pulling her to him. She let out a gasp as their bodies connected. His hands went to her face, grasping her gingerly as he kissed her ravenously, as if they were lovers reunited after a very long stay apart. Vince pulled back, holding her at arm's length as he stared at her longingly.

"You are so beautiful," he said, and he kissed her again. Slipping out of his coat, he let it fall to the floor. Raven backed up, Vince interlocked his fingers in hers, and their arms rose over her head as they bumped into the elevator wall. His released her, his hands finding her waist, and moving upward, following her curves until his fingers slipped underneath the fabric of her top, gliding over smooth flat meadows until he reached her mountainous breasts. Palming them gently, her squeezed her lovely mounds while Raven groaned.

Vince attacked her neck, first kissing, then sucking at the flesh of her clavicle, as one hand snaked down her torso and stomach. Downward it went, slipping underneath the fabric of her panties, until his fingers felt the rising flesh of her clit. Downward still, his fingers spread over her pubic hair and lips of her sex, before curling upward, finding her center, wet to his touch.

"Oh God!" Raven whispered, clutching at his neck as their mouths attacked each other. Panties slid down her thighs, her top bunched up until Vince retreated backwards to view her in all of her magnificence.

Bending forward, Vince traced a line of wet kisses from her neck on down until he reached the top of her breast. He cupped each one in hand, circling the rising flesh with his wet tongue, before taking each nipple in his mouth, biting down lightly, tugging at each one in a teasing kind of manner, as Raven moaned and grasped his head tightly, scrunching her eyes shut in tortuous pleasure.

His tongue meandered downward—circling her navel, painting a decreasingly wide swath until he met her sex, probing the hole lightly with a curled tongue.

Raven was a snake wriggling with delight as Vince kneeled down on his coat. Grasping her ankles, he ran his fingers lightly upward to the top of her thighs before quickly retreating the way he came, stroking her flesh with his fingernails. Vince moved his palms to her inner ankles and applied pressure, gently spreading her legs, before beginning his upstroke with his digits, but this time on the insides of her legs. His fingers traveled until they met at the apex of where her legs came together, that lovely spot of flesh that Vince drew himself to. Placing one hand on her pussy, Vince spread his fingers, and without fanfare, bent in, his tongue connecting with her gaping hole as he sucked her into his waiting mouth in one giant gulp.

Raven clutched at his head and moaned as Vince fed, licking the lips of her cunt and clit before swirling his tongue between her fleshes in a frenzy of activity that left Raven dizzy. He glanced upward and smiled, his tongue still connected to her saliva-coated clit, tickling it before swooping down, probing her insides deeply as he heard Raven gasp.

"Oh God, that tongue, yes! Don't stop," she moaned. Vince moved backwards, pulling her with him until he was prone atop his coat on the elevator floor, while Raven knelt over his face. He reached for her ass, took hold of her cheeks and forced them apart while sticking his nose into the interior of her cunt. He thrashed his head back and forth, side to side, his nose, lips, and teeth connecting with her wet pussy lips and engorged clit. He felt her spasm, as Raven sucked in a breath, clenching her thighs around his ears.

Vince continued his feeding without let-up, briefly allowing thoughts of Trey to bubble to the surface. Lord, his boy would be damn proud of him, if only he could witness him in action this very minute. The thought remained uncompleted, because Raven grabbed his hair, digging her fingernails into his scalp.

Vince spread her ass further apart, clutching at her flesh and pulling her downward as his tongue arced upward, slicing against the twitching opening of her anus. As his tongue flashed against it, Raven shuddered; her thighs tightened then opened. Vince curled his tongue and darted it against the puckered opening. Raven screamed: a short, high-pitched yell that reverberated along the steel walls of the elevator car.

Making his tongue flat, Vince licked her lengthwise, anus to cunt, and cunt back to anus, hearing her shriek and feeling her explode against his mouth with a force that pushed him into the car floor. Yet he held on, squeezing her ass cheeks and taking her drenched pussy lips between his teeth, slurping her sex into his mouth before turning attention to her clit and stimulating it with his teeth, gums, and frenzied tongue.

Her syrup oozed, warm and sticky on his face. It washed over his nose, lips and tongue, her juice injecting into his mouth as her body spasmed above him. After one final shudder that ended with Raven falling on top of him, exhausted, Vince reached for her breasts and tugged at her nipples, feeling the last of her orgasmic wave subside. After what seemed like several minutes of minimal silence and movement, save for the rise and fall of her breasts on his stomach, her head resting in the cleft of his thighs, his penis fully engorged and waiting to be unsheathed, Raven stirred. Silently, she unzipped him, extracting his thick member from the confines of his pants as Vince let his head fall to the floor. His eyes were unfocused as he glanced upward, past the curves of her ass, and dabs of love juice that was drying on her inner thighs. Vince sucked in a breath as Raven took him into her mouth, licking the shaft with her hot tongue as Vince squeezed his eyes tight, and tried to slow his breathing.

Fingers wrapped themselves around his meat, jerking up and down methodically as she took him deeper into her mouth. Vince fought the rising tide within as he felt the first inklings of an orgasm begin deep in his belly. He desperately wanted to implant himself inside of the sweetness he had just tasted, entomb his cock in her tight little cunt, fuck her from behind in the elevator of this five-star Omni. Vince bent over Raven as her lovely ass cheeks quivered, his cock slipping in and out her rapidly, dizzying her (and him) with the intensity of his fucking.

But it was not meant to be!

Vince groaned, feeling the dam burst, as he erupted into Raven's waiting mouth, trying as hard as he could to hold out, attempting to command his body to yield.

But Raven was too good, her mouth a lovely cavern that fit him like a form-fitting glove. Raven moaned, feeling Vince shudder underneath her. He squeezed his eyes shut, as his sap coated the insides of her mouth and ran down her throat, Vince shouting, "Oh God!" as every fiber of his being tightened simultaneously, and his toes, without being told, curled back like a wicked grin.

When he was done, when Vince was completely spent, Raven slipped his withering cock out of her mouth, and knelt up. Vince opened his eyes, as she rose, smiling as she came to him, her mouth an expanding orifice as their tongues intertwined. After a minute, Raven pulled back and stood up, releasing the STOP button as the car jerked upward in sudden movement.

"*Unconventional*," she whispered as the elevator chimed; the doors opened and Raven strode out, a satisfied smile adorning her pretty face.

Vince remained for a moment more on the floor before springing to his feet, grabbing his coat, and exiting the car. Raven sauntered down the hotel corridor naked, her decadent fur dragging on the floor behind her, Raven's bare ass and hips shaking seductively as she moved. When she had gone twenty yards, Raven turned her head back and smiled, a grin so hyper-erotic that Vince found himself growing hard again. She glanced down at his crotch and then back up at him, winked as she curled her finger beckoning him near. In that second, as Vince began to move, the elevator doors snapped shut behind him...

FORTY

They were led to a quiet table in the back, away from the din of the bar. Erika was grateful. She beamed at Naomi, while removing her coat and handing it to the maitre d'.

Two weeks into the New Year. They were dining at D.C. Coast, an upscale restaurant located at K and 14th Streets.

"Girl, you look *good*!" Erika exclaimed, while wiping flakes of moisture from her hair. A thin layer of snow blanketed the streets, making driving conditions hazardous. It always amazed Erika how a little bit of snow could shut down this metropolitan city.

Naomi grinned while smoothing back her short brown locks. She crossed her legs and folded her hands on the table. "Thank you, Erika—you ain't looking half-bad yourself!"

"Please, this 'do is tired, ya hear me? I need to do something with it."

"Well, you could always cut it all off like I did!"

"Girl, I'm too scared to try that shit. But it looks damn good on you." Erika glanced at the menu. "Seriously though, you've got a glow to you, sistah. What are you doing? Getting some on the regular?"

"Please, I wish!" Naomi exclaimed. "Just the opposite with me," she said softly.

"What do you mean?"

"Well, I told you the last time we hooked up that Michael and I had broken up."

"Yeah," Erika said, "I'm sorry to hear that."

"Don't be. That sorry specimen of a man was cheating on me—says he wasn't but you know what? I don't have time for that mess—having other women calling his cell or paging him at all hours of the night. I'm too old to be putting up with that shit!"

"I hear you, girl."

"I decided that it was time to focus on me—make me the number one priority instead of these crazy-ass niggas out here."

Erika nodded.

"It's only been a month or so, but I feel wonderful. I'm focusing on my relationship with God; I joined a gym, and am working out on the regular. And, check this out, I joined this really cool book club, *and* am taking an art history class!"

"A what?"

"You heard me right: an art history class. I wanted to stay busy and keep myself focused. So I signed up for this class. It's something I've always wanted to learn about, so I said, why not go for it. Let me tell you, girl, I love it! I spend my weekends going around town taking in the various museums, checking out the works of the Masters—it's intense."

"Dayum!"

"Yeah, it's all that. And this book club is the bomb. It's a bunch of professional sistahs who meet every few weeks to talk about black literature. Not this ghettofabulous drama that's out there, but real literature. Like Baldwin, Toomer, and Hurston."

"Wow. Well, you're doing your thing, girl, and it shows, 'cause you got this serious glow going on. You look rested and refreshed," Erika said.

"Thank you. I feel good. I'm putting it all into perspective—men are wonderful, but you've got to keep your priorities straight. Too many of us get it twisted and forget what's really important. We run ourselves ragged trying to keep our men so damn happy, that we lose a piece of ourselves in the process."

"I hear that!"

"So, what's new with you? I take it that you and James are still together?"

Erika nodded solemnly.

The waitress arrived with drinks. Naomi ordered the Caesar salad topped with grilled shrimp, Erika the broiled Atlantic salmon.

"Do tell…" Naomi encouraged.

Erika sighed. "Where do I begin?" She paused to sip at her chocolate martini, grimaced, and pushed the glass away. "Honestly, Naomi, I feel funny talking about it, because I'm not sure if I should be feeling this way."

"What do you mean?"

"Well, I've told you before about what's up."

"You mean about the sex?"

"Yeah—James is a wonderful man. And we have fun together. I shouldn't be complaining at all. So many women would give their left titty to be in my shoes. With a fine brutha like that? Shoot!"

"Looks ain't everything, you know."

"I know.

"Are things improving—in the bedroom?" Naomi asked.

"I don't know. I guess I'm having fun, but each time we make love and he doesn't come, it becomes even more difficult for me to relax and enjoy myself. I'm lying there, enjoying the sensations, but in the back of my mind, I can't help but wondering if he's going to come tonight. It preoccupies my mind and frankly, now it's beginning to interfere with *me* coming!"

"That's not good."

Erika shook her head.

"Then a few weeks ago, he comes over, I'm taking a bath, and he storms in with my dildo in his hand, freaking out and whatnot! 'What the fuck are you doing with this? Why you need this?' he yells. 'I'm not enough?' Girl—I told him to get the hell out of my damn apartment!"

"Good for you. The brutha shouldn't be rifling through your shit anyway. Serves his ass right for finding it!"

"Yup. But then he breaks down and tells me how much he loves me; how he's afraid of losing me…"

"Damn…" Naomi said, shaking her head.

"Yeah, damn is right. I mean, I dig James. He's a cool dude. We are having fun together. I'm comfortable with him. But lately, I can't help thinking about our relationship. I've been wondering if I'm being too judgmental—

no one is perfect, right? Women spend half their lives looking for Mr. Right. Well, perhaps James is Mr. Right, imperfections and all, and I'm just being unreasonable, insisting that my man be perfect, when I'm not."

Naomi nodded. "On the other hand, some imperfections are deal breakers. Some quirks you just can't get past. Only you can decide if James is one of those men."

"I know. Am I being too persnickety? I mean, who has a perfect relationship without issues? Every woman I know complains on some level about her man and his shit. Everyone!"

"Right."

"And what if I let James go because of his 'sexual' problems and then regret it. I mean, another man of James' caliber may not come along anytime soon, if ever."

"True," Naomi said. "I guess you need to just weigh both sides carefully. And take your time—'cause you don't need to rush things…especially when it comes to love."

"I wish that were true," Erika said. "But James is bugging me every other day. Calling me, e-mailing me, wanting to know how I feel. You know how it is when one person says, 'I love you' and the other one remains silent…"

"Yeah I do."

The food arrived. Erika was grateful for the lapse so she could collect her thoughts. She told the waitress to take away her chocolate martini and bring her an apple one. So much for daring to be different!

Erika took a bite of the salmon. It was delicious. Naomi attacked her salad with zeal.

"I just wish I could figure this shit out, girl!" Erika exclaimed. "It's driving me crazy."

"I know, but don't let it. You'll figure out what's best, in time," she said, patting her hand.

"Yeah, but in the meantime, it's bugging me big time!" She glanced up. "Can't I just get a sign? God, can't you show me the way to go?" she asked, gazing upward to the ceiling. "Is that asking too much? 'Cause I sure could use your counsel right now…"

✖✖✖

I heard the sharp rap at the door, and glanced up from working on my brief. That's when Bernard John Marshall waltzed in. I set down my fountain pen with an audible sigh.

"Bernard," I said, not wanting to deal with his shit first thing this morning.

"Trey. I have an assignment for you," he said, without preamble.

I stared at the mutha fucka in his starched white button-down shirt, yellow and blue striped power tie, hair wet with that slick-back shit he uses too much of, and let my expression remain flat and emotionless, not wanting him to sense my discontentment.

"I need you to meet with a client in New York. Day after tomorrow."

I didn't even blink.

"Can't, Bernie, I've got a deposition scheduled for Thursday at…"

"Cancel it."

"That's not how I do business…"

"Counselor, this isn't a request and I'm not seeking your permission!" He stood, smoothed out his slacks and turned for the door. "India has the details. I'll expect a full brief on your return." He reached the door and placed a hand on the knob. "This is an important client, Mr. Alexander. I'll expect your best work on this one."

"Last time I checked, we didn't have offices in New York City."

Bernard sighed. "I'll see you back here on Friday."

"Yessah mastah," I hissed.

Bernard turned.

"What did you say?" he barked.

I blinked but said nothing.

"You are this close," he said, showing me a quarter inch between thumb and forefinger, "from disciplinary action. Keep it up, counselor, and I will personally have the pleasure of escorting you from this office…"

The door slammed shut and I sat there, shaking my head morosely.

✖✖✖

The flight to LaGuardia was uneventful. Left on time, arrived on time. Imagine that!

I grabbed my garment bag and laptop, left the terminal quickly, and hailed a taxi for the thirty-five-minute ride into mid-town Manhattan. India had booked a room for me at the Marriott in Times Square. She had contacted the client, and made arrangements for her to meet me at the hotel for a breakfast meeting at 10. I glanced at my Breitling. Plenty of time to check in and even relax for a few minutes before we got started.

I recounted the conversation I had had with Calvin the previous evening. I had phoned him, pissed about my trip to New York, this interruption to my schedule, and the general way Bernard's style of micro-*fucking* management was creeping into my personal life.

Calvin counseled me to chill.

"Trey, I told you, you need to relax and stay focused. This guy is gunning for you; so don't give him the satisfaction of seeing you angry. That's what he wants—he desires to see you all up in a tizzy. So don't feed into it."

I grunted.

"Besides, is New York so bad? We all could use a diversion every so often. Think of this as a mini-vacation. You get out of here for a quick minute, you get to stay in a posh hotel on the firm's nickel—hell, go have a great dinner, take in a show or something, and come back refreshed, with a new attitude."

I grunted again...

"Trey, you need to stop letting him get to you. Here is my advice: Fuck Bernard John Marshall and the horse he rode in on...forget about him and move on with your life..."

I smiled at the thought of Calvin Figgs, Esq., Extraordinaire, cursing my boss' name. It made me feel better. Calvin was right. New York wasn't so bad. Hell, there was always something to do in this city, even in the midst of winter. Shit, if trouble wasn't around here somewhere, Trey Alexander would find it his damn self!

That's right. Flip the script, make this an outing. I hadn't gotten away from the office in a hot minute anyway. So now was my chance. Take advantage, as Calvin had suggested. Well, take advantage I would. Beginning this minute. Oh hell yeah, y'all!

Less than an hour later I was sitting at a table overlooking Broadway. I had checked in, finished reading *The Post*, and even watched a few minutes of *Regis and Kelly* before heading downstairs to the restaurant.

I sipped at my coffee while watching the people meander down the street. Cars and cabs (cabs mostly) whizzed past my view as obscenely large neon signs advertised everything from Calvin Klein underwear to Air Jordan kicks. A folded *Times* in hand, turned to the sports section, occupied most of my attention. I didn't hear her walk up until she cleared her throat.

"Mr. Alexander?" a sweet voice pronounced.

I placed my paper down and glanced up, almost dropping my cup in my lap.

DAYUM. I stood abruptly.

"Giovanna Marquis?"

"Yes." She smiled briefly. "May I sit down?"

"Of course. Please," I said, gesturing her to the seat across from me. She sat, and folded her legs. Her skin was caramel-colored and as smooth as syrup. She wore a dark pinstripe business suit, form-fitting jacket that displayed a hint of shapely cleavage, and a short skirt that showcased lovely long legs. Her hair was dark, and tied up in a bun. Her makeup was flawless. She was in a word, stunning.

My dick was growing hard by the second, and instantly I found myself forgetting about business, instead plotting a way into her soon-to-be-drenched-thanks-to-you-know-who panties.

"Have you been waiting long?" she asked, making eye contact with me. She was so fucking beautiful it almost hurt my eyes to stare back.

But I held her gaze.

"Not really, I checked in about half hour ago and just sat down a few minutes ago."

"How was your flight?" she asked while looking over the menu.

"Quick and uneventful. Just the way it's supposed to be." My hand instinctively went to my tie and readjusted the knot. I was so damn thankful for wearing this particular ensemble. Dark-gray Italian sports cut suit, polished shoes, and powder-blue tie! Funky fresh as only yours truly can do...I just know this honey was impressed.

The waiter came and we ordered breakfast.

"Where do we start?" she inquired when he had left.

"From the beginning, if you would," I said, all business-like, yet still wondering about how this chick would look straddling my dick. But then, like a blow striking the abdomen, I winced with the thought of Trey's Rules.

Those damn rules...

Trey's Rule Number 1—never *ever* fuck a client.

And so far, to date, I hadn't violated that rule. But damn, this chick was so *foine*, I was having trouble just sitting still.

Yet I persevered...

"Well, let's see," Giovanna said, "I was married seven years ago. Ali is a high-ranking diplomat working for the Qatar embassy. We separated about two months ago."

"Where were you married?" I asked.

"In Paris."

"And the marriage license is from..."

"New York."

"Go on," I said, reaching for my legal pad so I could scribble some notes.

"We divided our time mostly between New York City and Washington, maintaining two residences, sometimes traveling abroad. Since our separation, I've moved into an apartment on the Upper West Side, and use the Washington home on occasion."

I nodded, as I scribbled. "Have the two of you worked up any agreement concerning division of property?"

Giovanna shook her head.

"Good. Let me handle that. I'll need for you to put together a list of all marital assets and property amassed during the marriage so we can work up something for his attorney. Any idea whom that might be?"

She reached into her purse and pulled out a business card. Giovanna slid it across the table, and I took the opportunity to focus my attention on her slender fingers, nails polished to perfection. I swallowed involuntarily, suppressing the urge to suck those digits into my waiting mouth.

"Thank you," I said, glancing at the card and copying the information onto my legal pad. "So, you've been together seven years, then you split. Who made the decision?"

"I did."

"And can I assume you are seeking the divorce?"

She nodded.

"How is your husband reacting to all of this?" I asked delicately.

"Not well."

I nodded. "So I can assume he will not react well when we file for divorce?"

"Correct." She stared straight at me, an even expression, devoid of smiles or frowns.

"I can understand that," I replied.

"Why do you say that?" she exclaimed, her shoulders perking up.

My eyes grew wide for a split second. "No reason," I said, blinking. "I didn't mean anything by it."

"You had something on your mind when you uttered those words," she said coolly.

I smiled, holding up my hands up as in surrender. "You've misunderstood what I said. I only meant that you're a beautiful woman," I said, flashing her my pearly whites, "and that it is understandable for your husband to be hurt by your actions."

Giovanna sat back, arms folded across her chest as she glared at me. Suddenly I realized that things were not going well, and I couldn't, for the life of me, understand why.

"So, let me understand you," she replied. "You've known me for all of what—five minutes, you've never laid eyes on my husband, yet you profess to understand how he must have felt after I left him? That doesn't make sense."

"No, no, Mrs. Marquis—I didn't mean any disrespect. This is a difficult time…"

"Please, Mr. Alexander, don't patronize me. I know first-hand how difficult divorce can be. Can we get back on track?"

"Of course," I said, swallowing hard. "You are seeking to dissolve your marriage because of…?"

"I am no longer in love with my husband, Mr. Alexander. I was once, but not anymore. Therefore, I see no reason for the continued charade." Her eyes were brown unblinking orbs. I stared, unmoving for a moment before nodding quietly.

"Okay. Let's move on. Tell me, do you work? Any income?"

"No, Mr. Alexander, I do not work. I haven't since college."

I nodded and made a few notes. "So, I can assume we will be asking for alimony since…"

"That won't be necessary."

I looked up, pen poised above the yellow paper of my pad.

"And why not?" I asked, cocking my head to the side and eyeing her curiously.

"Because my family comes from wealth. So money is not the issue here."

"Okay," I said. I put my pen down and held both elbows close to my chest. "Mrs. Marquis, I think we have gotten off on the wrong foot. I want to apologize for that." I stared hard at her eyes. "I want to be your attorney, and I want to get everything that you deserve. To do that, we need to trust in each other and feel comfortable together."

She nodded but said nothing.

"I don't know what you've heard about me, but I am a damn good attorney. Divorce is all that I do—call it a specialty. I've handled all kind of clients from…"

"Mr. Alexander, let me stop you right there," Giovanna said, holding up a chiseled hand. "There is no need for you to relate the details of your accomplishments, for I can assure you that they are already known to me." She smiled, I think for the first time since we got started, and I felt my face flush.

"Alrighty then. What I'm trying to say, Mrs. Marquis, is that I don't want this to feel forced. I want you to relax and feed me any pertinent details about your married life and the financial situation of you and your husband, so that I can do the best job I can for you."

"I have no doubt in your abilities, Mr. Alexander, or you wouldn't be here…" she said, cracking a slight grin.

I smiled back. *Thank you, Lord! There's hope yet for getting into those panties.*

"Okay!" I sighed heavily while picking up my pen. "So tell me, Mrs. Marquis, what is it that you want out of this divorce?"

Giovanna glanced toward the window for a second, lost in thought. Even in profile this woman was beautiful. I rubbed my thighs together, attempting without success to quell the sexual tension I was feeling.

"I want my freedom back. I've been restrained for far too long. I don't like the way it makes me feel. It isn't me, Mr. Alexander. Can you understand that?"

"Yes," I replied, giving her my rapt attention, "of course I can." I have to confess that my "darker" side was thinking —*if it's release you want, baby, come on upstairs to my room right now—I will set your sexy ass free!*

"Material things are not important to me," she said, continuing. "We amassed some items of value during the marriage that I'd like to keep. I'm unsure about the properties and how they should be handled. I'm moving permanently to Washington, but have no desire to live in our home there."

"That's fine," I said, as thoughts of seeing Giovanna back on my home turf expanded my insides with desire. "I'll need a list of marital property so we can go over that. Item values, as best you can determine them, and all relevant information so that I can proceed." Giovanna nodded. "How quickly can you put this together?

"How long are you in town?"

"I return to Washington tomorrow."

"Then I'll have it ready in the morning." She pulled out a daytimer and jotted down some notes.

"Wonderful," I replied, "I'm looking forward to working with you." She nodded. "I'll try to make this as painless as possible, so you can get on track with your life…get your freedom back." I flashed a smile, and she returned a weak one.

The food arrived. We ate silently. My attempt at small talk was rebutted by more silence. Giovanna answered my questions, but didn't volunteer anything further. I was, in a word, perplexed. Frankly, I wasn't used to fine-ass, soon-to-be-single women acting toward me in this way. I was getting restless, wanting something to kick-start this thing between us into high gear. But it wasn't going to happen…not today anyway.

Giovanna pushed her half-eaten fruit plate away and dabbed her lips with a silk napkin.

I finished my omelet and took another sip of coffee before putting my mug down.

"Mrs. Marquis, can I get your contact information? I'm here the rest of the day and am anxious to begin working on your case. If something occurs to me, I'd like to be able to reach you."

She reached for her purse again and extracted a piece of paper.

"You will find all my numbers on there."

"Wonderful," I said, again, taking the paper and glancing at it quickly.

She stood, buttoning her jacket as she reached for her purse. I took the opportunity to scan the curves of her lovely form, the rise of her breasts, the fullness of her ass against the tight fabric of her skirt. Long, silky legs, high-heel fuck-me pumps…the entire package was speaking to me…

I swallowed…*hard*…

DAYUM!

"Thank you for breakfast, Mr. Alexander. I guess we will be in touch," Giovanna said pleasantly before turning on her heels and beginning to walk away.

I had to think fast—I cleared my throat audibly.

"Oh Mrs. Marquis?"

She paused in mid-step and turned. "Yes?"

"If you don't have plans tonight, I'd love to buy you dinner. We don't have to talk shop if you're not up to it. We can just kick it somewhere nice, and…"

"Mr. Alexander," she said, with a pained expression on her otherwise beautiful face, "I'm afraid that won't work." She stared at me for a long second as I felt my sails deflate and my mind whirl, contemplating my next response. I sucked in a breath and grinned.

"Perhaps another time…"

"Mr. Alexander," Giovanna said, buttoning her jacket with one hand. "I'd like to keep this strictly professional. I'm sure you can see the wisdom in that."

I swallowed and nodded slowly. Giovanna threw me a fake smile and walked away without further comment.

And I was left there, a stupid expression on my normally confident looking face.

FORTY-ONE

"**N**aomi, Hold that thought for a second," Erika said with a sigh, while reaching into her bag for her cell phone. This was the fourth ring in the past thirty minutes. She had let the others go to voice mail. Checking the Caller ID quickly, she huffed. "Damn, this boy is getting ridiculous!"

"Perhaps you should answer it…" Naomi said with a serious expression.

They had finished their dinner, their plates had been cleared away, and they were sitting enjoying the conversation and their espressos.

"James," she said into her cell sternly.

"Baby, I've been calling you for the past hour," he said, his voice harried.

"Stop exaggerating."

"So you purposely haven't been taking my calls?" he responded incredulously.

"James, I'm out with a friend having dinner. I'll call you later."

"Who's the friend?" he said quickly. "I don't recall you saying anything about having dinner tonight with any *friend*."

Erika stared at her phone as if it were a disgusting bug. "And *I* don't recall having to check in with your high-nASS. Now, if you will excuse me." Erika hung up before James could respond. She dropped the phone into her purse and looked up. "Can you believe this shit? Now the nigga's checking up on me, wanting to know my itinerary. Oh HELL NO!"

Naomi chuckled. "Can you blame him—the brutha's sprung—and hurting big time—first he finds your dildo, then he tells you he loves you and gets no response. Now his woman is out having dinner, for all he knows with some other nigga—come on—cut him some slack!"

"Trick, please!" Erika exclaimed. "Don't you dare take his side…"

"I'm not, Erika, I'm just saying—look at it from his perspective…"

Erika grew silent for a moment as she sipped her espresso.

"ERIKA?" a low male voice was rising in pitch from her nine o'clock position. Both women glanced up.

"OH MY GOODNESS, Erika!"

Erika dropped her jaw as the color drained from her normally rosy cheeks.

"Marcus?" she asked cautiously. A tall, athletic-built man appeared, dressed in an impeccable dark suit and gray tie. His hair was cut close to the scalp. He wore no facial hair and his baby face made him appear like a college student. He reached for Erika and gave her a bear hug. Behind him another man stood patiently, sharing his grin between the table of onlookers.

"I can't believe it—Erika," Marcus said, holding her at arm's length. "Look at you, girl. Damn, you look wonderful. It's so good to see you!"

Erika was blushing. She shook her head slowly from side to side, her lips pressed together as if attempting, without much success, to suppress a grin that threatened to erupt. Her hands remained in Marcus', who massaged her fingertips slowly. She pulled them away, pressed her hands to her jeans, and glanced at Naomi.

"Oh, my bad—Naomi—this is Marcus. Dr. Marcus Washington." Marcus reached out to take Naomi's hand in his.

"A pleasure," he said, showing her his straight white teeth. "And this is my boy, Dr. Harold Beasley."

Harold shook hands with the women.

Naomi was glancing rapidly between Marcus and Erika. "So where do you two know each other from?" she asked.

Erika was silent for a moment. Marcus was about to say something; he actually opened his mouth to speak but then thought better of it.

"I'll let Erika answer that," he said a split second later.

Erika smiled. "Well," she began, "Marcus and I dated for a while," she said, "but that was back in the day…" she added quickly.

Marcus turned to Erika and smiled. And at that moment, it seemed to Erika as if they were the only two people in this room. She smiled back, numerous thoughts and emotions welling to the surface. She felt herself grow weak, and sat down quickly to hide her disorientation. Marcus? She couldn't believe her own eyes…

"It is so good to see you, Erika," Marcus said again, and suddenly the thought occurred to her: was this the sign she'd been praying for???

✖✖✖

"Hey you!" Vince exclaimed while sitting back in his favorite chair.

"Hey yourself," Amber replied in an upbeat and welcoming voice. "Happy New Year!"

"Same to ya! I figured I better call you before half of the New Year flies by!"

"No chance of that happening," Amber said. "So what's up? How have you been?"

Vince could hear the enthusiasm filter through the connection loud and clear.

"Fine, can't complain—not a whole lot going on." Vince paused for a moment. "Actually, that's not true—a whole lot's been happening!"

"So, hook a sistah up!"

Vince laughed. "How's Angeliqué doing?" he asked.

"Fine," Amber responded. "She's been all busy getting ready for a new show. You need to make plans to come to the opening down here in March."

"We'll see—are you going to be in it?" he asked.

"Yup, bare ass and all!" Amber mused.

Vince grinned. His thoughts were transported back to the first time he spied Amber reclined on the floor of Angeliqué's studio, the hypnotic *veve* covering her nude form like lattice.

"In that case, count me in. I never turn down an opportunity to see a beautiful woman strut her bare ass!"

Amber laughed. "Hmmn," she said, "I wasn't sure you noticed…"

Vince got serious. "Excuse me? You don't need me to tell you that you're as fine as they come. I'm sure this isn't the first time you've heard that."

"Perhaps," Amber said quietly, "but it's nice to hear it from *you*."

Vince was silent for a moment.

"So, tell me what's been up, man?"

His thoughts shifted to Raven and the incredible time they had shared just a few weeks ago. Should he tell Amber? Vince was like a little kid in a candy store. He needed to tell anyone who would listen to his adventure. The thing he really dug about Amber was the way they jived—the two of them—being able to just talk about anything—conversation free-flowing. But could he talk to Amber about Raven, he wondered?

"Well, the holidays were nice. I spent them with my folks here in town. That was cool. No drama!"

"Yeah, us, too. Except we didn't get any snow—we never get any snow around here! Christmas and it's seventy-five degrees—that ain't right!" she said, pouting.

"Be happy you don't," Vince replied.

"So, Vince, now that you and Angeliqué are just friends, are you seeing anyone?"

Vince smiled. Here's the opening he'd been waiting for.

"Actually," he began, "I met this pretty cool lady a few weeks ago."

"Yeah? So, spill the tea. And don't leave out any details."

For the next fifteen minutes Vince recounted the story of how he met the mysterious and invigorating Raven, their initial encounter at his studio and the subsequent lunch where they discussed their adventure, to that fateful night in Philly, where he became a blind man, only to see her in a completely different light.

"Let me get this straight," Amber said. "Girlfriend pulls you into an empty elevator, presses the stop button and proceeds to seduce you?"

Vince laughed. "Yeah, something like that. But once I figured out what was going on, I took control of the situation…"

"Yeah, I bet. Vince—this chick was planning on seducing you from the moment she laid eyes on you. I've got to give homegirl credit—she's got skills!"

Vince had to agree with her on that point.

"So what happened next?" Amber asked.

"Well, we spent an incredible night in this very posh hotel. I have to say it was one of the most romantic moments of my life…" Vince said quietly.

"Boy, you know you did nothing more than wax that ass 'til daybreak. Please! Ain't no romance involved…"

"Oh you an expert now?" Vince yelled.

"Please—girlfriend ain't the only one with skills," she mused.

"Is that right?"

"That's a fact."

Vince chuckled along with Amber.

"So, you spent a romantic evening with Cat woman—yada yada—okay, I'm with you so far. So, you popped the question yet? Sounds like you popped everything else, man!"

"You ain't right." Vince became serious for a moment. "Here's the thing that I'm not understanding. The next morning, I woke up alone. Raven wasn't there…"

"Where'd she go?"

"Not sure. She left a note thanking me for the wonderful evening and telling me to order up whatever my heart desired from room service."

"What did you do?" Amber asked.

"What could I do—I had breakfast, showered, and left." Vince paused. "I haven't heard from her since…"

"WHAT?" Amber yelled, "How can that be? Did you at least call her?"

"Here's the thing. I don't have her number."

"Wait a minute—you guys kick it like that—spend the night swapping spit and God knows what else, and you didn't even exchange numbers???"

"Amber—I didn't expect to wake up alone," Vince replied a bit defensively.

"Okay, don't cut my head off—I hear you. But it's been what? Two weeks. She hasn't called?"

"Nope. Explain that one to me." Vince said dejectedly. "I don't get it. We spent this incredible night together. She wanted unconventional—well, I damn sure gave it to her, if I may say so myself. I blew her away—she told me herself. So why spend that kind of night with someone, becoming intimate, just to run away the next day? It just doesn't make any damn sense."

"To me neither. You can't get her number from information?"

"She called me on her cell phone—twice. I inadvertently erased my Caller ID. Like I said, I didn't expect for her to just *vanish*."

"Vince, perhaps with you guys hooking up so close to the holidays she just got busy with family and friends. I have a feeling she's gonna come around. Don't give up hope. She doesn't sound like the type to just play with a brutha like that."

"I hope not."

Vince's cell phone beeped. At first he thought it was Amber's line, but when it happened again, he glanced at his phone and paused in mid-breath.

"Amber—hold on, hold on." He clicked over.

"Hello?"

"Happy New Year," a smooth, sultry voice said.

"Raven." It was not a question, but a statement.

"Yes, baby—how are you? I've missed you." Vince felt his heart skip a beat. The mixture of frustration and passion collided inside his veins, making him tipsy. Vince was glad to be sitting down.

Ignoring the question, Vince replied: "Been a while, hasn't it?"

"Don't be mad at me."

Vince shut his eyes and said, "Raven, hold on, I'm on the other line." He clicked over before she could reply. "Amber—I'm back—you'll never guess who that is on the other line…"

Amber laughed. "Cat woman? As we live and breathe???"

"Yup."

"Thank you, Lord Jesus!" she replied, in her best phony church deacon voice, "Mah prayers have been answered!"

"You ain't right. I gotta go. Let me find out what this chick's been up to— why she's been dissin' me so!"

"Do your thang—I ain't mad at ya."

Vince turned serious. "Thank you, Amber—I consider you a true friend."

The warmth from Amber's smile could be felt through the phone close to a thousand miles away. She sung softly, "That's what friends are for…"

Vince grinned as he clicked over.

"I'm back."

"I'm glad."

Vince sucked in a breath. "So, Raven—it's been, what? Two weeks? No phone call, no nothing. Is that how you roll?"

"Vince, baby, don't be mad—okay?"

"And why shouldn't I?" Vince asked, purposely letting his irritation seep into his voice.

"Because, I'm gonna make it up to you. Gonna make it up to my *man*," she cooed.

That got Vince to pause.

"And how do you propose to do that?" he asked, the ice slowly thawing.

"I'm unconventional *and* resourceful. By now you should have no doubt in my abilities."

Vince grinned, but was careful not to let Raven hear him laugh.

"Whatever, Raven. At this point in time I am not impressed."

"That's too bad," Raven responded in a low, seductive voice. "I guess I made the trip here for nothing."

"Trip here *where*?" Vince said, feeling the pressure rise in his bowels.

"Look out your window, *baby*…"

FORTY-TWO

Glancing at her wristwatch, Erika was amazed at how time flies…

One minute she was greeting her ex-beau, Marcus Washington, a pediatrician whom she'd met when they both were doing their residency at Howard University Hospital; the next minute she, Naomi, Marcus, and his boy Harold were kicking it round a table at D.C. Coast, allowing the libations to flow freely as they conversed and caught up.

And damn, there was much catching up to be had!

It had been, what? More than four years…

Erika tempered her enthusiasm for seeing Marcus with thoughts of how he had left her, somewhat abruptly, with only so much as a half-hearted goodbye…

But that was a long time ago…

She'd grown up since then.

Meanwhile, Naomi and Harold were getting well acquainted. The two were both fresh from a breakup and not looking for anything serious beyond good conversation. So it was a nice surprise to find that each was enjoying the other being real and non-pretentious. What a surprise these days!

Erika didn't waste any time. As soon as the pleasantries were dispensed, she proceeded to grill Marcus point-blank, her low voice, discontent dripping from every syllable.

"So, Marcus," Erika said, eyeing him with disdain, "it's messed up when a girl has to find out from your mother that your sorry ass has left the country!"

Marcus looked at her sheepishly.

"Erika," he began, baring palms in forgiveness, "that was a long time ago—we were both young and naïve."

"Yeah, especially me," Erika declared. "Young and stupid. For thinking that you would act like a man…"

Marcus smiled, his white teeth a stark contrast to his rich dark skin. His closely cropped hair and smooth features caused Erika to shudder. But she would be damned if she'd let this brutha see her sweat…

He moved closer to the table, his elbows perched atop his knees so he could be eye level with her.

"I fucked up, Erika, no two ways about it," Marcus said, his eyes unblinking. "I should have come to you earlier. I should have told you of my plans."

"Oh, you told me, Marcus—yeah, you mentioned on several occasions your desire to go to Africa. I just never believed that it would happen so soon."

Marcus swallowed hard.

"Erika, believe me when I say I'm sorry. I know I should have discussed it with you. I was so wrong to up and leave like that. I don't know what else to say. I've never forgiven myself for that."

Erika stared at him, her insides warming. She could see the compassion and warmth that had originally attracted her to him.

That and his chocolate-covered smile.

"Well, I hope it was worth it—I hope your work in Africa was fruitful…"

Marcus and Erika had dated about nine months. Not a long time as far as relationships go, but there was something special about him that struck Erika deep to the core. His convictions. His passions. And his faith.

Unfortunately, she had never gotten the opportunity to truly know him well.

Their romance had come at a time when both of them were working insanely long hours, reeling from the intense stress that comes from working in a hospital, with little to no time for release. But when they found each other, they took those precious moments and made them last, relieving their stress together, the way young passionate lovers do—and what a wonderful release it had been…

Marcus smiled at her again, and Erika instinctively brought her hand to her forehead.

As Nelly would say, *It's getting hot in here…*

"Africa was a wonderful experience, Erika. Living and working among our people, experiencing them on their terms and not ours—what can I say? It was *intense*. But I have to be honest. I grew to really miss the things Americans take for granted—cable TV, Internet access, late-night lattes, McDonald's Big Macs…all those things began to weigh heavy on my mind. After four years, I knew I had had enough."

Erika nodded.

"It was a very difficult decision for me to leave—in the same way as it was incredibly hard for me to leave you…but ultimately I had to go, I felt as if I was losing myself and needed to regain my soul.

"So, enough about me, what is up with you? You look fantastic, have I told you that?"

She grinned. "About three times already, but don't slow your roll on my account!"

They talked for another hour and a half, as if their time apart had been compressed into a few weeks instead of a few years, the two settling easily into the rhythm of back and forth communication. Glancing to her left, Erika could see that Naomi and Harold were into their discussion as much as she. Naomi and Erika exchanged a quick grin. Erika took the opportunity to rise.

"Will you excuse me; I need to use the ladies room." Naomi took the cue and left her seat, too.

"I'll be back, Harold," she said seductively.

"I'll be waiting…" he cooed in response.

Once in the restroom, both women high-fived each other.

"Girl," Naomi exclaimed, "that Harold is fine. You hear me? I am loving his style—the way he actually gives a damn about what I'm saying! And a doctor no less??? SHOOT!"

Erika grinned. "Good for you, girl. Do your thing. Ain't nobody here mad at ya…"

"And how about you? Damn, Erika, Marcus with his fine self! I take it you two are catching up?"

"Yeah, girl, we are." Erika smiled but her mind was racing. So many different thoughts and emotions were rushing through her right now.

How to feel?

She was happy to see Marcus—actually, "happy" didn't do what she was feeling justice. There was a sentiment, deep inside of her that she didn't wish to acknowledge just yet.

On the other hand, Marcus had hurt her when he had left for Africa in search of a dream. Did she have a right to feel the way she had felt? It wasn't as if they had entered into a committed or exclusive relationship. That was something the two of them had never really talked about.

Why?

Because she had never felt the need to do so.

From her perspective, when Erika had had free time and wasn't working, she was spending it with Marcus.

Period.

Marcus had showed his true colors when he upped and left four years ago.

Then again, people change...folks make mistakes and then they learn from their mistakes.

Sometimes...

Some dogs can be taught new tricks, her mama used to say...

"I don't know, Naomi, this shit is too complicated even for me to consider. I mean, I don't even know how I should feel!" Erika glanced down into her open purse and the cell phone that laid there. James had called numerous times...

She'd powered off the phone after the fourth call, not wanting any further interruptions.

Not tonight.

Naomi touched her shoulder tenderly.

"Let me ask you something. Are you happy to see Marcus?"

Erika nodded.

"Did you feel something stir inside of you when you first saw him tonight?"

Erika exhaled.

"Yes, definitely."

"Then my advice is to enjoy the moment and go with the flow. You're entitled to rekindle an old flame. Nothing wrong with that. Nothing in the rule book that says you can't do that…"

"True, true," Erika responded, nodding, thinking.

"Besides," Naomi said softly, "this might be the sign you've been waiting for…"

✖✖✖

Fast forward two hours. Naomi yawned as she nuzzled against Harold. The two ladies exchanged a quick glance and a devilish smile. There were unspoken words that were lost, of course, on the men beside them.

The two couples had absconded to Bar Nun on U Street. They were sitting in the belowground level, on a plush couch and love-seat set against brick walls in mottled light. The DJ, a friend of a friend of Harold's was spinning acid-house-trance, whatever the hell that was, but it sounded damn good. The vibe was right, their drinks were on point, and the conversation bubbling along like a rain-laden stream.

Naomi yawned again as she covered her mouth. Erika laughed as Harold shook her shoulder. It was after 1 a.m. on a weekday…

"Wake up, baby girl," he said in a soothing voice. Erika and Marcus exchanged silent looks. For the past hour and a half, the conversation between them had intensified to the level where it felt as if they were the only ones there, regardless of the fact that Naomi and Harold were chatting away three feet away.

Naomi and Harold didn't seem to mind a bit.

They, too, were lost in their own little world. Naomi, it was obvious, had become enamored with Harold. Their bodies were pressed together on the love seat as if they had been intimate for months now.

Erika had to grin at her girl. It was all good!

Harold maneuvered Naomi off of his lap and stood up, attempting without much success to press out his wrinkled suit pants.

"I think I need to take this lady home," he said, pulling Naomi to her feet. She complied without so much as grunt. "It's getting late."

Erika eyed her friend.

"You gonna be okay?"

"Yup, I'm fine," Naomi said. The two stared at each other as more unspoken words were transmitted between them. Naomi nodded silently to her friend. Erika nodded back.

"Okay."

A few minutes later, when they were gone, Erika turned to Marcus and smiled.

"I think it's time for me to leave, too."

Marcus nodded.

"Let me drive you," he said.

Erika smiled, but shook her head. "No, it's late, Marcus. I can catch a cab—I have no problem with that."

Marcus stood. "I won't have that. Not at this time of night. I'll take you home." He reached for her arm and slipped on her coat. "It's settled and I won't hear anything else." He smiled as she brushed against him, his powerful athletic body soothing against her own.

"Okay."

They rode together in silence, the only sound coming from a Michael Franks CD. The early morning air was frigid, yet crystal clear. A piercing three-quarter moon shone down, illuminating the roadway where there was no light. At this time of morning, most of the downtown streets were completely desolate. It was an eerie feeling to be whizzing along Ninth Street, past Chinatown and the F.B.I. Headquarters, and not see folks milling about.

"Can I interest you in a nightcap?" he asked in a low voice, parting the silence the way a sharp knife does a stick of butter.

Erika was silent for a moment.

"I don't know, Marcus," she uttered, indecision etched into her normally smooth face.

"I do," he replied, "and I'm not ready to say goodnight just yet." He turned to her, just for a brief moment, and smiled. The interior of the car was dark, but his smile lit up the space, warming her heart.

Erika nodded silently, feeling a pang of guilt paw at her skin. She thought of James, knowing by now that he was beside himself with fear and raw jealousy. More than several hours had gone by without her returning his calls.

Marcus made a right and steered his vehicle over the bridge toward Rosslyn as she thought about the fact that she had never done this before.

James was a good man. What was she doing now, in an ex-lover's car, heading to his place at one something in the morning?

Erika didn't even know where he lived.

But then a calm overtook her as she closed her eyes, and let the music's haunting melody rock her to sleep.

He shook her gently awake minutes later.

"We're here," he said, taking her arm and leading her from the car. The wind bit at her face and neck as she intertwined her arms within his, attempting to fight the bitter cold.

They rode the elevator in silence, holding hands, Erika totally conscious of how his palm felt in hers, and the warmth that seemed to emanate from his hand and suffuse into hers. She tried to let go, but found she lacked the strength to do so.

No. It wasn't a weakness that interlocked their fingers together. It was desire.

Safely inside of his apartment, a tastefully decorated one-level overlooking the river and Georgetown, he removed her coat, set her on the couch facing the windows, and went to the kitchen to fire up some hot water for coffee.

When he returned with two steaming mugs, she rubbed her eyes and grinned.

Her eyes scanned the room, noticing the modern furniture, and eclectic artwork. "No way you did all of this yourself, Marcus. You had to have help!" She sniffed about, almost instinctively, for a female scent, noticing the coordination of colors. "No freaking way…"

Marcus grinned.

"You got me. It's a furnished place, courtesy of Georgetown Hospital, until I get settled in my own place."

"Must be nice…"

"It is. Here, let me warm things up." He reached for a remote and pointed it at the stone fireplace between the two large panes of windows. Flames instantly erupted, coating the logs with a bluish-yellowish glow.

"Oh my!" Erika exclaimed. "You trying to impress a girl, Dr. Washington?"

Marcus turned to her. "Why, is it working?"

He led her over to the fireplace where they lay down on the soft, cream-colored carpet. He reached for her boot and slipped it off, then did the same to the other one. Peeling her socks down until her toes wiggled free, Erika sipped at her mug of coffee.

"Be right back," Marcus said, rising from the ground. Erika watched him, feeling a dual pang of guilt/passion spike inside her. She glanced at her watch.

Close to 2 a.m.

She should leave.

Immediately.

Okay, you just got here—how about right after you finish your coffee???

But watching Marcus, the way he slipped in a Christian McBride CD, the manner in which he removed his jacket and flung it to the sofa in a slow, fluid motion, then removing his shoes and socks, the dark makeup of his feet in stark contrast to the bright carpet, she imagined his muscles flexing underneath his clothes as he moved. Erika had trouble deciding between what is right and what is wrong.

Marcus returned a few moments later. Gone was the suit. Replacing it—a pair of worn jeans, holes strategically placed; barefooted as before; a collared, button-down white shirt, un-ironed, hanging open, showing dark, supple skin and tight, fit muscle.

Erika couldn't help but stare as she sucked in a breath.

Leave…

Now.

Marcus was holding a tube of something in his hand.

He dropped down onto the floor, his white shirt fluttering as he moved. Erika took a gulp to hide her growing anxiety.

"Warming up?" he asked.

"Oh *yes*…"

Marcus held out his palm and squeezed a large dab of a clear, oily substance onto his skin.

"Give me your foot," he said, and Erika complied without so much as a second thought. He began to massage her, concentrating first on her toes, then moving to the underside, the ball of her foot and backwards to her heel before covering the top of her foot with the gel. When it was fully coated, he bent down and lightly blew on her skin. Instantly, Erika could feel the warmth; her eyes widened as her skin began to glow for a moment before fading.

An illusion?

Marcus did it again.

No, this was real.

"Oh my," she exclaimed, "that is wild!"

Marcus cocked his head in her direction, grinned before bending toward her toes and blowing on each one. Erika was beside herself—her skin was tingling and actually glowing. She wiggled her toes almost instinctively as Marcus continued his expert massage.

Erika sucked in a sharp breath and with one hand fanned herself. "Are you licensed to perform this procedure, Doctor?"

Marcus eyed her with a devilish grin.

"Why yes, Nurse. Of course I am."

Completing one foot, he reached for her other and repeated the entire process, massaging toes and flesh, the ball and heel of her foot before bending down and blowing lightly, setting her skin aglow.

Erika could feel herself becoming aroused.

Marcus lay prone beside her, his head to her feet, his open shirt fanned out on either side of him, the heat from the fireplace washing over them. She sipped at her coffee—the combination of experiences—the soft, yet hypnotic jazz, firelight and fire warmth, Marcus' expert hands, and his breath on her skin, utterly wondrous.

He reached for her shins and pushed the fabric of her jeans upward. Lathering up her calves, he massaged them with long strokes of his fingers, kneading the flesh before hovering his dark lips inches from her flesh and blowing gently, watching the skin come alive with color. Erika twitched involuntarily then lay back, her head resting on the carpet near the fireplace. Her eyelids fluttered momentarily before she shut her eyes with a sigh.

And opened them with alarm as Erika felt a set of hands tug at the clasp to her jeans.

The lights had been extinguished. The only illumination came from the open windows and the fireplace. Shadows danced over their prone forms. The music lingered.

"It's okay, Erika," Marcus whispered, his face suspended inches away from hers. "I can't do your legs with your jeans in the way…"

Erika stared for a moment, her heart racing, eyes darting across his soft features.

"Besides," he continued softly, "I'm a doctor, so there's nothing to fear…"

Erika shut her eyes without so much as a murmur as Marcus slipped down her jeans. For a brief moment her skin was cold, but Marcus' hands grazed her skin from ankle to thigh, instantly warming her.

"Turn over," he commanded.

Erika opened her eyes briefly; their eyes locked for a second or two before she silently obeyed.

He applied a liberal amount of the gel to her leg beginning at the back of her ankle and traced a line upward to the ridge where her ass cheek met her thigh. Erika was wearing a pair of black g-string panties. Simple yet elegant. She thanked God that she had chosen clean, un-tattered drawers.

Marcus began at her ankles, massaging the goo into her flesh as he worked her muscles. That feeling, in and of itself, would have been enough, but when he paused to blow on her skin, Erika felt herself ignite with heat and passion. Head resting gently on the carpet, eyes fluttering as firelight danced off of her smooth features, she let out a soft moan. Erika was now moist between her legs—in short time she would be damn near drenched, and Marcus, damn it, would know it, too!

Applying another line of gel from thigh to ankle, Marcus attacked the other leg with renewed vigor, massaging the goo into her skin with broad, strong strokes from his fingers and palms. This time, he straddled her below the knees, positioning each one of his hands by the insides of his thighs and pressing upward, his palms creating a wide trench in her skin as he moved toward her ass. When he reached the top of her thighs, he paused to apply more gel to his digits, before palming both cheeks and commencing a slow massage of that area. Erika opened her eyes and glanced back at him, observing the fire in his eyes. When he bent forward, his fingers still attached to the flesh of her ass, and blew on her skin, Erika groaned out loud, and without thought parted her legs.

"Damn, boy…" she managed to say in between her accelerated breathing. Erika found she couldn't find the strength to say much more.

Marcus didn't pause—he continued to blow across the soft curve of her ass, his nose inches from the cleft, blowing an arc of moist, hot air downward toward her core. Erika spread her legs farther, feeling Marcus coat the insides of her thighs, and work his magic there, closer and closer to her moistened sex, her moaning becoming incessant and a separate distinct melody to the soft jazz emanating around them, until his fingers brushed against the gate to her canal, the soft folds of her lips, the now drenched entrance to her cunt.

Erika sucked in a breath, knowing his fingers would enter her momentarily. Every sense was tuned to that single upcoming event. Her insides contracted, a quick spasm that sent a spike of electricity down her spinal cord, ending at the center of being, the locus of her passion, the entrance to her tunnel that ached for his passionate touch. Her torso even rose off the carpet and arched backward, another shudder of pleasure rippling down her spine as she felt his digits brush lightly against her wetness down there, anticipation driving her absolutely crazy.

But Marcus slid his hands upward instead, gliding over gel-lubricated skin as his fingers crept underneath the cotton of her top, feeling the power of her lower back muscles contract to his touch, as Erika nuzzled down against the carpet and let out a low lengthy sigh.

Her shirt was removed without words, his fingers reaching around and undoing the buttons. Erika's fingers assisted his own quietly; moments later, she was reclining on the rug, the curves of her opulent form silhouetted against the carpet as Marcus straddled her thighs, kneading her shoulders and arms, taking his time, ensuring ever muscle received its share of his attention. He even worked her fingers, first applying the gel before massaging it in to her skin and blowing on it, setting it momentarily aglow, just as sensually as before.

Erika lost track of the time—could fifteen minutes have passed by?

Twenty?

Thirty or forty?

She didn't know.

One thing for sure—her body was energized like never before, Marcus tuning the muscles and tendons of her insides to the point that she was smoldering and on fire, ready to ignite. He was purposely avoiding her sex, using broad brush strokes of his palms and fingers to go back over territory already touched by his talented hands, rushing downward toward the lovely rise of her ass and thighs, plunging down into the cleft of her ass cheeks, gliding by her now-wet inner thighs as Erika moaned with passion, no longer concerned by the volume of her outburst or what Marcus' reaction might be.

When she could no longer take it any further, when Erika reached the point of no return—when she *knew* what it was that she desired, and that, unequivocally meant Marcus inside of her, his sex deeply entombed in hers, she turned on her back, allowing Marcus an unencumbered view of her perked breasts.

Taking Marcus' hand in hers, Erika guided it to that sweet spot between her legs.

This time, it was Marcus' turn to moan.

✖✖✖

They made love on the carpet.

And in the bedroom.

And later, much later, in the bathtub, the sudsy water sloshing around them as they danced.

Erika lost count of how many times she came.

But she knew with precision just how many times Marcus came.

Yes.

Marcus came.

And came.

And came...

Erika felt a wave of calm overtake her.

For the first time in months, she felt at ease with herself and her sexuality.

It wasn't her.

It wasn't *anything* that she was doing wrong.

Marcus had come hard.

Three times by her count that night.

By 4:30 they lay exhausted on his bed, their skin reddened from the bath-water and the fervor of sexual passion that coursed between them.

She had enjoyed herself.

No question about that.

But now, as she shot a glance at the clock on the nightstand, she felt a pang of guilt attack her solar plexus. Erika had turned off her cell phone hours ago, not needing James or anyone else to interfere with her evening.

She needed this, she told herself.

She had prayed for a sign.

Well, she'd gotten one, that's for damn sure.

Except, now, Erika felt more confused then ever.

What to do?

First with James, and now with Marcus.

Perhaps it was too early to tell. Too early to make any lasting decisions. Let some time pass—and all things will become clear.

Erika untangled herself from Marcus' sleeping form—his arms and legs that bound her to him in a wondrous kind of way. She crept out of bed, not that she needed to do so—Marcus was so far gone, so deeply wrapped up in a slumber, that a jackhammer would not have awoken him.

Naked, she sauntered down the hall to the living room, where she stood by the large pane of cool glass and stared out at the expanse of river and city. Her nipples climbed to attention as she recounted the previous moments in Marcus' arms, the delicious way he had made her feel, his thick cock thrusting inside of her, filling her insides up with his well-oiled manhood, the two of them grooving to their own syncopated beat, their own music, their own kind of jazz, as she rode him hard, contracting around him, making Marcus feel her, as if for the very first time.

Making him remember what he had sorely missed…

Powering up her cell phone, she was not in the least bit alarmed to find her voice mail icon blinking, a swift reminder that brought her crashing back to reality. She positioned the phone to her ear and listened to the single message, her heart plummeting to the ground as she heard *his* voice and *his* words, which like an arctic wind blowing through a line of icy glaciers, cut straight to the bone.

Erika, it's James. It is now two-thirty-eight a.m. and I guess you do not intend to return my call tonight. That's fine. I trust you enjoyed your dinner with your friend. I'm sure you did—since I've been sitting outside your apartment, in your parking space actually, for over three hours now, and I see you have no intention of returning home. At least not tonight…

James paused, before letting a long, harried sigh escape from his lips.

I hope it was worth it, Erika…

She thought she heard a sniffle and her heart fell deeper still.

I hope it was worth everything you are giving up between us…Damn you, Erika.

And with that, the phone went silent, and Erika hung her head, listening to the sound of digital silence…

FORTY-THREE

Vince exploded inside of her with a grunt, with each and every muscle fiber of his being tensing in unison as his seed filled the condom. He held himself up as he squinted his eyes tightly shut, feeling the brush of flesh against flesh as he pulled out slowly, letting his cock linger at her pussy lips, Raven's hands kneading his chest and stomach as she wriggled underneath him in joyful ecstasy.

He rolled off onto the bed, and lay face up toward the ceiling, totally drained and exhausted. His left ankle found hers and they rubbed against one another, the flesh of his shoulder connecting against hers as well, feeling the perspiration slide from her flushed skin to his.

"Dayum, Raven," Vince exclaimed once his heart rate had returned to a comfortable level. He eyed his sheathed penis, which was cocked to one side of his inner thigh, withering like a flower in brilliant sunshine.

"So," she purred, "does this make up for me not calling?" Raven asked sardonically.

Vince turned to face her, searching her eyes for meaning behind her words.

"Perhaps," he replied. Vince sighed as he felt the rush of sensual satisfaction course through his veins. "But truthfully, I'd need another *dose* to be sure…"

Raven held herself up on one elbow as she eyed Vince curiously. Her breast hung boldly in the air as Vince traced around her nipple with his fingernail.

"Another dose?" she asked, seductively, while reaching for his shriveling penis, and slipping off the used condom. "Hmmn, perhaps it can be arranged…" Raven cooed as she clasped his cock between her fingers, taking his warm flesh into her hungry mouth.

Minutes later, Vince's lower half was slapping against hers, her long dark hair clutched tightly in one hand as he palmed her ass cheek in the other. Pummeling her from behind, Raven glanced backwards as their eyes met and locked, a look of pure delight drawn on her mouth, breasts swaying to his cadence while Vince fucked her *hard*.

The doorbell broke through the clamor and intensity of their lovemaking.

Vince paused in his movement, allowing himself to come to a rest deep inside of Raven's womb, posting his head to one side, unsure of the sound that he had just heard.

Then it resonated again.

Raven moved forward, Vince's cock slipping out of her as his lips twisted downward as if in pain.

"You expecting company?" she asked.

Vince swallowed hard, stealing a quick glance at the clock.

Ignoring Raven, Vince moved to the bathroom where he grabbed his bathrobe and donned it. He checked his reflection in the mirror and sniffed. A blind person could see that he'd been fucking…

Oh well. Serves them right for disturbing a brutha…

Vince moved to the door and opened it.

There stood Desiree.

Vince gulped.

Hard.

"Desiree," he said, awkwardly.

She nodded.

"I see you remember my name. Good start." She stared him up and down for a moment before continuing. "Now why don't you invite me in?" she asked. "It ain't summertime out here, you know!"

"Umm, look, now is not a good time…"

"Seems you've been quite busy these days, right, Vince? No time to call a sistah or to return her call, never mind stopping in to see a friend."

Desiree had one hand on her hip. Vince wore an uncomfortable expression on his face.

"It's not like we're in a relationship," she continued, waving her hand in front of his harried face. "I mean, we're only *fucking*, right, Vince?"

A movement behind him caught Vince's attention. He turned his head and dropped his jaw. Raven slid up to the door, completely naked, eyes glistening with that just-fucked look. She moved to the right of Vince and glanced quietly at Desiree whose eyes grew into quarters when she spotted the nude form.

"Oh, excuse me," Desiree said defensively. "Now I see why you haven't called." Her eyes traveled the length of Raven's body with disdain in her stare. Raven said nothing but smiled, her own stare unblinking.

"You know, little Miss Thing," Desiree belted out, clearly angered by Raven's presence and silence, "he's fucking me, *too*!"

Raven took her time responding. She nodded once.

"You mean he *was*, honey. 'Cause he just finished fucking me!" Raven briefly smiled at Desiree, whose eyes were wide with hatred. She glanced back at Vince and said: "Don't keep me waiting too long; this little kitty ain't finished with you yet…"

Raven reached down to his crotch and gave Vince a quick squeeze before turning away. Desiree huffed deeply before belting out: "Fuck you, *bitch*!"

Raven stopped dead in her tracks, pivoted on the balls of her bare feet and turned to face Desiree.

"Sorry, honey, but I like dicks, not chicks!"

Raven flashed Desiree a fake smile and turned away, leaving them both in shock, totally speechless.

✖✖✖

I was knee-deep in legal briefs, up to my ass in judicial bullshit between myself and opposing counsel, preparing for this big case that went to trial next month, but as they say, that's why I make the big bucks! It didn't bother me one bit—I live for this shit—the opportunity to stand in front of a judge and jury and pontificate for the court, weaving lurid tales of infidelity and injustice for all who will listen, garnishing as much support, and of course, money, for my clients as humanly possible. For in the end, it all comes down to cheddar, baby!

A knock at my door interrupted my concentration. I glanced up, and in strode Calvin Figgs.

I put down my fountain pen and grinned.

"To what do I owe this honor?" I asked enthusiastically, but my smile died on my lips as quickly as it had spread. I spotted his disconcerting look. I thought to myself, *oh shit, what have you done this time, Trey???*

"Trey," Calvin said, without preamble, "we have a problem."

I swallowed hard. "Okay," I said while gesturing to the couch, "have a seat." Calvin did.

"I received a disturbing call today. From one Giovanna Marquis. I believe she is your client."

My heart spiked. *I fucking knew it!*
Goddamn it!
Damn her!

"Trey—Mrs. Marquis was not amused by your gesture of sending flowers. Frankly, I'm quite surprised by your actions—you have to know that this is out of line, even for you, and potentially damaging to your career."

I held up my hands.

"Calvin—listen, I think you are taking my actions out of context," I said, thinking fast. "Mrs. Marquis is under an intense amount of stress. She is having a hard time with the separation, and it is affecting her thought process. I merely was trying to cheer her up, to show her that not all men are the bad guys, and that in my case, I'm on her side."

Calvin steepled his fingers together while nodding silently.

"Perhaps, but most folks won't see it that way. Surely not Bernard John Marshall."

He let the weight of that remark settle in.

"Trey—listen up—you probably don't know this, but I'm the one who suggested you to Mrs. Marquis."

I registered genuine shock.

"Yes, it was me. Her husband and I go way back. We've met socially a number of times, with her, of course. I heard that she was shopping for a good divorce attorney and gave her a call."

I shook my head.

"Damn, Calvin. All this time I thought it was Bernie."

"I made the suggestion to him also—figured I'd work both sides. You needed a change of pace. I knew Giovanna was a beautiful woman, but I figured that you could handle your emotions and keep it in your pants."

He glared at me.

"You have kept it in your pants, haven't you?"

"Yes, Calvin. Damn!" I replied again. "This feels like a setup."

Calvin shook his head forcefully.

"No setup, son. Believe that. I was trying to get you to focus on something new. You're in a rut—your output is down, and frankly, you're no longer in the zone. Trey—you're disenchanted with this place, which is understandable, given the circumstances. That is exactly why I was throwing you a bone. Something fresh, something new and exciting to stir your interest, get you back where you belong. But I didn't expect for you to break all the rules."

"Calvin," I said, my eyes pleading, "this is being blown way out of proportion. I've met with the woman once. I've talked to her on the phone several times. She's messengered documents over to me and I back to her. My conduct has been at all times professional. I am doing my job. However, I want my client to feel comfortable, and she is having a tough time. So I showed her some compassion. Is that really such a crime?"

Calvin stood up and went to the window. I followed him with my eyes.

"Does Bernard know?" I asked quickly, my anxiety evident.

"No, and he won't find out, unless you tell him. I counseled Mrs. Marquis to let me handle this, and she gave me her word that she would. I trust her to leave this in my hands." I nodded as Calvin clasped his hands behind him, staring out at the Capitol.

"Trey, you know as well as I do that if Bernard or any of the partners get wind of this, they will roast you alive. She's a beautiful woman, and you have, let's just say, a reputation with the ladies."

I exhaled a breath sharply. There wasn't any use taking my frustration out on Calvin. After all, he was covering for me. He was my friend.

Calvin turned to stare sharply at me.

"You need to tread lightly, Trey. Don't be messing this up, or Bernard will have all the ammunition he needs to boot you out of here. I'm serious. My advice is to give this woman a wide berth. Yes, she is gorgeous. Any man can see that! But she's not worth losing your job over."

Calvin was standing by my chair. Placing a hand on my shoulder he squeezed as he glanced down and smiled.

"You'll get through this—just keep your head clear and focused on the task at hand. You hear me?"

I swallowed hard, but nodded silently.

Calvin reached for the door.

"Good. I consider this case closed." He grinned like the old-school playa that he was, a man of class and distinction. He opened the door.

"Thank you, Calvin," I muttered morosely.

He turned. "Don't mention it. Just make sure you keep that thing of yours in your pants," he said, his voice dropping in pitch, "or I'll personally whip your ass my damn self!"

He waggled a finger at me.

"And you don't need this O.G. on your ass, you feel me???"

✖✖✖

I was so fucking pissed, I could barely see straight. I wanted to pick up the phone and scream at that goddamned woman for almost ruining my life, but thought better of it. I paced the office, staring obscenely at the phone as if I wanted to kill the thing with my fist. But it had done me no wrong.

Still...

Why had Giovanna misconstrued my intentions?

Hold up...who the hell was I kidding? I knew damn well what I was doing when I sent her those dozen roses two days ago! I was trying to get something going, since she'd been as cold as a fish from the first moment I'd laid eyes on her.

Every time I thought about Giovanna—her smooth dark skin, those haunting eyes, and ripe curves, I wanted to explode in sheer ecstasy.

That woman was fucking with me, big time!

I shook my head as I slumped down into my chair. I didn't fucking get it. Women are always complaining about not getting roses, but when a good-intentioned man tries to send them some, all of a sudden they get all jiggy on him!

Go figure!

My first reaction was to call her, and tell her that the shit with Calvin was completely uncalled for. But that would have made matters worse. I felt like I needed to speak to her, and talk with her about what I was feeling.

But probably not the best thing to do right now.

My hand poised over the phone a hundred times but didn't actually lift the receiver.

India came in to check on me, and I sent her away with a fling of my hand.

She vanished in a huff, her long braids waving behind her.

I skipped lunch. This shit was eating away at me.

Should I call her?

I had reason to. Business reasons...

I picked up the phone, dialed her cell (from memory) and listened to it ring.

My heart was thumping, but it relaxed a bit when I heard it switch over to voice mail.

Does anyone answer their phone these days???

"Mrs. Marquis, this is Trey Alexander." I took a deep breath. "I wanted to apologize for my behavior. Sending you flowers was inappropriate and out of line. It was not my intention to upset you. Merely, I wanted to cheer you up. Obviously, my actions were misconstrued. I'm sorry for that, and assure you that it won't happen again."

I took another deep breath.

"Good day, Mrs. Marquis." I hung up the phone.

A sudden thought occurred to me that gnawed at my skin.

I had just left incriminating evidence on the phone. If Giovanna wanted to really screw me, all she had to do was play the message…

How fucking stupid of me.

A lawyer no less…

I swore loudly as I picked up the receiver again and buzzed India.

"I'm leaving for the day. Cancel my appointments."

"Good idea," I heard her say as I slammed down the phone…

✖✖✖

I spent the next eight hours alone. Driving around for several hours in my coal-black Escalade, heat up, CD changer whirling as I rode up and down streets and neighborhoods I hadn't been on in years. Georgia Avenue, Takoma Park, New Hampshire Avenue, Glover Park, until that got boring. So I went home, only to stare at the walls of my condo. I sat on the couch, remote in hand, scanning channel after channel—it's fucked up when you've got over three hundred digital channels, and can't find a goddamn thing to watch on TV!

I wasn't used to sitting at home by myself. Especially not during the day. I was getting angrier by the minute. It seemed like everyone around me was getting more play than me. I couldn't understand it. I mean, I'm an intelligent guy, I'm good looking, and usually I never *ever* have a problem attracting the ladies. Usually, I have more pussy than I can shake a dick at…

My thoughts went back to Jamaica. Too much fun in the sun for a mere mortal. Rum, reggae, and tons of naked women…

But lately…

Vince was getting more play than me.

That was a first.

And even Erika was juggling James and getting some new strange!

Go figure that one!

A tremor shook my head.

This shit wasn't right. Ever since I'd gotten back from Jamaica things had been going downhill. It was as if God was mocking me—saying, oh yeah, you thought you were the big man down there, the head-nigga-in-charge, but back here among the normal folk you ain't shit!

That's what it was—he was taunting me, all 'cause a brutha had got his groove back.

Even God was hating!

Dayum…that's messed up…

By nine, I was totally annoyed and fed up. Not to mention famished. I had kept calling my voice mail at work, hoping and thinking that perhaps Giovanna had returned my call, thanking me for my phone call and the flowers, saying it was all a big mistake, and if she could come over and suck my dick…

Make it all feel better…

I even dialed-in to grab Aponi's contact info from my Outlook, giving her celly a ring. Hoping and dreaming that perhaps she was in town and in the mood for some Trey-*steak*…

She answered on the third ring.

"Who's this?" Aponi asked irritably.

"Trey Alexander, Esquire—your husband's lawyer, your lover, remember?" I was trying to sound cute, but I don't think she was in the mood to play.

"Yeah, what's up?" Total dismissal.

"Uh, well, I was wondering if you were in town. I thought perhaps we could get together. For dinner or something." I was so damn glad she couldn't see me sweat.

"No, Trey, I'm home."

Silence.

"Okay…"

Hanging up, I tried to remember the last time I'd gotten laid. I was horny, like a fucking toad, I kid you not, and finally decided that it was time to take matters into my own hands.

No, not that—I mean, I was gonna go out and get me some.

Wednesday night, mid-January, cold as hell. But fuck it. Trey was gonna get his cum-on.

Damn it, I was gonna get myself laid tonight! Come hell or high water. I refused to take this shit lying down.

Watch me work...

✖✖✖

My first stop was F Street. I pulled the Escalade up to VIP Club, but quickly frowned as I spied their windows dark. Across the street, Home was in the same sorry-ass state.

Onward up Connecticut Avenue, stopping briefly at 1223. I valeted my ride, and told the parking attendant to chill for a second while I ran in.

Not shit going on in there, so I handed the Mexican a ten-spot and moved on. Glancing to my left, Five looked dead and lame, too!

Damn, was any place open tonight???

I mean, come on now, this brutha was on a mission...

HELLO????

I knew bluespace would be open. I could always count on that place to be on point. Plus, by now I was famished and felt no need to be searching all over Chocolate City for food and companionship. So I steered my ride over to my favorite spot.

I pulled up in front of the awning. Me and the valet boys were on a first name basis, much as I frequented this place.

I got out, gave one of them, Hector, dap. We exchanged pleasantries, "How ya livin'?" "You know how we do!" "Right, right..."

I handed him a twenty and told him as always to keep the change.

Nikki, the stunning Ethiopian, met me at the door. We exchanged hugs and I kissed her on both cheeks, as her country custom dictates. I stepped back, holding her at arm's length.

"Check you out, girl!" I said, all animated. "Looking like a pork chop, good enough to eat!"

Nikki chuckled while displaying perfect white teeth. She was so fine I had to bite my knuckles.

Me love some Ethiopian women, ya hear me!

As with every time I came in, we exchanged small talk, and I attempted, once again without success to get her digits.

"What's the matter, Nikki, you don't like Americans?"

She waggled her finger in my face while shaking her head.

"For the thousandth time, Trey Alexander, I'm just not giving you any."

I radiated my infamous Trey smile.

"That's okie-doke with me, bab-ee. See, I'm gonna keep bugging you until them panties are mine, you hear me!"

Nikki smacked me on the arm and I moved on.

Inside, the restaurant was a kaleidoscope of colors. My man, Scott Chase, the owner, had, as of late, been bitten by the social consciousness bug. He'd been working on a new joint, a symphony of sorts—the theme being homelessness. He had solicited the help of black artists and photographers from up and down the East Coast: New York, Philly, Baltimore, Atlanta, Boston, and gotten them to photograph or paint images of homeless folk. These images were filtered through lenses of red, brown, orange, and blue/greens, the colors constantly shifting from bright to dark as jazzy/blues melodies of despair and heartbreak tracked along with the pictures.

I had to admit that the scenery made me pause. I stared up into the images, thinking to myself, these people looked just like me—a bit more worry lines in their brow, a touch of sweat mixed with ground in dirt around the edges of their eyes, but fundamentally, they were the same as me.

The idea was sobering indeed.

My thoughts went to the Nona E. Taylor Center and the women whom had passed through there. I had to watch the haunting images for a moment, making a mental note—I needed to get back there and cook for those ladies real soon.

The bar wasn't crowded. A scattering of folks, well-dressed men and women nursed their drinks. The mood was somber. I ordered a Hennessy and sat down as the cognac was poured into an oversized snifter. Can somebody explain to me why black folks order this shit? Not that I don't dig it, but it must be some heavy-duty subliminal marketing going on 'cause I didn't even blink when I sashayed up to the bar to order.

I took a sip, listening to Mary J. Blige's melodic voice, observing the grainy image of a woman pushing a shopping cart past the steps of the Lincoln Memorial, her two dirty children in tow. No words were needed— no subtitles required—the meaning was clear.

I glanced around. Most of the patrons were coupled up—a few women traveling in packs of two and three.

Like wolves…

I didn't see anything worth pursuing, although I was very horny and considered dropping my standards for one night until just *after* I secured some tang…

But that's always risky…I mean, someone could see me…and then my secret would be out!

Playa card confiscated…

NOT!

I watched the light show for a moment, slowly sipping the X.O. as it glided down my throat, smooth. Finally, I felt myself unwinding, courtesy of Hennessy and Scott Chase—his images and accompanying sounds made me relax and realize that life wasn't all that bad.

Lately, today in particular, I had been dwelling on my own situation—my deteriorating work environment, a dysfunctional asshole for a boss, my non-existent love life, my drying-up sex life…dayum…

My stomach churned.

I grabbed my drink and pushed off the bar, in search of a quiet table upstairs, hoping that a decent meal would bring me out of this funk.

✖✖✖

Pan-seared salmon with fresh asparagus, and mashed potatoes.

I tore into that bad boy like it was the Last Supper. The pink meat, all hot and moist, reminded me of—well, never mind, but trust me, I was enjoying the hell out of that fish! It was cooked to perfection, the mashed potatoes and asparagus so damn tasty that I was tempted to head to the kitchen just to pat Scott on the back.

I finished my dinner and pushed the plate away; the waiter cleared the table and offered up a dessert menu, which I half-heartedly looked over. I was sipping at my cognac when I heard someone utter my name.

"Mr. Alexander."

I glanced up into the beautiful face of Layla.

A cold wind suddenly whirled around my face, neck, and shoulders, instantly freezing my skin into hardened leather. Frowning, I said nothing.

I could feel my muscles tensing, my stomach, which was full with food suddenly replaced with a swarm of African killer bees. A range of emotions flooded through me, but I blinked them back as I sucked in a breath.

"Layla," I said, low-pitched.

"Happy New Year," she said.

I nodded.

Layla hovered over my table, but did not cross into my personal space…yet. She was dressed in hip-hugger jeans that flared at the bottom, black boots, a short midriff sweater that accentuated her large breasts. Her hair was tied back into a thick braid that ran down her back. It shined with blue and purple hues, reflecting stray light from the lightshow overhead. I gulped as I looked away. I hated to admit how damn good she looked—fine was an understatement—the thought alone, however, made me nauseous.

"It's been a while," she said, making no move to come closer.

I nodded again.

"You look well, Trey. You always did, no matter what the circumstance."

I grunted. "Good genes, I guess."

Layla smiled. "May I sit for a moment?"

I frowned. "No, Layla, that's not a good idea."

Layla ignored my remark and moved into the booth.

"I don't bite, you know. I just want to catch up, Trey. Is that so bad? Two old friends catching up."

"No, Layla, it's not okay. I'm asking you nicely, and I don't want to make a scene. Okay?"

"Trey, please…"

"Look, Layla—not everything is about you. You can't always get your way. I don't want you at my table. And that's my right!" I was hissing, trying to keep my voice low so as not to alert the other patrons, but it was getting difficult. I did not want *her* at my table.

"I just want you to talk to me…"

The look on her face was one of complete dismay.

"No, Layla. I said *no!*" My fists suddenly clenched. "Can't you get this through your thick head? I've had a shitty day, a shitty week, basically an entirely shitty fucking couple of months. My job sucks, I want to kill my fucking boss, and the only woman who turns me on is acting like I don't exist. Okay? I've stooped to fucking my own clients' wives, or ex-wives; I don't even give a shit any more, and to top it off, Vince and Erika are getting busy more than I am! Now if that doesn't signal an imbalance in the universe I don't know what does. I have my own problems, Layla, real problems, so I neither need nor do I want your support, guidance, or counsel. What I want, and what I am going to fucking *insist* on, is that you stop showing up conveniently at every fucking spot I choose to dine in, and stop for God's sake, these lame-ass games. Layla…"—and suddenly I could care less who heard my voice accelerate in pitch and in volume—"in summary, I want you to leave me the hell ALONE!"

I pushed myself up from the table, glaring down at her. She was weeping silently. Two tracks of tears ran down her cheeks. She did not look at me.

I clenched my fist, sighing deeply.

"Layla," I said quietly, glancing around. Thankfully, the place was darkened by the lightshow. I was grateful. "No need to cry. Please. Don't cry."

I couldn't help it. I hated to see her cry. After everything we had been through, I just couldn't find the strength to walk away, leaving her like this. Regardless of what she had done to me, I could no longer hate her.

This was a woman whom I had truly loved.

I hated to see her cry.

So, I shook my head and sat back down.

Handed Layla a cloth napkin from the booth behind us.

She wiped at her eyes.

"I'm not looking for your pity," she said softly. "I just miss what we had, Trey. Our friendship is what I miss the most."

I was silent.

She was staring into my eyes.

"I'm not stalking you, Trey; I'm not attempting to regain a place in your heart—I know that is impossible now. But it would be a crime if two people who used to be this close," she said, holding up two fingers curled together, "can't even have a drink and talk.

"Please, Trey," her voice had dropped to a whisper. "Do it for old-time's sake…"

I exhaled slowly. I felt dueling emotions tear at my heartstrings. Glancing downward, finding it difficult for me to hold her gaze with my own, I stared at my cognac. The golden liquid was still, no ripple upon its surface. It was like a quiet lake at sunset, peaceful and serene.

I took a sip, grateful for its invading warmth.

"One drink, Layla," I heard myself say in a voice that shocked me with its compassion.

Layla nodded silently. It took a moment, but her face gradually lit up, like a sunrise announcing a new day, and I found that I was trembling from the cold within.

Layla was back…and I was very much afraid…

FORTY-FOUR

Closing my eyes, I allowed the vapors to envelop me. The sweet smells of cooking penetrated my pores and circulated through blood vessels and nerve endings, entering my very being. It made me smile. This was me at my best—away from the pressures of the office, allowing my mind to free-fall, not prickled by minor distractions or daily annoyances—instead being free to create, the way a sculptor or painter does. Thin strips of freshly cut steak, marinating in my own spicy sauce I picked up from the natives in Jamaica; succulent lamb that was slow-cooking on a thirty-year-old rotisserie; stir-fried vegetables in my seasoned wok; fresh bread that I was baking myself; and of course, the piece de resistance—two pies—a chocolate bourbon pecan pie (I had never made this before, but had been dying to try)—sweet, chocolaty, crunchy, and downright decadent—and a cherry cheese pie made with cream cheese, cherries, and loads of whipped cream! My apron had been dusted with flour and stained with jerk sauce, my fingers and palms greased with virgin olive oil; my bald head streaked with brown sugar flecks—but it was all good. My friends were coming over tonight. After what seemed like a stretch of months without being seen, it was time for Vince, Erika, and yours truly to all crawl out of their respective caves and hook up!

It had been a while. A lot of shit had gone down. We'd all heard bits and pieces over the phone…

About Vince and his new beau, Raven.

About Erika and her old-fling, Marcus.

About yours truly and Layla…and the woman who kept me lying awake at night with perverse thoughts of her incredible form and splendor—Giovanna…

We'd talked about getting together at our usual spot—bluespace. But work and personal schedules conflicted. So, tonight, we were hooking up at my crib.

Tonight, I was gonna throw down for the family.

By now, y'all, you know how we do!

Erika arrived first.

She showed up looking fly, as usual, carrying an aluminum foil-covered pie she had baked. I had told them not to bring anything, but of course, these mutha fuckas never listen to me! Erika was in the kitchen checking out my goods, and relishing the vapors when the doorbell rang. It was Vince, dressed casual yet dapper, as he always did, carrying two bottles of wine. We hugged, longer than usual. It had been a while—we had all seen each other briefly a few days before Christmas—but that had been it. Now, weeks later, it was good to see old friends again.

"Damn, nigga, I can smell the cooking!" Vince exclaimed.

"You know how this playa do!" I responded, giving him dap. "Shoot, I'm not playing tonight—y'all my friends, and I don't fuck with my friends." Erika raised her eyebrows but said nothing.

"How's everybody?" I asked.

Erika nodded. "Busy at work," she replied, "but it's all good. If I can keep my personal life straight, I think I'll make it."

"Yeah, I heard about that shit," I said, laughingly. "You just a regular ole tramp, plain and simple—you getting more play than Vince and I combined!"

Vince shook his head.

"I'm not so sure about that," he added with a grin.

"Oh, so it's like that?" Erika inquired.

"Yeah, it's like that!" Vince said. "Don't hate the playa…"

I had to shake my head.

"Hate the game."

The table was already set. Vince opened the wines—one Merlot, the other a Chilean Chardonnay, while I pan-fried the steak. The aroma wafted out into the living room where Erika sat bare-footed on the couch.

"Damn that smells good," she said.

I served dinner and we ate.

(Pigged out was more like it!)

The conversation flowed as easily as the wine being poured. We were best friends, and it felt damn good to be in their presence again. After a way too-long hiatus, it truly warmed my heart to reconnect again.

"Where the fuck to begin!" Erika exclaimed while dabbing at the corner of her mouth with a cloth napkin, wiping away a fleck of my jerk sauce.

"Such language!" I noted, eyeing Vince. He nodded, sucking his teeth.

She told us about her chance encounter with Marcus, a person all too familiar to us. See, we had been there during their brief relationship, and dealt with his abrupt departure, leaving Erika to handle her emotions alone.

I, of course, couldn't believe that she had slept with him that same evening.

"Damn, Sassy, couldn't you have waited like one fucking day? I mean, why give him the keys to the castle so soon." I sat there shaking my head.

"Trey, please! We've been through this shit before. This is a new millennium—women are doing it just like men. I'm allowed to do my own thing, and if that means going to bed with an ex-lover, well, then that's my prerogative."

I held up my hands. "Okay. Whatever you say, ho."

Erika eyed me with disdain. In the background, Evelyn "Champagne" King's "Shame" was blaring through my Boston Acoustics speakers. Vince told us to pass the lamb down his way. That brutha was on a mission!

"You know what?" Erika exclaimed. "I enjoyed the *hell* out of myself. I mean, that shit was off the chain! Seriously though," she said, pausing to take a sip of her Merlot as she forked a piece of the lamb, "for the longest time I'd been thinking that something was wrong with me. That I couldn't please my man." She glanced up, making eye contact with both of us individually. "That shit is sobering—the fact that you may not have what it takes to please your lover…"

"Sassy—you know it wasn't you," Vince interjected, with food in his mouth.

"Yeah, in an intellectual sense you know. But when you're lying there and your man doesn't come, night after night, you begin to wonder. You can't help but wonder…"

I nodded. "Well, now you know," I said, somberly.

Vince smiled. "So, I hear James isn't taking it too well…"

"That's an understatement," Erika said. She smiled, but it was a weak one, devoid of any color, or any potency.

"He actually sat outside my apartment half the night—at some point he figured out that I wasn't coming home…"

"Ouch!" I responded, my shoulders flinching.

"So what did you say to him?" Vince asked.

"Well, I called him the next morning. It was the hardest thing I've ever done. Frankly I was scared shitless."

"How did he respond?"

Erika shook her head.

"He didn't—he didn't speak to me for three days. When he finally did return my call, he was very short. I guess that's to be expected."

Vince and I nodded in unison.

I helped myself to another helping of piquant, cooked-to-perfection steak and the lamb that would make a Middle Eastern eatery proud. Vince tore off another piece of piping hot bread and dipped it in a saucer filled with virgin olive oil.

"I toyed with making up some lie," Erika continued. "Telling him that it got late and I just stayed over one of my girlfriend's, but then realized that that story would eventually come back to haunt me. So I told the truth—that I had met Marcus, that one thing had led to another, and that I had slept with him." She paused. "And most importantly, that Marcus had *come*."

Erika nodded her head to the surprised looks from us.

"Yeah, Marcus came—and that he, James didn't—couldn't! James had a problem that I could no longer sweep under the rug."

"Oh no you didn't!" I said shockingly.

"Oh yes I did. I figured that the damage had already been done. So why not go ahead and spill all the damn tea!" She paused to remember the conversation. "Besides, it was time for James to hear the truth."

"Ouch!" I repeated, shaking my head forlornly.

"Yeah," Vince said, pitifully, "*very* ouch…"

"So," I said, trying to change the pitch and direction this conversation was taking, "what's next? I mean—are you going to see Marcus again? And what about James?"

Erika sighed heavily.

"I'm seeing Marcus, yes." She paused to the shocked stares around the table.

"You're kidding," Vince said, dropping his fork and putting down his glass of Chardonnay almost simultaneously.

"No, I'm not." Erika set her fork down, more perfunctorily than Vince had. "I'm enjoying seeing Marcus again. He's grown-up—I think his stint in Africa changed him—made him more respective of the things that are near and dear to his heart. I don't know if we have a future together or not—but right now, I don't care. There's too much uncertainty surrounding James and me. I don't know where the two of us are going. I don't know if my future includes him or not. And frankly, my head has been hurting from all the thinking going on."

Vince and I nodded silently.

"You know I was having a hard time with all of this—then Marcus appears—almost like a godsend. Sometimes I think he came into my life for a reason—like a test—to see if what James and I have is real. I don't know the answer to that, guys."

Erika paused, forked some of the stir-fry veggies into her mouth and chewed, the delight on her pallet evident from her smile. I shook my head.

"So, let me get this straight—you're just gonna let Marcus back into your panties and what? Kick James to the curb? After what that mutha fucka did to you?"

Erika gave me a hard look.

"Nigga, please. This girl is older and wiser. I'm not trippin' over Marcus—and I'm not expecting anything from him. To be honest, I don't know what

I even want from him—if anything. I'll tell you this, though—being with him makes me feel good—there's something between us—call it chemistry, that makes me feel alive. I dig being in his arms. And homeboy rocks in bed, so don't hate!"

"And James?" Vince asked cautiously.

"I guess we will have to see. James has a choice to make—whether he wants to continue seeing me, knowing that I am spending some time with Marcus or…"

"Hold up," I said. "He *knows* that you're gonna keep seeing Marcus?" I shook my head with distaste.

"Yeah, I figured that I would be completely honest with him. So I told him that I had no plans to stop seeing Marcus. James knows that I'm feeling torn—and that at this point I don't know what to do."

"What about the problem?" Vince asked. "Is he going to take some action to address his sexual issues?"

"Well," Erika said, holding up her glass so the light reflected red hues against the dark wood of the table, "I guess that remains to be seen. He is no longer denying there's a problem between us, but he has yet to admit his malady outright." She took a sip of her merlot. "According to James, his 'issue' is not a problem, but a fetish. Some people, according to him, are turned on by various things—for example, some folks get off on sucking other folks' toes, or having a large object shoved up their ass. James has a *fascination*, for lack of a better term, with his asshole." Erika shook her head. "That didn't come out right—what I meant is that James gets extremely turned on by anal stimulation."

Erika paused at my raised eyebrow.

"What?"

"Nothing—continue, please," I uttered.

"Some men can't come from a woman's blowjob. Others need a particular type of stimulation to orgasm. James falls into this category."

This time if was me who put my fork down with a *clank*.

"Hold up—who do you know who can't come from a blowjob? Even faggots can come that way!"

"Trey, sometimes you are so ignorant, it ain't even funny." She turned her attention back to Vince who was watching her closely. "James says that there is nothing wrong with him. He just happens to need this kind of stimulation in order to come. When he's stimulated in the right way, he comes. That's his story and he's sticking to it."

Vince nodded. He reached for his wine and took a sip, staring for a moment at the ceiling. Then he leveled his gaze at Erika.

"I would say that in one sense James is correct."

I threw up my hands. "Oh *Lord*!" I exclaimed.

"Trey—you have to admit that people are into all kinds of shit these days—I mean, just spend a few minutes on the Internet checking out the wide variety of porno sites—folks into all kinds of kinky shit—from bestiality, anal sex, and golden showers, to teens, fisting, and S&M—"

"Fisting???" Erika bellowed, interrupting. "Just what the fuck is *fisting*?"

Vince smiled. "That's when someone puts their entire hand in a woman's vagina—for some women it's an incredible turn-on."

"Damn, dawg, you sound like a mutha fucking expert rattling off all that shit!"

Vince ignored me.

Erika sat there shaking her head, the image of an entire hand, up to a wrist, or worse, rooted deep inside her. She winced uncontrollably.

"My point, Erika, is that there's a lot of variety out there. James is indeed correct when he points out that some people derive stimulation from sources that others might find objectionable. The fact that some men need an underaged child or teen just to get off proves my point."

"Yeah, but that's just plain sick," Erika exclaimed. She grabbed at a piece of bread, and soaked it in the olive oil before taking a huge bite.

"Of course it is. But let me serve up another example. How about someone who has a foot fetish? There are men (and women) who get off on seeing, stroking, and licking another's toes. While we might find this kind of behavior distasteful—I, for one, don't want anyone's toes, not even Halle's, in my mouth—that doesn't make it wrong."

I snapped my head at Vince.

"Are you out your goddamned mind? Dawg—Halle can put her funky ass toes between my teeth any goddamn day, ya heard me!"

Both Erika and Vince sighed audibly.

"To continue," Vince said, shifting his gaze to me for a moment before settling back on Erika, "the point is that folks respond to a variety of stimuli. I think that's what makes lovemaking between different couples so individual and unique. I mean, looking back on my share of lovers, no two have ever made love the same way. Each one had a different way of pleasing and being pleased—each one responding to different stimuli. That's what makes it so exciting and refreshing every single time…"

I shook my head vigorously.

"I can't believe you're taking up for the mutha fucka. Sassy—you need to drop-kick both of these knuckleheads and move on! For real!"

"Trey—I'm not taking up for him," Vince said. "But if James gets off from having his asshole licked or from someone sticking a banana up that shit (no pun intended), then more power to him. My philosophy is, and has always been, simple—as long as it doesn't hurt anybody, and it is consensual, then go for it. Life's too short to have certain folks telling other folks how to live their lives—and how to get off."

Vince picked up his fork and reached across the table for the last piece of steak that sat alone in its juices. He put it on his plate and attacked it with his steak knife. Half of the meat disappeared into his mouth within thirty seconds.

Erika was nodding slowly, digesting what he had said. She sipped at her wine as she draped her cloth napkin over her plate, signaling that she was done.

"I guess that's why you're the motivational speaker in the bunch," she said, "and the most cerebral one here—you always give us a fresh perspective, Vince—something to think about. That's why I love you."

Vince beamed as he chewed his food, reaching over to pat her hand.

"Do your thing, Ma," he said, as soon as he had finished swallowing. "If Marcus makes you feel good, then feel good with Marcus. But my advice to you is to not kick James to the curb just yet. You two have good history

together. It would be a shame to throw it all away, especially over something that perhaps could be fixed—or at least dealt with."

Erika nodded solemnly. I glanced rapidly from Erika to Vince, and back
again to my boo.

I had no choice but to nod solemnly as well...

✖✖✖

We retired to my living room after a scrumptious meal for coffee before
dessert.

Everyone was stuffed. Erika held her stomach as she lay on my buffalo-
brown couch, head back, eyes closed as if exhausted. Vince was by the
stereo, cranking up the volume on an old Con Funk Shun jam, "Ffun." For
three minutes, we all sang along with that old-school song, like it was
yesterday's number one hit. I was by the window, glancing downward, holding a steaming mug of coffee as I moved my head to the beat, completely
satisfied at the way the evening's meal had turned out.

The song died, segueing into another old-school classic from the Ohio
Players—"Skin Tight." I had burned a CD of my favorite songs from back
in the day. Lately I had that shit playing non-stop in my ride to the delight
of my passengers...

"So," Erika purred with her eyes closed, "that's definitely enough of me
and my drama for one evening. I believe the gentleman from the District of
Columbia is next..."

"Oh hell!" I exclaimed, turning away from the window and glancing
upward at the slanted ceiling and dual skylights. "I always go last..."

Erika and Vince exchanged a quick glance before giggling like school-
children.

"Y'all ain't right," I said as I sat by Erika dejectedly.

"Well," Vince said, sitting down across from us in the big dawg's love
seat. He moved his frame around until he was comfortable, took a sip of his
coffee, closed his eyes as if that act would assist in savoring the already
luscious flavor, before placing the mug down in the palm of his other hand.

"Man, I am blessed! Let me just say that."

"Okay," I said, feigning annoyance. "I can see where this conversation is going."

Erika's eyes snapped open. She cocked her head toward me, staring me up and down.

"What? When you are gloating about your latest wild-ass monkey sex conquest, we sit there and take it. Therefore, so will you!"

"Dayum, Sassy, cut a nigga some slack…"

"Whatever," she hissed. "Go on, playa—we're all ears…"

Vince cleared his throat. "As I was saying," he uttered with a grin. "Things are going *wonderfully* with Raven and me. I find it hard to even put into words what I've been experiencing. Raven is not like anyone I've ever been with before."

"So, I take it that she's been making up for not calling you those weeks," Erika said.

"Yeah, you can say that. I was pissed as all hell, and frankly, had written her off. But then, out of nowhere, she appeared, and what can I say? She made me forget any and all frustration that I was feeling. And trust me, it was all goodness!"

"I bet," I replied in an exasperated tone.

"Trey," Erika said, turning toward me, "can it be that you're jealous of your own boy? Say it ain't so!"

"Trick, please! I just wish I were getting as much as y'all seem to be getting. I hate it when you mutha fuckas get more stank than I do. That shit just ain't right. It ain't supposed to be like that, and y'all know it. Something is fucked up in the universe; the damn planets are *way* out of alignment, you hear me?"

Vince laughed.

"Listen, I refuse to feel sorry for your black ass—as much pussy as you command. But anywho—back to Raven. This chick is something else. I mean, she is strange—she keeps the details of her personal life close to her vest. I think there's been some drama in her life recently that she's desperately trying to run from. I'm not pushing her to open up. Not yet.

In time, I believe she will confide in me. In the meantime, we are having one hell of a time! This woman loves to do anything out of the ordinary. Whether it's meeting at a bar pretending to be complete strangers, or acting out these elaborate sexual fantasies of hers, she keeps things totally refreshing and passionate. I am loving life right now!"

"Good for you!" Erika exclaimed, raising her coffee mug to Vince. "Just be careful, Vince. I don't want you to put too much of yourself into this woman without knowing where she's coming from. Call me old-fashioned, but I tend not to trust a lover who isn't completely open with me from day one."

"Yeah, I hear you. But I get a very good vibe from this woman. I don't think she's out to deceive me. She's going through something right now, yet it is clear that she wants to spend her free time with me. And when she's in town, she's mine—I get all of her attention."

"Cool. So when are we going to meet her? I figure if homegirl is doing this kind of number on you, the least you can do is introduce her."

"Oh yeah—I've been trying to set that up for several weeks now. She's been pretty busy, running in and out of town on a frequent basis, plus I told you about her singing. She has an incredible voice and has this gig in Philly once a week."

"Well, girlfriend best make time to meet us, or I'm gonna put her on the shit-list! She doesn't want to be there, trust me."

"I will pass the word on—I expect to see her tomorrow night."

"Please do."

There was a pause in conversation. Vince glanced over at me and grinned.

"You okay, Dawg?"

"Never better," I responded.

"By the way, how are things between you, Angeliqué and Amber?" Erika inquired.

Vince's face glowed.

"Oh man, I've been talking to Amber on the regular. In fact, we're becoming quite close."

"Yeah?" I said. "And how's Angeliqué taking all of this?"

"In stride. She and I are cool—we've moved on to being just friends. She's doing her thing and I'm doing mine."

"So you and Amber are growing closer?" Erika asked, raised eyebrows and all.

"Yeah, she is good people—man, I dig her. So down-to-earth. It's amazing how I can talk to her about anything. When Raven first did this disappearing act after our night in Philly, I talked to Amber about it. She was so cool—she gave me a different perspective, and allowed me to vent without being judgmental."

"Doesn't surprise me," Erika said. "I picked up on her vibe when we were at bluespace—you wouldn't know about that, Trey—'cause your black ass wasn't there, as I recall..."

"Ouch," I said, a hurtful look painted across my face. "Is tonight 'fuck with Trey night'? I'm just wondering."

"That reminds me," Erika said, all excitedly, "I spoke to James about getting in touch with those people who help others find their birthparents. He called them and they said they'd be happy to assist." She put down her mug and directed her attention to Vince. "So you need to call your girl and tell her that if she's ready to do this, then to give me a call so I can get the ball rolling—get her in touch with these folks."

"Very cool!" Vince exclaimed. "I'll let her know. I'm sure she's anxious to get started. It sounds like this is something that's been on her mind for a while."

"So, big daddy," Vince said to me, "I think you're finally up. What's new, playa? Fill us in on your world."

I raised my hands in a mock shrug.

"Ah, you know me—I'm just a squirrel trying to get a nut..."

"Oh brother," Erika exclaimed, "it's gonna be a long night!"

✖✖✖

Back in my dining room with my guests seated around me, I waved my knife ceremoniously over dessert as if I were presiding over some Masai warrior initiation—Erika's homemade apple pie and my chocolate bourbon pecan and cherry cheese pies laid out majestically in front of us. The vapors wafted over the table, and for a moment I had to close my eyes to focus every nerve ending on what reached my nostrils. I could feel my dick swelling as my olfactory senses kicked into overdrive. DAYUM, those desserts smelled so fucking good!

Slicing into them, I handed over gleaming china filled to the brim with chocolate, cherry, apple, whipped cream, sugar, and pecans heavily doused with bourbon. Erika and Vince didn't wait for me, attacking their plates with a vengeance. There was pure unadulterated passion in their eyes as they licked their forks—you could see their crazed look, their don't-fuck-with-me-right-now-I'm-in-the-midst-of-ecstasy painted on *thick*. These weren't any old kind of pies—these mutha fuckas were to die for!

Pouring more coffee, I sat down and took a bite, relishing my own handiwork.

"You my dawg!" Vince said, in between bites. "This shit is the bomb!"

"For real, Trey—I take back every bad thing I've ever said 'bout you!"

I eyed her as I forked another bite.

"So, dawg," Vince said, pausing to slurp at his mug of coffee, "stop dilly-dallying and give us the 411 on your shit. How's the love life? Been kicking it with anyone new?"

"Nigga, please—I fucking wish!" I shouted. "This dry spell of mine is lasting way too long. This shit keeps up, my dick is gonna shrivel up and fall off, I kid you not!"

"You know, Trey," Erika said, seriously, "it's not a bad thing to abstain from sex for a time or two. Every now and then we need to clean the system out, so to speak—let our bodies rest from all of the impurities that come from intercourse."

"Trick, please—this coming from you? A woman who's boning two dudes at once? Take your own damn advice!"

Erika chuckled.

I continued.

"Things are so fucked up, I actually had a drink with Layla the other night."

Erika's jaw dropped; Vince bent forward explosively as if being shot in the back.

"WHAT?" they both barked simultaneously.

"What's the big deal?" I replied nonchalantly. I paused to fork another bite of pie into my mouth. Erika and Vince watched my every move, their mouths hanging open in shock.

"You can't be serious," Erika muttered.

"As a heart attack. Listen, I can take care of myself. Besides," I added boisterously, "Layla doesn't scare me…"

Vince and Erika exchanged looks as they remained silent.

"What? She came into bluespace while I was there having dinner alone. She came over to my booth to speak, and we ended up having a drink or two. No big deal."

I took a sip of coffee and glanced rapidly between Erika and Vince.

"WHAT?" I yelled.

It was Vince who spoke. Slowly, and with purpose.

"And you're okay with this—Layla back in your life?"

"She's not back in my life, Vince, just because I had a drink with her. Y'all are trippin'!"

Erika sighed.

"Okay, you're a big boy. Don't let us stop you."

"Thank you, momma!"

"One question though. What are your intentions with regard to her?" she asked.

I didn't even blink.

"Sassy—I have no fucking intentions when it comes to Layla. She walked over, we had a drink. End of discussion. Ain't nothing going down. Not then, not now, not in the future. Believe that!"

"Okay…"

"Besides," I said, scraping my plate clean with my shiny fork, before popping the warm sliver into my mouth, savoring the last bite, "I've got this other honey in my gun sights—Giovanna with her sexy ass. I know, I know," I said, holding up a hand, "I might lose my job over that fine heifer, but I'll tell you what, I swear I don't even care anymore—she's making me crazy, I can't tell you just how much. I am stone cold in lust with the thought of getting between those sultry-smooth thighs, and I refuse to stop the pursuit of little Ms. Thing until the fat lady sings!"

I glared at Erika and Vince, raising a finger in their faces before continuing.

"Bernard John *fucking* Marshall be damned! Y'all can put that in your peace pipe and smoke it! That *honey* is mine…"

FORTY-FIVE

I was sitting next to an angel. And nothing else in the world mattered ...

There was this long table of dark wood, polished to perfection. I was like a child, cognizant of my handprints leaving marks. So I folded, then unfolded my hands repeatedly, attempting to hover above the grain, feeling the sweat drip between palms, before finally giving in and resting my hands flat on the table, fingers outstretched, as if in surrender.

Next to me, Mrs. Giovanna Marquis sat rigid, the tendons in her face clenching as if they owned a pulse—otherwise she remained still. Her hair was pulled back into a single long braid that wound down her back. Not one strand of hair was out of place. She wore makeup, flawless: boysenberry lip-gloss that made her entire mouth shine, some rouge that roseyed up her high cheekbones, and a touch of eyeliner and eye shadow. An impeccable light green pantsuit—taut against flesh, was showing off sensuous curves, and tight-ass matching heels. I found myself stealing a glance over to my left every other minute or so. The outline of her breasts was hypnotic, the way they rose and fell with her steady breathing. I imagined where her nipples lay, and felt my craving for them burn inside of me. A fire was brewing; a volcano about to spew, and it took every ounce of strength to tear my gaze away. Shutting my eyes briefly during a lull in the conversation, I was transported to a place where her husband, a sand-colored man named Mr. Mubar, who sat directly across from me in a flawless double-breasted blue wool suit with a fiery look in his eyes, did not exist. Neither did his attorney, who also sat across the moat of dark, polished wood—a tall, gaunt man of Middle-Eastern decent, slightly balding on top, bespeckled, with the look of an authoritarian. Trying to scare me...

But I don't scare easily...

We were here, two days after the night of food and drink among friends at my crib, in a warmly lit conference room on the fourth floor of an office building a stone's throw from the United Nations. I had soured at the idea of meeting Giovanna's husband and attorney on their turf. But I wasn't going to argue, especially since I didn't have an office in New York.

The purpose of the meeting was to initiate a property settlement agreement. It hadn't gone well up to this point. Her husband, a high-ranking diplomat in the Qatar government, was pissed off and not afraid to show it. He leered at his soon-to-be ex-wife, raising his hands into the air every time I made a point about their impending divorce. Old boy wasn't taking it too well—that much was clear...

I had been corresponding with his attorney for over a week now. I was under the assumption that we were on the same page. Apparently, however, Mr. Mubar hadn't gotten the fax...

"As I was saying," I began, glancing between Mr. Mubar and his attorney, "At this point we just need to come to closure with regard to the main residence here in New York, and the secondary home in Washington. We have provided counsel with a proposal that we think is amicable."

Mr. Mubar threw up his hands again, a string of spittle flying from his mouth as he glared at his wife.

"I cannot for the life of me believe that you are actually going through with this!"

He turned to his attorney and began speaking rapidly in some language that was foreign to me. Slapping his hand hard on the table, he stood abruptly and went to the window. Pivoting, he glared for a moment at Giovanna before pointing in her direction.

"No!" he shouted boisterously. "I will not agree to this proposal. The apartment here in the city was furnished by my government and therefore not negotiable. As far as the Washington residence, I still use it when I'm in D.C. and therefore have no plans to give it up. *She*," he said with discontent dripping from his lips, "can find somewhere else to live, if she's not happy in our marriage!"

Giovanna's jaws clenched; I could see the muscles working beneath skin. She said nothing. I had counseled her to let me handle it.

I cleared my throat.

"Well, Mr. Mubar, I assure you that Mrs. Marquis is as distressed as you are—in fact, more so. Regardless, we need to reach an agreement on the property. Unfortunately this is a necessary step..."

"I am done with this!" he said, glaring at his attorney. "I am leaving this meeting and going home. To *our* home if she so chooses."

The attorney stood. Bent forward and whispered in the ear of his client. I took the opportunity to pat the hand of Giovanna, letting my hand stay on hers a microsecond more than custom would dictate. She glanced my way but remained silent. She was so beautiful, even when she was fuming. I fought the sudden urge to tongue-kiss her.

The two men's whispers pierced the air with their harsh language. I once again cleared my throat as I stood up.

"Excuse me. I have a question. Is it true that you will be returning to your native country for good next week?"

That got *everyone's* attention in the room...but quick...

Giovanna's husband spun around to glare at me. His eyes bore into my skull, yet I remained motionless, a smile painted on my face, unhurried in my breathing. I was not afraid. Just the opposite. I was galvanized with exhilaration.

Giovanna was getting out of her seat, a look of utter disbelief on her face. I used my palm to rest it on her shoulder, and apply slight pressure. I shook my head and she sat back down.

"How do you..."

"A simple yes or no will suffice," I said causally. I reached for my cell phone, flipped it up as I held it in my palm. "If yes, then we have nothing further to discuss—your actions will unfortunately be interpreted as fleeing the country in order to hide assets and..."

"That is preposterous!" his attorney yelled, his hands raised in the air. "I've never heard anything so ridiculous in all of my life!"

My eyebrow rose.

"I think not. Anyway, we will let the court decide. My job is to ensure that my client is not harmed in any way by his actions."

I pressed a few buttons, placing the phone to my ear. The two men stared at me in disbelief, jaws hanging open as if they could not believe what was transpiring.

"Yes, it's me. File the emergency injunction I drafted earlier per my instructions and have Mr. Mubar served within the hour. Yes. That is correct. Thank you. Goodbye."

I snapped the phone shut and palmed it away.

"Our business has concluded gentlemen," I said, reaching for Mrs. Marquis' shoulder. "Let's go," I whispered to her. "I'm sorry it had to come to this…"

Giovanna rose, her features stunned into slow motion as she wrestled to understand what was going on. Mr. Mubar was shrieking at his attorney, whose entire body was shaking with incredulity. I pressed my navy blue and mauve tie with a hand and buttoned the top two buttons of my suit.

"WAIT!" Mr. Mubar exclaimed, more froth alighting from his lips. "Wait—can we discuss this as civilized men?" he yelled, arms outstretched. The look on his face was priceless, and for a moment I actually felt sorry for him—first losing his wife, and now this.

I cocked my head sideways and said, "Yes?"

"Please!" he uttered, almost out of breath. "Let us sit and come to an agreement. I am not trying to hide anything. And I do not want to drag this out."

I motioned for Giovanna to sit.

Then I gestured for Mr. Mubar and his attorney to do the same.

My cell phone remained in my hand. I noticed that Mubar couldn't take his eyes off of it—as if it were a piece of steak that a Doberman was eyeing, or a petite young stripper on stage in front of a throng of anxious inebriated freshmen.

"Mr. Mubar—I hope you understand that my client has no desire to hold you here, especially if your official business has concluded." I paused for effect and to glance at Giovanna who stared straight ahead, her eyes boring laser holes into her husband. "But we will need to conclude all business related to the property settlement and the divorce, since as I'm sure your attorney here will tell you, once you leave the country, well, it will be difficult, if not impossible, for any jurisdiction here to enforce a ruling that the court may impose."

Mubar's jaw rattled, but he said nothing. He eyed his attorney as sweat broke out on his forehead. I took the opportunity to continue.

"Therefore, Mr. Mubar, I propose that, with your approval, we draft papers turning over ownership of the Washington residence to Mrs. Marquis immediately. And these other items that were highlighted here..." I slipped three typewritten pages across to them, "will need to be dealt with as well. ASAP, since we don't want to hold you up..."

I opened my hands, palms up. The cell phone lay in my right hand. Its closed shell looking like an oversized beetle.

"If this is agreeable to you, then we can forgo any further inconvenience to you and I will, of course, cancel any pending motions or emergency injunctions."

An audible sigh escaped from the lips of Mr. Mubar.

Forty-five minutes later, our business was concluded and Mrs. Marquis and I were escorted out. We stood on the corner, the curvature of the United Nations building to our backs, as Giovanna stood lost in thought.

"Walk with me. The fresh air will do you good."

I glanced at my watch. It was after three and my stomach was growling. I wondered if Giovanna could sense my hunger.

For food and something more primal...

She glared at me for a moment. I held out my hand, yet she refused to take it. I looked at her in earnest.

"What did I do?" I asked disbelievingly.

Giovanna fumed.

"You...have a..." She fought to find the right words. I stopped, letting well-dressed people meander around me, as I opened up my hands, palms up.

"What?"

"A certain *way* about you…"

I cocked my head to the side as I stood on a corner, cabs and pedestrians whizzing past me as if we were the only ones standing still.

"Meaning?" I asked with the birth of a smile.

Giovanna ignored me and began walking; I jogged to catch up. She glanced my way and said: "You can be one son-of-a-bitch when you want to."

"*Excuse me???*"

I stopped dead in my tracks, my irritation clearly evident.

"Don't get all up in a tizzy," she said. "I just meant that you were tough as nails in there."

I shook my head slowly.

"And how would you have me act?" I asked.

"Trey, calm down—I don't have a problem with what you did today. Actually I'm grateful. The son-o-a-bitch had it coming. I can't believe he's actually leaving…" she said, fuming.

Giovanna was shaking her head morosely as the lines around her mouth deepened.

"Listen, try not to dwell on that—the most important thing is that you've won—you got what you wanted and now you can go on with your life, free and clear from him. From this point forward, everything else will be just a technicality."

She nodded silently.

"I thank you for that," she said softly.

"It's what I do," I said, as if my performance in there was no big deal.

I could see the faint beginnings of a smile; her lines softening and her eyes beginning to brighten. I flashed a grin, and Giovanna grinned back.

"That's what I'm talking 'bout!" I exclaimed, watching her radiant smile. A wave of pleasure coursed through me and I'm sure she witnessed me shudder. I checked the Breitling again as my stomach groaned. "Listen, I'm famished; I'm sure you are, too. Let's grab some lunch, my treat, and celebrate."

Giovanna slowed her roll. We were halfway up a block of stately apartment buildings when she stopped and turned to me.

"Rain check—I need to be on my way."

I frowned.

"Hey, come on. You deserve this—you got what you wanted—to be free. And I want to take you out. It's just lunch, Giovanna—it's not a date, just lunch." I smiled, but I could feel the tension rising in my gut. There was no wind, but the temperature was cold. Regardless, I could feel beads of sweat below the surface of my forehead readying to appear. I hoped Giovanna couldn't see what I felt.

"Trey, I don't think so, but thank you just the same." She headed for the curb. "Actually, I think I'll catch a cab here." She raised her arm.

"Hey, wait a minute, am I missing something?" I asked, the frustration that had been bubbling to the surface finally erupting. I made no attempt to hide my resentment. "I really don't understand you, Giovanna. Have I done something to offend you? I mean, please tell me if I have, because ever since we've met, it seems like you've gone out of your way to avoid me. What is up with that?"

Giovanna sighed heavily.

"Correct me if I'm wrong, but our business has concluded. It's over. So, why can't two grown people get together and have lunch." I took a breath and moved forward into her space. "You're a beautiful woman," I said, my voice low as I eyed her, "and I'm not going to lie—I'm interested in you. I'd like to get to know you better. Is there something wrong with that? Tell me if there is…What am I missing here?"

Giovanna sighed again as her eyes locked onto mine. She made no move to retreat, our bodies deliciously close.

"Trey, you're a nice guy. Intelligent, successful, and very handsome. But…" her words faltered as she glanced downward.

I felt my sails deflate.

"But what? You're not attracted to me?"

"Trey—let's not do this. I'm not feeling this, okay? I don't know how else to say it."

"*Okay…*"

She glanced back at the curb, raising her hand as a cab ground to a halt.

I stared sheepishly at the driver. Giovanna stepped off the curb and into the cab. Once sequestered inside, she glanced my way.

"I never thanked you properly for the roses," she said with a timid smile. My pulse was racing as I stared into those eyes feeling my heart plummet. "They were lovely."

The cab sped up, leaving me on the sidewalk uttering, "Glad you liked them," to myself...

✖✖✖

Two-eighteen a.m. I know because the glaring ring of the telephone stung in my ears, yanking me away from a deep slumber. I struggled onto my side, glancing at the alarm clock as I reached for the phone, my eyes swimming inside my head.

"Hello?"

"Sorry to disturb you, Mr. Alexander; it's the front desk."

I sat up, rubbing my eyes as I fumbled for the light switch.

"Yes?" I responded, alarms going off in my head. What possibly could the front desk want with me at this late hour?

For a split second a horrific thought flooded through me—a terrorist attack was unfolding floors below, and I had minutes or even mere seconds to react before the mayhem and carnage kicked into high gear.

"You have a visitor, Mr. Alexander. I need to know whether to send her up."

Her.

My stomach tightened.

"Who is it?" I asked barely above a whisper, feeling my heart bounce.

"A Mrs. Marquis. She says she's a client of yours."

My mind hit a wall. For a moment I was speechless, unable to process what the desk clerk had just told me. Hours ago, the very same Mrs. Marquis had left me standing on a picturesque curb in midtown Manhattan, a sour look painted on my face as the epitome of perfection had left me standing there like a fool. Alone.

And now she was here…downstairs…

"Send her up," I said, my mind clearing.

"Right away, sir," the clerk responded, replacing the phone.

I stared at the receiver for a moment, then down at my half-naked form. I was clad only in a pair of black French Connection boxer briefs, *FCUK* written across the waistband in bold, block lettering; the fabric tight and form-fitting, showing off the package.

My package.

My mind continued to race—what to do, how to act?

But then a calm overtook me. I let my breathing return to normal. What was there to be concerned about? I was Trey Alexander, the *man*, and I needed to damn near start acting like him. I was in control—always had been. The fact that a fine-ass woman was in my sights should *never* throw me for a loop. I guess I was slipping…the past few months had taken a toll on me. With work and shit—not that that was any excuse, but I had slipped and lost sight of who I was for a moment…

But Trey was back in control!

And tonight, I would take no prisoners.

A rap at my door cut through the din of my concentration.

I rose from the bed, went to the door, and opened it.

Giovanna stood there in a red terry-cloth sweat suit, a pair of Nikes, and an oversized leather coat that hung to her mid-section. A Baltimore Orioles baseball cap adorned her head. I felt myself stirring, and did nothing to contain my swelling state.

I let my gaze scan over her body, my stare lingering at the curves of her hips.

"Did I wake you?" she asked, her voice not far above a whisper.

"You did," I answered.

She smiled seductively.

"Can you find it in your heart to forgive me?" she asked.

"Time will tell…"

Opening the door wider, she brushed past me, glancing down at my stomach and what lay below. I had not taken steps to cover my near-nakedness.

"Nice...abs," she said.

"Thank you," I said, following her as she sashayed into my room. "You will forgive the untidiness, but I wasn't expecting company this late."

Giovanna turned and eyed me as she threw off her cap and let her jacket fall to the bed. "I can leave if you'd prefer—come back another time when you're more...prepared."

"That won't be necessary."

She sat on the edge of the bed and I took the opportunity to view her ample breasts that strained against the terrycloth fabric. She had her top unzipped enough to show a hint of flesh and cleavage—I took it all in, her long, tight legs, and the cleft between her legs.

"So," I continued, "to what do I owe this pleasure?"

Giovanna stared at me without responding. Instead, she scanned me up and down in the same way as I had done moments before, paying close attention to my boxer/briefs, and to my chest. A grin was painted on her face. She nodded approvingly.

"Well," she finally said, after a moment of tense silence, "I didn't come here for small talk; I can tell you that."

I was standing a mere three feet from her, glancing downward at that most sacred of places—the point where her thighs met—when her hand went to her chest, manicured fingers hovering dangerously close to the zipper. She toyed with the thing as she closely monitored me. I was silent. Giovanna commanded me to sit. I took a seat on a couch that was positioned in front of the closed drapes. As I sat back, she stood, coming within a foot of me and glancing down, wearing a seductive smile.

"Trey Alexander," she began, with one hand on her hip. The other remained poised on the zipper to her top. My eyes were glued to that hand. I did not blink. "Esquire," she continued, "a man who commands attention whenever he speaks. Whenever he enters a room." Giovanna smiled. "I can just imagine how you command a courtroom—not a whisper nor sigh when Mr. Alexander is cross-examining a defendant!"

I nodded.

"Oh, but I wonder if you are man enough to command *this*," she said with a gleam in her eye.

Ever so slowly she began unzipping her top.

I was utterly speechless.

When it was down to her navel, she separated the two halves and let the top fall from her shoulders. I swallowed hard as my eyes bugged out. She was nude underneath. Her breasts were airbrush perfect, full, with small brown areolas—lovely pointed nipples that beckoned me, like a curled finger. I placed both hands on the couch, beginning to rise but Giovanna gestured for me to remain where I was.

I sat back down, as I was told.

Giovanna licked her lips seductively before kicking off her sneakers. Her palms went to her waist, hooking her fingers underneath the fabric of her sweatpants as she began to pull downward. I remained transfixed as her bare flesh came into view: a thin patch of hair between smooth, caramel thighs as her sex was unveiled. I sucked in a breath, my cock fully hard now, fighting against the fabric of my boxer/briefs. An audible moan escaped from my lips.

"Goddamn, Giovanna," was all I could muster.

"Are you, Trey?" she murmured, with a raised eyebrow. "Man enough to take this, making it yours?"

"God *yes*!"

The sweatpants pooled at her feet. She kicked them away as if they were a mere irritation.

Giovanna stood before me fully nude, the glory of her body a sight to behold.

"You best be sure. Because I don't need a man who's content just following along. I don't need a man who needs to be told. I could go to my husband if that's all I'm after."

She took a step closer. My hands reached forward, finding the soft curves of her waist. I pulled her into me, her breasts inches from my face. A nipple grazed my cheek. I closed my eyes, inhaled the essence of her being, the scent of her womanhood, as I exhaled forcefully.

"Why all the charades the past month?" I asked.

"Because I couldn't make it too easy—that would make me a slut, which I am not!"

I nodded, my insides burning. My head ached—but it was one of those damn good feelings...

"Tonight, Trey, I want a man who can take charge, command me with his power. I need this to be yours. I think you are *that* man. Don't prove me wrong..."

I enveloped the soft tissue of her breast with my mouth, reaching for her ass, palming each cheek as I massaged the taut flesh, circling each nipple with an erect tongue before some internal force consumed me, overtaking me with its fury, forcing both hands to ride the crease of her ass downward to her opening, finding her cavern, already moist, and plunging in, two fingers simultaneously attacking her slit as Giovanna arched her head back and cried out, "Oh *yes*, that's what I'm talking 'bout!"

My fingers shimmered with her juices; I spun her around, heart shaped ass inches from my face as I bent her forward forcefully, hair flying as I used the palm of my hand against the flat of her back, commanding her to spread her thighs, plunging my fingers in and out of her cave. Leaning forward, my tongue lashed out against the smooth darkness of her ass, tracing a swath downward, finding the cleft and riding it like a wave, downward still, past the tight puckering of flesh that made up her anus, licking that hole as she squirmed and groaned, inching downward still until tongue hit the fleshy folds of her sex.

"God *yes*!" Giovanna moaned, as I tongued her insides, tasting the sweet nectar that glistened against her pussy-juice laden skin.

Her head was almost to the ground, legs spread wider as I invaded her opening, using two fingers to spread her wings, attacking her clit with my teeth and gums, letting her feel my power and precision as I ran the length of her engorged sex, her lips glistening like fresh morning dew, the fleshy bulb of her clit pulsating as I sucked it into my waiting mouth, feeling the passion overtake me, giving into my desire of wanting to devour her whole, sex and all, leaving nothing but a wasteland in my wake.

As suddenly as I had begun, I shut it down, gently guiding her down onto the couch as I groped her breasts. Giovanna's chest was heaving, and her thighs were on fire. I could feel the heat on her skin.

I kissed her longingly.

Removing my briefs, I stood, naked, engorged, full of life, my thick cock dancing slothfully in front of me, as Giovanna tracked my every movement with glinting eyes. She licked her lips seductively as I brought my dick within feeding distance. Giovanna's hand raised up, her palms on my chest, twisting at my nipples, then gliding her hands down against the tautness of my stomach, one hand circling around to my tight ass that she gripped between clenched fingers as her other hand descended to the top of my sex, feeling the base of my stalk, running a hand up the shaft, encircling the girth, then tightening her grip, sliding upward, jerking as she went, until she reached the head, giving it a light squeeze before dropping her hand to my balls, which she cupped, *squeezed*, letting me know who was in charge...

There was a high-back chair—one of those old-fashioned things one found in rich white folk's homes—with a cream color seat set against richly stained wood. It sat off to the side, diagonally from the bed. I was eyeing it as Giovanna pulled me toward her, the pressure on my ass revving up, her lips parting, mouth opening, eyes closing as she prepared to consume my meat. But at the last second, just as the tip of my head, already speckled with precum, breached her opening and was grazing lightly against her teeth, I abruptly pulled out and went to the chair, leaving Giovanna bewildered and panting, a sour look on her face as she wondered just what I was up to!

Two neckties were draped across the back of the chair—the navy blue/mauve one that I had worn earlier in the day, and an aquamarine one with small rectangles that had been my alternate for the day—I grabbed them in one fist, the chair in the other as I dragged it over to Giovanna. I placed it in front of her, facing the draped windows, led her to it, and sat her down. Giovanna was silent as she stared at me. I took her hands and raised them over her head, following the lines of her arms with my fingers, stroking her smooth, caramel flesh in a seductive way, before I brought both of her hands down and behind the back of the chair. Interlocking her fingers, I used the blue and mauve tie to affix her wrists to the legs of the chair. Her eyes widened as she watched me, not with fear, but with delicious anticipation of things to come. Next, I spread her legs, slowly, purposefully, using the other tie to lash one ankle to the front leg of the chair. Her other leg remained free—I quickly glanced around the room and spied my Kenneth Cole belt on the floor. I scooped it up, and in a minute, Giovanna was completely bound to the chair—legs splayed, eyes wide, breasts heaving and skin quivering while her attorney stood nude before her.

I was silent for a moment, my cock swinging inches from her face. She was eyeing me before her gaze dropped to my member. Once again she licked her lips, but once again I moved away, this time behind her. Giovanna struggled to keep me in her sights, but she could not. Extinguishing the lights, the room was plunged into total darkness. For a moment neither of us moved. I listened to her breathing, my toes curling into the firm carpet as I tugged at the bulbous head of my cock and smiled.

Trey was back in the saddle, y'all.

For real!

Moving to the window in the obscurity of darkness, fingers stroking the edge of the bed for guidance, I found and grasped at the drapes. The fabric parted, revealing floor-to-ceiling windows and a spectacular view of the Hudson River with New Jersey beyond. Twinkling lights from streetlights, automobiles, and apartment buildings winked at us. A heavy rain had commenced. It pelted the glass, the sound therapeutic, as lightning flashed every few moments. I glanced back at Giovanna who was bound to the chair. She stared on in awe, the scene in front of her hauntingly beautiful. The river was an undulating mass of blackness. It was hypnotic. It was eerie. Had it not been for the sex-starved woman lashed to my chair, I would have taken a moment to take in the entire scene...with all of its splendor and glory.

Perhaps another time...

Returning back to Giovanna, I stood before her, hands on my hips. For a moment neither of us spoke. I tugged at my cock, using full long strokes, inches from her face. I waved it in front of her, my shaft tracing figure-eights above her cheek.

I allowed it to come to a rest above her lip, my fingers still wrapped around the shaft as I sucked in a deep breath. My stare bore into hers as I felt myself boiling. I could not put into words what I was feeling—everything these past months—the good, the bad, and the ugly—had rolled up into one considerable event that suddenly had been tossed away like an outdated magazine. Suddenly, tonight—this moment—*this* woman—overshadowed everything else. My eyes burned—with the anticipation of sexual release—it was right there, so close I swear to God I could taste it.

Reaching down with my free hand, my fingers grazed her pussy opening. I rubbed her clit, then shot a finger deep inside, feeling her suck me in, my flesh swishing against her own moist flesh.

She was wet.

She was ready.

And so was I…

But there was unfinished business between us.

"Whose pussy is this?" I asked, my voice slightly above a whisper. Yet there was no dithering in my pitch, no vacillation to my cadence.

Glancing upward into my face, Giovanna swallowed hard.

"Yours. No question …"

Her lips remained parted. She licked them nervously, the fleshy part of her mouth glistening. I entered her mouth slowly with the fullness of my cock, reaching for the back of her head as I guided my missile home, not stopping until the entire length of my shaft was entombed in her throat. Giovanna's eyes widened, and her body shifted unsteadily in the chair. But my hands remained locked onto her head. When I could feel the back of her throat rubbing against my tip, I ceased my thrust, gripping her head more tightly as I felt the pressure within me rise. Giovanna's eyes were locked onto mine.

"Are you ready?" I asked in a harried voice.

She could only nod.

She clamped down her jaws and I began a rhythmic thrusting of my cock in her mouth. I marveled at the way my length disappeared between her moist lips, only to reappear an instant later, shiny with saliva. I thrust harder and deeper, feeling the smoldering lava within me rise…

And then, almost without warning, my entire body convulsed and I was screaming and simultaneously coming, flooding her with my seed, my eye-balls rolling back into my head, toes forcing me to stand on end as light-ning flashed through my eyelids, thunder pounding around us, Giovanna lapping up my juice, not having any other choice, and I not giving her the chance for any other course of action. My cock quivered in her mouth, balls patting against her chin and neck as my orgasm rocked me.

"Oh FUCK!" I groaned before the wave subsided. After what seemed like perpetuity, my chest ceased to heavy, and I opened my eyes. Giovanna's stare was locked onto mine.

I slowly pulled out, watching my glistening shaft slide between her luscious lips, as I opened my mouth to speak.

"Swallow it," I murmured, and then as an afterthought I added with authority, "*bitch*!"

For a split second her eyes widened, but then grew soft, seeing my thin smile. So Giovanna did what I asked of her, silently and obediently…

When she was done, I wiped the last remnants of my juice on her mouth, smearing her top lip with a trail of still-warm semen. I suddenly grinned, for she and this scene reminded me of that dairy commercial. Giovanna must have sensed the same because she grinned back, too. She glanced upward, and said with an infectious beam: "Got *more* milk???"

✖✖✖

Fourteen days later, yours truly was in the office, head down, mug of steaming coffee by my side when the intercom buzzed.

It was India Jasmine Jackson.

"Mrs. Marquis is holding on line one."

I smiled eloquently as I laid down my fountain pen.

"Hey you!" I sat back in my leather chair, swiveling around to my win-dow as I grinned at the office buildings and the Capitol in the distance. I could feel my dick tingling in my pants. *He* always stirred when there was any mention of Giovanna…

"Hey, baby," she cooed in response. "The roses are sooooo wonderful, Trey! I can't believe you sent me two dozen!"

I clenched my fist in victory.

"You are quite welcome and you're more than worth it! Anywho—I was just thinking about you," I said, closing my eyes and re-running the delicious scenes of Giovanna and me in New York two weeks ago—her heart-shaped ass slapping against my pelvis, fucking her doggy style as thunder and lightning pounded the hotel. Outside, it was a storm of hurricane proportions—inside, the steamy passions were reaching similar magnitude…

"Oh really?" she said. "Do tell."

"I was wondering what kind of panties you were wearing today?" I mused.

"Oh baby," she replied playfully, "you *know* I don't wear panties…"

I grinned like Stevie Wonder.

"That's my girl!" I exclaimed.

For the past two weeks, I had been like a kid in a candy store—no, scratch that—like a child in the hood who's celebrating Christmas for the very first time! I was hooked on this woman like I don't know what. My friends hadn't seen me. My office mates were wondering if I was seriously ill with all the time off I had been taking. Even Bernard John Marshall had inquired as to my health.

But really, mutha fuckas were just jealous as hell 'cause they could see the glow in my mug…

Oh yeah.

They just *knew* I was getting some on the regular.

Giovanna and I had gotten together four more times since New York—twice more in Manhattan, and another two times here on my home turf. I was burning up those Frequent Flyer miles, but it was all good!

She was all I thought about—I was like someone with ADD—I couldn't wait to see her again.

Speaking of which…

"When am I gonna see you again?" I asked, my voice breathless.

"Listen to you. You sound like one of these bruthas who are pressed as hell. I LIKE THAT!"

"I *am* pressed. Shoot, this brutha's not afraid to admit it. I'm stuck on you like glue, bay-bee…"

She laughed.

"Well, Trey, I have some business to finish up tonight, but I'll be back in town tomorrow afternoon. We can get together anytime after that."

My mind was whirling. It conjured up a mouthwatering four-course meal; I would pull out all stops to impress the fuck out of this gal!

"Can't wait! I'm gonna—oooh, I can't even begin to tell you what I'm gonna do to you when I see you again!" I said, holding my clenched fist to my mouth.

The thoughts swirling inside my brain made me wince.

Giovanna laughed.

"Promises, promises. Just make sure you do that thing with your tongue I love so much."

"Anything you say, baby…"

"Oh, and tie me up again—I loved that!"

"If you're good…"

Giovanna purred.

"So, baby—what's on the agenda for tonight?" she asked.

"Oh, I don't know—I'm really not feeling work at the moment—what can I say; I can't seem to keep my mind focused on anything related to the office—anywho—I think I'll run to the gym and then swing by Blockbuster on the way home."

"Sounds like a plan!" she said. "Wish I could join you."

"You will," I said. "Tomorrow…"

She hung up and I grasped the phone for a moment more, as if holding the receiver, even after she had gone, would allow me some kind of continued connection with her.

There was a sudden rap at my door and Mitch Wagner waltzed in.

Mitch, like me, was an Associate Attorney, another fast-track guy who worked his white ass off, hoping to make partner before he was 40.

He was one of those guys who loved black people—he dated black women exclusively, he dressed like a brutha, and wore his hair combed forward to look like one of us, and he constantly was in my office looking for tips on everything from how black people talk to how we act in certain situations—we had a name for people like him—wigger!

But Mitch was good people.

And don't let the looks and lingo fool you—Mitch was one of the best litigators this firm had.

He was one of the good guys.

"What up, playa?" I said, returning the phone to its cradle.

"Same ole, same ole, Trey, how ya livin'?" he said.

I chuckled 'cause I'd taught him that shit, too!

"Large and in charge!" I replied, as he sat on the edge of my desk. Mitch was wearing a black pinstripe, single-breasted, four-button suit that was fly as hell. I told him so.

"So what can I do you for?"

"Last-minute thing, Trey—I got this ticket to this function tonight, but I can't go. Bernard's got me humping on this prelim—thought you could go in my stead. It's at the Mexican Embassy. Lots of fine-ass Latino honeys gonna be there, my man!" Mitch arched his eyebrows as if to say, "Dawg, you know how we do!"

"Yeah?"

My mind whirled. I didn't have anything going on tonight—it was a Thursday night and miraculously, I was free. Giovanna wasn't due in until tomorrow, and even though I missed her terribly, I still was the head-nigga-in-charge in this city—and the thought of surrounding myself with some Latino pussy did have a certain appeal…

"What's this thing?" I asked, giving Mitch my full attention.

"You gonna love this—the Ivy League Black & Latino MBA Society is holding their annual gala tonight. Gonna be some intelligent pussy up in there!"

I grinned.

"And how the fuck did you get an invite?"

Mitch feigned hurt.

"Trey, you know I'm an honorary member, cuz!"

I held out my hand.

"I'll go—and let you know how it turned out tomorrow!"

Mitch handed me an envelope as he waggled his tongue.

"Eat some of that hot spicy pussy for me, dawg, ya hear me?"

I just laughed as Mitch left me to my work...

✖✖✖

Nine hours later—I should have been tired, but instead I felt energized. I had spent an hour at the gym getting my workout on, and then swung by this really great West African place on 18th Street in Adams Morgan that did take-out. I came home, showered, ate, and chilled for a minute before putting on a fresh new suit that I had just picked up from Barneys the week before last while in New York, and headed out to the embassy. The invitation stated that the gala began at 7 p.m. So I figured I'd waltz in there at 9 and stop fucking traffic!

You know how we do!!!

Nine oh nine, to be exact (according to the Breitling) I showed my invitation to the doorman, a curly-headed, short, squat Latino with a badly tailored suit—but I wasn't mad at him. At least Juan was trying...

He waved me through and I took the stairs to the main reception hall.

The place was packed.

I grabbed a flute of champagne from a passing waiter (another Latino—a friendly faced middle-aged woman with dark hair and piercing eyes), stopped to nibble on some hors d'oeuvres—some smoked salmon rolled in cream cheese that was quite tasty, and delicious miniature crab cakes, and began to mingle.

There were a lot of college-aged faces, but a good number of thirty-something folks like myself. I was scanning the crowd, searching for fuckable honeys when I heard my name being raised above the din.

I swung around and wound up face-to-face with Vince Cannon, Jr.

"What's up, my nigga?" I exclaimed, slapping him on the shoulder.

Vince looked back at me with this stunned look.

"What are you doing here? You know Hoyas ain't exactly Ivy League," he replied.

"Ouch," I said, "that truly hurts."

I gave him dap anyway.

"Seriously, dawg," he said, "I didn't expect to see you here."

"Yeah, well, an associate gave me his invite—he was working late—I had no plans so I said, what the fuck!"

"I hear you. This is great, man—this is wonderful!"

Vince's eyes were blazing—he was on fire, and excitement oozed from his pores.

"What's up?" I asked, nodding to a pair of dark-skinned honeys that walked by, checking us out. They wore nametags with their school affiliation written with bright blue marker. Both of theirs read, "Cornell '02." I did the math and shook my head with a grin.

I bet that pussy is *tight*...

"You get to meet Raven tonight," Vince was saying.

"What?" I asked. Vince's words flew by me, my mind elsewhere, on the *hunt*.

"Raven—she's here, dawg—finally, after what seems like an eternity, you get to meet her—oh, I can't wait to introduce you. Your dick is gonna jump to attention when you..."

Vince lowered his voice as a movement off to his left caught his eye. He ceased speaking—instead a wide grin formed at his mouth. I stared at him for a second and then turned to search out the object of his affection.

I was taking a sip from my champagne stem when I spotted her.

I think she saw me at the exact same time.

Time suddenly ground to a halt.

Burgundy and gold print dress; knee-high brown-leather boots—sexy as all get-up—hair down free, diamond earrings that sparkled, flawless makeup, unmistakable beauty and sensuality.

I almost choked on my drink.

Giovanna stopped dead in her tracks when she spied me.

The smile that she had worn a microsecond ago was gone in the blink of an eye.

Her stare panned from Vince to me, and back again.

I saw her mouth the words, "Oh *shit*!"

Vince saw it, too.

His smile died on his face as he struggled to figure out what was happening.

We stood side by side, the two of us, men purporting to intermingle and socialize, as we wondered why this beauty wasn't advancing any closer.

I stared at her.

She stared at me.

Vince glared at her.

She seemed to be glaring back at Vince.

I called out her name.

"Giovanna," I yelled, gesturing at her to come closer.

Vince shot me a look.

"Raven," he called, gesturing the same.

"I'm sorry," she mouthed, as she crept closer.

And then, in an instant, all things became crystal *fucking* clear.

I glanced at Vince, my eyes wide. He wore the same comprehending look.

Raven and Giovanna were one and the same…

FORTY-SIX

"May I speak to Amber?"

"Speaking."

"Hey girl! It's Erika!" she said, leaning back into the folds of her comfortable chair. It was a frigid Sunday morning, but a beautiful one, blue sky, no wind, just down-right cold. Glancing outside of her picture window to the waiting street below, she just knew that looks were deceiving—that in fact it was freezing. But inside of her apartment with the heat cranked up, and wearing her flannel long johns and an oversized University of Southern California at Berkeley sweatshirt, she was feeling no pain…

"What's up, sistah?" Amber said enthusiastically. "It's been a while."

"Sure has. I hope I'm not catching you at a bad time."

"Not at all. It's good to hear from you. How's my buddy Vince doing?"

Erika grinned. "That fool is the same. Doing his thing. He tells me you two have been keeping in contact."

"Yeah, we have. I really dig Vince. He's got such a big heart. And so easy to talk to. I swear, sometimes we are on the phone for like hours, and I don't even know that the time is flying."

"I hear you. That's why Vince is so damn good at what he does. He has a gift for speaking and for listening. I think that's why we've been friends as long as we have."

"And how about you? What's new in your life?" Amber asked.

"Girl, I don't even know where to begin! My job is going really well, except for the long hours, but that's to be expected. It's just the male drama in my life that's got me jumping. Otherwise, I really can't complain."

"See, that's why I have to leave these Southern knuckleheads alone. 'Cause all they bring to the table is drama and more damn drama!"

"I hear ya! Sometimes I wish I was a damn lesbian!" The words slipped out effortlessly, and Erika instantly regretted it. "Ooops, I didn't mean it like that."

Amber chuckled.

"Hey, you're preaching to the choir."

"Yeah…well…"

Erika suddenly found herself thinking about Angeliqué. "Anywho—I called because I wanted to talk to you about something we briefly discussed when we all first met."

"I'm all ears," Amber replied.

"I remember that you mentioned you were raised by your great-grand-mother and that you never knew your father."

"Right." A pause.

"Well, perhaps Vince mentioned to you that my boyfriend, James, works at a local television station here in town, and he knows someone whose business it is to reconnect lost children with their parents. I thought you might be interested in pursuing this."

"Yes, Vince mentioned it to me a few weeks ago. And I told him I was very interested."

"Good. I thought you would be. Something about the way you spoke about not knowing your father told me that you were anxious to find him."

"I don't know if anxious is the right word," Amber said. "But I'm definitely interested in knowing who he is and whether or not he'd like to meet me. Growing up not knowing your father, what he looked like, or even his name, was extremely difficult, to say the least."

"I can't even imagine," Erika said.

"Yeah. I remember when I was little, probably no more than five or six, and being in school—this was in Houston. And we'd have these school activities where fathers and mothers would be invited to participate. And most of the kids would show up with their parents proudly in tow, except for this white girl and me. I'll never forget her name—Amy—she was just like me. She never knew her father. She didn't even know his name..." Amber paused in remembrance.

"I'm sorry," Erika offered.

"Don't be. That's life. After repeatedly questioning people about your father and not getting a response, you finally stop asking. But you never stop wondering..."

"Here's your opportunity to find out. These two people—they are a gay couple living in Washington—have started this foundation to reunite kids with the parents they never knew. They've approached James in the past about doing a piece for TV, in order to garner some financial support, but James put them off. When I told him your story he said he'd be willing to pursue it. So he spoke to the men, and they are more than willing to help."

Erika was getting excited about the prospects of assisting in Amber's search.

"That sounds great—but one thing," Amber said cautiously. "I don't have a lot of money—I've never had a steady income so I can't pay a lot."

"You don't have to worry about that at all," Erika exclaimed. "These folks are taking this case gratis, because James has said that he'll produce a segment on them if they do!"

"Wow—I don't know what to say!"

"Why don't you just start at the beginning? Tell me what you know about your family—and let's get this ball rolling!"

Amber sucked in a breath, then exhaled.

"Well, you know I was born in Houston. My mother is from New York. I'm not sure if she met my dad there or not. Anyway, she had me when she was real young—like fifteen. Her parents, my grandparents, sent her away to Texas to have me. From what I've been told, they were extremely upset by her getting pregnant so young. After my mother had me, she basically up and left. My great-grandmother, Stella, wound up caring for me. I don't know where my mother off and went to—I assume back to New York. All I know is that Stella raised me—*she* was the only mother I ever knew."

Erika nodded to herself as she reached for a legal pad and began to scribble furiously. "Okay. Can I ask a question?"

"Of course!"

"Why didn't your mother stay and raise you?"

"That's something I've wondered all my life," Amber said. "According to my great-grandmother, my mother wasn't really fit as a parent. She had issues of her own. And her family just wanted to pretend as if the whole thing never happened—as if I was never born..."

"I don't know what to say..." Erika said softly.

"Yeah, to say it was messed up is an understatement." Amber paused for a moment, as if in deep reflection. Erika let the silence waft over them both.

"Anyway, Stella was my mother. She was the one who put a roof over my head; she was the one who raised me. She and she alone put me in school down in Houston."

"What about your great-grandfather?"

"He had died of a heart attack years before I was born, so I never got a chance to meet him."

"And your grandparents? Did you interact with them?" Erika asked.

"Very little. They came basically once a year to visit Stella. Most times my mother didn't even accompany them. They always said she was preoccupied with something, like she was off doing something important—but Stella would tell me the truth—that she was down on her luck, moving from one loser to the next. My grandparents always blamed my father for the downturn in her behavior—as if it was his fault that she turned out the way she did."

Erika noted that Amber didn't use her mother's name.

"Amber, what did Stella say about your father?"

"Very little—supposedly, she had never met him. Whenever I asked about him, she just told me that he was a nobody. After a while, I stopped asking."

Erika scribbled.

"What happened to your mother?"

Amber sighed. "She died in a car accident when I was eight. She fell asleep at the wheel after leaving out of some guy's house at three in the morning; she hit a telephone pole and was killed instantly."

There was no bitterness in her voice. But it lacked any measure of emotion. She was reciting facts, nothing more.

"Amber, I'm sorry."

"Don't be. I refused to go to the funeral. That was one of the few times in my life that Stella and I really got into it. God, I'll never forget that!"

Erika remarked, "Go on."

"There's nothing more to tell—I continued to live with my great-grandmother until two years ago when she died."

"Damn, Amber, I'm really sorry about your loss."

She was silent for a moment. Erika could hear her controlling back the tears. After a moment she cleared her throat.

"Yeah, now *that* was hard on me. Losing Stella meant losing the only family I'd ever known."

"I understand."

"I went to the funeral. I had no choice but to go—I mean, she was my mother, right? My flesh and blood. Afterwards, I upped and left. There was nothing keeping me in Houston. I was done. I packed a suitcase and took a Greyhound out. Headed to New Orleans…but that's a whole 'nother story…"

"I hear you, girl," Erika exclaimed as she put the legal pad down.

"I'll need everyone's full name and addresses if you have them," she said. Amber recited what she knew. They chatted for a few moments more.

"I can't promise you anything; I hope you know that—but these folks are good at what they do. It's very possible that a name will turn up—and then we can go from there," Erika said.

"I know. I'm not getting my hopes up. But I do hope it happens. I've been waiting what seems like my entire life to meet my father—to look him in the eyes and hear his voice—I've spent years imagining what it would be like." Amber paused for a moment before continuing. "I just hope it's not too late," she said, quietly.

"Me neither, girl," Erika responded, "me neither…"

✖✖✖

"Hey you, It's me." Erika let the words sink in before venturing further.

"Hey…" There was a long pause as James processed what he was hearing, and what he would say next. "Long time no hear," he said.

That wasn't exactly true. It had only been four days. But it was like an eternity to him.

"How are you doing, James?" she asked tenderly. A big part of her missed him terribly. And she knew that her actions were hurting him deeply.

"Can't complain. Work's got me humping, as usual. You?"

"Same." Erika paused, waiting for him to chastise her for waiting four days to call—and letting most of the weekend pass without contact. But he remained silent. She was impressed.

Erika ventured forward. "I called, James, because I need to talk to you about my friend, Amber. Remember her? Vince's friend—the woman from New Orleans?"

"Yeah, the one who is searching for her father?"

"Right. I was hoping you could get things rolling. I've got the information you'll need from Amber."

James was silent. Erika knew his critical thinking mind was turning over like a twelve-cylinder engine.

"So, that's the only reason you called? Is this what it's come to? Just business between us?"

"Of course not, James. You know me better than that. I'm sorry—would it make a difference if I told you how much I missed you?"

James let out a breath.

"Yes."

"A lot. I've *definitely* missed you," she said, and she meant it.

There were several seconds of dead silence.

"Perhaps you can come over and show me just how much."

Erika was prepared for this.

"Is that an invite?" she teased.

"What does it sound like?" he replied.

"A booty call."

"You know me better than that, Erika. I miss you. Badly. Remember, I'm the one who said, 'I love you.'"

Erika found she couldn't respond.

James, thankfully, continued. "Why don't you come by around seven for dinner—I'll whip up something special; meanwhile, you can brief me on your friend Amber. Cool?"

Erika smiled.

"Way cool."

✖✖✖

"Hey you!" Erika exclaimed. She waited for the familiar response, but got none. "You there, Vince?" she asked.

"Yeah, Sassy, I'm here. What' up?" The way he said those six words made her heart sink.

"Hey, just checking on you. How you holding up?" she asked gingerly.

"I'm living."

Erika listened to the silence that seemed to envelop them. She took a breath and continued.

"I take it you haven't heard from Raven."

"Nope." The word popped off the top of his teeth. Erika cringed.

"Wow, I don't know what to say."

Vince emitted a grunt. "Haven't heard from Trey *either*." He let the weight of that statement fill the silence between them. Erika's mind raced.

"Now that's surprising. What's his problem?" she asked.

"Guess he doesn't want to fraternize with the enemy…" He spit a short laugh and then grew silent, contemplating the full meaning of those words.

Erika shook her head, making a mental note to call that fool and set his ass straight but quick. But first she needed to console Vince.

"I doubt that, Vince. I'm sure he's just busy. Working on some case, that's all." The words seemed hollow, however, even to her. "Listen, this thing is going to work out in the end, you'll see. You just need to have faith."

"Sassy, I just can't believe that I'm even in this mess in the first place. I mean, how does this shit happen? Raven is the first woman who's come along in a while that messed me up. This woman's got me hooked, and now look what's happened. She's fucking my best friend!"

"I know, Vince. I know. But as I said, things will work out for the best.

You just have to have faith in what the two of you shared. If it's meant to be, then it will be…" Erika didn't know what else to say.

Ever since Vince had called her in a panic, she had been in a state of shock—how the hell did two best friends end up dating the same woman, without even knowing it. This chick was playing a game on them; there was no doubt about that. And what the fuck was Trey thinking? She had spoken' to him only briefly a few days ago. He had sounded genuinely perplexed, as much as Vince, if not more so. He had ranted and raved for a good fifteen minutes, talking about how Giovanna, as she was known to him, was the best lay he'd had in a solid year! Trey wasn't about to give up that shit without a fight!

The whole mess made Erika sick.

Vince continued to air his thoughts. "Part of me doesn't even want to see her again, knowing that she's been with him. I mean, how can I continue to see Raven knowing that she's been doing things with Trey. God knows what things! Come on!"

"Have you tried to talk to her?" Erika ventured.

"Yeah, I had one really short conversation with her that night. She said she was sorry and that she needed some time and space to figure things out."

"I'm sure she does!" Erika shouted. "What did she think she was doing?"

"I don't know, Sassy. I honestly don't know."

"Well, I think the first priority has to be making sure your head is together; and that your friendship with your boy remains intact. No one should lose a friendship over a woman. No one."

"True dat! I just hope Trey feels the same," Vince responded.

"Me, too, Vince. Me, too…"

✖✖✖

Dinner was pan-fried tilapia with sweet potatoes and a fresh Caesar salad—Erika was extremely impressed. James was no Trey, that was for sure, but he tried hard, and got mega points for his efforts.

He served dinner in his oversized dining room. Conversation was relaxed and not forced. Erika was thankful. Over the past few weeks, their relationship had taken such a twisted, violent turn that Erika was unsure of where they stood now. And she knew James felt the same. But for some reason, James wasn't acting the way she had expected him to—gone was the incessant questioning of weeks before, and the condescending tone that had forced her to lash out at him when he burst into her bathroom that one evening, holding her prized chocolate dildo in hand!

James was holding a glass of Kendall Jackson Chardonnay as he spoke about the various assignments he was working on. He listened diligently as she recounted her work days and nights at the hospital—the critical cases that kept her late into the night, the patients who had gotten under her skin. James nodded as he forked the tilapia into his mouth, savoring the flavor of the sweet potatoes, and the crunchiness of the fresh Romaine lettuce.

The conversation shifted to Amber. James cleared the table as she talked, before retiring to the living room for coffee. Dessert would wait a bit further.

"You sound engaged with this whole thing," James remarked. "It's nice to see you getting involved."

"Yeah, I'm psyched, to tell you the truth. I don't know Amber all that well, but I feel a certain connection to her—I can't tell you why. Vince and I spoke about it—he had the same feeling when he first met her—as if they had met in a previous life or something. I can't put my finger on it, but something about her says 'family.'"

James nodded. He sat opposite her on the sofa—Erika placed her legs gently on his lap. James reached for her feet and began to massage them in turn.

"I'll give the foundation a call first thing tomorrow morning. They are anxious to begin working—I've already briefed them on the situation."

Erika smiled. She loved James' go-get-'em attitude.

"I really hope they can help," she said. "I hear the despair in Amber's voice when she talks about him. She truly wants to find her father. If only to bring some closure to her life."

They conversed for a few moments more. James continued his massage—his hands moving upward, gliding over her jeans to massage her calf muscles, knees, then thighs. He had put on a Brahms CD—it played softly and lazily in the background. By the time James reached for her breasts, Erika was moist beyond words. She hungrily took his tongue into her mouth, drinking in his familiar taste, like wine.

They groped each other for a moment further, mouths twisting about until James pulled back and looked at her longingly.

"Let me make love to you," he said, not bothering to hide his solid erection.

"What are you waiting for?" Erika replied softly, with a glint in her hazel-colored eyes.

✖✖✖

Flickers of candlelight danced over her prone form as she lay snuggled in James' terry-cloth robe. Erika's head was in her hands, her smooth, relaxed face turned to the side, cheek pressed against the thick blue-green comforter. She had come to love that thing—loved the way it felt on her skin, loved the way it shimmered and shined as they moved against it—she felt as if she were gliding underwater, the muted sea greens and blues comforting. The shower was raging in the next room. James had been in there for ten minutes now. He had invited her in, to wash away the remnants of their lovemaking, but Erika had declined. She wanted to savor this moment, alone.

Their lovemaking had been wonderful. Tender in the beginning, accelerating to a frenzied ending, like waves whipped up by gale-force winds; raw, primeval, and anima-like. James had surprised her with his actions. Normally so in control, so refined in everything he did, this night he seemed to lose control as the heat erupted between them. Perhaps he had lost himself within her slippery folds.

"Coming, baby?" he called from the next room.

Erika smiled but said nothing.

Her toes wiggled. As she shifted on the sea-green comforter, Erika could feel something stir inside her. She tightened the core of her being as it began to move. An imperceptible feeling, almost a silent thing, but she knew it was there—a trickle that began to seep, James' seed—slowly draining out of her, and that was what mattered to her most.

✖✖✖

Driving home, Erika reviewed their lovemaking in her mind as she checked messages. There was only one—from Marcus.

"Hey, Missy—it's me. I was hoping you didn't have plans tonight and would do me the honor of having dinner with me. I took the liberty of running by Blockbuster and picking out three must-see classics—hopefully one will catch your eye. Remember how we used to stay in for hours at a time watching movies, eating popcorn and pizza, and making what seemed back then like endless love? Well, I do. I suspect, and hope you do to. (Laughing). Okay, well, call me when you get this. I was thinking we could hook up around sixish…"

Erika's heart sank. The message was over five hours old. She glanced at the time: 11:40. Too late to call? Probably. She felt terrible, imagining Marcus, alone in his apartment with his movies, popcorn, and cold pizza.

For a few moments, indecision froze her. Then she hit speed-dial as she switched ears. He picked up on the fourth ring.

"Hey, you—I'm sorry for calling so late."

"That's okay," he responded, and she could hear him yawn as he stretched.

"I just got your message—I guess I missed dinner and a movie," she joked.

"That you did. Boy—I must have dozed off. What time is it?"

"Almost a quarter to midnight. So, what movies did you get, not that it matters now?" Erika asked.

"Well," she could hear the excitement in his voice. "I got a comedy, an action-adventure thriller, and a drama, because I didn't know what you'd be in the mood for. First there's *Romancing the Stone* with Michael Douglas, Kathleen Turner, and Danny DeVito—I just love that movie. Number two was *Top Gun* with Tom Cruise, and the third was *Ben-Hur*."

"*Ben-Hur?*"

"Yeah, *Ben-Hur*. That movie's the bomb. Charlton Heston is da man, you hear me?" Marcus said, laughing. He sighed before continuing. "It's too bad—I had a great evening planned—dinner, a movie, and a *special* massage for a special lady," he mused.

"Damn, damn, damn! So, what did you end up watching?"

"Two—*Romancing the Stone* and *Top Gun.*"

"No *Ben-Hur*?" Erika mused.

"Not enough time—I only had *five* hours…"

"I'm sorry, Marcus," she said softly. "Can a sistah get a rain check?" Erika pleaded.

"Nope."

"Marcus?"

"What?"

"I'll make it worth your while…"

Erika could feel his smile. She sighed heavily, thinking about her life at this very moment—having two good men who cared for her, both treating her right. She shook her head in amazement.

When it rains it sure does pour…

Marcus' voice interrupted her thoughts.

"Come sleep with me?"

"What?" She didn't think she had heard him correctly.

"Come sleep with me. I need to go to bed, and I suspect you do, too. But I'd love nothing more than to fall asleep with you in my arms. So come and sleep with me."

Erika thought about those powerful black arms surrounding her like a cocoon, holding her hostage, keeping her warm. She felt a shiver travel down her spine.

"Give me about twenty minutes," she heard herself say as she cut right, toward Rosslyn.

When it rains it sure does pour…

✖✖✖

I paced my office, jacket off, clad in my finest starched white cotton shirt with tiny black and purple stripes, dark wool suit pants, black onyx cuffs, suspenders, dressed to the nines, one thought coursing through my head: How the hell did I get myself into this mess?

I was pissed.

No. That was an understatement.

I was ready to put my size twelve up someone's ass, but quick.

An ass that I'd had the pleasure of getting to know intimately before this whole mess blew up in my face.

I cut a sharp glance at the phone. It sat on the edge of my desk, silent. I resisted the urge to bash its plastic shell with the underside of my hand. But that wouldn't accomplish anything. It wasn't the phone's fault.

Several more minutes of pacing before I stopped dead in front of my desk, glaring at the phone before snatching it up. Three days had gone by—I'd tried numerous times to reach Giovanna—on her cell, and at home. But my calls had been unanswered. I finally stopped calling, not wanting to seem like I was one of these bruthas who was sweating a woman. Shit, I sweated no one!

Fuck it, I thought as I punched in those numbers so hard I almost busted the damn phone. She picked up on the fourth ring.

"Trey," she said breathily.

"Oh, you're finally gonna take my call? How nice…" I let the sarcasm hang thick in the air. I was fuming and had no intentions of hiding it.

"I know you're angry with me…"

"Excuse me, Ms. Giovanna, or whatever the fuck your name is, but I only want to know one thing—is it gonna be him or me? The rest of what you have to say is excess baggage—frankly, I'm not fucking interested."

There was silence on the phone, and my heart spiked. I knew I was gambling with the best pussy I'd had in a long time. This was no way to talk to a lady. On the other hand, she had messed with my boy, Vince, and with me. And I wasn't having it. Trey was not about to go out like that!

"I was going to call you. Vince, too. I've arrived at a decision and need to tell you both. Can we meet?"

"Why don't you dispense with this formality bullshit and give it to me straight. I'm a big boy; I can handle it."

"Trey, please—you're not making this any easier. I didn't mean to hurt you or Vince."

"Well, I guess you should have thought about that before you began fucking my best friend."

"Trey, if I could take it back, I swear I would. I never would have done what I did knowing that the two of you had a friendship."

"Whatever. I just want to know what's up. 'Cause I sure as hell don't plan on sharing my pussy with anyone, least of all my best friend. I don't have to, you hear me?"

Silence.

I could feel my head throbbing, and my fists tightening. I don't know what was worse—finding out that the woman who you've been bedding down has been sexing someone else or finding out that that very person is your best friend. No, that wasn't true—it was *far* worse to learn that the pussy you'd thought belonged to you also belonged to your best friend. I loved Vince like a brother, but the thought of his dick sliding in and out of *my* baby's shit caused me to see red. I quickly reached out to my desk for support.

"Trey, this is difficult. For all of us," she replied. "Meet me tonight at eight. The bar in the Four Seasons, Georgetown. I'll let Vince know…"

I sighed, feeling the rush of blood as it pounded my forehead. "This shit better be worth my while…" I hissed.

But Giovanna's silence was unnerving…

✖✖✖

Mr. Lenitz will see you now," the stone-faced executive assistant uttered. I smoothed out my tie, buttoned the top two buttons of my jacket and strode inside.

Mr. Lenitz, the senior partner of the firm, was behind his mammoth desk. It was a huge thing, close to ten feet long and half that in width. Behind him were spacious floor-to-ceiling windows, with an amazing view of downtown Washington and the Capitol.

He rose, flung his bifocals to the table, and reached out his hand.

"Counselor, always good to see you," he said with an infectious grin. I smiled, took his hand and shook it, leveling my eyes with his.

"You, too, sir."

"Sit," he directed. I took a seat on a plush leather couch that seemed to envelop my entire lower half. I sat forward as the senior partner pulled up a chair directly across from me. "Coffee?"

"No, thank you, sir," I responded. I could feel the beads of sweat begin to form on my brow, but resisted the urge to wipe my forehead and bald head. That would show weakness, and I didn't want to convey that to the top dog.

"So," he said, spreading his hands wide, as his eyes took on a menacing glare, "what brings you here to the top floor?"

I smiled, briefly, as I reached into the interior breast pocket of my jacket. I grasped a folded document between my slender fingers.

I had contemplated this action for a while. Had even tried to get Calvin's take on the whole mess, but found out that old boy was on vacation.

Vacation???

Shit, Calvin Figgs *never* took a vacation. Things were indeed changing…

I took a breath, and spoke. "Sir, I'm filing an Equal Employment Opportunity complaint against the firm. I wanted to personally deliver a copy of the complaint to you, and answer any questions that you might have before I filed it."

"I see," Mr. Lenitz replied. His expression did not change and he mulled this over for a split second. "May I see the complaint?"

"Of course, sir," I said, handing over the folded document.

He took several minutes to read it. What I had given him was three single-spaced typewritten pages that outlined my complaint against my superior, Bernard John Marshall, and the firm. In it, I alleged discrimination based on race.

"Sir," I ventured to break the silence between us, "I've labored over this for quite some time now. As I'm sure you are aware, I have been a loyal servant to this firm for close to six years. I've worked hard, built up my clientele while bringing this firm a substantial amount of referral business, and most importantly, I'm very good at what I do. I love working here, and have every intention of remaining at the firm. But the actions of Bernard John Marshall are discriminatory and creating what I can only describe as a hostile work environment. I have never had a problem with a supervisor—

either at this firm, or in any work situation before Mr. Marshall. Simply put, he refuses to let me do my job. He harasses me, takes assignments away from me, questions my legal tactics, and interferes in my dealings with my clients. I cannot, for the life of me, understand why he would do this to me. It is not, I assure you, my work performance. The only explanation I'm left with is that he has a problem with my skin color, and that he is letting his discriminatory beliefs interfere with him managing me."

Mr. Lenitz steepled his hands as he listened intently. When I grew silent he nodded once and put down my memorandum to the EEOC. He sighed before speaking.

"Mr. Alexander, these are serious charges."

I nodded.

"Thank you for bringing this to my attention. I am shocked by these allegations, and want to assure you that this firm does not tolerate discriminatory practices of any kind." He paused as if to consider how to proceed next. Glancing up at the ceiling for a moment before leveling his gaze at me, he continued. "Let me ask you a question."

"Of course, sir."

"You've always known me to be a straightshooter, correct?"

"Absolutely, sir."

"Good. I would ask this of you. Give me seventy-two hours to personally investigate these allegations of racial discrimination before you go to the EEOC. Let me conduct my own discovery of the facts; let me talk to our managing partner and review whatever pertinent information you deem material to the case. Give me seventy-two hours to get back to you. I'm not asking you to forgo taking your complaint to the EEOC. Instead, I'm asking that you delay it, so that I can give it my full attention. First."

I considered his words. His eyes bore into me as I mulled over his proposal. I nodded once.

"Fair enough," I said, standing and attempting a half-smile. "I'll await your call on how to proceed next."

We shook hands.

"Thank you again, Trey, for bringing this to my attention. By all accounts you are a fine attorney with an exemplary work record. I'm sure that we can get to the bottom of this *misunderstanding*." Mr. Lenitz smiled as he let go of my hand. Unexpectedly, I was left with an uncomfortable feeling that began oozing through my veins. I was a black man in a white man's world. I was rocking the boat and the partners would definitely not appreciate that. I was messing with one of the top dogs—the new managing partner.

Did Mr. Lenitz care about me? Probably not. His allegiance was to the firm, first and foremost, ensuring that its pristine reputation remained intact.

Would he do anything regarding my complaint? Perhaps. But probably not.

Was I just being cynical?

No, I was a black man in a white man's world. I was just being *real*…

Suddenly, my anger flared. At my job, my boss, my personal life, my ex-girlfriend, my so-called-woman, and even my best friend. I felt my face flush, boiling rage meshed with red-hot heat.

Fuck them, I thought as I stood impatiently waiting for the down elevator. Fuck them *all*…

FORTY-SEVEN

Seven forty-five p.m. The lounge of the Four Seasons Hotel in Georgetown was moderately filled with patrons—out-of-towners and locals alike enjoying a cocktail, while Dennis, clad in his tuxedo, played softly on a Baldwin Grand piano. Trey swept in, the coattails of his long camelhair coat flaring behind him as he walked briskly, his eyes scanning the tables for his party. He slowed as he spied his best friend, Vince, who was already seated at a table off from mid-center. Trey wore a tight expression on his face as he reached the table. Vince didn't bother to stand up.

"Vince," Trey said.

"Trey." Gone was the normal back and forth banter between these two. The tension hung in the air, thick like cigarette smoke. Vince motioned for his friend to sit down.

"Waiting long?" Trey asked as he removed his coat and flung it on the chair beside him.

"Not really." Vince nursed a Corona. Trey could see that he had barely touched it. A waitress appeared to take Trey's drink order.

"I'll have the same," he said, motioning to Vince's beer. He rubbed his hands together vigorously to remove the chill as he flashed a fake smile.

"So, Dawg, here we are," Trey mused. Vince eyed him but did not smile.

"You think this is funny?" Vince asked, cocking his head to the side.

"Not at all. Actually, I think this is seriously fucked up."

Vince nodded.

"And you?" Trey asked. "What's your take on this whole thing?"

Vince glared at his best friend for a moment before clearing his throat.

"What I'm trying to figure out is a) how we let this woman do this to us—two grown-ass men, and b) where do we go from here?"

Trey steepled his fingers together and nodded silently. Vince continued.

"I mean, I met Raven several months ago and made no secret about it. I was pursuing her and let you and everyone know about it. So how is it that you end up with my woman?"

Trey's drink had arrived. He was placing the bottle to his lips when he stopped in mid-reach, putting the bottle down on the table. He looked at his friend incredulously.

"What are you saying, Vince? That I pursued this chick knowing she was dating you?"

"I'm trying to figure that out."

Trey forcefully exhaled.

"Nigga, please! Is that how you think I roll?"

"I don't know, Trey, you tell me..."

Vince's gaze was unwavering as he stared at Trey.

Trey fumed. "You know what, this shit is whacked. And you're whacked if you think that I somehow planned this. Vince, we go way back. I may have done a lot of messed-up things in my day, but fucking my best friend's woman ain't one of them!"

Vince took a swig of his beer and put the bottle down. He nodded to himself.

"That's good to hear, Trey. I needed to know."

"Yeah, well now you know." Trey took a swig of his own beer and shook his head.

"So, where do we go from here?" Vince repeated.

"That is a question you need to pose to Giovanna, or excuse me, Raven, as she's known to you."

Vince shook his head.

"I don't know, Trey. Do you think we should let her continue to control this situation, given what we've gone through? I've given this a lot of thought over the past few days and I'm very uncomfortable with having this woman who, obviously neither of us knows very well, pit two best friends against each other."

"How is she pitting us against each other?" Trey asked.

"Isn't it obvious?" Vince responded. "Here we are, sitting in this bar, waiting for her to render a verdict—it's either you or me. Don't you have a problem with that? Doesn't it bother you that we're letting a woman get between our friendship?"

Trey sighed.

"Vince, listen, I don't like this any more than you do. But I'm not sure what the proper course of action is. I mean, we can both walk away, but what would that solve? If we do that, we both lose out on a relationship that up to this point was pretty damn satisfying for both of us."

Vince exploded.

"I can't fucking believe what I'm hearing, although I shouldn't be surprised. Trey, what fucking relationship? The woman conned us. You and me. She played us. We thought she was someone else…"

"Hey," Trey said, raising his hands in self-defense, "I'm not condoning her behavior; I'm just saying, do we cut off our nose to spite our face, or…"

Vince waved him away as he leaned in, lowering his voice to a near whisper.

"You know what? This comes down to pussy, plain and simple. At the end of the day, you don't want to give up any fine snatch without a fight, your friendship be damned!" Vince took a swig of his beer while locking his gaze onto Trey. He shook his head slowly. "Well, I'm here to tell you, Trey Alexander, that my *so-called* friend, is *fucked up!*" Vince emptied his beer as someone cleared their throat. It caught both Vince's and Trey's attention. They both turned simultaneously and glanced up into the lovely face of Raven/Giovanna.

✖✖✖

"May I sit down, gentlemen," she uttered softly. Raven/Giovanna was covered in a luxurious fur wrap, which she draped over an empty chair.

Vince eyed her silently. She wore a beautiful print dress, in various shades of brown that hugged the contours of her voluptuous body. Trey nodded to her once as she sat next to him, across from Vince, whose lips were pressed together, draining all color from his flesh.

It was difficult to imagine that just a week ago this icon of beauty was his lover. Vince took a millisecond to remember their last lovemaking session—the passion; the fury that accompanied their conjoining was unlike anything he had ever experienced. This woman was something else; that's what he had told himself over and over again.

A gift from God.

Yes, he had been *that* blessed.

And then, like a heavy foot disturbing a puddle after a rain, all of what they had shared was shattered, like a fist hitting a pane of glass, and Vince was left with this deep-seated feeling of revulsion. He stared at her lips, thinking to himself, *Trey has kissed those same lips.* His eyes dropped unconsciously to her breasts as he thought, *Trey has caressed those very same breasts…*

Raven/Giovanna stared at each man for a moment before speaking.

"I honestly don't know what to say other than I am so very sorry for what I have done to both of you. I know my words must sound hollow, but I hope you will believe me when I say I never meant to hurt either of you."

"Question," Vince uttered, glaring at her. "Tell me your name, your real name—since I obviously don't know you."

Raven/Giovanna swallowed hard.

"It's Giovanna Marquis. I'm so sorry, Vince." She reached for his arm, but he pulled away.

"So, Giovanna, tell me. Why? Why run to another man, my best friend, no less? Was what we had not special?"

Vince's eyes seemed to water. Giovanna's lips quivered.

"Vince, what you and I had was special. Please believe me…"

"How the hell do you expect me to believe anything you say now?" Vince bellowed.

"And turning to me, Giovanna," Trey quipped, "why the game-playing? Why not come straight? Why not just tell me the real deal? Did you think you could just continue playing me like that? Playing the two of *us*?"

Giovanna was silent.

"You know what?" Vince exclaimed. "This is bullshit. There is no explanation. Nothing she can say will change anything. She dogged us. She dogged us both and now she stands here begging forgiveness. Well, she can't have it. Not from me."

There were several seconds of silence while all three stared each other down. The waitress arrived, Giovanna ordered a Johnnie Walker Black and Coke on the rocks, while Vince and Trey waved her away.

"Vince is right," Trey said, as he fondled his bottle. "This is bullshit. So why don't you tell us what you came here to tell us—and dispense with the rest of the formalities."

Giovanna nodded.

"Okay." She sucked in a deep breath. "Both of you are wonderful men in your own right. I'm lucky to have met both of you. Vince, what you and I had was indeed special—you took me to new heights that I'd never been to before, and for that I am immensely grateful. Trey," she said, turning to him, "I'm still getting to know you, but you have a side to you that I find extremely desirable."

Vince exhaled forcefully, but said nothing.

"As I stated, you both are wonderful men—but I can't date both of you," she remarked before pausing to gaze at each man in turn before leveling her stare at Vince. "Therefore, I would like to pursue things with, that is, if you'll have me," she said, eyes dropping momentarily to the table before flicking over to Trey and then resting on Vince, "what I'm trying to say, is that, Vince, you're a wonderful guy, but, I think I'm more compatible with…"

Vince was rising, reaching for his coat as he shook his head slowly. He refused to meet Giovanna's stare. Instead, he locked eyes with his best friend.

"Trey, you do what you want, dawg, but I'm done here. If you choose to allow this woman to get in the way of our friendship, then that's your prerogative. I can't stop you."

He glared at Giovanna for a moment.

"I've got *nothing* to say to you…"

Vince walked away briskly as Trey rose, calling out to him.

"Vince, dawg, hold up a second," he yelled, but Vince continued along, ignoring him. Trey sat, glowered at Giovanna for a moment as she followed Vince's retreat with her own gaze.

"You did a fucked-up thing, you hear me?" Trey exclaimed, leaning in to her.

She nodded silently. A minute passed.

"A real fucked up thing. So, the question becomes, what am I gonna do with your sorry ass?" Trey grabbed the bottle in front of him and downed the last of his beer. Giovanna reached for his arm and stroked it. She smiled weakly.

"Trey, I'm busted. What else can I say? I fucked up. But I want to be with you. And I hope you'll have me back." She made eye contact with him and smiled seductively as she dropped her voice to a near whisper. "I took the liberty of getting a suite here for the night. I thought that perhaps I could persuade you to come up for a…nightcap. Listen, I know I've been bad—very bad…and I'm hoping that you're willing to correct my dreadful behavior. I'm ready to be punished, Trey, any way you see fit. Just come upstairs with me, okay, baby? Teach mommy a lesson, Trey? The way you do so good…"

Trey sat back and frowned at her. He could feel his flesh stirring as he took in her lovely features. His thoughts were instantly transported back to those multitudes of moments where they shared each other intimately. He smiled, unconsciously, thinking about how fucking good she was. Giovanna set him free, like very few women before her had—brought him to that place where he was a sexual beast, a prince among men. Yes, Trey smiled at Giovanna as he eyed her seductively. Then his smile was erased.

"Key," he said.

"What?" she asked, her eyes blinking in confusion.

"I didn't stutter," he mused. "I said, 'key.'"

Giovanna rummaged through her purse. "It's suite 1211," she said before taking a deep breath. "Thank you, Trey, I'm…"

Trey cut her off with a wave of his hand as he leaned in and whispered, "Just do what I fucking say, okay?"

Giovanna blinked and nodded once.

"Go upstairs, remove your clothes, and get on the bed, on all fours, *doggie-style*, and wait for me to come. Are we clear?" His face was inches from hers. His eyes bore laser beams into her retinas. Giovanna swallowed and nodded silently.

"Good. Go on then," he said. "All I wanna see is ass and pussy when I come through that door. Comprende?"

Giovanna rose, grabbed her wrap, and turned to leave. Trey watched her retreat as he slapped some bills onto the table. He motioned for the waitress. "A celebration is in order," he mused, all teeth as he grinned. "So, bring me a glass of your finest Scotch, on the rocks, with a beer chaser."

"Of course, sir. I'd recommend the Ardbeg Provenance. It's the Holy Grail of scotches, with a sweet smoke flavor, and a multitude of layers."

"Perfect," Trey replied. "Bring me the bottle, if you would, thanks."

The waitress blinked. "I believe, sir, that the bottle is $875."

Trey didn't even blink. "I'll be charging it to Suite 1211…"

He hummed to himself as he watched her give his drink order to the bartender. Trey smiled before whispering, "Trey back in the saddle, y'all, for *real!*"

✖✖✖

The night was frigid, but Vince seemed not to feel it. Perhaps his body was on shutdown, after walking for over thirty minutes now, his extremities no longer feeling the cold, as if his limbs were lifeless, immune to the bone-chilling cold. He had taken a cab out of Georgetown; had hailed one immediately from the front entrance of the hotel, as if he were suffocating and could no longer stand being in this neck of the woods a minute longer.

He was now blocks from his home, and it was getting late. He knew better than to be out at this time of night—but the thought of getting mugged didn't even enter Vince's thoughts. Tonight, he had other things on his mind.

He had called Erika as soon as he had been deposited on the cold, dark sidewalk. Had flipped open his cell and speed-dialed her number. Thankfully, she had answered on the third ring.

"Hey, Sassy."

Erika could hear the misery in his voice.

"Vince. I take it things didn't go too well."

"An understatement. She chose Trey—no real surprise there. I upped and left the two lovebirds. I'm done with her and with *him*…"

"Oh, Vince," she exclaimed into the phone, "I'm real sorry to hear that." Her tone changed from soothing to hard. "But what the fuck is up with your boy? He can't be seriously contemplating dating her—not after everything she's put the two of you through."

"Sassy, please! This is Trey we're talking about. You know that nigga is only thinking with one head—and I ain't referring to the one on his shoulders…"

"I feel you, but damn! I'm gonna call his trifling ass…"

"You can do what you want, Erika, but I'm telling you. I'm done with his dumb-ass. Tonight was an eye-opener for me. Tonight I saw my best friend choose pussy over me…"

They had exchanged a few more minutes of conversation; Erika repeatedly told him that this was for the best—that she had gotten a bad feeling the first time he'd talked about Raven. There was something that wasn't quite right. And now, Raven's true colors had shone through, and the best thing Vince could do was move on and not look back.

Vince agreed.

But that didn't mean it wouldn't hurt for a while…

Immediately after hanging up with Vince, Erika called Trey on his cell. He answered on the second ring.

"What up, Boo?" he said, in a cocky, upbeat voice. Erika could hear the sound of a piano playing and distant chatter in the background.

"Oh, you're all full of yourself now that you've won your prize," she said, not bothering with pleasantries.

"Sassy, don't be calling up here with one of your lectures, 'cause I don't need it right now," he spat back.

"Oh, I see. You're in the zone right now, so nobody can tell you shit, is that it?"

"Na, it ain't…"

"You listen to me, Trey. I don't care what that *bitch* is saying to you, and I don't care how good her cootchie is, the shit ain't worth losing a friend-ship over! Use your head, man! She's gonna dog you until she's done with your sorry-ass, and then she's gonna up and leave. Where will you be then?"

Trey looked at the phone incredulously.

"I really don't know who you think you're talking to, but I'm tired of you trying to tell me how to lead my fucking life. It makes no sense to me that both Vince and I should come out losers in this game. Why not take advan-tage, Erika? Hell, one of us should, and guess what—I'm the chosen fucking one! So sorry to disappoint you, but damn it, I'm gonna take advantage. To *not* do so would be ludicrous!"

"And what about Vince? Do you care about his feelings, Trey? Or is it, as long as you get yours, it's every man for himself?" Erika exclaimed.

"Yeah," Trey snorted, "I care about him *and* his feelings. But he needs to take this shit like a man—if I was the loser I wouldn't be running off like a dog with its tail between its legs, and having my girlfriend call the winner to complain. I'd go out the way I came in—like the man that I am, not a bitch!"

Erika shook her head.

"So that's what Vince is to you—a bitch? You know what? Vince is done with you and so am I. You are one sorry-ass nigga."

Trey chuckled.

"And I'm going to tell you something else, smart-ass, whether you want to hear it or not," Erika continued. "You've changed. Your priorities are all fucked up. You used to be all about the friendship and family *first*. Now it's all about you—Trey getting his, regardless of the cost. Damn—now every fucking action of yours revolves around your dick—and that's messed up. Your life is so one-fucking dimensional, yet you can't see the forest for the trees. I just hope when things finally come crashing down you'll have someone to reach out to for support. Because it won't be Vince or me."

Trey sucked in a breath, felt his heart racing, and went off.

"And now let me tell you something, Sassy. You and your boy are just envious of the way I live. I'm living large, on my terms, by my own rules.

And you know what—y'all are just fucking jealous, because your lives don't match mine. I don't have your fucking problems. My dick works—I come. Yeah, Sassy—I said it. You know what your problem is, and that of your boys? You need to stop riding my jock!"

Erika fumed.

"You know what, Trey? Fuck *you* and the horse you rode in on!" she yelled, slamming down the phone.

"Not if I don't fuck you first," he replied as he snapped shut his cell.

Thankfully, Erika was no longer there to hear his reply.

✖✖✖

Vince was back in the confines of his warm house when he reached for the phone. He glanced at the clock—saw it was a little after 11:30 at night. He knew it was late, but he had to talk to her. And so he dialed and waited for the familiar voice to warm his heart.

"Hey you," he said easily into the receiver when she answered.

"Hey," Amber replied, sitting up in her bed. She immediately detected that something was wrong. Gone was the normal jovial tone in her friend's voice. "Vince, you okay?" she asked. The TV was on, volume muted as she listened to the new Erykah Badu CD. She pointed the remote at the stereo to cut the power. The silence was abrupt. She waited for Vince to respond.

"Sorry for calling so late," he said. Vince sounded winded, almost out of breath, like he was sick.

"You know it's cool. Always a pleasure to talk to you. So, what's up? You aren't your usual self—I can tell that."

"Yeah, I can't front with you, Amber." Vince paused.

"It's about that woman. Raven, right?"

"Damn, you're good." He attempted a smile, but it came out flat and subdued.

"Talk to *me*…"

Vince brought her up to speed on his situation. Amber listened patiently and without comment until he was finished. When he took a deep breath and sighed, Amber spoke.

"Oh, Vince, I am so sorry. Damn, that's messed up. I wish there was something I could do to make you feel better."

"Hearing your voice does that," he mused.

"Does Erika know?"

"Yeah, I spoke to her earlier. She was sorry, too, but told me to move on. And that it's for the best."

"Smart woman. Heed her words, young man!"

"I figured you'd say that."

There was an awkward moment of silence. Vince sighed heavily.

"So, what's new in N'awlins?" he asked, trying to change the subject.

"Same old, same old."

"How's the artist doing?" he asked, referring to Angeliqué.

"She's good. I haven't seen much of her lately—she's always on the go, doing something, you know how your girl is, all *flighty* and shit. Can't keep still for a minute! But she's always asking about you."

Vince smiled. "Tell her I said, 'Waz up!'"

Another pregnant pause.

"Vince," Amber said, "I've got an idea. Why don't you come down here for a few days? I know it's middle of the week and all, but it would be great to see you. We could hang out, do some stuff to get your mind off of this woman, or whatever. You promised you'd come down soon anyway. Well, now you've got a reason…"

Vince smiled.

"I don't know, Amber…"

"What's not to know? You need to get away. Staying in D.C. is only going to remind you of her and all you've been through. If you come down here, I'll play doctor and take care of you…make you forget all about that crazy-ass woman and her messed-up antics!"

Amber laughed, and Vince was filled with a feeling he wasn't yet prepared to comprehend. He smiled, laughed along with her, and heard himself saying, "Yeah, Amber, perhaps you're just what the doctor ordered…"

✖✖✖

Vince strolled up the incline of the jetway, lugging his carryon bag over his left shoulder as he made his way to the waiting area. He was tired and ill tempered. He hadn't slept well at all the previous evening. Vince had tossed and turned all night—images of Trey and Raven floated in and out of his consciousness, no matter how hard he tried to shoo them away. But thankfully, dawn had brought on a new day. Vince had risen at seven, showered and shaved, and grabbed a coffee and a bagel before heading to Reagan National Airport for his two-hour and fifty-two minute flight to New Orleans.

He entered the bright terminal and his eyes squinted as they took a moment to get used to the light. His gaze fell on a form to the left of the check-in counter. A woman was holding a placard with a name written in thick black magic marker.

Vince Cannon, Jr.

His name…

A lovely creature wearing a green and white Tulane University hooded sweatshirt, white sweatpants, and an engaging smile.

Vince smiled for the first time in twelve hours.

"Hey, you!" he said enthusiastically, sweeping Amber up into his arms and kissing her on the cheek. "What are you doing here?"

"I'm your official welcoming committee!" she replied, stroking his face with a fingernail before moving in and quickly kissing his lips. "Wanted to make sure there were no issues with your arrival."

She flashed Vince a smile as he thought: Amber is a sight for sore eyes. Her skin had a natural glow to its texture, and her eyes sparkled as they fell on his face. An aura presided over her, and Vince knew he had made the right decision in coming down here. He found himself staring once again at her facial appearance and her auburn-coated skin—not only beautiful on the outside, but her inner being as well—something familiar yet elusive stabbed at his insides—and as he did the first time he'd laid eyes on her lovely form, he tried to decipher where—but the answer alluded him.

"I took the liberty of picking up some java for you—that shit they serve on the plane is nasty…"

Vince beamed as she handed him a steaming cup of Starbucks.

"Bless you, my child," he said before pulling her to him and hugging her again. "Damn, it's good to see you, Amber. I feel better already."

"I guess my work here is done," she mused, feigning leaving.

"Not so fast," Vince replied, "I'm not done with you yet...we've only just begun..."

Vince noticed how her eyes sparkled when he uttered those words.

The ride into town went quickly. There was no traffic; besides Amber knew these streets like a native—Vince was impressed as she bypassed the interstate to cut through the city.

"Nice ride," he commented.

"It's Angelique's," Amber said. "You know I can't afford anything but a hooptie right now, and my ride's in the damn shop!" she mused.

"Hell, a hooptie gets you where you need to go, so don't knock it."

"I hear you...anyway, I just want you to sit back and relax—for the next few days it's all about you—it's your world, Vince. My job is to serve you," she said with a devilish grin. "I'm gonna make you forget all about your troubles up North—think of it as a soul cleansing," she said, eyeing him as she steered though the narrow streets of the Quarter, "washing away those negative toxins, leaving only positive energy in its place." She grinned over at him as he nodded to her. "You feel me, Vince?" she asked, in a tone that belied any seductive intent. Yet, as Vince stared back at her, he couldn't help but feel a fire being stoked.

"Yeah, for real, Amber," Vince replied, finding that he was having trouble breaking away from her stare.

"The woman up North is *history*," Amber said. "Poof—be gone, bitch," she uttered with a single flick of her wrist.

"You're *all* mine now..."

✖✖✖

How to describe the rest of the day?

One word said it all—*extraordinary*.

With the temperature hovering in the mid-fifties, and with no wind to create discomfort, it began with a walk through the Quarter to a salon where Vince had his first manicure and pedicure; he found the whole process energizing, and vowed to continue the practice once he returned home.

Next, they walked Jackson Square, taking in the Pontalba Buildings with their cast-iron galley railings and hanging ferns; the St. Louis Cathedral, which, Vince learned, was originally built in 1724, and was the oldest Cathedral in North America; and The Cablildo, the site of the signing of the historic Louisiana Purchase.

Walking down Pirate's Alley, Amber led Vince to Faulkner House, where William Faulkner rented a room on the ground floor close to eighty years ago. They perused the bookstore for thirty minutes before heading over to Café Du Monde on Decatur where they partook in dark roasted coffee and beignets. Vince was impressed with her knowledge of the city's history and its heritage.

"That's one thing I love about this place," she said while cupping her hands around the hot ceramic mug, "is that it has a richness that very few places can touch. And it is that richness of culture that hangs in the air here—you can sense it when you walk the Quarter, and I never grow tired of inhaling that scent."

A streetcar with mahogany seats and brass fittings took them along St. Charles Street to the Garden District, where Amber led Vince through Lafayette Cemetery No. 1 and the impressive aboveground tombs of the dead. Vince marveled at many of the eighteenth-century monuments, and the haunting emotions they evoked. After what seemed like hours, they hailed a cab back to the serene tranquility of St. Philip. There, they took a much-needed nap, Amber in her second-floor bedroom, while Vince made ready to recline on a futon in a room behind the gallery that overlooked the courtyard.

Vince felt a stab of guilt when he stared out from behind the wooden shutters, remembering with too much clarity, spying Angeliqué, the woman whom he had fallen hard for, in mid-embrace. That night seemed like eons ago. Yet, that night had changed him. He closed the shutters, muting the light, and sunk into the confines of the comfortable futon, like the arms of a beautiful woman, seeming to embrace and hold him captive. And he slept, dreaming of a time when things seemed less complicated and confused, and of Raven, the mysterious woman who had betrayed him.

✖✖✖

It was after dark when Vince was awakened. Angeliqué stood over him, hands folded across her breasts.

"Living the life of Riley, I see," she mused.

Vince jumped up and hugged her.

"How ya livin'?" he asked.

"Can't complain, Vince. Life is good," she said, all smiles. "I'm sorry to hear about your...*situation*," she added.

"Life goes on, Angeliqué," Vince responded as he stretched. Amber bounced in looking radiant in a pair of form-fitting black pants and an off-white sweater that highlighted her perky breasts. "Dayum—look at *you*!" he exclaimed.

Amber pirouetted for the pair as she grinned. "Don't hate the playa, Vince," she said with a gleam in her eye, "hate the *game*..."

"Are you hungry, Mister?" Angeliqué asked him. "Amber and I thought we'd take you out to eat, since you're gracing us with your presence."

"Bring it on, ladies!" he replied.

Vince took a quick shower and changed into a pair of corduroy slacks, dark sweater, tweed jacket, and boots. Amber told him he looked like a college professor, "but I mean that in a good sort of way!" Angeliqué looked like the artist that she was in a pair of brown leather pants, boots, and a funky '60s top.

The trio dined at Bacco on Chartres Street, a nice walk from St. Philip. Vince had the crawfish ravioli with sun-dried tomato pesto butter sauce. Amber selected the Foie Gras pizza topped with roasted Portobello mushrooms, caramelized Chianti onions, and house-made mozzarella cheese, while Angeliqué had the pistachio-crusted salmon. They shared a bottle of

Kendall Jackson Grand Reserve Chardonnay while they chatted and caught up.

The food was excellent; the conversation even better. Vince was so glad to have taken Amber up on her offer. And he was pleasantly surprised to see that there wasn't any tension between him and Angelique. She treated him like a good friend, with warmth and compassion.

Afterwards, they strolled the Quarter, stopping in at House of Blues to listen to some live music. By midnight, Angeliqué excused herself, and hailed a cab home. Amber and Vince stayed until 1:30 a.m., continuing to enjoy the libations and the conversation.

Vince followed up on their previous discussions surrounding Amber's goals, ambitions, and future plans. She always had many questions for Vince, considering this was his field of expertise.

"I don't know, Vince. I know I'm still young and all, but I feel as if I should be focusing on my passion and not the normal nine-to-five."

"I hear you, but don't beat up on yourself. Many people don't even know what their passion is, let alone how to turn it into a money-making endeavor," he replied. "You're doing what you need to do—one step at a time."

For months now, Amber had been talking to Vince about her love of writing—poetry, short-fiction, and of one day tackling the great American novel. Through her conversations with Vince, he had convinced her to keep a journal, and focus on honing her craft. She still held her administrative job at Tulane, largely so she could take classes at no cost to her.

Vince was proud of her, and let her know it every chance he got.

They took the stroll back hand-in-hand, taking their time, letting their silence envelop them, and enjoying the early morning chill and the night sounds. Vince was cognizant of the fact that not so long ago he and Angeliqué had walked the Quarter hand-in-hand as he did now. But he didn't dwell on the past. Amber made that impossible. There was only the here and now, and what was to come. Vince enjoyed her company—the closeness that they shared was something that had caught him off guard. But the more time he spent in her presence, the greater he felt the bond between them becoming.

They spoke little of Raven and Trey back in D.C. Vince found that he could go for hours before a thought of them whisked into his consciousness. But then, like one of those oversized horseflies, he waved the annoying thought away.

They made their way to the silent block of St. Philip and Angeliqué's home. It was close to 2 a.m. Amber opened the wrought-iron door and led Vince inside. They were quiet since they didn't want to disturb Angeliqué. On a hallway table was a note to Amber from Angeliqué. It said that she would be spending the night at a friend's, and would be home the following afternoon.

Amber grinned. "Uh-Oh, Vince, you better watch yourself, 'cause big momma's gone away. We've got the crib to ourselves!"

Vince yawned.

"Whatever, I ain't scared of you."

They laughed as they took the stairs.

"Thank you so much," Vince beamed when they reached the second-floor landing. He faced her and placed his hands on her shoulders. "This day has been something I can't put into words. You talked about healing. Well, I swear, I almost feel like my old self again."

"You're quite welcome. And it was my pleasure. That's what good friends do for their friends in need…"

He turned toward his room facing the courtyard. "Well, I'm gonna bid you goodnight," he said.

"Not so fast," Amber replied, following closely behind. "The night's not done yet."

Vince turned and stared at her, trying to read her expression. She wore a grin, but he couldn't decipher the meaning behind it. He raised an eyebrow.

"One more thing, before we both turn in. Something that I've planned for you. Part of the healing process, Mr. Cannon, Jr."

"Really?" Vince replied, suddenly feeling wide-awake.

"Trust me," she said, turning to head in the opposite direction. "Give me a few minutes, will you?" she said, with a gleam in her eye.

Just what is this woman up to? Vince pondered silently.

He was about to find out.

✖✖✖

Vince's legs were splayed across the open futon. Gone were his clothes—instead, he wore a pair of blue scrubs, courtesy of his dad, Dr. Vince Cannon, Sr., and Children's Hospital in D.C. His chest was bare. His gaze swept over the darkened ceiling, as Amber knocked on the door.

"Come," he said.

She strolled in. Gone were her earlier clothes, too—instead she wore a pair of gray sweat shorts, and a wifebeater. Her hair was pulled back and held with a scrunchie. Vince thought she looked wonderful, no matter what the attire.

"Your bath is ready, Sir!" she said, without preamble.

"Excuse me?" he said, rising quickly from the futon.

"Just follow me," she said, exiting the room.

She led him down the hallway to a small bathroom at the end. Vince entered, and was in awe at what awaited him.

The entire room was ablaze in candlelight—there must have been close to thirty candles placed on the black and white tile floor, on the lip of the old porcelain tub, and on the windowsill and commode top. His eyes swept to the filled tub—red and pink petals danced lazily among scented bubbles. There was no shower stall—just this ancient tub, a commode, and a small sink. Vince was, for a brief moment, speechless.

"Oh my God!" he exclaimed. He didn't know what else to say.

Amber grinned. "I take it you like?" she asked.

"Are you kidding?"

There was a folding chair leaning against the back wall. Amber unfolded it and scooted it up to the head of the tub. She sat down, tested the waters with her forearm as she locked her stare onto Vince.

"What are you waiting for? Get in!" It was a command.

Vince stood there, a look of incomprehension on his face. He swallowed involuntarily.

"Don't tell me you're scared?" Amber teased. "Big strapping hunk of a man like you? Say it ain't so…"

"Na..."

"As I recall, Mr. Cannon, Jr., you've already seen me in my birthday suit, and I didn't pitch a fit then, so neither should you." Amber splashed some water on her forearms and reached for a loofah and the soap, lathering up. "Come on, mister; don't want the water to get cold now, do we?"

Vince smiled. As he turned away to remove his pants, he felt his heart rate spike. He exhaled slowly, as the scrubs went down past his knees and onto the floor.

"Nice buns," Amber teased. "I love me a mans with nice buns!"

Vince lowered himself into the water, grateful for the thick bubbles that covered his growing erection. He sat back, letting the water envelop him, the scent of jasmine, Egyptian musk, and sandalwood, invading his senses. For a brief moment he shut his eyes, allowing the candlelight to flicker across his closed eyelids. Then Amber's hands were on his head, pouring water over his hair and massaging shampoo into his scalp. The feeling was indescribable: Vince lying in a tub of hot, scented water, rose petals lapping against his chest, being pampered like this as the flames from dozens of candles flickered around him. He began to speak, but Amber stopped him.

"Don't say anything," she said, continuing to run her fingers through his wet, soapy hair, "let the essence of this experience cleanse you."

Vince closed his eyes and focused on her hands.

She washed his hair with shampoo that smelled of lemongrass and eucalyptus. Let her fingers roam over his neck and shoulders, leaning him forward in order to soap up his back. She took her time, massaging the muscles in his skin with soap and hot water, cupping her hands and rinsing the flesh before moving onward, and down.

She told him to stand. Vince rose from the tub, his body dripping myriads of bubbles that meandered down his dark skin like a winding river. She took the loofah and soaped it up again, held it against his ass, coated his cheeks with a layer of soapy bubbles before using strong fingers to knead the flesh. Vince was fully hard now, his thick member facing away from her, but bobbing to its own rhythm as flickers of candlelight danced off the veined shaft. When she was done with his ass, she moved downward still, to his thighs, the back of his knees and onto his shins. Amber finished up by rinsing him clean with hot water, before urging him to turn around.

Vince did so, with only a single moment of hesitation, until his fully engorged state was in full view, directly in front of her.

Amber said nothing, eyeing him for a moment, her hands dipping lazily in the water, before she grabbed the loofah and soap, and stood.

Still silent, her eyes locked onto his dark skin, Amber washed his chest and stomach, lathering him up until not one inch of darkened flesh shone through. Then she rinsed him, slowly and methodically, watching the water cascade down and between his legs.

Vince remained silent, closing his eyes to the scene, allowing her touch and sound of her sighing to guide him.

Amber lathered his thighs and knees before rinsing. Vince remained standing, his eyes closed. He was breathing deeply, pulling air into his nostrils and letting it flow through his body before exhaling the same way it had come.

When she reached for him, Vince cut his breathing short.

Her fingers tentatively wrapped themselves around his penis, using her palm to stroke him from testicles to head. When she reached the tip, her fingers constricted, applying pressure, molding the bulbous flesh, almost twisting it out of shape.

Vince was about to lose his mind.

His eyes opened as she used her other hand to cup his balls lightly, pressing upward and around them, as if encasing them in her own wet cocoon. Vince groaned. Her eyes flicked upward for a brief moment, their eyes met and locked before dropping her gaze back down, concentrating on the task at hand...

He closed his eyes again as Amber washed him, using her hands, fingers, and the soap, alternating between gently stroking the sides of his shaft, and gripping the entire girth in her hand and squeezing.

Hard.

Feeling him pulse.

When Vince opened his eyes, she had joined him in the tub.

Gone were the shorts...

Gone was the wifebeater…

And her hair hung free.

She gazed into his eyes for a moment, one hand encircling his penis, the tip nudging between her well-toned thighs, inching forward. She tilted her head up, parted her lips, as Vince's mouth came down onto hers.

There were no words.

Only sounds as they explored each other with their tongues.

Their bodies pressed against one another, fingers and hands finding breasts and nipples, then descending down slender soap-covered backs to each other's asses, gripping the flesh, holding it firm, feeling the weight of the one rock against the other as candlelight flickered over their pulsating forms.

She rolled a condom onto him silently.

There were no words.

Only sounds as she gripped his head and neck tightly, climbing him the way an insect does a grass stem, rising before settling down, exhaling with a forceful sigh as Vince entered her cavern, plunging into the depths of her molten core.

There were no words.

Only sounds.

No foreplay.

The entire day had been just that—a preview of things to *come*.

Vince thrust into Amber with ambition.

As they rocked against one another, their bodies fusing as one, Vince thought about the first time he'd laid eyes on Amber's lovely prone form. It was at that moment, he mused, that the foreplay between them had begun—he hadn't considered it consciously, but he vividly recalled a quiver of excitement that ran down his spine as he watched her veve-covered flesh then.

And now, they were making love; passionately, completely, and without reservations, giving all to the other, as their tongues encircled the other like a slick vine.

And when they came, Amber and Vince came together.

Amber shouted, "Oh God!" and moaned before sucking his tongue into the recesses of her mouth. And for Vince, the explosion in his loins was the most powerful he'd ever experienced, like a wave of fireworks that roll overhead, a kaleidoscope of colors, cleansing his insides of anything that was bad, leaving only goodness behind...

And as he held her quaking form in his arms, legs encircling his ass, her chest heaving against his own, petal-laced water splashing around them, Vince found he had no choice but to give in to his emotions and let the tears flow down...

FORTY-EIGHT

Y'all don't know how damn good it felt to fire up the old Indian once April rolled around. I mean, February had been a mutha fucka—and March was just as bad. Windy, snowy, and downright bone-chilling cold, as if God was punishing us for a sin-filled year. It felt like we were living in Minneapolis and not the nation's capital. Dayum!

But once April hit, it was as if a light switch had been flipped. I swear! One day it was nasty-gray-cold. The next, April second to be exact, the sky turned ultra-blue, cloudless, with temperature rising into the forties. The following day—a bit warmer. The day after that—fifties! Can you believe it? Just like that! Me and everyone else in D.C. thought we'd died and gone to heaven!

For real!

So I pulled the Indian out, hosed her down for the first time in over six months, and spent the good part of a Saturday polishing that girl's chrome until she shined like I don't know what. That bad boy was looking so fly, I felt myself getting hard. Oh yeah, y'all, I couldn't' wait to get on the bike. And that's exactly what I did.

Took Giovanna out for a spin that turned into an all-day affair. Rode out Route 50 to Annapolis, spent some time walking Main Street before heading over the Chesapeake Bay Bridge and to the Red Eye's Dock Bar where we chilled, had lunch, and a few Coronas overlooking the bay. Finished off by heading up Route 13 into Delaware and looping back down into

Baltimore, stopping for dinner at the Inner Harbor. It turned out to be a wonderful day, and it felt so good to have the Indian once again between my legs.

Giovanna loved it, too.

For that day, I forgot all the trouble that seemed to have seeped into my life as of late. I can't even begin to explain where everything broke down, but damn it, things were, in a word, fucked the hell up!

Ever since...

Vince and I had become strangers the night Giovanna chose me over him. I'd given him some time to chill and get over it; had even called him a week later to see what was up, be he refused to take or return my calls. And I'm not one to beg, so I left it alone...

Same thing with Erika.

I know she's my boo and all, but damn, that last conversation really fucked with my head. I figured that like a woman, once she regained her composure, she'd come around.

Wrong.

I guess both she and Vince still had a stick up their ass...

Well, I wasn't going to lose any sleep over it.

At least that's what I told myself.

The truth is, I missed them both.

Missed them terribly.

But what was I to do?

Should I give up on a perfectly good relationship with a woman whom I was feeling just because my friends were in a tizzy?

I don't think so.

Then there was the situation at work. You will recall the initial meeting I had had with the Senior Partner, Mr. Lenitz. Although the follow-up meeting had occurred almost two months ago, it felt just like yesterday.

I clenched my jaws as I recalled that event...

Mr. Lenitz's executive assistant had buzzed India asking me to come up. No matter that I was in the midst of preparing a brief. This was the Senior Partner, and when he called, you jumped.

I grabbed my jacket off the back of my chair and headed for the elevator, heart thumping in my chest. A thousand thoughts flashed through my mind. What was he going to say to me? A part of me thought that Mr. Lenitz was as fair as they came—and that he would cut through the bureaucracy and bullshit of the firm and vindicate me.

I was a damn good attorney.

I kept my nose clean (for the most part, I told myself), and did what they asked of me.

I billed as many hours as most partners (okay, this was definitely the case *before* they ushered in Bernard John Marshall).

And I was held in high regard by my clients and associates alike (true).

Yet I couldn't shake the brooding feeling that had swept over me. Mr. Lenitz was going to blow me off. He was going to side with the managing partner, and that was that. How could he not do that? And then, what would I do? Move forward with my complaint to the EEOC? And let the chips fall where they may?

I arrived at the top floor and strode with a purposeful step toward his office. His exec assistant eyed me and told me to go on in.

I knocked once and entered.

Mr. Lenitz was already seated in a chair across from his couch. His legs were crossed and he was reading a document. He flung off his bifocals, as he was known for doing and glanced up.

"Do come in, Counselor," he said, gesturing for me to take a seat.

"Thank you, sir," I replied, taking a seat as I unbuttoned my jacket and flattened my tie.

"Trey," he began without preamble, "I've had a chance to investigate your allegations of racial discrimination as outlined in your memorandum," he said, staring directly at me. "I take these allegations extremely seriously, and want you to know that I appreciate you bringing this to my attention."

I nodded. "Yes, sir," I said, urging him to continue.

"I've spoken at length with the managing partner of this firm. I also talked with other partners and associates who are familiar with your work and work environment. Of course, these discussions were conducted in the strictest of confidence, I assure you."

"Okay," I said, and then held my breath.

"Trey, it is my conclusion that there is a lack of evidence of racial discrimination by Mr. Marshall and this firm."

I exhaled slowly, the color draining from my face.

Mr. Lenitz sat forward.

"I will tell you what I see, counselor—we have a new managing partner here. Bernard is damn good at what he does, but his methods may be construed by some as, how should I say this, *different*. Yes, that's a good word. I've spoken with him and with others—we are all in agreement that you are a damn fine attorney. And we don't want to lose you. I will tell you this—Bernard thinks that you're not working up to your potential—that you've," he paused for a brief moment to search for the right words, "you've slacked off a bit—I don't mean to imply that you aren't doing anything. No, that's not true at all. But the Trey Alexander that we've come to know and count on has taken a hiatus...and Bernard is working with you to bring that person back."

I was in a daze. I was having trouble focusing on the words that were being spoken.

"Trey, Bernard can be a bit bullish at times; I'll admit *that* (in confidence to you, of course). He pushes, hard sometimes, and he's pushing *you*. Is it racially motivated? No, not in my opinion. Is he creating a hostile work environment? No, I don't think so. He's attempting to get the best performance from one of our finest attorneys."

He sat back. Paused for a minute to let me take stock of what had been said. Then he leaned forward again and said to me, "Trey, does any of this make sense?"

I nodded slowly, silently.

Mr. Lenitz continued. "You know, Trey, sometimes we need to simply *adjust* the way we interact with our boss—even if the way we've dealt with him or her in the past has worked. I know it's not fair, but Bernard's a different kettle of fish, and it might make things a whole lot easier if you would just approach him differently. He is, I don't have to remind you, your supervisor..."

I took in a deep breath, letting the air swirl around my insides for a moment before exhaling. Lenitz watched me silently.

"Sir," I started and then shut down. There was so much I wanted to say, but suddenly I found that I had no words to say what I was actually feeling. My shoulders hunched. I exhaled again. "Okay," I began, "this is all—I don't know. I need some time to digest all of what you've said."

Mr. Lenitz was nodding as he rose from the chair, signaling that our meeting was over.

"Of course, counselor. Take the time you need. Remember what I've said. You are a damn fine attorney. Do consider changing the way you interact with Bernard. Perhaps then you'll see that he's really out to help, not hinder you, son."

"Okay," I said, rising and quickly turning on my heels so that Mr. Lenitz wouldn't see the redness that had enveloped my face. I was so angry I wanted to kill that fucking guy. Instead I nodded once and exited his office quietly. No sense in making a scene.

Where would that get me?

✖✖✖

Seven-ten p.m. on a Tuesday night at the office, and my freaking head throbbed. I popped two Aleve with water and pushed back from my desk. Behind me the evening sky was subdued. The stars were just beginning to shine. The moon would be rising soon, I knew, bathing the D.C. skyline with light.

What a day, I thought with despair. *When will it end? Will it ever?* Doubtful.

I toyed with the idea of packing up for the night, but lacked the energy to do so. In a minute, I decided, once my head cleared.

For the millionth time, I pondered why I even bothered with this shit anymore. Bernard John Marshall had not let up on me one single iota. I would have thought that my discrimination complaint would have, at the very least, slowed him down a bit. But not that mutha fucka. He was relentless. I think it amused him to think that he was getting to me. For a few days after my meeting with Lenitz I had no idea how to act. So I took some time off—called in sick, which I rarely did. In the end, I went back to work, and filed my fucking complaint. *Take that you pig*, I thought—and waited and waited for the EEOC to get back to me.

I was still waiting…

So what was I still doing here, working late?

Because it was my nature—besides, what else was there for me to do?

I had bills to pay like every other sorry-ass mutha fucka on earth!

Giovanna was busy tonight doing something, which was cool with me. We'd hook up later on this week—I knew that—at this point we were spending like three to four times a week together, which was damn near a record for yours truly. I mean, usually after I hit the punany a time or two, I got bored and moved on. Not so with Giovanna. She kept me occupied. Truth be told—that pussy was damn good! I kid you not! But the other reason was that I simply lacked the energy of my old self—the old Trey was in hibernation for the winter, or that's what it damn near felt like. Vince and Erika weren't around; I wasn't going out much, other than hanging with Giovanna…

I kneaded my temples while I contemplated my situation. I was the kind of guy who was used to staying busy. And, face it, I didn't do well just lounging around the crib, watching cable or waiting for some shit to happen. If I wasn't chasing tang, well then I was working or hanging with my friends—that's the way it had always been. But with my friends out of the picture as of late, well…

A sudden knock at my door burst through my psyche, causing me to flinch.

India had jetted, leaving me to fend for myself.

I glanced up, expecting to see Bernard John Marshall waltz in.

Instead, Layla flowed in, like mercury, and I felt myself wince.

"Hello, Trey."

She wore a to-the-knee, wraparound black and gray dress that tied on her left side. Shiny black knee-high boots. Her overcoat was draped over an arm. Hair worn down long as usual, sexy as all get-up. Her eyes sparkled as she locked her gaze with mine.

I felt myself flush.

"Layla," I responded, my palms reaching for my desktop as my fingers extended outwards. I could feel the perspiration on my skin. It was that quick.

"Been a while, Trey. You're a hard man to track down." Layla took a step forward, flinging down her coat onto my couch. "I hope you don't mind," she mused. I watched her silently, wondering to myself, *mind what? The fact that you're here, or the fact that you're laying down your overcoat…*

I swallowed. "To what do I owe the honor?" I asked.

Layla moved to the head of my desk, her thighs brushing against the polished wood. "Well, I've been reaching out to you for several months now, and you haven't returned any of my phone calls—that's not nice, Trey. So I decided to see if you're okay."

"I'm fine," I said hastily. "And how did you find me anyway? I don't recall providing you with my work address."

"Girl's gotta be resourceful in this day and age," she said, laughing. "Seriously though, Trey, you hurt my feelings by not calling back."

"Sorry, boo—been busy with work and all," I said, arms wide. I stood up, flattened my tie and moved around the table to the couch. I gestured for Layla to sit, and she took one of the upholstered chairs, crossing her legs. The move did not go unnoticed by me. As usual, Layla looked stunning. I controlled my breathing as I looked on nonchalantly. "So," I said, cheerfully, "what's new with you?"

"Missing you." The words emerged from her mouth so gracefully and purposefully that I had the feeling that she had rehearsed it many times.

"I bet," I exclaimed. "Seriously, Layla…"

"I am serious, Trey."

She brushed her hair from one side over to the other, a move so blatantly sexual that I had to laugh.

She continued. "I thought that after the last conversation at bluespace, that we were," and here she paused to find the right words, "vibing, Trey."

I nodded. "Yeah, we had some great conversation…"

"No, it was more than great conversation, Trey, and you know it—what we shared at bluespace…and what we always had was so different than anyone else—and that's what I miss most—what we shared years ago—that bond, that connection that exists between us. That special something that was on a different plane than everyone else. It was like we gelled in ways that most people don't. I know that now. Having had the years between us has given me the clarity to see…"

I held up my hands. "Whoa—Layla—don't you think you should slow down a bit? I mean, we aren't seeing each other *anymore*…"

She smiled. And just like that I felt my insides melt. The girl was good—I had to give her credit.

"Trey, I was hoping that after our last conversation we'd start moving toward something, call it a relationship—I don't mean that in the normal sense of the word—us dating—although you know I'd like nothing else. But I thought we connected that night—I felt it, and I know you did, too. So I was surprised and disappointed when you didn't call me back."

"Layla—as I said, I've been busy."

"Trey, save that shit for your clients. Okay? This is *me* you're talking to. I know you. The Trey I fell in love with made time for the things that mattered to him most. That much hasn't changed; I know that. So do you."

I was for a moment, speechless.

"Trey, I'm not asking for the world—but I want to be your friend. I see you now, and I can tell that you're hurting. Something is not right in your world. You don't have to say it, but it is there—as plain as day on your face."

"What?" I exclaimed, but I could feel the tension rising, blood curdling beneath my skin. The way she saw through my bullshit was uncanny.

"You need me as much as I need you, Trey Alexander. You know this to be the case. So why are you fighting it—why are you running away?"

I stood up, hand to my bald head as I wiped away the sweat. Heading to the window, I glanced outward, my mind racing. Turning back, I faced her again.

"Layla—we've been through this before. Things have changed. I've changed. I'm not the man I used to be. You've changed. You're not…"

I stopped.

Layla glared at me. She rose slowly as I caught my breath.

"Say it, Trey. Let's stop the charades and get to the heart of the matter."

She hadn't moved toward me, but the action of her standing forced me to stay in place. I took a breath and exhaled forcefully.

"I'm not in love with you, Layla. I'm sorry to burst your bubble, but I'm not. I was. Once upon a time. But not now."

Layla waved her hand away.

"Say what you were going to say, Trey. Get it out in the open."

I blinked.

"Let me help you. You're not...what? Go ahead—finish that sentence." Layla's eyes had diminished to mere slits.

I sighed heavily as I stared into her eyes.

"You're not the *woman*..." I said.

A pregnant pause.

Five, maybe ten seconds.

Layla's jaw worked. Otherwise she was still.

Her hands found her thighs.

"Not *the* woman, Trey, or not *a* woman?"

"Layla, please," I said. "Let's not..."

"Why stop now, Trey. Why not say what's been on your mind all these years...it's not like you were man enough to say it to my face back then!"

It felt as if a punch had been lobbed in my direction. I felt the wind drain out of me. I opened my mouth but no words emerged. My hands clenched as I sucked air.

"You don't want to go there," I said, seething.

"Why, what are you afraid of Trey—I mean, shit—why not bust it all out in the open? Now's as good a time as any. I don't have anywhere to go. How about you?"

I sighed again.

"You know what—I'm not playing your game, Layla—not now. So just drop it..."

"No, Trey, I won't drop it—because this is my life we're talking about— you were the only person who ever meant anything to me—and I lost you— and you won't even talk to me now, or look at me the way you used to; forget touching me, God forbid. What did I do that was so wrong, Trey?

Tell me. Was knowing the truth so damn horrid to you, to the point where you would give up everything that we had? That's something I could never understand."

"Yes, Layla—it was," I said, my voice taking on an air of authority. "Forgive me, but I couldn't live with you after that. I couldn't live with…"

Another pregnant pause.

"Say it, Trey. Don't stop now," Layla whispered.

"Fine," I said. My eyes locked onto hers. "A woman who's not a real woman. There, I said it," I yelled, hand going to my bald head again as my eyes blinked. "Happy?"

Layla emitted something resembling a laugh. She moved forward one step as she nodded, out and away from the confines of the low coffee table. I remained where I was, watching her silently.

"Not a real woman," she repeated, placing her hands on the tie by her waist. She stared at me—not threatening or with malice—but those eyes were alive, undulating in their own sea. I couldn't help but remain captivated.

Her fingers worked slowly. I followed them with my gaze, silently holding my breath.

"Am I not a woman, Trey?" Layla asked, tugging gently on the string. The effect was that her dress fell away, halves parted, like two hands moving away, revealing her jewels within.

Layla was naked. She wore no bra—none was needed. Her breasts were laying high just as I had remembered them, lovely orbs of flesh that jiggled as she moved. Nor panties—her crotch was bare save for a thin, dark patch of manicured pubic hair. I could see the lips of her cunt. They were distended and full. I had always marveled at the shape and form of her pussy lips—like the petals of a flower, so lovely, especially when drops of nectar glazed the sides.

My jaw had no choice but to drop.

"What does this look like?" she said, legs parted, holding the folds of her dress open so that I could see. I blinked rapidly, as I felt the stiffness in my suit pants. It was an immediate, automated response.

"For once and for all—answer the question you've been longing to answer—and be truthful, with yourself and with me. Tell me what you see, Trey. Look at me…"

And I did. I took her all in: the soft, curvy lines of her form; smooth, dark skin; the steep rise to her breasts; the scooping fall of her mid-section, the sensuous expanse to her hips; and slender yet strong legs. Nipples reaching out as if yearning for an embrace, and her sex—the core of her very essence—the draw on me overpowering. I could feel my legs going weak. Reaching out to the window for support, I continued to lock my stare on her lovely features, as I remained silent.

"Tell me what you see, Trey? Is this the body of a woman standing before you? Surely it's not that of a man's," she said. "If your eyes are playing tricks on you, come here and touch me. Take a feel. It's okay; I promise I won't bite."

I cleared my throat.

"I can't," I ventured, my whisper barely audible.

"Can't or won't?" Layla responded, moving until a foot of space separated us. I watched her flesh move. It was womanly flesh. Suddenly my entire being ached—feet to temples, spine to fingertips—and I longed to be swallowed up inside of her, tucked away safely where it was always warm.

The recognition of that feeling made me sick.

"I can't," I repeated, and then mumbled meekly, "I'm kind of seeing someone."

Layla's hands were on her hips. Her breasts reached out to me. They were now inches away. The scent of her was wafting over me, bringing me back to a time that I hadn't visited in ages. I closed my eyes, sucked in a quick breath, allowing the vapors to envelop me, consenting to this delicious sensation that swirled about before reopening my eyes to bear witness to Layla gazing upon me.

"Do you love her?" she asked tenderly. I watched her bite her lip, a response she couldn't control.

Another pregnant pause.

"I don't...I've just..." I stopped, seeing that any further effort would be fruitless.

"I'll take that as a 'no.'" She moved closer still. "Sure you don't wanna venture a feel? Just for old time's sake."

I blinked again.

"No, Layla, thanks."

My eyes were locked in a downward stare—catching her breasts, soft curve to her mid-section, and what lay beneath—all in the arc of my vision.

"There's just the simple question left to answer, then. So answer it," she commanded.

I swallowed forcefully and exhaled. I was fully hard now, my erection making no excuses for what it knew to be true.

I was angry with myself.

Irritated for allowing myself to be caught up in her magic. I so wanted to be dispassionate; hard and firm, but not in the sense that comes immediately to mind—I didn't want her to see me in this state. Just as I was contemplating all of this Layla glanced down, focusing her attention on this thing that jutted out at an ungodly angle from my pants.

She smiled, lips parting before coming together again, the flesh upturned as she reached for me. She brushed my erection with the tips of her fingers, and I felt myself implode—a silent explosion, almost coming on the spot.

"You've answered it," she said, "some things don't lie…"

I backed up, instinctively beyond reach, and into the window frame. I needed control. I needed to get out of her space.

Fast.

Layla smiled as she covered herself, the halves of dress fabric crossing over one another until she was no longer bare. Securing her dress, she turned away from me. I watched the swaying of those luscious hips, seducing me with her hypnotic rhythm.

Layla reached for her coat with one hand and headed for the door. Before exiting she turned, glancing over her shoulder at me as she said, "Some things never lie, Trey. He," she said, gesturing with a nod to my rock-hard dick, "knows a real woman when he sees one. The question is, do you????"

Then she left me alone, pondering the question, and all that it entailed…

✖✖✖

For the next several days, two thoughts rented out my psyche—Layla and love…

I can't help it, y'all, but the situation in my office forty-eight hours previously had me thinking about little else.

Layla—coming back into my life, pushing those buttons like only she can…hating myself for even contemplating her in *that* way—I had sworn off her a long time ago—but seeing her like that—exposed and vulnerable, her true beauty revealed—made me ponder some things that I wasn't prepared to deal with.

Layla and I had had our time—we've given it a healthy shot. I was ready to spend the rest of my life with her back then—but that was before she dropped the mother of all bombs on me, and left me changed. Forever.

Or had it?

I no longer could think straight. Nothing made sense to me anymore. I felt as if I was losing ground, slipping into the black abyss of a deep, dark hole, pawing my way to the surface, struggling to breath, straining to get my head above ground.

And then there was the question of love.

Was I in love?

Until Layla had posed the question to me, I hadn't given it a second thought. But after she uttered those words two days ago, I thought about little else.

Was I in love with Giovanna?

And how would I know?

See, this whole love thing was difficult for me. I had been in love before, what seemed like eons ago. Since then, I didn't let myself get attached to anyone. Why should I? I didn't want to run the risk of being hurt again. Besides, most relationships ended in a fucked-up sort of way, with folks yelling and screaming at each other, swearing that the last six or nine months of their lives had been one big fucking waste of time.

So I took a different approach.

Didn't let anyone into my space.

Kept them at a distance.

Romanced them, yes, but with the express purpose of getting them into my bed. Sample their wares and then move on!

Don't stay for a second longer than necessary.

Lest one gets hurt...

...or worse—burnt.

That's my story, y'all, and I'm sticking to it!

But over the past few months, everything seemed to be changing.

Giovanna came into my life—a woman who, for the first time in a long while, was my equal. I found someone whom I could vibe with. Yeah, the sex was the bomb—the best I'd had in a long, long time, but beyond that, I dug her company.

Was that love?

I didn't know.

I used to know.

But not now.

I wrestled with these questions in between meeting with clients, on the commute to and from the office, and at night at home in my crib, the television on but muted, the stereo on, either a Fourplay or a Jeff Lorber CD in the changer, funky jazz permeating the air as I contemplated my life. My *love* life...

If Erika were here, she'd tell me the deal.

Set me straight on this love thang.

I even contemplated picking up the phone and calling her—reached for it several times, but always, always ended up putting the receiver down. No, I couldn't just call Erika up out of the blue to ask her esoteric questions about love. We didn't have it like that anymore...

Talk to Giovanna?

No, she wasn't the kind of girl you had that kind of discussion with. Not yet, anyway.

Perhaps one day soon.

Once I sorted all of this shit out.

And while I attempted to do that, thoughts and images of Layla bubbled to the surface. The yin and yang of what I was feeling tore at my insides, tugging me in opposite directions. That night, seeing her there, laid open like a ripe grapefruit, ready to be taken, was so overpowering that just thinking about her made me hard. But then the opposite feeling would strike at my center—how could I feel the way I did? How could I even contemplate being stimulated by her after what went down?

The whole thing made me sick.

I shook my head morosely as I steered the Escalade onto River Road. It was a Thursday night, 7:30 in the evening and I was on my way to Giovanna's house. I had called first to tell her I was on my way.

She didn't sound overly happy to be receiving me, but I didn't ponder the deeper meaning of that very much.

I had other things on my mind.

I pulled into the driveway and as always when I visited here, marveled at her home and those in the neighborhood.

To call this house a mansion was an understatement.

Her car, a brand-new, jet-black Lexus SC convertible, was in the driveway. I pulled up next to it and got out, leaving my ride unlocked.

Who the fuck was gonna steal my shit in this neighborhood?

I had to ring the doorbell twice before Giovanna opened it.

I stepped back, surprise written all over my grille.

Giovanna wore a short white mini-skirt, matching top, and fuck-me pumps. Her hair was pulled up, done right, sparkling diamond studs in her ears, and face made up *thick*!

Girlfriend was not playing…

"Hey you," I said, reaching for her. I placed my arms around Giovanna's waist and pulled her to me, kissing her deeply on the mouth. She returned my kiss for a quick moment before pulling back and ushering me into the house.

I watched her maneuver down the hallway past dining room and sitting room into an enormous open-air living room. I paused as I always do, glancing left, then right at Vince's collection of masks—four pieces, two on each side, their vibrant colors leaping out from the whitewashed walls. Giovanna's attire, however, made me quickly squash any thoughts of Vince Cannon, Jr., and his artwork.

"Damn, baby—check you out all dressed up," I said, trying to contain the rising tension I felt in my gut. This wasn't home attire, that's for damn sure.

"Hey, yourself," she said, her back to me. I watched her ass flex against the taut fabric of her skirt as hips sashayed back and forth. I found myself growing hard. "Destiny just called," she said, "so I'm heading out with the girls. First nice evening in a long time, so they wanted to do a girls-night-out. Kind of an impromptu thing."

"I hear you," I said, but I didn't.

Joining her in the living room, I took a seat beside her on the sofa. She sat, legs together, hands on her lap, eyeing me closely.

"So," I ventured, looking sheepish, "what time you rolling out?" I asked, flashing one of my famous Trey smiles. I immediately sensed that my presentation was weak. These days I lacked the usual effort.

Giovanna checked her watch.

"Soon. Thirty minutes or so."

I nodded. Moving closer. Took her hand in mine, reaching forward, kissing her on her cheek. Tracing a line of kisses over her lips. Probing between the flesh of her lip gloss-covered mouth with my tongue, slipping it inside, sucking at hers like it was a strawberry, hands on her thighs, moving rapidly upward to her breasts, which I kneaded in my palms. Groaning lightly as I moved closer still, hand dropping to her lap, slipping in between her thighs, parting legs as I raced for that sweet spot.

"Trey, stop…" she whispered, turning her face away and leaning back.

"Why?" I asked, perplexed.

"Because, I can't," she said, removing my hand and fixing her skirt. Hands back on her lap. "Aunt Flo is visiting, that's why—sorry, baby," she added with a shrug.

It took me a second or two to catch on.

"Oh. You know what—I don't care," I said, moving in, reaching for her face and readying to kiss her again. "I need you so badly right now, baby. Just for a few minutes." I paused. "A few seconds," I added with a grin. "Just let me inside you, girl, for a split second—'cause I know it ain't gonna take me long!"

Giovanna gave me a stern look, and then relaxed her expression. She grinned at me and I found her so damn sexy I just had to lean back and drink her all in. *God, she was stunning*, I thought to myself.

"You are beautiful," I said, voicing what was on my mind. "I hope you know just how much you mean to me," I said, taking her hands in mine. Giovanna nodded, but remained silent. She watched me as I spoke, my eyes unwavering as I took in her features. "Truly beautiful," I repeated. Giovanna smiled.

I sucked in a breath while letting my gaze roam over her hard body. My mind was dizzy with thoughts swirling around me, my cock straining against my suit pants, feeling the pulse in my neck thud loudly as my gaze consumed her, Giovanna just sitting there, not moving, but every muscle fiber in her body speaking to me, singing its sensuous song—I wanted her so badly I could barely stand it. But it was more than just sheer physical longing. My eyes quivered along with my heart. So did the rest of my being.

"I think I'm falling in love with you, Giovanna," I heard myself say. Suddenly, it was as if I were a bystander watching the drama unfold from twenty feet away, standing on the other side of the room, staring at us sitting on the couch, holding hands, gazing into each other's eyes, the passion so thick that it was like fog hugging a valley.

The bystander in me observed my breath holding.

Had I just said that?

And where had that come from?

I hadn't fully analyzed my feelings and reached any conclusion yet...

Or had I?

Giovanna was silent for a moment. She rose quietly off the couch, disappearing into the kitchen. I leaned my head back, arms at my sides, eyes closed, mind racing.

Did my feelings jibe with my words?

My head hurt as the silence between us deepened.

Giovanna returned with two wine stems filled with Merlot. I accepted one with a smile and took a sip. She did the same and then put hers down on the coffee table in front of us.

"Trey, we need to talk," she began. I sat up and gave her my full attention, while feeling that my legs were like a rickety house of cards, about to blow over. Giovanna wore a strained expression before she continued. "The last few months have been stressful on you. You've lost good friends, at least in the short term; work's been a bitch—I recognize all of that." She paused to wipe a piece of invisible lint off of her lap. She took in a deep breath as she pondered her next words carefully. "Trey, what drew me to you when we first met was the way in which you carried yourself." Giovanna smiled in remembrance. "So cocky, so full of yourself, as if you were the bomb. Some girls might find that offensive and even a turn-off—but not me—just the opposite. It was an incredible turn-on. To find someone who had the balls to strut about the room as if they were the shit. I so dug that about you."

I nodded solemnly.

"I'll never forget the way you handled my property settlement in New York; the way you spoke with authority; the way you got my husband and his attorney all in a tizzy—you didn't know it, but your performance that day made me so damn wet. I had to run home and take care of business *myself*."

"Dayum," I uttered, eyes wide.

"Yeah, it was like that. That's why you and I clicked, Trey; that's why I gave myself to you that night in New York—'cause you and I were in the same zone—we vibed. We clicked. In case you haven't noticed, I'm a bit of a uppity bitch myself!"

I laughed. She did, too. Then her smile died.

"But over the past months, you've lost that swagger to your step. You're no longer the overconfident, arrogant brutha who turned me on with his in-your-face attitude."

I winced.

"I want—and I need—the old Trey back. I know you're going through a hard time right now. Lord knows, we all have those moments. But I need *that* guy back. Not this one sitting in front of me. You need to get back in the zone, Trey. Need to get back there and join me. Are you feeling me?"

I closed my eyes, and reopened them. Took a sip of wine, a bit too fast, splashing some on my chin. I wiped it away with the back of my hand.

"Yeah, Giovanna," I said cautiously, my brain sending commands to my mouth and face in way too slow motion. "I feel you."

Giovanna stood. Smoothed out her skirt and rubbed her palms together. She stole a glance at her watch and returned her gaze to me.

"Gotta go, baby," she said, softly. "Feel free to stay…"

But when she returned much later on that evening, I had been long gone.

✖✖✖

April's rain came down. Seemingly from out of nowhere, it fell with a vengeance, cleansing everything in its path. I drove around in the Escalade, nowhere to go, not wanting to head home and stare at my walls, wallowing in the self-pity I felt right now. So I drove on. Alone…

Driving cleared my head. The sheer act of steering and focusing on the road kept me from going insane.

Kept me from feeling sorry for myself.

I had made a mistake.

I had come to Giovanna when I was at my lowest, and reached out for her hand.

Bad move.

She wasn't one to help a drowning man…

I think I found that out way too late.

But my words continued to swirl around inside my head.

"I think I'm falling in love with you…"

In love with you.

Giovanna.

My jaws clenched.

I steered my ride up one street and down another, closed-up shops and government buildings flashing by me. The details were lost. I wasn't paying attention.

Once again I found myself longing for close friends. I needed Erika so badly right then. I even contemplated calling her up right that very minute, asking for her forgiveness and womanly advice. After close to fifteen years, she had always seen me through when times were rough.

But this time, picking up the phone to call her was easier said than done. Words had been spoken between us that couldn't be unspoken. And so I stared at my open cell phone in one hand, the blue light of the LCD bathing my forearm with eerie light as I rubbed the polished steel incessantly; snapping the thing shut only to reopen it again a moment later, bluish light returning to comfort me, as a Sting CD played on in the background.

Another thought poked through, but I pushed it back down, safely, for the moment, out of sight.

Across Florida Avenue, then up Georgia heading toward Silver Spring, fast-food restaurants and other establishments passing me by as I drove. My mind on things seven months previous, when life back then was simple and good. A sudden rush of images and emotions: A Caribbean sky—the fiery orange of a Jamaican sky. An enormous hot tub filled to capacity with writhing naked flesh, me in the prime of my existence, flowing from one sensuous encounter to another, dancing in the afterglow of rum-induced passion. Water bubbling underneath our hungered bodies that writhed as we touched, licked, and fed; bodies slicked with water, love juices, and desire as we played under a Jamaican moon; an envious crowd that longed to join in, but didn't dare interrupt this feast. I was the main course. And I had found heaven.

Fast forward in a blinding rush of imagery. Mutha fuckas chanting my name as I made way to center stage. *Trey, Trey, Trey, Trey, Trey, Trey!!!* At that point, everyone knew my name.

Month later, back home—rolling into a club dressed as fly as I don't know what. Women and men whispering as I glide on by. Who the fuck is that, they whisper? Oh, him—I hear he's some power attorney. Nigga is clean; I'll give him that…

And then, like a shockwave, I'm thrust back to the present. Two weeks ago, a Thursday night after work—Giovanna and I had been sitting at some bar, sipping a cocktail. Me harboring a serious case of the after-work blues. Giovanna suddenly rose off the bar stool and headed to the ladies room, exasperation painted on her face. I remember thinking to myself, *this place is close to capacity in here, and less than five percent of the female patronage were eyeing me like usual.* My averages were way the fuck down. It was as if I no longer existed.

It was as if these women could sense my discomfort.

It was as if they saw what Giovanna was seeing—that I was no longer in the zone.

Giovanna, I hated to admit, was right.

That thought weighed heavily on my mind.

Back to the present—tonight—the unfortunate here and now—I contemplated going to a strip club, Club 55, which I'd just passed a moment ago, where I'm sure some chocolate honey would (for the moment) take my heartache away. But the thought was indeed sobering.

I needed a friendly face—not that of a stranger.

The *other* thought—the one that kept popping up, like a piece of driftwood, refusing to become waterlogged and drown—once more revealed itself to me. And whether it was from sheer exhaustion or just finally being worn down, I do not know. But after glancing for the hundredth time at my open cell phone, fondling the plastic insert as if it were woman's flesh, I pressed some keys and waited for the phone to connect.

✖✖✖

"Trey?" her voice asked, rising in warmth and concern simultaneously.

"Yes," I responded, desperately trying to add some timbre to my volume, but simply lacking the energy to do so. "Caller ID's both a godsend and a mutha fucka," I added, my small attempt at humor.

She did not laugh. I stole a glance at the time: 11:40 p.m. It was late. Beyond that—I hadn't dialed her number in *years*...

"Is everything okay? You know I'm delighted to hear from you, but frankly, I'm surprised."

A pregnant pause as I considered how to respond. What to say to her? Open up to her, completely? Tell her what's really on my mind?

In the absence of words, I sighed heavily.

"I know it's late," I began, "but can we meet?" A whistle escaped from my lips. " I need to talk."

She didn't miss a beat.

"Of course, Trey. Where are you?" she asked.

"Driving. Up Georgia toward the Beltway."

"Come here." It wasn't open to debate. She gave me her address. I was approximately thirty minutes out.

"I'll be there in fifteen."

I closed my cell, eyes, for a moment boring into the metal like a laser, before I flipped a U-turn in the middle of the deserted street, and headed south.

On my way to see her.

To see *Layla*…

FORTY-NINE

When Layla met me at the door, she knew I was feeling down.

She could tell that from just my voice alone.

I would have bet anyone a thousand dollars that Layla would have come to the door clad in the latest Victoria's Secret fashion—something downright scandalous, sensuous, and revealing...

Yet she did nothing of the sort.

Layla was wearing flannel pajamas—down to her ankles and covering her forearms. The fit was loose—one could discern her curves, but it was clear that she was wearing these for comfort—and not for turning on a messed-up-in-da-head brutha.

"Hey you," I said sheepishly. Layla reached out and gave me a hug. She kissed my cheek. The warmth of her body felt good, but I pulled back, out of sudden discomfort.

How to act?

It was still unclear to me.

As I walked into her home, Layla took my overcoat and led me into a comfortable living room.

It was after midnight. For all I knew Layla had to get up in the morning for work. I sure as hell had to.

"Let me get you something to drink," Layla said, heading into the kitchen. I sat down on a couch. The television was on, BET on Jazz, concert footage of Sade singing "The Sweetest Taboo." I love Sade—she's one of the finest sisters on the planet, with an oh-so-sweet voice, so I settled back to watch.

"What can I get you? Water, juice, soda, or something stronger?" she asked, her face angling in from the next room.

"Stronger, please," I responded. "Do you have some rum?" I asked, my mind suddenly remembering better times under a Jamaican sky.

"Yeah mon!" she exclaimed, her dancing eyes and winning smile causing me to beam in reply.

Layla returned momentarily with my drink, a tumbler filled with clear ice cubes and dark rum.

"Merci," I replied.

Layla sat next to me as I sampled my drink, closing my eyes, grateful for the liquor that quelled my fears. Layla was relaxed, bare feet tucked underneath her on the couch as she faced me, throw pillow on her lap as she turned up the volume on the TV and began gyrating her upper body to the song.

"I just love this song," she said, and I had to smile at her. For a split second, it was like old times, just her and me, years ago, chilling at her crib, when life was simple back then, not the agonizing constant stress levels of today. I remember that smile—I remember how it used to get to me, make me stop what I was doing and reach for her, regardless of where I was or what I was doing; take her face in my hands, touch her lips tenderly with my fingertips, exploring the surface of her peaks and valleys as if for the very first time before covering her mouth with mine, invading her mouth with my tongue, letting her know just how special she was, just how much she moved me with just a smile.

Her smile.

"Earth to Trey," she said, bringing me back, "quarter for your thoughts." I smiled.

"Inflation," she added.

"Trey?"

"What?" I feigned ignorance before waving my hand at her. Taking a breath, I said, "It's just, I was recalling how we used to chill back in the day, your feet on my lap as we talked about everything under the sun—sometimes until four or five o'clock in the morning!" I emitted a short laugh;

took a sip of my rum before continuing. "Remember that? God—we were silly back then…"

Layla was silent for a moment. She glanced away, her own mind wandering before her gaze returned to me.

"There's nothing silly about being in love, Trey," she said, her voice low.

I nodded once and reached again for the comfort of my drink.

Sade's "No Ordinary Love" had come on. She was singing her heart out to a standing-room-only crowd. Layla gazed at the television for the rest of the song as I sipped my drink, watching closely, too. It wasn't until the crowd erupted in applause that Layla turned back to me and said, "So, Trey, tell me what brings you here?"

Until that moment, I hadn't been sure of what exactly I would say to Layla. Did I feel comfortable enough to fully vent, sharing with her the details of my life? As we sat there, Layla's feet curled up underneath her, clad in her flannel pajamas, I suddenly felt that I could tell her my woes— and that she would not judge me. I needed to speak—I needed to vent. Layla was, for now, all I had…

So I told her. Everything… Starting at the beginning.

Six, seven months ago, when I was on top of the world…when Trey was in the zone.

Taking her all the way up until tonight.

Tonight, only hours earlier, when I professed my love to another woman.

"I think I'm falling in love with you…"

Layla listened and did not judge. For two hours she let me speak. About Giovanna, Erika, Vince, and Bernard John Marshall. About everything that had affected me, causing me to slip out of the zone. Layla asked questions when what I was saying did not make any sense or required further clarification. When I asked for her opinion, she gave it. But mostly she just sat back and listened, pillow comfortably between her legs, nodding in a sympathetic way, urging me to go on, and to not be afraid of my feelings.

Layla refreshed my drink several times. At some point she poured herself a glass of white wine and twirled the stem between slender fingers as she listened to me.

When I was done, it was after 2 a.m.

"I messed up by telling her how I feel," I said, draining the last of my drink, the conclusion that summed up how I felt.

"No, you didn't mess up, Trey. You were vulnerable. You needed to be close to the woman whom you've been intimate with. It's natural to say and feel the way you do."

"Is it?" I asked.

"I'd say so. The question you need to ask yourself honestly is this: Were your words speaking the truth for you? Are you really falling in love with her, of is it something else?"

"Such as?" I inquired.

"Lust, Trey. Don't mistake love for lust."

I pondered her words for a moment.

Layla had something else on her mind, I could tell. I glanced over and nodded for her to continue. She pursed her lips as she twirled the wine stem.

"None of my business, of course, but I think you need to ask yourself if you are comfortable with Giovanna's response, or should I say, lack of response to your feelings. Are you cool with that? And what does that say about the type of person she is?"

"I know," I replied. "She fully admits that she's an 'uppity bitch'—her words, not mine, but your point is valid."

The Sade concert was long over. The television was still on, muted, to an all music video channel—rap and hip-hop videos dominating the late-night hour.

Layla had killed the lights. The window shades were open, and the rain had ceased. Clouds had swept in and back out again, leaving the fullness of the moon to shine down, illuminating the night. Some might say it was a romantic night.

The stereo was on. Playing in the background was a Sade CD—*Love Deluxe*—which Layla had put on because we were both still feeling Sade after the concert. The sounds were inviting, soothing, and comforting. There wasn't much talk between us. It was as if what needed to be said had been said, and dispensed with—we didn't broach the subject that was on both of our minds—when Layla had paid me a visit to my job and bared her all to me.

A woman who is not a real woman...

I was glad that issue remained under glass, out of sight, because I wasn't ready to discuss that just yet.

Things were cool between us—the tension that I had felt previously had evaporated. Just sitting there, next to her, was comforting—the silence was a friend. I remembered that about us—how we could go for hours without a sound between us—me on one end of the couch, her on the other, books or newspapers in hand, but some kind of connection between us—an ankle on the other's thigh, the back of a hand on a neck—something that let us know we were still there.

Not going anywhere.

I glanced at the Breitling, suddenly wincing as if in pain. It was very late. I yawned. Layla yawned back. She rose, left the room for a brief period before returning with a thick blanket, some sheets and a fluffy pillow. I yawned again, wondering how in the hell I'd get up in a few short hours for work.

"Don't even think about leaving," she said, shooing me off the couch so she could make it up into a bed. "It's late and you've had too much to drink— you'll stay here tonight."

I eyed her curiously, but said nothing. Once again, she wasn't open to debate.

"And don't worry, Trey—I pledge not to take advantage of you tonight, so don't worry your little head over it!"

I smiled, grateful for her hospitality.

But a sobering thought lingered.

It was exactly my small head that I was worried about...

✖✖✖

I awoke to the sounds of moaning. They were soft, discreet—the kind of noises that someone didn't want another soul to hear—but that somehow slipped out, while in the fury of passion, escaping like steam from a kettle. I sat up disoriented, cringing as I felt the taut muscles in my neck and back groan.

The sounds were coming from another room. Glancing at my Breitling, I saw it was just shy of 3:30 a.m. I'd been asleep for less than an hour. The lights were extinguished. The shades were drawn, making the room darkened but not pitch-black. I rose, careful to keep my weight from creaking against the hardwood floor.

Again, noises were emitted. They were soft whimpers, almost animal-like in form. Glancing down, I realized I was clad only in my boxer-briefs, black, and form fitting. I stole an opportunity to stretch toward the heavens, hearing my back creak. Suddenly my mind clicked into high gear, as I focused on the sounds and their possible meaning. A tingling sensation grew from my lower body, racing along my spine.

I inched forward, nose up—stopping for a moment as I cocked my head, first left, then right, like a dog sniffing for a scent. I moved on, into the hallway, pausing again to get my bearing. A restroom off to the left. Several bedrooms on the right. I passed one room, door closed. Braked again a foot shy of an open doorframe—the second bedroom. What I heard was a sharp intake of breath. Then a low, exhaling of breath, almost whistle-like. I filled my lungs slowly and silently before stepping forward into the open doorway.

Layla was on the queen-size bed, fully nude, her legs splayed across the mattress. The lights were off, but a lone candle burned on a nightstand to the left of the bed. Her eyes were closed, her fingers poised at the opening to her cunt. Entombed within her was a smooth dildo, white in color. The juxtaposition of those hues—bone white against her chocolate skin was striking—and an immediate turn-on. My heart thumped in my chest. She must have heard it, or sensed me near because Layla opened her eyes, her orbs sparkling as they focused on my darkened form.

The dildo was moving slowly in and out of her, commandeered by slender, dark fingers.

She did not slow her movements on my account. Her stare locked onto mine as her tongue clicked against her teeth. I found that I had to break the stare and glance away—following the movement of her fingers and that white plastic thing that traveled in and out of that tight cavern. Her nipples were distended, and her breasts swollen. A hand reached up to caress them, fingers gliding over darkened areolas before tracing a line back down, dipping into her navel, traversing the thin patch of pubic hair until she met the rising flesh of her clit.

Her fingers alighted from the dildo, leaving it sunken with only several inches showing as she reached for her nipples. For a moment she closed her eyes, pinching them as she gyrated her hips—and my eyes stayed glued to the plastic within her, watching as it moved in step with her—and there was a feeling that overtook me—not only of intense sensual passion and stimulation, but of admiration—for Layla—and the way she was so at peace, with herself and with me—the mere fact that she could pleasure herself, in full view of me, without missing a beat.

My breath was exhaled through dry lips. I had to re-wet them with my tongue.

Layla's eyes reopened. And she smiled.

"You can come in," Layla said, and I crossed the threshold apprehensively, candlelight flickering onto my taut form. Layla's eyes took me in, her gaze sweeping over my body, stopping when she spied my erection that strained against the cotton of my boxer-briefs. A grin transfixed her lips.

I was unsure of what to do next. Part of me wanted to go to her. She looked so…*womanly*…just lying there. The other—was terrified. I assumed that Layla would make a snide remark about my engorged state, but she didn't. Instead, her hand snaked back down to her sex, fingers massaging the cleft to her opening as she gripped the shiny white shaft and rotated it inside of her.

"I'm not trying to seduce you, Trey. So, don't be afraid to come closer." Layla pulled the dildo out excruciatingly slow, until the plastic head breached the lips of her pussy, wiping the glazed tip against her clit and moist thighs before plunging it back inside with a grunt.

"Ooooh, shit!" Layla hissed, eyes closing for a microsecond before training them back on me, her unwavering stare at cock-level.

I advanced slowly into the room, feeling more alive than I had in years. The yin and yang of emotions tugged at my insides—part of me was on fire—to the point where I felt ready to explode. The other—scared beyond words—this being something I had dreamt about—a nightmare that was suddenly coming true. Face-to-face with Layla once again—her secret no longer hidden, but bare and all-telling, as she was now before me.

And yet, as I stood there, toes curling into the thick carpet that for a moment soothed me, I marveled at Layla's dark writhing form before me. And discovered something that I found remarkable.

I had found myself thinking about Giovanna. And how different she was from the person lying before me.

Layla was sexual in a way that defied description.

It was innate for her—it was natural.

I suddenly realized this, and found that incredible.

Giovanna, with her intense physical beauty and desire to be queen-of-the-damned-sex-*bitch*, couldn't hold a candle to Layla in terms of sexual passion.

She just couldn't…

Layla wasn't playing. And she wasn't even trying.

She was just being herself. A woman…

Wasn't she?

I stepped closer to the bed, a calm bathing me like sunlight.

My heart was still thumping, yet I was tranquil inside…

I was thinking about Giovanna.

I think I'm falling in love with you.

That thought seized me as I sat on the bed, feet folding under my knees. Reclining on my left side, I reached for her. Connected with her ankles, sliding a hand up the smooth skin toward a thigh. Stroking the flesh, feeling her undulate, like a sea anemone, candlelight flickering over our bodies.

We were silent.

Words would have been wasted.

On my knees now, hovering above her, glancing downward at all that she revealed.

Her nakedness and her beauty.

Raw sensuality, unparalleled.

I was more scared than I'd been in years.

And yet, I pressed on…

Stroking both thighs, my fingers moved toward her hips, gripping the soft, supple flesh. Remembering with the blow of sudden intensity how good she used to feel.

I think I'm falling in love with you.

Reaching for her navel, ignoring the white protrusion at her cunt, circling the skin with a finger, tracing figure eights before gliding upward, Layla's eyes alternating between closing and opening, watching me fiercely, the passion in her like a storm brewing.

I think I'm falling in love with you.

Reaching for the mounds of flesh that were her breasts, slowly circling the areolas before giving each nipple my direct attention. As I bent forward, Layla tried to anticipate my movement and arch her back, pressing her tits toward me. Instead, I allowed my mouth to simply brush against her warm skin for a moment, my lips skirting the edges of the raised flesh that were her darkened nipples before suddenly racing upward and resting my mouth on hers.

I think I'm falling in love with you.

I kissed Layla, softly and tenderly; the years that had separated us seemed to suddenly contract until it was as if we had never been apart. Layla opened her mouth and gave her tongue to me, each of us exploring the other as if we were strangers. In a way we were.

There was no frenzied activity, no loss of control between us.

We each knew what the other was doing.

Layla was remembering...

Yet, for me, this was a sort of test, I realized all too suddenly. A test of my burgeoning love for Giovanna.

I considered this for a moment as I sucked on Layla's tongue. Pulling back, I gazed longingly at her features as I held her breasts in my hands.

I think I'm falling in love with you.

Snaking a hand downward to her core, I brushed against my own engorged sex-wand as I grasped the end of the white object between quivering fingers. Slowly I yanked the dildo out of her, feeling the strength of her cunt fighting against me to keep the plastic entombed. Rubbing the thing against the folds of her pussy lips, stretching her wide, probing her innards before sending the plastic rocket upward, to the smooth rise to her clit, pressuring the bulb as she swayed beneath me.

I think I'm falling in love with you.

That thought was sobering.

Was I?

For a moment I ceased all movement, contemplating my actions as the white dildo rested against her moistened thigh that quivered to my touch.

I'm think I'm falling in love with Giovanna...

And I'm readying to fuck Layla...

I exhaled forcefully feeling unsure. Layla felt the sudden change in my demeanor. She reached for my face, stroked a cheek with one hand passionately, while reaching for my cock with the other.

I closed my eyes, the yin and yang tormenting me, like a boxer in a lopsided boxing match. Pummeling me with the back and forth banter inside my head.

I think I'm falling in love with you.

And yet, I am here...

Settling against Layla's soft skin, her hands found my ass, gripping me tightly, guiding me as she rotated her hips underneath, her pelvis thrusting against me as my cock screamed against the fabric of my boxer briefs. The head butted against the opening to her cunt, stretching her out, my mouth on Layla's, our tongues now a frenzy of activity, as a single thought coursed through me.

Getting back into the zone.

Getting back into the zone.

That's what it all came down to, I realized suddenly. Getting back into the zone meant getting back to what was real to me.

Feeling like I had before.

Acting the way I used to act.

Becoming the man that I knew I could be.

Again.

I pulled back from Layla, gazing down into her dreamy eyes. She was reaching for my briefs; I felt them slide down my thighs, past my knees and calves. Unencumbered, suddenly free, the passion swelled in me like a monstrous tidal wave, readying to break upon shore.

Getting back into the zone.

Getting back into the zone.

I parted Layla's legs, and with a single arcing motion slid inside of her. She gasped—as I did, too—the feeling so out of this world—her cunt tightening around me, my flesh quivering inside of her as I began to move, rocking with her, holding her forearms as I fucked her, increasing the tempo and pressure of my thrusting, Layla's head thrashing from side to side as my rhythm met hers, my groove meshing with hers. And suddenly, it wasn't about Giovanna anymore. Nor was it about love. Gone were thoughts of Bernard John Marshall, Erika, and Vince. I ceased to care about those irritants that kept me awake at night.

Suddenly everything lifted away and became calm.

Just Layla and me.

I fucked Layla with abandonment. I fucked her good, matching whatever tempo she threw at me, sliding back into the warmth of her caress, as I had years ago, when things were simpler, when I was in love with this woman.

I fucked the woman I used to love, using long full strokes so she could feel my member's entire length and girth, licking the sides of her neck, gripping an earlobe between my teeth, sucking on her nipple, fingering her clit as she moaned and screamed my name, oh yeah, y'all, Trey was back in the saddle, doing his thing, hand gliding over her delicious ass, fingers flicking against her puckered asshole, making her flinch, feeling his woman about to cum, kissing, nibbling, massaging every inch of sweat-induced flesh, gripping her ass, stretching that opening, concentrating on each other's breathing, loving what was building as I pulled her off the bed, raising that ass up as I took her *hard* and fast, not missing a single beat, daring her to cum, again and again, the crazed look in my eyes as I worked it, toes and fingers curling, breathing strained as I took what had always been mine, drawing strength and power from each other's passion reserves, drinking it all in, delicious wine, intoxicating liquor, sweet mind-blowing drugs that felt so damn good, making one cry out, not in pain, but in pleasure, over-whelming intense pleasure, the feeling so overpowering, the emotion so strong, and Layla holding onto me tightly, riding me as a surfer rides a wave, hanging on, letting me do my thing, knowing that we both needed this release, but wanting so badly to fight the feeling, stem the tide, hold it back, yet powerless to do so, therefore welcoming it when it did come, the pressure mounting, the ride accelerating, no stopping this river that raged like a torrent, the floodgates opening until the pleasure was too much, the intensity on way too high, and there was nothing left to do but unleash as I screamed, my juice spraying forth, washing into her, cum spurting deep, insides bathed with my seed as I screamed her name again and again, Layla, Layla, oh fuck me God, Layla…

And her nails bit into my back and ass, a jagged trail of pain as she too unleashed; oh God, Trey, this feels so fucking good…

you got me so fucking tight

this shit is soooooooooooooooooooooooooooooooooooo fucking right

see what love feels like…

Both souls exhaling at the exact same time, gasping for air until our mouths clamped down upon one another, sucking out the screams, silencing our words, her name and mine, slowing our rhythm, chest heaving, hearts trembling, eyelids fluttering, lips shivering, bodies pressed against each other, sweat mingling, oh yes, baby, that shit was good…

you were good

everything I missed in you and more was good

every ounce of strength I mustered, ejected, infused into my baby was so fucking good…

My head resting against the warmth of her neck, kissing the soft spot, licking her earlobe as the frenzy subsided, heart beats returning to normal and I no longer gave a fuck 'cause I can feel you *clearly*…

that shit of yours is good

and I'm babbling baby

'cause I'm feeling no pain

life is about living

and if you ask how I'm livin'

I'm livin' large
everyting irie with me…

'Cause my body is screaming, but not in pain, toes flexing as the tingling ripples through me, lightning striking, from the top of my bald head, to the base of my feet, and baby, I'm singing to you quietly, can you hear me sing, thank you, Lord, 'cause this brutha is back, oh yeah, y'all, this brutha-man is back…

Layla's words stream into my consciousness, yet I'm having trouble focusing, still woozy, still high, from the Hypnotic, but I can hear music, her music, baby girl singing softly in my ear…

I feel you too
withering inside of me
like a flower after a sun-drenched day
ooooooooooooooooh yeah
ahhhhhhhhhhhhhh right there
that's it
that's it right there
no, like that
don't you dare stop
baby, keep it there, right there
let me feel you, just one minute more

Her eyes sparkling, begging, pleading for me to indulge her a moment's breath more, for old time's sake, please Trey, please…

ooooooooooooooooh
ahhhhhhhhhhhhhhhhh
I can feel your heartbeat
baby can you feel mine
your juices move me
your juices flow through me now…

And I can't help but smile 'cause this is livin, y'all, her eyelids brimmed with tears as we nuzzle, both of us crying, carrying on, 'cause this shit here is for real, and she's nodding and knowing, stroking my neck and shoulders as I tremble…

Layla knows

Layla's always known
She can feel me come alive
all over again
still wrapped inside of her
but expanding
filling those sugar walls
until I'm rock-hard again
engorged
ready to roll
slow moving now
but accelerating
increasing the force
and the power
as Layla begs me to take her
all over again
up and away
into the zone
where we used to live
where I can live again
will live again,
her repeating five simple words over and over
like a soundtrack stuck on loop
until everything is all mixed up
all good
just gravy
just soup—
see what love feels like
see what love feels like
see what love feels like
see what love feels like…

✗✗✗

There was a glow to Vince Cannon, Jr.'s face that couldn't be denied. Everyone noticed it—Lisa, the counter girl at Cosi on Capitol Hill, Erika, his parents, and even the folks at Sipp'ss Cafe, the new spot Vince frequented in Fort Washington, Maryland because of the hip atmosphere, eclectic clientele, live jazz, and exceptional service. His neighbors had asked about the new bounce to his step. Vince just smiled as he moseyed on up the street, thinking to himself, if only y'all knew...

Vince's book, *Finding Nirvana*, had been mentioned in *Essence* magazine. With a readership of close to eight-million African-American women and men—suddenly, his book was selling out from stores across the country.

Overnight, Vince was in high demand—his seminars were being sold out in several days. Other publications were also calling looking for interviews. And Vince found himself back on the road, heading to Houston, Dallas/Fort Worth, Chicago, and Cleveland in the space of one month. He had five other cities booked within the next sixty days.

But that wasn't the primary reason why folks noticed a pimp in his step! Nope.

There was a far more important reason...

He reached the Fat Boy, wiped her down before donning his helmet, glasses, and gloves, straddling the seat, and bringing the engine to life. He gunned it enthusiastically before taking off, in a trail of booming thunder.

Vince took his normal route, steering the Fat Boy across the Memorial Bridge, down Constitution Avenue past the State Department, Federal Reserve, White House, and museums, then across Seventh Street to Independence Avenue. He loved riding through D.C. on his bike—and here he was, the dawn of spring shining down upon him, hugging his skin like a warm blanket, the feeling of the open air and wind against his dark skin as he rode—something he always found hard to describe. Up Independence, past the sprawling curves of the brand new National Museum of the American Indian, the newly renovated U.S. Botanical Gardens Conservatory, and the Capitol on the left, speeding by the Library of Congress on the right, loving the Boy as it hummed and groaned beneath him, the Vance & Hines singing their rumbling bass tune in the morning air.

Into Capitol Hill and finally to the place which he continued to frequent several times a week even when it had turned cold outside: Cosi. Vince eyed the Indian motorcycle as he pulled alongside and cut the engine. He felt his chest tightening as he headed for the inside.

When he walked in, Trey was waiting for him.

Vince held out his hand and grinned, but Trey, to his astonishment, pulled him close, giving him a bear hug. They held each other for a moment before they both pulled back, eyeing one another carefully.

"Been a while," Trey began.

"Three months, sixteen days, but who's counting?" Vince quipped.

"Stop your lying! Damn, you haven't changed," Trey replied.

They settled down, Trey on the low couch in back, Vince across from him in a high-back upholstered chair.

"My nigga. How ya livin'?"

"Large and in charge," Vince responded. They both grinned.

Lisa, his favorite barista, brought him a steaming mug of coffee—Vince rose, embraced her, and sent her on her way with a quick peck to her cheek.

"You?" he asked, after stealing a sip from his coffee.

"Can't complain—wouldn't matter if I did!"

They settled back into the awkward silence. For a moment they sipped at their coffees before Trey cleared his throat.

"So, it's been a while…"

Vince nodded but let him continue.

"We haven't talked in a minute, so I wanted to holla at you. You know, make sure you're still living and shit."

Vince nodded again. He wondered if this was Trey's way of apologizing—if so, this was one hell of a way to start.

"Oh, I'm living, Trey. In fact, things with me have been all that!"

"It's like that?"

"Yeah, like that." Vince paused to sip at his coffee. Did he detect a bit of envy coming from his friend/former friend? He couldn't be sure. He pressed on regardless. "*Essence* magazine did a short piece on my book several months back—now bookstores can't keep copies on the shelf!"

"Dayum!"

Vince grinned. "Yeah. And my seminars are selling out. I mean, it's mad crazy—I've done more traveling in the last two months than in the previous year combined. And my schedule for the next four months is packed like sardines!"

"DAYUM!"

"So, life is good. This is what I've been waiting for. It's not Oprah—not yet anyway, but a brutha can bide his time. Girlfriend's gonna be calling any day now—I can feel it!"

"That's deep. I'm proud of you, man. You always was my nigga. My dawg!"

Trey grinned and gave Vince dap. But to Vince, his words seemed hollow, almost out of place. Yeah, Trey was happy for him. But damn it if it didn't appear as if his words were laced with sarcasm. Perhaps it was just Vince walking into this with preconceived notions.

He had gotten the call from Trey several days ago for them to meet. It had come out of the blue—and taken Vince by surprise. His first thought was that Trey was ready to apologize for his actions—*well, it was about damn time*, Vince surmised. But so far, no apology had been forthcoming.

"You look good, dawg," Trey was saying. "Well-rested or something—can't quite put my finger on it—but whatever it is, keep doing what you've been doing, playa!"

Vince laughed as he thought to himself: *Wish I could say the same for you, dawg...*

They drank some more coffee. Vince watched Trey carefully. He was edgy, shifting in his seat, glancing around the Cosi bar as if he were waiting for someone.

"So, what else is new in your world?" Trey asked quickly.

"Well...since you asked..." Vince paused, wondering if he should drop this golden nugget on him. Then he thought, *fuck it, why the hell not? The brutha asked...*

"I'm in love, man," Vince responded, his eyes unwavering as he stared at Trey. "Seriously in love…"

"What???" Trey sat back, putting down his mug of coffee. He seemed genuinely surprised, and perplexed at the sudden turn of events. He'd heard this kind of shit before, but this time, the eyes said it all—Vince was not playing.

"Oh yeah—I'm not even gonna front—this woman's got me hooked, line, and sinker. And I mean hooked for life!"

Trey's eyes narrowed. "WHAT???" His mind was racing.

"Who, Dawg? Who is this mystery woman?"

Vince grinned through perfectly straight white teeth.

"A lovely creature named Amber…"

✖✖✖

Erika was lying in bed when she heard her cell phone ring.

Marcus' bed.

It was late, after 11:30 on a weeknight. She wasn't used to her cell ringing this late—even work rarely called at this hour.

James…

It could only be James.

She shifted onto her side, rubbing against the hard mass of Marcus and his muscular body. He moved in without a sound, pelvis connecting ever so slightly with her ass that was bare. She felt a wave of energy surge through her—that simple action of spooning one another—pelvis to ass, his cock finding the soft crack of her ass, hardening the way it always did when he was within arms length of her, filling, expanding, moving ever so slowly against her caramel skin, heightening the intensity that they undoubtedly both felt, his hot breath on her neck as his hands moved in, wrapping around her thin waist and sliding upward, grasping at her upturned breasts.

She was already wet.

Marcus always did that to her.

And they had made love once already this evening.

But Marcus was insatiable when it came to her. He couldn't have her just once. No, he needed her time and time again.

Like a thirst that soda or juice just couldn't quench.

Erika felt the stirring and longing in Marcus. Heard it in his harried breathing. His frenzied hands. His sensuous yet impatient thrusting. And she gave into him and his carnal desires. Because her needs matched his.

Erika parted her legs, rubbing the head of his cock against her pussy lips and clit, sucking in a breath as she felt him enter her, instantly filling her up, Marcus embedded inside of her, thick stalk in the ground, connecting in a way that she marveled each time because of the intensity, the passion, the *electricity* that they both felt when they were making love this way, raw and primal, but with a tenderness that cut to the bone.

The ringing had ceased.

And then it began again.

And ceased.

Only to begin again.

Erika paid it no mind.

She refused to stop, letting *him* interfere with this thing that she and Marcus shared—for the moment as perfect as perfect could be.

It wasn't until she felt Marcus spasm, cry out, and wash his seed deep inside of her, astonishing herself each time she felt him come, that Erika focused once again on the incessant ringing.

She'd check her phone in a minute.

After the tremors subside...

✖✖✖

"James," she began with quiet diplomacy.

"Erika," he responded with guarded reserve.

"I see you called. Several times," Erika said, and then added, "What's up?"

She could sense the frustration in James' silence. He sighed before speaking.

"I thought you'd want to know that the foundation's making progress on your girl's case."

Erika perked up. She was by the window in the living room, staring out at the skyline. Marcus was in the next room, already asleep.

"Really? Oh wow, James. Tell me!" she exclaimed, trying to contain her enthusiasm.

James smiled. "A great deal of progress, actually." He paused, knowing the silence was killing her. After a few seconds she couldn't take it.

"James, stop fucking with me. Would you please just spill it!" she hissed as she felt Marcus' semen meander down her thigh. She glanced around frantically for a tissue or something to wipe it with—spying nothing, she used her fingers to scoop it up.

"I wish I *was* fucking with you, Erika," James responded morosely. There was a few seconds of dead air between them. "You there?" he asked.

"Yeah, just thinking about what you said," she answered, moving quietly into the kitchen where she reached for some paper towels.

James exhaled again. "Anyway, here's what they've dug up so far—pretty amazing, I think, considering they haven't been on the case that long." Erika could hear some papers ruffling in the background.

"Your friend, Amber, as you know, was born in Houston. Her maternal great-grandmother, Stella, who died a few years ago, raised her. Rich and Andy, who run the foundation, used her as their starting point and worked backwards. They got some information on her estate from county and state records. They were also able to locate a neighbor and friend of Stella's. To make a long story short, they tracked down Stella's daughter, Amber's grandmother, a woman named Lorna. She's still alive and living in Queens, Rockaway, to be exact."

"Wow," Erika said, sitting on the couch as she held a crushed paper towel between her legs.

"Yeah. Lorna was married to a cat named Harold, who is since deceased. Harold and Lorna had an only child, Michelle. Michelle is Amber's mother."

"They were able to gather all of this from records?" Erika asked.

"Yeah, most of it over the Internet, if you can believe that shit! Isn't technology grand?" James mused. "Stella had an executor of her will for the purposes of probate. That person was her daughter, Lorna. All of that is a matter of public record."

"Damn."

"Yeah. Rich and Andy contacted Lorna in New York. She's an old biddy—nasty as all hell—a real bitch, from what they tell me. Didn't want to give them shit about Amber or the identity of the father. What they did find out was that her only daughter, Michelle, died thirteen years ago in a car accident. She was only 23 when she died. Michelle had problems all of her short life. Seems she got into drugs, alcohol, and God knows what else. She acknowledged that Michelle had a daughter, and that Amber was sent to live and be raised by the great-grand mother, Stella."

"Did she say why?" Erika asked.

"Basically she said that Michelle wasn't capable of raising a child that young. She and Harold thought it was best."

"Okay."

"Moving on—we now know Michelle attended high school right there in Rockaway. Beach Channel High School. She was in the class of 1984."

"Wow—so if they know her high school and graduating class, perhaps they can track down some of her friends…"

"Exactly! That's exactly what they did." James chuckled. "Once again technology comes to the rescue."

"What do you mean?"

"Ever heard of Classmates.com?"

"Of course. A website that reconnects students, classmates, and teachers from schools and colleges regardless of when they attended."

"Right. Rich and Andy go online. Put in Beach Channel H.S., class of 1984. Guess what? There's like hundreds of former students that are on Classmates.com for that graduating class alone!"

"You're shitting me?" Erika whispered incredulously.

"I shit you not! So, what is Rich and Andy's next move? They proceed to post a message to the entire class—anyone remembers Michelle? And of course they get like thirty responses back!"

"Oh man."

"Yup." James chuckles again. "You gotta love this shit—I mean, this is coming together like a damn first-rate detective novel. Anyway, they ask some more questions. Anyone remember that Michelle got pregnant?

Anyone know whom she was dating? Of course, at this point they are discreet—dealing one-on-one with some of her closer friends. They find one girl in particular, Soli, who was in her class and lived not too far from Michelle's family. According to Soli, Michelle was dating this guy from another high school. This guy lived in Brooklyn. Also went to school in Brooklyn. Get this—she even recalls the name of the cat's high school: Brooklyn Tech!"

"DAYUM. What's his name? Please tell me you got a name???"

"Hold your horses, Erika," James quipped. "Soli says that Michelle met this dude at an intramural track meet. You see, Michelle was on the track team—ran the relays. So did old boy, but for Tech. Soli says they met when they were both sophomores, which would make them around 15, and that they had a hot and heavy romance. Everyone knew they were dating. Michelle's mother and father were so incredibly strict, that dating in high school was forbidden. But Michelle didn't care. She was smitten with old boy and took the subway practically every day to Brooklyn to be with him after school."

"James—okay, give me the name. Don't play games any further. What's the dude's name?"

James sighed. "Soli doesn't have a name. Or she can't recall it. But—she does know that old dude had a nickname—what Michelle and all of her friends referred to him by. Rich and Andy says that even with a nickname and a positive hit on the high school, it's a matter of days or weeks at the most before they learn the identify of Amber's father."

"And? The suspense, James, is fucking killing me."

"Okay, precious—I've kept you waiting long enough—the dude's nickname is Peacock."

"Peacock?" Erika yells. "What kind of name is that?"

James was laughing now. "Beats the hell out of me! Soli says old boy pranced around back in the day like he was the shit—like he owned the entire school. Can you believe that? Amber's father was a peacock!" James was in stitches. "Peacock…Jesus Christ!" he exclaimed. "Old boy just knew he was the shit!"

FIFTY

Erika was tapping an elderly woman's vein when her co-worker walked in.

"This shouldn't hurt a bit," Erika said to the woman, while sliding the needle under her mottled skin. Setting the I.V., she glanced back at Carmen, who held a bemused look on her face.

"What?" Erika asked as Carmen stood there, arms folded across her chest.

"Nothing. I just want to know what you got?" Carmen said.

"Excuse me?" Erika asked, as the elderly woman's stare panned between them two, trying to figure out what was going on.

"Well, let's see," Carmen said holding up a finger. "You have this very handsome man who just happens to be on Channel Four every single night."

The elderly woman grinned, showing her very stained yellow teeth.

Carmen's second finger came up.

"And you've stolen the fancy of this tall, well-built chocolate doctor *thing* who obviously still makes house calls!"

Erika blushed as the elderly woman let out a cackle, slapping her thin hands together.

"And now, to add insult to injury," Carmen exclaimed, pressing her third finger into the air, "you've got this heavenly, and I do mean *heavenly* man at the front desk, dressed to the nines, holding a bouquet of roses, looking and smelling all good, like one of them delectable Nestle's Crunch bars, and Girl, I swear if you don't get down there within two minutes, I'm gonna head down there myself and take a bite!"

"I know that's right!" the elderly woman yelled, a bit too loud for the small room. Erika glanced rapidly at her watch, and frowned. Close to noon on a Tuesday. She wasn't expecting anyone, she was sure of that. Regardless, she was out the door, and heading for the steps as the laughter of her elderly patient and Carmen echoed in her ears. Just who could it be, Erika wondered?

When she came 'round the corner, clad in her yellow scrubs and tennis sneakers, she came face-to-face with Trey Alexander.

A smirk was painted on his face. As Carmen had accurately reported, Trey was dressed in his usual style: well-tailored, double-breasted suit, power tie, and lace-up shoes buffed to perfection. She ignored the way he smelled: oh so good. Trey was holding a dozen red roses, which he thrust in her direction when she came near.

"I come in peace," he said, one hand to his heart, all loud so that the staff behind the front desk couldn't help but hearing. He then added, "And to fall on my sword if I must—anything, Sassy, to beg your forgiveness and ask for your hand in friendship once again." He ended this with a flourish, raising his free hand to the heavens, as if he were some kind of Shakespearean actor. Every set of eyes was glued to the scene as if this were the daytime soaps.

Erika folded her arms across her chest and shook her head, yet a smile peeked out. After a moment of silence on Trey's part, and a few words of encouragement from behind the desk:

"Get him, girl, go handle yo' business!"

"I'll take him back, shoot! With his fine self?"

"Testify!"

Erika broke into a grin and went to Trey, snatching the flowers from his hand.

"Trying to embarrass me at my job," she said. "That's low, Trey. Even for you."

"Desperate times call for desperate measures…"

"Let's go," she said, pulling on his arm, "before the entire hospital knows my damn business!"

Erika led Trey outside. The morning had given way to a beautiful cloudless day. The temperature hovered in the mid-sixties, and after a long, chilling winter, folks absolutely loved the springtime air.

"Do you have time for me?" Trey asked, once they had cleared the automatic doors.

"Yes, Trey," Erika responded as if she were weary.

There was a park not too far from the hospital. They found a bench underneath a large tree that was already in bloom, white and pink flowers hanging over their heads. A light breeze hung in the air.

"It's been a while," Erika said, once they were seated. "To what do I owe this honor?"

Actually, she had been expecting Trey's call for a few days now. Erika was well aware of the fact that Vince and Trey had gotten together a few days ago. That had gone well, according to Vince. Trey was making an effort to reconnect with those friends he had pushed aside a few months back.

"What can I say, Sassy?" Trey began. "I messed up with you and Vince. And I'm sorry for that. Sorry, especially, for what I said to you. We go back too far for me to be treating you like that."

"I agree."

"Damn. Are you gonna cut this brutha some slack?"

"Maybe. Maybe not! You'll just have to wait and see."

Trey eyed Erika for a moment. She inhaled the fragrance of her roses and smiled.

"These are nice. Thank you for them." Erika leaned over and kissed Trey on the cheek.

Trey's eyes misted up.

"I've missed you, boo," he said quietly.

He blinked away a few tears and used the back of his hand to wipe at one eye. Erika watched him for a moment before nodding and saying: "Me, too, Trey, me too."

They sat for a moment staring out at the expanse of tree and grass. A nice image, especially for a city the scale and like of Washington.

Trey cleared his throat. He stared straight ahead as he spoke.

"Things have been really…" he paused to search for the right word, "*trying* for me over the past few months. A lot of shit that I don't understand, stuff that's not making a whole lot of sense. You know?" he said, glancing over at Erika.

"Yeah, I do," she replied. "Life's like that sometimes, Trey. We can't have blue sky and eighty-degree weather all the time."

Trey nodded, considered her words.

"This thing with Giovanna's gotten complicated," he said.

"I was wondering if you were still seeing her," Erika responded.

"Yeah, but you don't know the half of it. Giovanna's not even the crazy part. You won't believe me if I told you," Trey added.

"Believe what?" Erika asked, turning her body so that she faced him.

Trey swallowed.

"It's Layla," he said.

"Okay," she said, cautiously.

He glanced over at her for a second before sweeping his gaze away. His chest billowed before he shocked her with his quiet words.

"I slept with her," he admitted. When Erika didn't respond, he glanced up and locked his stare onto hers. Neither blinked for a moment.

Erika nodded. Placing her hand on his leg, she squeezed it once before grinning.

"See what happens when you dis your friends and end up alone? You do stupid shit. That's what your monkey-ass gets!"

They shared a chuckle over that one.

"Seriously, Trey, you wanna talk about it?" Erika asked. Her voice lowered. "I mean, this is a subject that we haven't spoken of in like *years*…"

"I know, Sassy," Trey responded, scratching at his bald head. "Lord knows *I* know."

"Okay."

Trey sighed, and brought Erika up-to-date.

"The truth?" he said. "No fronting on this one, Sassy—that evening with her left me feeling incredible, so absolutely wonderful, as if we were the only two people in this whole galaxy. She was digging me and I was digging her, and all the negative energy that had been in my life just got sucked out into the vacuum of outer space, you feel me? All that was left was the two of us and this wonderful, most incredibly erotic sensation, which has stayed with me for *days*…"

Trey sighed again and continued. "Does any of this make sense?"

Erika considered his question and his words.

"Yeah," she said. "You loved Layla once. She loved you. And she still does, trust me on that one. So the two of you got together and shared something intimate and special. Nothing strange or mystical about that."

"But…"

Erika watched Trey. He was sweating, his hand rising to his bald head to wipe away the perspiration that had beaded there.

"But?" she asked gingerly. She knew what came next but was afraid to raise the dead.

Sometimes better to let sleeping dogs lie…

Trey stared at her.

"There's Giovanna smack in the middle of my life, who for the first time in a long while has me feeling stuff I haven't felt in ages. I'm digging her, Sassy; I'm not afraid to admit it. Feeling her for real—she's good people, we have mad fun, one hundred and fifty percent compatible, and the sex is da bomb! But then, out of the blue, Layla waltzes back into my life, and I can't help it if I'm feeling her vibe, too. More than that—the girl's got me thinking about shit that I thought I'd left buried…"

Erika nodded for him to continue.

"And then I go to Layla. Fuck! I mean, how could I do that?" Trey asked. "Knowing what I know. Knowing what she is/was?"

It was Erika's turn to sigh.

"Trey…"

"No, Sassy, what the hell does that make me? A closet homosexual or a no-good faggot? Me, Trey Alexander, sleeping with someone who used to be a fucking dude? A fucking *man*…"

All Trey could do was hang his head low.

Erika waited for the moment to pass. In her usual consoling manner, she reached over and rubbed Trey's back, attempting to soothe him. She moved closer until their knees were touching.

"Trey—why are you doing this to yourself? You put yourself through plenty of pain and anguish when you first learned the truth about Layla. No one should have to endure the pain and suffering you experienced. I don't think you ever fully got over her and what she did to you. So please, Trey, think long and hard about what you're doing this time."

"Sassy, trust me, I know. But I can't help what I felt that night. I wanted her, Sassy. I'm not gonna even front. I knew what I was doing when I went to her that night. I knew that what went down between the two of us was ultimately up to me and me alone—and yet, I still went to her apartment that evening. Knowing what I know. Knowing that Layla was born a man. And what the fuck does that say about what I have with Giovanna? Oh God!" Trey exclaimed, crushing his eyes shut.

Erika held him as he quietly sobbed into her shoulder. She said nothing. Words were not what Trey needed right now.

After a moment, he raised his head, wiping away the tears.

"I'm sorry, boo," he whispered, and attempted a smile.

"For what? Ruining my scrubs?"

Erika grinned and rubbed his shoulder.

"You'll be a'ight," she said.

There was the beginning of a grin.

"Let me ask you a question, Trey?"

He nodded.

"Are you ashamed of what transpired between the two of you?"

He glanced at Erika as if he'd seen a ghost.

"Wouldn't you? If you were a man—sleeping with another man? Men fucking men. Come on, Boo, you know that shit's disgusting."

Erika sucked in a breath.

"Trey, do you remember the conversation we had years ago when you first found out—when Layla told you about her operation? Do you remember what I said to you then?"

Trey was silent, remembering.

Erika continued.

"I said that Layla was no longer a man. Do you remember that?"

"So? What does it matter?" Trey responded.

"It matters a great deal. Why? Because it gets to the heart of the matter. You don't believe that Layla is a woman, and therein lies the conflict within you."

Trey grunted but said nothing.

"Do you?"

"Do I what?"

"What do you think Layla is?"

Trey didn't have to ponder his answer.

"She was born a man," he said. "That's all I need to know."

Erika shook her head.

"I beg to differ. Layla, in my opinion, is one hundred percent woman."

"Please, Sassy, you don't know shit!"

Erika's stare locked onto Trey's.

"Listen to me—when you first told me she revealed her operation to you, I did some digging. I spoke to some folks at the hospital who had experience with this sort of thing. Furthermore I did some research on the Internet. I'll tell you this—actually I tried to tell you back then, but you wouldn't listen—Layla may have been born a man, but when she woke up from that final operation, there was nothing left but all woman. Layla, and there are many others like her, was born a woman inside of a man's body. Surgery can correct those things, thank goodness. And judging from how long you dated Layla, falling in love and loving her the way you did all those years, the surgery went quite well. If you pardon my saying so, it sure as hell fooled you…"

Trey said nothing.

"And after all those years of knowing the truth, you still went back a few nights ago. Why, Trey? That's the question that haunts you. That's what keeps you awake at night."

"Yes," Trey whispered.

"Because your mind is saying one thing that differs considerably from what your heart and your own eyes confirm. That Layla is all woman. She's affected you in a way that defies description. She seduced you, in the same way she did years ago—instead, this time you knew the truth—yet you still went to her. You still made love to her.

"Trey, listen up—you need to accept Layla for what she is: a woman who loves you. And judging from your reaction to everything that's happened, I suspect you still love her, too."

Trey, for a long while, was silent. He pondered Erika's words carefully, staring out at the expanse of blue sky, greenery, and passers-by. Erika let him simmer in the juices of his silence for a moment. She knew that Trey needed to think this through on his own. When he turned to her, their knees once again touching as she raised her gaze to meet his, Trey took in a deep breath and spoke.

"It's all a mess…" he said, hoarsely.

"Doesn't have to be, Trey," Erika responded.

"Really? I don't see it that way. I'm sleeping with a man. Or a woman who used to be a man. Either way, what the fuck does that make me?"

Erika touched his shoulder.

"And where does this leave me and Giovanna? I was really feeling her before I ran into Layla again. Still am…"

Erika avoided his last question. Instead she had a question of her own.

"What constitutes a woman?"

Trey stared at her.

"Is it physical beauty? If so, Layla's got that. I'm a woman, and not ashamed to say that Layla is one of the most beautiful women I've ever met. Not only does she possess outer beauty, Trey, but inner beauty as well—you'll agree that she has one of the sweetest hearts around.

"What constitutes a woman, I ask you? Is it those womanly instincts that set us apart from those horrible creatures we have to share the planet with—men? If so, you have to agree that Layla possesses those in abundance, too.

"What about those other assorted feminine characteristics: compassion, strength, nurturing, sheltering, giving, loving…Layla has all of those and more. She is a woman, Trey. You fell in love with a woman once, and now, years later, you've made love to her once again after being presented with the truth. Why? Because your heart and eyes know what your mind has been struggling to accept. Because you were drawn back into the warmth of that womanly embrace, which once captivated you. She stimulated you then and she does so now."

Trey was silent.

"Close your eyes, Trey—tell me about the night she bared her all to you in your office—what did you see?"

"I'll tell you. Swear to God, Sassy, that night I wanted Layla so bad I could taste it. I had never been more scared of anything in my entire life—and more turned on! Those two emotions—fear and seduction—two opposite ends of the spectrum—were tugging at me like I was a kite on a windy day. And yet, all I could think about when Layla let the folds of her dress hang free, exposing herself to me, allowing me in to stare at her exquisiteness, was this: As I took in the fullness of her, all inviting, drawing me in like some kind of magic spell, I remember thinking: Her entire being is so beautiful and awe-inspiring, it had to be carved from the hand of God..."

His eyes locked onto hers.

"That was the single thread that raced through my consciousness—her entire being was art—that no man could have created that kind of beauty. No matter what my mind told me, no matter what devilish tricks it attempted to play on me, I knew better. I so much wanted what my eyes spoke to be true. Because my own eyes could not lie—Layla was created by the hand of God. Even in the face of what I knew to be the truth..."

Erika nodded solemnly.

"Yes, Trey. You saw a woman who threw herself off a cliff without the benefit of a safety net. You saw in her all of her splendor and rare glory. You saw raw nakedness and striking imperfections spread before you. You were aroused. And finally, when you could stand it no longer, you went to her, and satisfied, what I suspect, was a long-held craving. You took her, all of her womanly virtues, made love to her, in a way that spoke to you, in a way that left the indelible mark of her on you. It's here now, as plain as the nose on your face."

Trey continued to remain silent.

"You made love to a woman. A woman inside and out. Your mind is playing games with you—but you know better, Trey. Hearts don't lie. Neither do these," Erika said, pointing to his eyes.

"Tell your mind to quit its silly games, Trey," Erika exclaimed, taking his hand in hers. "Take control, show your brain who's the boss, and put this thing to bed once and for all. Layla's all woman, Trey. It's perfectly fine to respond the way you do."

Erika loosened her grip.

Trey's gaze swept up past the colorful flowers that hung in the air to the sky that captivated his attention.

"Never be ashamed of love, Trey," Erika added, patting his thigh twice. "Never..."

Trey sighed.

"So where does all of this leave Giovanna? The woman whom I'm falling in love with?" he asked morosely.

Erika waited a half-second before answering.

"I think we *both* know the answer to that one..."

✖✖✖

The next day Erika was back at the hospital racing around florescent-lit corridors in her yellow scrubs and tennis shoes when her pager went off. She swept her gaze down to her hip, reading the number with its 911 suffix, and frowned.

James rarely paged her.

Come to think of it, in the entire time they'd been dating he'd never paged her before.

Erika took the elevator to her station, picked up an available phone and dialed his cell.

James answered on the second ring.

"It's me, what's up?" she asked, heart thumping, wondering what was so pressing that it couldn't wait until after work.

James' response was short and to the point.

"I need you to get to a fax machine. Now. And give me the number!"

Erika's mind raced.

"What? James, what's going…"

"Erika—fax machine. You've got those in the hospital, right?" She glanced around, frantic now.

"Yes…" There was one on the far side of the desk. She moved over, reading the number rapidly into the phone.

"Got it," he replied forcefully. "Stand by."

"James, what is this about?" Erika asked skeptically. "You're scaring me."

"Erika. Are you sitting down? Because if not, you ought to be. Rich and Andy found your man. I'm sending over the identity of Amber's father *now*."

"Oh my God—who is it, James. Just tell me!"

"My fax is on its way. You'll know in a minute. Besides, you know what they say: A picture's worth a thousand words."

The phone went dead. Erika stared at it, frowned and replaced it as the fax machine rang, making a series of shrilling noises. She moved over to it and huddled close by. Thirty seconds later a single page emerged. Erika snatched it from the paper tray, stared at it: a page from a high school yearbook, photograph circled in thick black ink. Name underneath. Nickname underneath that. Her eyes bugged out as her mouth dropped. The fax fluttered to the cold hard floor without a sound.

"Oh my God!" she howled as her hand flew to her trembling mouth; yet no one was there to hear the anguish behind her words…

FIFTY-ONE

I couldn't understand what all the clamor was about? India Jasmine Jackson had text-messaged me on my cell while I was in a meeting with a client—she rarely did that. She could have just interrupted; hell, we were only two floors down in one of the conference rooms, yet she chose to leave me an electronic message.

Because if was personal.

"Erika+Vince Insist U Meet @ Vince Crib 8PM Tonight. 911"

After my meeting I inquired as to what was the emergency.

"Don't know," India informed me. The braids were gone. Instead, she had little twists the color of copper. Actually, they looked quite good. And I told her so!

"Can you get them on the line for me?" I asked, striding into my office. "Either one!" I yelled.

Flinging down my jacket, I checked messages as I waited for India to connect me.

After four minutes, I buzzed her.

"No answer from either one," she informed me.

"Keep trying, please," I issued.

Forty-five minutes later I glanced up from my work, checked the time and buzzed India again.

"Anything?" I asked.

"Not yet. I'll keep trying…"

I whipped out my cell and speed-dialed Vince first, then Erika.

No answer.

"Damn!" I exclaimed. "What gives?"

Then a smile creased my face.

"Ahhh," I said to the empty room. "I bet I know what's going on," I mused. The two of them are planning a bit of a reunion; just the three of us, for old time's sake. I sat back in my chair, swiveled around so I could face the window and stare out at the Capitol.

How long has it been since we've been to bluespace to shoot the shit and enjoy the food?

I didn't even know.

Too long...

Okay, so now I know what the deal is, I told myself.

So relax, and get through the rest of the day.

Which is exactly what I did.

Had another client meeting, finished several briefs, filed a motion with the court, and returned a bunch of phone calls. Billed the hell out of every-one like it was going out of style!

I called Giovanna since I hadn't seen or heard from her in a few days.

The last time we'd spoken was the day after Layla and I had gotten together.

We were supposed to have dinner, but she had called to cancel. Citing not being hungry.

Whatever.

I asked her to swing by instead, but she wasn't feeling that plan either. So, I ended up in her crib, spending twenty minutes in her bed having emotionless sex, you know the kind that is just all right, like when it's all said and done, the shit wasn't even worth the effort of getting dressed and driving the hell over...

Giovanna didn't answer my call now either.

Damn, were the Nextel and AT&T networks down for maintenance today???

I left the office at 7, wanting to stop by a liquor store to pick up a bottle of wine. Didn't want to show up at my reunion empty-handed, ya know?

I arrived promptly at 8. Got out of my car and walked up to ring Vince's doorbell. There was a light breeze in the air. Temp's still on the rise, air still feeling good. Yet something tugged at my insides.

I was still unresolved about being with Layla.

And Giovanna and I seemed to be on the crest of a downturn in our relationship. Lately, I had gotten the distinct feeling that she was losing interest in me.

Didn't know what to do about that.

Getting back into the zone.

Anyway…

The door opened and the first thing I noticed was that Vince's smile was strained.

"How ya livin'?" I asked boisterously, giving him dap.

"Trey, come in," he responded.

I frowned as I entered, antennae going up.

Erika got up from the couch and gave me a hug and a squeeze.

"Brought Kendall's finest," I announced, thrusting the bottle into her hand.

"That was sweet. Thank you, Trey."

Immediately my antennae went on full alert. Something here was definitely wrong. I could feel the tension in the air. One could cut it with a switchblade.

"What up, y'all—India said this was important. Everything okay?" I shot a glance between Erika, who had taken a seat; and Vince, who was standing, hands clasped together in front of him.

I caught the look that the two of them exchanged.

"Seriously, what's up? Erika—your ass pregnant or something?"

"Trey, why don't you have a seat." This came from Vince.

"Okay, dawg. It's your party." I removed my jacket, folded it over the end of the couch, and sat down. Vince took a seat across from me. Erika was to my left. He sighed and began to speak.

"This is kind of serious, Trey. And it's difficult for both of us."

"What's difficult?" I asked, glancing between the two of them.

Erika sucked in a breath.

"Trey—you went to Brooklyn Tech, didn't you?"

I stared at Erika hard.

"As in the high school? Yeah. What of it?"

"You dated a girl named Michelle who ran track for Beach Channel?"

I glared at Vince for a moment, turned my attention to Erika giving her two seconds of my ocular wrath before glancing back at Vince again. Unexpectedly I felt the muscles in my neck constrict. I was suddenly extremely thirsty, as if my entire throat was being baked over an open flame.

"Can a brutha get something to drink?" I asked, grasping my throat with both hands in mock strangulation.

"Of course, my bad," Vince replied, rising to pour me a glass of something. "Corona do?"

"Yeah."

I pivoted toward Erika who remained seated, hands clasped in her lap. She wore a disturbing scowl on her face. I smiled, attempting to hide the rising tide I felt in my gut.

My Lord…

I hadn't thought about Michelle in close to twenty fucking years…

Erika's expression remained fixed.

"Michelle," she repeated, as if I hadn't heard her the first time. Vince returned with a cold Corona topped off with a sliver of lime. I took my time twisting the lime into the bottle, tipping it over, thumb covering the hole before righting it, and taking a sip. I swallowed several healthy swigs.

"What is this about, Erika? Vince?" I asked, putting the cold beer between my legs.

Vince returned to his seat.

"You dated a girl named Michelle in high school." It was a statement, not a question.

"Perhaps. Perhaps not," I replied in a cavalier tone. "I dated a lot of honeys in high school. That was over twenty years ago. You expect me to remember the name of each one?"

I swung my glare over to Erika whose stare locked onto mine.

"Only the ones you got pregnant," she replied softly.

Immediately I took a swig of my beer and placed it on the coffee table in front of me. I said to no one in particular, "This *bullshit* inquisition is coming to an end right the fuck now." I did not yell, but there was sufficient depth to my voice to let everyone in the room know that I was to be taken seriously.

Neither Erika nor Vince said a word.

"Anybody gonna tell me why the fuck y'all are up in my business?"

Still they were silent.

"Fine." I stood, grabbed my suit jacket and flung it over my shoulder. "Nice party, Vince. See ya!" I said, strolling for the door.

Reaching for the handle, I heard Erika clear her throat and say: "Peacock. They called you Peacock, Trey, didn't they? Says right here."

I froze. Spun around on my heels and glared at her. Crossed the room to where she sat and snatched up the paper that was being held gingerly between her fingers. I bore my laser stare into it, a faxed page from my high school yearbook. The picture was twenty plus years old. Me with my foot-high fro! Trey Alexander. Nickname "Peacock."

My expression glowered.

"Hmmn, let's see," I said, holding the paper at arm's length. "Says here 'track team, chess club, astronomy club, debate team. Nickname Peacock. Voted most likely to sue a non-profit organization or government agency!'" I threw up my hands in mock surrender. "You got me, dawg—I can't deny this shit!"

I tossed the paper aside.

"This is bullshit!" I hollered and headed toward the front door.

"You dated Michelle when you were a sophomore," Erika began. "She got pregnant by you in the winter of 1981. She had a child, a girl…"

I spun around.

"YOU DON'T KNOW WHAT THE FUCK YOU'RE TALKING ABOUT!" I yelled, no longer able to contain the anguish. "Just who the fuck do you think you are—bringing me here for what? Depose me like a fucking criminal. I don't think so!"

My hand went to the knob.

"For the record, and since you've done a shitty job of fact-finding," and here I spun and glared at Vince for a moment, "both of you suck at this— I'll set the record straight.

"One—Michelle and I did in fact date, not that it's any of your fucking business.

"Two—she did in fact get pregnant, but her parents found out, and forced her to have an abortion.

"Three—once she aborted the child, and it is a *fact* that she in fact aborted said child—she remained in Texas for six months or whatever, finally returning to New York to move on with her life. There was no baby—no child—no little girl. You are mis-*fucking* informed!"

Erika stood as I snatched the door open and strolled outside. She once again cleared her throat.

"I'm sorry, Trey," she said softly, but with enough conviction that I had zero trouble hearing her clearly. "It is you who is misinformed. Michelle did have the baby. Her great-grandmother raised the child. She's all grown up now. And she's *your* daughter."

I stopped in mid-stride and turned around slowly as I shook my head so rapidly I became faint.

"No, no, no, no, NO. You're wrong."

Erika moved to the door.

"I'm sorry, Trey, but I'm right. You have a daughter; her name is Amber."

That froze me in my tracks. I glared at her for what seemed like ten minutes. Seconds flew by before I began to grin. Leaning to the side, I caught the stare of Vince who stood behind Erika in the front door.

"Oh, I get it now," I said slowly, nodding my head. "Amber—the one you're dating, right, Vince?"

Vince swallowed hard and nodded.

"That's right, Trey."

"I see…" I said, but I didn't.

Suddenly the ground felt as if it were moving under my feet. I felt myself sliding and reached out to the doorframe for support.

"So, that's what this is all about!" I snapped. "I fucked your woman, so you're gonna fuck my little girl, is that it?"

Vince was shaking his head, "No, Trey—it's not…"

"FUCK YOU!" I screamed so loud I'm sure the entire block heard me. "Y'ALL DON'T KNOW JACK!"

✖✖✖

Driving straight over to Giovanna's, on my cell the entire time, relentlessly hitting redial, not taking no answer for an answer until I steered the M3 next to her Lexus, and braked to a halt, hard.

I was furious.

I knew Giovanna was home. Her car in the driveway told me that.

She wasn't taking my calls.

I had left her a message, saying it was an emergency.

Then another one.

And another one after that...

Pick up, Giovanna, pick up now!!!

Yet, she refused to answer my pleas.

Exiting the car, I hit the steps two at a time until I was banging on the door, ignoring the ruckus I was creating. After a minute and a half I began to yell.

"Giovanna, I know you are in there. OPEN THE DOOR. Giovanna. OPEN THE FUCKING DOOR."

A family of four was walking by, their toddlers on bright Big Wheels. I paid them no mind, using the heel of my palm to crash against the stained wood.

Giovanna opened the door and ushered me inside.

"Just what the fuck is wrong with you, Trey? Jesus..."

I pushed past her, ignoring the artwork on the walls courtesy of Vince Cannon, Jr., and went to the bar, pouring myself a stiff drink.

Three-quarters rum. One-quarter ice.

Giovanna followed me into the room, the smoke coming off her head in waves. She was pissed.

No doubt.

I could give a fuck.

"What's gotten into you?" Giovanna cried, hand in my face as I downed my drink in several gulps. "Are you wigging out, Trey? Where do you get off coming over here..."

I had poured myself a second and was exiting the room when she paused in mid-sentence.

"Hey—where the fuck do you think you're going?" Giovanna yelled.

"Hey—I'm talking to you!"

Taking the stairs, two at a time, I hit the top-floor landing and turned to the right into the master bedroom before Giovanna could figure out what was going on.

I strolled in, taking in the clothes that were strewn over her bed—outfits, undergarments, at least four sets of bikinis—not that I was counting.

She pushed me aside as I stood there in disbelief.

"Get the fuck out!" she cried.

"Going somewhere?" I asked slowly, my stare panning over the disarray. I spied travel documents on the bedside table. She followed my stare but I was too quick—scooping up the tickets before she had even moved a muscle.

Placing my back to her, discounting the pummel of fists to my kidneys, I examined them.

Two airline tickets.

Destination—Hawaii.

Her name and her travel companion.

David Morrison.

Departure: Tomorrow morning.

I placed the tickets back where I found them and turned around. Giovanna instinctively jumped back.

"How nice," I uttered.

"It's not what you think," she muttered.

I headed for the open door. Stopped. Spun around. Glared at her.

"All I wanted was for you to support me during my down time. Was that too much to ask?" I said in disbelief.

Giovanna's hand was at her breast.

"Oh please. Spare me the performance. We aren't having a relationship, Counselor. We're fuck buddies. What part of *that* didn't you understand?"

I had to laugh.

"And David what's his name? Is he a fuck buddy, too?" I exclaimed.

Giovanna didn't miss a beat.

"No, Trey—he's just a friend."

I stood their shaking my head.

After everything I'd gone through: losing my mentor and my friends, my roller-coaster ride at my job, Bernard John Marshall, telling Giovanna I was falling for her, making love to Layla, reconnecting with Vince and Erika only to find out they were backstabbing me, and the latest—that single nugget of critical information that caused my heart to go into palpitations every few moments now—learning the truth about Michelle and our *daughter*—this is what it all came down to.

Fuck buddies.

Fuck buddies.

"I came here to tell you about my daughter, Giovanna," I whispered, trying to contain the rising anger that threatened to spark out of control. "Because I'm scared. And because I have nowhere else to go."

A single tear meandered down my cheek. I quickly wiped it away with my wrist.

"But that's okay. You go on. You and your *friend* have a wonderful trip. Don't worry about me, baby. I'll deal with this shit on my own. 'Cause I'm a trooper, Giovanna. I'll find my way back into the zone. On my own…"

Fuck buddies.

I laughed again as I descended the stairs.

The sad part was that Giovanna let me go.

And why wouldn't she?

After all, that's all I was to her, these past few months. A fuck buddy.

Nothing more.

I exited the house, got into my car, and drove away, heading to the only place I had left.

To the only one who would have me…

FIFTY-TWO

James and Erika sat facing each other, a bottle of just-opened Merlot between them. The restaurant was Tony and Joe's, a seafood place located in Georgetown Harbour facing the water. They had a cozy table by the window, nice view and quiet, away from the din of other patrons.

They picked at their appetizer: lightly fried calamari.

Three days had passed since the time Erika and Vince had "broken" the news to Trey, and neither had heard a peep from him. Their calls had gone unanswered.

Erika was worried, but there wasn't much else she could do.

Vince felt bad also, but he, too, was powerless to intervene until Trey came around.

"I can't say I blame the man," James was saying as he squeezed fresh lemon onto the plate of calamari. Erika stared at him. "I mean, come on, I don't like old dude, you know that, but I can't help but feeling sorry for him. You dropped this on him kind of suddenly. Think about it—you've been proceeding along with your life for the past twenty years and then one day you wake up to find you have a grown-up child!"

Erika nodded.

"Yeah, but why take it out on us. We didn't do anything."

James smiled.

"'Cause you're the messenger. In time he'll come around. He's confused right now. He needs time to sort this out—what it means, having an adult-aged daughter in his life, and worse, having his best friend dating her. Ouch! I feel sorry for the man!"

Their food arrived. James had the grilled swordfish, while Erika tried the pan-seared crabcakes. For the first few minutes, they ate their food in silence.

James broke the silence first.

"It's good to see you, Erika. It's been a minute since we've gotten together."

Erika glanced up.

"I know, James. Work and stuff. You know how it is."

He did.

"But we're here now," she added earnestly.

"That we are—I'm happy for that." He patted her arm and Erika enjoyed the sensation.

She had genuinely missed James. Their respective schedules had them both hopping. Plus, she'd been spending more time with Marcus lately— something she felt quite guilty about—but not enough to stop seeing him.

That was one of the reasons why she was here tonight with James.

Erika stared across the table at her date and once again felt the anguish flood her insides. *I'm so confused*, she thought.

Sitting right across from her was a wonderful man: intelligent, confident, and good looking. Great job, stable, and let's not forget wonderful lover. Most women would give their right ovary for a man like James. And yet, Erika felt unfulfilled by their relationship.

And then there was Marcus—tall, muscular, handsome, a woman's true fantasy. A wonderful lover in ways that defied description. Also intelligent, confident, with a great job, and stable (well, that remained to be seen.)

So what was the problem? Most women struggled to find and keep one man, let alone two. Here she was, nitpicking over *two* men and their some-times seemingly inconsequential issues.

Still, she couldn't help feeling the way she did.

Erika was never one to just brush aside her emotions.

An intense shoot-from-the-hip kind of gal, Erika had always trusted her instincts—and for the most part, they hadn't steered her wrong yet.

So what did her instincts tell her about James? And Marcus?

That was the part she was unsure about...

James' fingers were lightly tracing figure-eights on the back of her hand, following the path of opaque veins that glided beneath the skin.

Erika watched him silently, feeling the tickles transmit pulses of minute pleasure bombs that were discreetly going off inside her. She crossed and uncrossed her legs absentmindedly.

"Erika, there's a party tonight north of Baltimore that I'd really like to check out." He glanced up, his eyes meeting hers.

"Where? What kind of party is it?" she asked. "I'm not really dressed for a party, James."

He smiled.

"Sure you are. It's not that far from the Inner Harbor. And it's a party thrown by some friends of mine."

James could read the indecision on her forehead.

"It's a *fetish* ball, Erika," he added. James let the words sink in before venturing forward.

Erika had been poised to fork a piece of crabcake into her mouth. When she heard the word "fetish" her hand froze, stopping all action in mid-stream.

"WHAT?" she exclaimed.

James glanced around.

"Erika, keep it down."

"James—please tell me this is a joke."

James sighed.

"No joke, Erika. What's the big deal? It's a fetish ball, where some folks get dressed up in various outfits. Some go to check out the toys. Others go to just watch. Regardless, it's harmless fun for consenting adults. It's something I've been meaning to check out for some time, if you don't mind. We wouldn't have to stay long."

"Let me get this straight. You want to take *me* to a fetish party? James, you know I'm not into that shit. Come on, what am I supposed to do while a bunch of S&M-loving freaks get it on. Are there going to be swingers there?"

"I don't know. There probably will be some, but that's not why we're going."

"Jesus!" Erika said, exhaling loudly.

"You know what, Erika? Forget it!" He sipped his wine and then added, "I really don't understand you!"

"What do you mean?"

"This," he exclaimed, holding up his hands. "For the entire time we've been dating we've been doing what you want to do—I'm always the one who compromises. I'm always the one who seems to be adjusting this or that in order to make sure you are happy. I'm not complaining, but I thought relationships were about compromises—on both sides. Therefore, is it asking too much for you to bend and do what I want? Just this once, can you indulge me, instead of the other way around?"

Erika opened her mouth to spew a retort, but quickly shut down.

James, she mused, was right.

"Okay James. Tell me this—how am I supposed to act at one of these things? It's not as if I'm an expert in this kind of activity. I don't practice this stuff every day!"

"Erika," James said, smiling, seeing he had won some ground, "it's okay. Just be yourself. No one's going to force you to do anything you don't want to do. Just come with me and keep an open mind. Okay? Maybe, just maybe you'll actually have a good time. And maybe, you'll get turned onto something that you've never even dreamt of before…"

Doubtful, Erika thought, but kept her comments to herself…

✗✗✗

It wasn't forty minutes. It was more like an hour forty. Or that's what it seemed like to Erika. When they arrived at the party, she was ready to exit the car and go anywhere—just not a fetish ball.

They found themselves in some kind of warehouse district. Lots of huge windowless buildings out in the middle of nowhere, low lighting, trash strewn about the sidewalk, the smell of piss suspended in the air. A lot of cars parked on both sides of the wide street, which was a good sign.

But that didn't change the way Erika felt.

They entered the non-descript building on the first floor, paid the cover and were immediately assaulted by the heavy bass of house music. An enormous dance floor was littered with partygoers—most dressed in various stages of undress or leather, others completely nude or adorned only with body paint. Erika held her tongue as she followed James to one of a half-dozen bars edging the dance floor. She spied a tall Amazonian black woman with flaming red hair down to her ass dancing in front of two men with dog collars—and she was holding both leashes; women wearing leather lace-up corsets skirted against others in baby-doll outfits; a few pre-op transsexuals wearing PVC dresses or short skirts; men wearing only thongs and pouches, rubber vests; and the list went on and on…

Erika pulled at her Corona as they took the wide metal stairs to the second floor. Mid-center on a raised platform there was an auction taking place.

A human auction.

Both scantily clad men and women, black folks along with whites, Erika noted, were being auctioned off to the highest bidder. Audience participants were huddled close to the stage, holding up their hand when they wanted to bid on human flesh.

Erika was shocked to see a throng of black people standing by the front row, hands constantly erupting into the air as if they were at a rap concert.

James stopped to make introductions to several people and a few couples. Erika smiled automatically and shook a few hands—feeling out of place in her non-descript black dress and knee-high boots. James had chosen a pair of black leather pants and a tight sweater for this evening's activities. Now Erika understood why he had dressed the way he did.

Moving onward, they passed what could only be described as a field of pup tents—over two dozen set on this plot of warehouse floor half the size of a football field. James maneuvered past them like a serpent, while Erika to her chagrin noticed that there were couples inside, having sex. Voyeurs stood outside the tent flaps, their mouths agape as they watched the various love scenes unfold. Some of the inhabitants chose to close their tents in order to make their copulating private—or as private as one could get here, in the midst of this tent forest, while the pulsating sound of techno invaded every space.

James led Erika to the third floor. Thankfully, it was quieter here. A few couples were paired off in dimly lit areas with curved walls, showcasing their talents. A small crowd had formed in front of a pair of performers, watching in silence as the man fitted his woman with a leather hood, restrained her hands and feet with gleaming handcuffs, and then proceeded to flog her with a leather-studded paddle. A second performer twenty yards away was demonstrating the proper use and fit of cock rings, aided by his large-breasted assistant who jerked him incessantly, a thick tube of KY Jelly in her left hand. James didn't seem to show much interest in these kinds of activities, so they moved onwards. Further ahead was an Indian or Pakistani vendor selling adult movies in VHS and DVD formats. An entire wall of products, Erika observed. James perused the selection while Erika hung back, nursing her Corona, other folks wandering by, attempting to catch her eye, especially the women. Thankfully, they moved on when Erika didn't acknowledge a single solitary one.

Off in the distance, Erika spied what appeared to be a mock jail cell. She whispered to James that she'd return in a minute. Walking off, moving closer, she noticed the twenty-foot square cell situated against one wall of red brick. The bars appeared to be made of steel and ran about eight feet in height. Inside, sitting on a lone wooden bench by himself was a muscle-bound black man. He was as dark as midnight, smooth black skin that reflected not a wink of light. He was fully nude, sitting there in his lone cell, a single naked light bulb hanging over him, light cascading down like an invigorating shower, highlighting his long black cock that he held between thick fingers.

Erika moved to within spitting distance of the cell door, acknowledging the thick metal padlock on the outside, and paused as they made eye contact. He was stroking himself, and when he spied Erika he neither smiled nor changed his expression. Nor did he miss a single stroke. The only subtle change was the increased pressure of his hand around his dick, and the change in tempo.

She swore she sensed him beginning to move faster.

Erika continued to watch him, taking slow swigs of her Corona as he masturbated for her. After several moments he was fully hard and over eleven inches in length. Erika was enthralled. She watched his eyes for a moment that were locked onto hers. They were sad eyes. Erika felt sorry for him. Yet she couldn't pull herself away.

Erika felt a tug at her side, turned to see James in her space, watching her silently. He gestured for them to go, but she shook her head. She returned her gaze to the man who tipped his head up to the light bulb for a moment, eyes squinting before settling back on Erika.

James, she could tell, was bored. He shifted on his heels, but Erika was determined to see this through...to completion.

And she did.

When the black man came, he groaned, spurting his hot liquid onto his smooth dark stomach. Erika watched with a detached sort of fascination—the act didn't turn her on, not exactly, but she knew that she was instrumental in helping him get off. And that brought a wave of satisfaction to her.

With his hand in the small of her back, exerting an increasing amount of pressure, James moved Erika along. They passed another bar against a wall, tended by a thin Asian woman with the largest set of fake tits she'd ever seen. Cold Coronas in hand, they moved off toward the opposite end of the floor.

And came to an area made up of large drab green army tents.

Tent city.

Each tent was the size of a small room, and they were placed together in rows, with little more than a foot or two between them. James led Erika over to one, pushed open the flap—empty; moved on between a row of tents to a second row standing in the shadows of the first—they stopped in front of another, hauling back the flap—spied a white woman in a Super Girl costume astride a nude black man on an army cot.

He was facing away from her, ass up, his face buried in a thick white pillow. She wore a strap on, and was thrusting the thing into his behind.

Immediately Erika could feel James tense up. He dropped her hand that he had been holding and sucked in a breath.

This is what he had been after.

The woman's face turned while in mid-stroke, and a smile formed on her lips; she mouthed something to James and he nodded once, then took Erika's hand and retreated quietly.

Erika stood outside the tent, wide-eyed.

"I've seen enough, James. I want to go home."

James had a glazed look in his eyes. Erika had seen that look before. Once before.

"Not yet, Erika. Just a few minutes more..." he said, almost groggily.

Erika stood, arms folded as she eyed him.

"Just what's going on, James?"

"I want you to meet someone..."

The rest of his sentence was cut off by the high-pitched scream coming from inside the tent.

Erika noted with certainty that it had emanated from the male. She took a long swig from her beer, glanced at the empty bottle as if she'd just witnessed a carjacking and said, "I think I need another."

Walking away, leaving James in front of the drab green tent alone, she wondered just what had possessed her to come. She knew she was trying to compromise, but this shit took the cake. There wasn't a single individual inside here that turned her on—okay, that wasn't exactly true—there were a few nice-looking bruthas she'd eyed downstairs on the dance floor, but they had their sights set on other dudes!

What a waste!

She found the Asian chick with the big tits a moment later, paid for a fresh Corona and leaned against the bar as she pondered her next move. She couldn't very well leave. She had come with James. It was his car that was parked outside. Hell, she had no idea where she was; let alone how to get home. A burning anger rose inside of her. Would Marcus put her in this kind of position?

Absolutely not...

She turned back to the bartender, eyed her silently, pondering if making small talk was a smart move, then thought better of it.

Bet she's a dyke, Erika mused.

On the other hand, I'm not feeling that vibe.

She spun around.

"Some freaky shit up in here," Erika barked, attempting to break the ice.

"Yes and no," the bartender answered, reaching for her water with a lipstick-painted straw, "depends on the kind of shit you're into."

Erika grinned.

"I guess. But what happened to straight sex, no onlookers, just you and your man?"

"Or your woman…" the Asian added with a grin, "not that I'm down like that, just so you know…"

"Na," Erika exclaimed, "never crossed my mind!"

"Yeah right!"

They made small talk for ten minutes. Erika finished her beer and ordered another. Instead the Asian offered to make her a specialty drink, on the house.

The chick was bored.

So Erika got something called a Hummingbird, which turned out to be one fine-tasting beverage.

They conversed for a few moments more before Erika slapped a ten on the bar and said she had to go find her man.

"God knows what trouble he's getting into," she said with a wink.

The bartender pocketed the tip, thanked Erika, and told her it was probably way too late for that.

Erika headed back to tent city, thinking, *I'm gonna find my freaky-ass man and haul his high-yellow ass home! That's what I'm gonna do!*

She came to the first set of tents and maneuvered her way over to the second row where she had left James. The particular tent where they had stopped before was closed. Erika reached for the flap and pulled. What she saw caused her to almost faint.

James was on the cot, face up, and naked. He was holding his knees in his hands. The woman in the Super Girl outfit was sitting on the floor behind the cot, facing Erika. In her latex glove-covered hand she grasped a slender dildo. The dildo was half embedded in his ass. James' eyes were closed. When the woman paused her tender thrusting, James opened his eyes and turned, seeing Erika. The woman beckoned for her to enter. Yet she just stood there, unable to breathe or move a muscle.

"It's okay, honey," the woman offered softly in her down-home Southern drawl that made Erika's skin raise. "He's been waiting for you." The woman gestured for Erika to move forward, and Erika felt her feet move slightly. Suddenly she found herself sucked inside the tent, flap caressing her back, standing less than ten feet from the prone form of James, her boyfriend and local television anchorman, and this stranger, with a dildo stuck up his ass. She glanced down. That's when she noted that James was fully hard. In fact, she had never seen him harder. His cock seemed to be expanding as she stared at it.

An optical illusion she hoped, but the effect did little to settle her almost burnt nerves.

The woman's hand returned to the dildo, pressing it forward. James grimaced for a moment; head coming forward in an automatic reaction before settling back and closing his eyes with a sigh.

"Come forward," the woman intoned, eyeing Erika, "help him get off."

The woman jutted her chin toward his hardened cock.

Erika shook her head imperceptibly.

The woman gestured her chin toward his belly again.

Erika stood her ground.

The woman shrugged. Reached for James with one hand, the other holding the dildo, rotating it clockwise, then counter, tugging on it gently until several inches emerged before plunging it back inside with fury. Wrapping her fingers around his member's girth, she proceed to commence jerking him off, slowly at first, then with an increased tempo, her two hands operating independently in the beginning before finding their groove, a rhythm, becoming coordinated and synchronized, a symphony of erotica.

Erika was too far-gone to notice.

She stared at the scene unfolding before her, feeling her heart race. At this point she wasn't really seeing…

Hands and knees began to move in a flurry of activity, James' caramel skin and the woman's white hands, the vibrant blue and red of her Super Girl's suit, tits jiggling in the tight top as James' chest heaved while he moaned, pressure and intensity increasing until he cried out, sputtering like a car running out of gas, the woman ceasing her movements, opening her hand, latex covered palm up toward the ceiling, like in offering, his cock spasming against her warm flesh as he came, hot liquid shooting onto smooth dark skin.

It took several more minutes for James to complete and wind down, painful, agonizing minutes as Erika clutched her dress, listening to his rapid breathing and decelerating moans, watching his toes twitch like a chicken without a head, dead and unknowing, still believing there's a bit of life left. Finally, James came to a rest, opened his eyes, turned toward Erika and presented her with a satisfied smile.

Erika could only watch on in horror, realizing in that second with absolute clarity that she had never witnessed James in that kind of blissful peace before.

He had never been this happy.

The thought cut straight to the bone, racking her like a spasm; the truth appalled her.

Suddenly Erika found herself clawing at the cloth of drab green tent flap, racing away from the tent city throng, past the Asian with the big tits who winked as she flew by, her breath stinging in her throat, wide-eyed like a terrified child, down a dank corridor that led past the cold steel cell with its midnight-black inhabitant, down the metal staircase, cell phone out, clutched in hand as she passed the mob of semi-naked partygoers, out the front door, the damp rancid air catching in her throat as she refused to look back.

Not even once…

✖✖✖

It wasn't until she was speeding away in a cab that Erika slowed her breathing. She had been on her cell, trying frantically to reach Marcus. She left messages at home, on his cell, and even had his service page him. But Erika never reached him that night.

James, on the other hand, had called her a million times, frantic and out of breath.

She refused to take his calls.

Three days later, Marcus finally returned hers.

Some lame excuse about being out of town.

By that time, Erika had made up her mind.

Both men in her life were *history*.

And this time, she made a promise not to look back.

Not even once...

FIFTY-THREE

The structure stood majestically in the dizzying brilliance of a summer sun against a yawning line of dark poplar trees. From the log cabin exterior, with its thick deep brown and beige polished woods, to its expansive upper deck that skirted the entire length and faced the setting sun, its size was deceiving. For once one ventured inside, their first reaction was to marvel at the enormity of the great room, with its huge stone fireplace, high ceilings with thick blackened cross-beams, and the four spacious bedrooms.

He had done so the first time he'd set foot in this space close to three months ago.

Outside, to the right of the cabin, if viewed from the waterline, was an enclosed area, where firewood was stored. As large as a two-car garage, the space was filled to the ceiling with seasoned split wood. But that did not stop him from rising every morning to stoke the still-burning wood stove in the kitchen, brew his first cup of coffee before donning his frayed jeans, worn tee shirt, and black boots, to spend forty minutes to an hour outdoors halving logs with an axe.

The work was hard and tedious, and not at all needed. It was late June, seasonable and quite warm. Regardless he followed this regiment to the letter. The result was a honing of his upper body; muscles, which had lain dormant, rose to the surface like a submarine, giving way to sinewy forearms and a ropy back. The tattoos shown like neon on a darkened street.

He actually considered more ink, now that his body was being grinded into shape.

Perhaps he would.

Behind this wood shed that was cut into the cabin was a garage. A single vehicle in width. It was here that he kept his auto, free from the sun's penetrating rays.

To the left and right of the cabin were stands of apple trees, their scent hanging in the air. Frequently, he'd pick a half-bushel, disappearing into the kitchen to bake pies that he was never able to finish.

Directly in front of the set of French double doors that opened out onto the narrow patio, and several yards down from where the last flagstone ended, lay a motorcycle in various stages of disassembly. The front and back tires were off. The fenders and tank had been dismantled and were sitting together on the grass under the sun. He had just gotten them back from being repainted—a vibrant reddish orange with singes of bluish flames at the edges. Later on today, he'd put the machine back together. Tomorrow perhaps, he'd put on the new set of Sampson pipes. By the following day or the day after that, he'd be feeling the wind on his scalp once again.

Of course, he was in the midst of a fine book—several actually; he'd turned into a voracious reader during the past few months, especially the classics—Charles Dickens, Bram Stoker, James Baldwin, Jack London, Alexandre Dumas, Mark Twain. So perhaps the schedule he'd outlined for himself would slip. It didn't matter. Time was something he had plenty of out here.

Looking out from either the upper deck or French doors, one was assaulted by the expanse of lake that was reached by a thin line of weathered dock. This rickety contraption that was used to tether a seventeen-foot skiff had been hand built almost ten years ago. Sections were in disrepair and rotting. Others sported fresh dark wood that lacked the grayish washed-out expression of its neighbors. Regardless, he'd sit, sometimes for hours, at the end, toes dipping in the dark water, watching the sun go down, or counting the stars, imagining if there are worlds beyond our reach, or simply wondering what was lurking beneath his feet.

The boat he was in laid less than two-thousand yards from the cabin, in deep water, cool to the touch. It was motionless, motor off. He was fishing or napping or reading, depending on when you chose to glance his way—the pole was in the water, and he was reacting to the nibbles every few minutes. A leafy novel lay at his side—Herman Melville's *Moby Dick*, fingers tracing the curled edges of acid paper—khaki waterman's hat with the wide brim sheltering his eyes from the relentless sunbeams. What time it was, he could not tell; no timepiece adorned his wrists. But he knew in general terms, by noting the location of the sun.

Way passed the noontime hour, less than halfway toward the horizon to the west; close to three or four o'clock. That was when he spotted the glint coming from the vehicle as it rounded the gravel road. As it ground to a halt, a second vehicle appeared. Both were Jeeps or SUVs—it was difficult to discern the details this far out.

He watched, almost in a detached, amused kind of way, neither shifting forward nor bothering to stand up. He wasn't expecting visitors and he had no friends. Not here in West Virginia anyway. He watched a form emerge from the lead vehicle: tall, male, and black. Something made him sit slightly forward. A second form, definitely female, emerged a moment later.

His chest began its slow tightening.

He squinted his eyes, attempting to see more clearly.

Finally, he gave up, stood and stretched, while holding a tan forearm to his forehead.

He glanced down, his two pails almost full with fish, gills still flapping—a good day, he mused as he regarded them silently—and decided to bring it on in.

As he got closer, he made out the appearance of Calvin Figgs, Esq.

It was as he had remembered, he noted as he pulled up to the dock, tossing a bowline silently—infectious smile, low-cropped hair and thin beard peppered with gray.

Still looking good.

Still the fire in his eyes.

Erika stood behind him, the radiance from a picturesque blue sky doing little to diminish her beauty.

Behind her, Vince Cannon, Jr., watched silently.

He cut the motor and stood, feeling the boat shift lazily under his weight. He wore, they noted, torn jeans, black boots, a faded blue bandanna tied tightly against his bald head. His upper body was bare, tanned, and well developed. Erika was amazed at the transformation. But what was most noticeable, she considered, were his eyes—he wore a look of completeness about him—he was not the person she remembered and last seen months ago: shifty, nervous, seemingly out of place—no, here he was at peace.

He was home.

Passing Calvin the pails of fresh fish, he accepted the proffered hand, climbed onto the dock, and stared silently at all of them.

Calvin broke the silence first.

"You're a hard one to track down."

"Some don't want to be found," he replied.

"But found you we did. So, you gonna stare us down for the rest of the afternoon, son, or you gonna give us our proper greeting?"

And for the first time, Trey smiled.

He reached out for Calvin's hand, but Figgs shook his head angrily as he grabbed him, embracing Trey in a bear hug.

"Good to see you, son."

"You too, sir."

Erika stood holding her hands in front of her. She wore an uneasy expression; Trey stepped up to her, stared for a moment, before he broke into a grin as he stretched out his arms. She went to him and hugged him tight.

Vince was next. They embraced silently, words not needed.

Trey moved back, allowing everyone to stare at each other.

Trey settled his gaze upon Calvin. It was clear he was the leader.

"How'd you find me?" Trey asked.

Calvin nodded in Erika's direction.

"Ask her. She's the one who did all the dirty work—been at it for close to a month—tracked you here even though you were as slick as they come—as you said, some people don't want to be found."

Trey was staring at Erika.

She wore a painted-on smile that she shot back at him.

"Resigned from the firm, condo locked up good and tight, bills paid through the fall—nice move, especially not telling anyone where you were going…"

There was a sparkle in her eyes.

"But you messed up, son," Calvin declared. "Yes, indeed—giving that woman at the Nona E. Taylor Women's Center a P.O. Box where you could be reached in an emergency—like Erika here wouldn't find out sooner or later? Please!"

Trey sucked his teeth as he scratched his bald head through the damp bandanna.

"Why are you here?" he asked.

Calvin's face turned serious.

"Because an intervention was needed."

Trey's stare wavered between the three. For a moment they were all silent.

"Intervention?" he asked cautiously.

"I'm here, Trey, because you've lost sight of those things that are most important to you."

Trey glared back at him. "I suppose you're going to tell me what those are?"

"Don't catch an attitude with me, son—I may be old, but I can still kick your ass—you forget I'm the O.G.—Original Gangster!"

Erika attempted to contain her laugher.

Calvin continued.

"Life, when it comes down to it, Trey; when you strip away all the bull-shit—what's *only* important is family."

Trey nodded.

"You say you understand, but do you?" Calvin asked. "Do you grasp the significance of these people standing before you? I wonder if you've forgotten."

Trey sucked in air to speak. He glanced down at the weathered wood of the dock, the ripples in the lake, and blinked. Calvin forged ahead.

"Doesn't matter, son. I'm not here to pass judgment on you or anyone else. I've driven the three hours with these folks because I believe in family." He looked at Erika and then at Vince. Reached out to take their hands. "And this here's your family, Trey. I'm here because today, the past disappears into the past, and what's only important is the glorious future. A future with the folks standing beside me who love you and care about you, just as I do. As my daughter is fond of saying, 'ya feel me,' son?"

Trey's eyes watered. He nodded once. Then nodded again.

"Yes," Trey replied softly, showing his white teeth, "I feel ya!"

"Excellent!" Calvin quipped. "My job here is *almost* done."

Trey's stare went to him.

"Almost, sir?"

Calvin smiled and turned toward the second vehicle. Trey heard the car door slam. He glanced up, past Vince and Erika, who parted so that he could see.

A figure emerged, a shock of lovely brown hair and auburn skin caught by the sun, illuminating the space around her like a halo. Trey shook his head as if to ward off the aberration. She moved toward him in slow motion, and Trey inhaled a sharp breath, witnessing his daughter for the very first time.

They met at the dock's edge where hard wood met soft grass. She glanced up into his eyes, searching for recognition. He smiled, and she found it.

"Hello, baby," Trey ventured, his arms spread wide.

She stared for a moment.

"Can I call you 'daddy'?" she asked hesitantly.

Trey pulled Amber to him, wrapping his arms around her body, engulfing her with all the warmth and love he could muster. At that moment, all emotions were funneled into the sheer joy he felt at holding his little girl for the very first time. He kissed her tear-streaked cheek as his own tears fell. He took her face in his hands and stepped back, staring longingly at her beautiful features. Trey touched her cheeks, ran a finger along the bridge of her nose, and felt her eyebrows. He pressed her against him, stroking her hair and whispered, "You're beautiful, Amber, and you're my baby girl..."

Amber sobbed loudly, but Trey held her until her quivering stilled. Erika and Vince hovered around them and together, all four people reunited, arms and fingers intertwining until it was difficult to tell where one ended and the other began.

Amber wiped the underside of one eye with a fingernail and Trey took care of the other. He stared at her, smiled, and said, "You remind me completely of your mother. Would you like me to tell you about her?"

Amber beamed as she nodded her head.

Vince cleared his throat. As he patted Trey on the back, he said, "I knew from the very first time I laid eyes on this lady that there was something vaguely familiar—something about her that reminded me of something or someone—it took me a while to figure out just what it was." He paused, locking eyes with Trey before saying, "It's you, Trey. Amber has your features, especially your smile. Can you see it, Erika? Can you see it in their eyes?"

"Oh yes," she said. "A wonderful smile, just like your daddy's."

Calvin cleared his throat as everyone turned.

"My job here is done," he boasted, arms held wide. At that moment he felt like a preacher after a heartfelt sermon on a Sunday morning. He flashed a warm smile as he smacked Trey on the shoulder. "Just one thing, counselor, if I may?"

"That's ex-counselor, if you please."

Calvin ignored the comment.

"Well, I don't know about you, but driving three hours makes me damn hungry. What you got to eat up in this piece?"

Trey grinned showing his vibrant white teeth.

"Anyone for some fried fish???"

✖✖✖

They ate until well after sundown. Actually, the rest of the afternoon and evening turned into a celebration as they ate, drank, napped, and ate again. For Trey, it was a dream come true. This morning he woke up thinking he would be spending his day quietly fishing, doing some reading, working on the bike or perhaps spending time in the kitchen concocting some new recipe—instead, he was reunited with his family, seeing his little girl for the very first time. Amber, he was convinced, had similar thoughts and feelings about this special day.

Vince and Erika knew that things between him and Amber were going smoothly. As soon as they had settled in, Trey had asked Amber to assist him in the kitchen. While Erika and Vince were relegated to the dock to gut and clean the fish, Trey supervised Amber cutting up vegetables. Pretty soon there was laughter and carryings on emanating from the kitchen. Vince and Erika kept coming in to check on things, but they were shooed away—first by Trey and then by Amber.

"Vince, leave me alone!" she said, as she cut up potatoes into thin slivers for later. "My daddy is schooling me and I need to pay attention!"

"That's my baby girl!" Trey added with a chuckle.

Vince just shook his head and left.

They ate in the Great Room, on couches, comfortable leather chairs, and on the floor in front of the stone fireplace—fried fish that Trey had caught in the lake that day, scrambled eggs stuffed with onions, ham, and cheese; and potatoes, cut sliver-thin and deep-fried in oil. After nightfall, Trey lit a fire—not that one was needed, but the effect of having one going after the sun went down was too good to ignore. He pulled out a bottle of Johnnie Walker Black and poured a round of drinks before serving hot apple pie baked from the apples they had picked that very afternoon.

"Are you legal?" he asked with a smirk as he held the bottle in front of Amber.

"Yes, Daddy! Please!"

Calvin made the toast once everyone held a glass.

"To family and good friends. May they both be in our hearts forever."

"Oh my God, this pie is soooooo good!" Erika exclaimed after taking a bite.

"Compliments to Amber—she made it!" Trey quipped.

"With your help!" she quickly added.

They settled down to talk and reflect on the past year.

"Why did you resign from the firm, Trey?" Erika asked as she sipped her drink.

Trey was lying on the floor, his head on an oversized throw rug. Amber's head lay in his lap.

"I got to the point where my work was no longer fun. And that felt wrong to me. I was spending far too much time thinking about negative things—

what I'd say to my boss the next time he barged into my office, how I'd structure my appeal letter to the EEOC, stuff like that. I woke up one morning and said—Trey, no more!"

Calvin nodded.

"So, what are your plans now that you are no longer working?" Vince asked from the couch.

"Honestly, I don't know. I came here to figure out just what my priorities are. I didn't put myself on a time schedule. I knew that when I was ready to go back to work and home, I would. I've got enough money saved to keep me here for a year or more, if need be. When I go back I'll figure out what I want to do. Whether its law or something else, when the time is right, I'll know."

Vince grinned. "Your head is on straight, and that is what matters most. I applaud you for recognizing when it's time to move on—most folks just stay in a dead-end job, a marriage, or what have you until they are so damn bitter they just give up on life or go postal, whichever comes first!"

Amber turned to stare at her father.

"I have a question."

"Shoot."

"Any females in your life?" she asked. "Love life, I mean," she added.

Amber was asking the question everyone else in the room dared not ask.

Trey cleared his throat and smiled, sitting up.

"Not at this time," he responded, his eyes clear and unblinking. "Part of why I came here was to take control of my life—get back to where I was before—to regain what I had lost along the way. I think that in the past year I've spent too much time focusing on the wrong things, instead of what's truly important. Right, Erika?"

Erika grinned.

Vince and Calvin nodded in unison.

"There was someone special in my life. But what we had was complicated. I need time to figure out just what the future holds, if there's a future for us. I think there is, but I need to be sure."

Trey took in a breath.

"I felt that I needed space to contemplate all of this—alone."

They were silent for a moment before Amber opened her mouth and spoke.

"I feel you," she said, returning her head to her father's lap. "I was just wondering—I mean, if Vince over there can get a girl, surely you can, too!"

✖✖✖

The fire had been reduced to simmering coals that sparked a warm red-orange glow. The five of them, Trey, Vince, Amber, Erika, and Calvin had consumed more liquor in one night than Trey had drunk in the entire year! Additionally, they finished off the rest of the apple pie until each of them lay around the Great Room holding full stomachs in hand as they frowned and groaned.

Erika lay in front of the fire asleep. Calvin was in a chair engrossed in a novel he hadn't read since college.

Vince gestured for Trey to follow him outside onto the upper deck. They toasted one another as they stared at the stars. Out here, with no lights from the city to impair their vision, the night was crystal clear and the stars brilliant, almost dizzying in their intensity. Vince stared for a moment, engrossed with how black the sky had become. The lake was still and ink-black, too—eerie, yet hauntingly beautiful.

Trey broke the silence first.

"How ya livin'?" he said simply.

"Having you back in my life, and Amber, too—man, I'm living large. And that's no lie!" He eyed his best friend. "It's good to have you back, Trey. I missed you, dawg."

Trey gave his friend dap and nodded.

"I feel the same," he uttered.

"There's one thing I need to ask," Vince continued quietly, glancing back through the glass at the Great Room and its inhabitants.

"Anything," Trey said.

Vince leaned forward and whispered in his ear.

Trey listened to his best friend, nodded and turned to him, considering his words for a moment before rewarding him with a smile.

"Nothing would please me more, dawg," he said, and reached over to give him a hug. They embraced silently. Vince had tears in his eyes that Trey could not see.

"You know what this means," Trey added with a gleam in his eyes.

"What?"

Trey leaned in and whispered. Vince's eyes rolled back in his head as he laughed out loud.

"Oh Lord!" he exclaimed, "I sure as hell didn't consider that!"

"That's right," Trey boasted, raising his glass to the heavens. "I'm gonna be your freaking *daddy*-in-law!!!"

✖✖✖

"There's way too much mischief going on out here!"

They both turned, and saw Erika joining them on the deck. She had wrapped herself in a blanket, the same one she had covering her by the fire. Only her hands were visible, and one held a fresh drink. She nuzzled between Vince and Trey and stared out at the stars.

"God, it's beautiful here. I can see why you came."

"It does wonders for cleansing the mind," Trey said.

"No question."

Vince rubbed her back while Trey draped an arm around her shoulder. The three of them stayed like that, no one speaking for a while, the trio enjoying the warmth and love that radiated from this place.

Erika raised her glass to the others.

"I want to say something. You two are the most important people in my life. You are my family. We've been through shit and thin together and we're still standing strong." She gazed upon Trey for a moment. "And we've had our share of troubling times—but regardless, we were always there for each other. That's what best friends do—they never turn their back on each other."

Trey and Vince nodded.

"I want for us to pledge right now that we will forever and always be here for each other—in sickness and in health…you know the drill, so raise your damn glass!"

Vince grinned.

"Well said."

"I'll drink to that," Trey said.

And they did, on a warm summer night, somewhere in West Virginia, nuzzling against each other as they held their glasses high.

✖✖✖

They had gone to bed—finally unable to keep their eyes open a second longer. It was way past 1 a.m., Erika had crashed a while ago, and then Amber turned in followed by Vince. Trey remained awake, unable to sleep. He stood on the deck by the railing, observing the stars. The remains of a drink laid in his palm. He swished the contents around, over and over in a circular motion, the action repetitive and comfortable, before tossing the remains over the rail.

Calvin joined him on the deck, bringing him a fresh glass of Johnnie Walker Black.

"Thought you could use a nightcap."

"Thank you, sir."

They sipped at their drinks in silence before Calvin set his down on the wooden rail. He turned to Trey.

"You have a wonderful family, Trey."

"Yes, I do."

"Don't forget that," he added.

"I won't."

"Good."

They drank a moment more.

"Trey—concerning your law career."

"Yes, sir?"

"I've started a new firm." Calvin's eyes reflected stray moonlight.

Trey's jaw went slack.

"I thought you were retiring—that's what you told me!"

"Yes—and after a lengthy trip with the missus and way too much time at home, it became apparent to both of us that I needed to get back to work! So I decided to start my own firm. I want to specialize in high-profile clients and cases, the kind I've spent my career negotiating."

Trey nodded, waiting for what came next.

"I'd like for you to come work for me, son—I want you with me."

Trey exhaled forcefully.

"Sir, I don't know what to say." Trey beamed. "Thank you, sir, thank you for thinking of me."

Calvin waved him away.

"Counselor—I've always been one of your biggest fans, you know that. You do great work, that is when your head isn't in the clouds, or up someone's skirt!" He gave Trey a wink. "Seriously, I think you'd be a valuable asset, especially with the contacts you have in Washington."

Trey grinned, shaking his head. Suddenly, everything was falling back into place, right where it belonged.

"I'm not going to lie to you, son—it'll be hard work—we're starting from scratch—I can't pay you what you were making—but the money will come in time. Just keep your nose clean and work your ass off!"

"I will, sir."

"One thing, Trey—and this is vital, so pay attention." He pointed a finger at Trey's nose. Trey put down his drink and gave Calvin Figgs his utmost attention.

"Take whatever time you need to consider my offer, but get your family in order *first*. When you come work for me—that is *if* you decide to work for me—I want no less than two hundred percent from you. I won't accept anything less. Do I make myself clear?"

"Understood sir," Trey responded.

"Good. Remember what I said, counselor—take your time but get your family in order first—then come, ready and willing, and together we'll kick some serious ass. Bernard John Marshall be damned!"

Trey grinned and held up his drink.

"With all due respect, sir, *fuck* Bernard John Marshall…"

Calvin finished the sentence for me: "…And the horse he rode in on!"

EPILOGUE

(One year later...)

I can't begin to tell you just how wonderful Vince and Amber's wedding day turned out to be. Simply put, it was one of the most incredible moments of my life!

My little girl, Amber, was dolled-up in this fabulous wedding gown, hand-beaded with sequins and pearls, intricate lace and matte satin, with a flowing train and matching headpiece. Her brown hair was straightened and worn long, makeup flawless, skin beyond radiant as she emerged from the white limousine on a cloudless day in June to stand in front of this majestic black church in Northwest D.C. Oh, my God! I took her hand, me looking dapper, funky *fresh* in my tuxedo; oh yeah, y'all, the honeys were clocking a brutha, and why wouldn't they as I walked her up the steps and down the aisle.

Yours truly walked my baby girl down the aisle!

There was so much pride in me that day as hundreds of onlookers turned in their pews to watch this icon of loveliness, my baby girl, walk to her husband, Vince Cannon, Jr., my best friend. Vince was looking as fly as he wanna be in his tux, GQ-*down*, you hear me, waiting to say, "I do!"

I don't mean to get choked up, but this is my baby girl we're talking about. The ceremony was wonderful, not too long, and filled with singing, music, and spoken word—oh yeah, y'all, we got down like that, for real!

Black folks in the house! So holla if ya hear me!

Get this—everybody that was anybody in D.C. was there—I mean,

Vince's parents, Dr. and Mrs. Vince Cannon, are well connected, so the elite were all up in this piece! But more importantly, all of our family and friends were there to support us on this most auspicious day.

A wedding invitation had gone out to Amber's grandmother, Lorna, but as expected, she had declined to attend. Soli, her mother's good friend from high school, made it down with a few other high school chums in tow.

Amber was also successful in reconnecting with some of her friends from Houston, and a contingent of ladies came to D.C. for the wedding. Amber couldn't have been more pleased.

It was great to finally meet Angeliqué, Vince's old flame. She came and stayed an entire week, seeing how she was one of the bridesmaids.

Erika, it turned out, was the Maid of Honor. She, too, looked radiant, but of course, my boo always does.

Always has—always will!

Guess who else was in the wedding party?

Okay, I've made you wait long enough.

You guessed right.

Layla!

My girl!

My boo boo!

Damn that woman looked so fine in her sensuously tight bridesmaid's dress, I swear to God I couldn't wait to fuck her after church! But let me get back to moi!

I held the dual role of being the best man *and* giving away the bride.

How cool is that?

Plus, I had fine-ass Layla on my arm so you know I was the *man* that day, prancing around like some spring chicken, all cocky and shit—yeah y'all know by now how I do; this brutha's back in the zone, way up in the ooooooooooo-zone!

I gotta tell you this, though, the absolute highlight of the day/evening, was at the reception when guess who strolls in???

(Drum roll, please).

Yup, y'all guessed it.

Giovanna!

That heifer had the *nerve* to show her face on Amber's wedding day. Check this—I hadn't heard a peep—and I do mean peep from girlfriend since April of the *previous* year! After she went on her trip to Hawaii with old dude—I cut her ass loose.

Had to!

You know you can't pimp this brutha and get away with it!

She did try and contact me a few times, but by then I'd had enough of her shit.

If I wasn't good enough for her then, I surely didn't want any part of her now!

Anywho, back to the story—girlfriend rolls in, looking, I must say, as tasty as one of those Hostess Twinkies! I mean, she was not playing in her tight-ass dress, fuck-me pumps, hair done all up, like she owned this mutha fucka!

Listen, I may be in love, but I damn sure ain't blind.

I had to give girlfriend credit—she was trying to make a scene and *succeeding*, with her fine self, every mutha fucka turning in their chairs, straining their necks, trying to get a closer look.

Vince just shook his head and sighed.

The truth is, next to my girls—Amber and Layla—Giovanna ain't shit!

At the reception I spotted her out of the corner of my eye. I did a double take (I'm not gonna even front), and decided to pay her ass no mind!

Later on, when folks were dancing, I got up from the head table to go to the bar. Guess what? She was clocking the hell out of brutha—and I just tipped my head back and laughed out loud!

She actually had the audacity to join me at the bar, away from the stares of Layla and Vince, where she could say her hello.

"Damn, Trey, you are looking *foine*; I guess a girl really fucked up by letting your smooth ass go," she began, and I just stood there, tugging at my mustache, while she proceeded to brush invisible lint off the lapel of my jacket.

I was grinning like my numbers just came in!

"Yeah, you sure did fuck up," I said, as I flashed my best Trey-smile, "but it's all good, girl, so enjoy the party, cause I'm sure gonna!" And then I waltzed away, fresh drink in hand, snickering my ass off.

Giovanna's hand reached for my shoulder and spun me around, whispering low, eyes wide, "Trey, you can have this," her stare dropping seductively to my crotch, "why don't you take this, for old time's sake...

My pussy is wet,

my sex box is hot,

you got me twitching,

like an addict on rock..."

Cocking her head to the side, gesturing upstairs to one of the private rooms, she told me, "You can take this right now, wedding day be damned; I'll let you hike up my dress, and you won't find any panties to get in your way...

"Remember that, baby? Do you???"

I just smirked as I walked away.

I didn't even give her the satisfaction of responding.

End of story, y'all.

Poof! Giovanna's gone...

Later, as I sat with my woman drinking champagne, Layla's elbow resting comfortably in my lap, teasing my fly in a luring yet tasteful kind of way, I pondered the past year as I watched Vince dance with his new bride.

I had regained my friends.

I found my family.

The job was going remarkable well—better than expected—we had pulled in some big name clients, and in the short time that we had been in business, Figgs & Associates had created quite a stir within the D.C. community.

And...

(Another drum roll, please).

Layla moved in with me!

Yeah, you heard right. Okay, y'all can get up off the damn floor now, 'cause I ain't playing. Your boy, Trey decided, why the hell not—I mean, I'm feeling her something terrible—actually, she's the best thing that's ever happened to me, other than finding my daughter, or should I say, her finding me.

Simply put: I'm in love, y'all, and I'm not ashamed to admit it!

Dayum.

I guess momma was right.

You can teach old dogs new tricks...

Vince's book, *Finding Nirvana*, has been on the *Essence* bestseller list for the past nine months in a row. That brutha's seminars are sold out wherever he travels to; he's working on a sequel to the book, and is frequently on television and radio shows. He's waiting for Oprah to call any minute now...

You go, boy!

Vince is livin' large!

Angeliqué's art show took to the road to rave reviews. After doing a short stint in Dallas and Atlanta, she came to New York where her vibrant, colorful, live show featuring Amber, Jacques, and a handful of other nude models covered in *veve* netted her a feature in *Heart & Soul*. Turns out, a very successful video director saw the show while it was in New York, and fell in love with Amber's looks. Next thing we knew, my baby girl was cast in several of his video projects.

All of a sudden, Amber's face, wonderful smile, and body were gracing the screen of BET and MTV.

My girl, Erika, too, is doing quite well.

After kicking both James and Marcus to the curb, she took some time off to be alone—to chill, and enjoy being by herself.

After her experience with the foundation run by Rich and Andy, she decided that she wanted to start her own not-for-profit group to assist people of color with finding their birthparents.

So, homegirl put her head down and started her own shit! It takes up all of her time; we barely see her ass anymore, and then only at fund-raisers, but she's doing her thing, and she's happy. Girl's finally found her passion— and y'all know just how important that is!

I'm damn proud of my boo!

She's an independent black woman doing her own thing, in control of her own destiny! And nobody's gonna get in her way!

By the way, Sassy came to the wedding with this dude she'd just started dating—this local author, tall, bald, light-skinned, thin goatee; guy by the name of Jonathan Somefuckingbody. Okay, the brutha's good-looking; I'll give him that. I expected him to bend my fucking ear with talk about his novels like he was Eric Jerome Dickey, but he didn't. He was way cool. We spoke for a while about all kinds of eclectic stuff: jazz, politics, classic literature, the rebuilding of Iraq, funding for NASA explorations to Mars—the brutha's quite deep! And I must admit he and Erika do look good together.

Hmmn…I might have to start hanging with him…you know, two good-looking, bald-headed bruthas with an intellect and something to say—oh hell no! But I digress…

Let's see—what else can I tell you?

Oh, yeah—India Jasmine Jackson followed me to Figgs & Associates. And of course, she's working out great. She's keeping my black ass in check every single day!

Quentin Hues, who incidentally was traded to the Miami Heat, also followed me to my new firm. We still see each other when he's in town, we stay in touch, and I'm still his lawyer for any mess he finds himself in.

Aponi—I left that fine shit alone.

I'm still doing my volunteer thing at the Nona E. Taylor Women's Center—I try to get there every other month or so, since work's been taking up most of my time. It's always a pleasure to cook for those ladies, and Yolanda Taylor hasn't changed a bit! She still hugs me to death whenever I stop by, and we can sit for hours just shooting the shit and telling lies. She's good people…

I ran into Allison some months back at a reception held at the new D.C. Convention Center—real hoity-toity affair—spied her at the bar—didn't go over—didn't want to make a scene—she saw me, though—our eyes connected and locked, I winked and she didn't smile back—so I went on my way!

Get this—I also ran into Bernard John Marshall a few months ago at Angelo & Maxi's. We both were there dining with our respective clients. He was leaving when I was coming in, and he had no choice but to shake my hand and ask how things were going. You could see the seething anger dripping from his fangs when I told him about a high-profile client I had just nabbed—a client I had actually stolen from the old firm! It was so good to see him outside of work, where he no longer controls me.

My, how things change...

So, here I am, standing with a champagne flute in my hand, Erika and Jonathan sitting to my left, engaged in some serious conversation about God-knows what; Sassy hanging on every word this bald-head brutha utters, head tipped back as she laughs at his corny-ass jokes. My boo boo to my right, eyes sparkling like diamonds, dress fitting her like driving gloves, her plunging neckline, curvy hips, and heart-shaped ass speaking to me in volumes; her loveliness shining like a beacon so damn bright that I have to resist her potion with every ounce of strength I can muster. Amber and Vince slow-dancing a few feet away; her eyes and mine connecting, her mouthing over the din of the slow jam, "Daddy, I love you," and my eyes watering because it's at times like this that I realize that I'm the luckiest damn guy in the world...

And I think to myself, back when I was in Jamaica, a time now that seems like eons ago, down among the throng of naked partygoers, I thought I'd died and gone to heaven. But now, as I stand here tonight, my family and close friends all around me, I realize that, naw bro, you were wrong. Heaven is right here on earth—with your family, with your friends, and with the ones you love.

Yeah, y'all, Trey Alexander is one of the lucky ones...

Yeah mon!

The End

November 2001—February 2004
Accokeek, Maryland

AUTHOR'S NOTE

Let me take a moment to explain the journey I undertook in writing this novel. In late 2001, I was doing the 9-5 thing and had just self-published my novella, *Feeding Frenzy*. While promoting it around town, I was also dabbling in writing erotica. In October I went to Jamaica for a long overdue vacation. I took my journal with me and decided that while I was down there, I'd sketch out an idea or two for some hot new stuff. A month later I posted a thirty-five-page piece entitled *Trey in Play*. It was about this guy who goes down to Jamaica and parties his ass off—has wild sex with all of these women only to see this chick who reminds him of his ex—he freaks out right as the story ends. Recognize it???

After completing this piece I got to thinking—this could be the beginning of something bigger. I discussed it with several of my good friends to get their advice. Zodie Makonnen, in particular, was instrumental in helping me see this as more than just a piece of erotica—and together we began to shape the story that you hold in your hands now. What I was enjoying the most were the characters—Trey and his best friends Vince and Erika. I wanted to write a book about single people and their wacky experiences in and out of relationships. Of course I wanted to make it hot and drama-filled—shit, most of our relationships are exactly that! But what I was most interested in doing was to make this book a character novel. Develop the folks within these pages and the depth of their quirky personalities until they were so detailed and life-like that it felt as if you actually knew them. As if they were family. So that's exactly what I set out to do…

Besides penning a drama-infested, sex-choked character novel, I also wanted to do something a bit different (as if the preceding stuff wasn't enough!)—I was interested in getting feedback from readers *as I wrote it*—so I decided to post significant portions of the unedited manuscript on my website, and solicit feedback from people. For close to six months I posted a chapter a month on my site—receiving comments about everything from the sex (too much, too little, too detailed, not enough detail, and thanks for using condoms) to the drama (Trey is an ass; Vince, on the other hand, is my kind of man; what the hell is wrong with that boy? He's just plain stupid)!

As I wrote *How Ya Livin'* (HYL) the story grew. The characters leapt off the pages and found a home in my soul, and it got to the point where I was thinking about Trey, Vince, and Erika all the time. I mean, I'd go out to dinner and think to myself, how would Trey act in this situation? I'd run into someone I knew in a club and ponder, how would Vince handle himself here?

Some of you know (from reading the author's note in *Jasminium*, my last novel), that I was laid off from my job in 2002. Instead of going back to work, I decided to focus on my creative side, and take the summer to pen *Jasminium*. It forced me to put HYL on hold for close to six months.

By the beginning of 2003, I was back to HYL full-time, promising myself (and my publisher) that I'd finish it by the end of the year! The entire process from beginning to end wound up taking two years and change, but I finally completed it in February of 2004.

So many things have happened to me since I first wrote about Trey having the time of his life down in Jamaica. During the past year, I think what has been most remarkable is the fact that I've settled into this new author lifestyle, and I couldn't be happier. Honestly, when I first lost my job, I had no idea how I'd pay the bills and take care of my kids. But you know what? You learn to adjust to new situations. When you earn less, you spend less. And I found that it wasn't very difficult to cut out those things that were draining my wallet on the regular, but actually provided little value to me. In the past twelve months my lifestyle and spending habits have changed— I make do with less than before (although I'm not gonna front—my Indian

Motorcycle is *still* sitting in my garage and it ain't going nowhere, so fuck you, repo man!) Seriously, I've learned that there's more to life than the trappings of corporate existence. Inner peace and happiness are where I'm at now, because I'm doing what I've always dreamed of doing. I've found my passion, and I'm living my dreams. Like Trey, Vince, and Erika, I'm livin' large, y'all…

Additionally, a remarkable thing has happened to me. I've become more spiritual. Losing one's livelihood will do that to you! Believe that! I've come to realize that things, whether good or bad, really do happen for a reason; that when one door closes another one opens! I heard that countless times growing up, but never truly understood the power of its meaning until now. Today, when I converse with people about my writing and my new lifestyle, I tell them "I'm blessed." And I truly believe that. My friends, some of whom seemingly have everything, tell me how much they envy me and the inner peace I have found. I'm grateful for the doors that have been opened to me. I'm humbled that I've been allowed to follow my passion when so many folks out there don't even know what their passion looks like.

The moral of this story? It's simple.

Be careful what you wish for, because you just might get it!

There are a few people I'd like to thank for inspiring me during the writing of this novel. First and foremost—to Zodie—I dedicate this book to you because you had the vision to lay out the possibilities of this story to me. You've been with me from day one on this incredible journey—and you've helped me bring these characters to life. I thank you for all that you've contributed.

To my family: my mom and dad, and siblings: Emily and Michael, thanks for being there. To my children: Alexandra and Julian—you continue to be the center of my life—that will never change. Daddy loves you with all of his heart!

To my close circle of friends—you know who you are—thanks for all your support. A special shout-out to Hayes Fountain III and Ed Mulrenin for staying the course after all these years. It's good to know you have my back!

To my Jamaica crew—Mike and Debbie, John and Patricia, Ron and Paula,

Doug and MaryAnn, and Michael and Patty—thanks for the memories, the island adventures, and most importantly, the friendship—yeah mon! P.S. No more flaming Bob Marleys for me, ya hear?!?

To the Hedonism II staff, especially the entertainment coordinators who work ungodly hours without so much as a frown, thanks for making a brutha feel like a king!

To my attorney, Mike Danels, thank you for the legal advice over the years, before this book was even a fleeting thought in my mind, and during the writing of this manuscript.

To the spinning queens at World's Gym, Fort Washington, Maryland—Steffani, Veronica, Bobette, Joyce, Tianna, Tomeka, Nechelle, Candace, Natasha, Monique, Dana, and Holly—you know y'all my boos. Thanks for the support and the luv.

To Sipp's Café—Steven, Sheila, Tanya, Nathan, and the rest of the staff—thanks for opening up your establishment and letting me move my shit in…you've made me feel extremely comfortable these past six months, (at least a third of HYL was penned there.)

To Zane—you continue to support and nurture your authors, even when you clearly don't have to. Thank you for that, and for believing in us. To Charmaine, the hardest-working person in the publishing industry—you are amazing. I'm blessed to be working with you. To the rest of the Strebor Books International staff, thank you for your hard work, and for making your authors shine.

Speaking of my fellow Strebor authors, I'm proud to be part of the family—all of you keep doing your thing! A special shout-out goes to my road dawg, Rique Johnson, the hardest-working author I know.

To the wonderful people in book clubs up and down the East Coast—thank you for inviting me into your living room for good conversation and great food!

And finally, to all of the wonderful people I've met at book signings, in bookstores, in the mall, at book club events, and online, thank you for taking the time to read and comment on my work. From Stephanie who called me all the way from Iraq to tell me that she and her fellow soldiers were loving my book (girl, you didn't just make my day, you made my entire month!) to Angelyne in the U.K., Tanya in Delaware, Brendesha in Cali, Gwen in B-More, (yeah, I haven't forgotten your ride), Queen Nita, and finally, Nicole (Philly), just to name a few...thank you all for your kind words.

Okay, I've bent your ear long enough!

Until next time, keep reading—and I'll keep writing!

Peace and love,

Jonathan
March 15, 2004
Accokeek, Maryland

Author's Bio

Jonathan Luckett is a native of Brooklyn, New York and has been writing since he was in the seventh grade. Now residing in the Washington, D.C. area, he was educated at Cornell and Johns Hopkins universities. Jonathan is the author of the novel *Jasminium* (2003), and the self-published novella *Feeding Frenzy* (2002). His latest work is featured in *Chocolate Flava* (2004), a collection of erotica. Jonathan has also written various short stories, poetry, and erotic fiction. His work is available on-line at www.jonathanluckett.com.

HOW YA LIVIN'

BOOK CLUB QUESTIONS/READER'S GUIDE

- Who were your favorite characters in the book and why? Who were your least favorites and why?
- What did you think of Vince's relationship with Maxi, Desiree, Angeliqué, and Raven? Do you think he gave each woman enough time in his relationships with them before moving on?
- When Erika first discovered James' problem, what do you think she should have done? Was she right to stay with him and try to work through his issues?
- How did you feel when Trey pursued Allison at the club?
- How did you react when Vince traveled to New Orleans, only to find Angelique involved with someone else? Do you think he should have pursued her regardless of what he found there?
- What do you think of Vince's principles balancing Personal, Professional, and Self? Do you agree with his concept? Can you apply these principles to your own life?
- How do you feel about Trey's Rules and did he violate them when he had sex with Allison, Aponi, and Giovanna?
- What do you think of Bernard John Marshall? Do you think Trey's reaction to him and his management style was understandable and justifiable? Can you relate to his situation at work?
- What was your reaction when Trey chose Raven over Vince? How did that scene make you feel?
- Do you think Erika made the right decision in dumping both men in her life? Why or why not?
- Were Trey, Vince, and Erika all searching for the same thing? How were their methods similar or different?
- If you were Trey, would you get back together with Layla, knowing what he knew? Why or why not?

- What were your feelings regarding Trey's reaction to learning about his daughter? What do you think of the way his friends broke the news to him? Would you have done the same? Why or why not?
- What do you think of the sex scenes in *How Ya Livin'*? Do you feel they added to or detracted from the overall storyline?
- Were you satisfied with the ending of this novel? Why or why not?
- Do you think there should be a sequel to the book? What characters and situations would you like to see covered next?

Johnson, Keith Lee
Sugar & Spice 1-59309-013-7
Pretenses 1-59309-018-8

Johnson, Rique
Love & Justice 1-59309-002-1
Whispers From a Troubled Heart (July 2004) 1-59309-020-X
Every Woman's Man (November 2004) 1-59309-036-6
Sistergirls.com 1-59309-004-8

Lee, Darrien
All That and a Bag of Chips 0-9711953-0-7
Been There, Done That 1-59309-001-3
What Goes Around Comes Around (July 2004) 1-59309-024-2

Luckett, Jonathan
Jasminium 1-59309-007-2
How Ya Livin' 1-59309-025-0

McKinney, Tina Brooks
All That Drama (December 2004) 1-59309-033-1

Quartay, Nane
Feenin 0-9711953-7-4

Rivers, V. Anthony
Daughter by Spirit 0-9674601-4-X
Everybody Got Issues 1-59309-003-X
Sistergirls.com 1-59309-004-8

Roberts, J. Deotis
Roots of a Black Future: Family and Church 0-9674601-6-6
Christian Beliefs 0-9674601-5-8

Stephens, Sylvester
Our Time Has Come (September 2004) 1-59309-026-9

Turley II, Harold L.
Love's Game (November 2004) 1-59309-029-3

Valentine, Michelle
Nyagra's Falls 0-9711953-4-X

White, A.J.
Ballad of a Ghetto Poet 1-59309-009-9

White, Franklin
Money for Good 1-59309-012-9
Potentially Yours 1-59309-027-7

Zane (Editor)
Breaking the Cycle (September 2004) 1-59309-021-8